The Miss Billy Trilogy

Eleanor H. Porter

TABLE OF CONTENTS

MISS BILLY

MISS BILLY'S DECISION

MISS BILLY MARRIED

MISS BILLY

CHAPTER I

BILLY WRITES A LETTER

Billy Neilson was eighteen years old when the aunt, who had brought her up from babyhood, died. Miss Benton's death left Billy quite alone in the world—alone, and peculiarly forlorn. To Mr. James Harding, of Harding & Harding, who had charge of Billy's not inconsiderable property, the girl poured out her heart in all its loneliness two days after the funeral.

"You see, Mr. Harding, there isn't any one—not any one who—cares," she choked.

"Tut, tut, my child, it's not so bad as that, surely," remonstrated the old man, gently. "Why, I—I care."

Billy smiled through tear-wet eyes.

"But I can't LIVE with you," she said.

"I'm not so sure of that, either," retorted the man. "I'm thinking that Letty and Ann would LIKE to have you with us."

The girl laughed now outright. She was thinking of Miss Letty, who had "nerves," and of Miss Ann, who had a "heart"; and she pictured her own young, breezy, healthy self attempting to conform to the hushed and shaded thing that life was, within Lawyer Harding's home.

"Thank you, but I'm sure they wouldn't," she objected. "You don't know how noisy I am."

The lawyer stirred restlessly and pondered.

"But, surely, my dear, isn't there some relative, somewhere?" he demanded. "How about your mother's people?"

Billy shook her head. Her eyes filled again with tears.

"There was only Aunt Ella, ever, that I knew anything about. She and mother were the only children there were, and mother died when I was a year old, you know."

"But your father's people?"

"It's even worse there. He was an only child and an orphan when mother married him. He died when I was but six months old. After that there was only mother and Aunt Ella, then Aunt Ella alone; and now—no one."

"And you know nothing of your father's people?"

"Nothing; that is—almost nothing."

"Then there is some one?"

Billy smiled. A deeper pink showed in her cheeks.

"Why, there's one—a man but he isn't really father's people, anyway. But I—I have been tempted to write to him."

"Who is he?"

"The one I'm named for. He was father's boyhood chum. You see that's why I'm 'Billy' instead of being a proper 'Susie,' or 'Bessie,' or 'Sally Jane.' Father had made up his mind to name his baby 'William' after his chum, and when I came, Aunt Ella said, he was quite broken-hearted until somebody hit upon the idea of naming me Billy.' Then he was content, for it seems that he always called his chum 'Billy' anyhow. And so—'Billy' I am to-day."

"Do you know this man?"

"No. You see father died, and mother and Aunt Ella knew him only very slightly. Mother knew his wife, though, Aunt Ella said, and SHE was lovely."

"Hm—; well, we might look them up, perhaps. You know his address?"

"Oh, yes unless he's moved. We've always kept that. Aunt Ella used to say sometimes that she was going to write to him some day about me, you know."

"What's his name?"

"William Henshaw. He lives in Boston."

Lawyer Harding snatched off his glasses, and leaned forward in his chair.

"William Henshaw! Not the Beacon Street Henshaws!" he cried.

It was Billy's turn to be excited. She, too, leaned forward eagerly.

"Oh, do you know him? That's lovely! And his address IS Beacon Street! I know because I saw it only to-day. You see, I HAVE been tempted to write him."

"Write him? Of course you'll write him," cried the lawyer. "And we don't need to do much 'looking up' there, child. I've known the family for years, and this William was a college mate of my boy's. Nice fellow, too. I've heard Ned speak of him. There were three sons, William, and two others much younger than he. I've forgotten their names."

"Then you do know him! I'm so glad," exclaimed Billy. "You see, he never seemed to me quite real."

"I know about him," corrected the lawyer, smilingly, "though I'll confess I've rather lost track of him lately. Ned will know. I'll ask Ned. Now go home, my dear, and dry those pretty eyes of yours. Or, better still, come home with me to tea. I—I'll telephone up to the house." And he rose stiffly and went into the inner office.

Some minutes passed before he came back, red of face, and plainly distressed.

"My dear child, I—I'm sorry, but—but I'll have to take back that invitation," he blurted out miserably. "My sisters are—are not well this afternoon. Ann has been having a turn with her heart—you know Ann's heart is—is bad; and Letty—Letty is always nervous at such times—very nervous. Er—I'm so sorry! But you'll—excuse it?"

"Indeed I will," smiled Billy, "and thank you just the same; only"—her eyes twinkled mischievously—"you don't mind if I do say that it IS lucky that we hadn't gone on planning to have me live with them, Mr. Harding!"

"Eh? Well—er, I think your plan about the Henshaws is very good," he interposed hurriedly. "I'll speak to Ned—I'll speak to Ned," he finished, as he ceremoniously bowed the girl from the office.

James Harding kept his word, and spoke to his son that night; but there was little, after all, that Ned could tell him. Yes, he remembered Billy Henshaw well, but he had not heard of him for years, since Henshaw's marriage, in fact. He must be forty years old, Ned said; but he was a fine fellow, an exceptionally fine fellow, and would be sure to deal kindly and wisely by his little orphan namesake; of that Ned was very sure.

"That's good. I'll write him," declared Mr. James Harding. "I'll write him tomorrow."

He did write—but not so soon as Billy wrote; for even as he spoke, Billy, in her lonely little room at the other end of the town, was laying bare all her homesickness in four long pages to "Dear Uncle William."

CHAPTER II

"THE STRATA"

Bertram Henshaw called the Beacon Street home "The Strata." This annoyed Cyril, and even William, not a little; though they reflected that, after all, it was "only Bertram." For the whole of Bertram's twenty-four years of life it had been like this—"It's only Bertram," had been at once the curse and the salvation of his existence.

In this particular case, however, Bertram's vagary of fancy had some excuse. The Beacon Street house, the home of the three brothers, was a "Strata."

"You see, it's like this," Bertram would explain airily to some new acquaintance who expressed surprise at the name; "if I could slice off the front of the house like a loaf of cake, you'd understand it better. But just suppose that old Bunker Hill should suddenly spout fire and brimstone and bury us under tons of ashes—only fancy the condition of mind of those future archaeologists when they struck our house after their months of digging!

"What would they find? Listen. First: stratum number one, the top floor; that's Cyril's, you know. They'd note the bare floors, the sparse but heavy furniture, the piano, the violin, the flute, the book-lined walls, and the absence of every sort of curtain, cushion, or knickknack. 'Here lived a plain man,' they'd say; 'a scholar, a musician, stern, unloved and unloving; a monk.'

"And what next? They'd strike William's stratum next, the third floor. Imagine it! You know William as a State Street broker, well-off, a widower, tall, angular, slow of speech, a little bald, very much nearsighted, and the owner of the kindest heart in the world. But really to know William, you must know his rooms. William collects things. He has always collected things—and he's saved every one of them. There's a tradition that at the age of one year he crept into the house with four small round white stones. Anyhow, if he did, he's got them now. Rest assured of that—and he's forty this year. Miniatures, carved ivories, bugs, moths, porcelains, jades, stamps, postcards, spoons, baggage tags, theatre programs, playing-cards—there isn't anything that he doesn't collect. He's on teapots, now. Imagine it—William and teapots! And they're all there in his rooms—one glorious mass of confusion. Just fancy those archaeologists trying to make their 'monk' live there!

"But when they reach me, my stratum, they'll have a worse time yet. You see, I like cushions and comfort, and I have them everywhere. And I like—well, I like lots of things. My rooms don't belong to that monk, not a little bit. And so you see," Bertram would finish merrily, "that's why I call it all 'The Strata.'"

And "The Strata" it was to all the Henshaws' friends, and even to William and Cyril themselves, in spite of their objection to the term.

From babyhood the Henshaw boys had lived in the handsome, roomy house, facing the Public Garden. It had been their father's boyhood home, as well, and he and his wife had died there, soon after Kate, the only daughter, had married. At the age of twenty-two, William Henshaw, the eldest son, had brought his bride to the house, and together they had striven to make a home for the two younger orphan boys, Cyril, twelve, and Bertram, six. But Mrs. William, after a short five years of married life, had died; and since then, the house had known almost nothing of a woman's touch or care.

Little by little as the years passed, the house and its inmates had fallen into what had given Bertram his excuse for the name. Cyril, thirty years old now, dignified, reserved, averse to cats, dogs, women, and confusion, had early taken himself and his music to the peace and exclusiveness of the fourth floor. Below him, William had long discouraged any meddling with his precious chaos of possessions, and had finally come to spend nearly all his spare time among them. This left Bertram to undisputed ownership of the second floor, and right royally did he hold sway there with his paints and brushes and easels, his old armor, rich hangings, rugs, and cushions, and everywhere his specialty—his "Face of a Girl." From canvas, plaque, and panel they looked out—those girlish faces: winsome, wilful, pert, demure, merry, sad, beautiful, even almost ugly—they were all there; and they were growing famous, too. The world of art was beginning to take notice, and to adjust its spectacles for a more critical glance. This "Face of a Girl" by Henshaw bade fair to be worth while.

Below Bertram's cheery second floor were the dim old library and drawing-rooms, silent, stately, and almost never used; and below them were the dining-room and the kitchen. Here ruled Dong Ling, the Chinese cook, and Pete.

Pete was—indeed, it is hard telling what Pete was. He said he was the butler; and he looked the part when he answered the bell at the great front door. But at other times, when he swept a room, or dusted Master William's curios, he looked—like nothing so much as what he was: a fussy, faithful old man, who expected to die in the service he had entered fifty years before as a lad.

Thus in all the Beacon Street house, there had not for years been the touch of a woman's hand. Even Kate, the married sister, had long since given up trying to instruct Dong Ling or to chide Pete, though she still walked across the Garden from her Commonwealth Avenue home and tripped up the stairs to call in turn upon her brothers, Bertram, William, and Cyril.

CHAPTER III

THE STRATA—WHEN THE LETTER COMES

It was on the six o'clock delivery that William Henshaw received the letter from his namesake, Billy. To say the least, the letter was a great shock to him. He had not quite forgotten Billy's father, who had died so long ago, it is true, but he had forgotten Billy, entirely. Even as he looked at the disconcerting epistle with its round, neatly formed letters, he had great difficulty in ferreting out the particular niche in his memory which contained the fact that Walter Neilson had had a child, and had named it for him.

And this child, this "Billy," this unknown progeny of an all but forgotten boyhood friend, was asking a home, and with him! Impossible! And William Henshaw peered at the letter as if, at this second reading, its message could not be so monstrous.

"Well, old man, what's up?" It was Bertram's amazed voice from the hall doorway; and indeed, William Henshaw, red-faced and plainly trembling, seated on the lowest step of the stairway, and gazing, wild-eyed, at the letter in his hand, was somewhat of an amazing sight.

"What IS up?"

"What's up!" groaned William, starting to his feet, and waving the letter frantically in the air. "What's up! Young man, do you want us to take in a child to board?—a CHILD?" he repeated in slow horror.

"Well, hardly," laughed the other. "Er, perhaps Cyril might like it, though; eh?"

"Come, come, Bertram, be sensible for once," pleaded his brother, nervously. "This is serious, really serious, I tell you!"

"What is serious?" demanded Cyril, coming down the stairway. "Can't it wait? Pete has already sounded the gong twice for dinner."

William made a despairing gesture.

"Well, come," he groaned. "I'll tell you at the table.... It seems I've got a namesake," he resumed in a shaking voice, a few moments later; "Walter Neilson's child."

"And who's Walter Neilson?" asked Bertram.

"A boyhood friend. You wouldn't remember him. This letter is from his child."

"Well, let's hear it. Go ahead. I fancy we can stand the—LETTER; eh, Cyril?"

Cyril frowned. Cyril did not know, perhaps, how often he frowned at Bertram.

The eldest brother wet his lips. His hand shook as he picked up the letter.

"It—it's so absurd," he muttered. Then he cleared his throat and read the letter aloud.

"DEAR UNCLE WILLIAM: Do you mind my calling you that? You see I want SOME one, and there isn't any one now. You are the nearest I've got. Maybe you've forgotten, but I'm named for you. Walter Neilson was my father, you know. My Aunt Ella has just died.

"Would you mind very much if I came to live with you? That is, between times—I'm going to college, of course, and after that I'm going to be—well, I haven't decided that part yet. I think I'll consult you. You may have some preference, you know. You can be thinking it up until I come.

"There! Maybe I ought not to have said that, for perhaps you won't want me to come. I AM noisy, I'll own, but not so I think you'll mind it much unless some of you have 'nerves' or a 'heart.' You see, Miss Letty and Miss Ann—they're Mr. Harding's sisters, and Mr. Harding is our lawyer, and he will write to you. Well, where was I? Oh, I know—on Miss Letty's nerves. And, say, do you know, that is where I do get—on Miss Letty's nerves. I do, truly. You see, Mr. Harding very kindly suggested that I live with them, but, mercy! Miss Letty's nerves won't let you walk except on tiptoe, and Miss Ann's heart won't let you speak except in whispers. All the chairs and tables have worn little sockets in the carpets, and it's a crime to move them. There isn't a window-shade in the house that isn't pulled down EXACTLY to the middle sash, except where the sun shines, and those are pulled way down. Imagine me and Spunk living there! Oh, by the way, you don't mind my bringing Spunk, do you? I hope you don't, for I couldn't live without Spunk, and he couldn't live without me.

"Please let me hear from you very soon. I don't mind if you telegraph; and just 'come' would be all you'd have to say. Then I'd get ready right away and let you know what train to meet me on. And, oh, say—if you'll wear a pink in your buttonhole I will, too. Then we'll know each other. My address is just 'Hampden Falls.'

"Your awfully homesick namesake,

"BILLY HENSHAW NEILSON"

For one long minute there was a blank silence about the Henshaw dinner-table; then the eldest brother, looking anxiously from one man to the other, stammered:

"W-well?"

"Great Scott!" breathed Bertram.

Cyril said nothing, but his lips were white with their tense pressure against each other.

There was another pause, and again William broke it anxiously.

"Boys, this isn't helping me out any! What's to be done?"

"'Done'!" flamed Cyril. "Surely, you aren't thinking for a moment of LETTING that child come here, William!"

Bertram chuckled.

"He WOULD liven things up, Cyril; wouldn't he? Such nice smooth floors you've got upstairs to trundle little tin carts across!"

"Tin nonsense!" retorted Cyril. "Don't be silly, Bertram. That letter wasn't written by a baby. He'd be much more likely to make himself at home with your paint box, or with some of William's junk."

"Oh, I say," expostulated William, "we'll HAVE to keep him out of those things, you know."

Cyril pushed back his chair from the table.

"'We'll have to keep him out'! William, you can't be in earnest! You aren't going to let that boy come here," he cried.

"But what can I do?" faltered the man.

"Do? Say 'no,' of course. As if we wanted a boy to bring up!"

"But I must do something. I—I'm all he's got. He says so."

"Good heavens! Well, send him to boarding-school, then, or to the penitentiary; anywhere but here!"

"Shucks! Let the kid come," laughed Bertram. "Poor little homesick devil! What's the use? I'll take him in. How old is he, anyhow?"

William frowned, and mused aloud slowly.

"Why, I don't know. He must be—er—why, boys, he's no child," broke off the man suddenly. "Walter himself died seventeen or eighteen years ago, not more than a year or two after he was married. That child must be somewhere around eighteen years old!"

"And only think how Cyril WAS worrying about those tin carts," laughed Bertram. "Never mind—eight or eighteen—let him come. If he's that age, he won't bother much."

"And this—er—'Spunk'; do you take him, too? But probably he doesn't bother, either," murmured Cyril, with smooth sarcasm.

"Gorry! I forgot Spunk," acknowledged Bertram. "Say, what in time is Spunk, do you suppose?"

"Dog, maybe," suggested William.

"Well, whatever he is, you will kindly keep Spunk down-stairs," said Cyril with decision. "The boy, I suppose I shall have to endure; but the dog—!"

"Hm-m; well, judging by his name," murmured Bertram, apologetically, "it may be just possible that Spunk won't be easily controlled. But maybe he isn't a dog, anyhow. He—er—sounds something like a parrot to me."

Cyril rose to his feet abruptly. He had eaten almost no dinner.

"Very well," he said coldly. "But please remember that I hold you responsible, Bertram. Whether it's a dog, or a parrot, or—or a monkey, I shall expect you to keep Spunk down-stairs. This adopting into the family an unknown boy seems to me very absurd from beginning to end. But if you and William will have it so, of course I've nothing to say. Fortunately my rooms are at the TOP of the house," he finished, as he turned and left the dining-room.

For a moment there was silence. The brows of the younger man were uplifted quizzically.

"I'm afraid Cyril is bothered," murmured William then, in a troubled voice.

Bertram's face changed. Stern lines came to his boyish mouth.

"He is always bothered—with anything, lately."

The elder man sighed.

"I know, but with his talent—"

"'Talent'! Great Scott!" cut in Bertram. "Half the world has talent of one sort or another; but that doesn't necessarily make them unable to live with any one else! Really, Will, it's becoming serious—about Cyril. He's getting to be, for all the world, like those finicky old maids that that young namesake of yours wrote about. He'll make us whisper and walk on tiptoe yet!"

The other smiled.

"Don't you worry. You aren't in any danger of being kept too quiet, young man."

"No thanks to Cyril, then," retorted Bertram. "Anyhow, that's one reason why I was for taking the kid—to mellow up Cyril. He needs it all right."

"But I had to take him, Bert," argued the elder brother, his face growing anxious again. "But Heaven only knows what I'm going to do with him when I get him. What shall I say to him, anyway? How shall I write? I don't know how to get up a letter of that sort!"

"Why not take him at his word and telegraph? I fancy you won't have to say 'come' but once before you see him. He doesn't seem to be a bashful youth."

"Hm-m; I might do that," acquiesced William, slowly. "But wasn't there somebody—a lawyer—going to write to me?" he finished, consulting the letter by his plate. "Yes," he added, after a moment, "a Mr. Harding. Wonder if he's any relation to Ned Harding. I used to know Ned at Harvard, and seems as if he came from Hampden Falls. We'll soon see, at all events. Maybe I'll hear to-morrow."

"I shouldn't wonder," nodded Bertram, as he rose from the table. "Anyhow, I wouldn't do anything till I did hear."

CHAPTER IV

BILLY SENDS A TELEGRAM

James Harding's letter very promptly followed Billy's, though it was not like Billy's at all. It told something of Billy's property, and mentioned that, according to Mrs. Neilson's will, Billy would not come into control of her fortune until the age of twenty-one years was reached. It dwelt at some length upon the fact of Billy's loneliness in the world, and expressed the hope that her father's friend could find it in his heart to welcome the orphan into his home. It mentioned Ned, and the old college friendship, and it closed by saying that the writer, James Harding, was glad to renew his acquaintance with the good old Henshaw family that he had known long years ago; and that he hoped soon to hear from William Henshaw himself.

It was a good letter—but it was not well written. James Harding's handwriting was not distinguished for its legibility, and his correspondents rejoiced that the most of his letters were dictated to his stenographer. In this case, however, he had elected to use the more personal pen; and it was because of this that William Henshaw, even after reading the letter, was still unaware of his mistake in supposing his namesake, Billy, to be a boy.

In the main the lawyer had referred to Billy by name, or as "the orphan," or as that "poor, lonely child." And whenever the more distinctive feminine "her" or "herself" had occurred, the carelessly formed letters had made them so much like "his" and "himself" that they carried no hint of the truth to a man who had not the slightest reason for thinking himself in the wrong. It was therefore still for the "boy," Billy, that William Henshaw at once set about making a place in the home.

First he telegraphed the single word "Come" to Billy.

"I'll set the poor lad's heart at rest," he said to Bertram. "I shall answer Harding's letter more at length, of course. Naturally he wants to know something about me now before he sends Billy along; but there is no need for the boy to wait before he knows that I'll take him. Of course he won't come yet, till Harding hears from me."

It was just here, however, that William Henshaw met with a surprise, for within twenty-four hours came Billy's answer, and by telegraph.

"I'm coming to-morrow. Train due at five P. M."

"BILLY."

William Henshaw did not know that in Hampden Falls Billy's trunk had been packed for days. Billy was desperate. The house, even with the maid, and with the obliging neighbor and his wife who stayed there nights, was to Billy nothing but a dismal tomb. Lawyer Harding had fallen suddenly ill; she could not even tell him that the blessed telegram "Come" had arrived. Hence Billy, lonely, impulsive, and always used to pleasing herself, had taken matters in hand with a confident grasp, and had determined to wait no longer.

That it was a fearsomely unknown future to which she was so jauntily pledging herself did not trouble the girl in the least. Billy was romantic. To sally gaily forth with a pink in the buttonhole of her coat to find her father's friend who was a "Billy" too, seemed to Billy Neilson not only delightful, but eminently sensible, and an excellent way out of her present homesick loneliness. So she bought the pink and her ticket, and impatiently awaited the time to start.

To the Beacon Street house, Billy's cheerful telegram brought the direst consternation. Even Kate was hastily summoned to the family conclave that immediately resulted.

"There's nothing—simply nothing that I can do," she declared irritably, when she had heard the story. "Surely, you don't expect ME to take the boy!"

"No, no, of course not," sighed William. "But you see, I supposed I'd have time to—to get used to things, and to make arrangements; and this is so—so sudden! I hadn't even answered Harding's letter until to-day; and he hasn't got that—much less replied to it."

"But what could you expect after sending that idiotic telegram?" demanded the lady. "'Come,' indeed!"

"But that's what Billy told me to do."

"What if it was? Just because a foolish eighteen-year-old boy tells you to do something, must you, a supposedly sensible forty-year-old man obey?"

"I think it tickled Will's romantic streak," laughed Bertram. "It seemed so sort of alluring to send that one word 'Come' out into space, and watch what happened."

"Well, he's found out, certainly," observed Cyril, with grim satisfaction.

"Oh, no; it hasn't happened yet," corrected Bertram, cheerfully. "It's just going to happen. William's got to put on the pink first, you know. That's the talisman."

William reddened.

"Bertram, don't be foolish. I sha'n't wear any pink. You must know that."

"How'll you find him, then?"

"Why, he'll have one on; that's enough," settled William.

"Hm-m; maybe. Then he'll have Spunk, too," murmured Bertram, mischievously.

"Spunk!" cried Kate.

"Yes. He wrote that he hoped we wouldn't mind his bringing Spunk with him."

"Who's Spunk?"

"We don't know." Bertram's lips twitched.

"You don't know! What do you mean?"

"Well, Will thinks it's a dog, and I believe Cyril is anticipating a monkey. I myself am backing it for a parrot."

"Boys, what have you done!" groaned Kate, falling back in her chair. "What have you done!"

To William her words were like an electric shock stirring him to instant action. He sprang abruptly to his feet.

"Well, whatever we've done, we've done it," he declared sternly; "and now we must do the rest—and do it well, too. He's the son of my boyhood's dearest friend, and he shall be made welcome. Now to business! Bertram, you said you'd take him in. Did you mean it?"

Bertram sobered instantly, and came erect in his chair. William did not often speak like this; but when he did—

"Yes, Will. He shall have the little bedroom at the end of the hall. I never used the room much, anyhow, and what few duds I have there shall be cleared out to-morrow."

"Good! Now there are some other little details to arrange, then I'll go down-stairs and tell Pete and Dong Ling. And, please to understand, we're going to make this lad welcome—welcome, I say!"

"Yes, sir," said Bertram. Neither Kate nor Cyril spoke.

CHAPTER V

GETTING READY FOR BILLY

The Henshaw household was early astir on the day of Billy's expected arrival, and preparations for the guest's comfort were well under way before breakfast. The center of activity was in the little room at the end of the hall on the second floor; though, as Bertram said, the whole Strata felt the "upheaval."

By breakfast time Bertram with the avowed intention of giving "the little chap half a show," had the room cleared for action; and after that the whole house was called upon for contributions toward the room's adornment. And most generously did most of the house respond. Even Dong Ling slippered up-stairs and presented a weird Chinese banner which he said he was "velly much glad" to give. As to Pete—Pete was in his element. Pete loved boys. Had he not served them nearly all his life? Incidentally it may be mentioned that he did not care for girls.

Only Cyril held himself aloof. But that he was not oblivious of the proceedings below him was evidenced by the somber bass that floated down from his piano strings. Cyril always played according to the mood that was on him; and when Bertram heard this morning the rhythmic beats of mournfulness, he chuckled and said to William:

"That's Chopin's Funeral March. Evidently Cy thinks this is the death knell to all his hopes of future peace and happiness."

"Dear me! I wish Cyril would take some interest," grieved William.

"Oh, he takes interest all right," laughed Bertram, meaningly. "He takes INTEREST!"

"I know, but—Bertram," broke off the elder man, anxiously, from his perch on the stepladder, "would you put the rifle over this window, or the fishing-rod?"

"Why, I don't think it makes much difference, so long as they're somewhere," answered Bertram. "And there are these Indian clubs and the swords to be disposed of, you know."

"Yes; and it's going to look fine; don't you think?" exulted William. "And you know for the wall-space between the windows I'm going to bring down that case of mine, of spiders."

Bertram raised his hands in mock surprise.

"Here—down here! You're going to trust any of those precious treasures of yours down here!"

William frowned.

"Nonsense, Bertram, don't be silly! They'll be safe enough. Besides, they're old, anyhow. I was on spiders years ago—when I was Billy's age, in fact. I thought he'd like them here. You know boys always like such things."

"Oh, 'twasn't Billy I was worrying about," retorted Bertram. "It was you—and the spiders."

"Not much you worry about me—or anything else," replied William, good-humoredly. "There! how does that look?" he finished, as he carefully picked his way down the stepladder.

"Fine!—er—only rather warlike, maybe, with the guns and that riotous confusion of knives and scimitars over the chiffonier. But then, maybe you're intending Billy for a soldier; eh?"

"Do you know? I AM getting interested in that boy," beamed William, with some excitement. "What kind of things do you suppose he does like?"

"There's no telling. Maybe he's a sissy chap, and will howl at your guns and spiders. Perhaps he'll prefer autumn leaves and worsted mottoes for decoration."

"Not much he will," contested the other. "No son of Walter Neilson's could be a sissy. Neilson was the best half-back in ten years at Harvard, and he was always in for everything going that was worth while. 'Autumn leaves and worsted mottoes' indeed! Bah!"

"All right; but there's still a dark horse in the case, you know. We mustn't forget—Spunk."

The elder man stirred uneasily.

"Bert, what do you suppose that creature is? You don't think Cyril can be right, and that it's a—monkey?"

"'You never can tell,'" quoted Bertram, merrily. "Of course there ARE other things. If it were you, now, we'd only have to hunt up the special thing you happened to be collecting at the time, and that would be it: a snake, a lizard, a toad, or maybe a butterfly. You know you were always lugging those things home when you were his age."

"Yes, I know," sighed William. "But I can't think it's anything like that," he finished, as he turned away.

There was very little done in the Beacon Street house that day but to "get ready for Billy." In the kitchen Dong Ling cooked. Everywhere else, except in Cyril's domain, Pete dusted and swept and "puttered" to his heart's content. William did not go to the office at all that day, and Bertram did not touch his brushes. Only Cyril attended to his usual work:

practising for a coming concert, and correcting the proofs of his new book, "Music in Russia."

At ten minutes before five William, anxious-eyed and nervous, found himself at the North Station. Then, and not till then, did he draw a long breath of relief.

"There! I think everything's ready," he sighed to himself. "At last!"

He wore no pink in his buttonhole. There was no need that he should accede to that silly request, he told himself. He had only to look for a youth of perhaps eighteen years, who would be alone, a little frightened, possibly, and who would have a pink in his buttonhole, and probably a dog on a leash.

As he waited, the man was conscious of a curious warmth at his heart. It was his namesake, Walter Neilson's boy, that he had come to meet; a homesick, lonely orphan who had appealed to him—to him, out of all the world. Long years ago in his own arms there had been laid a tiny bundle of flannel holding a precious little red, puckered face. But in a month's time the little face had turned cold and waxen, and the hopes that the white flannel bundle had carried had died with the baby boy;—and that baby would have been a lad grown by this time, if he had lived—a lad not far from the age of this Billy who was coming to-day, reflected the man. And the warmth in his heart deepened and glowed the more as he stood waiting at the gate for Billy to arrive.

The train from Hampden Falls was late. Not until quite fifteen minutes past five did it roll into the train-shed. Then at once its long line of passengers began to sweep toward the iron gate.

William was just inside the gate now, anxiously scanning every face and form that passed. There were many half-grown lads, but there was not one with a pink in his buttonhole until very near the end. Then William saw him—a pleasant-faced, blue-eyed boy in a neat gray suit. With a low cry William started forward; but he saw at once that the gray-clad youth was unmistakably one of a merry family party. He looked to be anything but a lad that was lonely and forlorn.

William hesitated and fell back. This debonair, self-reliant fellow could not be Billy! But as a hasty glance down the line revealed only half a dozen straggling women, and beyond them, no one, William decided that it must be Billy; and taking brave hold of his courage, he hurried after the blue-eyed youth and tapped him on the shoulder.

"Er—aren't you Billy?" he stammered.

The lad stopped and stared. He shook his head slowly.

"No, sir," he said.

"But you must be! Are you sure?"

The boy laughed this time.

"Sorry, sir, but my name is 'Frank'; isn't it, mother?" he added merrily, turning to the lady at his side, who was regarding William very unfavorably through a pair of gold-bowed spectacles.

William did not wait for more. With a stammered apology and a flustered lifting of his hat he backed away.

But where was Billy?

William looked about him in helpless dismay. All around was a wide, empty space. The long aisle to the Hampden Falls train was deserted save for the baggage-men loading the trunks and bags on to their trucks. Nowhere was there any one who seemed forlorn or ill at ease except a pretty girl with a suit-case, and with a covered basket on her arm, who stood just outside the gate, gazing a little nervously about her.

William looked twice at this girl. First, because the splash of color against her brown coat had called his attention to the fact that she was wearing a pink; and secondly because she was very pretty, and her dark eyes carried a peculiarly wistful appeal.

"Too bad Bertram isn't here," thought William. "He'd be sketching that face in no time on his cuff."

The pink had given William almost a pang. He had been so longing to see a pink—though in a different place. He wondered sympathetically if she, too, had come to meet some one who had not appeared. He noticed that she walked away from the gate once or twice, toward the waiting-room, and peered anxiously through the glass doors; but always she came back to the gate as if fearful to be long away from that place. He forgot all about her very soon, for her movements had given him a sudden idea: perhaps Billy was in the waiting-room. How stupid of him not to think of it before! Doubtless they had missed each other in the crowd, and Billy had gone straight to the waiting-room to look for him. And with this thought William hurried away at once, leaving the girl still standing by the gate alone.

He looked everywhere. Systematically he paced up and down between the long rows of seats, looking for a boy with a pink. He even went out upon the street, and gazed anxiously in all directions. It occurred to him after a time that possibly Billy, like himself, had changed his mind at the last moment, and not worn the pink. Perhaps he had forgotten it, or lost it, or even not been able to get it at all. Very bitterly William blamed himself then for disregarding his own part of the suggested plan. If only he had worn the pink himself!—but he had not; and it was useless to repine. In the meantime, where was Billy, he wondered frantically.

CHAPTER VI

THE COMING OF BILLY

After another long search William came back to the train-shed, vaguely hoping that Billy might even then be there. The girl was still standing alone by the gate. There was another train on the track now, and the rush of many feet had swept her a little to one side. She looked frightened now, and almost ready to cry. Still, William noticed that her chin was lifted bravely, and that she was making a stern effort at self-control. He hesitated a moment, then went straight toward her.

"I beg your pardon," he said kindly, lifting his hat, "but I notice that you have been waiting here some time. Perhaps there is something I can do for you."

A rosy color swept to the girl's face. Her eyes lost their frightened appeal, and smiled frankly into his.

"Oh, thank you, sir! There IS something you can do for me, if you will be so kind. You see, I can't leave this place, I'm so afraid he'll come and I'll miss him. But—I think there's some mistake. Could you telephone for me?" Billy Neilson was country-bred, and in Hampden Falls all men served all other men and women, whether they were strangers or not; so to Billy this was not an extraordinary request to make, in the least.

William Henshaw smiled.

"Certainly; I shall be very glad to telephone for you. Just tell me whom you want, and what you want to say."

"Thank you. If you'll call up Mr. William Henshaw, then, of Beacon Street, please, and tell him Billy's come. I'll wait here."

"Oh, then Billy did come!" cried the man in glad surprise, his face alight. "But where is he? Do YOU know Billy?"

"I should say I did," laughed Billy, with the lightness of a long-lost child who has found a friend. "Why, I am Billy, myself!"

To William Henshaw the world swam dizzily, and went suddenly mad. The floor rose, and the roof fell, while cars and people performed impossible acrobatic feats above, below, and around him. Then, from afar off, he heard his own voice stammer:

"You—are—B-Billy!"

"Yes; and I'll wait here, if you'll just tell him, please. He's expecting me, you know, so it's all right, only perhaps he made a mistake in the time. Maybe you know him, anyhow."

With one mighty effort William Henshaw pulled himself sharply together. He even laughed, and tossed his head in a valiant imitation of Billy herself; but his voice shook.

"Know him!—I should say I did!" he cried. "Why, I am William Henshaw, myself."

"You!—Uncle William! Why, where's your pink?"

The man's face was already so red it could not get any redder—but it tried to do so.

"Why, er—I—it—er—if you'll just come into the waiting-room a minute, my dear," he stuttered miserably, "I—I'll explain—about that. I shall have to leave you—for a minute," he plunged on frenziedly, as he led the way to a seat; "A—matter of business that I must attend to. I'll be—right back. Wait here, please!" And he almost pushed the girl into a seat and hurried away.

At a safe distance William Henshaw turned and looked back. His knees were shaking, and his fingers had grown cold at their tips. He could see her plainly, as she bent over the basket in her lap. He could see even the pretty curve of her cheek, and of her slender throat when she lifted her head.

And that was Billy—a GIRL!

People near him at that moment saw a flushed-faced, nervous-appearing man throw up his hands with a despairing gesture, roll his eyes heavenward, and then plunge into the nearest telephone booth.

In due time William Henshaw had his brother Bertram at the other end of the wire.

"Bertram!" he called shakily.

"Hullo, Will; that you? What's the matter? You're late! Didn't he come?"

"Come!" groaned William. "Good Lord! Bertram—Billy's a GIRL!"

"A wh-what?"

"A girl."

"A GIRL!"

"Yes, yes! Don't stand there repeating what I say in that idiotic fashion, Bertram. Do something—do something!"

"'Do something'!" gasped Bertram. "Great Scott, Will! If you want me to do something, don't knock me silly with a blow like that. Now what did you say?"

"I said that Billy is—a—girl. Can't you get that?" demanded William, despairingly.

"Well, by Jove!" breathed Bertram.

"Come, come, think! What shall we do?"

"Why, bring her home, of course."

"Home—home!" chattered William. "Do you think we five men can bring up a distractingly pretty eighteen-year-old girl with curly cheeks and pink hair?"

"With wha-at?"

"No, no. I mean curly hair and pink cheeks. Bertram, do be sensible," begged the man. "This is serious!"

"Serious! I should say it was! Only fancy what Cy will say! A girl! Holy smoke! Tote her along—I want to see her!"

"But I say we can't keep her there with us, Bertram. Don't you see we can't?"

"Then take her to Kate's, or to—to one of those Young Women's Christian Union things."

"No, no, I can't do that. That's impossible. Don't you understand? She's expecting to go home with me—HOME! I'm her Uncle William."

"Lucky Uncle William!"

"Be still, Bertram!"

"Well, doesn't she know your—mistake?—that you thought she was a boy?"

"Heaven forbid!—I hope not," cried the man, fervently. "I 'most let it out once, but I think she didn't notice it. You see, we—we were both surprised."

"Well, I should say!"

"And, Bertram, I can't turn her out—I can't, I tell you. Only fancy my going to her now and saying: 'If you please, Billy, you can't live at my house, after all. I thought you were a boy, you know!' Great Scott! Bert, if she'd once turned those big brown eyes of hers on you as she has on me, you'd see!"

"I'd be delighted, I'm sure," sung a merry voice across the wires. "Sounds real interesting!"

"Bertram, can't you be serious and help me out?"

"But what CAN we do?"

"I don't know. We'll have to think; but for now, get Kate. Telephone her. Tell her to come right straight over, and that she's got to stay all night."

"All night!"

"Of course! Billy's got to have a chaperon; hasn't she? Now hurry. We shall be up right away."

"Kate's got company."

"Never mind—leave 'em. Tell her she's got to leave 'em. And tell Cyril, of course, what to expect. And, look a-here, you two behave, now. None of your nonsense! Now mind. I'm not going to have this child tormented."

"I won't bat an eyelid—on my word, I won't," chuckled Bertram. "But, oh, I say,—Will!"

"Yes."

"What's Spunk?"

"Eh?—oh—Great Scott! I forgot Spunk. I don't know. She's got a basket. He's in that, I suppose. Anyhow, he can't be any more of a bombshell than his mistress was. Now be quick, and none of your fooling, Bertram. Tell them all—Pete and Dong Ling. Don't forget. I wouldn't have Billy find out for the world! Fix it up with Kate. You'll have to fix it up with her; that's all!" And there came the sharp click of the receiver against the hook.

CHAPTER VII

INTRODUCING SPUNK

In the soft April twilight Cyril was playing a dreamy waltz when Bertram knocked, and pushed open the door.

"Say, old chap, you'll have to quit your mooning this time and sit up and take notice."

"What do you mean?" Cyril stopped playing and turned abruptly.

"I mean that Will has gone crazy, and I think the rest of us are going to follow suit."

Cyril shrugged his shoulders and whirled about on the piano stool. In a moment his fingers had slid once more into the dreamy waltz.

"When you get ready to talk sense, I'll listen," he said coldly.

"Oh, very well; if you really want it broken gently, it's this: Will has met Billy, and Billy is a girl. They're due here now 'most any time."

The music stopped with a crash.

"A—GIRL!"

"Yes, a girl. Oh, I've been all through that, and I know how you feel. But as near as I can make out, it's really so. I've had instructions to tell everybody, and I've told. I got Kate on the telephone, and she's coming over. You KNOW what SHE'LL be. Dong Ling is having what I suppose are Chinese hysterics in the kitchen; and Pete is swinging back and forth like a pendulum in the dining-room, moaning 'Good Lord, deliver us!' at every breath. I would suggest that you follow me down-stairs so that we may be decently ready for—whatever comes." And he turned about and stalked out of the room, followed by Cyril, who was too stunned to open his lips.

Kate came first. She was not stunned. She had a great deal to say.

"Really, this is a little the most absurd thing I ever heard of," she fumed. "What in the world does your brother mean?"

That she quite ignored her own relationship to the culprit was not lost on Bertram. He made instant response.

"As near as I can make out," he replied smoothly, "YOUR brother has fallen under the sway of a pair of great dark eyes, two pink cheeks, and an unknown quantity of curly hair, all of which in its entirety is his namesake, is lonesome, and is in need of a home."

"But she can't live—here!"

"Will says she shall."

"But that is utter nonsense," cut in Cyril.

"For once I agree with you, Cyril," laughed Bertram; "but William doesn't."

"But how can she do it?" demanded Kate.

"Don't know," answered Bertram. "He's established a petticoat propriety in you for a few hours, at least. Meanwhile, he's going to think. At least, he says he is, and that we've got to help him."

"Humph!" snapped Kate. "Well, I can prophesy we sha'n't think alike—so you'd notice it!"

"I know that," nodded Bertram; "and I'm with you and Cyril on this. The whole thing is absurd. The idea of thrusting a silly, eighteen-year-old girl here into our lives in this fashion! But you know what Will is when he's really roused. You might as well try to move a nice good-natured mountain by saying 'please,' as to try to stir him under certain circumstances. Most of the time, I'll own, we can twist him around our little fingers. But not now. You'll see. In the first place, she's the daughter of his dead friend, and she DID write a pathetic little letter. It got to the inside of me, anyhow, when I thought she was a boy."

"A boy! Who wouldn't think she was a boy?" interposed Cyril. "'Billy,' indeed! Can you tell me what for any sane man should have named a girl 'Billy'?"

"For William, your brother, evidently," retorted Bertram, dryly. "Anyhow, he did it, and of course our mistake was a very natural one. The dickens of it is now that we've got to keep it from her, so Will says; and how—hush! here they are," he broke off, as there came the sound of wheels stopping before the house.

There followed the click of a key in the lock and the opening of a heavy door; then, full in the glare of the electric lights stood a plainly nervous man, and a girl with startled, appealing eyes.

"My dear," stammered William, "this is my sister, Kate, Mrs. Hartwell; and here are Cyril and Bertram, whom I've told you of. And of course I don't need to say to them that you are Billy."

It was over. William drew a long breath, and gave an agonized look into his brothers' eyes. Then Billy turned from Mrs. Hartwell and held out a cordial hand to each of the men in turn.

"Oh, you don't know how lovely this is—to me," she cried softly. "And to think that you were willing I should come!" The two younger men caught their breath sharply, and tried not to see each other's eyes. "You look so good—all of you; and I don't believe there's one of you that's got nerves or a heart," she laughed.

Bertram rallied his wits to respond to the challenge.

"No heart, Miss Billy? Now isn't that just a bit hard on us—right at first?"

"Not a mite, if you take it the way I mean it," dimpled Billy. "Hearts that are all right just keep on pumping, and you never know they are there. They aren't worth mentioning. It's the other kind—the kind that flutters at the least noise and jumps at the least bang! And I don't believe any of you mind noises and bangs," she finished merrily, as she handed her hat and coat to Mrs. Hartwell, who was waiting to receive them.

Bertram laughed. Cyril scowled, and occupied himself in finding a chair. William had already dropped himself wearily on to the sofa near his sister. Billy still continued to talk.

"Now when Spunk and I get to training—oh, and you haven't seen Spunk!" she interrupted herself suddenly. "Why, the introductions aren't half over. Where is he, Uncle William—the basket?"

"I—I put it in—in the hall," mumbled William, starting to rise.

"No, no; I'll get him," cried Billy, hurrying from the room. She returned in a moment, the green covered basket in her hand. "He's been asleep, I guess. He's slept 'most all the way down, anyhow. He's so used to being toted 'round in this basket that he doesn't mind it a bit. I take him everywhere in it at the Falls."

There was an electric pause. Four pairs of startled, questioning, fearful eyes were on the basket while Billy fumbled at the knot of the string. The next moment, with a triumphant flourish, Billy lifted from the basket and placed on the floor a very small gray kitten with a very large pink bow.

"There, ladies and gentlemen, may I present to you, Spunk."

The tiny creature winked and blinked, and balanced for a moment on sleepy legs; then at the uncontrollable shout that burst from Bertram's throat, he faced the man, humped his tiny back, bristled his diminutive tail to almost unbelievable fluffiness, and spit wrathfully.

"And so that is Spunk!" choked Bertram.

"Yes," said Billy. "This is Spunk."

CHAPTER VIII

THE ROOM—AND BILLY

For the first fifteen minutes after Billy's arrival conversation was a fitful thing made up mostly of a merry monologue on the part of Billy herself, interspersed with somewhat dazed replies from one after another of her auditors as she talked to them in turn. No one thought to ask if she cared to go up to her room, and during the entire fifteen minutes Billy sat on the floor with Spunk in her lap. She was still there when the funereal face of Pete appeared in the doorway. Pete's jaw dropped. It was plain that only the sternest self-control enabled him to announce dinner, with anything like dignity. But he managed to stammer out the words, and then turn loftily away. Bertram, who sat near the door, however, saw him raise his hands in horror as he plunged through the hall and down the stairway.

With a motion to Bertram to lead the way with Billy, William frenziedly gripped his sister's arm, and hissed in her ear for all the world like a villain in melodrama:

"Listen! You'll sleep in Bert's room to-night, and Bert will come up-stairs with me. Get Billy to bed as soon as you can after dinner, and then come back down to us. We've got to plan what's got to be done. Sh-h!" And he dragged his sister downstairs.

In the dining-room there was a slight commotion. Billy stood at her chair with Spunk in her arms. Before her Pete was standing, dumbly staring into her eyes. At last he stammered:

"Ma'am?"

"A chair, please, I said, for Spunk, you know. Spunk always sits at the table right next to me."

It was too much for Bertram. He fled chokingly to the hall. William dropped weakly into his own place. Cyril stared as had Pete; but Mrs. Hartwell spoke.

"You don't mean—that that cat—has a chair—at the table!" she gasped.

15

"Yes; and isn't it cute of him?" beamed Billy, entirely misconstruing the surprise in the lady's voice. "His mother always sat at table with us, and behaved beautifully, too. Of course Spunk is little, and makes mistakes sometimes. But he'll learn. Oh, there's a chair right here," she added, as she spied Bertram's childhood's high-chair, which for long years had stood unused in the corner. "I'll just squeeze it right in here," she finished gleefully, making room for the chair at her side.

When Bertram, a little red of face, but very grave, entered, the dining-room a moment later, he found the family seated with Spunk snugly placed between Billy and a plainly disgusted and dismayed brother, Cyril. The kitten was alert and interested; but he had settled back in his chair, and was looking as absurdly dignified as the flaring pink bow would let him.

"Isn't he a dear?" Billy was saying. But Bertram noticed that there was no reply to this question.

It was a peculiar dinner-party. Only Billy did not feel the strain. Even Spunk was not entirely happy—his efforts to investigate the table and its contents were too frequently curbed by his mistress for his unalloyed satisfaction. William, it is true, made a valiant attempt to cause the conversation to be general; but he failed dismally. Kate was sternly silent, while Cyril was openly repellent. Bertram talked, indeed—but Bertram always talked; and very soon he and Billy had things pretty much to themselves—that is, with occasional interruptions caused by Spunk. Spunk had an inquisitive nose or paw for each new dish placed before his mistress; and Billy spent much time admonishing him. Billy said she was training him; that it was wonderful what training would do, and, of course, Spunk WAS little, now.

Dinner was half over when there was a slight diversion created by Spunk's conclusion to get acquainted with the silent man at his left. Cyril, however, did not respond to Spunk's advances. So very evident, indeed, was the man's aversion that Billy turned in amazement.

"Why, Mr. Cyril, don't you see? Spunk is trying to say 'How do you do'?"

"Very likely; but I'm not fond of cats, Miss Billy."

"You're not fond—of—cats!" repeated the girl, as if she could not have heard aright. "Why not?"

Cyril changed his position.

"Why, just because I—I'm not," he retorted lamely. "Isn't there anything that—that you don't like?"

Billy considered.

"Why, not that I know of," she began, after a moment, "only rainy days and—tripe. And Spunk isn't a bit like those."

Bertram chuckled, and even Cyril smiled—though unwillingly.

"All the same," he reiterated, "I don't like cats."

"Oh, I'm so sorry," lamented Billy; and at the grieved hurt in her dark eyes Bertram came promptly to the rescue.

"Never mind, Miss Billy. Cyril is only ONE of us, and there is all the rest of the Strata besides."

"The—what?"

"The Strata. You don't know, of course, but listen, and I'll tell you." And he launched gaily forth into his favorite story.

Billy was duly amused and interested. She laughed and clapped her hands, and when the story was done she clapped them again.

"Oh, what a funny house! And how perfectly lovely that I'm going to live in it," she cried. Then straight at Mrs. Hartwell she hurled a bombshell. "But where is your stratum?" she demanded. "Mr. Bertram didn't mention a thing about you!"

Cyril said a sharp word under his breath. Bertram choked over a cough. Kate threw into William's eyes a look that was at once angry, accusing, and despairing. Then William spoke.

"Er—she—it isn't anywhere, my dear," he stammered; "or rather, it isn't here. Kate lives up on the Avenue, you see, and is only here for—for a day or two—just now."

"Oh!" murmured Billy. And there was not one in the room at that moment who did not bless Spunk—for Spunk suddenly leaped to the table before him; and in the ensuing confusion his mistress quite forgot to question further concerning Mrs. Hartwell's stratum.

Dinner over, the three men, with their sister and Billy, trailed up-stairs to the drawing-rooms. Billy told them, then, of her life at Hampden Falls. She cried a little at the mention of Aunt Ella; and she portrayed very vividly the lonely life from which she herself had so gladly escaped. She soon had every one laughing, even Cyril, over her stories of the lawyer's home that might have been hers, with its gloom and its hush and its socketed chairs.

As soon as possible, however, Mrs. Hartwell, with a murmured "I know you must be tired, Billy," suggested that the girl go up-stairs to her room. "Come," she added, "I will show you the way."

There was some delay, even then, for Spunk had to be provided with sleeping quarters; and it was not without some hesitation that Billy finally placed the kitten in the reluctant hands of Pete, who had been hastily summoned. Then she turned and followed Mrs. Hartwell up-stairs.

It seemed to the three men in the drawing-room that almost immediately came the piercing shriek, and the excited voice of their sister in expostulation. Without waiting for more they leaped to the stairway and hurried up, two steps at a time.

"For heaven's sake, Kate, what is it?" panted William, who had been outdistanced by his more agile brothers.

Kate was on her feet, her face the picture of distressed amazement. In the low chair by the window Billy sat where she had flung herself, her hands over her face. Her shoulders were shaking, and from her throat came choking little cries.

"I don't know," quavered Kate. "I haven't the least idea. She was all right till she got up-stairs here, and I turned on the lights. Then she gave one shriek and—you know all I know."

William advanced hurriedly.

"Billy, what is the matter? What are you crying for?" he demanded.

Billy dropped her hands then, and they saw her face. She was not crying. She was laughing. She was laughing so she could scarcely speak.

"Oh, you did, you did!" she gurgled. "I thought you did, and now I know!"

"Did what? What do you mean?" William's usually gentle voice was sharp. Even William's nerves were beginning to feel the strain of the last few hours.

"Thought I was a—b-boy!" choked Billy. "You called me 'he' once in the station—I thought you did; but I wasn't sure—not till I saw this room. But now I know—I know!"

And off she went into another hysterical gale of laughter—Billy's nerves, too, were beginning to respond to the excitement of the last few hours.

As to the three men and the woman, they stood silent, helpless, looking into each other's faces with despairing eyes.

In a moment Billy was on her feet, fluttering about the room, touching this thing, looking at that. Nothing escaped her.

"I'm to fish—and shoot—and fence!" she crowed. "And, oh!—look at those knives! U-ugh!... And, my! what are these?" she cried, pouncing on the Indian clubs. "And look at the spiders! Dear, dear, I AM glad they're dead, anyhow," she shuddered with a nervous laugh that was almost a sob.

Something in Billy's voice stirred Mrs. Hartwell to sudden action.

"Come, come, this will never do," she protested authoritatively, motioning her brothers to leave the room. "Billy is quite tired out, and needs rest. She mustn't talk another bit to-night."

"Of c-course not," stammered William. And only too glad of an excuse to withdraw from a very embarrassing situation, the three men called back a faltering good-night, and precipitately fled down-stairs.

CHAPTER IX

A FAMILY CONCLAVE

"Well, William," greeted Kate, grimly, when she came into the drawing-room, after putting her charge to bed, "have you had enough, now?"
"'Enough'! What do you mean?"
Kate raised her eyebrows.
"Why, surely, you're not thinking NOW that you can keep this girl here; are you?"
"I don't know why not."
"William!"
"Well, where shall she go? Will you take her?"
"I? Certainly not," declared Kate, with decision. "I'm sure I see no reason why I should."
"No more do I see why William should, either," cut in Cyril.
"Oh, come, what's the use," interposed Bertram. "Let her stay. She's a nice little thing, I'm sure."
Cyril and Kate turned sharply.
"Bertram!" The cry was a duet of angry amazement. Then Kate added: "It seems that you, too, have come under the sway of dark eyes, pink cheeks, and an unknown quantity of curly hair!"
Bertram laughed.
"Oh, well, she would be nice to—er—paint," he murmured.
"See here, children," demurred William, a little sternly, "all this is wasting time. There is no way out of it. I wouldn't be seen turning that homeless child away now. We must keep her; that's settled. The question is, how shall it be done? We must have some woman friend here to be her companion, of course; but whom shall we get?"
Kate sighed, and looked her dismay. Bertram threw a glance into Cyril's eyes, and made an expressive gesture.
"You see," it seemed to say. "I told you how it would be!"
"Now whom shall we get?" questioned William again. "We must think."
Unattached gentlewomen of suitable age and desirable temper did not prove to be so numerous among the Henshaws' acquaintances, however, as to make the selection of a chaperon very easy. Several were thought of and suggested; but in each case the candidate was found to possess one or more characteristics that made the idea of her presence utterly abhorrent to some one of the brothers. At last William expostulated:
"See here, boys, we aren't any nearer a settlement than we were in the first place. There isn't any woman, of course, who would exactly suit all of us; and so we shall just have to be willing to take some one who doesn't."
"The trouble is," explained Bertram, airily, "we want some one who will be invisible to every one except the world and Billy, and who will be inaudible always."
"I don't know but you are right," sighed William. "But suppose we settle on Aunt Hannah. She seems to be the least objectionable of the lot, and I think she'd come. She's alone in the world, and I believe the comfortable roominess of this house would be very grateful to her after the inconvenience of her stuffy little room over at the Back Bay."
"You bet it would!" murmured Bertram, feelingly; but William did not appear to hear him.

"She's amiable, fairly sensible, and always a lady," he went on; "and to-morrow morning I believe I'll run over and see if she can't come right away."

"And may I ask which—er—stratum she—they—will occupy?" smiled Bertram.

"You may ask, but I'm afraid you won't find out very soon," retorted William, dryly, "if we take as long to decide that matter as we have the rest of it."

"Er—Cyril has the most—UNOCCUPIED space," volunteered Bertram, cheerfully.

"Indeed!" retaliated Cyril. "Suppose you let me speak for myself! Of course, so far as truck is concerned, I'm not in it with you and Will. But as for the USE I put my rooms to—! Besides, I already have Pete there, and would have Dong Ling probably, if he slept here. However, if you want any of my rooms, don't let my petty wants and wishes interfere—"

"No, no," interrupted William, in quick conciliation. "We don't want your rooms, Cyril. Aunt Hannah abhors stairs. Of course I might move, I suppose. My rooms are one flight less; but if I only didn't have so many things!"

"Oh, you men!" shrugged Kate, wearily. "Why don't you ask my opinion sometimes? It seems to me that in this case a woman's wit might be of some help!"

"All right, go ahead!" nodded William.

Kate leaned forward eagerly—Kate loved to "manage."

"Go easy, now," cautioned Bertram, warily. "You know a strata, even one as solid as ours, won't stand too much of an earthquake!"

"It isn't an earthquake at all," sniffed Kate. "It's a very sensible move all around. Here are these two great drawing-rooms, the library, and the little reception-room across the hall, and not one of them is ever used but this. Of course the women wouldn't like to sleep down here, but why don't you, Bertram, take the back drawing-room, the library, and the little reception-room for yours, and leave the whole of the second floor for Billy and Aunt Hannah?"

"Good for you, Kate," cried Bertram, appreciatively. "You've hit it square on the head, and we'll do it. I'll move to-morrow. The light down here is just as good as it is up-stairs—if you let it in!"

"Thank you, Bertram, and you, too, Kate," breathed William, fervently. "Now, if you don't mind, I believe I'll go to bed. I am tired!"

CHAPTER X

AUNT HANNAH

As soon as possible after breakfast William went to see Aunt Hannah.

Hannah Stetson was not really William's aunt, though she had been called Aunt Hannah for years. She was the widow of a distant cousin, and she lived in a snug little room in a Back Bay boarding-house. She was a slender, white-haired woman with kind blue eyes, and a lovable smile. Her cheeks were still faintly pink, and her fine silver-white hair broke into little kinks and curls about her ears. According to Bertram she always made one think of "lavender and old lace."

She welcomed William cordially this morning, though with faint surprise in her eyes.

"Yes, I know I'm an early caller, and an unexpected one," began William, hurriedly. "And I shall have to plunge straight into the matter, too, for there isn't time to preamble. I've taken an eighteen-year-old girl to bring up, Aunt Hannah, and I want you to come down and live with us to chaperon her."

"My grief and conscience, WILLIAM!" gasped the little woman, agitatedly.

"Yes, yes, I know, Aunt Hannah, everything you would say if you could. But please skip the hysterics. We've all had them, and Kate has already used every possible adjective that you could think up. Now it's just this." And he hurriedly gave Mrs. Stetson a full account of the case, and told her plainly what he hoped and expected that she would do for him.

"Why, yes, of course—I'll come," acquiesced the lady, a little breathlessly, "if—if you are sure you're going to—keep her."

"Good! And remember I said 'now,' please—that I wanted you to come right away, to-day. Of course Kate can't stay. Just get in half a dozen women to help you pack, and come."

"Half a dozen women in that little room, William—impossible!"

"Well, I only meant to get enough so you could come right off this morning."

"But I don't need them, William. There are only my clothes and books, and such things. You know it is a FURNISHED room."

"All right, all right, Aunt Hannah. I wanted to make sure you hurried, that's all. You see, I don't want Billy to suspect just how much she's upsetting us. I've asked Kate to take her over to her house for the day, while Bertram is moving down-stairs, and while we're getting you settled. I—I think you'll like it there, Aunt Hannah," added William, anxiously. "Of course Billy's got Spunk, but—" he hesitated, and smiled a little.

"Got what?" faltered the other.

"Spunk. Oh, I don't mean THAT kind," laughed William, in answer to the dismayed expression on his aunt's face. "Spunk is a cat."

"A cat!—but such a name, William! I—I think we'll change that."

"Eh? Oh, you do," murmured William, with a curious smile. "Very well; be that as it may. Anyhow, you're coming, and we shall want you all settled by dinner time," he finished, as he picked up his hat to go.

With Kate, Billy spent the long day very contentedly in Kate's beautiful Commonwealth Avenue home. The two boys, Paul, twelve years old, and Egbert, eight, were a little shy, it is true, and not really of much use as companions; but there was a little Kate, four years old, who proved to be wonderfully entertaining.

Billy was not much used to children, and she found this four-year-old atom of humanity to be a great source of interest and amusement. She even told Mrs. Hartwell at parting that little Kate was almost as nice as Spunk—which remark, oddly enough, did not appear to please Mrs. Hartwell to the extent that Billy thought that it would.

At the Beacon Street house Billy was presented at once to Mrs. Stetson.

"And you are to call me 'Aunt Hannah,' my dear," said the little woman, graciously, "just as the boys do."

"Thank you," dimpled Billy, "and you don't know, Aunt Hannah, how good it seems to me to come into so many relatives, all at once!"

Upon going up-stairs Billy found her room somewhat changed. It was far less warlike, and the case of spiders had been taken away.

"And this will be your stratum, you know," announced Bertram from the stairway, "yours and Aunt Hannah's. You're to have this whole floor. Will and Cyril are above, and I'm down-stairs."

"You are? Why, I thought you—were—here." Billy's face was puzzled.

"Here? Oh, well, I did have—some things here," he retorted airily; "but I took them all away to-day. You see, my stratum is down-stairs, and it doesn't do to mix the layers. By the way, you haven't been up-stairs yet; have you? Come on, and I'll show you—and you, too, Aunt Hannah."

Billy clapped her hands; but Aunt Hannah shook her head.

"I'll leave that for younger feet than mine," she said; adding whimsically: "It's best sometimes that one doesn't try to step too far off one's own level, you know."

"All right," laughed the man. "Come on, Miss Billy."

On the door at the head of the stairs he tapped twice, lightly.

"Well, Pete," called Cyril's voice, none too cordially.

"Pete, indeed!" scoffed Bertram. "You've got company, young man. Open the door. Miss Billy is viewing the Strata."

The bare floor echoed to a quick tread, then the door opened and Cyril faced them with a forced smile on his lips.

"Come in—though I fear there will be little—to see," he said.

Bertram assumed a pompous attitude.

"Ladies and gentlemen; you behold here the lion in his lair."

"Be still, Bertram," ordered Cyril.

"He is a lion, really," confided Bertram, in a lower voice; "but as he prefers it, we'll just call him 'the Musical Man.'"

"I should think I was some sort of music-box that turned with a crank," bristled Cyril.

Bertram grinned.

"A—CRANK, did you say? Well, even I wouldn't have quite dared to say that, you know!"

With an impatient gesture Cyril turned on his heel. Bertram fell once more into his pompous attitude.

"Before you is the Man's workshop," he orated. "At your right you see his instruments of tor—I mean, his instruments: a piano, flute, etc. At your left is the desk with its pens, paper, erasers, ink and postage stamps. I mention these because there are—er—so few things to mention here. Beyond, through the open door, one may catch glimpses of still other rooms; but they hold even less than this one holds. Tradition doth assert, however, that in one is a couch-bed, and in another, two chairs."

Billy listened silently. Her eyes were questioning. She was not quite sure how to take Bertram's words; and the bare rooms and their stern-faced master filled her with a vague pity. But the pause that followed Bertram's nonsense seemed to be waiting for her to fill it.

"Oh, I should like to hear you—play, Mr. Cyril," she stammered. Then, gathering courage. "CAN you play 'The Maiden's Prayer'?"

Bertram gave a cough, a spasmodic cough that sent him, red-faced, out into the hall. From there he called:

"Can't stop for the animals to perform, Miss Billy. It's 'most dinner time, and we've got lots to see yet."

"All right; but—sometime," nodded Billy over her shoulder to Cyril as she turned away. "I just love that 'Maiden's Prayer'!"

"Now this is William's stratum," announced Bertram at the foot of the stairs. "You will perceive that there is no knocking here; William's doors are always open."

"By all means! Come in—come in," called William's cheery voice.

"Oh, my, what a lot of things!" exclaimed Billy. "My—my—what a lot of things! How Spunk will like this room!"

Bertram chuckled; then he made a great display of drawing a long breath.

"In the short time at our disposal," he began loftily, "it will be impossible to point out each particular article and give its history from the beginning; but somewhere you will find four round white stones, which—"

"Er—yes, we know all about those white stones," interrupted William, "and you'll please let me talk about my own things myself!" And he beamed benevolently on the wondering-eyed girl at Bertram's side.

"But there are so many!" breathed Billy.

"All the more chance then," smiled William, "that somewhere among them you'll find something to interest you. Now these Chinese ceramics, and these bronzes—maybe you'd like those," he suggested. And with a resigned sigh and an exaggerated air of submission, Bertram stepped back and gave way to his brother.

"And there are these miniatures, and these Japanese porcelains. Or perhaps you'd like stamps, or theatre programs better," William finished anxiously.

Billy did not reply. She was turning round and round, her eyes wide and amazed. Suddenly she pounced on a beautifully decorated teapot, and held it up in admiring hands.

"Oh, what a pretty teapot! And what a cute little plate it sets in!" she cried.

The collector fairly bubbled over with joy.

"That's a Lowestoft—a real Lowestoft!" he crowed. "Not that hard-paste stuff from the Orient that's CALLED Lowestoft, but the real thing—English, you know. And that's the tray that goes with it, too. Wonderful—how I got them both! You know they 'most always get separated. I paid a cool hundred for them, anyhow."

"A hundred dollars for a teapot!" gasped Billy.

"Yes; and here's a nice little piece of lustre-ware. Pretty—isn't it? And there's a fine bit of black basalt. And—"

"Er—Will," interposed Bertram, meekly.

"Oh, and here's a Castleford," cried William, paying no attention to the interruption. "Marked, too; see? 'D. D. & Co., Castleford.' You know there isn't much of that ware marked. This is a beauty, too, I think. You see this pitted surface—they made that with tiny little points set into the inner side of the mold. The design stands out fine on this. It's one of the best I ever saw. And, oh—"

"Er—William," interposed Bertram again, a little louder this time. "May I just say—"

"And did you notice this 'Old Blue'?" hurried on William, eagerly. "Lid sets down in, you see—that's older than the kind where it sets over the top. Now here's one—"

"William," almost shouted Bertram, "DINNER IS READY! Pete has sounded the gong twice already!"

"Eh? Oh, sure enough—sure enough," acknowledged William, with a regretful glance at his treasures. "Well, we must go, we must go."

"But I haven't seen your stratum at all," demurred Billy to her guide, as they went down the stairway.

"Then there's something left for to-morrow," promised Bertram; "but you must remember, I haven't got any beautiful 'Old Blues' and 'black basalts,' to say nothing of stamps and baggage tags. But I'll make you some tea—some real tea—and that's more than William has done, with all his hundred and one teapots!"

CHAPTER XI

BERTRAM HAS VISITORS

Spunk did not change his name; but that was perhaps the only thing that did not meet with some sort of change during the weeks that immediately followed Billy's arrival. Given a house, five men, and an ironbound routine of life, and it is scarcely necessary to say that the advent of a somewhat fussy elderly woman, an impulsive young girl, and a very-much-alive small cat will make some difference. As to Spunk's name—it was not Mrs. Stetson's fault that even that was left undisturbed.

Mrs. Stetson early became acquainted with Spunk. She was introduced to him, indeed, on the night of her arrival—though fortunately not at table: William had seen to it that Spunk did not appear at dinner, though to accomplish this the man had been obliged to face the amazed and grieved indignation of the kitten's mistress.

"But I don't see how any one CAN object to a nice clean little cat at the table," Billy had remonstrated tearfully.

"I know; but—er—they do, sometimes," William had stammered; "and this is one of the times. Aunt Hannah would never stand for it—never!"

"Oh, but she doesn't know Spunk," Billy had observed then, hopefully. "You just wait until she knows him."

Mrs. Stetson began to "know" Spunk the next day. The immediate source of her knowledge was the discovery that Spunk had found her ball of black knitting yarn, and had delightedly captured it. Not that he was content to let it remain where it was—indeed, no. He rolled it down the stairs, batted it through the hall to the drawing-room, and then proceeded to 'chasse' with it in and out among the legs of various chairs and tables, ending in one grand whirl that wound the yarn round and round his small body, and keeled him over half upon his back. There he blissfully went to sleep.

Billy found him after a gleeful following of the slender woollen trail. Mrs. Stetson was with her—but she was not gleeful.

"Oh, Aunt Hannah, Aunt Hannah," gurgled Billy, "isn't he just too cute for anything?"

Aunt Hannah shook her head.

"I must confess I don't see it," she declared. "My dear, just look at that hopeless snarl!"

"Oh, but it isn't hopeless at all," laughed Billy. "It's like one of those strings they unwind at parties with a present at the end of it. And Spunk is the present," she added, when she had extricated the small gray cat. "And you shall hold him," she finished, graciously entrusting the sleepy kitten to Mrs. Stetson's unwilling arms.

"But, I—it—I can't—Billy! I don't like that name," blurted out the indignant little lady with as much warmth as she ever allowed herself to show. "It must be changed to—to 'Thomas.'"

"Changed? Spunk's name changed?" demanded Billy, in a horrified voice. "Why, Aunt Hannah, it can't be changed; it's HIS, you know." Then she laughed merrily. "'Thomas,' indeed! Why, you old dear!—just suppose I should ask YOU to change your name! Now I like 'Helen Clarabella' lots better than 'Hannah,' but I'm not going to ask you to change that—and I'm going to love you just as well, even if you are 'Hannah'—see if I don't! And you'll love Spunk, too, I'm sure you will. Now watch me find the end of this snarl!" And she danced over to the dumbfounded little lady in the big chair, gave her an affectionate kiss, and then attacked the tangled mass of black with skilful fingers.

"But, I—you—oh, my grief and conscience!" finished the little woman whose name was not Helen Clarabella.—"Oh, my grief and conscience," according to Bertram, was Aunt Hannah's deadliest swear-word.

In Aunt Hannah's black silk lap Spunk stretched luxuriously, and blinked sleepy eyes; then with a long purr of content he curled himself for another nap—still Spunk.

It was some time after luncheon that day that Bertram heard a knock at his studio door. Bertram was busy. His particular pet "Face of a Girl" was to be submitted soon to the judges of a forthcoming Art Exhibition, and it was not yet finished. He was trying to make up now for the many hours lost during the last few days; and even Bertram, at times, did not like interruptions. His model had gone, but he was still working rapidly when the knock came. His tone was not quite cordial when he answered.

"Well?"

"It's I—Spunk and I. May we come in?" called a confident voice.

Bertram said a sharp word behind his teeth—but he opened the door.

"Of course! I was—painting," he announced.

"How lovely! And I'll watch you. Oh, my—what a pretty room!"

"I'm glad you like it."

"Indeed I do; I like it ever so much. I shall stay here lots, I know."

"Oh, you—will!" For once even Bertram's ready tongue failed to find fitting response.

"Yes. Now paint. I want to see you. Aunt Hannah has gone out anyway, and I'm lonesome. I think I'll stay."

"But I can't—that is, I'm not used to spectators."

"Of course you aren't, you poor old lonesomeness! But it isn't going to be that way, any more, you know, now that I've come. I sha'n't let you be lonesome."

"I could swear to that," declared the man, with sudden fervor; and for Billy's peace of mind it was just as well, perhaps, that she did not know the exact source of that fervency.

"Now paint," commanded Billy again.

Because he did not know what else to do, Bertram picked up a brush; but he did not paint. The first stroke of his brush against the canvas was to Spunk a challenge; and Spunk never refused a challenge. With a bound he was on Bertram's knee, gleeful paw outstretched, batting at the end of the brush.

"Tut, tut—no, no—naughty Spunk! Say, but wasn't that cute?" chuckled Billy. "Do it again!"

The artist gave an exasperated sigh.

"My dear girl," he protested, "cruel as it may seem to you, this picture is not a kindergarten game for the edification of small cats. I must politely ask Spunk to desist."

"But he won't!" laughed Billy. "Never mind; we will take it some day when he's asleep. Let's not paint any more, anyhow. I've come to see your rooms." And she sprang blithely to her feet. "Dear, dear, what a lot of faces!—and all girls, too! How funny! Why don't you paint other things? Still, they are rather nice."

"Thank you," accepted Bertram; dryly.

Bertram did not paint any more that afternoon. Billy found much to interest her, and she asked numberless questions. She was greatly excited when she understood the full significance of the omnipresent "Face of a Girl"; and she graciously offered to pose herself for the artist. She spent, indeed, quite half an hour turning her head from side to side, and demanding "Now how's that?—and that?" Tiring at last of this, she suggested Spunk as a substitute, remarking that, after all, cats—pretty cats like Spunk—were even nicer to paint than girls.

She rescued Spunk then from the paint-box where he had been holding high carnival with Bertram's tubes of paint, and demanded if Bertram ever saw a more delightful, more entrancing, more altogether-to-be-desired model. She was so artless, so merry, so frankly charmed with it all that Bertram could not find it in his heart to be angry, notwithstanding his annoyance. But when at four o'clock, she took herself and her cat cheerily up-stairs, he lifted his hands in despair.

"Great Scott!" he groaned. "If this is a sample of what's coming—I'm GOING, that's all!"

CHAPTER XII

CYRIL TAKES HIS TURN

Billy had been a member of the Beacon Street household a week before she repeated her visit to Cyril at the top of the house. This time Bertram was not with her. She went alone. Even Spunk was left behind—Billy remembered her prospective host's aversion to cats.

Billy did not feel that she knew Cyril very well. She had tried several times to chat with him; but she had made so little headway, that she finally came to the conclusion—privately expressed to Bertram—that Mr. Cyril was bashful. Bertram had only laughed. He had laughed the harder because at that moment he could hear Cyril pounding out his angry annoyance on the piano upstairs—Cyril had just escaped from one of Billy's most determined "attempts," and Bertram knew it. Bertram's laugh had puzzled Billy—and it had not quite pleased her. Hence to-day she did not tell him of her plan to go up-stairs and see what she could do herself, alone, to combat this "foolish bashfulness" on the part of Mr. Cyril Henshaw.

In spite of her bravery, Billy waited quite one whole minute at the top of the stairs before she had the courage to knock at Cyril's door.

The door was opened at once.

"Why—Billy!" cried the man in surprise.

"Yes, it's Billy. I—I came up to—to get acquainted," she smiled winningly.

"Why, er—you are very kind. Will you—come in?"

"Thank you; yes. You see, I didn't bring Spunk. I—remembered."

Cyril bowed gravely.

"You are very kind—again," he said.

Billy fidgeted in her chair. To her mind she was not "getting on" at all. She determined on a bold stroke.

"You see, I thought if—if I should come up here, where there wouldn't be so many around, we might get acquainted," she confided; "then I would get to like you just as well as I do the others."

At the odd look that came into the man's face, the girl realized suddenly what she had said. Her cheeks flushed a confused red.

"Oh, dear! That is, I mean—I like you, of course," she floundered miserably; then she broke off with a frank laugh. "There! you see I never could get out of anything. I might as well own right up. I DON'T like you as well as I do Uncle William and Mr. Bertram. So there!"

Cyril laughed. For the first time since he had seen Billy, something that was very like interest came into his eyes.

"Oh, you don't," he retorted. "Now that is—er—very UNkind of you."

Billy shook her head.

"You don't say that as if you meant it," she accused him, her eyes gravely studying his face. "Now I'M in earnest. I really want to like YOU!"

"Thank you. Then perhaps you won't mind telling me why you don't like me," he suggested.

Again Billy flushed.

"Why, I—I just don't; that's all," she faltered. Then she cried aggrievedly: "There, now! you've made me be impolite; and I didn't mean to be, truly."

"Of course not," assented the man; "and it wasn't impolite, because I asked you for the information, you know. I may conclude then," he went on with an odd twinkle in his eyes, "that I am merely classed with tripe and rainy days."

"With—wha-at?"

"Tripe and rainy days. Those are the only things, if I remember rightly, that you don't like."

The girl stared; then she chuckled.

"There! I knew I'd like you better if you'd only SAY something," she beamed. "But let's not talk any more about that. Play to me; won't you? You know you promised me 'The Maiden's Prayer.'"

Cyril stiffened.

"Pardon me, but you must be mistaken," he replied coldly. "I do not play 'The Maiden's Prayer.'"

"Oh, what a shame! And I do so love it! But you play other things; I've heard you a little, and Mr. Bertram says you do—in concerts and things."

"Does he?" murmured Cyril, with a slight lifting of his eyebrows.

"There! Now off you go again all silent and horrid!" chaffed Billy. "What have I said now? Mr. Cyril—do you know what I think? I believe you've got NERVES!" Billy's voice was so tragic that the man could but laugh.

"Perhaps I have, Miss Billy."

"Like Miss Letty's?"

"I'm not acquainted with the lady."

"Gee! wouldn't you two make a pair!" chuckled Billy unexpectedly. "No; but, really, I mean—do you want people to walk on tiptoe and speak in whispers?"

"Sometimes, perhaps."

The girl sprang to her feet—but she sighed.

"Then I'm going. This might be one of the times, you know." She hesitated, then walked to the piano. "My, wouldn't I like to play on that!" she breathed.

Cyril shuddered. Cyril could imagine what Billy would play—and Cyril did not like "rag-time," nor "The Storm."

"Oh, do you play?" he asked constrainedly.

Billy shook her head.

"Not much. Only little bits of things, you know," she said wistfully, as she turned toward the door.

For some minutes after she had gone, Cyril stood where she had left him, his eyes moody and troubled.

"I suppose I might have played—something," he muttered at last; "but—'The Maiden's Prayer'!—good heavens!"

Billy was a little shy with Cyril when he came down to dinner that night. For the next few days, indeed, she held herself very obviously aloof from him. Cyril caught himself wondering once if she were afraid of his "nerves." He did not try to find out, however; he was too emphatically content that of her own accord she seemed to be leaving him in peace. It must have been a week after Billy's visit to the top of the house that Cyril stopped his playing very abruptly one day, and opened his door to go down-stairs. At the first step he started back in amazement.

"Why, Billy!" he ejaculated.

The girl was sitting very near the top of the stairway. At his appearance she got to her feet shamefacedly.

"Why, Billy, what in the world are you doing there?"

"Listening."

"Listening!"

"Yes. Do you mind?"

The man did not answer. He was too surprised to find words at once, and he was trying to recollect what he had been playing.

"You see, listening to music this way isn't like listening to—to talking," hurried on Billy, feverishly. "It isn't sneaking like that; is it?"

"Why—no."

"And you don't mind?"

"Why, surely, I ought not to mind—that," he admitted.

"Then I can keep right on as I have done. Thank you," sighed Billy, in relief.

"Keep right on! Have you been here before?"

"Why, yes, lots of days. And, say, Mr. Cyril, what is that—that thing that's all chords with big bass notes that keep saying something so fine and splendid that it marches on and on, getting bigger and grander, just as if there couldn't anything stop it, until it all ends in one great burst of triumph? Mr. Cyril, what is that?"

"Why, Billy!"—the interest this time in the man's face was not faint—"I wish I might make others catch my meaning as I have evidently made you do it! That's something of my own—that I'm writing, you understand; and I've tried to say—just what you say you heard."

"And I did hear it—I did! Oh, won't you play it, please, with the door open?"

"I can't, Billy. I'm sorry, indeed I am. But I've an appointment, and I'm late now. You shall hear it, though, I promise you, and with the door wide open," continued the man, as, with a murmured apology, he passed the girl and hurried down the stairs.

Billy waited until she heard the outer hall door shut; then very softly she crept through Cyril's open doorway, and crossed the room to the piano.

CHAPTER XIII

A SURPRISE ALL AROUND

May came, and with it warm sunny days. There was a little balcony at the rear of the second floor, and on this Mrs. Stetson and Billy sat many a morning and sewed. There were occupations that Billy liked better than sewing; but she was dutiful, and she was really fond of Aunt Hannah; so she accepted as gracefully as possible that good lady's dictum that a woman who could not sew, and sew well, was no lady at all.

One of the things that Billy liked to do so much better than to sew was to play on Cyril's piano. She was very careful, however, that Mr. Cyril himself did not find this out. Cyril was frequently gone from the house, and almost as frequently Aunt Hannah took naps. At such times it was very easy to slip up-stairs to Cyril's rooms, and once at the piano, Billy forgot everything else.

One day, however, the inevitable happened: Cyril came home unexpectedly. The man heard the piano from William's floor, and with a surprised ejaculation he hurried upstairs two steps at a time. At the door he stopped in amazement.

Billy was at the piano, but she was not playing "rag-time," "The Storm," nor yet "The Maiden's Prayer." There was no music before her, but under her fingers "big bass notes" very much like Cyril's own, were marching on and on to victory. Billy's face was rapturously intent and happy.

"By Jove—Billy!" gasped the man.

Billy leaped to her feet and whirled around guiltily.

"Oh, Mr. Cyril—I'm so sorry!"

"Sorry!—and you play like that!"

"No, no; I'm not sorry I played. It's because you—found me."

Billy's cheeks were a shamed red, but her eyes were defiantly brilliant, and her chin was at a rebellious tilt. "I wasn't doing any—harm; not if you weren't here—with your NERVES!"

The man laughed and came slowly into the room.

"Billy, who taught you to play?"

"No one. I can't play. I can only pick out little bits of things in C."

"But you do play. I just heard you."

Billy shrugged her shoulders.

"That was nothing. It was only what I had heard. I was trying to make it sound like—yours."

"And, by George! you succeeded," muttered Cyril under his breath; then aloud he asked: "Didn't you ever study music?"

Billy's eyes dimmed.

"No. That was the only thing Aunt Ella and I didn't think alike about. She had an old square piano, all tin-panny and thin, you know. I played some on it, and wanted to take lessons; but I didn't want to practise on that. I wanted a new one. That's what she wouldn't do—get me a new piano, or let me do it. She said SHE practised on that piano, and that it was quite good enough for me, especially to learn on. I—I'm afraid I got stuffy. I hated that piano so! But I was almost ready to give in when—when Aunt Ella died."

"And all you play then is just by ear?"

"By—ear? I suppose so—if you mean what I hear. Easy things I can play quick, but—but those chords ARE hard; they skip around so!"

Cyril smiled oddly.

"I should say so," he agreed. "But perhaps there is something else that I play—that you like. Is there?"

"Oh, yes. Now there's that little thing that swings and sways like this," cried Billy, dropping herself on to the piano stool and whisking about. Billy was not afraid now, nor defiant. She was only eager and happy again. In a moment a dreamy waltz fell upon Cyril's ears—a waltz that he often played himself. It was not played correctly, it is true. There were notes, and sometimes whole measures, that were very different from the printed music. But the tune, the rhythm, and the spirit were there.

"And there's this," said Billy; "and this," she went on, sliding into one little strain after another—all of which were recognized by the amazed man at her side.

"Billy," he cried, when she had finished and whirled upon him again, "Billy, would you like to learn to play—really play from notes?"

"Oh, wouldn't I!"

"Then you shall! We'll have a piano tomorrow in your rooms for you to practise on. And—I'll teach you myself."

"Oh, thank you, Mr. Cyril—you don't know how I thank you!" exulted Billy, as she danced from the room to tell Aunt Hannah of this great and good thing that had come into her life. To Billy, this promise of Cyril's to be her teacher was very kind, very delightful; but it was not in the least a thing at which to marvel. To Bertram, however, it most certainly was.

"Well, guess what's happened," he said to William that night, after he had heard the news. "I'll believe anything now—anything: that you'll raffle off your collection of teapots at the next church fair, or that I shall go to Egypt as a 'Cooky' guide. Listen; Cyril is going to give piano lessons to Billy!—CYRIL!"

CHAPTER XIV

AUNT HANNAH SPEAKS HER MIND

Bertram said that the Strata was not a strata any longer. He declared that between them, Billy and Spunk had caused such an upheaval that there was no telling where one stratum left off and another began. What Billy had not attended to, Spunk had, he said.

"You see, it's like this," he explained to an amused friend one day. "Billy is taking piano lessons of Cyril, and she is posing for one of my heads. Naturally, then, such feminine belongings as fancy-work, thread, thimbles, and hairpins are due to show up at any time either in Cyril's apartments or mine—to say nothing of William's; and she's in William's lots—to look for Spunk, if for no other purpose.

"You must know that Spunk likes William's floor the best of the bunch, there are so many delightful things to play with. Not that Spunk stays there—dear me, no. He's a sociable little chap, and his usual course is to pounce on a shelf, knock off some object that tickles his fancy, then lug it in his mouth to—well, anywhere that he happens to feel like going. Cyril has found him up-stairs with a small miniature, battered and chewed almost beyond recognition. And Aunt Hannah nearly had a fit one day when he appeared in her room with an enormous hard-shelled black bug—dead, of course—that he had fished from a case that Pete had left open. As for me, I can swear that the little round white stone he was playing with in my part of the house was one of William's Collection Number One.

"And that isn't all," Bertram continued. "Billy brings her music down to show to me, and lugs my heads all over the rest of the house to show to other folks. And there is always everywhere a knit shawl, for Aunt Hannah is sure to feel a draught, and Billy keeps shawls handy. So there you are! We certainly aren't a strata any longer," he finished.

Billy was, indeed, very much at home in the Beacon Street house—too much so, Aunt Hannah thought. Aunt Hannah was, in fact, seriously disturbed. To William one evening, late in May, she spoke her mind.

"William, what are you going to do with Billy?" she asked abruptly.

"Do with her? What do you mean?" returned William with the contented smile that was so often on his lips these days. "This is Billy's home."

"That's the worst of it," sighed the woman, with a shake of her head.

"The worst of it! Aunt Hannah, what do you mean? Don't you like Billy?"

"Yes, yes, William, of course I like Billy. I love her! Who could help it? That's not what I mean. It's of Billy I'm thinking, and of the rest of you. She can't stay here like this. She must go away, to school, or—or somewhere."

"And she's going in September," replied the man. "She'll go to preparatory school first, and to college, probably."

"Yes, but now—right away. She ought to go—somewhere."

"Why, yes, for the summer, of course. But those plans aren't completed yet. Billy and I were talking of it last evening. You know the boys are always away more or less, but I seldom go until August, and we let Pete and Dong Ling off then for a month and close the house. I told Billy I'd send you and her anywhere she liked for the whole summer, but she says no. She prefers to stay here with me. But I don't quite fancy that idea—through all the hot June and July—so I don't know but I'll get a cottage somewhere near at one of the beaches, where I can run back and forth night and morning. Of course, in that case, we take Pete and Dong Ling with us and close the house right away. I fear Cyril would not fancy it much; but, after all, he and Bertram would be off more or less. They always are in the summer."

"But, William, you haven't yet got my idea at all," demurred Aunt Hannah, with a discouraged shake of her head. "It's away!—away from all this—from you—that I want to get Billy."

"Away! Away from me," cried the man, with an odd intonation of terror, as he started forward in his chair. "Why, Aunt Hannah, what are you talking about?"

"About Billy. This is no place in which to bring up a young girl—a young girl who has not one shred of relationship to excuse it."

"But she is my namesake, and quite alone in the world, Aunt Hannah; quite alone—poor child!"

"My dear William, that is exactly it—she is a child, and yet she is not. That's where the trouble lies."

"What do you mean?"

"William, Billy has been brought up in a little country town with a spinster aunt and a whole good-natured, tolerant village for company. Well, she has accepted you and your entire household, even down to Dong Ling, on the same basis."

"Well, I'm sure I'm glad," asserted the man with genial warmth. "It's good for us to have her here. It's good for the boys. She's already livened Cyril up and toned Bertram down. I may as well confess, Aunt Hannah, that I've been more than a little disturbed about Bertram of late. I don't like that Bob Seaver that he is so fond of; and some other fellows, too, that have been coming here altogether too much during the last year. Bertram says they're only a little 'Bohemian' in their tastes. And to me that's the worst of it, for Bertram himself is quite too much inclined that way."

"Exactly, William. And that only goes to prove what I said before. Bertram is not a spinster aunt, and neither are any of the rest of you. But Billy takes you that way."

"Takes us that way—as spinster aunts!"

"Yes. She makes herself as free in this house as she was in her Aunt Ella's at Hampden Falls. She flies up to Cyril's rooms half a dozen times a day with some question about her lessons; and I don't know how long she'd sit at his feet and adoringly listen to his playing if he didn't sometimes get out of patience and tell her to go and practise herself. She makes nothing of tripping into Bertram's studio at all hours of the day; and he's sketched her head at every conceivable angle—which certainly doesn't tend to make Billy modest or retiring. As to you—you know how much she's in your rooms, spending evening after evening fussing over your collections."

"I know; but we're—we're sorting them and making a catalogue," defended the man, anxiously. "Besides, I—I like to have her there. She doesn't bother me a bit."

"No; I know she doesn't," replied Aunt Hannah, with a curious inflection. "But don't you see, William, that all this isn't going to quite do? Billy's too young—and too old."

"Come, come, Aunt Hannah, is that exactly logical?"

"It's true, at least."

"But, after all, where's the harm? Don't you think that you are just a little bit too—fastidious? Billy's nothing but a care-free child."

"It's the 'free' part that I object to, William. She has taken every one of you into intimate companionship—even Pete and Dong Ling."

"Pete and Dong Ling!"

"Yes." Mrs. Stetson's chin came up, and her nostrils dilated a little. "Billy went to Pete the other day to have him button her shirt-waist up in the back; and yesterday I found her down-stairs in the kitchen instructing Dong Ling how to make chocolate fudge!"

William fell back in his chair.

"Well, well," he muttered, "well, well! She is a child, and no mistake!" He paused, his brows drawn into a troubled frown. "But, Aunt Hannah, what CAN I do? Of course you could talk to her, but—I don't seem to quite like that idea."

"My grief and conscience—no, no! That isn't what is needed at all. It would only serve to make her self-conscious; and that's her one salvation now—that she isn't self-conscious. You see, it's only the fault of her environment and training, after all. It isn't her heart that's wrong."

"Indeed it isn't!"

"It will be different when she is older—when she has seen a little more of the world outside Hampden Falls. She'll go to school, of course, and I think she ought to travel a little. Meanwhile, she mustn't live—just like this, though; certainly not for a time, at least."

"No, no, I'm afraid not," agreed William, perplexedly, rising to his feet. "But we must think—what can be done." His step was even slower than usual as he left the room, and his eyes were troubled.

CHAPTER XV

WHAT BERTRAM CALLS "THE LIMIT"

At half past ten o'clock on the evening following Mrs. Stetson's very plain talk with William, the telephone bell at the Beacon Street house rang sharply. Pete answered it.

"Well?"—Pete never said "hello."

"Hello. Is that you, Pete?" called Billy's voice agitatedly. "Is Uncle William there?"

"No, Miss Billy."

"Oh dear! Well, Mr. Cyril, then?"

"He's out, too, Miss Billy. And Mr. Bertram—they're all out."

"Yes, yes, I know HE'S out," almost sobbed Billy. "Dear, dear, what shall I do! Pete, you'll have to come. There isn't any other way!"

"Yes, Miss; where?" Pete's voice was dubious, but respectful.

"To the Boylston Street subway—on the Common, you know—North-bound side. I'll wait for you—but HURRY! You see, I'm all alone here."

"Alone! Miss Billy—in the subway at this time of night! But, Miss Billy, you shouldn't—you can't—you mustn't—" stuttered the old man in helpless horror.

"Yes, yes, Pete, but never mind; I am here! And I should think if 'twas such a dreadful thing you would hurry FAST to get here, so I wouldn't be alone," appealed Billy.

With an inarticulate cry Pete jerked the receiver on to the hook, and stumbled away from the telephone. Five minutes later he had left the house and was hurrying through the Common to the Boylston Street subway station.

Billy, a long cloak thrown over her white dress, was waiting for him. Her white slippers tapped the platform nervously, and her hair, under the light scarf of lace, fluffed into little broken curls as if it had been blown by the wind.

"Miss Billy, Miss Billy, what can this mean?" gasped the man. "Where is Mrs. Stetson?"

"At Mrs. Hartwell's—you know she is giving a reception to-night. But come, we must hurry! I'm after Mr. Bertram."

"After Mr. Bertram!"

"Yes, yes."

"Alone?—like this?"

"But I'm not alone now; I have you. Don't you see?"

At the blank stupefaction in the man's face, the girl sighed impatiently.

"Dear me! I suppose I'll have to explain; but we're losing time—and we mustn't—we mustn't!" she cried feverishly. "Listen then, quick. It was at Mrs. Hartwell's tonight. I'd been watching Mr. Bertram. He was with that horrid Mr. Seaver, and I never liked him, never! I overheard something they said, about some place they were going to, and I didn't like what Mr. Seaver said. I tried to speak to Mr. Bertram, but I didn't get a chance; and the next thing I knew he'd gone with that Seaver man! I saw them just in time to snatch my cloak and follow them."

"FOLLOW them! MISS BILLY!"

"I had to, Pete; don't you see? There was no one else. Mr. Cyril and Uncle William had gone—home, I supposed. I sent back word by the maid to Aunt Hannah that I'd gone ahead; you know the carriage was ordered for eleven; but I'm afraid she won't have sense to tell Aunt Hannah, she looked so dazed and frightened when I told her. But I COULDN'T wait to say more. Well, I hurried out and caught up with Mr. Bertram just as they were crossing Arlington Street to the Garden. I'd heard them say they were going to walk, so I knew I could do it. But, Pete, after I got there, I didn't dare to speak—I didn't DARE to! So I just—followed. They went straight through the Garden and across the Common to Tremont Street, and on and on until they stopped and went down some stairs, all marble and lights and mirrors. 'Twas a restaurant, I think. I saw just where it was, then I flew back here to telephone for Uncle William. I knew HE could do something. But—well, you know the rest. I had to take you. Now come, quick; I'll show you."

"But, Miss Billy, I can't! You mustn't; it's impossible," chattered old Pete. "Come, let me take ye home, Miss Billy, do!"

"Home—and leave Mr. Bertram with that Seaver man? No, no!"

"What CAN ye do?"

"Do? I can get him to come home with me, of course."

The old man made a despairing gesture and looked about him as if for help. He saw then the curious, questioning eyes on all sides; and with a quick change of manner, he touched Miss Billy's arm.

"Yes; we'll go. Come," he apparently agreed. But once outside on the broad expanse before the Subway entrance he stopped again. "Miss Billy, please come home," he implored. "Ye don't know—ye can't know what yer a-doin'!"

The girl tossed her head. She was angry now.

"Pete, if you will not go with me I shall go alone. I am not afraid."

"But the hour—the place—you, a young girl! Miss Billy!" remonstrated the old man agitatedly.

"It isn't so very late. I've been out lots of times later than this at home. And as for the place, it's all light and bright, and lots of people were going in—ladies and gentlemen. Nothing could hurt me, Pete, and I shall go; but I'd rather you were with me. Why, Pete, we mustn't leave him. He isn't—he isn't HIMSELF, Pete. He—he's been DRINKING!" Billy's voice broke, and her face flushed scarlet. She was almost crying. "Come, you won't refuse now!" she finished, resolutely turning toward the street.

And because old Pete could not pick her up bodily and carry her home, he followed close at her heels. At the head of the marble stairs "all lights and mirrors," however, he made one last plea.

"Miss Billy, once more I beg of ye, won't ye come home? Ye don't know what yer a-doin', Miss Billy, ye don't—ye don't!"

"I can't go home," persisted Billy. "I must get Mr. Bertram away from that man. Now come; we'll just stand at the door and look in until we see him. Then I'll go straight to him and speak to him." And with that she turned and ran down the steps.

Billy blinked a little at the lights which, reflected in the great plate-glass mirrors, were a million dazzling points that found themselves again repeated in the sparkling crystal and glittering silver on the flower-decked tables. All about her Billy saw flushed-faced men, and bright-eyed women, laughing, chatting, and clinking together their slender-stemmed wine glasses. But nowhere, as she looked about her, could Billy descry the man she sought.

The head waiter came forward with uplifted hand, but Billy did not see him. A girl at her left laughed disagreeably, and several men stared with boldly admiring eyes; but to them, too, Billy paid no heed. Then, halfway across the room she spied Bertram and Seaver sitting together at a small table alone.

Simultaneously her own and Bertram's eyes met.

With a sharp word under his breath Bertram sprang to his feet. His befogged brain had cleared suddenly under the shock of Billy's presence.

"Billy, for Heaven's sake what are you doing here?" he demanded in a low voice, as he reached her side.

"I came for you. I want you to go home with me, please, Mr. Bertram," whispered Billy, pleadingly.

The man had not waited for an answer to his question. With a deft touch he had turned Billy toward the door; and even as she finished her sentence she found herself in the marble hallway confronting Pete, pallid-faced, and shaking.

"And you, too, Pete! Great Scott! what does this mean?" he exploded angrily.

Pete could only shake his head and glance imploringly at Billy. His dry lips and tongue refused to articulate even one word.

"We came—for—you," choked Billy. "You see, I don't like that Seaver man."

"Well, by Jove! this is the limit!" breathed Bertram.

CHAPTER XVI

KATE TAKES A HAND

Undeniably Billy was in disgrace, and none knew it better than Billy herself. The whole family had contributed to this knowledge. Aunt Hannah was inexpressibly shocked; she had not breath even to ejaculate "My grief and conscience!" Kate was disgusted; Cyril was coldly reserved; Bertram was frankly angry; even William was vexed, and showed it. Spunk, too, as if in league with the rest, took this opportunity to display one of his occasional fits of independence; and when Billy, longing for some sort of comfort, called him to her, he settled back on his tiny haunches and imperturbably winked and blinked his indifference.

Nearly all the family had had something to say to Billy on the matter, with not entirely satisfactory results, when Kate determined to see what she could do. She chose a time when she could have the girl quite to herself with small likelihood of interruption.

"But, Billy, how could you do such an absurd thing?" she demanded. "The idea of leaving my house alone, at half-past ten at night, to follow a couple of men through the streets of Boston, and then with my brothers' butler make a scene like that in a—a public dining-room!"

Billy sighed in a discouraged way.

"Aunt Kate, can't I make you and the rest of them understand that I didn't start out to do all that? I meant just to speak to Mr. Bertram, and get him away from that man."

"But, my dear child, even that was bad enough!"

Billy lifted her chin.

"You don't seem to think, Aunt Kate; Mr. Bertram was—was not sober."

"All the more reason then why you should NOT have done what you did!"

"Why, Aunt Kate, you wouldn't leave him alone in that condition with that man!"

It was Mrs. Hartwell's turn to sigh.

"But, Billy," she contested, wearily, "can't you understand that it wasn't YOUR place to interfere—you, a young girl?"

"I'm sure I don't see what difference that makes. I was the only one that could do it! Besides, afterward, I did try to get some one else, Uncle William and Mr. Cyril. But when I found I couldn't get them, I just had to do it alone—that is, with Pete."

"Pete!" scoffed Mrs. Hartwell. "Pete, indeed!"

Billy's head came up with a jerk. Billy was very angry now.

"Aunt Kate, it seems I've done a very terrible thing, but I'm sure I don't see it that way. I wasn't afraid, and I wasn't in the least bit of danger anywhere. I knew my way perfectly, and I did NOT make any 'scene' in that restaurant. I just asked Mr. Bertram to come home with me. One would think you WANTED Mr. Bertram to go off with that man and—and drink too much. But Uncle William hasn't liked him before, not one bit! I've heard him talk about him—that Mr. Seaver."

Mrs. Hartwell raised both her hands, palms outward.

"Billy, it is useless to talk with you. You are quite impossible. It is even worse than I expected!" she cried, with wrathful impatience.

"Worse than you—expected? What do you mean, please?"

"Worse than I thought it would be—before you came. The idea of those five men taking a girl to bring up!"

Billy sat very still. She was even holding her breath, though Mrs. Hartwell did not know that.

"You mean—that they did not—want me?" she asked quietly, so quietly that Mrs. Hartwell did not realize the sudden tension behind the words. For that matter, Mrs. Hartwell was too angry now to realize anything outside of herself.

"Want you! Billy, it is high time that you understand just how things are, and have been, at the house; then perhaps you will conduct yourself with an eye a little more to other people's comfort. Can you imagine three young men like my brothers WANTING to take a strange young woman into their home to upset everything?"

"To—upset—everything!" echoed Billy, faintly. "And have I done—that?"

"Of course you have! How could you help it? To begin with, they thought you were a boy, and that was bad enough; but William was so anxious to do right by his dead friend that he insisted upon taking you, much against the will of all the rest of us. Oh, I know this isn't pleasant for you to hear," admitted Mrs. Hartwell, in response to the dismayed expression in Billy's eyes; "but I think it's high time you realize something of what those men have sacrificed for you. Now, to resume. When they found you were a girl, what did they do? Did they turn you over to some school or such place, as they should have done? Certainly not! William would not hear of it. He turned Bertram out of his rooms, put you into them, and established Aunt Hannah as chaperon and me as substitute until she arrived. But because, through it all, he smiled blandly, you have been blind to the whole thing.

"And what is the result? His entire household routine is shattered to atoms. You have accepted the whole house as if it were your own. You take Cyril's time to teach you music, and Bertram's to teach you painting, without a thought of what it means to them. There! I suppose I ought not to have said all this, but I couldn't help it, Billy. And surely now, NOW you appreciate a little more what your coming to this house has meant, and what my brothers have done for you."

"I do, certainly," said Billy, still in that voice that was so oddly smooth and emotionless.

"And you'll try to be more tractable, less headstrong, less assertive of your presence?"

The girl sprang to her feet now.

"More tractable! Less assertive of my presence!" she cried. "Mrs. Hartwell, do you mean to say you think I'd STAY after what you've told me?"

"Stay? Why, of course you'll stay! Don't be silly, child. I didn't tell you this to make you go. I only wanted you to understand how things were—and are."

"And I do understand—and I'm going."

Mrs. Hartwell frowned. Her face changed color.

"Come, come, Billy, this is nonsense. William wants you here. He would never forgive me if anything I said should send you away. You must not be angry with, him."

Billy turned now like an enraged little tigress.

"Angry with him! Why, I love him—I love them all! They are the dearest men ever, and they've been so good to me!" The girl's voice broke a little, then went on with a more determined ring. "Do you think I'd have them know why I'm going?—that I'd hurt them like that? Never!"

"But, Billy, what are you going to do?"

"I don't know. I've got to plan it out. I only know now that I'm going, sure!" And with a choking little cry Billy ran from the room.

In her own chamber a minute later the tears fell unrestrained.

"It's home—all the home there is—anywhere!" she sobbed. "But it's got to go—it's got to go!"

CHAPTER XVII

A PINK-RIBBON TRAIL

Mrs. Stetson wore an air of unmistakable relief as she stepped into William's sitting-room. Even her knock at the half-open door had sounded almost triumphant.

"William, it does seem as if Fate itself had intervened to help us out," she began delightedly. "Billy, of her own accord, came to me this morning, and said that she wanted to go away with me for a little trip. So you see that will make it easier for us."

"Good! That is fortunate, indeed," cried William; but his voice did not carry quite the joy that his words expressed. "I have been disturbed ever since your remarks the other day," he continued wearily; "and of course her extraordinary escapade the next evening did not help matters any. It is better, I know, that she shouldn't be here—for a time. Though I shall miss her terribly. But, tell me, what is it—what does she want to do?"

"She says she guesses she is homesick for Hampden Falls; that she'd like to go back there for a few weeks this summer if I'll go with her. The—the dear child seems suddenly to have taken a great fancy to me," explained Aunt Hannah, unsteadily. "I never saw her so affectionate."

"She is a dear girl—a very dear girl; and she has a warm heart." William cleared his throat sonorously, but even that did not clear his voice. "It was her heart that led her wrong the other night," he declared. "Hers was a brave and fearless act—but a very unwise one. Much as I deplore Bertram's intimacy with Seaver, I should hesitate to take the course marked out by Billy. Bertram is not a child. But tell me more of this trip of yours. How did Billy happen to suggest it?"

"I don't know. I noticed yesterday that she seemed strangely silent—unhappy, in fact. She sat alone in her room the greater part of the day, and I could not get her out of it. But this morning she came to my door as bright as the sun itself and made me the proposition I told you of. She says her aunt's house is closed, awaiting its sale; but that she would like to open it for awhile this summer, if I'd like to go. Naturally, you can understand that I'd very quickly fall in with a plan like that—one which promised so easily to settle our difficulties."

"Yes, of course, of course," muttered William. "It is very fine, very fine indeed," he concluded. And again his voice failed quite to match his words in enthusiasm.

"Then I'll go and begin to see to my things," murmured Mrs. Stetson, rising to her feet. "Billy seems anxious to get away."

Billy did, indeed, seem anxious to get away. She announced her intended departure at once to the family. She called it a visit to her old home, and she seemed very glad in her preparations. If there was anything forced in this gayety, no one noticed it, or at least, no one spoke of it. The family saw very little of Billy, indeed, these days. She said that she was busy; that she had packing to do. She stopped taking lessons of Cyril, and visited Bertram's studio only once during the whole three days before she went away, and then merely to get some things that belonged to her. On the fourth day, almost before the family realized what was happening, she was gone; and with her had gone Mrs. Stetson and Spunk.

The family said they liked it—the quiet, the freedom. They said they liked to be alone—all but William. He said nothing.

And yet—

When Bertram went to his studio that morning he did not pick up his brushes until he had sat for long minutes before the sketch of a red-cheeked, curly-headed young girl whose eyes held a peculiarly wistful appeal; and Cyril, at his piano up-stairs, sat with idle fingers until they finally drifted into a simple little melody—the last thing Billy had been learning.

It was Pete who brought in the kitten; and Billy had been gone a whole week then.

"The poor little beast was cryin' at the alleyway door, sir," he explained. "I—I made so bold as to bring him in."

"Of course," said William. "Did you feed it?"

"Yes, sir; Ling did."

There was a pause, then Pete spoke, diffidently.

"I thought, sir, if ye didn't mind, I'd keep it. I'll try to see that it stays down-stairs, sir, out of yer way."

"That's all right, Pete; keep it, by all means, by all means," approved William.

"Thank ye, sir. Ye see, it's a stray. It hasn't got any home. And, did ye notice, sir? it looks like Spunk."

"Yes, I noticed," said William, stirring with sudden restlessness. "I noticed."

"Yes, sir," said Pete. And he turned and carried the small gray cat away.

The new kitten did not stay down-stairs. Pete tried, it is true, to keep his promise to watch it; but after he had seen the little animal carried surreptitiously up-stairs in Mr. William's arms, he relaxed his vigilance. Some days later the kitten appeared with a huge pink bow behind its ears, somewhat awkwardly tied, if it must be confessed. Where it came from, or who put it there was not known—until one day the kitten was found in the hall delightedly chewing at the end of what had been a roll of pink ribbon. Up the stairs led a trail of pink ribbon and curling white paper—and the end of the trail was in William's room.

CHAPTER XVIII

BILLY WRITES ANOTHER LETTER

By the middle of June only William and the gray kitten were left with Pete and Dong Ling in the Beacon Street house. Cyril had sailed for England, and Bertram had gone on a sketching trip with a friend.

To William the house this summer was unusually lonely; indeed, he found the silent, deserted rooms almost unbearable. Even the presence of the little gray cat served only to accentuate the loneliness—it reminded him of Billy.

William missed Billy. He owned that now even to Pete. He said that he would be glad when she came back. To himself he said that he wished he had not fallen in quite so readily with Aunt Hannah's notion of getting the child away. It was all nonsense, he declared. All she needed was a little curbing and directing, both of which could just as well have been done there at home. But she had gone, and it could not be helped now. The only thing left for him to do was to see that it did not occur again. When Billy came back she should stay, except for necessary absences for school, of course. All this William settled in his own mind quite to his own satisfaction, entirely forgetting, strange to say, that it had been Billy's own suggestion that she go away.

Very promptly William wrote to Billy. He told her how he missed her, and said that he had stopped trying to sort and catalogue his collections until she should be there to help him. He told her, too, after a time, of the gray kitten, "Spunkie," that looked so much like Spunk. In reply he received plump white envelopes directed in the round, schoolboy hand that he remembered so well. In the envelopes were letters, cheery and entertaining, like Billy herself. They thanked him for all his many kindnesses, and they told him something of what Billy was doing. They showed unbounded interest in the new kitten, and in all else that William wrote about; but they hinted very plainly that he had better not wait for her to help him out on the catalogue, for it would soon be autumn, and she would be in school.

William frowned at this, and shook his head; yet he knew that it was true.

In August William closed the Beacon street house and went to the Rangeley Lakes on a camping trip. He told himself that he would not go had it not been for a promise given to an old college friend months before. True, he had been anticipating this trip all winter; but it occurred to him now that it would be much more interesting to go to Hampden Falls and see Billy. He had been to the Rangeley Lakes, and he had not been to Hampden Falls; besides, there would be Ned Harding and those queer old maids with their shaded house and socketed chairs to see. In short, to William, at the moment, there seemed no place quite so absorbingly interesting as was Hampden Falls. But he went to the Rangeley Lakes.

In September Cyril came back from Europe, and Bertram from the Adirondacks where he had been spending the month of August. William already had arrived, and with Pete and Dong Ling had opened the house.

"Where's Billy? Isn't Billy here?" demanded Bertram.

"No. She isn't back yet," replied William.

"You don't mean to say she's stayed up there all summer!" exclaimed Cyril.

"Why, yes, I—I suppose so," hesitated William. "You see, I haven't heard but once for a month. I've been down in Maine, you know."

William wrote to Billy that night.

"My dear:—" he said in part. "I hope you'll come home right away. We want to see SOMETHING of you before you go away again, and you know the schools will be opening soon.

"By the way, it has just occurred to me as I write that perhaps, after all, you won't have to go quite away. There are plenty of good schools for young ladies right in and near Boston, which I am sure you could attend, and still live at home. Suppose you come back then as soon as you can, and we'll talk it up. And that reminds me, I wonder how Spunk will get along with Spunkie. Spunkie has been boarding out all August at a cat home, but he seems glad to get back to us. I am anxious to see the two little chaps together, just to find out how much alike they really do look."

Very promptly came Billy's answer; but William's face, after he had read the letter, was almost as blank as it had been on that April day when Billy's first letter came—though this time for a far different reason.

"Why, boys, she—isn't—coming," he announced in dismay.

"Isn't coming!" ejaculated two astonished Voices.

"No."

"Not—at—ALL?"

"Why, of course, later," retorted William, with unwonted sharpness. "But not now. This is what she says." And he read aloud:

"DEAR UNCLE WILLIAM:—You poor dear man! Did you think I'd really let you spend your time and your thought over hunting up a school for me, after all the rest you have done for me? Not a bit of it! Why, Aunt Hannah and I have been buried under school catalogues all summer, and I have studied them all until I know just which has turkey dinners on Sundays, and which ice cream at least twice a week. And it's all settled, too, long ago. I'm going to a girls' school up the Hudson a little way—a lovely place, I'm sure, from the pictures of it.

"Oh, and another thing; I shall go right from here. Two girls at Hampden Falls are going, and I shall go with them. Isn't that a fine chance for me? You see it would never do, anyway, for me to go alone—me, a 'Billy'—unless I sent a special courier ahead to announce that 'Billy' was a girl.

"Aunt Hannah has decided to stay here this winter in the old house. She likes it ever so much, and I don't think I shall sell the place just yet, anyway. She will go back, of course, to Boston (after I've gone) to get some things at the house that she'll want, and also to do some shopping. But she'll let you know when she'll be there.

"I'll write more later, but just now I'm in a terrible rush. I only write this note to set your poor heart at rest about having to hunt up a school for me.

"With love to all,

"BILLY."

As had happened once before after a letter from Billy had been read, there was a long pause.

"Well, by Jove!" breathed Bertram.

"It's very sensible, I'm sure," declared Cyril. "Still, I must confess, I would have liked to pick out her piano teacher for her."

William said nothing—perhaps because he was reading Billy's letter again.

At eight o'clock that night Bertram tapped on Cyril's door.

"What's the trouble?" demanded Cyril in answer to the look on the other's face.

Bertram lifted his eyebrows oddly.

"I'm not sure whether you'll call it 'trouble' or not," he replied; "but I think it's safe to say that Billy is gone—for good."

"For good! What do you mean?—that she's not coming back—ever?"

"Exactly that."

"Nonsense! What's put that notion into your head?"

"Billy's letter first; after that, Pete."

"Pete!"

"Yes. He came to me a few minutes ago, looking as if he had seen a ghost. It seems he swept Billy's rooms this morning and put them in order against her coming; and tonight William told him that she wouldn't be here at present. Pete came straight to me. He said he didn't dare tell Mr. William, but he'd got to tell some one: there wasn't one single thing of Miss Billy's left in her rooms nor anywhere else in the house—not so much as a handkerchief or a hairpin."

"Hm-m; that does look—suspicious," murmured Cyril. "What's up, do you think?"

"Don't know; but something, sure. Still, of course we may be wrong. We won't say anything to Will about it, anyhow. Poor old chap, 'twould worry him, specially if he thought Billy's feelings had been hurt."

"Hurt?—nonsense! Why, we did everything for her—everything!"

"Yes, I know—and she tried to do EVERYTHING for us, too," retorted Bertram, quizzically, as he turned away.

CHAPTER XIX

SEEING BILLY OFF

Early in October Mrs. Stetson arrived at the Beacon Street house, but she did not stay long.

"I've come for just a few things I want, and to do some shopping," she explained.

"But Aunt Hannah," remonstrated William, "what is the meaning of this? Why are you staying up there at Hampden Falls?"

"I like it there, William; and why shouldn't I stay? Surely there's no need for me to be here now, with Billy away!"

"But Billy's coming back!"

"Of course she's coming back," laughed Aunt Hannah, "but not this winter, certainly. Why, William, what's the matter? I'm sure, I think it's a beautiful arrangement. Why, don't you remember? It's just what we said we wanted—to keep Billy away for awhile. And the best part of it is, it's her own idea from the start."

"Yes, I know, I know," frowned William: "but I'm not sure, after all, that that idea of ours wasn't a mistake,—a mistake that she needed to get away."

"Never! We were just right about it," declared Aunt Hannah, with conviction.

"And is Billy—happy?"

"She seems to be."

"Hm-m; well, THAT'S good," said William, as he turned to go up to his room. But as he climbed the stairs he sighed; and to hear him, one would have thought it anything but good to him—that Billy was happy.

One by one the weeks passed. Mrs. Stetson had long since gone back to Hampden Falls; and Bertram said that the Strata was beginning to look natural again. There remained now, indeed, only Spunkie, the small gray cat, to remind any one of the days that were gone—though, to be sure, there were Billy's letters, if they might be called a reminder.

Billy did not write often. She said that she was "too busy to breathe." Such letters as did come from her were addressed to William, though they soon came to be claimed by the entire family. Bertram and Cyril frankly demanded that William read them aloud; and even Pete always contrived to have some dusting or "puttering" within earshot—a subterfuge quite well understood, but never reproved by any of the brothers.

When the Christmas vacation drew near, William wrote that he hoped Billy and Aunt Hannah would spend it with them; but Billy answered that although she appreciated their kindness and thanked them for it, yet she must decline their invitation, as she had already invited several of the girls to go home with her to Hampden Falls for a country Christmas.

For the Easter vacation William was even more insistent—but so was Billy: she had already accepted an invitation to go home with one of the girls, and she did not think it would be at all polite to change her plans now.

William fretted not a little. Even Cyril and Bertram said that it was "too bad"; that they themselves would like to see the girl—so they would!

It was in the spring, at the close of school, however, that the heaviest blow fell: Billy was not coming to Boston even then. She wrote that she and Aunt Hannah were going to "run across the water for a little trip through the British Isles"; and that their passage was already engaged.

"And so you see," she explained, "I shall not have a minute to spare. There'll be only time to skip home for Aunt Hannah, and to pack the trunks before it'll be time to start."

Bertram looked at Cyril significantly when this letter was read aloud; and afterward he muttered in Cyril's ear:

"You see! It's Hampden Falls she calls 'home' now—not the Strata."

"Yes, I see," frowned Cyril. "It does look suspicious."

Two days before the date of Billy's expected sailing, William announced at the breakfast table that he was going away on business; might be gone until the end of the week.

"You don't say," commented Bertram. "I'M going to-morrow, but I'm coming back in a couple of days."

"Hm-m;" murmured William, abstractedly. "Oh, well, I may be back before the end of the week."

Only one meal did Cyril eat alone after his brothers had gone; then he told Pete that he had decided to take the night boat for New York. There was a little matter that called him there, he said, and he believed the trip by water would be a pleasure, the night was so fine and warm.

In New York Cyril had little trouble in finding Billy, as he knew the steamship she was to take.

"I thought as long as I was in New York to-day I'd just come and say good-by to you and Aunt Hannah," he informed her, with an evident aim toward making his presence appear to be casual.

"That was good of you!" exclaimed Billy. "And how are Uncle William and Mr. Bertram?"

"Very well, I fancy, though they weren't there when I left," replied the man.

"Oh!—gone away?"

"Yes. A little matter of business they said; but—well, by Jove!" he broke off, his gaze on a familiar figure hurrying at that moment toward them. "There's William now!"

William, with no eyes but for Billy, came rapidly forward.

"Well, well, Billy! I thought as long as I happened to be in New York to-day I'd just run down to the boat and see you and Aunt Hannah off, and wish—CYRIL! Where did YOU come from?"

Billy laughed.

"He just happened to be in town, too, Uncle William, like you," she explained. "And I'm sure I think it's lovely of you to be so kind. Aunt Hannah'll be up right away. She went down to the stateroom to—" This time it was Billy who stopped abruptly. The two men facing her could not see what she saw, and not until their brother Bertram's merry greeting fell on their ears did they understand her sudden silence.

"And is this the way you meant to run away from us, young lady?" cried Bertram. "Not so fast! You see, I happened to be in New York this morning, and so I—" Something in Billy's face sent a pause to his words just as his eyes spied the two men at the girl's side. For a moment he stared dumbly; then he gave a merry gesture of defeat.

"It's all up! I might as well confess. I'VE been planning this thing for three weeks, Billy, ever since your letter came, in fact. As for my two fellow-sinners here, I'll wager they weren't two days behind me in their planning. So now, own up, boys!"

William and Cyril, however, did not have to "own up." Mrs. Stetson appeared at the moment and created, for them, a very welcome diversion.

Long minutes later, when the good-byes had become nothing but a flutter of white handkerchiefs from deck to shore, and shore to deck, William drew a long sigh.

"That's a nice little girl, boys, a nice little girl!" he exclaimed. "I declare! I didn't suppose I'd mind so much her going so far away."

CHAPTER XX

BILLY, THE MYTH

To all appearances it came about very naturally that Billy did not return to America for some time. During the summer she wrote occasionally to William, and gave glowing accounts of their travels. Then in September came the letter telling him that they had concluded to stay through the winter in Paris. Billy wrote that she had decided not to go to college. She would take up some studies there in Paris, she said, but she would devote herself more particularly to her music.

When the next summer came there was still something other than America to claim her attention: the Calderwells had invited her to cruise with them for three months. Their yacht was a little floating palace of delight, Billy declared, not to mention the charm of the unknown lands and waters that she and Aunt Hannah would see.

Of all this Billy wrote to William—at occasional intervals—but she did not come home. Even when the next autumn came, there was still Paris to detain her for another long winter of study.

In the Henshaw house on Beacon Street, William mourned not a little as each recurring season brought no Billy.

"The idea! It's just as if one didn't have a namesake!" he fumed.

"Well, did you have one?" Bertram demanded one day. "Really, Will, I'm beginning to think she's a myth. Long years ago, from the first of April till June we did have two frolicsome sprites here that announced themselves as 'Billy' and 'Spunk,' I'll own. And a year later, by ways devious and secret, we three managed to see the one called 'Billy' off on a great steamship. Since then, what? A word—a message—a scrap of paper. Billy's a myth, I say!" William sighed.

"Sometimes I don't know but you are right," he admitted. "Why, it'll be three years next June since Billy was here. She must be nearly twenty-one—and we know almost nothing about her."

"That's so. I wonder—" Bertram paused, and laughed a little, "I wonder if NOW she'd play guardian angel to me through the streets of Boston."

William threw a keen glance into his brother's face.

"I don't believe it would be quite necessary, NOW, Bert," he said quietly.

The other flushed a little, but his eyes softened.

"Maybe not, Will; still—one can always find some use for—a guardian angel, you know," he finished, almost under his breath.

To Cyril Bertram had occasionally spoken, during the last two years, of their first suspicions concerning Billy's absence. They speculated vaguely, too, as to why she had gone, and if she would ever come back; and they wondered if anything could have wounded her and sent her away. To William they said nothing of all this, however; though they agreed that they would have asked Kate for her opinion, had she been there. But Kate was not there. As it chanced, a good business opportunity had called Kate's husband to a Western town very soon after Billy herself had gone to Hampden Falls; and since the family's removal to the West, Mrs. Hartwell had not once returned to Boston.

It was in April, three years since Billy's first appearance in the Beacon Street house, that Bertram met his friend, Hugh Calderwell, on the street one afternoon, and brought him home to dinner.

Hugh Calderwell was a youth who, Bertram said, had been born with a whole dozen silver spoons in his mouth. And, indeed, it would seem so, if present prosperity were any indication. He was a good-looking young fellow with a frank manliness that appealed to men, and a deferential chivalry that appealed to women; a combination that brought him many friends—and some enemies. With plenty of money to indulge a passion for traveling, young Calderwell had spent the most of his time since graduation in daring trips into the heart of almost impenetrable forests, or to the top of almost inaccessible mountains, with an occasional more ordinary trip to give variety. He had now come to the point, however, where he was determined to "settle down to something that meant something," he told the Henshaws, as the four men smoked in Bertram's den after dinner.

"Yes, sir, I have," he iterated. "And, by the way, the little girl that has set me to thinking in such good earnest is a friend of yours, too,—Miss Neilson. I met her in Paris. She was on our yacht all last summer."

Three men sat suddenly erect in their chairs.

"Billy?" cried three voices. "Do you know Billy?"

"To be sure! And you do, too, she says."

"Oh, no, we don't," disputed Bertram, emphatically. "But we WISH we did!"

His guest laughed.

"Well, I fancy you DO know her, or you wouldn't have answered like that," he retorted. "For you just begin to know Miss Billy when you find out that you DON'T know her. She is a charming girl—a very charming girl."

"She is my namesake," announced William, in what Bertram called his "finest ever" voice that he used only for the choicest bits in his collections.

"Yes, she told me," smiled Calderwell. "'Billy' for 'William.' Odd idea, too, but clever. It helps to distinguish her even more—though she doesn't need it, for that matter."

"'Doesn't need it,'" echoed William in a puzzled voice.

"No. Perhaps you don't know, Mr. Henshaw, but Miss Billy is a very popular young woman. You have reason to be proud of your namesake."

"I have always been that," declared William, with just a touch of hauteur.

"Tell us about her," begged Bertram. "You remember I said that we wished we did know her."

Calderwell smiled.

"I don't believe, after all, that you do know much about her," he began musingly. "Billy is not one who talks much of herself, I fancy, in her letters."

William frowned. This time there was more than a touch of hauteur in his voice.

"MISS NEILSON is not one to show vanity anywhere," he said, with suggestive emphasis on the name.

"Indeed she isn't," agreed Calderwell, heartily. "She is a fine girl—quite one of the finest I know, in fact."

There was an uncomfortable silence. Over in the corner Cyril puffed at his cigar with an air almost of boredom. He had not spoken since his first surprised questioning with the others, "Do you know Billy?" William was still frowning. Even Bertram wore a look that was not quite satisfied.

"Miss Neilson has spent two winters in Paris now, you know," resumed Calderwell, after a moment; "and she is very popular both with the American colony, and with the other students. As for her 'Aunt Hannah'—they all make a pet of her; but that is, perhaps, because Billy herself is so devoted."

Again William frowned at the familiar "Billy"; but Calderwell talked on unheeding.

"After all, I'm not sure but some of us regard 'Aunt Hannah' with scant favor, occasionally," he laughed; "something as if she were the dragon that guarded the princess, you know. Miss Billy IS popular with the men, and she has suitors enough to turn any girl's head—but her own."

"Suitors!" cried William, plainly aghast. "Why, Billy's nothing but a child!"

Calderwell gave an odd smile.

"How long is it since you've seen—Miss Neilson?" he asked.

"Two years."

"And then only for a few minutes just before she sailed," amended Bertram. "We haven't really seen much of her since three years ago."

"Hm-m; well, you'll see for yourself soon. You know she's coming home next month."

Not one of the brothers did know it—but not one of them intended that Calderwell should find out that they did not.

"Yes, she's coming home," said William, lifting his chin a little.

"Oh, yes, next month," added Bertram, nonchalantly.

Even Cyril across the room was not to be outdone.

"Yes. Miss Neilson comes home next month," he said.

CHAPTER XXI

BILLY, THE REALITY

Very early in May came the cheery letter from Billy herself announcing the news of her intended return.

"And I shall be so glad to see you all," she wrote in closing. "It seems so long since I left America." Then she signed her name with "kindest regards to all"—Billy did not send "love to all" any more.

William at once began to make plans for his namesake's comfort.

"But, Will, she didn't say she was coming here," Bertram reminded him.

"She didn't need to," smiled William, confidently. "She just took it for granted, of course. This is her home."

"But it hasn't been—for years. She's called Hampden Falls 'home.'"

"I know, but that was before," demurred William, his eyes a little anxious. "Besides, they've sold the house now, you know. There's nowhere for her to go but here, Bertram."

"All right," acquiesced the younger man, still doubtingly. "Maybe that's so; maybe! But—" he did not finish his sentence, and his eyes were troubled as he watched his brother begin to rearrange Billy's rooms. In time, however, so sure was William of Billy's return to the Beacon Street house, that Bertram ceased to question; and, with almost as much confidence as William himself displayed, he devoted his energies to the preparations for Billy's arrival.

And what preparations they were! Even Cyril helped this time to the extent of placing on Billy's piano a copy of his latest book, and a pile of new music. Nor were the melodies that floated down from the upper floor akin to funeral marches; they were perilously near to being allied to "ragtime."

At last everything was ready. There was not one more bit of dust to catch Pete's eye, nor one more adornment that demanded William's careful hand to adjust. In Billy's rooms new curtains graced the windows and new rugs the floors. In Mrs. Stetson's, too, similar changes had been made. The latest and best "Face of a Girl" smiled at one from above Billy's piano, and the very rarest of William's treasures adorned the mantelpiece. No guns nor knives nor fishing-rods met the eyes now. Instead, at every turn, there was a hint of feminine tastes: a mirror, a workbasket, a low sewing-chair, a stand with a tea tray. And everywhere were roses, up-stairs and down-stairs, until the air was heavy with their perfume. In the dining-room Pete was again "swinging back and forth like a pendulum," it is true; but it was a cheerful pendulum to-day, anxious only that no time should be lost. In the kitchen alone was there unhappiness, and there because Dong Ling had already spoiled a whole cake of chocolate in a vain attempt to make Billy's favorite fudge. Even Spunkie, grown now to be sleek, lazy, and majestically indifferent, was in holiday attire, for a brand-new pink bow of huge dimensions adorned his fat neck—for the first time in many months.

"You see," William had explained to Bertram, "I put on that ribbon again because I thought it would make Spunkie seem more homelike, and more like Spunk. You know there wasn't anything Billy missed so much as that kitten when she went abroad. Aunt Hannah said so."

"Yes, I know," Bertram had laughed; "but still, Spunkie isn't Spunk, you understand!" he had finished, with a vision in his eyes of Billy as she had looked that first night when she had triumphantly lifted from the green basket the little gray kitten with its enormous pink bow. This time there was no circuitous journeying, no secrecy in the trip to New York. Quite as a matter of course the three brother made their plans to meet Billy, and quite as a matter of course they met her. Perhaps the only cloud in the horizon of their happiness was the presence of Calderwell. He, too, had come to meet Billy—and all the Henshaw brothers were vaguely conscious of a growing feeling of dislike toward Calderwell.

Billy was unmistakably glad to see them—and to see Calderwell. It was while she was talking to Calderwell, indeed, that William and Cyril and Bertram had an opportunity really to see the girl, and to note what time had done for her. They knew then, at once, that time had been very kind.

It was a slim Billy that they saw, with a head royally poised, and a chin that was round and soft, and yet knew well its own mind. The eyes were still appealing, in a way, yet behind the appeal lay unsounded depths of—not one of the brothers could quite make up his mind just what, yet all the brothers determined to find out. The hair still curled distractingly behind the pretty ears, and fluffed into burnished bronze where the wind had loosened it. The cheeks were paler now, though the rose-flush still glowed warmly through the clear, smooth skin. The mouth—Billy's mouth had always been fascinating, Bertram suddenly decided, as he watched it now. He wanted to paint it—again. It was not too large for beauty nor too small for strength. It curved delightfully, and the lower lip had just the fullness and the color that he liked—to paint, he said to himself.

William, too, was watching Billy's mouth; in fact—though he did not know it—one never was long near Billy without noticing her mouth, if she talked. William thought it pretty, merry, and charmingly kissable; but just now he wished that it would talk to him, and not to Calderwell any longer. Cyril—indeed, Cyril was paying little attention to Billy. He had turned to Aunt Hannah. To tell the truth, it seemed to Cyril that, after all, Billy was very much like other merry, thoughtless, rather noisy young women, of whom he knew—and disliked—scores. It had occurred to him suddenly that perhaps it would not be unalloyed bliss to take this young namesake of William's home with them.

It was not until an hour later, when Billy, Aunt Hannah, and the Henshaws had reached the hotel where they were to spend the night, that the Henshaw brothers began really to get acquainted with Billy. She seemed then more like their own Billy—the Billy that they had known.

"And I'm so glad to be here," she cried; "and to see you all. America IS the best place, after all!"

"And of America, Boston is the Hub, you know," Bertram reminded her.

"It is," nodded Billy.

"And it hasn't changed a mite, except to grow better. You'll see to-morrow."

"As if I hadn't been counting the days!" she exulted. "And now what have you been doing—all of you?"

"Just wait till you see," laughed Bertram. "They're all spread out for your inspection."

"A new 'Face of a Girl'?"

"Of course—yards of them!"

"And heaps of 'Old Blues' and 'black basalts'?" she questioned, turning to William.

"Well, a—few," hesitated William, modestly.

"And—the music; what of that?" Billy looked now at Cyril.

"You'll see," he shrugged. "There's very little, after all—of anything."

Billy gave a wise shake of her head.

"I know better; and I want to see it all so much. We've talked and talked of it; haven't we, Aunt Hannah?—of what we would do when we got to Boston?"

"Yes, my dear; YOU have."

The girl laughed.

"I accept the amendment," she retorted with mock submission. "I suppose it is always I who talk."

"It was—when I painted you," teased Bertram. "By the way, I'll LET you talk if you'll pose again for me," he finished eagerly.

Billy uptilted her nose.

"Do you think, sir, you deserve it, after that speech?" she demanded.

"But how about YOUR art—your music?" entreated William. "You have said so little of that in your letters."

Billy hesitated. For a brief moment she glanced at Cyril. He did not appear to have heard his brother's question. He was talking with Aunt Hannah.

"Oh, I play—some," murmured the girl, almost evasively. "But tell me of yourself, Uncle William, and of what you are doing." And William needed no second bidding.

It was some time later that Billy turned to him with an amazed exclamation in response to something he had said.

"Home with you! Why, Uncle William, what do you mean? You didn't really think you'd got to be troubled with ME any longer!" she cried merrily.

William's face paled, then flushed.

"I did not call it 'trouble,' Billy," he said quietly. His grieved eyes looked straight into hers and drove the merriment quite away.

"Oh, I'm so sorry," she said gently. "And I appreciate your kindness, indeed I do; but I couldn't—really I couldn't think of such a thing!"

"And you don't have to think of it," cut in Bertram, who considered that the situation was becoming much too serious. "All you have to do is to come."

Billy shook her head.

"You are so good, all of you! But you didn't—you really didn't think I WAS—coming!" she protested.

"Indeed we did," asserted Bertram, promptly; "and we have done everything to get ready for you, too, even to rigging up Spunkie to masquerade as Spunk. I'll warrant that Pete's nose is already flattened against the window-pane, lest we should HAPPEN to come to-night; and there's no telling how many cakes of chocolate Dong Ling has spoiled by this time. We left him trying to make fudge, you know."

Billy laughed—but she cried, too; at least, her eyes grew suddenly moist. Bertram tried to decide afterward whether she laughed till she cried, or cried till she laughed.

"No, no," she demurred tremulously. "I couldn't. I really have never intended that."

"But why not? What are you going to do?" questioned William in a voice that was dazed and hurt.

The first question Billy ignored. The second she answered with a promptness and a gayety that was meant to turn the thoughts away from the first.

"We are going to Boston, Aunt Hannah and I. We've got rooms engaged for just now, but later we're going to take a house and live together. That's what we're going to do."

CHAPTER XXII

HUGH CALDERWELL

In the Beacon Street house William mournfully removed the huge pink bow from Spunkie's neck, and Bertram threw away the roses. Cyril marched up-stairs with his pile of new music and his book; and Pete, in obedience to orders, hid the workbasket, the tea table, and the low sewing-chair. With a great display of a "getting back home" air, Bertram moved many of his belongings upstairs—but inside of a week he had moved them down again, saying that, after all, he believed he liked the first floor better. Billy's rooms were closed then, and remained as they had for years—silent and deserted.

Billy with Aunt Hannah had gone directly to their Back Bay hotel. "This is for just while I'm house-hunting," the girl had said. But very soon she had decided to go to Hampden Falls for the summer and postpone her house-buying until the autumn. Billy was twenty-one now, and there were many matters of business to arrange with Lawyer Harding, concerning her inheritance. It was not until September, therefore, when Billy once more returned to Boston, that the Henshaw brothers had the opportunity of renewing their acquaintance with William's namesake.

"I want a home," Billy said to Bertram and William on the night of her arrival. (As before, Mrs. Stetson and Billy had gone directly to a hotel.) "I want a real home with a furnace to shake—if I want to—and some dirt to dig in."

"Well, I'm sure that ought to be easy to find," smiled Bertram.

"Oh, but that isn't all," supplemented Billy. "It must be mostly closets and piazza. At least, those are the important things."

"Well, you might run across a snag there. Why don't you build?"

Billy gave a gesture of dissent.

"Too slow. I want it now."

Bertram laughed. His eyes narrowed quizzically.

"From what Calderwell says," he bantered, "I should judge that there are plenty of sighing swains who are only too ready to give you a home—and now."

The pink deepened in Billy's cheeks.

"I said closets and a piazza, dirt to dig, and a furnace to shake," she retorted merrily. "I didn't say I wanted a husband."

"And you don't, of course," interposed William, decidedly. "You are much too young for that."

"Yes, sir," agreed Billy demurely; but Bertram was sure he saw a twinkle under the downcast lashes.

"And where is Cyril?" asked Mrs. Stetson, coming into the room at that moment.

William stirred restlessly.

"Well, Cyril couldn't—couldn't come," stammered William with an uneasy glance at his brother.

Billy laughed unexpectedly.

"It's too bad—about Mr. Cyril's not coming," she murmured. And again Bertram caught the twinkle in the downcast eyes.

To Bertram the twinkle looked interesting, and worth pursuit; but at the very beginning of the chase Calderwell's card came up, and that ended—everything, so Bertram declared crossly to himself.

Billy found her dirt to dig in, and her furnace to shake, in Brookline. There were closets, too, and a generous expanse of veranda. They all belonged to a quaint little house perched on the side of Corey Hill. From the veranda in the rear, and from many of the windows, one looked out upon a delightful view of many-hued, many-shaped roofs nestling among towering trees, with the wide sweep of the sky above, and the haze of faraway hills at the horizon.

"In fact, it's as nearly perfect as it can be—and not take angel-wings and fly away," declared Billy. "I have named it 'Hillside.'"

Very early in her career as house-owner, Billy decided that however delightful it might be to have a furnace to shake, it would not be at all delightful to shake it; besides, there was the new motor car to run. Billy therefore sought and found a good, strong man who had not only the muscle and the willingness to shake the furnace, but the skill to turn chauffeur at a moment's notice. Best of all, this man had also a wife who, with a maid to assist her, would take full charge of the house, and thus leave Billy and Mrs. Stetson free from care. All these, together with a canary, and a kitten as near like Spunk as could be obtained, made Billy's household.

"And now I'm ready to see my friends," she announced.

"And I think your friends will be ready to see you," Bertram assured her.

And they were—at least, so it appeared. For at once the little house perched on the hillside became the Mecca for many of the Henshaws' friends who had known Billy as William's merry, eighteen-year-old namesake. There were others, too, whom Billy had met abroad; and there were soft-stepping, sweet-faced old women and an occasional white-whiskered old man—Aunt Hannah's friends—who found that the young mistress of Hillside was a charming hostess. There were also the Henshaw "boys," and there was always Calderwell—at least, so Bertram declared to himself sometimes.

Bertram came frequently to the little house on the hill, even more frequently than William; but Cyril was not seen there so often. He came once at first, it is true, and followed Billy from room to room as she proudly displayed her new home. He showed polite interest in her view, and a perfunctory enjoyment of the tea she prepared for him. But he did not come again for some time, and when he did come, he sat stiffly silent, while his brothers did most of the talking.

As to Calderwell—Calderwell seemed suddenly to have lost his interest in impenetrable forests and unclimbable mountains. Nothing more intricate than the long Beacon Street boulevard, or more inaccessible than Corey Hill seemed worth exploring, apparently. According to Calderwell's own version of it, he had "settled down"; he was going to "be something that was something." And he did spend sundry of his morning hours in a Boston law office with ponderous, calf-bound volumes spread in imposing array on the desk before him. Other hours—many hours—he spent with Billy.

One day, very soon, in fact, after she arrived in Boston, Billy asked Calderwell about the Henshaws.

"Tell me about them," she said. "Tell me what they have been doing all these years."

"Tell you about them! Why, don't you know?"

She shook her head.

"No. Cyril says nothing. William little more—about themselves; and you know what Bertram is. One can hardly separate sense from nonsense with him."

"You don't know, then, how splendidly Bertram has done with his art?"

"No; only from the most casual hearsay. Has he done well then?"

"Finely! The public has been his for years, and now the critics are tumbling over each other to do him honor. They rave about his 'sensitive, brilliant, nervous touch,'—whatever that may be; his 'marvelous color sense'; his 'beauty of line and pose.' And they quarrel over whether it's realism or idealism that constitutes his charm."

"I'm so glad! And is it still the 'Face of a Girl'?"

"Yes; only he's doing straight portraiture now as well. It's got to be quite the thing to be 'done' by Henshaw; and there's many a fair lady that has graciously commissioned him to paint her portrait. He's a fine fellow, too—a mighty fine fellow. You may not know, perhaps, but three or four years ago he was—well, not wild, but 'frolicsome,' he would probably have called it. He got in with a lot of fellows that—well, that weren't good for a chap of Bertram's temperament."

"Like—Mr. Seaver?"

Calderwell turned sharply.

"Did YOU know Seaver?" he demanded in obvious surprise.

"I used to SEE him—with Bertram."

"Oh! Well, he WAS one of them, unfortunately. But Bertram shipped him years ago."

Billy gave a sudden radiant smile—but she changed the subject at once.

"And Mr. William still collects, I suppose," she observed.

"Jove! I should say he did! I've forgotten the latest; but he's a fine fellow, too, like Bertram."

"And—Mr. Cyril?"

Calderwell frowned.

"That chap's a poser for me, Billy, and no mistake. I can't make him out!"

"What's the matter?"

"I don't know. Probably I'm not 'tuned to his pitch.' Bertram told me once that Cyril was very sensitively strung, and never responded until a certain note was struck. Well, I haven't ever found that note, I reckon."

Billy laughed.

"I never heard Bertram say that, but I think I know what he means; and he's right, too. I begin to realize now what a jangling discord I must have created when I tried to harmonize with him three years ago! But what is he doing in his music?"

The other shrugged his shoulders.

"Same thing. Plays occasionally, and plays well, too; but he's so erratic it's difficult to get him to do it. Everything must be just so, you know—air, light, piano, and audience. He's got another book out, I'm told—a profound treatise on somebody's something or other—musical, of course."

"And he used to write music; doesn't he do that any more?"

"I believe so. I hear of it occasionally through musical friends of mine. They even play it to me sometimes. But I can't stand for much of it—his stuff—really, Billy."

"'Stuff' indeed! And why not?" An odd hostility showed in Billy's eyes.

Again Calderwell shrugged his shoulders.

"Don't ask me. I don't know. But they're always dead slow, somber things, with the wail of a lost spirit shrieking through them."

"But I just love lost spirits that wail," avowed Billy, with more than a shade of reproach in her voice.

Calderwell stared; then he shook his head.

"Not in mine, thank you;" he retorted whimsically. "I prefer my spirits of a more sane and cheerful sort."

The girl laughed, but almost instantly she fell silent.

"I've been wondering," she began musingly, after a time, "why some one of those three men does not—marry."

"You wouldn't wonder—if you knew them better," declared Calderwell. "Now think. Let's begin at the top of the Strata—by the way, Bertram's name for that establishment is mighty clever! First, Cyril: according to Bertram Cyril hates 'all kinds of women and other confusion'; and I fancy Bertram hits it about right. So that settles Cyril. Then there's William—you know William. Any girl would say William was a dear; but William isn't a MARRYING man. Dad says,"—Calderwell's voice softened a little—"dad says that William and his young wife were the most devoted couple that he ever saw; and that when she died she seemed to take with her the whole of William's heart—that is, what hadn't gone with the baby a few years before. There was a boy, you know, that died."

"Yes, I know," nodded Billy, quick tears in her eyes. "Aunt Hannah told me."

"Well, that counts out William, then," said Calderwell, with an air of finality.

"But how about Bertram? You haven't settled Bertram," laughed Billy, archly.

"Bertram!" Calderwell's eyes widened. "Billy, can you imagine Bertram's making love in real earnest to a girl?"

"Why, I—don't—know; maybe!" Billy tipped her head from side to side as if she were viewing a picture set up for her inspection.

"Well, I can't. In the first place, no girl would think he was serious; or if by any chance she did, she'd soon discover that it was the turn of her head or the tilt of her chin that he admired—TO PAINT. Now isn't that so?"

Billy laughed, but she did not answer.

"It is, and you know it," declared Calderwell. "And that settles him. Now you can see, perhaps, why none of these men—will marry."

It was a long minute before Billy spoke.

"Not a bit of it. I don't see it at all," she declared with roguish merriment. "Moreover, I think that some day, some one of them—will marry, Sir Doubtful!"

Calderwell threw a quick glance into her eyes. Evidently something he saw there sent a swift shadow to his own. He waited a moment, then asked abruptly:

"Billy, WON'T you marry me?"

Billy frowned, though her eyes still laughed.

"Hugh, I told you not to ask me that again," she demurred.

"And I told you not to ask impossibilities of me," he retorted imperturbably. "Billy, won't you, now—seriously?"

"Seriously, no, Hugh. Please don't let us go all over that again when we've done it so many times."

"No, let's don't," agreed the man, cheerfully. "And we don't have to, either, if you'll only say 'yes,' now right away, without any more fuss."

Billy sighed impatiently.

"Hugh, won't you understand that I'm serious?" she cried; then she turned suddenly, with a peculiar flash in her eyes.

"Hugh, I don't believe Bertram himself could make love any more nonsensically than you can!"

Calderwell laughed, but he frowned, too; and again he threw into Billy's face that keenly questioning glance. He said something—a light something—that brought the laugh to Billy's lips in spite of herself; but he was still frowning when he left the house some minutes later, and the shadow was not gone from his eyes.

CHAPTER XXIII

BERTRAM DOES SOME QUESTIONING

Billy's time was well occupied. There were so many, many things she wished to do, and so few, few hours in which to do them. First there was her music. She made arrangements at once to study with one of Boston's best piano teachers, and she also made plans to continue her French and German. She joined a musical club, a literary club, and a more strictly social club; and to numerous church charities and philanthropic enterprises she lent more than her name, giving freely of both time and money.

Friday afternoons, of course, were to be held sacred to the Symphony concerts; and on certain Wednesday mornings there was to be a series of recitals, in which she was greatly interested.

For Society with a capital S, Billy cared little; but for sociability with a small s, she cared much; and very wide she opened her doors to her friends, lavishing upon them a wealth of hospitality. Nor did they all come in carriages or automobiles—these friends. A certain pale-faced little widow over at the South End knew just how good Miss Neilson's tea tasted on a crisp October afternoon and Marie Hawthorn, a frail young woman who gave music lessons, knew just how restful was Miss Neilson's couch after a weary day of long walks and fretful pupils.

"But how in the world do you discover them all—these forlorn specimens of humanity?" queried Bertram one evening, when he had found Billy entertaining a freckled-faced messenger-boy with a plate of ice cream and a big square of cake.

"Anywhere—everywhere," smiled Billy.

"Well, this last candidate for your favor, who has just gone—who's he?"

"I don't know, beyond that his name is 'Tom,' and that he likes ice cream."

"And you never saw him before?"

"Never."

"Humph! One wouldn't think it, to see his charming air of nonchalant accustomedness."

"Oh, but it doesn't take much to make a little fellow like that feel at home," laughed Billy.

"And are you in the habit of feeding every one who comes to your house, on ice cream and chocolate cake? I thought that stone doorstep of yours was looking a little worn."

"Not a bit of it," retorted Billy. "This little chap came with a message just as I was finishing dinner. The ice cream was particularly good to-night, and it occurred to me that he might like a taste; so I gave it to him."

Bertram raised his eyebrows quizzically.

"Very kind, of course; but—why ice cream?" he questioned. "I thought it was roast beef and boiled potatoes that was supposed to be handed out to gaunt-eyed hunger."

"It is," nodded Billy, "and that's why I think sometimes they'd like ice cream and chocolate frosting. Besides, to give sugar plums one doesn't have to unwind yards of red tape, or worry about 'pauperizing the poor.' To give red flannels and a ton of coal, one must be properly circumspect and consult records and city missionaries, of course; and that's why it's such a relief sometimes just to hand over a simple little sugar plum and see them smile."

For a minute Bertram was silent, then he asked abruptly:

"Billy, why did you leave the Strata?"

Billy was taken quite by surprise. A pink flush spread to her forehead, and her tongue stumbled at first over her reply.

"Why, I—it seemed—you—why, I left to go to Hampden Falls, to be sure. Don't you remember?" she finished gaily.

"Oh, yes, I remember THAT," conceded Bertram with disdainful emphasis. "But why did you go to Hampden Falls?"

"Why, it—it was the only place to go—that is, I WANTED to go there," she corrected hastily. "Didn't Aunt Hannah tell you that I—I was homesick to get back there?"

"Oh, yes, Aunt Hannah SAID that," observed the man; "but wasn't that homesickness a little—sudden?"

Billy blushed pink again.

"Why, maybe; but—well, homesickness is always more or less sudden; isn't it?" she parried.

Bertram laughed, but his eyes grew suddenly almost tender.

"See here, Billy, you can't bluff worth a cent," he declared. "You are much too refreshingly frank for that. Something was the trouble. Now what was it? Won't you tell me, please?"

Billy pouted. She hesitated and gazed anywhere but into the challenging eyes before her. Then very suddenly she looked straight into them.

"Very well, there WAS a reason for my leaving," she confessed a little breathlessly. "I—didn't want to—bother you any more—all of you."

"Bother us!"

"No. I found out. You couldn't paint; Mr. Cyril couldn't play or write; and—and everything was different because I was there. But I didn't blame you—no, no!" she assured him hastily. "It was only that I—found out."

"And may I ask HOW you obtained this most extraordinary information?" demanded Bertram, savagely.

Billy shook her head. Her round little chin looked suddenly square and determined.

"You may ask, but I shall not tell," she declared firmly.

If Bertram had known Billy just a little better he would have let the matter drop there; but he did not know Billy, so he asked:

"Was it anything I did—or said?"

The girl did not answer.

"Billy, was it?" Bertram's voice showed terror now.

Billy laughed unexpectedly.

"Do you think I'm going to say 'no' to a series of questions, and then give the whole thing away by my silence when you come to the right one?" she demanded merrily. "No, sir!"

"Well, anyhow, it wasn't I, then," sighed the man in relief; "for you just observed that you were not going to say 'no to a series of questions'—and that was the first one. So I've found out that much, anyhow," he concluded triumphantly.

The girl eyed him for a moment in silence; then she shook her head.

"I'm not going to be caught that way, either," she smiled. "You know—just what you did in the first place about it: nothing."

The man stirred restlessly and pondered. After a long pause he adopted new tactics. With a searching study of her face to note the slightest change, he enumerated:

"Was it Cyril, then? Will? Aunt Hannah? Kate? It couldn't have been Pete, or Dong Ling!"

Billy still smiled inscrutably. At no name had Bertram detected so much as the flicker of an eyelid; and with a glance half-admiring, half-chagrined, he fell back into his chair.

"I'll give it up. You've won," he acknowledged. "But, Billy,"—his manner changed suddenly—"I wonder if you know just what a hole you left in the Strata when you went away."

"But I couldn't have—in the whole Strata," objected Billy. "I occupied only one stratum, and a stratum doesn't go up and down, you know, only across; and mine was the second floor."

Bertram gave a slow shake of his head.

"I know; but yours was a freak formation," he maintained gravely. "It DID go up and down. Honestly, Billy, we did care—lots. Will and I were inconsolable, and even Cyril played dirges for a week."

"Did he?" gurgled Billy, with sudden joyousness. "I'm so glad!"

"Thank you," murmured Bertram, disapprovingly. "We hadn't considered it a subject for exultation."

"What? Oh, I didn't mean that! That is—" she stopped helplessly.

"Oh, never mind about trying to explain," interposed Bertram. "I fancy the remedy would be worse than the disease, in this case."

"Nonsense! I only meant that I like to be missed—sometimes," retorted Billy, a little nettled.

"And you rejoice then to have me mope, Cyril play dirges, and Will wander mournfully about the house with Spunkie in his arms! You should have seen William. If his forlornness did not bring tears to your eyes, the grace of the pink bow that lopped behind Spunkie's left ear would surely have brought a copious flow."

Billy laughed, but her eyes grew tender.

"Did Uncle William do—that?" she asked.

"He did—and he did more. Pete told me after a time that you had not left one thing in the house, anywhere; but one day, over behind William's most treasured Lowestoft, I found a small shell hairpin, and a flat brown silk button that I recognized as coming from one of your dresses."

"Oh!" said Billy, softly. "Dear Uncle William—and how good he was to me!"

CHAPTER XXIV

CYRIL, THE ENIGMA

Perhaps it was because Billy saw so little of Cyril that it was Cyril whom she wished particularly to see. William, Bertram, Calderwell—all her other friends came frequently to the little house on the hill, Billy told herself; only Cyril held aloof—and it was Cyril that she wanted.

Billy said that it was his music; that she wanted to hear him play, and that she wanted him to hear her. She felt grieved and chagrined. Not once since she had come had he seemed interested—really interested in her music. He had asked her, it is true, in a perfunctory way what she had done, and who her teachers had been. But all the while she was answering she had felt that he was not listening; that he did not care. And she cared so much! She knew now that all her practising through the long hard months of study, had been for Cyril. Every scale had been smoothed for his ears, and every phrase had been interpreted with his approbation in view. Across the wide waste of waters his face had shone like a star of promise, beckoning her on and on to heights unknown... And now she was here in Boston, but she could not even play the scale, nor interpret the phrase for the ear to which they had been so laboriously attuned; and Cyril's face, in the flesh, was no beckoning star of promise, but was a thing as cold and relentless as was the waste of waters across which it had shone in the past.

Billy did not understand it. She knew, it is true, of Cyril's reputed aversion to women in general and to noise; but she was neither women in general nor noise, she told herself indignantly. She was only the little maid, grown three years older, who had sat at his feet and adoringly listened to all that he had been pleased to say in the old days at the top of the Strata. And he had been kind then—very kind, Billy declared stoutly. He had been patient and interested, too, and he had seemed not only willing, but glad to teach her, while now—

Sometimes Billy thought she would ask him candidly what was the matter. But it was always the old, frank Billy that thought this; the impulsive Billy, that had gone up to Cyril's rooms years before and cheerfully announced that she had come to get acquainted. It was never the sensible, circumspect Billy that Aunt Hannah had for three years been shaping and coaxing into being. But even this Billy frowned rebelliously, and declared that sometime something should be said that would at least give him a chance to explain.

In all the weeks since Billy's purchase of Hillside, Cyril had been there only twice, and it was nearly Thanksgiving now. Billy had seen him once or twice, also, at the Beacon Street house, when she and Aunt Hannah had dined there; but on all these occasions he had been either the coldly reserved guest or the painfully punctilious host. Never had he been in the least approachable.

"He treats me exactly as he treated poor little Spunk that first night," Billy declared hotly to herself.

Only once since she came had Billy heard Cyril play, and that was when she had shared the privilege with hundreds of others at a public concert. She had sat then entranced, with her eyes on the clean-cut handsome profile of the man who played with so sure a skill and power, yet without a note before him. Afterward she had met him face to face, and had tried to tell him how moved she was; but in her agitation, and because of a strange shyness that had suddenly come to her, she had ended only in stammering out some flippant banality that had brought to his face merely a bored smile of acknowledgment.

Twice she had asked him to play for her; but each time he had begged to be excused, courteously, but decidedly.

"It's no use to tease," Bertram had interposed once, with an airy wave of his hands. "This lion always did refuse to roar to order. If you really must hear him, you'll have to slip upstairs and camp outside his door, waiting patiently for such crumbs as may fall from his table."

"Aren't your metaphors a little mixed?" questioned Cyril irritably.

"Yes, sir," acknowledged Bertram with unruffled temper, "but I don't mind if Billy doesn't. I only meant her to understand that she'd have to do as she used to do—listen outside your door."

Billy's cheeks reddened.

"But that is what I sha'n't do," she retorted with spirit. "And, moreover, I still have hopes that some day he'll play to me."

"Maybe," conceded Bertram, doubtfully; "if the stool and the piano and the pedals and the weather and his fingers and your ears and my watch are all just right—then he'll play."

"Nonsense!" scowled Cyril. "I'll play, of course, some day. But I'd rather not today." And there the matter had ended. Since then Billy had not asked him to play.

CHAPTER XXV

THE OLD ROOM—AND BILLY

Thanksgiving was to be a great day in the Henshaw family. The Henshaw brothers were to entertain. Billy and Aunt Hannah had been invited to dinner; and so joyously hospitable was William's invitation that it would have included the new kitten and the canary if Billy would have consented to bring them.

Once more Pete swept and garnished the house, and once more Dong Ling spoiled uncounted squares of chocolate trying to make the baffling fudge. Bertram said that the entire Strata was a-quiver. Not but that Billy and Aunt Hannah had visited there before, but that this was different. They were to come at noon this time. This visit was not to be a tantalizing little piece of stiffness an hour and a half long. It was to be a satisfying, whole-souled matter of half a day's comradeship, almost like old times. So once more the roses graced the rooms, and a flaring pink bow adorned Spunkie's fat neck; and once more Bertram placed his latest "Face of a Girl" in the best possible light. There was still a difference, however, for this time Cyril did not bring any music down to the piano, nor display anywhere a copy of his newest book.

The dinner was to be at three o'clock, but by special invitation the guests were to arrive at twelve; and promptly at the appointed hour they came.

"There, this is something like," exulted Bertram, when the ladies, divested of their wraps, toasted their feet before the open fire in his den.

"Indeed it is, for now I've time to see everything—everything you've done since I've been gone," cried Billy, gazing eagerly about her.

"Hm-m; well, THAT wasn't what I meant," shrugged Bertram.

"Of course not; but it's what I meant," retorted Billy. "And there are other things, too. I expect there are half a dozen new 'Old Blues' and black basalts that I want to see; eh, Uncle William?" she finished, smiling into the eyes of the man who had been gazing at her with doting pride for the last five minutes.

"Ho! Will isn't on teapots now," quoth Bertram, before his brother had a chance to reply. "You might dangle the oldest 'Old Blue' that ever was before him now, and he'd pay scant attention if he happened at the same time to get his eyes on some old pewter chain with a green stone in it."

Billy laughed; but at the look of genuine distress that came into William's face, she sobered at once.

"Don't you let him tease you, Uncle William," she said quickly. "I'm sure pewter chains with green stones in them sound just awfully interesting, and I want to see them right away now. Come," she finished, springing to her feet, "take me up-stairs, please, and show them to me."

William shook his head and said, "No, no!" protesting that what he had were scarcely worth her attention; but even while he talked he rose to his feet and advanced half eagerly, half reluctantly, toward the door.

"Nonsense," said Billy, fondly, as she laid her hand on his arm. "I know they are very much worth seeing. Come!" And she led the way from the room. "Oh, oh!" she exclaimed a few moments later, as she stood before a small cabinet in one of William's rooms. "Oh, oh, how pretty!"

"Do you like them? I thought you would," triumphed William, quick joy driving away the anxious fear in his eyes. "You see, I—I thought of you when I got them—every one of them. I thought you'd like them. But I haven't very many, yet, of course. This is the latest one." And he tenderly lifted from its black velvet mat a curious silver necklace made of small, flat, chain-linked disks, heavily chased, and set at regular intervals with a strange, blue-green stone.

Billy hung above it enraptured.

"Oh, what a beauty! And this, I suppose, is Bertram's 'pewter chain'! 'Pewter,' indeed!" she scoffed. "Tell me, Uncle William, where did you get it?"

And uncle William told, happily, thirstily, drinking in Billy's evident interest with delight. There were, too, a quaintly-set ring and a cat's-eye brooch; and to each belonged a story which William was equally glad to tell. There were other treasures, also: buckles, rings, brooches, and necklaces, some of dull gold, some of equally dull silver; but all of odd design and curious workmanship, studded here and there with bits of red, green, yellow, blue, and flame-colored stones. Very learnedly then from William's lips fell the new vocabulary that had come to him with his latest treasures: chrysoprase, carnelian, girasol, onyx, plasma, sardonyx, lapis lazuli, tourmaline, chrysolite, hyacinth, and carbuncle.

"They are lovely, perfectly lovely!" breathed Billy, when the last chain had slipped through her fingers into William's hand. "I think they are the very nicest things you ever collected."

"So do I," agreed the man, emphatically. "And they are—different, too."

"They are," said Billy, "very—different." But she was not looking at the jewelry: her eyes were on a small shell hairpin and a brown silk button half hidden behind a Lowestoft teapot.

On the way down-stairs William stopped a moment at Billy's old rooms.

"I wish you were here now," he said wistfully. "They're all ready for you—these rooms."

"Oh, but why don't you use them?—such pretty rooms!" cried Billy, quickly.

William gave a gesture of dissent.

"We have no use for them; besides, they belong to you and Aunt Hannah. You left your imprint long ago, my dear—we should not feel at home in them."

"Oh, but you should! You mustn't feel like that!" objected Billy, hurriedly crossing the room to the window to hide a sudden nervousness that had assailed her. "And here's my piano, too, and open!" she finished gaily, dropping herself upon the piano stool and dashing into a brilliant mazourka.

Billy, like Cyril, had a way of working off her moods at her finger tips; and to-day the tripping notes and crashing chords told of a nervous excitement that was not all joy. From the doorway William watched her flying fingers with fond pride, and it was very reluctantly that he acceded to Pete's request to go down-stairs for a moment to settle a vexed question concerning the table decorations.

Billy, left alone, still played, but with a difference. The tripping notes slowed into a weird melody that rose and fell and lost itself in the exquisite harmony that had been born of the crashing chords. Billy was improvising now, and into her music had crept something of her old-time longing when she had come to that house a lonely, orphan girl, in search of a home. On and on she played; then with a discordant note, she suddenly rose from the piano. She was thinking of Kate, and wondering if, had Kate not "managed" the little room would still be home.

So swiftly did Billy cross to the door that the man on the stairs outside had not time to get quite out of sight. Billy did not see his face, however; she saw only a pair of gray-trousered legs disappearing around the curve of the landing above. She thought nothing of it until later when dinner was announced, and Cyril came down-stairs; then she saw that he, and he only, that afternoon wore trousers of that particular shade of gray.

The dinner was a great success. Even the chocolate fudge in the little cut glass bonbon dishes was perfect; and it was a question whether Pete or Dong Ling tried the harder to please.

After dinner the family gathered in the drawing-room and chatted pleasantly. Bertram displayed his prettiest and newest pictures, and Billy played and sung—bright, tuneful little things that she knew Aunt Hannah and Uncle William liked. If Cyril was pleased or displeased, he did not show it—but Billy had ceased to play for Cyril's ears. She told herself that she did not care; but she did wonder: was that Cyril on the stairs, and if so—what was he doing there?

CHAPTER XXVI

"MUSIC HATH CHARMS"

Two days after Thanksgiving Cyril called at Hillside.
"I've come to hear you play," he announced abruptly.
Billy's heart sung within her—but her temper rose. Did he think then that he had but to beckon and she would come—and at this late day, she asked herself. Aloud she said:
"Play? But this is 'so sudden'! Besides, you have heard me."
The man made a disdainful gesture.
"Not that. I mean play—really play. Billy, why haven't you played to me before?"
Billy's chin rose perceptibly.
"Why haven't you asked me?" she parried.
To Billy's surprise the man answered this with calm directness.
"Because Calderwell said that you were a dandy player, and I don't care for dandy players."
Billy laughed now.
"And how do you know I'm not a dandy player, Sir Impertinent?" she demanded.
"Because I've heard you—when you weren't."
"Thank you," murmured Billy.
Cyril shrugged his shoulders.
"Oh, you know very well what I mean," he defended. "I've heard you; that's all."
"When?"
"That doesn't signify."
Billy was silent for a moment, her eyes gravely studying his face. Then she asked:
"Were you long—on that stairway?"
"Eh? What? Oh!" Cyril's forehead grew suddenly pink. "Well?" he finished a little aggressively.
"Oh, nothing," smiled the girl. "Of course people who live in glass houses must not throw stones."
"Very well then, I did listen," acknowledged the man, testily. "I liked what you were playing. I hoped, down-stairs later, that you'd play it again; but you didn't. I came to-day to hear it."
Again Billy's heart sung within her—but again her temper rose, too.
"I don't think I feel like it," she said sweetly, with a shake of her head. "Not to-day."
For a brief moment Cyril stared frowningly; then his face lighted with his rare smile.
"I'm fairly checkmated," he said, rising to his feet and going straight to the piano.
For long minutes he played, modulating from one enchanting composition to another, and finishing with the one "all chords with big bass notes" that marched on and on—the one Billy had sat long ago on the stairs to hear.
"There! Now will you play for me?" he asked, rising to his feet, and turning reproachful eyes upon her.
Billy, too, rose to her feet. Her face was flushed and her eyes were shining. Her lips quivered with emotion. As was always the case, Cyril's music had carried her quite out of herself.
"Oh, thank you, thank you," she sighed. "You don't know—you can't know how beautiful it all is—to me!"
"Thank you. Then surely now you'll play to me," he returned.

A look of real distress came to Billy's face.

"But I can't—not what you heard the other day," she cried remorsefully. "You see, I was—only improvising."

Cyril turned quickly.

"Only improvising! Billy, did you ever write it down—any of your improvising?"

An embarrassed red flew to Billy's face.

"Not—not that amounted to—well, that is, some—a little," she stammered.

"Let me see it."

"No, no, I couldn't—not YOU!"

Again the rare smile lighted Cyril's eyes.

"Billy, let me see that paper—please."

Very slowly the girl turned toward the music cabinet. She hesitated, glanced once more appealingly into Cyril's face, then with nervous haste opened the little mahogany door and took from one of the shelves a sheet of manuscript music. But, like a shy child with her first copy book, she held it half behind her back as she came toward the piano.

"Thank you," said Cyril as he reached far out for the music. The next moment he seated himself again at the piano.

Twice he played the little song through carefully, slowly.

"Now, sing it," he directed.

Falteringly, in a very faint voice, and with very many breaths taken where they should not have been taken, Billy obeyed.

"When we want to show off your song, Billy, we won't ask you to sing it," observed the man, dryly, when she had finished.

Billy laughed and dimpled into a blush.

"When I want to show off my song I sha'n't be singing it to you for the first time," she pouted.

Cyril did not answer. He was playing over and over certain harmonies in the music before him.

"Hm-m; I see you've studied your counterpoint to some purpose," he vouchsafed, finally; then: "Where did you get the words?"

The girl hesitated. The flush had deepened on her face.

"Well, I—" she stopped and gave an embarrassed laugh. "I'm like the small boy who made the toys. 'I got them all out of my own head, and there's wood enough to make another.'"

"Hm-m; indeed!" grunted the man. "Well, have you made any others?"

"One—or two, maybe."

"Let me see them, please."

"I think—we've had enough—for today," she faltered.

"I haven't. Besides, if I could have a couple more to go with this, it would make a very pretty little group of songs."

"'To go with this'! What do you mean?"

"To the publishers, of course."

"The PUBLISHERS!"

"Certainly. Did you think you were going to keep these songs to yourself?"

"But they aren't worth it! They can't be—good enough!" Unbelieving joy was in Billy's voice.

"No? Well, we'll let others decide that," observed Cyril, with a shrug. "All is, if you've got any more wood—like this—I advise you to make it up right away."

"But I have already!" cried the girl, excitedly. "There are lots of little things that I've—that is, there are—some," she corrected hastily, at the look that sprang into Cyril's eyes.

"Oh, there are," laughed Cyril. "Well, we'll see what—" But he did not see. He did not even finish his sentence; for Billy's maid, Rosa, appeared just then with a card.

"Show Mr. Calderwell in here," said Billy. Cyril said nothing—aloud; which was well. His thoughts, just then, were better left unspoken.

CHAPTER XXVII

MARIE, WHO LONGS TO MAKE PUDDINGS

Wonderful days came then to Billy. Four songs, it seemed, had been pronounced by competent critics decidedly "worth it"—unmistakably "good enough"; and they were to be brought out as soon as possible.

"Of course you understand," explained Cyril, "that there's no 'hit' expected. Thank heaven they aren't that sort! And there's no great money in it, either. You'd have to write a masterpiece like 'She's my Ju-Ju Baby' or some such gem to get the 'hit' and the money. But the songs are fine, and they'll take with cultured hearers. We'll get them introduced by good singers, of course, and they'll be favorites soon for the concert stage, and for parlors."

Billy saw a good deal of Cyril now. Already she was at work rewriting and polishing some of her half-completed melodies, and Cyril was helping her, by his interest as well as by his criticism. He was, in fact, at the house very frequently—too frequently, indeed, to suit either Bertram or Calderwell. Even William frowned sometimes when his cozy chats with Billy were interrupted by Cyril's appearing with a roll of new music for her to "try"; though William told himself that he ought to be thankful if there was anything that could make Cyril more companionable, less reserved and morose. And Cyril WAS different—there was no disputing that. Calderwell said that he had come "out of his shell"; and Bertram told Billy that she must have "found his note and struck it good and hard."

Billy was very happy. To the little music teacher, Marie Hawthorn, she talked more freely, perhaps, than she did to any one else.

"It's so wonderful, Marie—so wonderfully wonderful," she said one day, "to sit here in my own room and sing a little song that comes from somewhere, anywhere, out of the sky itself. Then by and by, that little song will fly away, away, over land and sea; and some day it will touch somebody's heart just as it has touched mine. Oh, Marie, is it not wonderful?"

"It is, dear—and it is not. Your songs could not help reaching somebody's heart. There's nothing wonderful in that."

"Sweet flatterer!"

"But I mean it. They are beautiful; and so is—Mr. Henshaw's music."

"Yes, it is," murmured Billy, abstractedly.

There was a long pause, then Marie asked with shy hesitation:

"Do you think, Miss Billy—that he would care? I listened yesterday when he was playing to you. I was up here in your room, but when I heard the music I—I went out, on the stairs and sat down. Was it very—bad of me?"

Billy laughed happily.

"If it was, he can't say anything," she reassured her. "He's done the same thing himself—and so have I."

"HE has done it!"

"Yes. It was at his home last Thanksgiving. It was then that he found out—about my improvising."

"Oh-h!" Marie's eyes were wistful. "And he cares so much now for your music!"

"Does he? Do you think he does?" demanded Billy.

"I know he does—and for the one who makes it, too."

"Nonsense!" laughed Billy, with pinker cheeks. "It's the music, not the musician, that pleases him. Mr. Cyril doesn't like women."

"He doesn't like women!"

"No. But don't look so shocked, my dear. Every one who knows Mr. Cyril knows that."

"But I don't think—I believe it," demurred Marie, gazing straight into Billy's eyes. "I'm sure I don't believe it."

Under the little music teacher's steady gaze Billy flushed again. The laugh she gave was an embarrassed one, but through it vibrated a pleased ring.

"Nonsense!" she exclaimed, springing to her feet and moving restlessly about the room. With the next breath she had changed the subject to one far removed from Mr. Cyril and his likes and dislikes.

Some time later Billy played, and it was then that Marie drew a long sigh.

"How beautiful it must be to play—like that," she breathed.

"As if you, a music teacher, could not play!" laughed Billy.

"Not like that, dear. You know it is not like that."

Billy frowned.

"But you are so accurate, Marie, and you can read at sight so rapidly!"

"Oh, yes, like a little machine, I know!" scorned the usually gentle Marie, bitterly. "Don't they have a thing of metal that adds figures like magic? Well, I'm like that. I see g and I play g; I see d and I play d; I see f and I play f; and after I've seen enough g's and d's and f's and played them all, the thing is done. I've played."

"Why, Marie! Marie, my dear!" The second exclamation was very tender, for Marie was crying.

"There! I knew I should some day have it out—all out," sobbed Marie. "I felt it coming."

"Then perhaps you'll—you'll feel better now," stammered Billy. She tried to say more—other words that would have been a real comfort; but her tongue refused to speak them. She knew so well, so woefully well, how very wooden and mechanical the little music teacher's playing always had been. But that Marie should realize it herself like this—the tragedy of it made Billy's heart ache. At Marie's next words, however, Billy caught her breath in surprise.

"But you see it wasn't music—it wasn't ever music that I wanted—to do," she confessed.

"It wasn't music! But what—I don't understand," murmured Billy.

"No, I suppose not," sighed the other. "You play so beautifully yourself."

"But I thought you loved music."

"I do. I love it dearly—in others. But I can't—I don't want to make it myself."

"But what do you want to do?"

Marie laughed suddenly.

"Do you know, my dear, I have half a mind to tell you what I do like to do—just to make you stare."

"Well?" Billy's eyes were wide with interest.

"I like best of anything to—darn stockings and make puddings."

"Marie!"

"Rank heresy, isn't it?" smiled Marie, tearfully. "But I do, truly. I love to weave the threads evenly in and out, and see a big hole close. As for the puddings I don't mean the common bread-and-butter kind, but the ones that have whites of eggs and fruit, and pretty quivery jellies all ruby and amber lights, you know."

"You dear little piece of domesticity," laughed Billy. "Then why in the world don't you do these things?"

"I can't, in my own kitchen; I can't afford a kitchen to do them in. And I just couldn't do them—right along—in other people's kitchens."

"But why do you—play?"

"I was brought up to it. You know we had money once, lots of it," sighed Marie, as if she were deploring a misfortune. "And mother was determined to have me musical. Even then, as a little tot, I liked pudding-making, and after my mud-pie days I was always begging mother to let me go down into the kitchen, to cook. But she wouldn't allow it, ever. She engaged the most expensive masters and set me practising, always practising. I simply had to learn music; and I learned it like the adding machine. Then afterward, when father died, and then mother, and the money flew away, why, of course I had to do something, so naturally I turned to the music. It was all I could do. But—well, you know how it is, dear. I teach, and teach well, perhaps, so far as the mechanical part goes; but as for the rest—I am always longing for a cozy corner with a basket of stockings to mend, or a kitchen where there is a pudding waiting to be made."

"You poor dear!" cried Billy. "I've a pair of stockings now that needs attention, and I've been just longing for one of your 'quivery jellies all ruby and amber lights' ever since you mentioned them. But—well, is there anything I could do to help?"

"Nothing, thank you," sighed Marie, rising wearily to her feet, and covering her eyes with her hand for a moment. "My head aches shockingly, but I've got to go this minute and instruct little Jennie Knowls how to play the wonderful scale of G with a black key in it. Besides, you do help me, you have helped me, you are always helping me, dear," she added remorsefully; "and it's wicked of me to make that shadow come to your eyes. Please don't think of it, or of me, any more." And with a choking little sob she hurried from the room, followed by the amazed, questioning, sorrowful eyes of Billy.

CHAPTER XXVIII

"I'M GOING TO WIN"

Nearly all of Billy's friends knew that Bertram Henshaw was in love with Billy Neilson before Billy herself knew it. Not that they regarded it as anything serious—"it's only Bertram" was still said of him on almost all occasions. But to Bertram himself it was very serious.

The world to Bertram, indeed, had come to assume a vastly different aspect from what it had displayed in times past. Heretofore it had been a plaything which like a juggler's tinsel ball might be tossed from hand to hand at will. Now it was no plaything—no glittering bauble. It was something big and serious and splendid—because Billy lived in it; something that demanded all his powers to do, and be—because Billy was watching; something that might be a Hades of torment or an Elysium of bliss—according to whether Billy said "no" or "yes."

Since Thanksgiving Bertram had known that it was love—this consuming fire within him; and since Thanksgiving he had known, too, that it was jealousy—this fierce hatred of Calderwell. He was ashamed of the hatred. He told himself that it was unmanly, unkind, and unreasonable; and he vowed that he would overcome it. At times he even fancied that he had overcome it; but always the sight of Calderwell in Billy's little drawing-room or of even the man's card on Billy's silver tray was enough to show him that he had not.

There were others, too, who annoyed Bertram not a little, foremost of these being his own brothers. Still he was not really worried about William and Cyril, he told himself. William he did not consider to be a marrying man; and Cyril—every one knew that Cyril was a woman-hater. He was doubtless attracted now only by Billy's music. There was no real rivalry to be feared from William and Cyril. But there was always Calderwell, and Calderwell was serious. Bertram decided, therefore, after some weeks of feverish unrest, that the only road to peace lay through a frank avowal of his feelings, and a direct appeal to Billy to give him the great boon of her love.

Just here, however, Bertram met with an unexpected difficulty. He could not find words with which to make his avowal or to present his appeal. He was surprised and annoyed. Never before had he been at a loss for words—mere words. And it was not that he lacked opportunity. He walked, drove, and talked with Billy, and always she was companionable, attentive to what he had to say. Never was she cold or reserved. Never did she fail to greet him with a cheery smile.

Bertram concluded, indeed, after a time, that she was too companionable, too cheery. He wished she would hesitate, stammer, blush; be a little shy. He wished that she would display surprise, annoyance, even—anything but that eternal air of comradeship. And then, one afternoon in the early twilight of a January day, he freed his mind, quite unexpectedly.

"Billy, I wish you WOULDN'T be so—so friendly!" he exclaimed in a voice that was almost sharp.

Billy laughed at first, but the next moment a shamed distress drove the merriment quite out of her face.

"You mean that I presume on—on our friendship?" she stammered. "That you fear that I will again—shadow your footsteps?" It was the first time since the memorable night itself that Billy had ever in Bertram's presence referred to her young guardianship of his welfare. She realized now, suddenly, that she had just been giving the man before her some very "sisterly advice," and the thought sent a confused red to her cheeks.

Bertram turned quickly.

"Billy, that was the dearest and loveliest thing a girl ever did—only I was too great a chump to appreciate it!" finished Bertram in a voice that was not quite steady.

"Thank you," smiled the girl, with a slow shake of her head and a relieved look in her eyes; "but I'm afraid I can't quite agree to that." The next moment she had demanded mischievously: "Why, then, pray, this unflattering objection to my—friendliness now?"

"Because I don't want you for a friend, or a sister, or anything else that's related," stormed Bertram, with sudden vehemence. "I don't want you for anything but—a wife! Billy, WON'T you marry me?"

Again Billy laughed—laughed until she saw the pained anger leap to the gray eyes before her; then she became grave at once.

"Bertram, forgive me. I didn't think you could—you can't be—serious!"

"But I am."

Billy shook her head.

"But you don't love me—not ME, Bertram. It's only the turn of my head or—or the tilt of my chin that you love—to paint," she protested, unconsciously echoing the words Calderwell had said to her weeks before. "I'm only another 'Face of a Girl.'"

"You're the only 'Face of a girl' to me now, Billy," declared the man, with disarming tenderness.

"No, no, not that," demurred Billy, in distress. "You don't mean it. You only think you do. It couldn't be that. It can't be!"

"But it is, dear. I think I have loved you ever since that night long ago when I saw your dear, startled face appealing to me from beyond Seaver's hateful smile. And, Billy, I never went once with Seaver again—anywhere. Did you know that?"

"No; but—I'm glad—so glad!"

"And I'm glad, too. So you see, I must have loved you then, though unconsciously, perhaps; and I love you now."

"No, no, please don't say that. It can't be—it really can't be. I—I don't love you—that way, Bertram."

The man paled a little.

"Billy—forgive me for asking, but it's so much to me—is it that there is—some one else?" His voice shook.

"No, no, indeed! There is no one."

"It's not—Calderwell?"

Billy's forehead grew pink. She laughed nervously.

"No, no, never!"

"But there are others, so many others!"

"Nonsense, Bertram; there's no one—no one, I assure you!"

"It's not William, of course, nor Cyril. Cyril hates women."

A deeper flush came to Billy's face. Her chin rose a little; and an odd defiance flashed from her eyes. But almost instantly it was gone, and a slow smile had come to her lips.

"Yes, I know. Every one—says that Cyril hates women," she observed demurely.

"Then, Billy, I sha'n't give up!" vowed Bertram, softly. "Sometime you WILL love me!"

"No, no, I couldn't. That is, I'm not going to—to marry," stammered Billy.

"Not going to marry!"

"No. There's my music—you know how I love that, and how much it is to me. I don't think there'll ever be a man—that I'll love better."

Bertram lifted his head. Very slowly he rose till his splendid six feet of clean-limbed strength and manly beauty towered away above the low chair in which Billy sat. His mouth showed new lines about the corners, and his eyes looked down very tenderly at the girl beside him; but his voice, when he spoke, had a light whimsicality that deceived even Billy's ears.

"And so it's music—a cold, senseless thing of spidery marks on clean white paper—that is my only rival," he cried. "Then I'll warn you, Billy, I'll warn you. I'm going to win!" And with that he was gone.

CHAPTER XXIX

"I'M NOT GOING TO MARRY"

Billy did not know whether to be more amazed or amused at Bertram's proposal of marriage. She was vexed; she was very sure of that. To marry Bertram? Absurd!... Then she reflected that, after all, it was only Bertram, so she calmed herself.

Still, it was annoying. She liked Bertram, she had always liked him. He was a nice boy, and a most congenial companion. He never bored her, as did some others; and he was always thoughtful of cushions and footstools and cups of tea when one was tired. He was, in fact, an ideal friend, just the sort she wanted; and it was such a pity that he must spoil it all now with this silly sentimentality! And of course he had spoiled it all. There was no going back now to their old friendliness. He would be morose or silly by turns, according to whether she frowned or smiled; or else he would take himself off in a tragic sort of way that was very disturbing. He had said, to be sure, that he would "win." Win, indeed! As if she could marry Bertram! When she married, her choice would fall upon a man, not a boy; a big, grave, earnest man to whom the world meant something; a man who loved music, of course; a man who would single her out from all the world, and show to her, and to her only, the depth and tenderness of his love; a man who—but she was not going to marry, anyway, remembered Billy, suddenly. And with that she began to cry. The whole thing was so "tiresome," she declared, and so "absurd."

Billy rather dreaded her next meeting with Bertram. She feared—she knew not what. But, as it turned out, she need not have feared anything, for he met her tranquilly, cheerfully, as usual; and he did nothing and said nothing that he might not have done and said before that twilight chat took place.

Billy was relieved. She concluded that, after all, Bertram was going to be sensible. She decided that she, too, would be sensible. She would accept him on this, his chosen plane, and she would think no more of his "nonsense."

Billy threw herself then even more enthusiastically into her beloved work. She told Marie that after all was said and done, there could not be any man that would tip the scales one inch with music on the other side. She was a little hurt, it is true, when Marie only laughed and answered:

"But what if the man and the music both happen to be on the same side, my dear; what then?"

Marie's voice was wistful, in spite of the laugh—so wistful that it reminded Billy of their conversation a few weeks before.

"But it is you, Marie, who want the stockings to darn and the puddings to make," she retorted playfully. "Not I! And, do you know? I believe I shall turn matchmaker yet, and find you a man; and the chiefest of his qualifications shall be that he's wretchedly hard on his hose, and that he adores puddings."

"No, no, Miss Billy, don't, please!" begged the other, in quick terror. "Forget all I said the other day; please do! Don't tell—anybody!"

She was so obviously distressed and frightened that Billy was puzzled.

"There, there, 'twas only a jest, of course," she soothed her. "But, really Marie, it is the dear, domestic little mouse like yourself that ought to be somebody's wife—and that's the kind men are looking for, too."

Marie gave a slow shake of her head.

"Not the kind of man that is somebody, that does something," she objected; "and that's the only kind I could—love. HE wants a wife that is beautiful and clever, that can do things like himself—LIKE HIMSELF!" she iterated feverishly.

Billy opened wide her eyes.

"Why, Marie, one would think—you already knew—such a man," she cried.

The little music teacher changed her position, and turned her eyes away.

"I do, of course," she retorted in a merry voice, "lots of them. Don't you? Come, we've discussed my matrimonial prospects quite long enough," she went on lightly. "You know we started with yours. Suppose we go back to those."

"But I haven't any," demurred Billy, as she turned with a smile to greet Aunt Hannah, who had just entered the room. "I'm not going to marry; am I, Aunt Hannah?"

"Er—what? Marry? My grief and conscience, what a question, Billy! Of course you're going to marry—when the time comes!" exclaimed Aunt Hannah.

Billy laughed and shook her head vigorously. But even as she opened her lips to reply, Rosa appeared and announced that Mr. Calderwell was waiting down-stairs. Billy was angry then, for after the maid was gone, the merriment in Aunt Hannah's laugh only matched that in Marie's—and the intonation was unmistakable.

"Well, I'm not!" declared Billy with pink cheeks and much indignation, as she left the room. And as if to convince herself, Marie, Aunt Hannah, and all the world that such was the case, she refused Calderwell so decidedly that night when he, for the half-dozenth time, laid his hand and heart at her feet, that even Calderwell himself was convinced—so far as his own case was concerned—and left town the next day.

Bertram told Aunt Hannah afterward that he understood Mr. Calderwell had gone to parts unknown. To himself Bertram shamelessly owned that the more "unknown" they were, the better he himself would be pleased.

CHAPTER XXX

MARIE FINDS A FRIEND

It was on a very cold January afternoon, and Cyril was hurrying up the hill toward Billy's house, when he was startled to see a slender young woman sitting on a curbstone with her head against an electric-light post. He stopped abruptly.
"I beg your pardon, but—why, Miss Hawthorn! It is Miss Hawthorn; isn't it?"
Under his questioning eyes the girl's pale face became so painfully scarlet that in sheer pity the man turned his eyes away. He thought he had seen women blush before, but he decided now that he had not.
"I'm sure—haven't I met you at Miss Neilson's? Are you ill? Can't I do something for you?" he begged.
"Yes—no—that is, I AM Miss Hawthorn, and I've met you at Miss Neilson's," stammered the girl, faintly. "But there isn't anything, thank you, that you can do—Mr. Henshaw. I stopped to—rest."
The man frowned.
"But, surely—pardon me, Miss Hawthorn, but I can't think it your usual custom to choose an icy curbstone for a resting place, with the thermometer down to zero. You must be ill. Let me take you to Miss Neilson's."
"No, no, thank you," cried the girl, struggling to her feet, the vivid red again flooding her face. "I have a lesson—to give."
"Nonsense! You're not fit to give a lesson. Besides, they are all folderol, anyway, half of them. A dozen lessons, more or less, won't make any difference; they'll play just as well—and just as atrociously. Come, I insist upon taking you to Miss Neilson's."
"No, no, thank you! I really mustn't. I—" She could say no more. A strong, yet very gentle hand had taken firm hold of her arm in such a way as half to support her. A force quite outside of herself was carrying her forward step by step—and Miss Hawthorn was not used to strong, gentle hands, nor yet to a force quite outside of herself. Neither was she accustomed to walk arm in arm with Mr. Cyril Henshaw to Miss Billy's door. When she reached there her cheeks were like red roses for color, and her eyes were like the stars for brightness. Yet a minute later, confronted by Miss Billy's astonished eyes, the stars and the roses fled, and a very white-faced girl fell over in a deathlike faint in Cyril Henshaw's arms.
Marie was put to bed in the little room next to Billy's, and was peremptorily hushed when faint remonstrance was made. The next morning, white-faced and wide-eyed, she resolutely pulled herself half upright, and announced that she was all well and must go home—home to Marie was a six-by-nine hall bed-room in a South End lodging house.
Very gently Billy pushed her back on the pillow and laid a detaining hand on her arm.
"No, dear. Now, please be sensible and listen to reason. You are my guest. You did not know it, perhaps, for I'm afraid the invitation got a little delayed. But you're to stay—oh, lots of weeks."
"I—stay here? Why, I can't—indeed, I can't," protested Marie.
"But that isn't a bit of a nice way to accept an invitation," disapproved Billy. "You should say, 'Thank you, I'd be delighted, I'm sure, and I'll stay.'"
In spite of herself the little music teacher laughed, and in the laugh her tense muscles relaxed.
"Miss Billy, Miss Billy, what is one to do with you? Surely you know—you must know that I can't do what you ask!"
"I'm sure I don't see why not," argued Billy. "I'm merely giving you an invitation and all you have to do is to accept it."

"But the invitation is only the kind way your heart has of covering another of your many charities," objected Marie; "besides, I have to teach. I have my living to earn."

"But you can't," demurred the other. "That's just the trouble. Don't you see? The doctor said last night that you must not teach again this winter."

"Not teach—again—this winter! No, no, he could not be so cruel as that!"

"It wasn't cruel, dear; it was kind. You would be ill if you attempted it. Now you'll get better. He says all you need is rest and care—and that's exactly what I mean my guest shall have."

Quick tears came to the sick girl's eyes.

"There couldn't be a kinder heart than yours, Miss Billy," she murmured, "but I couldn't—I really couldn't be a burden to you like this. I shall go to some hospital."

"But you aren't going to be a burden. You are going to be my friend and companion."

"A companion—and in bed like this?"

"Well, THAT wouldn't be impossible," smiled Billy; "but, as it happens you won't have to put that to the test, for you'll soon be up and dressed. The doctor says so. Now surely you will stay."

There was a long pause. The little music teacher's eyes had left Billy's face and were circling the room, wistfully lingering on the hangings of filmy lace, the dainty wall covering, and the exquisite water colors in their white-and-gold frames. At last she drew a deep sigh.

"Yes, I'll stay," she breathed rapturously; "but—you must let me help."

"Help? Help what?"

"Help you; your letters, your music-copying, your accounts—anything, everything. And if you don't let me help,"—the music teacher's voice was very stern now—"if you don't let me help, I shall go home just—as—soon—as—I—can—walk!"

"Dear me!" dimpled Billy. "And is that all? Well, you shall help, and to your heart's content, too. In fact, I'm not at all sure that I sha'n't keep you darning stockings and making puddings all the time," she added mischievously, as she left the room.

Miss Hawthorn sat up the next day. The day following, in one of Billy's "fluttery wrappers," as she called them, she walked all about the room. Very soon she was able to go downstairs, and in an astonishingly short time she fitted into the daily life as if she had always been there. She was, moreover, of such assistance to Billy that even she herself could see the value of her work; and so she stayed, content.

The little music teacher saw a good deal of Billy's friends then, particularly of the Henshaw brothers; and very glad was Billy to see the comradeship growing between them. She had known that William would be kind to the orphan girl, but she had feared that Marie would not understand Bertram's nonsense or Cyril's reserve. But very soon Bertram had begged, and obtained, permission to try to reproduce on canvas the sheen of the fine, fair hair, and the veiled bloom of the rose-leaf skin that were Marie's greatest charms; and already Cyril had unbent from his usual stiffness enough to play to her twice. So Billy's fears on that score were at an end.

CHAPTER XXXI

THE ENGAGEMENT OF ONE

Many times during those winter days Billy thought of Marie's words: "But what if the man and the music both happen to be on the same side?" They worried her, to some extent, and, curiously, they pleased and displeased her at the same time.

She told herself that she knew very well, of course, what Marie meant: it was Cyril; he was the man, and the music. But was Cyril beginning to care for her; and did she want him to? Very seriously one day Billy asked herself these questions; very calmly she argued the matter in her mind—as was Billy's way.

She was proud, certainly, of what her influence had apparently done for Cyril. She was gratified that to her he was showing the real depth and beauty of his nature. It WAS flattering to feel that she, and only she, had thus won the regard of a professional woman-hater. Then, besides all this, there was his music—his glorious music. Think of the bliss of living ever with that! Imagine life with a man whose soul would be so perfectly attuned to hers that existence would be one grand harmony! Ah, that, truly, would be the ideal marriage! But she had planned not to marry. Billy frowned now, and tapped her foot nervously. It was, indeed, most puzzling—this question, and she did not want to make a mistake. Then, too, she did not wish to wound Cyril. If the dear man HAD come out of his icy prison, and were reaching out timid hands to her for her help, her interest, her love—the tragedy of it, if he met with no response!.... This vision of Cyril with outstretched hands, and of herself with cold, averted eyes was the last straw in the balance with Billy. She decided suddenly that she did care for Cyril—a little; and that she probably could care for him a great deal. With this thought, Billy blushed—already in her own mind she was as good as pledged to Cyril.

It was a great change for Billy—this sudden leap from girlhood and irresponsibility to womanhood and care; but she took it fearlessly, resolutely. If she was to be Cyril's wife she must make herself fit for it—and in pursuance of this high ideal she followed Marie into the kitchen the very next time the little music teacher went out to make one of her dainty desserts that the family liked so well.

"I'll just watch, if you don't mind," announced Billy.

"Why, of course not," smiled Marie, "but I thought you didn't like to make puddings."

"I don't," owned Billy, cheerfully.

"Then why this—watchfulness?"

"Nothing, only I thought it might be just as well if I knew how to make them. You know how Cyril—that is, ALL the Henshaw boys like every kind you make."

The egg in Marie's hand slipped from her fingers and crashed untidily on the shelf. With a gleeful laugh Billy welcomed the diversion. She had not meant to speak so plainly. It was one thing to try to fit herself to be Cyril's wife, and quite another to display those efforts so openly before the world.

The pudding was made at last, but Marie proved to be a nervous teacher. Her hand shook, and her memory almost failed her at one or two critical points. Billy laughingly said that it must be stage fright, owing to the presence of herself as spectator; and with this Marie promptly, and somewhat effusively, agreed.

So very busy was Billy during the next few days, acquiring her new domesticity, that she did not notice how little she was seeing of Cyril. Then she suddenly realized it, and asked herself the reason for it. Cyril was at the house certainly, just as frequently as he had been; but she saw that a new shyness in herself had developed which was causing her to be restless in his presence, and was leading her to like better to have Marie or Aunt Hannah in the room when he called. She discovered, too, that she welcomed William, and even Bertram, with peculiar enthusiasm—if they happened to interrupt a tete-a-tete with Cyril.

Billy was disturbed at this. She told herself that this shyness was not strange, perhaps, inasmuch as her ideas in regard to love and marriage had undergone so abrupt a change; but it must be overcome. If she was to be Cyril's wife, she must like to be with him—and of course she really did like to be with him, for she had enjoyed his companionship very much during all these past weeks. She set herself therefore, now, determinedly to cultivating Cyril. It was then that Billy made a strange and fearsome discovery: there were some things about Cyril that she did—not—like!

Billy was inexpressibly shocked. Heretofore he had been so high, so irreproachable, so godlike!—but heretofore he had been a friend. Now he was appearing in a new role—though unconsciously, she knew. Heretofore she had looked at him with eyes that saw only the delightful and marvelous unfolding of a coldly reserved nature under the warmth of her own encouraging smile. Now she looked at him with eyes that saw only the possibilities of that same nature when it should have been unfolded in a lifelong companionship. And what she saw frightened her. There was still the music—she acknowledged that; but it had come to Billy with overwhelming force that music, after all, was not everything. The man counted, as well. Very frankly then Billy stated the case to herself.

"What passes for 'fascinating mystery' in him now will be plain moroseness—sometime. He is 'taciturn' now; he'll be—cross, then. It is 'erratic' when he won't play the piano to-day; but a few years from now, when he refuses some simple request of mine, it will be—stubbornness. All this it will be—if I don't love him; and I don't. I know I don't. Besides, we aren't really congenial. I like people around; he doesn't. I like to go to plays; he doesn't. He likes rainy days; I abhor them. There is no doubt of it—life with him would not be one grand harmony; it would be one jangling discord. I simply cannot marry him. I shall have to break the engagement!"

Billy spoke with regretful sorrow. It was evident that she grieved to bring pain to Cyril. Then suddenly the gloom left her face: she had remembered that the "engagement" was just three weeks old—and was a profound secret, not only to the bridegroom elect, but to all the world as well—save herself!

Billy was very happy after that. She sang about the house all day, and she danced sometimes from room to room, so light were her feet and her heart. She made no more puddings with Marie's supervision, but she was particularly careful to have the little music teacher or Aunt Hannah with her when Cyril called. She made up her mind, it is true, that she had been mistaken, and that Cyril did not love her; still she wished to be on the safe side, and she became more and more averse to being left alone with him for any length of time.

CHAPTER XXXII

CYRIL HAS SOMETHING TO SAY

Long before spring Billy was forced to own to herself that her fancied security from lovemaking on the part of Cyril no longer existed. She began to suspect that there was reason for her fears. Cyril certainly was "different." He was more approachable, less reserved, even with Marie and Aunt Hannah. He was not nearly so taciturn, either, and he was much more gracious about his playing. Even Marie dared to ask him frequently for music, and he never refused her request. Three times he had taken Billy to some play that she wanted to see, and he had invited Marie, too, besides Aunt Hannah, which had pleased Billy very much. He had been at the same time so genial and so gallant that Billy had declared to Marie afterward that he did not seem like himself at all, but like some one else. Marie had disagreed with her, it is true, and had said stiffly:

"I'm sure I thought he seemed very much like himself." But that had not changed Billy's opinion at all.

To Billy's mind, nothing but love could so have softened the stern Cyril she had known. She was, therefore, all the more careful these days to avoid a tete-a-tete with him, though she was not always successful, particularly owing to Marie's unaccountable perverseness in so often having letters to write or work to do, just when Billy most wanted her to make a safe third with herself and Cyril. It was upon such an occasion, after Marie had abruptly left them alone together, that Cyril had observed, a little sharply:

"Billy, I wish you wouldn't say again what you said ten minutes ago when Miss Marie was here."

"What was that?"

"A very silly reference to that old notion that you and every one else seem to have that I am a 'woman-hater.'"

Billy's heart skipped a beat. One thought, pounded through her brain and dinned itself into her ears—at all costs Cyril must not be allowed to say that which she so feared; he must be saved from himself.

"Woman-hater? Why, of course you're a woman-hater," she cried merrily. "I'm sure, I—I think it's lovely to be a woman-hater."

The man opened wide his eyes; then he frowned angrily.

"Nonsense, Billy, I know better. Besides, I'm in earnest, and I'm not a woman-hater."

"Oh, but every one says you are," chattered Billy. "And, after all, you know it IS distinguishing!"

With a disdainful exclamation the man sprang to his feet. For a time he paced the room in silence, watched by Billy's fearful eyes; then he came back and dropped into the low chair at Billy's side. His whole manner had undergone a complete change. He was almost shamefaced as he said:

"Billy, I suppose I might as well own up. I don't think I did think much of women until I saw—you."

Billy swallowed and wet her lips. She tried to speak; but before she could form the words the man went on with his remarks; and Billy did not know whether to be the more relieved or frightened thereat.

"But you see now it's different. That's why I don't like to sail any longer under false colors. There's been a change—a great and wonderful change that I hardly understand myself."

"That's it! You don't understand it, I'm sure," interposed Billy, feverishly. "It may not be such a change, after all. You may be deceiving yourself," she finished hopefully.

The man sighed.

"I can't wonder you think so, of course," he almost groaned. "I was afraid it would be like that. When one's been painted black all one's life, it's not easy to change one's color, of course."

"Oh, but I didn't say that black wasn't a very nice color," stammered Billy, a little wildly.

"Thank you." Cyril's heavy brows rose and fell the fraction of an inch. "Still, I must confess that just now I should prefer another shade."

He paused, and Billy cast distractedly about in her mind for a simple, natural change of subject. She had just decided to ask him what he thought of the condition of the Brittany peasants, when he questioned abruptly, and in a voice that was not quite steady:

"Billy, what should you say if I should tell you that the avowed woman-hater had strayed so far from the prescribed path as to—to like one woman well enough as to want to—marry her?"

The word was like a match to the gunpowder of Billy's fears. Her self-control was shattered instantly into bits.

"Marry? No, no, you wouldn't—you couldn't really be thinking of that," she babbled, growing red and white by turns. "Only think how a wife would—would b-bother you!"

"Bother me? When I loved her?"

"But just think—remember! She'd want cushions and rugs and curtains, and you don't like them; and she'd always be talking and laughing when you wanted quiet; and she—she'd want to drag you out to plays and parties and—and everywhere. Indeed, Cyril, I'm sure you'd never like a wife—long!" Billy stopped only because she had no breath with which to continue.

Cyril laughed a little grimly.

"You don't draw a very attractive picture, Billy. Still, I'm not afraid. I don't think this particular—wife would do any of those things—to trouble me."

"Oh, but you don't know, you can't tell," argued the girl. "Besides, you have had so little experience with women that you'd just be sure to make a mistake at first. You want to look around very carefully—very carefully, before you decide."

"I have looked around, and very carefully, Billy. I know that in all the world there is just one woman for me."

Billy struggled to her feet. Mingled pain and terror looked from her eyes. She began to speak wildly, incoherently. She wondered afterward just what she would have said if Aunt Hannah had not come into the room at that moment and announced that Bertram was at the door to take her for a sleigh-ride if she cared to go.

"Of course she'll go," declared Cyril, promptly, answering for her. "It is time I was off anyhow." To Billy, he said in a low voice: "You haven't been very encouraging, little girl—in fact, you've been mighty discouraging. But some day—some other day, I'll try to make clear to you—many things."

Billy greeted Bertram very cordially. It was such a relief—his cheery, genial companionship! The air, too, was bracing, and all the world lay under a snow-white blanket of sparkling purity. Everything was so beautiful, so restful!

It was not surprising, perhaps, that the very frankness of Billy's joy misled Bertram a little. His blood tingled at her nearness, and his eyes grew deep and tender as he looked down at her happy face. But of all the eager words that were so near his lips, not one reached the girl's ears until the good-byes were said; then wistfully Bertram hazarded:

"Billy, don't you think, sometimes, that I'm gaining—just a little on that rival of mine—that music?"

Billy's face clouded. She shook her head gently.

"Bertram, please don't—when we've had such a beautiful hour together," she begged. "It troubles me. If you do, I can't go—again."

"But you shall go again," cried Bertram, bravely smiling straight into her eyes. "And there sha'n't ever anything in the world trouble you, either—that I can help!"

CHAPTER XXXIII

WILLIAM IS WORRIED

Billy's sleigh-ride had been due to the kindness of a belated winter storm that had surprised every one the last of March. After that, March, as if ashamed of her untoward behavior, donned her sweetest smiles and "went out" like the proverbial lamb. With the coming of April, and the stirring of life in the trees, Billy, too, began to be restless; and at the earliest possible moment she made her plans for her long anticipated "digging in the dirt."

Just here, much to her surprise, she met with wonderful assistance from Bertram. He seemed to know just when and where and how to dig, and he displayed suddenly a remarkable knowledge of landscape gardening. (That this knowledge was as recent in its acquirement as it was sudden in its display, Billy did not know.) Very learnedly he talked of perennials and annuals; and without hesitation he made out a list of flowering shrubs and plants that would give her a "succession of bloom throughout the season." His words and phrases smacked loudly of the very newest florists' catalogues, but Billy did not notice that. She only wondered at the seemingly exhaustless source of his wisdom.

"I suspect 'twould have been better if we'd begun things last fall," he told her frowningly one day. "But there's plenty we can do now anyway; and we'll put in some quick-growing things, just for this season, until we can get the more permanent things established."

And so they worked together, studying, scheming, ordering plants and seeds, their two heads close together above the gaily colored catalogues. Later there was the work itself to be done, and though strong men did the heavier part, there was yet plenty left for Billy's eager fingers—and for Bertram's. And if sometimes in the intimacy of seed-sowing and plant-setting, the touch of the slenderer fingers sent a thrill through the browner ones, Bertram made no sign. He was careful always to be the cheerful, helpful assistant—and that was all.

Billy, it is true, was a little disturbed at being quite so much with Bertram. She dreaded a repetition of some such words as had been uttered at the end of the sleigh-ride. She told herself that she had no right to grieve Bertram, to make it hard for him by being with him; but at the very next breath, she could but question; did she grieve him? Was it hard for him to have her with him? Then she would glance at his eager face and meet his buoyant smile—and answer "no." After that, for a time, at least, her fears would be less.

Systematically Billy avoided Cyril these days. She could not forget his promise to make many things clear to her some day. She thought she knew what he meant—that he would try to convince her (as she had tried to convince herself) that she would make a good wife for him.

Billy was very sure that if Cyril could be prevented from speaking his mind just now, his mind would change in time; hence her determination to give his mind that opportunity.

Billy's avoidance of Cyril was the more easily accomplished because she was for a time taking a complete rest from her music. The new songs had been finished and sent to the publishers. There was no excuse, therefore, for Cyril's coming to the house on that score; and, indeed, he seemed of his own accord to be making only infrequent visits now. Billy was pleased, particularly as Marie was not there to play third party. Marie had taken up her teaching again, much to Billy's distress.

"But I can't stay here always, like this," Marie had protested.

"But I should like to keep you!" Billy had responded, with no less decision.

Marie had been firm, however, and had gone, leaving the little house lonely without her.

Aside from her work in the garden Billy as resolutely avoided Bertram as she did Cyril. It was natural, therefore, that at this crisis she should turn to William with a peculiar feeling of restfulness. He, at least, would be safe, she told herself. So she frankly welcomed his every appearance, sung to him, played to him, and took long walks with him to see some wonderful bracelet or necklace that he had discovered in a dingy little curio-shop.

William was delighted. He was very fond of his namesake, and he had secretly chafed a little at the way his younger brothers had monopolized her attention. He was rejoiced now that she seemed to be turning to him for companionship; and very eagerly he accepted all the time she could give him.

William had, in truth, been growing more and more lonely ever since Billy's brief stay beneath his roof years before. Those few short weeks of her merry presence had shown him how very forlorn the house was without it. More and more sorrowfully during past years, his thoughts had gone back to the little white flannel bundle and to the dear hopes it had carried so long ago. If the boy had only lived, thought William, mournfully, there would not now have been that dreary silence in his home, and that sore ache in his heart.

Very soon after William had first seen Billy, he began to lay wonderful plans, and in every plan was Billy. She was not his child by flesh and blood, he acknowledged, but she was his by right of love and needed care. In fancy he looked straight down the years ahead, and everywhere he saw Billy, a loving, much-loved daughter, the joy of his life, the solace of his declining years.

To no one had William talked of this—and to no one did he show the bitterness of his grief when he saw his vision fade into nothingness through Billy's unchanging refusal to live in his home. Only he himself knew the heartache, the loneliness, the almost unbearable longing of the past winter months while Billy had lived at Hillside; and only he himself knew now the almost overwhelming joy that was his because of what he thought he saw in Billy's changed attitude toward himself.

Great as was William's joy, however, his caution was greater. He said nothing to Billy of his new hopes, though he did try to pave the way by dropping an occasional word about the loneliness of the Beacon Street house since she went away. There was something else, too, that caused William to be silent—what he thought he saw between Billy and Bertram. That Bertram was in love with Billy, he guessed; but that Billy was not in love with Bertram he very much feared. He hesitated almost to speak or move lest something he should say or do should, just at the critical moment, turn matters the wrong way. To William this marriage of Bertram and Billy was an ideal method of solving the problem, as of course Billy would come there to the house to live, and he would have his "daughter" after all. But as the days passed, and he could see no progress on Bertram's part, no change in Billy, he began to be seriously worried—and to show it.

CHAPTER XXXIV

CLASS DAY

Early in June Billy announced her intention of not going away at all that summer.

"I don't need it," she declared. "I have this cool, beautiful house, this air, this sunshine, this adorable view. Besides, I've got a scheme I mean to carry out."

There was some consternation among Billy's friends when they found out what this "scheme" was: sundry of Billy's humbler acquaintances were to share the house, the air, the sunshine, and the adorable view with her.

"But, my dear Billy," Bertram cried, aghast, "you don't mean to say that you are going to turn your beautiful little house into a fresh-air place for Boston's slum children!"

"Not a bit of it," smiled the girl, "though I'd like to, really, if I could," she added, perversely. "But this is quite another thing. It's no slum work, no charity. In the first place my guests aren't quite so poor as that, and they're much too proud to be reached by the avowed charity worker. But they need it just the same."

"But you haven't much spare room; have you?" questioned Bertram.

"No, unfortunately; so I shall have to take only two or three at a time, and keep them maybe a week or ten days. It's just a sugar plum, Bertram. Truly it is," she added whimsically, but with a tender light in her eyes.

"But who are these people?" Bertram's face had lost its look of shocked surprise, and his voice expressed genuine interest.

"Well, to begin with, there's Marie. She'll stay all summer and help me entertain my guests; at the same time her duties won't be arduous, and she'll get a little playtime herself. One week I'm going to have a little old maid who keeps a lodging house in the West End. For uncounted years she's been practically tied to a doorbell, with never a whole day to breathe free. I've made arrangements there for a sister to keep house a whole week, and I'm going to show this little old maid things she hasn't seen for years: the ocean, the green fields, and a summer play or two, perhaps.

"Then there's a little couple that live in a third-story flat in South Boston. They're young and like good times; but the man is on a small salary, and they have had lots of sickness.

He's been out so much he can't take any vacation, and they wouldn't have any money to go anywhere if he could. Well, I'm going to have them a week. She'll be here all the time, and he'll come out at night, of course.

"Another one is a widow with six children. The children are already provided for by a fresh-air society, but the woman I'm going to take, and—and give her a whole week of food that she didn't have to cook herself. Another one is a woman who is not so very poor, but who has lost her baby, and is blue and discouraged. There are some children, too, one crippled, and a boy who says he's 'just lonesome.' And there are—really, Bertram, there is no end to them."

"I can well believe that," declared Bertram, with emphasis, "so far as your generous heart is concerned."

Billy colored and looked distressed.

"But it isn't generosity or charity at all, Bertram," she protested. "You are mistaken when you think it is—really! Why, I shall enjoy every bit of it just as well as they do—and better, perhaps."

"But you stay here—in the city—all summer for their sakes."

"What if I do? Besides, this isn't the real city," argued Billy, "with all these trees and lawns about one. And another thing," she added, leaning forward confidentially, "I might as well confess, Bertram, you couldn't hire me to leave the place this summer—not while all these things I planted are coming up!"

Bertram laughed; but for some reason he looked wonderfully happy as he turned away.

On the fifteenth of June Kate and her husband arrived from the West. A young brother of Mr. Hartwell's was to be graduated from Harvard, and Kate said they had come on to represent the family, as the elder Mr. and Mrs. Hartwell were not strong enough to undertake the journey. Kate was looking well and happy. She greeted Billy with effusive cordiality, and openly expressed her admiration of Hillside. She looked very keenly into her brothers' face, and seemed well pleased with the appearance of Cyril and Bertram, but not so much so with William's countenance.

"William does NOT look well," she declared one day when she and Billy were alone together.

"Sick? Uncle William sick? Oh, I hope not!" cried the girl.

"I don't know whether it's 'sick' or not," returned Mrs. Hartwell. "But it's something. He's troubled. I'm going to speak to him. He's worried over something; and he's grown terribly thin."

"But he's always thin," reasoned Billy.

"I know, but not like this—ever. You don't notice it, perhaps, or realize it, seeing him every day as you do. But I know something troubles him."

"Oh, I hope not," murmured Billy, with anxious eyes. "We don't want Uncle William troubled: we all love him too well."

Mrs. Hartwell did not at once reply; but for a long minute she thoughtfully studied Billy's face as it was bent above the sewing in Billy's hand. When she did speak she had changed the subject.

Young Hartwell was to deliver the Ivy Oration in the Stadium on Class Day, and all the Henshaws were looking eagerly forward to the occasion.

"You have seen the Stadium, of course," said Bertram to Billy, a few days before the anticipated Friday.

"Only from across the river."

"Is that so? And you've never been here Class Day, either. Good! Then you've got a treat in store. Just wait and see!"

And Billy waited—and she saw. Billy began to see, in fact, before Class Day. Young Hartwell was a popular fellow, and he was eager to have his friends meet Billy and the Henshaws. He was a member of the Institute of 1770, D. K. E., Stylus, Signet, Round

Table, and Hasty Pudding Clubs, and nearly every one of these had some sort of function planned for Class-Day week. By the time the day itself arrived Billy was almost as excited as was young Hartwell himself.

It rained Class-Day morning, but at nine o'clock the sun came out and drove the clouds away, much to every one's delight. Billy's day began at noon with the spread given by the Hasty Pudding Club. Billy wondered afterward how many times that day remarks like these were made to her:

"You've been here Class Day before, of course. You've seen the confetti-throwing!... No? Well, you just wait!"

At ten minutes of four Billy and Mrs. Hartwell, with Mr. Hartwell and Bertram as escorts, entered the cool, echoing shadows under the Stadium, and then out in the sunlight they began to climb the broad steps to their seats.

"I wanted them high up, you see," explained Bertram, "because you can get the effect so much better. There, here we are!"

For the first time Billy turned and looked about her. She gave a low cry of delight.

"Oh, oh, how beautiful—how wonderfully beautiful!"

"You just wait!" crowed Bertram. "If you think this is beautiful, you just wait!"

Billy did not seem to hear him. Her eyes were sweeping the wonderful scene before her, and her face was aglow with delight.

First there was the great amphitheater itself. Only the wide curve of the horseshoe was roped off for to-day's audience. Beyond lay the two sides with their tier above tier of empty seats, almost dazzling in the sunshine. Within the roped-off curve the scene was of kaleidoscopic beauty. Charmingly gowned young women and carefully groomed young men were everywhere, stirring, chatting, laughing. Gay-colored parasols and flower-garden hats made here and there brilliant splashes of rainbow tints. Above was an almost cloudless canopy of blue, and at the far horizon, earth and sky met and made a picture that was like a wondrous painted curtain hung from heaven itself.

At the first sound of the distant band that told of the graduates' coming, Bertram said almost wistfully:

"Class Day is the only time when I feel 'out of it.' You see I'm the first male Henshaw for ages that hasn't been through Harvard; and to-day, you know, is the time when the old grads come back and do stunts like the kids—if they can (and some of them can all right!). They march in by classes ahead of the seniors, and vie with each other in giving their yells. You'll see Cyril and William, if your eyes are sharp enough—and you'll see them as you never saw them before."

Far down the green field Billy spied now the long black line of moving figures with a band in the lead. Nearer and nearer it came until, greeted by a mighty roar from thousands of throats, the leaders swept into the great bowl of the horseshoe curve.

And how they yelled and cheered—those men whose first Class Day lay five, ten, fifteen, even twenty or more years behind them, as told by the banners which they so proudly carried. How they got their heads together and gave the "Rah! Rah! Rah!" with unswerving eyes on their leader! How they beat the air with their hats in time to their lusty shouts! And how the throngs above cheered and clapped in answer, until they almost split their throats—and did split their gloves—especially when the black-gowned seniors swept into view.

And when the curving line of black had become one solid mass of humanity that filled the bowl from side to side, the vast throng seated themselves, and a great hush fell while the Glee Club sang.

Young Hartwell proved to be a good speaker, and his ringing voice reached even the topmost tier of seats. Billy was charmed and interested. Everything she saw and heard was but a new source of enjoyment, and she had quite forgotten the thing for which she was to "wait," when she saw the ushers passing through the aisles with their baskets of many-hued packages of confetti and countless rolls of paper ribbon.

It began then, the merry war between the students below and the throng above. In a trice the air was filled with shimmering bits of red, blue, white, green, purple, pink, and yellow. From all directions fluttering streamers that showed every color of the rainbow, were flung to the breeze until, upheld by the supporting wires, they made a fairy lace work of marvelous beauty.

"Oh, oh, oh!" cried Billy, her eyes misty with emotion. "I think I never saw anything in my life so lovely!"

"I thought you'd like it," gloried Bertram. "You know I said to wait!"

But even with this, Class Day for Billy was not finished. There was still Hartwell's own spread from six to eight, and after that there were the President's reception, and dancing in the Memorial Hall and in the Gymnasium. There was the Fairyland of the yard, too, softly aglow with moving throngs of beautiful women and gallant men. But what Billy remembered best of all was the exquisite harmony that came to her through the hushed night air when the Glee Club sang Fair Harvard on the steps of Holworthy Hall.

CHAPTER XXXV

SISTER KATE AGAIN

It was on the Sunday following Class Day that Mrs. Hartwell carried out her determination to "speak to William." The West had not taken from Kate her love of managing, and she thought she saw now a matter that sorely needed her guiding hand.

William's thin face, anxious looks, and nervous manner had troubled her ever since she came. Then one day, very suddenly, had come enlightenment: William was in love—and with Billy.

Mrs. Hartwell watched William very closely after that. She saw his eyes follow Billy fondly, yet anxiously. She saw his open joy at being with her, and at any little attention, word, or look that the girl gave him. She remembered, too, something that Bertram had said about William's grief because Billy would not live at the Strata. She thought she saw something else, also: that Billy was fond of William, but that William did not know it; hence his frequent troubled scrutiny of her face. Why these two should play at cross purposes Sister Kate could not understand. She smiled, however, confidently: they should not play at cross purposes much longer, she declared.

On Sunday afternoon Kate asked her eldest brother to take her driving.

"Not a motor car; I want a horse—that will let me talk," she said.

"Certainly," agreed William, with a smile; but Bertram, who chanced to hear her, put in the sly comment: "As if ANY horse could prevent—that!"

On the drive Kate began to talk at once, but she did not plunge into the subject nearest her heart until she had adroitly led William into a glowing enumeration of Billy's many charming characteristics; then she said:

"William, why don't you take Billy home with you?"

William stirred uneasily as he always did when anything annoyed him.

"My dear Kate, there is nothing I should like better to do," he replied.

"Then why don't you do it?"

"I—hope to, sometime."

"But why not now?"

"I'm afraid Billy is not quite—ready."

"Nonsense! A young girl like that does not know her own mind lots of times. Just press the matter a little. Love will work wonders—sometimes."

William blushed like a girl. To him her words had but one meaning—Bertram's love for Billy. William had never spoken of this suspected love affair to any one. He had even thought that he was the only one that had discovered it. To hear his sister refer thus lightly to it came therefore in the nature of a shock to him.

"Then you have—seen it—too?" he stammered

"'Seen it, too,'" laughed Kate, with her confident eyes on William's flushed face, "I should say I had seen it! Any one could see it."

William blushed again. Love to him had always been something sacred; something that called for hushed voices and twilight. This merry discussion in the sunlight of even another's love was disconcerting.

"Now come, William," resumed Kate, after a moment; "speak to Billy, and have the matter settled once for all. It's worrying you. I can see it is."

Again William stirred uneasily.

"But, Kate, I can't do anything. I told you before; I don't believe Billy is—ready."

"Nonsense! Ask her."

"But Kate, a girl won't marry against her will!"

"I don't believe it is against her will."

"Kate! Honestly?"

"Honestly! I've watched her."

"Then I WILL speak," cried the man, his face alight, "if—if you think anything I can say would—help. There is nothing—nothing in all this world that I so desire, Kate, as to have that little girl back home. And of course that would do it. She'd live there, you know."

"Why, of—course," murmured Kate, with a puzzled frown. There was something in this last remark of William's that she did not quite understand. Surely he could not suppose that she had any idea that after he had married Billy they would go to live anywhere else;—she thought. For a moment she considered the matter vaguely; then she turned her attention to something else. She was the more ready to do this because she believed that she had said enough for the present: it was well to sow seeds, but it was also well to let them have a chance to grow, she told herself.

Mrs. Hartwell's next move was to speak to Billy, and she was careful to do this at once, so that she might pave the way for William.

She began her conversation with an ingratiating smile and the words:

"Well, Billy, I've been doing a little detective work on my own account."

"Detective work?"

"Yes; about William. You know I told you the other day how troubled and anxious he looked to me. Well, I've found out what's the matter."

"What is it?"

"Yourself."

"Myself! Why, Mrs. Hartwell, what can you mean?"

The elder lady smiled significantly.

"Oh, it's merely another case, my dear, of 'faint heart never won fair lady.' I've been helping on the faint heart; that's all."

"But I don't understand."

"No? I can't believe you quite mean that, my dear. Surely you must know how earnestly my brother William is longing for you to go back and live with him."

Like William, Billy flushed scarlet.

"Mrs. Hartwell, certainly no one could know better than YOURSELF why that is quite impossible," she frowned.

The other colored confusedly.

"I understand, of course, what you mean. And, Billy, I'll confess that I've been sorry lots of times, since, that I spoke as I did to you, particularly when I saw how it grieved my brother William to have you go away. If I blundered then, I'm sorry; and perhaps I did blunder. At all events, that is only the more reason now why I am so anxious to do what I can to rectify that old mistake, and plead William's suit."

To Mrs. Hartwell's blank amazement, Billy laughed outright.

"'William's suit'!" she quoted merrily. "Why, Mrs. Hartwell, there isn't any 'suit' to it. Uncle William doesn't want me to marry him!"

"Indeed he does."

Billy stopped laughing, and sat suddenly erect.

"MRS. HARTWELL!"

"Billy, is it possible that you did not know this?"

"Indeed I don't know it, and—excuse me, but I don't think you do, either."

"But I do. I've talked with him, and he's very much in earnest," urged Mrs. Hartwell, speaking very rapidly. "He says there's nothing in all the world that he so desires. And, Billy, you do care for him—I know you do!"

"Why, of course I care for him—but not—that way."

"But, Billy, think!" Mrs. Hartwell was very earnest now, and a little frightened. She felt that she must bring Billy to terms in some way now that William had been encouraged to put his fate to the test. "Just remember how good William has always been to you, and think what you have been, and may BE—if you only will—in his lonely life. Think of his great sorrow years ago. Think of this dreary waste of years between. Think how now his heart has turned to you for love and comfort and rest. Billy, you can't turn away!—you can't find it in your heart to turn away from that dear, good man who loves you so!" Mrs. Hartwell's voice shook effectively, and even her eyes looked through tears. Mentally she was congratulating herself: she had not supposed she could make so touching an appeal.

In the chair opposite the girl sat very still. She was pale, and her eyes showed a frightened questioning in their depths. For a long minute she said nothing, then she rose dazedly to her feet.

"Mrs. Hartwell, please do not speak of this to any one," she begged in a low voice. "I—I am taken quite by surprise. I shall have to think it out—alone."

Billy did not sleep well that night. Always before her eyes was the vision of William's face; and always in her ears was the echo of Mrs. Hartwell's words: "Remember how good William has always been to you. Think of his great sorrow years ago. Think of this dreary waste of years between. Think how now his heart has turned to you for love and comfort and rest."

For a time Billy tossed about on her bed trying to close her eyes to the vision and her ears to the echo. Then, finding that neither was possible, she set herself earnestly to thinking the matter out.

William loved her. Extraordinary as it seemed, such was the fact; Mrs. Hartwell said so. And now—what must she do; what could she do? She loved no one—of that she was very sure. She was even beginning to think that she would never love any one. There were Calderwell, Cyril, Bertram, to say nothing of sundry others, who had loved her, apparently, but whom she could not love. Such being the case, if she were, indeed, incapable of love herself, why should she not make the sacrifice of giving up her career, her independence, and in that way bring this great joy to Uncle William's heart?... Even as she said the "Uncle William" to herself, Billy bit her lip and realized that she must no longer say "Uncle" William—if she married him.

"If she married him." The words startled her. "If she married him."... Well, what of it? She would go to live at the Strata, of course; and there would be Cyril and Bertram. It might be awkward, and yet—she did not believe Cyril was in love with anything but his music; and as to Bertram—it was the same with Bertram and his painting, and he would soon forget that he had ever fancied he loved her. After that he would be simply a congenial friend and companion—a good comrade. As Billy thought of it, indeed, one of the pleasantest features of this marriage with William would be the delightful comradeship of her "brother," Bertram.

Billy dwelt then at some length on William's love for her, his longing for her presence, and his dreary years of loneliness.... And he was so good to her, she recollected; he had always been good to her. He was older, to be sure—much older than she; but, after all, it would not be so difficult, so very difficult, to learn to love him. At all events, whatever happened, she would have the supreme satisfaction of knowing that at least she had brought into dear Uncle—that is, into William's life the great peace and joy that only she could give.

It was almost dawn when Billy arrived at this not uncheerful state of prospective martyrdom. She turned over then with a sigh, and settled herself to sleep. She was relieved that she had decided the question. She was glad that she knew just what to say when William should speak. He was a dear, dear man, and she would not make it hard for him, she promised herself. She would be William's wife.

CHAPTER XXXVI

WILLIAM MEETS WITH A SURPRISE

In spite of his sister's confident assurance that the time was ripe for him to speak to Billy, William delayed some days before broaching the matter to her. His courage was not so good as it had been when he was talking with Kate. It seemed now, as it always had, a fearsome thing to try to hasten on this love affair between Billy and Bertram. He could not see, in spite of Kate's words, that Billy showed unmistakable evidence at all of being in love with his brother. The more he thought of it, in fact, the more he dreaded the carrying out of his promise to speak to his namesake.

What should he say, he asked himself. How could he word it? He could not very well accost her with: "Oh, Billy, I wish you'd please hurry up and marry Bertram, because then you'd come and live with me." Neither could he plead Bertram's cause directly. Quite probably Bertram would prefer to plead his own. Then, too, if Billy really was not in love with Bertram—what then? Might not his own untimely haste in the matter forever put an end to the chance of her caring for him?

It was, indeed, a delicate matter, and as William pondered it he wished himself well out of it, and that Kate had not spoken. But even as he formed the wish, William remembered with a thrill Kate's positive assertion that a word from him would do wonders, and that now was the time to utter it. He decided then that he would speak; that he must speak; but that at the same time he would proceed with a caution that would permit a hasty retreat if he saw that his words were not having the desired effect. He would begin with a frank confession of his grief at her leaving him, and of his longing for her return; then very gradually, if wisdom counseled it, he would go on to speak of Bertram's love for her, and of his own hope that she would make Bertram and all the Strata glad by loving him in return.

Mrs. Hartwell had returned to her Western home before William found just the opportunity for his talk with Billy. True to his belief that only hushed voices and twilight were fitting for such a subject, he waited until he found the girl early one evening alone on her vine-shaded veranda. He noticed that as he seated himself at her side she flushed a little and half started to rise, with a nervous fluttering of her hands, and a murmured "I'll call Aunt Hannah." It was then that with sudden courage, he resolved to speak.

"Billy, don't go," he said gently, with a touch of his hand on her arm. "There is something I want to say to you. I—I have wanted to say it for some time."

"Why, of—of course," stammered the girl, falling back in her seat. And again William noticed that odd fluttering of the slim little hands.

For a time no one spoke, then William began softly, his eyes on the distant sky-line still faintly aglow with the sunset's reflection.

"Billy, I want to tell you a story. Long years ago there was a man who had a happy home with a young wife and a tiny baby boy in it. I could not begin to tell you all the plans that man made for that baby boy. Such a great and good and wonderful being that tiny baby was one day to become. But the baby—went away, after a time, and carried with him all the plans—and he never came back. Behind him he left empty hearts that ached, and great bare rooms that seemed always to be echoing sighs and sobs. And then, one day, such a few years after, the young wife went to find her baby, and left the man all alone with the heart that ached and the great bare rooms that echoed sighs and sobs.

"Perhaps it was this—the bareness of the rooms—that made the man turn to his boyish passion for collecting things. He wanted to fill those rooms full, full!—so that the sighs and sobs could not be heard; and he wanted to fill his heart, too, with something that would still the ache. And he tried. Already he had his boyish treasures, and these he lined up in brave array, but his rooms still echoed, and his heart still ached; so he built more shelves and bought more cabinets, and set himself to filling them, hoping at the same time that he might fill all that dreary waste of hours outside of business—hours which once had been all too short to devote to the young wife and the baby boy.

"One by one the years passed, and one by one the shelves and the cabinets were filled. The man fancied, sometimes, that he had succeeded; but in his heart of hearts he knew that the ache was merely dulled, and that darkness had only to come to set the rooms once more to echoing the sighs and sobs. And then—but perhaps you are tired of the story, Billy." William turned with questioning eyes.

"No, oh, no," faltered Billy. "It is beautiful, but so—sad!"

"But the saddest part is done—I hope," said William, softly. "Let me tell you. A wonderful thing happened then. Suddenly, right out of a dull gray sky of hopelessness, dropped a little brown-eyed girl and a little gray cat. All over the house they frolicked, filling every nook and cranny with laughter and light and happiness. And then, like magic, the man lost the ache in his heart, and the rooms lost their echoing sighs and sobs. The man knew, then, that never again could he hope to fill his heart and life with senseless things of clay and metal. He knew that the one thing he wanted always near him was the little brown-eyed girl; and he hoped that he could keep her. But just as he was beginning to bask in this new light—it went out. As suddenly as they had come, the little brown-eyed girl and the gray cat went away. Why, the man did not know. He knew only that the ache had come back, doubly intense, and that the rooms were more gloomy than ever. And now, Billy,"—William's voice shook a little—"it is for you to finish the story. It is for you to say whether that man's heart shall ache on and on down to a lonely old age, and whether those rooms shall always echo the sighs and sobs of the past."

"And I will finish it," choked Billy, holding out both her hands. "It sha'n't ache—they sha'n't echo!"

The man leaned forward eagerly, unbelievingly, and caught the hands in his own.

"Billy, do you mean it? Then you will—come?"

"Yes, yes! I didn't know—I didn't think. I never supposed it was like that! Of course I'll come!" And in a moment she was sobbing in his arms.

"Billy!" breathed William rapturously, as he touched his lips to her forehead. "My own little Billy!"

It was a few minutes later, when Billy was more calm, that William started to speak of Bertram. For a moment he had been tempted not to mention his brother, now that his own point had been won so surprisingly quick; but the new softness in Billy's face had encouraged him, and he did not like to let the occasion pass when a word from him might do so much for Bertram. His lips parted, but no words came—Billy herself had begun to speak.

"I'm sure I don't know why I'm crying," she stammered, dabbing her eyes with her round moist ball of a handerchief. "I hope when I'm your wife I'll learn to be more self-controlled. But you know I am young, and you'll have to be patient."

As once before at something Billy said, the world to William went suddenly mad. His head swam dizzily, and his throat tightened so that he could scarcely breathe. By sheer force of will he kept his arm about Billy's shoulder, and he prayed that she might not know how numb and cold it had grown. Even then he thought he could not have heard aright.

"Er—you said—" he questioned faintly.

"I say when I'm your wife I hope I'll learn to be more self-controlled," laughed Billy, nervously. "You see I just thought I ought to remind you that I am young, and that you'll have to be patient."

William stammered something—a hurried something; he wondered afterward what it was. That it must have been satisfactory to Billy was evident, for she began laughingly to talk again. What she said, William scarcely knew, though he was conscious of making an occasional vague reply. He was still floundering in a hopeless sea of confusion and dismay. His own desire was to get up and say good night at once. He wanted to be alone to think. He realized, however, with sickening force, that men do not propose and run away—if they are accepted. And he was accepted; he realized that, too, overwhelmingly. Then he tried to think how it had happened, what he had said; how she could so have misunderstood his meaning. This line of thought he abandoned quickly, however; it could do no good. But what could do good, he asked himself. What could he do?

With blinding force came the answer: he could do nothing. Billy cared for him. Billy had said "yes." Billy expected to be his wife. As if he could say to her now: "I beg your pardon, but 'twas all a mistake. I did not ask you to marry me."

Very valiantly then William summoned his wits and tried to act his part. He told himself, too, that it would not be a hard one; that he loved Billy dearly, and that he would try to make her happy. He winced a little at this thought, for he remembered suddenly how old he was—as if he, at his age, were a fit match for a girl of twenty-one!

And then he looked at Billy. The girl was plainly nervous. There was a deep flush on her cheeks and a brilliant sparkle in her eyes. She was talking rapidly—almost incoherently at times—and her voice was tremulous. Frequent little embarrassed laughs punctuated her sentences, and her fingers toyed with everything that came within reach. Some time before she had sprung to her feet and had turned on the electric lights; and when she came back she had not taken her old position at William's side, but had seated herself in a chair near by. All of which, according to William's eyes, meant the maidenly shyness of a girl who has just said "yes" to the man she loves.

William went home that night in a daze. To himself he said that he had gone out in search of a daughter, and had come back with a wife.

CHAPTER XXXVII

"WILLIAM'S BROTHER"

It was decided that for the present, the engagement should not be known outside the family. The wedding would not take place immediately, William said, and it was just as well to keep the matter to themselves until plans were a little more definite.

The members of the family were told at once. Aunt Hannah said "Oh, my grief and conscience!" three times, and made matters scarcely better by adding apologetically: "Oh, of course it's all right, it's all right, only—" She did not finish her sentence, and William, who had told her the news, did not know whether he would have been more or less pleased if she had finished it.

Cyril received the information moodily, and lapsed at once into a fit of abstraction from which he roused himself hardly enough to offer perfunctory congratulations and best wishes.

Billy was a little puzzled at Cyril's behavior. She had been sure for some time that Cyril had ceased to care specially for her, even if he ever did fancy that he loved her. She had hoped to keep him for a friend, but of late she had been forced to question even his friendliness. He had, in fact, gone back almost to his old reserve and taciturn aloofness.

From the West, in response to William's news of the engagement, came a cordially pleased note in Kate's scrawling handwriting. Kate, indeed, seemed to be the only member of the family who was genuinely delighted with the coming marriage. As to Bertram—Bertram appeared to have aged years in a single night, so drawn and white was his face the morning after William had told him his plans.

William had dreaded most of all to tell Bertram. He was very sure that Bertram himself cared for Billy; and it was doubly hard because in William's own mind was a strong conviction that the younger man was decidedly the one for her. Realizing, however, that Bertram must be told, William chose a time for the telling when Bertram was smoking in his den in the twilight, with his face half hidden from sight.

Bertram said little—very little, that night; but in the morning he went straight to Billy.

Billy was shocked. She had never seen the smiling, self-reliant, debonair Bertram like this.

"Billy, is this true?" he demanded. The dull misery in his voice told Billy that he knew the answer before he asked the question.

"Yes, yes; but, Bertram, please—please don't take it like this!" she implored.

"How would you have me take it?"

"Why, just—just sensibly. You know I told you that—that the other never could be—never."

"I know YOU said so; but I—believed otherwise."

"But I told you—I did not love you—that way."

Bertram winced. He rose to his feet abruptly.

"I know you did, Billy. I'm a fool, of course, to think that I could ever—change it. I shouldn't have come here, either, this morning. But I—had to. Good-by!" His face, as he held out his hand, was tragic with renunciation.

"Why, Bertram, you aren't going—now—like this!" cried the girl. "You've just come!"

The man turned almost impatiently.

"And do you think I can stay—like this? Billy, won't you say good-by?" he asked in a softer voice, again with outstretched hand.

Billy shook her head. She ignored the hand, and resolutely backed away.

"No, not like that. You are angry with me," she grieved. "Besides, you make it sound as if—if you were going away."

"I am going away."

"Bertram!" There was terror as well as dismay in Billy's voice.

Again the man turned sharply.

"Billy, why are you making this thing so hard for me?" he asked in despair. "Can't you see that I must go?"

"Indeed, I can't. And you mustn't go, either. There isn't any reason why you should," urged Billy, talking very fast, and working her fingers nervously. "Things are just the same as they were before—for you. I'm just going to marry William, but I wasn't ever going to marry you, so that doesn't change things any for you. Don't you see? Why, Bertram, you mustn't go away! There won't be anybody left. Cyril's going next week, you know; and if you go there won't be anybody left but William and me. Bertram, you mustn't go; don't you see? I should feel lost without—you!" Billy was almost crying now.

Bertram looked up quickly. An odd change had come to his face. For a moment he gazed silently into Billy's agitated countenance; then he asked in a low voice:

"Billy, did you think that after you and William were married I should still continue to live at—the Strata?"

"Why, of course you will!" cried the girl, indignantly. "Why, Bertram, you'll be my brother then—my real brother; and one of the very chiefest things I'm anticipating when I go there to live is the good times you and I will have together when I'm William's wife!"

Bertram drew in his breath audibly, and caught his lower lip between his teeth. With an abrupt movement he turned his back and walked to the window. For a full minute he stayed there, watched by the amazed, displeased eyes of the girl. When he came back he sat down quietly in the chair facing Billy. His countenance was grave and his eyes were a little troubled; but the haggard look of misery was quite gone.

"Billy," he began gently, "you must forgive my saying this, but—are you quite sure you—love William?"

Billy flushed with anger.

"You have no right to ask such a question. Of course I love William."

"Of course you do—we all love William. William is, in fact, a most lovable man. But William's wife should, perhaps, love him a little differently from—all of us."

"And she will, certainly," retorted the girl, with a quick lifting of her chin. "Bertram, I don't think you have any right to—to make such insinuations."

"And I won't make them any more," replied Bertram, gravely. "I just wanted you to make sure that you—knew."

"I shall make sure, and I shall know," said Billy, firmly—so firmly that it sounded almost as if she were trying to convince herself as well as others.

There was a long pause, then the man asked diffidently:

"And so you are very sure that—that you want me to—stay?"

"Indeed I do! Besides,—don't you remember?—there are all my people to be entertained. They must be taken to places, and given motor rides and picnics. You told me last week that you'd love to help me; but, of course, if you don't want to—"

"But I do want to," cried Bertram, heartily, a gleam of the old cheerfulness springing to his eyes. "I'm dying to!"

The girl looked up with quick distrust. For a moment she eyed him with bent brows. To her mind he had gone back to his old airy, hopeful light-heartedness. He was once more "only Bertram." She hesitated, then said with stern decision:

"Bertram, you know I want you, and you must know that I'm delighted to have you drop this silly notion of going away. But if this quick change means that you are staying with any idea that—that I shall change, then—then you must go. But if you will stay as WILLIAM'S BROTHER then—I'll be more than glad to have you."

"I'll stay—as William's brother," agreed Bertram; and Billy did not notice the quick indrawing of his breath nor the close shutting of his lips after the words were spoken.

CHAPTER XXXVIII

THE ENGAGEMENT OF TWO

By the middle of July the routine of Billy's days was well established. Marie had been for a week a welcome addition to the family, and she was proving to be of invaluable aid in entertaining Billy's guests. The overworked widow and the little lodging-house keeper from the West End were enjoying Billy's hospitality now; and just to look at their beaming countenances was an inspiration, Billy said.

Cyril had gone abroad. Aunt Hannah was spending a week at the North Shore with friends. Bertram, true to his promise, was playing the gallant to Billy's guests; and so assiduous was he in his attentions that Billy at last remonstrated with him.

"But I didn't mean them to take ALL your time," she protested.

"Don't they like it? Do they see too much of me?" he demanded.

"No, no! They love it, of course. You must know that. Nobody else could give such beautiful times as you've given us. But it's yourself I'm thinking of. You're giving up all your time. Besides, I didn't mean to keep you here all summer, of course. You always go away some, you know, for a vacation."

"But I'm having a vacation here, doing this," laughed Bertram. "I'm sure I'm getting sea air down to the beaches and mountain air out to the Blue Hills. And as for excitement—if you can find anything more wildly exciting than it was yesterday when Miss Marie and I took the widow and the spinster lady on the Roller-coaster—just show it to me; that's all!"

Billy laughed.

"They told me about it—Marie in particular. She said you were lovely to them, and let them do every single thing they wanted to; and that half an hour after they got there they were like two children let out of school. Dear me, I wish I'd gone. I never stay at home that I don't miss something," she finished regretfully.

Bertram shrugged his shoulders.

"If it's Roller-coasters and Chute-the-chutes that you want, I fancy you'll get enough before the week is out," he sighed laughingly. "They said they'd like to go there to-morrow, please, when I asked them what we should do next. What surprises me is that they like such things—such hair-raising things. When I first saw them, black-gowned and stiff-backed, sitting in your little room here, I thought I should never dare offer them anything more wildly exciting than a church service or a lecture on psychology, with perhaps a band concert hinted at, provided the band could be properly instructed beforehand as to tempo and selections. But now—really, Billy, why do you suppose they have taken such a fancy to these kiddish stunts—those two staid women?"

Billy laughed, but her eyes softened.

"I don't know unless it's because all their lives they've been tied to such dead monotony that just the exhilaration of motion is bliss to them. But you won't always have to risk your neck and your temper in this fashion, Bertram. Next week my little couple from South Boston comes. She adores pictures and stuffed animals. You'll have to do the museums with her. Then there's little crippled Tommy—he'll be perfectly contented if you'll put him down where he can hear the band play. And all you'll have to do when that one stops is to pilot him to the next one. This IS good of you, Bertram, and I do thank you for it," finished Billy, fervently, just as Marie, the widow, and the "spinster lady" entered the room.

Billy told herself these days that she was very happy—very happy indeed. Was she not engaged to a good man, and did she not also have it in her power to make the long summer days a pleasure to many people? The fact that she had to tell herself that she was happy in order to convince herself that she was so, did not occur to Billy—yet.

Not long after Marie arrived, Billy told her of the engagement. William was at the house very frequently, and owing to the intimacy of Marie's relationship with the family Billy decided to tell her how matters stood. Marie's reception of the news was somewhat surprising. First she looked frightened.

"To William?—you are engaged to William?"

"Why—yes."

"But I thought—surely it was—don't you mean—Mr. Cyril?"

"No, I don't," laughed Billy. "And certainly I ought to know."

"And you don't—care for him?"

"I hope not—if I'm going to marry William."

So light was Billy's voice and manner that Marie dared one more question.

"And he—doesn't care—for you?"

"I hope not—if William is going to marry me," laughed Billy again.

"Oh-h!" breathed Marie, with an odd intonation of relief. "Then I'm glad—so glad! And I hope you'll be very, very happy, dear."

Billy looked into Marie's glowing face and was pleased: there seemed to be so few, so very few faces into which she had looked and found entire approbation of her engagement to William.

Billy saw a great deal of William now. He was always kind and considerate, and he tried to help her entertain her guests; but Billy, grateful as she was to him for his efforts, was relieved when he resigned his place to Bertram. Bertram did, indeed, know so much better how to do it. William tried to help her, too, about training her vines and rosebushes; but of course, even in this, he could not be expected to show quite the interest that Bertram manifested in every green shoot and opening bud, for he had not helped her plant them, as Bertram had.

Billy was a little troubled sometimes, that she did not feel more at ease with William. She thought it natural that she should feel a little diffident with him, in the face of his sudden change from an "uncle" to an accepted lover; but she did not see why she should be afraid of him—yet she was. She owned that to herself unhappily. And he was so good!—she owned that, too. He seemed not to have a thought in the world but for her comfort and happiness; and there was no end to the tactful little things he was always doing for her pleasure. He seemed, also, to have divined that she did not like to be kissed and caressed; and only occasionally did he kiss her, and then it was merely a sort of fatherly salute on her forehead—for which consideration Billy was grateful: Billy decided that she would not like to be kissed on the lips.

After some days of puzzling over the matter Billy concluded that it was self-consciousness that caused all the trouble. With William she was self-conscious. If she could only forget that she was some day to be William's wife, the old delightful comradeship would return, and she would be at ease again with him. In time, after she had become accustomed to the idea of marriage, it would not so confuse her, of course. She loved him dearly, and she wanted to make him happy; but for the present—just while she was "getting used to things"—she would try to forget, sometimes, that she was going to be William's wife.

Billy was happier now. She was always happier after she had thought things out to her own satisfaction. She turned with new zest to the entertainment of her guests; and with Bertram she planned many delightful trips for their pleasure. Bertram was a great comfort to her these days. Never, in word or look, could she see that he overstepped the role which he had promised to play—William's brother.

Billy went back to her music, too. A new melody was running through her head, and she longed to put it on paper. Already her first little "Group of Songs" had found friends, and Billy, to a very modest extent, was beginning to taste the sweets of fame.

Thus, by all these interests, did Billy try "to get used to things."

CHAPTER XXXIX

A LITTLE PIECE OF PAPER

Of all Billy's guests, Marie was very plainly the happiest. She was a permanent guest, it is true, while the others came for only a week or two at a time; but it was not this, Billy decided, that had brought so brilliant a sparkle to Marie's eyes, so joyous a laugh to her lips. The joyousness was all the more noticeable, because heretofore Marie, while very sweet, had been also sad. Her big blue eyes had always carried a haunting shadow, and her step had lacked the spring belonging to youth and happiness. Certainly, Billy had never seen her like this before.

"Verily, Marie," she teased one day, "have you found an exhaustless supply of stockings to mend, or a never-done pudding to make—which?"

"Why? What do you mean?"

"Oh, nothing. I was only wondering just what had brought that new light to your eyes."

"Is there a new light?"

"There certainly is."

"It must be because I'm so happy, then," sighed Marie; "because you're so good to me."

"Is that all?"

"Isn't that enough?" Marie's tone was evasive.

"No." Billy shook her head mischievously. "Marie, what is it?"

"It's nothing—really, it's nothing," protested Marie, hurrying out of the room with a nervous laugh.

Billy frowned. She was suspicious before; she was sure now. In less than twelve hours' time came her opportunity. She was alone again with Marie.

"Marie, who is he?" she asked abruptly.

"He? Who?"

"The man who is to wear the stockings and eat the pudding."

The little music teacher flushed very red, but she managed to display something that might pass for surprise.

"BILLY!"

"Come, dear," coaxed Billy, winningly. "Tell me about it. I'm so interested!"

"But there isn't anything to tell—really there isn't."

"Who is he?"

"He isn't anybody—that is, he doesn't know he's anybody," amended Marie.

Billy laughed softly.

"Oh, doesn't he! Hasn't he ever shown—that he cared?"

"No; that is—perhaps he has, only I thought then—that it was—another girl."

"Another girl! So there's another girl in the case?"

"Yes. I mean, no," corrected Marie, suddenly beginning to realize what she was saying. "Really, it wasn't anything—it isn't anything!" she protested.

"Hm-m," murmured Billy, archly. "Oh, I'm getting on some! He did show, once, that he cared; but you thought it was another girl, and you coldly looked the other way. Now, there ISN'T any other girl, you find, and—Marie, tell me the rest!"

Marie shook her head emphatically, and pulled herself gently away from Billy's grasp.

"No, no, please!" she begged. "It really isn't anything. I'm sure I'm imagining it all!" she cried, as she ran away.

During the days that followed, Billy speculated not a little on Marie's half-told story, and wondered interestedly who the man might be. She questioned Marie once again, but the girl would tell nothing more; and, indeed, Billy was so occupied with her own perplexities that she had little time for those of other people.

To herself Billy was forced to own that she was not "getting used to things." She was still self-conscious with William; she could not forget that she was one day to be his wife. She could not bring back the dear old freedom of comradeship with him.

Billy was alarmed now. She had begun to ask herself searching questions. What should she do if never, never should she get used to the idea of marrying William? How could she marry him if he was still "Uncle William," and never her dear lover in her eyes? Why had she not been wise enough and brave enough to tell him in the first place that she was not at all sure that she loved him, but that she would try to do so? Then when she had tried—as she had now—and failed, she could have told him honestly the truth, and it would not have been so great a shock to him as it must be now, if she should tell him.

Billy had remorsefully come to the conclusion that she could never love any man well enough to marry him, when one day so small a thing as a piece of paper fluttered into her vision, and showed her the fallacy of that idea.

It was a half-sheet of note paper, and it blew from Marie's balcony to the lawn below. Billy found it there later, and as she picked it up her eyes fell on a single name in Marie's handwriting inscribed half a dozen times as if the writer had musingly accompanied her thoughts with her pen; and the name was, "Marie Henshaw."

For a moment Billy stared at the name perplexedly—then in a flash came the remembrance of Marie's words; and Billy breathed: "Henshaw!—the man—BERTRAM!"

Billy dropped the paper then and fled. In her own room, behind locked doors, she sat down to think.

Bertram! It was he for whom Marie cared—HER Bertram! And then it came to Billy with staggering force that he was not HER Bertram at all. He never could be her Bertram now. He was—Marie's.

Billy was frightened then, so fierce was this strange new something that rose within her—this overpowering something that seemed to blot out all the world, and leave only—Bertram. She knew then, that it had always been Bertram to whom she had turned, though she had been blind to the cause of that turning. Always her plans had included him. Always she had been the happiest in his presence; never had she pictured him anywhere else but at her side. Certainly never had she pictured him as the devoted lover of another woman!... And she had not known what it all meant—poor blind child that she was!

Very resolutely now Billy set herself to looking matters squarely in the face. She understood it quite well. All summer Marie and Bertram had been thrown together. No wonder Marie had fallen in love with Bertram, and that he—Billy thought she comprehended now why Bertram had found it so easy for the last few weeks to be William's brother. She, of course, had been the "other girl" whom Marie had once feared that the man loved. It was all so clear—so woefully clear!

With an aching heart Billy asked herself what now was to be done. For herself, turn whichever way she could, she could see nothing but unhappiness. She determined, therefore, with Spartan fortitude, that to no one else would she bring equal unhappiness. She would be silent. Bertram and Marie loved each other. That matter was settled. As to William—Billy thought of the story William had told her of his lonely life,—of the plea he had made to her; and her heart ached. Whatever happened, William must be made happy. William must not be told. Her promise to William must be kept.

CHAPTER XL

WILLIAM PAYS A VISIT

Before September passed all Billy's friends said that her summer's self-appointed task had been too hard for her. In no other way could they account for the sad change that had come to her.

Undeniably Billy looked really ill. Always slender, she was shadow-like now. Her eyes had found again the wistful appeal of her girlhood, only now they carried something that was almost fear, as well. The rose-flush had gone from her cheeks, and pathetic little hollows had appeared, making the round young chin below look almost pointed. Certainly Billy did seem to be ill.

Late in September William went West on business. Incidentally he called to see his sister, Kate.

"Well, and how is everybody?" asked Kate, cheerily, after the greetings were over.

William sighed.

"Well, 'everybody,' to me, Kate, is pretty badly off. We're worried about Billy."

"Billy! You don't mean she's sick? Why, she's always been the picture of health!"

"I know she has; but she isn't now."

"What's the trouble?"

"That's what we don't know."

"You've had the doctor?"

"Of course; two or three of them—though much against Billy's will. But—they didn't help us."

"What did they say?"

"They could find nothing except perhaps a little temporary stomach trouble, or something of that kind, which they all agreed was no just cause for her present condition."

"But what did they say it was?"

"Why, they said it seemed like nervousness, or as if something was troubling her. They asked if she weren't under some sort of strain."

"Well, is she? Does anything trouble her?"

"Not that I know of. Anyhow, if there is anything, none of us can find out what it is."

Kate frowned. She threw a quick look into her brother's face.

"William," she began hesitatingly, "forgive me, but—Billy is quite happy in—her engagement, I suppose."

The man flushed painfully, and sighed.

"I've thought of that, of course. In fact, it was the first thing I did think of. I even began to watch her rather closely, and once I—questioned her a little."

"What did she say?"

"She seemed so frightened and distressed that I didn't say much myself. I couldn't. I had but just begun when her eyes filled with tears, and she asked me in a frightened little voice if she had done anything to displease me, anything to make me unhappy; and she seemed so anxious and grieved and dismayed that I should even question her, that I had to stop."

"What has she done this summer? Where has she been?"

"She hasn't been anywhere. Didn't I write you? She's kept open house for a lot of her less fortunate friends—a sort of vacation home, you know; and—and I must say she's given them a world of happiness, too."

"But wasn't that hard for her?"

"It didn't seem to be. She appeared to enjoy it immensely, particularly at first. Of course she had plenty of help, and that wonderful little Miss Hawthorn has been a host in herself. They're all gone now, anyway, except Miss Hawthorn."

"But Billy must have had the care and the excitement."

"Perhaps—to a certain extent. Though not much, after all. You see Bertram, too, has given up his summer to them, and has been playing the devoted escort to the whole bunch. Indeed, for the last few weeks of it, since Billy began to seem so ill, he and Miss Hawthorn have schemed to take all the care from Billy, and they have done the whole thing together."

"But what HAS Billy done to make her like this?"

"I don't know. She's done lots for me, in all sorts of ways—cataloguing my curios, you know, and going with me to hunt up things. In fact, she seems the happiest when she IS doing something for me. It's come to be a sort of mania with her, I'm afraid—to do something for me. Kate, I'm really worried. What do you suppose is the matter?"

Kate shook her head. The puzzled frown had come back to her face.

"I can't imagine," she began slowly. "Of course, when I told her you loved her and—"

"When you told her wha-at?" exploded the usually low-voiced William, with sudden sharpness.

"When I told her that you loved her, William. You see, I—"

William sprang to his feet.

"Told her that I loved her!" he cried, aghast. "Good heavens, Kate, do you mean to say that YOU told her THAT."

"Why, y-yes."

"And may I ask where you got your information?"

"Why, William Henshaw, what a question! I got it from yourself, of course," defended Kate.

"From ME!" William's face expressed sheer amazement.

"Certainly; on that drive when I was East in June," returned Kate, with dignity. "YOU evidently have forgotten it, but I have not. You told me very frankly how much you thought of her, and how you longed to have her back there with you, but that she didn't seem to be ready to come. I was sorry for you, and I wanted to do something to help, particularly as it might have been my fault, partly, that she went away, in the first place."

William lifted his head.

"What do you mean?"

"Why, nothing, only that I—I told her a little of how—how upsetting her arrival had been to everything, and of how much you had done for her, and put yourself out. I said it so she'd appreciate things, of course, but she took it quite differently from what I had intended she should take it, and seemed quite cut up about it. Then she went away in that wily, impulsive fashion."

William bit his lip, but he did not speak. Kate was plunging on feverishly, and in the face of the greater revelation he let the lesser one drop.

"And so that's why I was particularly anxious to bring things around right again," continued Kate. "And that's why I spoke. I thought I'd seen how things were, and on the drive I said so. Then is when I advised you to speak to Billy; but you declared that Billy wasn't ready, and that you couldn't make a girl marry against her will. NOW don't you recollect it?"

A great light of understanding broke over William's face. He started to speak, but something evidently stayed the words on his lips. With controlled deliberation he turned and sat down. Then he said:

"Kate, will you kindly tell me just what you DID do?"

"Why, I didn't do so very much. I just tried to help, that's all. After I talked with you, and advised you to ask Billy right away to marry you, I went to her. I thought she cared for you already, anyway; but I just wanted to tell her how very much it was to you, and so sort of pave the way. And now comes the part that I started to tell you a little while ago when you caught me up so sharply. I was going to say that when I told Billy this, she appeared to be surprised, and almost frightened. You see, she hadn't known you cared for her, after all, and so I had a chance to help and make it plain to her how you did love her, so that when you spoke everything would be all right. There, that's all. You see I didn't do so very much."

"'So very much'!" groaned William, starting to his feet. "Great Scott!"

"Why, William, what do you mean? Where are you going?"

"I'm going—to—Billy," retorted William with slow distinctness. "And I'm going to try to get there—before—you—CAN!" And with this extraordinary shot—for William—he left the house.

William went to Billy as fast as steam could carry him. He found her in her little drawing-room listlessly watching with Aunt Hannah the game of chess that Bertram and Marie were playing.

"Billy, you poor, dear child, come here," he said abruptly, as soon as the excitement of his unexpected arrival had passed. "I want to talk to you." And he led the way to the veranda which he knew would be silent and deserted.

"To talk to—me?" murmured Billy, as she wonderingly came to his side, a startled questioning in her wide dark eyes.

CHAPTER XLI

THE CROOKED MADE STRAIGHT

William did not re-enter the house after his talk with Billy on the veranda.

"I will go down the steps and around by the rose garden to the street, dear," he said. "I'd rather not go in now. Just make my adieus, please, and say that I couldn't stay any longer. And now—good-by." His eyes as they looked down at her, were moist and very tender. His lips trembled a little, but they smiled, and there was a look of new-born peace and joy on his face.

Billy, too, was smiling, though wistfully. The frightened questioning had gone from her eyes, leaving only infinite tenderness.

"You are sure it—is all right—now?" she stammered.

"Very sure, little girl; and it's the first time it has been right for weeks. Billy, that was very dear of you, and I love you for it; but think how near—how perilously near you came to lifelong misery!"

"But I thought—you wanted me—so much," she smiled shyly.

"And I did, and I do—for a daughter. You don't doubt that NOW?"

"No, oh, no," laughed Billy, softly; and to her face came a happy look of relief as she finished: "And I'll be so glad to be—the daughter!"

For some minutes after the man had gone, Billy stood by the steps where he had left her. She was still there when Bertram came to the veranda door and spoke to her.

"Billy, I saw William go by the window, so I knew you were alone. May I speak to you?"

The girl turned with a start.

"Why, of course! What is it?—but I thought you were playing. Where is Marie?"

"The game is finished; besides—Billy, why are you always asking me lately where Marie is, as if I were her keeper, or she mine?" he demanded, with a touch of nervous irritation.

"Why, nothing, Bertram," smiled Billy, a little wearily; "only that you were playing together a few minutes ago, and I wondered where she had gone."

"'A few minutes ago'!" echoed Bertram with sudden bitterness. "Evidently the time passed swiftly with you, Billy. William was out here MORE than an hour."

"Why—Bertram!"

"Yes, I know. I've no business to say that, of course," sighed the man; "but, Billy, that's why I came out—because I must speak to you this once. Won't you come and sit down, please?" he implored despairingly.

"Why, Bertram," murmured Billy again, faintly, as she turned toward the vine-shaded corner and sat down. Her eyes were startled. A swift color had come to her cheeks.

"Billy," began the man, in a sternly controlled voice, "please let me speak this once, and don't try to stop me. You may think, for a moment, that it's disloyal to William if you listen; but it isn't. There's this much due to me—that you let me speak now. Billy, I can't stand it. I've tried, but it's no use. I've got to go away, and it's right that I should. I'm not the only one that thinks so, either. Marie does, too."

"MARIE!"

"Yes. I talked it all over with her. She's known for a long time how it's been with me; how I cared—for you."

"Marie! You've told Marie that?" gasped Billy.

"Yes. Surely you don't mind Marie's knowing," went on Bertram, dejectedly. "And she's been so good to me, and tried to—help me."

Bertram was not looking at Billy now. If he had been he would have seen the incredulous joy come into her face. His eyes were moodily fixed on the floor.

"And so, Billy, I've come to tell you. I'm going away," he continued, after a moment. "I've got to go. I thought once, when I first talked with you of William, that you didn't know your own heart; that you didn't really care for him. I was even fool enough to think that—that it would be I to whom you'd turn—some day. And so I stayed. But I stayed honorably, Billy! YOU know that! You know that I haven't once forgotten—not once, that I was only William's brother. I promised you I'd be that—and I have been; haven't I?"

Billy nodded silently. Her face was turned away.

"But, Billy, I can't do it any longer. I've got to ask for my promise back, and then, of course, I can't stay."

"But you—you don't have to go—away," murmured the girl, faintly.

Bertram sprang to his feet. His face was white.

"Billy," he cried, standing tall and straight before her, "Billy, I love every touch of your hand, every glance of your eye, every word that falls from your lips. Do you think I can stay—now? I want my promise back! When I'm no longer William's brother—then I'll go!"

"But you don't have to have it back—that is, you don't have to have it at all," stammered Billy, flushing adorably. She, too, was on her feet now.

"Billy, what do you mean?"

"Don't you see? I—I HAVE turned," she faltered breathlessly, holding out both her hands. Even then, in spite of the great light that leaped to his eyes, Bertram advanced only a single step.

"But—William?" he questioned, unbelievingly.

"It WAS a mistake, just as you thought. We know now—both of us. We don't either of us care for the other—that way. And—Bertram, I think it HAS been you—all the time, only I didn't know!"

"Billy, Billy!" choked Bertram in a voice shaken with emotion. He opened his arms then, wide—and Billy walked straight into them.

CHAPTER XLII

THE "END OF THE STORY"

It was two days after Billy's new happiness had come to her that Cyril came home. He went very soon to see Billy.

The girl was surprised at the change in his appearance. He had grown thin and haggard looking, and his eyes were somber. He moved restlessly about the room for a time, finally seating himself at the piano and letting his fingers slip from one mournful little melody to another. Then, with a discordant crash, he turned.

"Billy, do you think any girl would marry—me?" he demanded.

"Why, Cyril!"

"There, now, please don't begin that," he begged fretfully. "I realize, of course, that I'm a very unlikely subject for matrimony. You made me understand that clearly enough last winter!"

"Last—winter?"

Cyril raised his eyebrows.

"Oh, I came to you for a little encouragement, and to make a confession," he said. "I made the confession—but I didn't get the encouragement."

Billy changed color. She thought she knew what he meant, but at the same time she couldn't understand why he should wish to refer to that conversation now.

"A—confession?" she repeated, hesitatingly.

"Yes. I told you that I'd begun to doubt my being such a woman-hater, after all. I intimated that YOU'D begun the softening process, and that then I'd found a certain other young woman who had—well, who had kept up the good work."

"Oh!" cried Billy suddenly, with a peculiar intonation. "Oh-h!" Then she laughed softly.

"Well, that was the confession," resumed Cyril. "Then I came out flat-footed and said that I wanted to marry her—but there is where I didn't get the encouragement!"

"Indeed! I'm afraid I wasn't very considerate," stammered Billy.

"No, you weren't," agreed Cyril, moodily. "I didn't know but now—" his voice softened a little—"with this new happiness of yours and Bertram's that—you might find a little encouragement for me."

"And I will," cried Billy, promptly. "Tell me about her."

"I did—last winter," reproached the man, "and you were sure I was deceiving myself. You drew the gloomiest sort of picture of the misery I would take with a wife."

"I did?" Billy was laughing very merrily now.

"Yes. You said she'd always be talking and laughing when I wanted to be quiet, and that she'd want to drag me out to parties and plays when I wanted to stay at home; and—oh, lots of things. I tried to make it clear to you that—that this little woman wasn't that sort. But I couldn't," finished Cyril, gloomily.

"But of course she isn't," declared Billy, with quick sympathy. "I—I didn't know—WHAT—I was—talking about," she added with emphatic distinctness. Then she smiled to think how little Cyril knew how very true those words were. "Tell me about her," she begged again. "I know she must be very lovely and brilliant, and of course a wonderful musician. YOU couldn't choose any one else!"

To her surprise Cyril turned abruptly and began to play again. A nervous little staccato scherzo fell from his fingers, but it dropped almost at once into a quieter melody, and ended with something that sounded very much like the last strain of "Home, Sweet Home." Then he wheeled about on the piano stool.

"Billy, that's exactly where you're wrong—I DON'T want that kind of wife. I don't want a brilliant one, and—now, Billy, this sounds like horrible heresy, I know, but it's true—I don't care whether she can play, or not; but I should prefer that she shouldn't play—much!"

"Why, Cyril Henshaw!—and you, with your music! As if you could be contented with a woman like that!"

"Oh, I want her to like music, of course," modified Cyril; "but I don't care to have her MAKE it. Billy, do you know? You'll laugh, of course, but my picture of a wife is always one thing: a room with a table and a shaded lamp, and a little woman beside it with the light on her hair, and a great, basket of sewing beside her. You see I AM domestic!" he finished a little defiantly.

"I should say you were," laughed Billy. "And have you found her?—this little woman who is to do nothing but sit and sew in the circle of the shaded lamp?"

"Yes, I've found her, but I'm not at all sure she's found me. That's where I want your help. Oh, I don't mean, of course," he added, "that she's got to sit under that lamp all the time. It's only that—that I hope she likes that sort of thing."

"And—does she?"

"Yes; that is, I think she does," smiled Cyril. "Anyhow, she told me once that—that the things she liked best to do in all the world were to mend stockings and to make puddings."

Billy sprang to her feet with a little cry. Now, indeed, had Cyril kept his promise and made "many things clear" to her.

"Cyril, come here," she cried tremulously, leading the way to the open veranda door. The next moment Cyril was looking across the lawn to the little summerhouse in the midst of Billy's rose garden. In full view within the summerhouse sat Marie—sewing.

"Go, Cyril; she's waiting for you," smiled Billy, mistily. "The light's only the sun, to be sure, and maybe there isn't a whole basket of sewing there. But—SHE'S there!"

"You've—guessed, then!" breathed Cyril.

"I've not guessed—I know. And—it's all right."

"You mean—?" Only Cyril's pleading eyes finished the question.

"Yes, I'm sure she does," nodded Billy. And then she added under her breath as the man passed swiftly down the steps: "'Marie Henshaw' indeed! So 'twas Cyril all the time—and never Bertram—who was the inspiration of that bit of paper give-away!"

When she turned back into the room she came face to face with Bertram.

"I spoke, dear, but you didn't hear," he said, as he hurried forward with outstretched hands.

"Bertram," greeted Billy, with surprising irrelevance, "'and they all lived happily ever after'—they DID! Isn't that always the ending to the story—a love story?"

"Of course," said Bertram with emphasis;—"OUR love story!"

"And theirs," supplemented Billy, softly; but Bertram did not hear that.

CHAPTER I. CALDERWELL DOES SOME TALKING

Calderwell had met Mr. M. J. Arkwright in London through a common friend; since then they had tramped half over Europe together in a comradeship that was as delightful as it was unusual. As Calderwell put it in a letter to his sister, Belle:
"We smoke the same cigar and drink the same tea (he's just as much of an old woman on that subject as I am!), and we agree beautifully on all necessary points of living, from tipping to late sleeping in the morning; while as for politics and religion—we disagree in those just enough to lend spice to an otherwise tame existence."

Farther along in this same letter Calderwell touched upon his new friend again.

"I admit, however, I would like to know his name. To find out what that mysterious 'M. J.' stands for has got to be pretty nearly an obsession with me. I am about ready to pick his pocket or rifle his trunk in search of some lurking 'Martin' or 'John' that will set me at peace. As it is, I confess that I have ogled his incoming mail and his outgoing baggage shamelessly, only to be slapped in the face always and everlastingly by that bland 'M. J.' I've got my revenge, now, though. To myself I call him 'Mary Jane'—and his broad-shouldered, brown-bearded six feet of muscular manhood would so like to be called 'Mary Jane'! By the way, Belle, if you ever hear of murder and sudden death in my direction, better set the sleuths on the trail of Arkwright. Six to one you'll find I called him 'Mary Jane' to his face!"

Calderwell was thinking of that letter now, as he sat at a small table in a Paris café. Opposite him was the six feet of muscular manhood, broad shoulders, pointed brown beard, and all—and he had just addressed it, inadvertently, as "Mary Jane."

During the brief, sickening moment of silence after the name had left his lips, Calderwell was conscious of a whimsical realization of the lights, music, and laughter all about him.

"Well, I chose as safe a place as I could!" he was thinking. Then Arkwright spoke.

"How long since you've been in correspondence with members of my family?"

"Eh?"

Arkwright laughed grimly.

"Perhaps you thought of it yourself, then—I'll admit you're capable of it," he nodded, reaching for a cigar. "But it so happens you hit upon my family's favorite name for me."

"Mary Jane! You mean they actually call you that?"

"Yes," bowed the big fellow, calmly, as he struck a light. "Appropriate!—don't you think?"

Calderwell did not answer. He thought he could not.

"Well, silence gives consent, they say," laughed the other. "Anyhow, you must have had some reason for calling me that."

"Arkwright, what does 'M. J.' stand for?" demanded Calderwell.

"Oh, is that it?" smiled the man opposite. "Well, I'll own those initials have been something of a puzzle to people. One man declares they're 'Merely Jokes'; but another, not so friendly, says they stand for 'Mostly Jealousy' of more fortunate chaps who have real names for a handle. My small brothers and sisters, discovering, with the usual perspicacity of one's family on such matters, that I never signed, or called myself anything but 'M. J.,' dubbed me 'Mary Jane.' And there you have it."

"Mary Jane! You!"

Arkwright smiled oddly.

"Oh, well, what's the difference? Would you deprive them of their innocent amusement? And they do so love that 'Mary Jane'! Besides, what's in a name, anyway?" he went on, eyeing the glowing tip of the cigar between his fingers. "'A rose by any other name—'—you've heard that, probably. Names don't always signify, my dear fellow. For instance, I know a 'Billy'—but he's a girl."

Calderwell gave a sudden start.

"You don't mean Billy—Neilson?"

The other turned sharply.

"Do you know Billy Neilson?"

Calderwell gave his friend a glance from scornful eyes.

"Do I know Billy Neilson?" he cried. "Does a fellow usually know the girl he's proposed to regularly once in three months? Oh, I know I'm telling tales out of school, of course," he went on, in response to the look that had come into the brown eyes opposite. "But what's the use? Everybody knows it—that knows us. Billy herself got so she took it as a matter of course—and refused as a matter of course, too; just as she would refuse a serving of apple pie at dinner, if she hadn't wanted it."

"Apple pie!" scouted Arkwright.

Calderwell shrugged his shoulders.

"My dear fellow, you don't seem to realize it, but for the last six months you have been assisting at the obsequies of a dead romance."

"Indeed! And is it—buried, yet?"

"Oh, no," sighed Calderwell, cheerfully. "I shall go back one of these days, I'll warrant, and begin the same old game again; though I will acknowledge that the last refusal was so very decided that it's been a year, almost, since I received it. I think I was really convinced, for a while, that—that she didn't want that apple pie," he finished with a whimsical lightness that did not quite coincide with the stern lines that had come to his mouth.

For a moment there was silence, then Calderwell spoke again.

"Where did you know—Miss Billy?"

"Oh, I don't know her at all. I know of her—through Aunt Hannah."

Calderwell sat suddenly erect.

"Aunt Hannah! Is she your aunt, too? Jove! This is a little old world, after all; isn't it?"

"She isn't my aunt. She's my mother's third cousin. None of us have seen her for years, but she writes to mother occasionally; and, of course, for some time now, her letters have been running over full of Billy. She lives with her, I believe; doesn't she?"

"She does," rejoined Calderwell, with an unexpected chuckle. "I wonder if you know how she happened to live with her, at first."

"Why, no, I reckon not. What do you mean?"

Calderwell chuckled again.

"Well, I'll tell you. You, being a 'Mary Jane,' ought to appreciate it. You see, Billy was named for one William Henshaw, her father's chum, who promptly forgot all about her. At eighteen, Billy, being left quite alone in the world, wrote to 'Uncle William' and asked to come and live with him."

"Well?"

"But it wasn't well. William was a forty-year-old widower who lived with two younger brothers, an old butler, and a Chinese cook in one of those funny old Beacon Street houses in Boston. 'The Strata,' Bertram called it. Bright boy—Bertram!"

"The Strata!"

"Yes. I wish you could see that house, Arkwright. It's a regular layer cake. Cyril—he's the second brother; must be thirty-four or five now—lives on the top floor in a rugless, curtainless, music-mad existence—just a plain crank. Below him comes William. William collects things—everything from tenpenny nails to teapots, I should say, and they're all there in his rooms. Farther down somewhere comes Bertram. He's the Bertram Henshaw, you understand; the artist."

"Not the 'Face-of-a-Girl' Henshaw?"

"The same; only of course four years ago he wasn't quite so well known as he is now. Well, to resume and go on. It was into this house, this masculine paradise ruled over by Pete and Dong Ling in the kitchen, that Billy's naïve request for a home came."

"Great Scott!" breathed Arkwright, appreciatively.

"Yes. Well, the letter was signed 'Billy.' They took her for a boy, naturally, and after something of a struggle they agreed to let 'him' come. For his particular delectation they fixed up a room next to Bertram with guns and fishing rods, and such ladylike specialties; and William went to the station to meet the boy."

"With never a suspicion?"

"With never a suspicion."

"Gorry!"

"Well, 'he' came, and 'she' conquered. I guess things were lively for a while, though. Oh, there was a kitten, too, I believe, 'Spunk,' who added to the gayety of nations."

"But what did the Henshaws do?"

"Well, I wasn't there, of course; but Bertram says they spun around like tops gone mad for a time, but finally quieted down enough to summon a married sister for immediate propriety, and to establish Aunt Hannah for permanency the next day."

"So that's how it happened! Well, by George!" cried Arkwright.

"Yes," nodded the other. "So you see there are untold possibilities just in a name. Remember that. Just suppose you, as Mary Jane, should beg a home in a feminine household—say in Miss Billy's, for instance!"

"I'd like to," retorted Arkwright, with sudden warmth.

Calderwell stared a little.

The other laughed shamefacedly.

"Oh, it's only that I happen to have a devouring curiosity to meet that special young lady. I sing her songs (you know she's written some dandies!), I've heard a lot about her, and I've seen her picture." (He did not add that he had also purloined that same picture from his mother's bureau—the picture being a gift from Aunt Hannah.) "So you see I would, indeed, like to occupy a corner in the fair Miss Billy's household. I could write to Aunt Hannah and beg a home with her, you know; eh?"

"Of course! Why don't you—'Mary Jane'?" laughed Calderwell. "Billy'd take you all right. She's had a little Miss Hawthorn, a music teacher, there for months. She's always doing stunts of that sort. Belle writes me that she's had a dozen forlornites there all this last summer, two or three at a time-tired widows, lonesome old maids, and crippled kids—just to give them a royal good time. So you see she'd take you, without a doubt. Jove! what a pair you'd make: Miss Billy and Mr. Mary Jane! You'd drive the suffragettes into conniption fits—just by the sound of you!"

Arkwright laughed quietly; then he frowned.

"But how about it?" he asked. "I thought she was keeping house with Aunt Hannah. Didn't she stay at all with the Henshaws?"

"Oh, yes, a few months. I never knew just why she did leave, but I fancied, from something Billy herself said once, that she discovered she was creating rather too much of an upheaval in the Strata. So she took herself off. She went to school, and travelled considerably. She was over here when I met her first. After that she was with us all one summer on the yacht. A couple of years ago, or so, she went back to Boston, bought a house and settled down with Aunt Hannah."

"And she's not married—or even engaged?"

"Wasn't the last I heard. I haven't seen her since December, and I've heard from her only indirectly. She corresponds with my sister, and so do I—intermittently. I heard a month ago from Belle, and she had a letter from Billy in August. But I heard nothing of any engagement."

"How about the Henshaws? I should think there might be a chance there for a romance—a charming girl, and three unattached men."

Calderwell gave a slow shake of the head.

"I don't think so. William is—let me see—nearly forty-five, I guess, by this time; and he isn't a marrying man. He buried his heart with his wife and baby years ago. Cyril, according to Bertram, 'hates women and all other confusion,' so that ought to let him out. As for Bertram himself—Bertram is 'only Bertram.' He's always been that. Bertram loves girls—to paint; but I can't imagine him making serious love to any one. It would always be the tilt of a chin or the turn of a cheek that he was admiring—to paint. No, there's no chance for a romance there, I'll warrant."

"But there's—yourself."

Calderwell's eyebrows rose the fraction of an inch.

"Oh, of course. I presume January or February will find me back there," he admitted with a sigh and a shrug. Then, a little bitterly, he added: "No, Arkwright. I shall keep away if I can. I know there's no chance for me—now."

"Then you'll leave me a clear field?" bantered the other.

"Of course—'Mary Jane,'" retorted Calderwell, with equal lightness.

"Thank you."

"Oh, you needn't," laughed Calderwell. "My giving you the right of way doesn't insure you a thoroughfare for yourself—there are others, you know. Billy Neilson has had sighing swains about I her, I imagine, since she could walk and talk. She is a wonderfully fascinating little bit of femininity, and she has a heart of pure gold. All is, I envy the man who wins it—for the man who wins that, wins her."

There was no answer. Arkwright sat with his eyes on the moving throng outside the window near them. Perhaps he had not heard. At all events, when he spoke some time later, it was of a matter far removed from Miss Billy Neilson, or the way to her heart. Nor was the young lady mentioned between them again that day.

Long hours later, just before parting for the night, Arkwright said:

"Calderwell, I'm sorry, but I believe, after all, I can't take that trip to the lakes with you. I—I'm going home next week."

"Home! Hang it, Arkwright! I'd counted on you. Isn't this rather sudden?"

"Yes, and no. I'll own I've been drifting about with you contentedly enough for the last six months to make you think mountain-climbing and boat-paddling were the end and aim of my existence. But they aren't, you know, really."

"Nonsense! At heart you're as much of a vagabond as I am; and you know it."

"Perhaps. But unfortunately I don't happen to carry your pocketbook."

"You may, if you like. I'll hand it over any time," grinned Calderwell.

"Thanks. You know well enough what I mean," shrugged the other.

There was a moment's silence; then Calderwell queried:

"Arkwright, how old are you?"

"Twenty-four."

"Good! Then you're merely travelling to supplement your education, see?"

"Oh, yes, I see. But something besides my education has got to be supplemented now, I reckon."

"What are you going to do?"

There was an almost imperceptible hesitation; then, a little shortly, came the answer:

"Hit the trail for Grand Opera, and bring up, probably—in vaudeville."

Calderwell smiled appreciatively.

"You can sing like the devil," he admitted.

"Thanks," returned his friend, with uplifted eyebrows. "Do you mind calling it 'an angel'—just for this occasion?"

"Oh, the matinée-girls will do that fast enough. But, I say, Arkwright, what are you going to do with those initials then?"

"Let 'em alone."

"Oh, no, you won't. And you won't be 'Mary Jane,' either. Imagine a Mary Jane in Grand Opera! I know what you'll be. You'll be 'Señor Martini Johnini Arkwrightino'! By the way, you didn't say what that 'M. J.' really did stand for," hinted Calderwell, shamelessly.

"'Merely Jokes'—in your estimation, evidently," shrugged the other. "But my going isn't a joke, Calderwell. I'm really going. And I'm going to work."

"But—how shall you manage?"

"Time will tell."

Calderwell frowned and stirred restlessly in his chair.

"But, honestly, now, to—to follow that trail of yours will take money. And—er—" a faint red stole to his forehead—"don't they have—er—patrons for these young and budding geniuses? Why can't I have a hand in this trail, too—or maybe you'd call it a foot, eh? I'd be no end glad to, Arkwright."

"Thanks, old man." The red was duplicated this time above the brown silky beard. "That was mighty kind of you, and I appreciate it; but it won't be necessary. A generous, but perhaps misguided bachelor uncle left me a few thousands a year or so ago; and I'm going to put them all down my throat—or rather, into it—before I give up."

"Where you going to study? New York?"

Again there was an almost imperceptible hesitation before the answer came.

"I'm not quite prepared to say."

"Why not try it here?"

Arkwright shook his head.

"I did plan to, when I came over but I've changed my mind. I believe I'd rather work while longer in America."

"Hm-m," murmured Calderwell.

There was a brief silence, followed by other questions and other answers; after which the friends said good night.

In his own room, as he was dropping off to sleep, Calderwell muttered drowsily:

"By George! I haven't found out yet what that blamed 'M. J.' stands for!"

CHAPTER II. AUNT HANNAH GETS A LETTER

In the cozy living-room at Hillside, Billy Neilson's pretty home on Corey Hill, Billy herself sat writing at the desk. Her pen had just traced the date, "October twenty-fifth," when Mrs. Stetson entered with a letter in her hand.

"Writing, my dear? Then don't let me disturb you." She turned as if to go.

Billy dropped her pen, sprang to her feet, flew to the little woman's side and whirled her half across the room.

"There!" she exclaimed, as she plumped the breathless and scandalized Aunt Hannah into the biggest easy chair. "I feel better. I just had to let off steam some way. It's so lovely you came in just when you did!"

"Indeed! I—I'm not so sure of that," stammered the lady, dropping the letter into her lap, and patting with agitated fingers her cap, her curls, the two shawls about her shoulders, and the lace at her throat. "My grief and conscience, Billy! Wors't you ever grow up?"

"Hope not," purred Billy cheerfully, dropping herself on to a low hassock at Aunt Hannah's feet.

"But, my dear, you—you're engaged!"

Billy bubbled into a chuckling laugh.

"As if I didn't know that, when I've just written a dozen notes to announce it! And, oh, Aunt Hannah, such a time as I've had, telling what a dear Bertram is, and how I love, love, love him, and what beautiful eyes he has, and such a nose, and—"

"Billy!" Aunt Hannah was sitting erect in pale horror.

"Eh?" Billy's eyes were roguish.

"You didn't write that in those notes!"

"Write it? Oh, no! That's only what I wanted to write," chuckled Billy. "What I really did write was as staid and proper as—here, let me show you," she broke off, springing to her feet and running over to her desk. "There! this is about what I wrote to them all," she finished, whipping a note out of one of the unsealed envelopes on the desk and spreading it open before Aunt Hannah's suspicious eyes.

"Hm-m; that is very good—for you," admitted the lady.

"Well, I like that!—after all my stern self-control and self-sacrifice to keep out all those things I wanted to write," bridled Billy. "Besides, they'd have been ever so much more interesting reading than these will be," she pouted, as she took the note from her companion's hand.

"I don't doubt it," observed Aunt Hannah, dryly.

Billy laughed, and tossed the note back on the desk.

"I'm writing to Belle Calderwell, now," she announced musingly, dropping herself again on the hassock. "I suppose she'll tell Hugh."

"Poor boy! He'll be disappointed."

Billy sighed, but she uptilted her chin a little.

"He ought not to be. I told him long, long ago, the very first time, that—that I couldn't."

"I know, dear; but—they don't always understand." Aunt Hannah sighed in sympathy with the far-away Hugh Calderwell, as she looked down at the bright young face near her.

There was a moment's silence; then Billy gave a little laugh.

"He will be surprised," she said. "He told me once that Bertram wouldn't ever care for any girl except to paint. To paint, indeed! As if Bertram didn't love me—just me!—if he never saw another tube of paint!"

"I think he does, my dear."

Again there was silence; then, from Billy's lips there came softly:

"Just think; we've been engaged almost four weeks—and to-morrow it'll be announced. I'm so glad I didn't ever announce the other two!"

"The other two!" cried Aunt Hannah.

Billy laughed.

"Oh, I forgot. You didn't know about Cyril."

"Cyril!"

"Oh, there didn't anybody know it, either not even Cyril himself," dimpled Billy, mischievously. "I just engaged myself to him in imagination, you know, to see how I'd like it. I didn't like it. But it didn't last, anyhow, very long—just three weeks, I believe. Then I broke it off," she finished, with unsmiling mouth, but dancing eyes.

"Billy!" protested Aunt Hannah, feebly.

"But I am glad only the family knew about my engagement to Uncle William—oh, Aunt Hannah, you don't know how good it does seem to call him 'Uncle' again. It was always slipping out, anyhow, all the time we were engaged; and of course it was awful then."

"That only goes to prove, my dear, how entirely unsuitable it was, from the start."

A bright color flooded Billy's face.

"I know; but if a girl will think a man is asking for a wife when all he wants is a daughter, and if she blandly says 'Yes, thank you, I'll marry you,' I don't know what you can expect!"

"You can expect just what you got—misery, and almost a tragedy," retorted Aunt Hannah, severely.

A tender light came into Billy's eyes.

"Dear Uncle William! What a jewel he was, all the way through! And he'd have marched straight to the altar, too, with never a flicker of an eyelid, I know—self-sacrificing martyr that he was!"

"Martyr!" bristled Aunt Hannah, with extraordinary violence for her. "I'm thinking that term belonged somewhere else. A month ago, Billy Neilson, you did not look as if you'd live out half your days. But I suppose you'd have gone to the altar, too, with never a flicker of an eyelid!"

"But I thought I had to," protested Billy. "I couldn't grieve Uncle William so, after Mrs. Hartwell had said how he—he wanted me."

Aunt Hannah's lips grew stern at the corners.

"There are times when—when I think it would be wiser if Mrs. Kate Hartwell would attend to her own affairs!" Aunt Hannah's voice fairly shook with wrath.

"Why-Aunt Hannah!" reproved Billy in mischievous horror. "I'm shocked at you!"

Aunt Hannah flushed miserably.

"There, there, child, forget I said it. I ought not to have said it, of course," she murmured agitatedly.

Billy laughed.

"You should have heard what Uncle William said! But never mind. We all found out the mistake before it was too late, and everything is lovely now, even to Cyril and Marie. Did you ever see anything so beatifically happy as that couple are? Bertram says he hasn't heard a dirge from Cyril's rooms for three weeks; and that if anybody else played the kind of music he's been playing, it would be just common garden ragtime!"

"Music! Oh, my grief and conscience! That makes me think, Billy. If I'm not actually forgetting what I came in here for," cried Aunt Hannah, fumbling in the folds of her dress for the letter that had slipped from her lap. "I've had word from a young niece. She's going to study music in Boston."

"A niece?"

"Well, not really, you know. She calls me 'Aunt,' just as you and the Henshaw boys do. But I really am related to her, for her mother and I are third cousins, while it was my husband who was distantly related to the Henshaw family."

"What's her name?"

"'Mary Jane Arkwright.' Where is that letter?"

"Here it is, on the floor," reported Billy. "Were you going to read it to me?" she asked, as she picked it up.

"Yes—if you don't mind."

"I'd love to hear it."

"Then I'll read it. It—it rather annoys me in some ways. I thought the whole family understood that I wasn't living by myself any longer—that I was living with you. I'm sure I thought I wrote them that, long ago. But this sounds almost as if they didn't understand it—at least, as if this girl didn't."

"How old is she?"

"I don't know; but she must be some old, to be coming here to Boston to study music, alone—singing, I think she said."

"You don't remember her, then?"

Aunt Hannah frowned and paused, the letter half withdrawn from its envelope.

"No—but that isn't strange. They live West. I haven't seen any of them for years. I know there are several children—and I suppose I've been told their names. I know there's a boy—the eldest, I think—who is quite a singer, and there's a girl who paints, I believe; but I don't seem to remember a 'Mary Jane.'"

"Never mind! Suppose we let Mary Jane speak for herself," suggested Billy, dropping her chin into the small pink cup of her hand, and settling herself to listen.

"Very well," sighed Aunt Hannah; and she opened the letter and began to read.

"DEAR AUNT HANNAH:—This is to tell you that I'm coming to Boston to study singing in the school for Grand Opera, and I'm planning to look you up. Do you object? I said to a friend the other day that I'd half a mind to write to Aunt Hannah and beg a home with her; and my friend retorted: 'Why don't you, Mary Jane?' But that, of course, I should not think of doing.

"But I know I shall be lonesome, Aunt Hannah, and I hope you'll let me see you once in a while, anyway. I plan now to come next week —I've already got as far as New York, as you see by the address—and I shall hope to see you soon.

"All the family would send love, I know.
"M. J. ARKWRIGHT."

"Grand Opera! Oh, how perfectly lovely," cried Billy.
"Yes, but Billy, do you think she is expecting me to invite her to make her home with me? I shall have to write and explain that I can't—if she does, of course."
Billy frowned and hesitated.
"Why, it sounded—a little—that way; but—" Suddenly her face cleared. "Aunt Hannah, I've thought of the very thing. We will take her!"
"Oh, Billy, I couldn't think of letting you do that," demurred Aunt Hannah. "You're very kind—but, oh, no; not that!"
"Why not? I think it would be lovely; and we can just as well as not. After Marie is married in December, she can have that room. Until then she can have the little blue room next to me."
"But—but—we don't know anything about her."
"We know she's your niece, and she's lonesome; and we know she's musical. I shall love her for every one of those things. Of course we'll take her!"
"But—I don't know anything about her age."
"All the more reason why she should be looked out for, then," retorted Billy, promptly. "Why, Aunt Hannah, just as if you didn't want to give this lonesome, unprotected young girl a home!"
"Oh, I do, of course; but—"
"Then it's all settled," interposed Billy, springing to her feet.
"But what if we—we shouldn't like her?"
"Nonsense! What if she shouldn't like us?" laughed Billy. "However, if you'd feel better, just ask her to come and stay with us a month. We shall keep her all right, afterwards. See if we don't!"
Slowly Aunt Hannah got to her feet.
"Very well, dear. I'll write, of course, as you tell me to; and it's lovely of you to do it. Now I'll leave you to your letters. I've hindered you far too long, as it is."
"You've rested me," declared Billy, flinging wide her arms.
Aunt Hannah, fearing a second dizzying whirl impelled by those same young arms, drew her shawls about her shoulders and backed hastily toward the hall door.
Billy laughed.

"Oh, I won't again—to-day," she promised merrily. Then, as the lady reached the arched doorway: "Tell Mary Jane to let us know the day and train and we'll meet her. Oh, and Aunt Hannah, tell her to wear a pink—a white pink; and tell her we will, too," she finished gayly.

CHAPTER III. BILLY AND BERTRAM

Bertram called that evening. Before the open fire in the living-room he found a pensive Billy awaiting him—a Billy who let herself be kissed, it is true, and who even kissed back, shyly, adorably; but a Billy who looked at him with wide, almost frightened eyes.

"Why, darling, what's the matter?" he demanded, his own eyes growing wide and frightened.

"Bertram, it's—done!"

"What's done? What do you mean?"

"Our engagement. It's—announced. I wrote stacks of notes to-day, and even now there are some left for to-morrow. And then there's—the newspapers. Bertram, right away, now, everybody will know it." Her voice was tragic.

Bertram relaxed visibly. A tender light came to his eyes.

"Well, didn't you expect everybody would know it, my dear?"

"Y-yes; but—"

At her hesitation, the tender light changed to a quick fear.

"Billy, you aren't—sorry?"

The pink glory that suffused her face answered him before her words did.

"Sorry! Oh, never, Bertram! It's only that it won't be ours any longer—that is, it won't belong to just our two selves. Everybody will know it. And they'll bow and smile and say 'How lovely!' to our faces, and 'Did you ever?' to our backs. Oh, no, I'm not sorry, Bertram; but I am—afraid."

"Afraid—Billy!"

"Yes."

Billy sighed, and gazed with pensive eyes into the fire.

Across Bertram's face swept surprise, consternation, and dismay. Bertram had thought he knew Billy in all her moods and fancies; but he did not know her in this one.

"Why, Billy!" he breathed.

Billy drew another sigh. It seemed to come from the very bottoms of her small, satin-slippered feet.

"Well, I am. You're the Bertram Henshaw. You know lots and lots of people that I never even saw. And they'll come and stand around and stare and lift their lorgnettes and say: 'Is that the one? Dear me!'"

Bertram gave a relieved laugh.

"Nonsense, sweetheart! I should think you were a picture I'd painted and hung on a wall."

"I shall feel as if I were—with all those friends of yours. Bertram, what if they don't like it?" Her voice had grown tragic again.

"Like it!"

"Yes. The picture—me, I mean."

"They can't help liking it," he retorted, with the prompt certainty of an adoring lover.

Billy shook her head. Her eyes had gone back to the fire.

"Oh, yes, they can. I can hear them. 'What, she—Bertram Henshaw's wife?—a frivolous, inconsequential "Billy" like that?' Bertram!"—Billy turned fiercely despairing eyes on her lover—"Bertram, sometimes I wish my name were 'Clarissa Cordelia,' or 'Arabella Maud,' or 'Hannah Jane'—anything that's feminine and proper!"

Bertram's ringing laugh brought a faint smile to Billy's lips. But the words that followed the laugh, and the caressing touch of the man's hands sent a flood of shy color to her face.

"'Hannah Jane,' indeed! As if I'd exchange my Billy for her or any Clarissa or Arabella that ever grew! I adore Billy—flame, nature, and—"

"And naughtiness?" put in Billy herself.

"Yes—if there be any," laughed Bertram, fondly. "But, see," he added, taking a tiny box from his pocket, "see what I've brought for this same Billy to wear. She'd have had it long ago if she hadn't insisted on waiting for this announcement business."

"Oh, Bertram, what a beauty!" dimpled Billy, as the flawless diamond in Bertram's fingers caught the light and sent it back in a flash of flame and crimson.

"Now you are mine—really mine, sweetheart!" The man's voice and hand shook as he slipped the ring on Billy's outstretched finger.

Billy caught her breath with almost a sob.

"And I'm so glad to be—yours, dear," she murmured brokenly. "And—and I'll make you proud that I am yours, even if I am just 'Billy,'" she choked. "Oh, I know I'll write such beautiful, beautiful songs now."

The man drew her into a close embrace.

"As if I cared for that," he scoffed lovingly.

Billy looked up in quick horror.

"Why, Bertram, you don't mean you don't—care?"

He laughed lightly, and took the dismayed little face between his two hands.

"Care, darling? of course I care! You know how I love your music. I care about everything that concerns you. I meant that I'm proud of you now—just you. I love you, you know."

There was a moment's pause. Billy's eyes, as they looked at him, carried a curious intentness in their dark depths.

"You mean, you like—the turn of my head and the tilt of my chin?" she asked a little breathlessly.

"I adore them!" came the prompt answer.

To Bertram's utter amazement, Billy drew back with a sharp cry.

"No, no—not that!"

"Why, Billy!"

Billy laughed unexpectedly; then she sighed.

"Oh, it's all right, of course," she assured him hastily. "It's only—" Billy stopped and blushed. Billy was thinking of what Hugh Calderwell had once said to her: that Bertram Henshaw would never love any girl seriously; that it would always be the turn of her head or the tilt of her chin that he loved—to paint.

"Well; only what?" demanded Bertram.

Billy blushed the more deeply, but she gave a light laugh.

"Nothing, only something Hugh Calderwell said to me once. You see, Bertram, I don't think Hugh ever thought you would—marry."

"Oh, didn't he?" bridled Bertram. "Well, that only goes to show how much he knows about it. Er—did you announce it—to him?" Bertram's voice was almost savage now.

Billy smiled.

"No; but I did to his sister, and she'll tell him. Oh, Bertram, such a time as I had over those notes," went on Billy, with a chuckle. Her eyes were dancing, and she was seeming more like her usual self, Bertram thought. "You see there were such a lot of things I wanted to say, about what a dear you were, and how much I—I liked you, and that you had such lovely eyes, and a nose—"

"Billy!" This time it was Bertram who was sitting erect in pale horror.

Billy threw him a roguish glance.

"Goosey! You are as bad as Aunt Hannah! I said that was what I wanted to say. What I really said was—quite another matter," she finished with a saucy uptilting of her chin.

Bertram relaxed with a laugh.

"You witch!" His admiring eyes still lingered on her face. "Billy, I'm going to paint you sometime in just that pose. You're adorable!"

"Pooh! Just another face of a girl," teased the adorable one.

Bertram gave a sudden exclamation.

"There! And I haven't told you, yet. Guess what my next commission is."

"To paint a portrait?"

"Yes."

"Can't. Who is it?"

"J. G. Winthrop's daughter."

"Not the J. G. Winthrop?"

"The same."

"Oh, Bertram, how splendid!"

"Isn't it? And then the girl herself! Have you seen her? But you haven't, I know, unless you met her abroad. She hasn't been in Boston for years until now."

"No, I haven't seen her. Is she so very beautiful?" Billy spoke a little soberly.

"Yes—and no." The artist lifted his head alertly. What Billy called his "painting look" came to his face. "It isn't that her features are so regular—though her mouth and chin are perfect. But her face has so much character, and there's an elusive something about her eyes—Jove! If I can only catch it, it'll be the best thing yet that I've ever done, Billy."

"Will it? I'm so glad—and you'll get it, I know you will," claimed Billy, clearing her throat a little nervously.

"I wish I felt so sure," sighed Bertram. "But it'll be a great thing if I do get it—J. G. Winthrop's daughter, you know, besides the merit of the likeness itself."

"Yes; yes, indeed!" Billy cleared her throat again. "You've seen her, of course, lately?"

"Oh, yes. I was there half the morning discussing the details—sittings and costume, and deciding on the pose."

"Did you find one—to suit?"

"Find one!" The artist made a despairing gesture. "I found a dozen that I wanted. The trouble was to tell which I wanted the most."

Billy gave a nervous little laugh.

"Isn't that—unusual?" she asked.

Bertram lifted his eyebrows with a quizzical smile.

"Well, they aren't all Marguerite Winthrops," he reminded her.

"Marguerite!" cried Billy. "Oh, is her name Marguerite? I do think Marguerite is the dearest name!" Billy's eyes and voice were wistful.

"I don't—not the dearest. Oh, it's all well enough, of course, but it can't be compared for a moment to—well, say, 'Billy'!"

Billy smiled, but she shook her head.

"I'm afraid you're not a good judge of names," she objected.

"Yes, I am; though, for that matter, I should love your name, no matter what it was."

"Even if 'twas 'Mary Jane,' eh?" bantered Billy. "Well, you'll have a chance to find out how you like that name pretty quick, sir. We're going to have one here."

"You're going to have a Mary Jane here? Do you mean that Rosa's going away?"

"Mercy! I hope not," shuddered Billy. "You don't find a Rosa in every kitchen—and never in employment agencies! My Mary Jane is a niece of Aunt Hannah's,—or rather, a cousin. She's coming to Boston to study music, and I've invited her here. We've asked her for a month, though I presume we shall keep her right along."

Bertram frowned.

"Well, of course, that's very nice for—Mary Jane," he sighed with meaning emphasis.

Billy laughed.

"Don't worry, dear. She won't bother us any."

"Oh, yes, she will," sighed Bertram. "She'll be 'round—lots; you see if she isn't. Billy, I think sometimes you're almost too kind—to other folks."

"Never!" laughed Billy. "Besides, what would you have me do when a lonesome young girl was coming to Boston? Anyhow, you're not the one to talk, young man. I've known you to take in a lonesome girl and give her a home," she flashed merrily.

Bertram chuckled.

"Jove! What a time that was!" he exclaimed, regarding his companion with fond eyes. "And Spunk, too! Is she going to bring a Spunk?"

"Not that I've heard," smiled Billy; "but she is going to wear a pink."

"Not really, Billy?"

"Of course she is! I told her to. How do you suppose we could know her when we saw her, if she didn't?" demanded the girl, indignantly. "And what is more, sir, there will be two pinks worn this time. I sha'n't do as Uncle William did, and leave off my pink. Only think what long minutes—that seemed hours of misery—I spent waiting there in that train-shed, just because I didn't know which man was my Uncle William!"

Bertram laughed and shrugged his shoulders.

"Well, your Mary Jane won't probably turn out to be quite such a bombshell as our Billy did—unless she should prove to be a boy," he added whimsically. "Oh, but Billy, she can't turn out to be such a dear treasure," finished the man. And at the adoring look in his eyes Billy blushed deeply—and promptly forgot all about Mary Jane and her pink.

CHAPTER IV. FOR MARY JANE

"I have a letter here from Mary Jane, my dear," announced Aunt Hannah at the luncheon table one day.

"Have you?" Billy raised interested eyes from her own letters. "What does she say?"

"She will be here Thursday. Her train is due at the South Station at four-thirty. She seems to be very grateful to you for your offer to let her come right here for a month; but she says she's afraid you don't realize, perhaps, just what you are doing—to take her in like that, with her singing, and all."

"Nonsense! She doesn't refuse, does she?"

"Oh, no; she doesn't refuse—but she doesn't accept either, exactly, as I can see. I've read the letter over twice, too. I'll let you judge for yourself by and by, when you have time to read it."

Billy laughed.

"Never mind. I don't want to read it. She's just a little shy about coming, that's all. She'll stay all right, when we come to meet her. What time did you say it was, Thursday?"

"Half past four, South Station."

"Thursday, at half past four. Let me see—that's the day of the Carletons' 'At Home,' isn't it?"

"Oh, my grief and conscience, yes! But I had forgotten it. What shall we do?"

"Oh, that will be easy. We'll just go to the Carletons' early and have John wait, then take us from there to the South Station. Meanwhile we'll make sure that the little blue room is all ready for her. I put in my white enamel work-basket yesterday, and that pretty little blue case for hairpins and curling tongs that I bought at the fair. I want the room to look homey to her, you know."

"As if it could look any other way, if you had anything to do with it," sighed Aunt Hannah, admiringly.

Billy laughed.

"If we get stranded we might ask the Henshaw boys to help us out, Aunt Hannah. They'd probably suggest guns and swords. That's the way they fixed up my room."
Aunt Hannah raised shocked hands of protest.
"As if we would! Mercy, what a time that was!"
Billy laughed again.
"I never shall forget, never, my first glimpse of that room when Mrs. Hartwell switched on the lights. Oh, Aunt Hannah, I wish you could have seen it before they took out those guns and spiders!"
"As if I didn't see quite enough when I saw William's face that morning he came for me!" retorted Aunt Hannah, spiritedly.
"Dear Uncle William! What an old saint he has been all the way through," mused Billy aloud. "And Cyril—who would ever have believed that the day would come when Cyril would say to me, as he did last night, that he felt as if Marie had been gone a month. It's been just seven days, you know."
"I know. She comes to-morrow, doesn't she?"
"Yes, and I'm glad. I shall tell Marie she needn't leave Cyril on my hands again. Bertram says that at home Cyril hasn't played a dirge since his engagement; but I notice that up here—where Marie might be, but isn't—his tunes would never be mistaken for ragtime. By the way," she added, as she rose from the table, "that's another surprise in store for Hugh Calderwell. He always declared that Cyril wasn't a marrying man, either, any more than Bertram. You know he said Bertram only cared for girls to paint; but—" She stopped and looked inquiringly at Rosa, who had appeared at that moment in the hall doorway.
"It's the telephone, Miss Neilson. Mr. Bertram Henshaw wants you."
A few minutes later Aunt Hannah heard Billy at the piano. For fifteen, twenty, thirty minutes the brilliant scales and arpeggios rippled through the rooms and up the stairs to Aunt Hannah, who knew, by the very sound of them, that some unusual nervousness was being worked off at the finger tips that played them. At the end of forty-five minutes Aunt Hannah went down-stairs.
"Billy, my dear, excuse me, but have you forgotten what time it is? Weren't you going out with Bertram?"
Billy stopped playing at once, but she did not turn her head. Her fingers busied themselves with some music on the piano.
"We aren't going, Aunt Hannah," she said.
"Bertram can't."
"Can't!"
"Well, he didn't want to—so of course I said not to. He's been painting this morning on a new portrait, and she said he might stay to luncheon and keep right on for a while this afternoon, if he liked. And—he did like, so he stayed."
"Why, how—how—" Aunt Hannah stopped helplessly.
"Oh, no, not at all," interposed Billy, lightly. "He told me all about it the other night. It's going to be a very wonderful portrait; and, of course, I wouldn't want to interfere with—his work!" And again a brilliant scale rippled from Billy's fingers after a crashing chord in the bass.
Slowly Aunt Hannah turned and went up-stairs. Her eyes were troubled. Not since Billy's engagement had she heard Billy play like that.
Bertram did not find a pensive Billy awaiting him that evening. He found a bright-eyed, flushed-cheeked Billy, who let herself be kissed—once—but who did not kiss back; a blithe, elusive Billy, who played tripping little melodies, and sang jolly little songs, instead of sitting before the fire and talking; a Billy who at last turned, and asked tranquilly:
"Well, how did the picture go?"
Bertram rose then, crossed the room, and took Billy very gently into his arms.

"Sweetheart, you were a dear this noon to let me off like that," he began in a voice shaken with emotion. "You don't know, perhaps, exactly what you did. You see, I was nearly wild between wanting to be with you, and wanting to go on with my work. And I was just at that point where one little word from you, one hint that you wanted me to come anyway—and I should have come. But you didn't say it, nor hint it. Like the brave little bit of inspiration that you are, you bade me stay and go on with my work."

The "inspiration's" head drooped a little lower, but this only brought a wealth of soft bronze hair to just where Bertram could lay his cheek against it—and Bertram promptly took advantage of his opportunity. "And so I stayed, Billy, and I did good work; I know I did good work. Why, Billy,"—Bertram stepped back now, and held Billy by the shoulders at arms' length—"Billy, that's going to be the best work I've ever done. I can see it coming even now, under my fingers."

Billy lifted her head and looked into her lover's face. His eyes were glowing. His cheeks were flushed. His whole countenance was aflame with the soul of the artist who sees his vision taking shape before him. And Billy, looking at him, felt suddenly—ashamed.

"Oh, Bertram, I'm proud, proud, proud of you!" she breathed. "Come, let's go over to the fire-and talk!"

CHAPTER V. MARIE SPEAKS HER MIND

Billy with John and Peggy met Marie Hawthorn at the station. "Peggy" was short for "Pegasus," and was what Billy always called her luxurious, seven-seated touring car.

"I simply won't call it 'automobile,'" she had declared when she bought it. "In the first place, it takes too long to say it, and in the second place, I don't want to add one more to the nineteen different ways to pronounce it that I hear all around me every day now. As for calling it my 'car,' or my 'motor car'—I should expect to see a Pullman or one of those huge black trucks before my door, if I ordered it by either of those names. Neither will I insult the beautiful thing by calling it a 'machine.' Its name is Pegasus. I shall call it 'Peggy.'"

And "Peggy" she called it. John sniffed his disdain, and Billy's friends made no secret of their amused tolerance; but, in an astonishingly short time, half the automobile owners of her acquaintance were calling their own cars "Peggy"; and even the dignified John himself was heard to order "some gasoline for Peggy," quite as a matter of course.

When Marie Hawthorn stepped from the train at the North Station she greeted Billy with affectionate warmth, though at once her blue eyes swept the space beyond expectantly and eagerly.

Billy's lips curved in a mischievous smile.

"No, he didn't come," she said. "He didn't want to—a little bit."

Marie grew actually pale.

"Didn't want to!" she stammered.

Billy gave her a spasmodic hug.

"Goosey! No, he didn't—a little bit; but he did a great big bit. As if you didn't know he was dying to come, Marie! But he simply couldn't—something about his concert Monday night. He told me over the telephone; but between his joy that you were coming, and his rage that he couldn't see you the first minute you did come, I couldn't quite make out what was the trouble. But he's coming to dinner to-night, so he'll doubtless tell you all about it."

Marie sighed her relief.

"Oh, that's all right then. I was afraid he was sick—when I didn't see him."

Billy laughed softly.

"No, he isn't sick, Marie; but you needn't go away again before the wedding—not to leave him on my hands. I wouldn't have believed Cyril Henshaw, confirmed old bachelor and avowed woman-hater, could have acted the part of a love-sick boy as he has the last week or two."

The rose-flush on Marie's cheek spread to the roots of her fine yellow hair.

"Billy, dear, he—he didn't!"

"Marie, dear—he—he did!"

Marie laughed. She did not say anything, but the rose-flush deepened as she occupied herself very busily in getting her trunk-check from the little hand bag she carried.

Cyril was not mentioned again until the two girls, veils tied and coats buttoned, were snugly ensconced in the tonneau, and Peggy's nose was turned toward home. Then Billy asked:

"Have you settled on where you're going to live?"

"Not quite. We're going to talk of that to-night; but we do know that we aren't going to live at the Strata."

"Marie!"

Marie stirred uneasily at the obvious disappointment and reproach in her friend's voice.

"But, dear, it wouldn't be wise, I'm sure," she argued hastily. "There will be you and Bertram—"

"We sha'n't be there for a year, nearly," cut in Billy, with swift promptness. "Besides, I think it would be lovely—all together."

Marie smiled, but she shook her head.

"Lovely—but not practical, dear."

Billy laughed ruefully.

"I know; you're worrying about those puddings of yours. You're afraid somebody is going to interfere with your making quite so many as you want to; and Cyril is worrying for fear there'll be somebody else in the circle of his shaded lamp besides his little Marie with the light on her hair, and the mending basket by her side."

"Billy, what are you talking about?"

Billy threw a roguish glance into her friend's amazed blue eyes.

"Oh, just a little picture Cyril drew once for me of what home meant for him: a room with a table and a shaded lamp, and a little woman beside it with the light on her hair and a great basket of sewing by her side."

Marie's eyes softened.

"Did he say—that?"

"Yes. Oh, he declared he shouldn't want her to sit under that lamp all the time, of course; but he hoped she'd like that sort of thing."

Marie threw a quick glance at the stolid back of John beyond the two empty seats in front of them. Although she knew he could not hear her words, instinctively she lowered her voice.

"Did you know—then—about—me?" she asked, with heightened color.

"No, only that there was a girl somewhere who, he hoped, would sit under the lamp some day. And when I asked him if the girl did like that sort of thing, he said yes, he thought so; for she had told him once that the things she liked best of all to do were to mend stockings and make puddings. Then I knew, of course, 'twas you, for I'd heard you say the same thing. So I sent him right along out to you in the summer-house."

The pink flush on Marie's face grew to a red one. Her blue eyes turned again to John's broad back, then drifted to the long, imposing line of windowed walls and doorways on the right. The automobile was passing smoothly along Beacon Street now with the Public Garden just behind them on the left. After a moment Marie turned to Billy again.

"I'm so glad he wants—just puddings and stockings," she began a little breathlessly. "You see, for so long I supposed he wouldn't want anything but a very brilliant, talented wife who could play and sing beautifully; a wife he'd be proud of—like you."

"Me? Nonsense!" laughed Billy. "Cyril never wanted me, and I never wanted him—only once for a few minutes, so to speak, when I thought, I did. In spite of our music, we aren't a mite congenial. I like people around; he doesn't. I like to go to plays; he doesn't. He likes rainy days, and I abhor them. Mercy! Life with me for him would be one long jangling discord, my love, while with you it'll be one long sweet song!"

Marie drew a deep breath. Her eyes were fixed on a point far ahead up the curveless street.

"I hope it will, indeed!" she breathed.

Not until they were almost home did Billy say suddenly:

"Oh, did Cyril write you? A young relative of Aunt Hannah's is coming to-morrow to stay a while at the house."

"Er—yes, Cyril told me," admitted Marie.

Billy smiled.

"Didn't like it, I suppose; eh?" she queried shrewdly.

"N-no, I'm afraid he didn't—very well. He said she'd be—one more to be around."

"There, what did I tell you?" dimpled Billy. "You can see what you're coming to when you do get that shaded lamp and the mending basket!"

A moment later, coming in sight of the house, Billy saw a tall, smooth-shaven man standing on the porch. The man lifted his hat and waved it gayly, baring a slightly bald head to the sun.

"It's Uncle William—bless his heart!" cried Billy. "They're all coming to dinner, then he and Aunt Hannah and Bertram and I are going down to the Hollis Street Theatre and let you and Cyril have a taste of what that shaded lamp is going to be. I hope you won't be lonesome," she finished mischievously, as the car drew up before the door.

CHAPTER VI. AT THE SIGN OF THE PINK

After a week of beautiful autumn weather, Thursday dawned raw and cold. By noon an east wind had made the temperature still more uncomfortable.

At two o'clock Aunt Hannah tapped at Billy's chamber door. She showed a troubled face to the girl who answered her knock.

"Billy, would you mind very much if I asked you to go alone to the Carletons' and to meet Mary Jane?" she inquired anxiously.

"Why, no—that is, of course I should mind, dear, because I always like to have you go to places with me. But it isn't necessary. You aren't sick; are you?"

"N-no, not exactly; but I have been sneezing all the morning, and taking camphor and sugar to break it up—if it is a cold. But it is so raw and Novemberish out, that—"

"Why, of course you sha'n't go, you poor dear! Mercy! don't get one of those dreadful colds on to you before the wedding! Have you felt a draft? Where's another shawl?" Billy turned and cast searching eyes about the room—Billy always kept shawls everywhere for Aunt Hannah's shoulders and feet. Bertram had been known to say, indeed, that a room, according to Aunt Hannah, was not fully furnished unless it contained from one to four shawls, assorted as to size and warmth. Shawls, certainly, did seem to be a necessity with Aunt Hannah, as she usually wore from one to three at the same time—which again caused Bertram to declare that he always counted Aunt Hannah's shawls when he wished to know what the thermometer was.

"No, I'm not cold, and I haven't felt a draft," said Aunt Hannah now. "I put on my thickest gray shawl this morning with the little pink one for down-stairs, and the blue one for breakfast; so you see I've been very careful. But I have sneezed six times, so I think 'twould be safer not to go out in this east wind. You were going to stop for Mrs. Granger, anyway, weren't you? So you'll have her with you for the tea."

"Yes, dear, don't worry. I'll take your cards and explain to Mrs. Carleton and her daughters."

"And, of course, as far as Mary Jane is concerned, I don't know her any more than you do; so I couldn't be any help there," sighed Aunt Hannah.

"Not a bit," smiled Billy, cheerily. "Don't give it another thought, my dear. I sha'n't have a bit of trouble. All I'll have to do is to look for a girl alone with a pink. Of course I'll have mine on, too, and she'll be watching for me. So just run along and take your nap, dear, and be all rested and ready to welcome her when she comes," finished Billy, stooping to give the soft, faintly pink cheek a warm kiss.

"Well, thank you, my dear; perhaps I will," sighed Aunt Hannah, drawing the gray shawl about her as she turned away contentedly.

Mrs. Carleton's tea that afternoon was, for Billy, not an occasion of unalloyed joy. It was the first time she had appeared at a gathering of any size since the announcement of her engagement; and, as she dolefully told Bertram afterwards, she had very much the feeling of the picture hung on the wall.

"And they did put up their lorgnettes and say, 'Is that the one?'" she declared; "and I know some of them finished with 'Did you ever?' too," she sighed.

But Billy did not stay long in Mrs. Carleton's softly-lighted, flower-perfumed rooms. At ten minutes past four she was saying good-by to a group of friends who were vainly urging her to remain longer.

"I can't—I really can't," she declared. "I'm due at the South Station at half past four to meet a Miss Arkwright, a young cousin of Aunt Hannah's, whom I've never seen before. We're to meet at the sign of the pink," she explained smilingly, just touching the single flower she wore.

Her hostess gave a sudden laugh.

"Let me see, my dear; if I remember rightly, you've had experience before, meeting at this sign of the pink. At least, I have a very vivid recollection of Mr. William Henshaw's going once to meet a boy with a pink, who turned out to be a girl. Now, to even things up, your girl should turn out to be a boy!"

Billy smiled and reddened.

"Perhaps—but I don't think to-day will strike the balance," she retorted, backing toward the door. "This young lady's name is 'Mary Jane'; and I'll leave it to you to find anything very masculine in that!"

It was a short drive from Mrs. Carleton's Commonwealth Avenue home to the South Station, and Peggy made as quick work of it as the narrow, congested cross streets would allow. In ample time Billy found herself in the great waiting-room, with John saying respectfully in her ear:

"The man says the train comes in on Track Fourteen, Miss, an' it's on time."

At twenty-nine minutes past four Billy left her seat and walked down the train-shed platform to Track Number Fourteen. She had pinned the pink now to the outside of her long coat, and it made an attractive dash of white against the dark-blue velvet. Billy was looking particularly lovely to-day. Framing her face was the big dark-blue velvet picture hat with its becoming white plumes.

During the brief minutes' wait before the clanging locomotive puffed into view far down the long track, Billy's thoughts involuntarily went back to that other watcher beside a train gate not quite five years before.

"Dear Uncle William!" she murmured tenderly. Then suddenly she laughed—so nearly aloud that a man behind her gave her a covert glance from curious eyes. "My! but what a jolt I must have been to Uncle William!" Billy was thinking.

The next minute she drew nearer the gate and regarded with absorbed attention the long line of passengers already sweeping up the narrow aisle between the cars.

Hurrying men came first, with long strides, and eyes that looked straight ahead. These Billy let pass with a mere glance. The next group showed a sprinkling of women—women whose trig hats and linen collars spelled promptness as well as certainty of aim and accomplishment. To these, also, Billy paid scant attention. Couples came next—the men anxious-eyed, and usually walking two steps ahead of their companions; the women plainly flustered and hurried, and invariably buttoning gloves or gathering up trailing ends of scarfs or boas.

The crowd was thickening fast, now, and Billy's eyes were alert. Children were appearing, and young women walking alone. One of these wore a bunch of violets. Billy gave her a second glance. Then she saw a pink—but it was on the coat lapel of a tall young fellow with a brown beard; so with a slight frown she looked beyond down the line.

Old men came now, and old women; fleshy women, and women with small children and babies. Couples came, too—dawdling couples, plainly newly married: the men were not two steps ahead, and the women's gloves were buttoned and their furs in place.

Gradually the line thinned, and soon there were left only an old man with a cane, and a young woman with three children. Yet nowhere had Billy seen a girl wearing a white carnation, and walking alone.

With a deeper frown on her face Billy turned and looked about her. She thought that somewhere in the crowd she had missed Mary Jane, and that she would find her now, standing near. But there was no one standing near except the good-looking young fellow with the little pointed brown beard, who, as Billy noticed a second time, was wearing a white carnation.

As she glanced toward him, their eyes met. Then, to Billy's unbounded amazement, the man advanced with uplifted hat.

"I beg your pardon, but is not this—Miss Neilson?"

Billy drew back with just a touch of hauteur.

"Y-yes," she murmured.

"I thought so—yet I was expecting to see you with Aunt Hannah. I am M. J. Arkwright, Miss Neilson."

For a brief instant Billy stared dazedly.

"You don't mean—Mary Jane?" she gasped.

"I'm afraid I do." His lips twitched.

"But I thought—we were expecting—" She stopped helplessly. For one more brief instant she stared; then, suddenly, a swift change came to her face. Her eyes danced.

"Oh—oh!" she chuckled. "How perfectly funny! You have evened things up, after all. To think that Mary Jane should be a—" She paused and flashed almost angrily suspicious eyes into his face. "But mine was 'Billy,'" she cried. "Your name isn't really—Mary Jane'?"

"I am often called that." His brown eyes twinkled, but they did not swerve from their direct gaze into her own.

"But—" Billy hesitated, and turned her eyes away. She saw then that many curious glances were already being flung in her direction. The color in her cheeks deepened. With an odd little gesture she seemed to toss something aside. "Never mind," she laughed a little hysterically. "If you'll pick up your bag, please, Mr. Mary Jane, and come with me. John and Peggy are waiting. Or—I forgot—you have a trunk, of course?"

The man raised a protesting hand.

"Thank you; but, Miss Neilson, really—I couldn't think of trespassing on your hospitality—now, you know."

"But we—we invited you," stammered Billy.

He shook his head.

"You invited Miss Mary Jane."

Billy bubbled into low laughter.

"I beg your pardon, but it is funny," she sighed. "You see I came once just the same way, and now to have the tables turned like this! What will Aunt Hannah say—what will everybody say? Come, I want them to begin—to say it," she chuckled irrepressibly.

"Thank you, but I shall go to a hotel, of course. Later, if you'll be so good as to let me call, and explain—!"

"But I'm afraid Aunt Hannah will think—" Billy stopped abruptly. Some distance away she saw John coming toward them. She turned hurriedly to the man at her side. Her eyes still danced, but her voice was mockingly serious. "Really, Mr. Mary Jane, I'm afraid you'll have to come to dinner; then you can settle the rest with Aunt Hannah. John is almost upon us—and I don't want to make explanations. Do you?"

"John," she said airily to the somewhat dazed chauffeur (who had been told he was to meet a young woman), "take Mr. Arkwright's bag, please, and show him where Peggy is waiting. It will be five minutes, perhaps, before I can come—if you'll kindly excuse me," she added to Arkwright, with a flashing glance from merry eyes. "I have some—telephoning to do."

All the way to the telephone booth Billy was trying to bring order out of the chaos of her mind; but all the way, too, she was chuckling.

"To think that this thing should have happened to me!" she said, almost aloud. "And here I am telephoning just like Uncle William—Bertram said Uncle William did telephone about me!"

In due course Billy had Aunt Hannah at the other end of the wire.

"Aunt Hannah, listen. I'd never have believed it, but it's happened. Mary Jane is—a man."

Billy heard a dismayed gasp and a muttered "Oh, my grief and conscience!" then a shaking "Wha-at?"

"I say, Mary Jane is a man." Billy was enjoying herself hugely.

"A ma-an!"

"Yes; a great big man with a brown beard. He's waiting now with John and I must go."

"But, Billy, I don't understand," chattered an agitated voice over the line. "He—he called himself 'Mary Jane.' He hasn't any business to be a big man with a brown beard! What shall we do? We don't want a big man with a brown beard—here!"

Billy laughed roguishly.

"I don't know. You asked him! How he will like that little blue room—Aunt Hannah!" Billy's voice turned suddenly tragic. "For pity's sake take out those curling tongs and hairpins, and the work-basket. I'd never hear the last of it if he saw those, I know. He's just that kind!"

A half stifled groan came over the wire.

"Billy, he can't stay here."

Billy laughed again.

"No, no, dear; he won't, I know. He says he's going to a hotel. But I had to bring him home to dinner; there was no other way, under the circumstances. He won't stay. Don't you worry. But good-by. I must go. Remember those curling tongs!" And the receiver clicked sharply against the hook.

In the automobile some minutes later, Billy and Mr. M. J. Arkwright were speeding toward Corey Hill. It was during a slight pause in the conversation that Billy turned to her companion with a demure:

"I telephoned Aunt Hannah, Mr. Arkwright. I thought she ought to be—warned."

"You are very kind. What did she say?—if I may ask."

There was a brief moment of hesitation before Billy answered.

"She said you called yourself 'Mary Jane,' and that you hadn't any business to be a big man with a brown beard."

Arkwright laughed.

"I'm afraid I owe Aunt Hannah an apology," he said. He hesitated, glanced admiringly at the glowing, half-averted face near him, then went on decisively. He wore the air of a man who has set the match to his bridges. "I signed both letters 'M. J. Arkwright,' but in the first one I quoted a remark of a friend, and in that remark I was addressed as 'Mary Jane.' I did not know but Aunt Hannah knew of the nickname." (Arkwright was speaking a little slowly now, as if weighing his words.) "But when she answered, I saw that she did not; for, from something she said, I realized that she thought I was a real Mary Jane. For the joke of the thing I let it pass. But—if she noticed my letter carefully, she saw that I did not accept your kind invitation to give 'Mary Jane' a home."

"Yes, we noticed that," nodded Billy, merrily. "But we didn't think you meant it. You see we pictured you as a shy young thing. But, really," she went on with a low laugh, "you see your coming as a masculine 'Mary Jane' was particularly funny—for me; for, though perhaps you didn't know it, I came once to this very same city, wearing a pink, and was expected to be Billy, a boy. And only to-day a lady warned me that your coming might even things up. But I didn't believe it would—a Mary Jane!"

Arkwright laughed. Again he hesitated, and seemed to be weighing his words.

"Yes, I heard about that coming of yours. I might almost say—that's why I—let the mistake pass in Aunt Hannah's letter," he said.

Billy turned with reproachful eyes.

"Oh, how could—you? But then—it was a temptation!" She laughed suddenly. "What sinful joy you must have had watching me hunt for 'Mary Jane.'"

"I didn't," acknowledged the other, with unexpected candor. "I felt—ashamed. And when I saw you were there alone without Aunt Hannah, I came very near not speaking at all—until I realized that that would be even worse, under the circumstances."

"Of course it would," smiled Billy, brightly; "so I don't see but I shall have to forgive you, after all. And here we are at home, Mr. Mary Jane. By the way, what did you say that 'M. J.' did stand for?" she asked, as the car came to a stop.

The man did not seem to hear; at least he did not answer. He was helping his hostess to alight. A moment later a plainly agitated Aunt Hannah—her gray shawl topped with a huge black one—opened the door of the house.

CHAPTER VII. OLD FRIENDS AND NEW

At ten minutes before six on the afternoon of Arkwright's arrival, Billy came into the living-room to welcome the three Henshaw brothers, who, as was frequently the case, were dining at Hillside.

Bertram thought Billy had never looked prettier than she did this afternoon with the bronze sheen of her pretty house gown bringing out the bronze lights in her dark eyes and in the soft waves of her beautiful hair. Her countenance, too, carried a peculiar something that the artist's eye was quick to detect, and that the artist's fingers tingled to put on canvas.

"Jove! Billy," he said low in her ear, as he greeted her, "I wish I had a brush in my hand this minute. I'd have a 'Face of a Girl' that would be worth while!"

Billy laughed and dimpled her appreciation; but down in her heart she was conscious of a vague unrest. Billy wished, sometimes, that she did not so often seem to Bertram—a picture.

She turned to Cyril with outstretched hand.

"Oh, yes, Marie's coming," she smiled in answer to the quick shifting of Cyril's eyes to the hall doorway. "And Aunt Hannah, too. They're up-stairs."

"And Mary Jane?" demanded William, a little anxiously

"Will's getting nervous," volunteered Bertram, airily. "He wants to see Mary Jane. You see we've told him that we shall expect him to see that she doesn't bother us four too much, you know. He's expected always to remove her quietly but effectually, whenever he sees that she is likely to interrupt a tête-á-tête. Naturally, then, Will wants to see Mary Jane."

Billy began to laugh hysterically. She dropped into a chair and raised both her hands, palms outward.

"Don't, don't—please don't!" she choked, "or I shall die. I've had all I can stand, already."

"All you can stand?"

"What do you mean?"

"Is she so—impossible?" This last was from Bertram, spoken softly, and with a hurried glance toward the hall.

Billy dropped her hands and lifted her head. By heroic effort she pulled her face into sobriety—all but her eyes—and announced:

"Mary Jane is—a man."

"Wha-at?"

"A man!"

"Billy!"

Three masculine forms sat suddenly erect.

"Yes. Oh, Uncle William, I know now just how you felt—I know, I know," gurgled Billy, incoherently. "There he stood with his pink just as I did—only he had a brown beard, and he didn't have Spunk—and I had to telephone to prepare folks, just as you did. And the room—the room! I fixed the room, too," she babbled breathlessly, "only I had curling tongs and hair pins in it instead of guns and spiders!"

"Child, child! what are you talking about?" William's face was red.

"A man!—Mary Jane!" Cyril was merely cross.

"Billy, what does this mean?" Bertram had grown a little white.

Billy began to laugh again, yet she was plainly trying to control herself.

"I'll tell you. I must tell you. Aunt Hannah is keeping him up-stairs so I can tell you," she panted. "But it was so funny, when I expected a girl, you know, to see him with his brown beard, and he was so tall and big! And, of course, it made me think how I came, and was a girl when you expected a boy; and Mrs. Carleton had just said to-day that maybe this girl would even things up. Oh, it was so funny!"

"Billy, my-my dear," remonstrated Uncle William, mildly.

"But what is his name?" demanded Cyril.

"Did the creature sign himself 'Mary Jane'?" exploded Bertram.

"I don't know his name, except that it's 'M. J.'—and that's how he signed the letters. But he is called 'Mary Jane' sometimes, and in the letter he quoted somebody's speech—I've forgotten just how—but in it he was called 'Mary Jane,' and, of course, Aunt Hannah took him for a girl," explained Billy, grown a little more coherent now.

"Didn't he write again?" asked William.

"Yes."

"Well, why didn't he correct the mistake, then?" demanded Bertram.

Billy chuckled.

"He didn't want to, I guess. He thought it was too good a joke."

"Joke!" scoffed Cyril.

"But, see here, Billy, he isn't going to live here—now?" Bertram's voice was almost savage.

"Oh, no, he isn't going to live here—now," interposed smooth tones from the doorway.

"Mr.—Arkwright!" breathed Billy, confusedly.

Three crimson-faced men sprang to their feet. The situation, for a moment, threatened embarrassed misery for all concerned; but Arkwright, with a cheery smile, advanced straight toward Bertram, and held out a friendly hand.

"The proverbial fate of listeners," he said easily; "but I don't blame you at all. No, 'he' isn't going to live here," he went on, grasping each brother's hand in turn, as Billy murmured faint introductions; "and what is more, he hereby asks everybody's pardon for the annoyance his little joke has caused. He might add that he's heartily-ashamed of himself, as well; but if any of you—" Arkwright turned to the three tall men still standing by their chairs—"if any of you had suffered what he has at the hands of a swarm of youngsters for that name's sake, you wouldn't blame him for being tempted to get what fun he could out of Mary Jane—if there ever came a chance!"

Naturally, after this, there could be nothing stiff or embarrassing. Billy laughed in relief, and motioned Mr. Arkwright to a seat near her. William said "Of course, of course!" and shook hands again. Bertram and Cyril laughed shamefacedly and sat down. Somebody said: "But what does the 'M. J.' stand for, anyhow?" Nobody answered this, however; perhaps because Aunt Hannah and Marie appeared just then in the doorway.

Dinner proved to be a lively meal. In the newcomer, Bertram met his match for wit and satire; and "Mr. Mary Jane," as he was promptly called by every one but Aunt Hannah, was found to be a most entertaining guest.

After dinner somebody suggested music.

Cyril frowned, and got up abruptly. Still frowning, he turned to a bookcase near him and began to take down and examine some of the books.

Bertram twinkled and glanced at Billy.

"Which is it, Cyril?" he called with cheerful impertinence; "stool, piano, or audience that is the matter to-night?"

Only a shrug from Cyril answered.

"You see," explained Bertram, jauntily, to Arkwright, whose eyes were slightly puzzled, "Cyril never plays unless the piano and the pedals and the weather and your ears and my watch and his fingers are just right!"

"Nonsense!" scorned Cyril, dropping his book and walking back to his chair. "I don't feel like playing to-night; that's all."

"You see," nodded Bertram again.

"I see," bowed Arkwright with quiet amusement.

"I believe—Mr. Mary Jane—sings," observed Billy, at this point, demurely.

"Why, yes, of course," chimed in Aunt Hannah with some nervousness. "That's what she—I mean he—was coming to Boston for—to study music."

Everybody laughed.

"Won't you sing, please?" asked Billy. "Can you—without your notes? I have lots of songs if you want them."

For a moment—but only a moment—Arkwright hesitated; then he rose and went to the piano.

With the easy sureness of the trained musician his fingers dropped to the keys and slid into preliminary chords and arpeggios to test the touch of the piano; then, with a sweetness and purity that made every listener turn in amazed delight, a well-trained tenor began the "Thro' the leaves the night winds moving," of Schubert's Serenade.

Cyril's chin had lifted at the first tone. He was listening now with very obvious pleasure. Bertram, too, was showing by his attitude the keenest appreciation. William and Aunt Hannah, resting back in their chairs, were contentedly nodding their approval to each other. Marie in her corner was motionless with rapture. As to Billy—Billy was plainly oblivious of everything but the song and the singer. She seemed scarcely to move or to breathe till the song's completion; then there came a low "Oh, how beautiful!" through her parted lips.

Bertram, looking at her, was conscious of a vague irritation.

"Arkwright, you're a lucky dog," he declared almost crossly. "I wish I could sing like that!"

"I wish I could paint a 'Face of a Girl,'" smiled the tenor as he turned from the piano.

"Oh, but, Mr. Arkwright, don't stop," objected Billy, springing to her feet and going to her music cabinet by the piano. "There's a little song of Nevin's I want you to sing. There, here it is. Just let me play it for you." And she slipped into the place the singer had just left.

It was the beginning of the end. After Nevin came De Koven, and after De Koven, Gounod. Then came Nevin again, Billy still playing the accompaniment. Next followed a duet. Billy did not consider herself much of a singer, but her voice was sweet and true, and not without training. It blended very prettily with the clear, pure tenor.

William and Aunt Hannah still smiled contentedly in their chairs, though Aunt Hannah had reached for the pink shawl near her—the music had sent little shivers down her spine. Cyril, with Marie, had slipped into the little reception-room across the hall, ostensibly to look at some plans for a house, although—as everybody knew—they were not intending to build for a year.

Bertram, still sitting stiffly erect in his chair, was not conscious of a vague irritation now. He was conscious of a very real, and a very decided one—an irritation that was directed against himself, against Billy, and against this man, Arkwright; but chiefly against music, per se. He hated music. He wished he could sing. He wondered how long it took to teach a man to sing, anyhow; and he wondered if a man could sing—who never had sung.

At this point the duet came to an end, and Billy and her guest left the piano. Almost at once, after this, Arkwright made his very graceful adieus, and went off with his suit-case to the hotel where, as he had informed Aunt Hannah, his room was already engaged.

William went home then, and Aunt Hannah went up-stairs. Cyril and Marie withdrew into a still more secluded corner to look at their plans, and Bertram found himself at last alone with Billy. He forgot, then, in the blissful hour he spent with her before the open fire, how he hated music; though he did say, just before he went home that night:

"Billy, how long does it take—to learn to sing?"

"Why, I don't know, I'm sure," replied Billy, abstractedly; then, with sudden fervor: "Oh, Bertram, hasn't Mr. Mary Jane a beautiful voice?"

Bertram wished then he had not asked the question; but all he said was:

"'Mr. Mary Jane,' indeed! What an absurd name!"

"But doesn't he sing beautifully?"

"Eh? Oh, yes, he sings all right," said Bertram's tongue. Bertram's manner said: "Oh, yes, anybody can sing."

CHAPTER VIII. M. J. OPENS THE GAME

On the morning after Cyril's first concert of the season, Billy sat sewing with Aunt Hannah in the little sitting-room at the end of the hall upstairs. Aunt Hannah wore only one shawl this morning,—which meant that she was feeling unusually well.

"Marie ought to be here to mend these stockings," remarked Billy, as she critically examined a tiny break in the black silk mesh stretched across the darning-egg in her hand; "only she'd want a bigger hole. She does so love to make a beautiful black latticework bridge across a yawning white china sea—and you'd think the safety of an army depended on the way each plank was laid, too," she concluded.

Aunt Hannah smiled tranquilly, but she did not speak.

"I suppose you don't happen to know if Cyril does wear big holes in his socks," resumed Billy, after a moment's silence. "If you'll believe it, that thought popped into my head last night when Cyril was playing that concerto so superbly. It did, actually—right in the middle of the adagio movement, too. And in spite of my joy and pride in the music I had all I could do to keep from nudging Marie right there and then and asking her whether or not the dear man was hard on his hose."

"Billy!" gasped the shocked Aunt Hannah; but the gasp broke at once into what—in Aunt Hannah—passed for a chuckle. "If I remember rightly, when I was there at the house with you at first, my dear, William told me that Cyril wouldn't wear any sock after it came to mending."

"Horrors!" Billy waved her stocking in mock despair. "That will never do in the world. It would break Marie's heart. You know how she dotes on darning."

"Yes, I know," smiled Aunt Hannah. "By the way, where is she this morning?"

Billy raised her eyebrows quizzically.

"Gone to look at an apartment in Cambridge, I believe. Really, Aunt Hannah, between her home-hunting in the morning, and her furniture-and-rug hunting in the afternoon, and her poring over house-plans in the evening, I can't get her to attend to her clothes at all. Never did I see a bride so utterly indifferent to her trousseau as Marie Hawthorn—and her wedding less than a month away!"

"But she's been shopping with you once or twice, since she came back, hasn't she? And she said it was for her trousseau."

Billy laughed.

"Her trousseau! Oh, yes, it was. I'll tell you what she got for her trousseau that first day. We started out to buy two hats, some lace for her wedding gown, some crêpe de Chine and net for a little dinner frock, and some silk for a couple of waists to go with her tailored suit; and what did we get? We purchased a new-style egg-beater and a set of cake tins. Marie got into the kitchen department and I simply couldn't get her out of it. But the next day I was not to be inveigled below stairs by any plaintive prayer for a nutmeg-grater or a soda spoon. She shopped that day, and to some purpose. We accomplished lots."

Aunt Hannah looked a little concerned.

"But she must have some things started!"

"Oh, she has—'most everything now. I've seen to that. Of course her outfit is very simple, anyway. Marie hasn't much money, you know, and she simply won't let me do half what I want to. Still, she had saved up some money, and I've finally convinced her that a trousseau doesn't consist of egg-beaters and cake tins, and that Cyril would want her to look pretty. That name will fetch her every time, and I've learned to use it beautifully. I think if I told her Cyril approved of short hair and near-sightedness she'd I cut off her golden locks and don spectacles on the spot."

Aunt Hannah laughed softly.

"What a child you are, Billy! Besides, just as if Marie were the only one in the house who is ruled by a magic name!"

The color deepened in Billy's cheeks.

"Well, of course, any girl—cares something—for the man she loves. Just as if I wouldn't do anything in the world I could for Bertram!"

"Oh, that makes me think; who was that young woman Bertram was talking with last evening—just after he left us, I mean?"

"Miss Winthrop—Miss Marguerite Winthrop. Bertram is—is painting her portrait, you know."

"Oh, is that the one?" murmured Aunt Hannah. "Hm-m; well, she has a beautiful face."

"Yes, she has." Billy spoke very cheerfully. She even hummed a little tune as she carefully selected a needle from the cushion in her basket.

"There's a peculiar something in her face," mused Aunt Hannah, aloud.

The little tune stopped abruptly, ending in a nervous laugh.

"Dear me! I wonder how it feels to have a peculiar something in your face. Bertram, too, says she has it. He's trying to 'catch it,' he says. I wonder now—if he does catch it, does she lose it?" Flippant as were the words, the voice that uttered them shook a little.

Aunt Hannah smiled indulgently—Aunt Hannah had heard only the flippancy, not the shake.

"I don't know, my dear. You might ask him this afternoon."

Billy made a sudden movement. The china egg in her lap rolled to the floor.

"Oh, but I don't see him this afternoon," she said lightly, as she stooped to pick up the egg.

"Why, I'm sure he told me—" Aunt Hannah's sentence ended in a questioning pause.

"Yes, I know," nodded Billy, brightly; "but he's told me something since. He isn't going. He telephoned me this morning. Miss Winthrop wanted the sitting changed from to-morrow to this afternoon. He said he knew I'd understand."

"Why, yes; but—" Aunt Hannah did not finish her sentence. The whir of an electric bell had sounded through the house. A few moments later Rosa appeared in the open doorway.

"It's Mr. Arkwright, Miss. He said as how he had brought the music," she announced.

"Tell him I'll be down at once," directed the mistress of Hillside.

As the maid disappeared, Billy put aside her work and sprang lightly to her feet.

"Now wasn't that nice of him? We were talking last night about some duets he had, and he said he'd bring them over. I didn't know he'd come so soon, though."

Billy had almost reached the bottom of the stairway, when a low, familiar strain of music drifted out from the living-room. Billy caught her breath, and held her foot suspended. The next moment the familiar strain of music had become a lullaby—one of Billy's own—and sung now by a melting tenor voice that lingered caressingly and understandingly on every tender cadence.

Motionless and almost breathless, Billy waited until the last low "lul-la-by" vibrated into silence; then with shining eyes and outstretched hands she entered the living-room.

"Oh, that was—beautiful," she breathed.

Arkwright was on his feet instantly. His eyes, too, were alight.

"I could not resist singing it just once—here," he said a little unsteadily, as their hands met.

"But to hear my little song sung like that! I couldn't believe it was mine," choked Billy, still plainly very much moved. "You sang it as I've never heard it sung before."

Arkwright shook his head slowly.

"The inspiration of the room—that is all,", he said. "It is a beautiful song. All of your songs are beautiful."

Billy blushed rosily.

"Thank you. You know—more of them, then?"

"I think I know them all—unless you have some new ones out. Have you some new ones, lately?"

Billy shook her head.

"No; I haven't written anything since last spring."

"But you're going to?"

She drew a long sigh.

"Yes, oh, yes. I know that now—" With a swift biting of her lower lip Billy caught herself up in time. As if she could tell this man, this stranger, what she had told Bertram that night by the fire—that she knew that now, now she would write beautiful songs, with his love, and his pride in her, as incentives. "Oh, yes, I think I shall write more one of these days," she finished lightly. "But come, this isn't singing duets! I want to see the music you brought."

They sang then, one after another of the duets. To Billy, the music was new and interesting. To Billy, too, it was new (and interesting) to hear her own voice blending with another's so perfectly—to feel herself a part of such exquisite harmony.

"Oh, oh!" she breathed ecstatically, after the last note of a particularly beautiful phrase. "I never knew before how lovely it was to sing duets."

"Nor I," replied Arkwright in a voice that was not quite steady.

Arkwright's eyes were on the enraptured face of the girl so near him. It was well, perhaps, that Billy did not happen to turn and catch their expression. Still, it might have been better if she had turned, after all. But Billy's eyes were on the music before her. Her fingers were busy with the fluttering pages, searching for another duet.

"Didn't you?" she murmured abstractedly. "I supposed you'd sung them before; but you see I never did—until the other night. There, let's try this one!"

"This one" was followed by another and another. Then Billy drew a long breath.

"There! that must positively be the last," she declared reluctantly. "I'm so hoarse now I can scarcely croak. You see, I don't pretend to sing, really."

"Don't you? You sing far better than some who do, anyhow," retorted the man, warmly.

"Thank you," smiled Billy; "that was nice of you to say so—for my sake—and the others aren't here to care. But tell me of yourself. I haven't had a chance to ask you yet; and—I think you said Mary Jane was going to study for Grand Opera."

Arkwright laughed and shrugged his shoulders.

"She is; but, as I told Calderwell, she's quite likely to bring up in vaudeville."

"Calderwell! Do you mean—Hugh Calderwell?" Billy's cheeks showed a deeper color.

The man gave an embarrassed little laugh. He had not meant to let that name slip out just yet.

"Yes." He hesitated, then plunged on recklessly. "We tramped half over Europe together last summer."

"Did you?" Billy left her seat at the piano for one nearer the fire. "But this isn't telling me about your own plans," she hurried on a little precipitately. "You've studied before, of course. Your voice shows that."

"Oh, yes; I've studied singing several years, and I've had a year or two of church work, besides a little concert practice of a mild sort."

"Have you begun here, yet?"

"Y-yes, I've had my voice tried."

Billy sat erect with eager interest.

"They liked it, of course?"

Arkwright laughed.

"I'm not saying that."

"No, but I am," declared Billy, with conviction. "They couldn't help liking it."

Arkwright laughed again. Just how well they had "liked it" he did not intend to say. Their remarks had been quite too flattering to repeat even to this very plainly interested young woman—delightful and heart-warming as was this same show of interest, to himself.

"Thank you," was all he said.

Billy gave an excited little bounce in her chair.

"And you'll begin to learn rôles right away?"

"I already have, some—after a fashion—before I came here."

"Really? How splendid! Why, then you'll be acting them next right on the Boston Opera House stage, and we'll all go to hear you. How perfectly lovely! I can hardly wait."

Arkwright laughed—but his eyes glowed with pleasure.

"Aren't you hurrying things a little?" he ventured.

"But they do let the students appear," argued Billy. "I knew a girl last year who went on in 'Aida,' and she was a pupil at the School. She sang first in a Sunday concert, then they put her in the bill for a Saturday night. She did splendidly—so well that they gave her a chance later at a subscription performance. Oh, you'll be there—and soon, too!"

"Thank you! I only wish the powers that could put me there had your flattering enthusiasm on the matter," he smiled.

"I don't worry any," nodded Billy, "only please don't 'arrive' too soon—not before the wedding, you know," she added jokingly. "We shall be too busy to give you proper attention until after that."

A peculiar look crossed Arkwright's face.

"The—wedding?" he asked, a little faintly.

"Yes. Didn't you know? My friend, Miss Hawthorn, is to marry Mr. Cyril Henshaw next month."

The man opposite relaxed visibly.

"Oh, Miss Hawthorn! No, I didn't know," he murmured; then, with sudden astonishment he added: "And to Mr. Cyril, the musician, did you say?"

"Yes. You seem surprised."

"I am." Arkwright paused, then went on almost defiantly. "You see, Calderwell was telling me only last September how very unmarriageable all the Henshaw brothers were. So I am surprised—naturally," finished Arkwright, as he rose to take his leave.

A swift crimson stained Billy's face.

"But surely you must know that—that—"

"That he has a right to change his mind, of course," supplemented Arkwright smilingly, coming to her rescue in the evident confusion that would not let her finish her sentence. "But Calderwell made it so emphatic, you see, about all the brothers. He said that William had lost his heart long ago; that Cyril hadn't any to lose; and that Bertram—"

"But, Mr. Arkwright, Bertram is—is—" Billy had moistened her lips, and plunged hurriedly in to prevent Arkwright's next words. But again was she unable to finish her sentence, and again was she forced to listen to a very different completion from the smiling lips of the man at her side.

"Is an artist, of course," said Arkwright. "That's what Calderwell declared—that it would always be the tilt of a chin or the curve of a cheek that the artist loved—to paint."

Billy drew back suddenly. Her face paled. As if now she could tell this man that Bertram Henshaw was engaged to her! He would find it out soon, of course, for himself; and perhaps he, like Hugh Calderwell, would think it was the curve of her cheek, or the tilt of her chin—

Billy lifted her chin very defiantly now as she held out her hand in good-by.

CHAPTER IX. A RUG, A PICTURE, AND A GIRL AFRAID

Thanksgiving came. Once again the Henshaw brothers invited Billy and Aunt Hannah to spend the day with them. This time, however, there was to be an additional guest present in the person of Marie Hawthorn.

And what a day it was, for everything and everybody concerned! First the Strata itself: from Dong Ling's kitchen in the basement to Cyril's domain on the top floor, the house was as spick-and-span as Pete's eager old hands could make it. In the drawing-room and in Bertram's den and studio, great clusters of pink roses perfumed the air, and brightened the sombre richness of the old-time furnishings. Before the open fire in the den a sleek gray cat—adorned with a huge ribbon bow the exact shade of the roses (Bertram had seen to that!)—winked and blinked sleepy yellow eyes. In Bertram's studio the latest "Face of a Girl" had made way for a group of canvases and plaques, every one of which showed Billy Neilson in one pose or another. Up-stairs, where William's chaos of treasures filled shelves and cabinets, the place of honor was given to a small black velvet square on which rested a pair of quaint Battersea enamel mirror knobs. In Cyril's rooms—usually so austerely bare— a handsome Oriental rug and several curtain-draped chairs hinted at purchases made at the instigation of a taste other than his own.

When the doorbell rang Pete admitted the ladies with a promptness that was suggestive of surreptitious watching at some window. On Pete's face the dignity of his high office and the delight of the moment were fighting for mastery. The dignity held firmly through Mrs. Stetson's friendly greeting; but it fled in defeat when Billy Neilson stepped over the threshold with a cheery "Good morning, Pete."

"Laws! But it's good to be seein' you here again," stammered the man,—delight now in sole possession.

"She'll be coming to stay, one of these days, Pete," smiled the eldest Henshaw, hurrying forward.

"I wish she had now," whispered Bertram, who, in spite of William's quick stride, had reached Billy's side first.

From the stairway came the patter of a man's slippered feet.

"The rug has come, and the curtains, too," called a "householder" sort of voice that few would have recognized as belonging to Cyril Henshaw. "You must all come up-stairs and see them after dinner." The voice, apparently, spoke to everybody; but the eyes of the owner of the voice plainly saw only the fair-haired young woman who stood a little in the shadow behind Billy, and who was looking about her now as at something a little fearsome, but very dear.

"You know—I've never been—where you live—before," explained Marie Hawthorn in a low, vibrant tone, when Cyril bent over her to take the furs from her shoulders.

In Bertram's den a little later, as hosts and guests advanced toward the fire, the sleek gray cat rose, stretched lazily, and turned her head with majestic condescension.

"Well, Spunkie, come here," commanded Billy, snapping her fingers at the slow-moving creature on the hearthrug. "Spunkie, when I am your mistress, you'll have to change either your name or your nature. As if I were going to have such a bunch of independent moderation as you masquerading as an understudy to my frisky little Spunk!"

Everybody laughed. William regarded his namesake with fond eyes as he said:

"Spunkie doesn't seem to be worrying." The cat had jumped into Billy's lap with a matter-of-course air that was unmistakable—and to Bertram, adorable. Bertram's eyes, as they rested on Billy, were even fonder than were his brother's.

"I don't think any one is—worrying," he said with quiet emphasis.

Billy smiled.

"I should think they might be," she answered. "Only think how dreadfully upsetting I was in the first place!"

William's beaming face grew a little stern.

"Nobody knew it but Kate—and she didn't know it; she only imagined it," he said tersely.

Billy shook her head.

"I'm not so sure," she demurred. "As I look back at it now, I think I can discern a few evidences myself—that I was upsetting. I was a bother to Bertram in his painting, I am sure."

"You were an inspiration," corrected Bertram. "Think of the posing you did for me."

A swift something like a shadow crossed Billy's face; but before her lover could question its meaning, it was gone.

"And I know I was a torment to Cyril." Billy had turned to the musician now.

"Well, I admit you were a little—upsetting, at times," retorted that individual, with something of his old imperturbable rudeness.

"Nonsense!" cut in William, sharply. "You were never anything but a comfort in the house, Billy, my dear—and you never will be."

"Thank you," murmured Billy, demurely. "I'll remember that—when Pete and I disagree about the table decorations, and Dong Ling doesn't like the way I want my soup seasoned."

An anxious frown showed on Bertram's face.

"Billy," he said in a low voice, as the others laughed at her sally, "you needn't have Pete nor Dong Ling here if you don't want them."

"Don't want them!" echoed Billy, indignantly. "Of course I want them!"

"But—Pete is old, and—"

"Yes; and where's he grown old? For whom has he worked the last fifty years, while he's been growing old? I wonder if you think I'd let Pete leave this house as long as he wants to stay! As for Dong Ling—"

A sudden movement of Bertram's hand arrested her words. She looked up to find Pete in the doorway.

"Dinner is served, sir," announced the old butler, his eyes on his master's face.

William rose with alacrity, and gave his arm to Aunt Hannah.

"Well, I'm sure we're ready for dinner," he declared.

It was a good dinner, and it was well served. It could scarcely have been otherwise with Dong Ling in the kitchen and Pete in the dining-room doing their utmost to please. But even had the turkey been tough instead of tender, and even had the pies been filled with sawdust instead of with delicious mincemeat, it is doubtful if four at the table would have known the difference: Cyril and Marie at one end were discussing where to put their new sideboard in their dining-room, and Bertram and Billy at the other were talking of the next Thanksgiving, when, according to Bertram, the Strata would have the "dearest little mistress that ever was born." As if, under these circumstances, the tenderness of the turkey or the toothsomeness of the mince pie mattered! To Aunt Hannah and William, in the centre of the table, however, it did matter; so it was well, of course, that the dinner was a good one.

"And now," said Cyril, when dinner was over, "suppose you come up and see the rug."

In compliance with this suggestion, the six trailed up the long flights of stairs then, Billy carrying an extra shawl for Aunt Hannah—Cyril's rooms were always cool.

"Oh, yes, I knew we should need it," she nodded to Bertram, as she picked up the shawl from the hall stand where she had left it when she came in. "That's why I brought it."

"Oh, my grief and conscience, Cyril, how can you stand it?—to climb stairs like this," panted Aunt Hannah, as she reached the top of the last flight and dropped breathlessly into the nearest chair—from which Marie had rescued a curtain just in time.

"Well, I'm not sure I could—if I were always to eat a Thanksgiving dinner just before," laughed Cyril. "Maybe I ought to have waited and let you rest an hour or two."

"But 'twould have been too dark, then, to see the rug," objected Marie. "It's a genuine Persian—a Kirman, you know; and I'm so proud of it," she added, turning to the others. "I wanted you to see the colors by daylight. Cyril likes it better, anyhow, in the daytime."

"Fancy Cyril liking any sort of a rug at any time," chuckled Bertram, his eyes on the rich, softly blended colors of the rug before him. "Honestly, Miss Marie," he added, turning to the little bride elect, "how did you ever manage to get him to buy any rug? He won't have so much as a ravelling on the floor up here to walk on."

A startled dismay came into Marie's blue eyes.

"Why, I thought he wanted rugs," she faltered. "I'm sure he said—"

"Of course I want rugs," interrupted Cyril, irritably. "I want them everywhere except in my own especial den. You don't suppose I want to hear other people clattering over bare floors all day, do you?"

"Of course not!" Bertram's face was preternaturally grave as he turned to the little music teacher. "I hope, Miss Marie, that you wear rubber heels on your shoes," he observed solicitously.

Even Cyril laughed at this, though all he said was:

"Come, come, I got you up here to look at the rug."

Bertram, however, was not to be silenced.

"And another thing, Miss Marie," he resumed, with the air of a true and tried adviser. "Just let me give you a pointer. I've lived with your future husband a good many years, and I know what I'm talking about."

"Bertram, be still," growled Cyril.

Bertram refused to be still.

"Whenever you want to know anything about Cyril, listen to his playing. For instance: if, after dinner, you hear a dreamy waltz or a sleepy nocturne, you may know that all is well. But if on your ears there falls anything like a dirge, or the wail of a lost spirit gone mad, better look to your soup and see if it hasn't been scorched, or taste of your pudding and see if you didn't put in salt instead of sugar."

"Bertram, will you be still?" cut in Cyril, testily, again.

"After all, judging from what Billy tells me," resumed Bertram, cheerfully, "what I've said won't be so important to you, for you aren't the kind that scorches soups or uses salt for sugar. So maybe I'd better put it to you this way: if you want a new sealskin coat or an extra diamond tiara, tackle him when he plays like this!" And with a swift turn Bertram dropped himself to the piano stool and dashed into a rollicking melody that half the newsboys of Boston were whistling.

What happened next was a surprise to every one. Bertram, very much as if he were a naughty little boy, was jerked by a wrathful brother's hand off the piano stool. The next moment the wrathful brother himself sat at the piano, and there burst on five pairs of astonished ears a crashing dissonance which was but the prelude to music such as few of the party often heard.

Spellbound they listened while rippling runs and sonorous harmonies filled the room to overflowing, as if under the fingers of the player there were—not the keyboard of a piano—but the violins, flutes, cornets, trombones, bass viols and kettledrums of a full orchestra.

Billy, perhaps, of them all, best understood. She knew that in those tripping melodies and crashing chords were Cyril's joy at the presence of Marie, his wrath at the flippancy of Bertram, his ecstasy at that for which the rug and curtains stood—the little woman sewing in the radiant circle of a shaded lamp. Billy knew that all this and more were finding voice at Cyril's finger tips. The others, too, understood in a way; but they, unlike Billy, were not in the habit of finding on a few score bits of wood and ivory a vent for their moods and fancies.

The music was softer now. The resounding chords and purling runs had become a bell-like melody that wound itself in and out of a maze of exquisite harmonies, now hiding, now coming out clear and unafraid, like a mountain stream emerging into a sunlit meadow from the leafy shadows of its forest home.

In a breathless hush the melody quivered into silence. It was Bertram who broke the pause with a long-drawn:

"By George!" Then, a little unsteadily: "If it's I that set you going like that, old chap, I'll come up and play ragtime every day!"

Cyril shrugged his shoulders and got to his feet.

"If you've seen all you want of the rug we'll go down-stairs," he said nonchalantly.

"But we haven't!" chorussed several indignant voices. And for the next few minutes not even the owner of the beautiful Kirman could find any fault with the quantity or the quality of the attention bestowed on his new possession. But Billy, under cover of the chatter, said reproachfully in his ear:

"Oh, Cyril, to think you can play like that—and won't—on demand!"

"I can't—on demand," shrugged Cyril again.

On the way down-stairs they stopped at William's rooms.

"I want you to see a couple of Batterseas I got last week," cried the collector eagerly, as he led the way to the black velvet square. "They're fine—and I think she looks like you," he finished, turning to Billy, and holding out one of the knobs, on which was a beautifully executed miniature of a young girl with dark, dreamy eyes.

"Oh, how pretty!" exclaimed Marie, over Billy's shoulder. "But what are they?"

The collector turned, his face alight.

"Mirror knobs. I've got lots of them. Would you like to see them—really? They're right here."

The next minute Marie found herself looking into a cabinet where lay a score or more of round and oval discs of glass, porcelain, and metal, framed in silver, gilt, and brass, and mounted on long spikes.

"Oh, how pretty," cried Marie again; "but how—how queer! Tell me about them, please."

William drew a long breath. His eyes glistened. William loved to talk—when he had a curio and a listener.

"I will. Our great-grandmothers used them, you know, to support their mirrors, or to fasten back their curtains," he explained ardently. "Now here's another Battersea enamel, but it isn't so good as my new ones—that face is almost a caricature."

"But what a beautiful ship—on that round one!" exclaimed Marie. "And what's this one?—glass?"

"Yes; but that's not so rare as the others. Still, it's pretty enough. Did you notice this one, with the bright red and blue and green on the white background?—regular Chinese mode of decoration, that is."

"Er—any time, William," began Bertram, mischievously; but William did not seem to hear.

"Now in this corner," he went on, warming to his subject, "are the enamelled porcelains. They were probably made at the Worcester works—England, you know; and I think many of them are quite as pretty as the Batterseas. You see it was at Worcester that they invented that variation of the transfer printing process that they called bat printing, where they used oil instead of ink, and gelatine instead of paper. Now engravings for that kind of printing were usually in stipple work—dots, you know—so the prints on these knobs can easily be distinguished from those of the transfer printing. See? Now, this one is—"

"Er, of course, William, any time—" interposed Bertram again, his eyes twinkling.

William stopped with a laugh.

"Yes, I know. 'Tis time I talked of something else, Bertram," he conceded.

"But 'twas lovely, and I was interested, really," claimed Marie. "Besides, there are such a lot of things here that I'd like to see," she finished, turning slowly about.

"These are what he was collecting last year," murmured Billy, hovering over a small cabinet where were some beautiful specimens of antique jewelry brooches, necklaces, armlets, Rajah rings, and anklets, gorgeous in color and exquisite in workmanship.

"Well, here is something you will enjoy," declared Bertram, with an airy flourish. "Do you see those teapots? Well, we can have tea every day in the year, and not use one of them but five times. I've counted. There are exactly seventy-three," he concluded, as he laughingly led the way from the room.

"How about leap year?" quizzed Billy.

"Ho! Trust Will to find another 'Old Blue' or a 'perfect treasure of a black basalt' by that time," shrugged Bertram.

Below William's rooms was the floor once Bertram's, but afterwards given over to the use of Billy and Aunt Hannah. The rooms were open to-day, and were bright with sunshine and roses; but they were very plainly unoccupied.

"And you don't use them yet?" remonstrated Billy, as she paused at an open door.

"No. These are Mrs. Bertram Henshaw's rooms," said the youngest Henshaw brother in a voice that made Billy hurry away with a dimpling blush.

"They were Billy's—and they can never seem any one's but Billy's, now," declared William to Marie, as they went down the stairs.

"And now for the den and some good stories before the fire," proposed Bertram, as the six reached the first floor again.

"But we haven't seen your pictures, yet," objected Billy.

Bertram made a deprecatory gesture.

"There's nothing much—" he began; but he stopped at once, with an odd laugh. "Well, I sha'n't say that," he finished, flinging open the door of his studio, and pressing a button that flooded the room with light. The next moment, as they stood before those plaques and panels and canvases—on each of which was a pictured "Billy"—they understood the change in his sentence, and they laughed appreciatively.

"'Much,' indeed!" exclaimed William.

"Oh, how lovely!" breathed Marie.

"My grief and conscience, Bertram! All these—and of Billy? I knew you had a good many, but—" Aunt Hannah paused impotently, her eyes going from Bertram's face to the pictures again.

"But how—when did you do them?" queried Marie.

"Some of them from memory. More of them from life. A lot of them were just sketches that I did when she was here in the house four or five years ago," answered Bertram; "like this, for instance." And he pulled into a better light a picture of a laughing, dark-eyed girl holding against her cheek a small gray kitten, with alert, bright eyes. "The original and only Spunk," he announced.

"What a dear little cat!" cried Marie.

"You should have seen it—in the flesh," remarked Cyril, dryly. "No paint nor painter could imprison that untamed bit of Satanic mischief on any canvas that ever grew!"

Everybody laughed—everybody but Billy. Billy, indeed, of them all, had been strangely silent ever since they entered the studio. She stood now a little apart. Her eyes were wide, and a bit frightened. Her fingers were twisting the corners of her handkerchief nervously. She was looking to the right and to the left, and everywhere she saw—herself.

Sometimes it was her full face, sometimes her profile; sometimes there were only her eyes peeping from above a fan, or peering from out brown shadows of nothingness. Once it was merely the back of her head showing the mass of waving hair with its high lights of burnished bronze. Again it was still the back of her head with below it the bare, slender neck and the scarf-draped shoulders. In this picture the curve of a half-turned cheek showed plainly, and in the background was visible a hand holding four playing cards, at which the pictured girl was evidently looking. Sometimes it was a merry Billy with dancing eyes; sometimes a demure Billy with long lashes caressing a flushed cheek. Sometimes it was a wistful Billy with eyes that looked straight into yours with peculiar appeal. But always it was—Billy.

"There, I think the tilt of this chin is perfect." It was Bertram speaking.

Billy gave a sudden cry. Her face whitened. She stumbled forward.

"No, no, Bertram, you—you didn't mean the—the tilt of the chin," she faltered wildly.

The man turned in amazement.

"Why—Billy!" he stammered. "Billy, what is it?"

The girl fell back at once. She tried to laugh lightly. She had seen the dismayed questioning in her lover's eyes, and in the eyes of William and the others.

"N-nothing," she gesticulated hurriedly. "It was nothing at all, truly."

"But, Billy, it was something." Bertram's eyes were still troubled. "Was it the picture? I thought you liked this picture."

Billy laughed again—this time more naturally.

"Bertram, I'm ashamed of you—expecting me to say I 'like' any of this," she scolded, with a wave of her hands toward the omnipresent Billy. "Why, I feel as if I were in a room with a thousand mirrors, and that I'd been discovered putting rouge on my cheeks and lampblack on my eyebrows!"

William laughed fondly. Aunt Hannah and Marie gave an indulgent smile. Cyril actually chuckled. Bertram only still wore a puzzled expression as he laid aside the canvas in his hands.

Billy examined intently a sketch she had found with its back to the wall. It was not a pretty sketch; it was not even a finished one, and Billy did not in the least care what it was. But her lips cried interestedly:

"Oh, Bertram, what is this?"

There was no answer. Bertram was still engaged, apparently, in putting away some sketches. Over by the doorway leading to the den Marie and Aunt Hannah, followed by William and Cyril, were just disappearing behind a huge easel. In another minute the merry chatter of their voices came from the room beyond. Bertram hurried then straight across the studio to the girl still bending over the sketch in the corner.

"Bertram!" gasped Billy, as a kiss brushed her cheek.

"Pooh! They're gone. Besides, what if they did see? Billy, what was the matter with the tilt of that chin?"

Billy gave an hysterical little laugh—at least, Bertram tried to assure himself that it was a laugh, though it had sounded almost like a sob.

"Bertram, if you say another word about—about the tilt of that chin, I shall scream!" she panted.

"Why, Billy!"

With a nervous little movement Billy turned and began to reverse the canvases nearest her.

"Come, sir," she commanded gayly. "Billy has been on exhibition quite long enough. It is high time she was turned face to the wall to meditate, and grow more modest."

Bertram did not answer. Neither did he make a move to assist her. His ardent gray eyes were following her slim, graceful figure admiringly.

"Billy, it doesn't seem true, yet, that you're really mine," he said at last, in a low voice shaken with emotion.

Billy turned abruptly. A peculiar radiance shone in her eyes and glorified her face. As she stood, she was close to a picture on an easel and full in the soft glow of the shaded lights above it.

"Then you do want me," she began, "—just me!—not to—" she stopped short. The man opposite had taken an eager step toward her. On his face was the look she knew so well, the look she had come almost to dread—the "painting look."

"Billy, stand just as you are," he was saying. "Don't move. Jove! But that effect is perfect with those dark shadows beyond, and just your hair and face and throat showing. I declare, I've half a mind to sketch—" But Billy, with a little cry, was gone.

CHAPTER X. A JOB FOR PETE—AND FOR BERTRAM

The early days in December were busy ones, certainly, in the little house on Corey Hill. Marie was to be married the twelfth. It was to be a home wedding, and a very simple one—according to Billy, and according to what Marie had said it was to be. Billy still serenely spoke of it as a "simple affair," but Marie was beginning to be fearful. As the days passed, bringing with them more and more frequent evidences either tangible or intangible of orders to stationers, caterers, and florists, her fears found voice in a protest.

"But Billy, it was to be a simple wedding," she cried.

"And so it is."

"But what is this I hear about a breakfast?"

Billy's chin assumed its most stubborn squareness.

"I don't know, I'm sure, what you did hear," she retorted calmly.

"Billy!"

Billy laughed. The chin was just as stubborn, but the smiling lips above it graced it with an air of charming concession.

"There, there, dear," coaxed the mistress of Hillside, "don't fret. Besides, I'm sure I should think you, of all people, would want your guests fed!"

"But this is so elaborate, from what I hear."

"Nonsense! Not a bit of it."

"Rosa says there'll be salads and cakes and ices—and I don't know what all."

Billy looked concerned.

"Well, of course, Marie, if you'd rather have oatmeal and doughnuts," she began with kind solicitude; but she got no farther.

"Billy!" besought the bride elect. "Won't you be serious? And there's the cake in wedding boxes, too."

"I know, but boxes are so much easier and cleaner than—just fingers," apologized an anxiously serious voice.

Marie answered with an indignant, grieved glance and hurried on.

"And the flowers—roses, dozens of them, in December! Billy, I can't let you do all this for me."

"Nonsense, dear!" laughed Billy. "Why, I love to do it. Besides, when you're gone, just think how lonesome I'll be! I shall have to adopt somebody else then—now that Mary Jane has proved to be nothing but a disappointing man instead of a nice little girl like you," she finished whimsically.

Marie did not smile. The frown still lay between her delicate brows.

"And for my trousseau—there were so many things that you simply would buy!"

"I didn't get one of the egg-beaters," Billy reminded her anxiously.

Marie smiled now, but she shook her head, too.

"Billy, I cannot have you do all this for me."

"Why not?"

At the unexpectedly direct question, Marie fell back a little.

"Why, because I—I can't," she stammered. "I can't get them for myself, and—and—"

"Don't you love me?"

A pink flush stole to Marie's face.

"Indeed I do, dearly."

"Don't I love you?"

The flush deepened.

"I—I hope so."

"Then why won't you let me do what I want to, and be happy in it? Money, just money, isn't any good unless you can exchange it for something you want. And just now I want pink roses and ice cream and lace flounces for you. Marie,"—Billy's voice trembled a little—"I never had a sister till I had you, and I have had such a good time buying things that I thought you wanted! But, of course, if you don't want them—" The words ended in a choking sob, and down went Billy's head into her folded arms on the desk before her.

Marie sprang to her feet and cuddled the bowed head in a loving embrace.

"But I do want them, dear; I want them all—every single one," she urged. "Now promise me—promise me that you'll do them all, just as you'd planned! You will, won't you?"

There was the briefest of hesitations, then came the muffled reply:

"Yes—if you really want them."

"I do, dear—indeed I do. I love pretty weddings, and I—I always hoped that I could have one—if I ever married. So you must know, dear, how I really do want all those things," declared Marie, fervently. "And now I must go. I promised to meet Cyril at Park Street at three o'clock." And she hurried from the room—and not until she was half-way to her destination did it suddenly occur to her that she had been urging, actually urging Miss Billy Neilson to buy for her pink roses, ice cream, and lace flounces.

Her cheeks burned with shame then. But almost at once she smiled.

"Now wasn't that just like Billy?" she was saying to herself, with a tender glow in her eyes.

It was early in December that Pete came one day with a package for Marie from Cyril. Marie was not at home, and Billy herself went downstairs to take the package from the old man's hands.

"Mr. Cyril said to give it to Miss Hawthorn," stammered the old servant, his face lighting up as Billy entered the room; "but I'm sure he wouldn't mind your taking it."

"I'm afraid I'll have to take it, Pete, unless you want to carry it back with you," she smiled. "I'll see that Miss Hawthorn has it the very first moment she comes in."

"Thank you, Miss. It does my old eyes good to see your bright face." He hesitated, then turned slowly. "Good day, Miss Billy."

Billy laid the package on the table. Her eyes were thoughtful as she looked after the old man, who was now almost to the door. Something in his bowed form appealed to her strangely. She took a quick step toward him.

"You'll miss Mr. Cyril, Pete," she said pleasantly.

The old man stopped at once and turned. He lifted his head a little proudly.

"Yes, Miss. I—I was there when he was born. Mr. Cyril's a fine man."

"Indeed he is. Perhaps it's your good care that's helped, some—to make him so," smiled the girl, vaguely wishing that she could say something that would drive the wistful look from the dim old eyes before her.

For a moment Billy thought she had succeeded. The old servant drew himself stiffly erect. In his eyes shone the loyal pride of more than fifty years' honest service. Almost at once, however, the pride died away, and the wistfulness returned.

"Thank ye, Miss; but I don't lay no claim to that, of course," he said. "Mr. Cyril's a fine man, and we shall miss him; but—I cal'late changes must come—to all of us."

Billy's brown eyes grew a little misty.

"I suppose they must," she admitted.

The old man hesitated; then, as if impelled by some hidden force, he plunged on:

"Yes; and they'll be comin' to you one of these days, Miss, and that's what I was wantin' to speak to ye about. I understand, of course, that when you get there you'll be wantin' younger blood to serve ye. My feet ain't so spry as they once was, and my old hands blunder sometimes, in spite of what my head bids 'em do. So I wanted to tell ye—that of course I shouldn't expect to stay. I'd go."

As he said the words, Pete stood with head and shoulders erect, his eyes looking straight forward but not at Billy.

"Don't you want to stay?" The girlish voice was a little reproachful.

Pete's head drooped.

"Not if—I'm not wanted," came the husky reply.

With an impulsive movement Billy came straight to the old man's side and held out her hand.

"Pete!"

Amazement, incredulity, and a look that was almost terror crossed the old man's face; then a flood of dull red blotted them all out and left only worshipful rapture. With a choking cry he took the slim little hand in both his rough and twisted ones much as if he were possessing himself of a treasured bit of eggshell china.

"Miss Billy!"

"Pete, there aren't a pair of feet in Boston, nor a pair of hands, either, that I'd rather have serve me than yours, no matter if they stumble and blunder all day! I shall love stumbles and blunders—if you make them. Now run home, and don't ever let me hear another syllable about your leaving!"

They were not the words Billy had intended to say. She had meant to speak of his long, faithful service, and of how much they appreciated it; but, to her surprise, Billy found her own eyes wet and her own voice trembling, and the words that she would have said she found fast shut in her throat. So there was nothing to do but to stammer out something—anything, that would help to keep her from yielding to that absurd and awful desire to fall on the old servant's neck and cry.

"Not another syllable!" she repeated sternly.

"Miss Billy!" choked Pete again. Then he turned and fled with anything but his usual dignity.

Bertram called that evening. When Billy came to him in the living-room, her slender self was almost hidden behind the swirls of damask linen in her arms.

Bertram's eyes grew mutinous.

"Do you expect me to hug all that?" he demanded.

Billy flashed him a mischievous glance.

"Of course not! You don't have to hug anything, you know."

For answer he impetuously swept the offending linen into the nearest chair and drew the girl into his arms.

"Oh! And see how you've crushed poor Marie's table-cloth!" she cried, with reproachful eyes.

Bertram sniffed imperturbably.

"I'm not sure but I'd like to crush Marie," he alleged.

"Bertram!"

"I can't help it. See here, Billy." He loosened his clasp and held the girl off at arm's length, regarding her with stormy eyes. "It's Marie, Marie, Marie—always. If I telephone in the morning, you've gone shopping with Marie. If I want you in the afternoon for something, you're at the dressmaker's with Marie. If I call in the evening—"

"I'm here," interrupted Billy, with decision.

"Oh, yes, you're here," admitted Bertram, aggrievedly, "and so are dozens of napkins, miles of table-cloths, and yards upon yards of lace and flummydiddles you call 'doilies.' They all belong to Marie, and they fill your arms and your thoughts full, until there isn't an inch of room for me. Billy, when is this thing going to end?"

Billy laughed softly. Her eyes danced.

"The twelfth;—that is, there'll be a—pause, then."

"Well, I'm thankful if—eh?" broke off the man, with a sudden change of manner. "What do you mean by 'a pause'?"

Billy cast down her eyes demurely.

"Well, of course this ends the twelfth with Marie's wedding; but I've sort of regarded it as an—understudy for one that's coming next October, you see."

"Billy, you darling!" breathed a supremely happy voice in a shell-like ear—Billy was not at arm's length now.

Billy smiled, but she drew away with gentle firmness.

"And now I must go back to my sewing," she said.

Bertram's arms did not loosen. His eyes had grown mutinous again.

"That is," she amended, "I must be practising my part of—the understudy, you know."

"You darling!" breathed Bertram again; this time, however, he let her go.

"But, honestly, is it all necessary?" he sighed despairingly, as she seated herself and gathered the table-cloth into her lap. "Do you have to do so much of it all?"

"I do," smiled Billy, "unless you want your brother to run the risk of leading his bride to the altar and finding her robed in a kitchen apron with an egg-beater in her hand for a bouquet."

Bertram laughed.

"Is it so bad as that?"

"No, of course not—quite. But never have I seen a bride so utterly oblivious to clothes as Marie was till one day in despair I told her that Cyril never could bear a dowdy woman."

"As if Cyril, in the old days, ever could bear any sort of woman!" scoffed Bertram, merrily.
"I know; but I didn't mention that part," smiled Billy. "I just singled out the dowdy one."
"Did it work?"
Billy made a gesture of despair.
"Did it work! It worked too well. Marie gave me one horrified look, then at once and immediately she became possessed with the idea that she was a dowdy woman. And from that day to this she has pursued every lurking wrinkle and every fold awry, until her dressmaker's life isn't worth the living; and I'm beginning to think mine isn't, either, for I have to assure her at least four times every day now that she is not a dowdy woman."
"You poor dear," laughed Bertram. "No wonder you don't have time to give to me!"
A peculiar expression crossed Billy's face.
"Oh, but I'm not the only one who, at times, is otherwise engaged, sir," she reminded him.
"What do you mean?"
"There was yesterday, and last Monday, and last week Wednesday, and—"
"Oh, but you let me off, then," argued Bertram, anxiously. "And you said—"
"That I didn't wish to interfere with your work—which was quite true," interrupted Billy in her turn, smoothly. "By the way,"—Billy was examining her stitches very closely now—"how is Miss Winthrop's portrait coming on?"
"Splendidly!—that is, it was, until she began to put off the sittings for her pink teas and folderols. She's going to Washington next week, too, to be gone nearly a fortnight," finished Bertram, gloomily.
"Aren't you putting more work than usual into this one—and more sittings?"
"Well, yes," laughed Bertram, a little shortly. "You see, she's changed the pose twice already."
"Changed it!"
"Yes. Wasn't satisfied. Fancied she wanted it different."
"But can't you—don't you have something to say about it?"
"Oh, yes, of course; and she claims she'll yield to my judgment, anyhow. But what's the use? She's been a spoiled darling all her life, and in the habit of having her own way about everything. Naturally, under those circumstances, I can't expect to get a satisfactory portrait, if she's out of tune with the pose. Besides, I will own, so far her suggestions have made for improvement—probably because she's been happy in making them, so her expression has been good."
Billy wet her lips.
"I saw her the other night," she said lightly. (If the lightness was a little artificial Bertram did not seem to notice it.) "She is certainly—very beautiful."
"Yes." Bertram got to his feet and began to walk up and down the little room. His eyes were alight. On his face the "painting look" was king. "It's going to mean a lot to me—this picture, Billy. In the first place I'm just at the point in my career where a big success would mean a lot—and where a big failure would mean more. And this portrait is bound to be one or the other from the very nature of the thing."
"I-is it?" Billy's voice was a little faint.
"Yes. First, because of who the sitter is, and secondly because of what she is. She is, of course, the most famous subject I've had, and half the artistic world knows by this time that Marguerite Winthrop is being done by Henshaw. You can see what it'll be—if I fail."
"But you won't fail, Bertram!"
The artist lifted his chin and threw back his shoulders.
"No, of course not; but—" He hesitated, frowned, and dropped himself into a chair. His eyes studied the fire moodily. "You see," he resumed, after a moment, "there's a peculiar, elusive something about her expression—" (Billy stirred restlessly and gave her thread so savage a jerk that it broke)"—a something that isn't easily caught by the brush. Anderson and Fullam—big fellows, both of them—didn't catch it. At least, I've understood that

neither her family nor her friends are satisfied with their portraits. And to succeed where Anderson and Fullam failed—Jove! Billy, a chance like that doesn't come to a fellow twice in a lifetime!" Bertram was out of his chair, again, tramping up and down the little room.

Billy tossed her work aside and sprang to her feet. Her eyes, too, were alight, now.

"But you aren't going to fail, dear," she cried, holding out both her hands. "You're going to succeed!"

Bertram caught the hands and kissed first one then the other of their soft little palms.

"Of course I am," he agreed passionately, leading her to the sofa, and seating himself at her side.

"Yes, but you must really feel it," she urged; "feel the 'sure' in yourself. You have to!—to doing things. That's what I told Mary Jane yesterday, when he was running on about what he wanted to do—in his singing, you know."

Bertram stiffened a little. A quick frown came to his face.

"Mary Jane, indeed! Of all the absurd names to give a full-grown, six-foot man! Billy, do, for pity's sake, call him by his name—if he's got one."

Billy broke into a rippling laugh.

"I wish I could, dear," she sighed ingenuously.

"Honestly, it bothers me because I can't think of him as anything but 'Mary Jane.' It seems so silly!"

"It certainly does—when one remembers his beard."

"Oh, he's shaved that off now. He looks rather better, too."

Bertram turned a little sharply.

"Do you see the fellow—often?"

Billy laughed merrily.

"No. He's about as disgruntled as you are over the way the wedding monopolizes everything. He's been up once or twice to see Aunt Hannah and to get acquainted, as he expresses it, and once he brought up some music and we sang; but he declares the wedding hasn't given him half a show."

"Indeed! Well, that's a pity, I'm sure," rejoined Bertram, icily.

Billy turned in slight surprise.

"Why, Bertram, don't you like Mary Jane?"

"Billy, for heaven's sake! Hasn't he got any name but that?"

Billy clapped her hands together suddenly.

"There, that makes me think. He told Aunt Hannah and me to guess what his name was, and we never hit it once. What do you think it is? The initials are M. J."

"I couldn't say, I'm sure. What is it?"

"Oh, he didn't tell us. You see he left us to guess it."

"Did he?"

"Yes," mused Billy, abstractedly, her eyes on the dancing fire. The next minute she stirred and settled herself more comfortably in the curve of her lover's arm. "But there! who cares what his name is? I'm sure I don't."

"Nor I," echoed Bertram in a voice that he tried to make not too fervent. He had not forgotten Billy's surprised: "Why, Bertram, don't you like Mary Jane?" and he did not like to call forth a repetition of it. Abruptly, therefore, he changed the subject. "By the way, what did you do to Pete to-day?" he asked laughingly. "He came home in a seventh heaven of happiness babbling of what an angel straight from the sky Miss Billy was. Naturally I agreed with him on that point. But what did you do to him?"

Billy smiled.

"Nothing—only engaged him for our butler—for life."

"Oh, I see. That was dear of you, Billy."

"As if I'd do anything else! And now for Dong Ling, I suppose, some day."

Bertram chuckled.

"Well, maybe I can help you there," he hinted. "You see, his Celestial Majesty came to me himself the other day, and said, after sundry and various preliminaries, that he should be 'velly much glad' when the 'Little Missee' came to live with me, for then he could go back to China with a heart at rest, as he had money 'velly much plenty' and didn't wish to be 'Melican man' any longer."

"Dear me," smiled Billy, "what a happy state of affairs—for him. But for you—do you realize, young man, what that means for you? A new wife and a new cook all at once? And you know I'm not Marie!"

"Ho! I'm not worrying," retorted Bertram with a contented smile; "besides, as perhaps you noticed, it wasn't Marie that I asked—to marry me!"

CHAPTER XI. A CLOCK AND AUNT HANNAH

Mrs. Kate Hartwell, the Henshaw brothers' sister from the West, was expected on the tenth. Her husband could not come, she had written, but she would bring with her, little Kate, the youngest child. The boys, Paul and Egbert, would stay with their father.

Billy received the news of little Kate's coming with outspoken delight.

"The very thing!" she cried. "We'll have her for a flower girl. She was a dear little creature, as I remember her."

Aunt Hannah gave a sudden low laugh.

"Yes, I remember," she observed. "Kate told me, after you spent the first day with her, that you graciously informed her that little Kate was almost as nice as Spunk. Kate did not fully appreciate the compliment, I fear."

Billy made a wry face.

"Did I say that? Dear me! I was a terror in those days, wasn't I? But then," and she laughed softly, "really, Aunt Hannah, that was the prettiest thing I knew how to say, for I considered Spunk the top-notch of desirability."

"I think I should have liked to know Spunk," smiled Marie from the other side of the sewing table.

"He was a dear," declared Billy. "I had another 'most as good when I first came to Hillside, but he got lost. For a time it seemed as if I never wanted another, but I've about come to the conclusion now that I do, and I've told Bertram to find one for me if he can. You see I shall be lonesome after you're gone, Marie, and I'll have to have something," she finished mischievously.

"Oh, I don't mind the inference—as long as I know your admiration of cats," laughed Marie.

"Let me see; Kate writes she is coming the tenth," murmured Aunt Hannah, going back to the letter in her hand.

"Good!" nodded Billy. "That will give time to put little Kate through her paces as flower girl."

"Yes, and it will give Big Kate time to try to make your breakfast a supper, and your roses pinks—or sunflowers," cut in a new voice, dryly.

"Cyril!" chorussed the three ladies in horror, adoration, and amusement—according to whether the voice belonged to Aunt Hannah, Marie, or Billy.

Cyril shrugged his shoulders and smiled.

"I beg your pardon," he apologized; "but Rosa said you were in here sewing, and I told her not to bother. I'd announce myself. Just as I got to the door I chanced to hear Billy's speech, and I couldn't resist making the amendment. Maybe you've forgotten Kate's love of managing—but I haven't," he finished, as he sauntered over to the chair nearest Marie.

"No, I haven't—forgotten," observed Billy, meaningly.

"Nor I—nor anybody else," declared a severe voice—both the words and the severity being most extraordinary as coming from the usually gentle Aunt Hannah.

"Oh, well, never mind," spoke up Billy, quickly. "Everything's all right now, so let's forget it. She always meant it for kindness, I'm sure."

"Even when she told you in the first place what a—er—torment you were to us?" quizzed Cyril.

"Yes," flashed Billy. "She was being kind to you, then."

"Humph!" vouchsafed Cyril.

For a moment no one spoke. Cyril's eyes were on Marie, who was nervously trying to smooth back a few fluffy wisps of hair that had escaped from restraining combs and pins.

"What's the matter with the hair, little girl?" asked Cyril in a voice that was caressingly irritable. "You've been fussing with that long-suffering curl for the last five minutes!"

Marie's delicate face flushed painfully.

"It's got loose—my hair," she stammered, "and it looks so dowdy that way!"

Billy dropped her thread suddenly. She sprang for it at once, before Cyril could make a move to get it. She had to dive far under a chair to capture it—which may explain why her face was so very red when she finally reached her seat again.

On the morning of the tenth, Billy, Marie, and Aunt Hannah were once more sewing together, this time in the little sitting-room at the end of the hall up-stairs.

Billy's fingers, in particular, were flying very fast.

"I told John to have Peggy at the door at eleven," she said, after a time; "but I think I can finish running in this ribbon before then. I haven't much to do to get ready to go."

"I hope Kate's train won't be late," worried Aunt Hannah.

"I hope not," replied Billy; "but I told Rosa to delay luncheon, anyway, till we get here. I—" She stopped abruptly and turned a listening ear toward the door of Aunt Hannah's room, which was open. A clock was striking. "Mercy! that can't be eleven now," she cried. "But it must be—it was ten before I came up-stairs." She got to her feet hurriedly.

Aunt Hannah put out a restraining hand.

"No, no, dear, that's half-past ten."

"But it struck eleven."

"Yes, I know. It does—at half-past ten."

"Why, the little wretch," laughed Billy, dropping back into her chair and picking up her work again. "The idea of its telling fibs like that and frightening people half out of their lives! I'll have it fixed right away. Maybe John can do it—he's always so handy about such things."

"But I don't want it fixed," demurred Aunt Hannah.

Billy stared a little.

"You don't want it fixed! Maybe you like to have it strike eleven when it's half-past ten!" Billy's voice was merrily sarcastic.

"Y-yes, I do," stammered the lady, apologetically. "You see, I—I worked very hard to fix it so it would strike that way."

"Aunt Hannah!"

"Well, I did," retorted the lady, with unexpected spirit. "I wanted to know what time it was in the night—I'm awake such a lot."

"But I don't see." Billy's eyes were perplexed. "Why must you make it tell fibs in order to—to find out the truth?" she laughed.

Aunt Hannah elevated her chin a little.

"Because that clock was always striking one."

"One!"

"Yes—half-past, you know; and I never knew which half-past it was."

"But it must strike half-past now, just the same!"

"It does." There was the triumphant ring of the conqueror in Aunt Hannah's voice. "But now it strikes half-past on the hour, and the clock in the hall tells me then what time it is, so I don't care."

For one more brief minute Billy stared, before a sudden light of understanding illumined her face. Then her laugh rang out gleefully.

"Oh, Aunt Hannah, Aunt Hannah," she gurgled. "If Bertram wouldn't call you the limit—making a clock strike eleven so you'll know it's half-past ten!"

Aunt Hannah colored a little, but she stood her ground.

"Well, there's only half an hour, anyway, now, that I don't know what time it is," she maintained, "for one or the other of those clocks strikes the hour every thirty minutes. Even during those never-ending three ones that strike one after the other in the middle of the night, I can tell now, for the hall clock has a different sound for the half-hours, you know, so I can tell whether it's one or a half-past."

"Of course," chuckled Billy.

"I'm sure I think it's a splendid idea," chimed in Marie, valiantly; "and I'm going to write it to mother's Cousin Jane right away. She's an invalid, and she's always lying awake nights wondering what time it is. The doctor says actually he believes she'd get well if he could find some way of letting her know the time at night, so she'd get some sleep; for she simply can't go to sleep till she knows. She can't bear a light in the room, and it wakes her all up to turn an electric switch, or anything of that kind."

"Why doesn't she have one of those phosphorous things?" questioned Billy.

Marie laughed quietly.

"She did. I sent her one,—and she stood it just one night."

"Stood it!"

"Yes. She declared it gave her the creeps, and that she wouldn't have the spooky thing staring at her all night like that. So it's got to be something she can hear, and I'm going to tell her Mrs. Stetson's plan right away."

"Well, I'm sure I wish you would," cried that lady, with prompt interest; "and she'll like it, I'm sure. And tell her if she can hear a town clock strike, it's just the same, and even better; for there aren't any half-hours at all to think of there."

"I will—and I think it's lovely," declared Marie.

"Of course it's lovely," smiled Billy, rising; "but I fancy I'd better go and get ready to meet Mrs. Hartwell, or the 'lovely' thing will be telling me that it's half-past eleven!" And she tripped laughingly from the room.

Promptly at the appointed time John with Peggy drew up before the door, and Billy, muffled in furs, stepped into the car, which, with its protecting top and sides and glass wind-shield, was in its winter dress.

"Yes'm, 'tis a little chilly, Miss," said John, in answer to her greeting, as he tucked the heavy robes about her.

"Oh, well, I shall be very comfortable, I'm sure," smiled Billy. "Just don't drive too rapidly, specially coming home. I shall have to get a limousine, I think, when my ship comes in, John."

John's grizzled old face twitched. So evident were the words that were not spoken that Billy asked laughingly:

"Well, John, what is it?"

John reddened furiously.

"Nothing, Miss. I was only thinkin' that if you didn't 'tend ter haulin' in so many other folks's ships, yours might get in sooner."

"Why, John! Nonsense! I—I love to haul in other folks's ships," laughed the girl, embarrassedly.

"Yes, Miss; I know you do," grunted John.

Billy colored.

"No, no—that is, I mean—I don't do it—very much," she stammered.

John did not answer apparently; but Billy was sure she caught a low-muttered, indignant "much!" as he snapped the door shut and took his place at the wheel.

To herself she laughed softly. She thought she possessed the secret now of some of John's disapproving glances toward her humble guests of the summer before.

CHAPTER XII. SISTER KATE

At the station Mrs. Hartwell's train was found to be gratifyingly on time; and in due course Billy was extending a cordial welcome to a tall, handsome woman who carried herself with an unmistakable air of assured competence. Accompanying her was a little girl with big blue eyes and yellow curls.

"I am very glad to see you both," smiled Billy, holding out a friendly hand to Mrs. Hartwell, and stooping to kiss the round cheek of the little girl.

"Thank you, you are very kind," murmured the lady; "but—are you alone, Billy? Where are the boys?"

"Uncle William is out of town, and Cyril is rushed to death and sent his excuses. Bertram did mean to come, but he telephoned this morning that he couldn't, after all. I'm sorry, but I'm afraid you'll have to make the best of just me," condoled Billy. "They'll be out to the house this evening, of course—all but Uncle William. He doesn't return until to-morrow."

"Oh, doesn't he?" murmured the lady, reaching for her daughter's hand.

Billy looked down with a smile.

"And this is little Kate, I suppose," she said, "whom I haven't seen for such a long, long time. Let me see, you are how old now?"

"I'm eight. I've been eight six weeks."

Billy's eyes twinkled.

"And you don't remember me, I suppose."

The little girl shook her head.

"No; but I know who you are," she added, with shy eagerness. "You're going to be my Aunt Billy, and you're going to marry my Uncle William—I mean, my Uncle Bertram."

Billy's face changed color. Mrs. Hartwell gave a despairing gesture.

"Kate, my dear, I told you to be sure and remember that it was your Uncle Bertram now. You see," she added in a discouraged aside to Billy, "she can't seem to forget the first one. But then, what can you expect?" laughed Mrs. Hartwell, a little disagreeably. "Such abrupt changes from one brother to another are somewhat disconcerting, you know."

Billy bit her lip. For a moment she said nothing, then, a little constrainedly, she rejoined:

"Perhaps. Still—let us hope we have the right one, now."

Mrs. Hartwell raised her eyebrows.

"Well, my dear, I'm not so confident of that. My choice has been and always will be—William."

Billy bit her lip again. This time her brown eyes flashed a little.

"Is that so? But you see, after all, you aren't making the—the choice." Billy spoke lightly, gayly; and she ended with a bright little laugh, as if to hide any intended impertinence.

It was Mrs. Hartwell's turn to bite her lip—and she did it.

"So it seems," she rejoined frigidly, after the briefest of pauses.

It was not until they were on their way to Corey Hill some time later that Mrs. Hartwell turned with the question:

"Cyril is to be married in church, I suppose?"

"No. They both preferred a home wedding."

"Oh, what a pity! Church weddings are so attractive!"

"To those who like them," amended Billy in spite of herself.

"To every one, I think," corrected Mrs. Hartwell, positively.

Billy laughed. She was beginning to discern that it did not do much harm—nor much good—to disagree with her guest.

"It's in the evening, then, of course?" pursued Mrs. Hartwell.

"No; at noon."

"Oh, how could you let them?"

"But they preferred it, Mrs. Hartwell."

"What if they did?" retorted the lady, sharply. "Can't you do as you please in your own home? Evening weddings are so much prettier! We can't change now, of course, with the guests all invited. That is, I suppose you do have guests!"

Mrs. Hartwell's voice was aggrievedly despairing.

"Oh, yes," smiled Billy, demurely. "We have guests invited—and I'm afraid we can't change the time."

"No, of course not; but it's too bad. I conclude there are announcements only, as I got no cards.

"Announcements only," bowed Billy.

"I wish Cyril had consulted me, a little, about this affair."

Billy did not answer. She could not trust herself to speak just then. Cyril's words of two days before were in her ears: "Yes, and it will give Big Kate time to try to make your breakfast supper, and your roses pinks—or sunflowers."

In a moment Mrs. Hartwell spoke again.

"Of course a noon wedding is quite pretty if you darken the rooms and have lights—you're going to do that, I suppose?"

Billy shook her head slowly.

"I'm afraid not, Mrs. Hartwell. That isn't the plan, now."

"Not darken the rooms!" exclaimed Mrs. Hartwell. "Why, it won't—" She stopped suddenly, and fell back in her seat. The look of annoyed disappointment gave way to one of confident relief. "But then, that can be changed," she finished serenely.

Billy opened her lips, but she shut them without speaking. After a minute she opened them again.

"You might consult—Cyril—about that," she said in a quiet voice.

"Yes, I will," nodded Mrs. Hartwell, brightly. She was looking pleased and happy again. "I love weddings. Don't you? You can do so much with them!"

"Can you?" laughed Billy, irrepressibly.

"Yes. Cyril is happy, of course. Still, I can't imagine him in love with any woman."

"I think Marie can."

"I suppose so. I don't seem to remember her much; still, I think I saw her once or twice when I was on last June. Music teacher, wasn't she?"

"Yes. She is a very sweet girl."

"Hm-m; I suppose so. Still, I think 'twould have been better if Cyril could have selected some one that wasn't musical—say a more domestic wife. He's so terribly unpractical himself about household matters."

Billy gave a ringing laugh and stood up. The car had come to a stop before her own door.

"Do you? Just you wait till you see Marie's trousseau of—egg-beaters and cake tins," she chuckled.

Mrs. Hartwell looked blank.

"Whatever in the world do you mean, Billy?" she demanded fretfully, as she followed her hostess from the car. "I declare! aren't you ever going to grow beyond making those absurd remarks of yours?"

"Maybe—sometime," laughed Billy, as she took little Kate's hand and led the way up the steps.

Luncheon in the cozy dining-room at Hillside that day was not entirely a success. At least there were not present exactly the harmony and tranquillity that are conceded to be the best sauce for one's food. The wedding, of course, was the all-absorbing topic of conversation; and Billy, between Aunt Hannah's attempts to be polite, Marie's to be sweet-tempered, Mrs. Hartwell's to be dictatorial, and her own to be pacifying as well as firm, had a hard time of it. If it had not been for two or three diversions created by little Kate, the meal would have been, indeed, a dismal failure.

But little Kate—most of the time the personification of proper little-girlhood—had a disconcerting faculty of occasionally dropping a word here, or a question there, with startling effect. As, for instance, when she asked Billy "Who's going to boss your wedding?" and again when she calmly informed her mother that when she was married she was not going to have any wedding at all to bother with, anyhow. She was going to elope, and she should choose somebody's chauffeur, because he'd know how to go the farthest and fastest so her mother couldn't catch up with her and tell her how she ought to have done it.

After luncheon Aunt Hannah went up-stairs for rest and recuperation. Marie took little Kate and went for a brisk walk—for the same purpose. This left Billy alone with her guest.

"Perhaps you would like a nap, too, Mrs. Hartwell," suggested Billy, as they passed into the living-room. There was a curious note of almost hopefulness in her voice.

Mrs. Hartwell scorned naps, and she said so very emphatically. She said something else, too.

"Billy, why do you always call me 'Mrs. Hartwell' in that stiff, formal fashion? You used to call me 'Aunt Kate.'"

"But I was very young then." Billy's voice was troubled. Billy had been trying so hard for the last two hours to be the graciously cordial hostess to this woman—Bertram's sister.

"Very true. Then why not 'Kate' now?"

Billy hesitated. She was wondering why it seemed so hard to call Mrs. Hartwell "Kate."

"Of course," resumed the lady, "when you're Bertram's wife and my sister—"

"Why, of course," cried Billy, in a sudden flood of understanding. Curiously enough, she had never before thought of Mrs. Hartwell as her sister. "I shall be glad to call you 'Kate'—if you like."

"Thank you. I shall like it very much, Billy," nodded the other cordially. "Indeed, my dear, I'm very fond of you, and I was delighted to hear you were to be my sister. If only—it could have stayed William instead of Bertram."

"But it couldn't," smiled Billy. "It wasn't William—that I loved."

"But Bertram!—it's so absurd."

"Absurd!" The smile was gone now.

"Yes. Forgive me, Billy, but I was about as much surprised to hear of Bertram's engagement as I was of Cyril's."

Billy grew a little white.

"But Bertram was never an avowed—woman-hater, like Cyril, was he?"

"'Woman-hater'—dear me, no! He was a woman-lover, always. As if his eternal 'Face of a Girl' didn't prove that! Bertram has always loved women—to paint. But as for his ever taking them seriously—why, Billy, what's the matter?"

Billy had risen suddenly.

"If you'll excuse me, please, just a few minutes," Billy said very quietly. "I want to speak to Rosa in the kitchen. I'll be back—soon."

In the kitchen Billy spoke to Rosa—she wondered afterwards what she said. Certainly she did not stay in the kitchen long enough to say much. In her own room a minute later, with the door fast closed, she took from her table the photograph of Bertram and held it in her two hands, talking to it softly, but a little wildly.

"I didn't listen! I didn't stay! Do you hear? I came to you. She shall not say anything that will make trouble between you and me. I've suffered enough through her already! And she doesn't know—she didn't know before, and she doesn't now. She's only imagining. I will not not—not believe that you love me—just to paint. No matter what they say—all of them! I will not!"

Billy put the photograph back on the table then, and went down-stairs to her guest. She smiled brightly, though her face was a little pale.

"I wondered if perhaps you wouldn't like some music," she said pleasantly, going straight to the piano.

"Indeed I would!" agreed Mrs. Hartwell.

Billy sat down then and played—played as Mrs. Hartwell had never heard her play before.

"Why, Billy, you amaze me," she cried, when the pianist stopped and whirled about. "I had no idea you could play like that!"

Billy smiled enigmatically. Billy was thinking that Mrs. Hartwell would, indeed, have been surprised if she had known that in that playing were herself, the ride home, the luncheon, Bertram, and the girl—whom Bertram did not love only to paint!

CHAPTER XIII. CYRIL AND A WEDDING

The twelfth was a beautiful day. Clear, frosty air set the blood to tingling and the eyes to sparkling, even if it were not your wedding day; while if it were—

It was Marie Hawthorn's wedding day, and certainly her eyes sparkled and her blood tingled as she threw open the window of her room and breathed long and deep of the fresh morning air before going down to breakfast.

"They say 'Happy is the bride that the sun shines on,'" she whispered softly to an English sparrow that cocked his eye at her from a neighboring tree branch. "As if a bride wouldn't be happy, sun or no sun," she scoffed tenderly, as she turned to go down-stairs.

As it happens, however, tingling blood and sparkling eyes are a matter of more than weather, or even weddings, as was proved a little later when the telephone bell rang.

Kate answered the ring.

"Hullo, is that you, Kate?" called a despairing voice.

"Yes. Good morning, Bertram. Isn't this a fine day for the wedding?"

"Fine! Oh, yes, I suppose so, though I must confess I haven't noticed it—and you wouldn't, if you had a lunatic on your hands."

"A lunatic!"

"Yes. Maybe you have, though. Is Marie rampaging around the house like a wild creature, and asking ten questions and making twenty threats to the minute?"

"Certainly not! Don't be absurd, Bertram. What do you mean?"

"See here, Kate, that show comes off at twelve sharp, doesn't it?"

"Show, indeed!" retorted Kate, indignantly. "The wedding is at noon sharp—as the best man should know very well."

"All right; then tell Billy, please, to see that it is sharp, or I won't answer for the consequences."

"What do you mean? What is the matter?"

"Cyril. He's broken loose at last. I've been expecting it all along. I've simply marvelled at the meekness with which he has submitted himself to be tied up with white ribbons and topped with roses."

"Nonsense, Bertram!"

"Well, it amounts to that. Anyhow, he thinks it does, and he's wild. I wish you could have heard the thunderous performance on his piano with which he woke me up this morning. Billy says he plays everything—his past, present, and future. All is, if he was playing his future this morning, I pity the girl who's got to live it with him."

"Bertram!"

Bertram chuckled remorselessly.

"Well, I do. But I'll warrant he wasn't playing his future this morning. He was playing his present—the wedding. You see, he's just waked up to the fact that it'll be a perfect orgy of women and other confusion, and he doesn't like it. All the samee,{sic} I've had to assure him just fourteen times this morning that the ring, the license, the carriage, the minister's fee, and my sanity are all O. K. When he isn't asking questions he's making threats to snake the parson up there an hour ahead of time and be off with Marie before a soul comes."

"What an absurd idea!"

"Cyril doesn't think so. Indeed, Kate, I've had a hard struggle to convince him that the guests wouldn't think it the most delightful experience of their lives if they should come and find the ceremony over with and the bride gone."

"Well, you remind Cyril, please, that there are other people besides himself concerned in this wedding," observed Kate, icily.

"I have," purred Bertram, "and he says all right, let them have it, then. He's gone now to look up proxy marriages, I believe."

"Proxy marriages, indeed! Come, come, Bertram, I've got something to do this morning besides to stand here listening to your nonsense. See that you and Cyril get here on time—that's all!" And she hung up the receiver with an impatient jerk.

She turned to confront the startled eyes of the bride elect.

"What is it? Is anything wrong—with Cyril?" faltered Marie.

Kate laughed and raised her eyebrows slightly.

"Nothing but a little stage fright, my dear."

"Stage fright!"

"Yes. Bertram says he's trying to find some one to play his rôle, I believe, in the ceremony."

"Mrs. Hartwell!"

At the look of dismayed terror that came into Marie's face, Mrs. Hartwell laughed reassuringly.

"There, there, dear child, don't look so horror-stricken. There probably never was a man yet who wouldn't have fled from the wedding part of his marriage if he could; and you know how Cyril hates fuss and feathers. The wonder to me is that he's stood it as long as he has. I thought I saw it coming, last night at the rehearsal—and now I know I did."

Marie still looked distressed.

"But he never said—I thought—" She stopped helplessly.

"Of course he didn't, child. He never said anything but that he loved you, and he never thought anything but that you were going to be his. Men never do—till the wedding day. Then they never think of anything but a place to run," she finished laughingly, as she began to arrange on a stand the quantity of little white boxes waiting for her.

"But if he'd told me—in time, I wouldn't have had a thing—but the minister," faltered Marie.

"And when you think so much of a pretty wedding, too? Nonsense! It isn't good for a man, to give up to his whims like that!"

Marie's cheeks grew a deeper pink. Her nostrils dilated a little.

"It wouldn't be a 'whim,' Mrs. Hartwell, and I should be glad to give up," she said with decision.

Mrs. Hartwell laughed again, her amused eyes on Marie's face.

"Dear me, child! don't you know that if men had their way, they'd—well, if men married men there'd never be such a thing in the world as a shower bouquet or a piece of wedding cake!"

There was no reply. A little precipitately Marie turned and hurried away. A moment later she was laying a restraining hand on Billy, who was filling tall vases with superb long-stemmed roses in the kitchen.

"Billy, please," she panted, "couldn't we do without those? Couldn't we send them to some—some hospital?—and the wedding cake, too, and—"

"The wedding cake—to some hospital!"

"No, of course not—to the hospital. It would make them sick to eat it, wouldn't it?" That there was no shadow of a smile on Marie's face showed how desperate, indeed, was her state of mind. "I only meant that I didn't want them myself, nor the shower bouquet, nor the rooms darkened, nor little Kate as the flower girl—and would you mind very much if I asked you not to be my maid of honor?"

"Marie!"

Marie covered her face with her hands then and began to sob brokenly; so there was nothing for Billy to do but to take her into her arms with soothing little murmurs and pettings. By degrees, then, the whole story came out.

Billy almost laughed—but she almost cried, too. Then she said:

"Dearie, I don't believe Cyril feels or acts half so bad as Bertram and Kate make out, and, anyhow, if he did, it's too late now to—to send the wedding cake to the hospital, or make any other of the little changes you suggest." Billy's lips puckered into a half-smile, but her eyes were grave. "Besides, there are your music pupils trimming the living-room this minute with evergreen, there's little Kate making her flower-girl wreath, and Mrs. Hartwell stacking cake boxes in the hall, to say nothing of Rosa gloating over the best china in the dining-room, and Aunt Hannah putting purple bows into the new lace cap she's counting on wearing. Only think how disappointed they'd all be if I should say: 'Never mind—stop that. Marie's just going to have a minister. No fuss, no feathers!' Why, dearie, even the roses are hanging their heads for grief," she went on mistily, lifting with gentle fingers one of the full-petalled pink beauties near her. "Besides, there's your—guests."

"Oh, of course, I knew I couldn't—really," sighed Marie, as she turned to go up-stairs, all the light and joy gone from her face.

Billy, once assured that Marie was out of hearing, ran to the telephone.

Bertram answered.

"Bertram, tell Cyril I want to speak to him, please."

"All right, dear, but go easy. Better strike up your tuning fork to find his pitch to-day. You'll discover it's a high one, all right."

A moment later Cyril's tersely nervous "Good morning, Billy," came across the line.

Billy drew in her breath and cast a hurriedly apprehensive glance over her shoulder to make sure Marie was not near.

"Cyril," she called in a low voice, "if you care a shred for Marie, for heaven's sake call her up and tell her that you dote on pink roses, and pink ribbons, and pink breakfasts—and pink wedding cake!"

"But I don't."

"Oh, yes, you do—to-day! You would—if you could see Marie now."

"What do you mean?"

"Nothing, only she overheard part of Bertram's nonsensical talk with Kate a little while ago, and she's ready to cast the last ravelling of white satin and conventionality behind her, and go with you to the justice of the peace."

"Sensible girl!"

"Yes, but she can't, you know, with fifty guests coming to the wedding, and twice as many more to the reception. Honestly, Cyril, she's broken-hearted. You must do something. She's—coming!" And the receiver clicked sharply into place.

Five minutes later Marie was called to the telephone. Dejectedly, wistful-eyed, she went. Just what were the words that hummed across the wire into the pink little ear of the bride-to-be, Billy never knew; but a Marie that was anything but wistful-eyed and dejected left the telephone a little later, and was heard very soon in the room above trilling merry snatches of a little song. Contentedly, then, Billy went back to her roses.

It was a pretty wedding, a very pretty wedding. Every one said that. The pink and green of the decorations, the soft lights (Kate had had her way about darkening the rooms), the pretty frocks and smiling faces of the guests all helped. Then there were the dainty flower girl, little Kate, the charming maid of honor, Billy, the stalwart, handsome best man, Bertram, to say nothing of the delicately beautiful bride, who looked like some fairy visitor from another world in the floating shimmer of her gossamer silk and tulle. There was, too, not quite unnoticed, the bridegroom; tall, of distinguished bearing, and with features that were clear cut and-to-day-rather pale.

Then came the reception—the "women and confusion" of Cyril's fears—followed by the going away of the bride and groom with its merry warfare of confetti and old shoes.

At four o'clock, however, with only William and Bertram remaining for guests, something like quiet descended at last on the little house.

"Well, it's over," sighed Billy, dropping exhaustedly into a big chair in the living-room.

"And well over," supplemented Aunt Hannah, covering her white shawl with a warmer blue one.

"Yes, I think it was," nodded Kate. "It was really a very pretty wedding."

"With your help, Kate—eh?" teased William.

"Well, I flatter myself I did do some good," bridled Kate, as she turned to help little Kate take the flower wreath from her head.

"Even if you did hurry into my room and scare me into conniption fits telling me I'd be late," laughed Billy.

Kate tossed her head.

"Well, how was I to know that Aunt Hannah's clock only meant half-past eleven when it struck twelve?" she retorted.

Everybody laughed.

"Oh, well, it was a pretty wedding," declared William, with a long sigh.

"It'll do—for an understudy," said Bertram softly, for Billy's ears alone.

Only the added color and the swift glance showed that Billy heard, for when she spoke she said:

"And didn't Cyril behave beautifully? 'Most every time I looked at him he was talking to some woman."

"Oh, no, he wasn't—begging your pardon, my dear," objected Bertram. "I watched him, too, even more closely than you did, and it was always the woman who was talking to Cyril!"

Billy laughed.

"Well, anyhow," she maintained, "he listened. He didn't run away."

"As if a bridegroom could!" cried Kate.

"I'm going to," avowed Bertram, his nose in the air.

"Pooh!" scoffed Kate. Then she added eagerly: "You must be married in church, Billy, and in the evening."

Bertram's nose came suddenly out of the air. His eyes met Kate's squarely.

"Billy hasn't decided yet how she does want to be married," he said with unnecessary emphasis.

Billy laughed and interposed a quick change of subject.

"I think people had a pretty good time, too, for a wedding, don't you?" she asked. "I was sorry Mary Jane couldn't be here—'twould have been such a good chance for him to meet our friends."

"As—Mary Jane?" asked Bertram, a little stiffly.

"Really, my dear," murmured Aunt Hannah, "I think it would be more respectful to call him by his name."

"By the way, what is his name?" questioned William.

"That's what we don't know," laughed Billy.

"Well, you know the 'Arkwright,' don't you?" put in Bertram. Bertram, too, laughed, but it was a little forcedly. "I suppose if you knew his name was 'Methuselah,' you wouldn't call him that—yet, would you?"

Billy clapped her hands, and threw a merry glance at Aunt Hannah.

"There! we never thought of 'Methuselah,'" she gurgled gleefully. "Maybe it is 'Methuselah,' now—'Methuselah John'! You see, he's told us to try to guess it," she explained, turning to William; "but, honestly, I don't believe, whatever it is, I'll ever think of him as anything but 'Mary Jane.'"

"Well, as far as I can judge, he has nobody but himself to thank for that, so he can't do any complaining," smiled William, as he rose to go. "Well, how about it, Bertram? I suppose you're going to stay a while to comfort the lonely—eh, boy?"

"Of course he is—and so are you, too, Uncle William," spoke up Billy, with affectionate cordiality. "As if I'd let you go back to a forlorn dinner in that great house to-night! Indeed, no!"

William smiled, hesitated, and sat down.

"Well, of course—" he began.

"Yes, of course," finished Billy, quickly. "I'll telephone Pete that you'll stay here—both of you."

It was at this point that little Kate, who had been turning interested eyes from one brother to the other, interposed a clear, high-pitched question.

"Uncle William, didn't you want to marry my going-to-be-Aunt Billy?"

"Kate!" gasped her mother, "didn't I tell you—" Her voice trailed into an incoherent murmur of remonstrance.

Billy blushed. Bertram said a low word under his breath. Aunt Hannah's "Oh, my grief and conscience!" was almost a groan.

William laughed lightly.

"Well, my little lady," he suggested, "let us put it the other way and say that quite probably she didn't want to marry me."

"Does she want to marry Uncle Bertram?" "Kate!" gasped Billy and Mrs. Hartwell together this time, fearful of what might be coming next.

"We'll hope so," nodded Uncle William, speaking in a cheerfully matter-of-fact voice, intended to discourage curiosity.

The little girl frowned and pondered. Her elders cast about in their minds for a speedy change of subject; but their somewhat scattered wits were not quick enough. It was little Kate who spoke next.

"Uncle William, would she have got Uncle Cyril if Aunt Marie hadn't nabbed him first?"

"Kate!" The word was a chorus of dismay this time.

Mrs. Hartwell struggled to her feet.

"Come, come, Kate, we must go up-stairs—to bed," she stammered.

The little girl drew back indignantly.

"To bed? Why, mama, I haven't had my supper yet!"

"What? Oh, sure enough—the lights! I forgot. Well, then, come up—to change your dress," finished Mrs. Hartwell, as with a despairing look and gesture she led her young daughter from the room.

CHAPTER XIV. M. J. MAKES ANOTHER MOVE

Billy came down-stairs on the thirteenth of December to find everywhere the peculiar flatness that always follows a day which for weeks has been the focus of one's aims and thoughts and labor.

"It's just as if everything had stopped at Marie's wedding, and there wasn't anything more to do," she complained to Aunt Hannah at the breakfast table. "Everything seems so—queer!"

"It won't—long, dear," smiled Aunt Hannah, tranquilly, as she buttered her roll, "specially after Bertram comes back. How long does he stay in New York?"

"Only three days; but I'm just sure it's going to seem three weeks, now," sighed Billy. "But he simply had to go—else he wouldn't have gone."

"I've no doubt of it," observed Aunt Hannah. And at the meaning emphasis of her words, Billy laughed a little. After a minute she said aggrievedly:

"I had supposed that I could at least have a sort of 'after the ball' celebration this morning picking up and straightening things around. But John and Rosa have done it all. There isn't so much as a rose leaf anywhere on the floor. Of course most of the flowers went to the hospital last night, anyway. As for Marie's room—it looks as spick-and-span as if it had never seen a scrap of ribbon or an inch of tulle."

"But—the wedding presents?"

"All carried down to the kitchen and half packed now, ready to go over to the new home. John says he'll take them over in Peggy this afternoon, after he takes Mrs. Hartwell's trunk to Uncle William's."

"Well, you can at least go over to the apartment and work," suggested Aunt Hannah, hopefully.

"Humph! Can I?" scoffed Billy. "As if I could—when Marie left strict orders that not one thing was to be touched till she got here. They arranged everything but the presents before the wedding, anyway; and Marie wants to fix those herself after she gets back. Mercy! Aunt Hannah, if I should so much as move a plate one inch in the china closet, Marie would know it—and change it when she got home," laughed Billy, as she rose from the table. "No, I can't go to work over there."

"But there's your music, my dear. You said you were going to write some new songs after the wedding."

"I was," sighed Billy, walking to the window, and looking listlessly at the bare, brown world outside; "but I can't write songs—when there aren't any songs in my head to write."

"No, of course not; but they'll come, dear, in time. You're tired, now," soothed Aunt Hannah, as she turned to leave the room.

"It's the reaction, of course," murmured Aunt Hannah to herself, on the way up-stairs. "She's had the whole thing on her hands—dear child!"

A few minutes later, from the living-room, came a plaintive little minor melody. Billy was at the piano.

Kate and little Kate had, the night before, gone home with William. It had been a sudden decision, brought about by the realization that Bertram's trip to New York would leave William alone. Her trunk was to be carried there to-day, and she would leave for home from there, at the end of a two or three days' visit.

It began to snow at twelve o'clock. All the morning the sky had been gray and threatening; and the threats took visible shape at noon in myriads of white snow feathers that filled the air to the blinding point, and turned the brown, bare world into a thing of fairylike beauty. Billy, however, with a rare frown upon her face, looked out upon it with disapproving eyes.

"I was going in town—and I believe I'll go now," she cried.

"Don't, dear, please don't," begged Aunt Hannah. "See, the flakes are smaller now, and the wind is coming up. We're in for a blizzard—I'm sure we are. And you know you have some cold, already."

"All right," sighed Billy. "Then it's me for the knitting work and the fire, I suppose," she finished, with a whimsicality that did not hide the wistful disappointment of her voice.

She was not knitting, however, she was sewing with Aunt Hannah when at four o'clock Rosa brought in the card.

Billy glanced at the name, then sprang to her feet with a glad little cry.

"It's Mary Jane!" she exclaimed, as Rosa disappeared. "Now wasn't he a dear to think to come to-day? You'll be down, won't you?"

Aunt Hannah smiled even while she frowned.

"Oh, Billy!" she remonstrated. "Yes, I'll come down, of course, a little later, and I'm glad Mr. Arkwright came," she said with reproving emphasis.

Billy laughed and threw a mischievous glance over her shoulder.

"All right," she nodded. "I'll go and tell Mr. Arkwright you'll be down directly."

In the living-room Billy greeted her visitor with a frankly cordial hand.

"How did you know, Mr. Arkwright, that I was feeling specially restless and lonesome to-day?" she demanded.

A glad light sprang to the man's dark eyes.

"I didn't know it," he rejoined. "I only knew that I was specially restless and lonesome myself."

Arkwright's voice was not quite steady. The unmistakable friendliness in the girl's words and manner had sent a quick throb of joy to his heart. Her evident delight in his coming had filled him with rapture. He could not know that it was only the chill of the snowstorm that had given warmth to her handclasp, the dreariness of the day that had made her greeting so cordial, the loneliness of a maiden whose lover is away that had made his presence so welcome.

"Well, I'm glad you came, anyway," sighed Billy, contentedly; "though I suppose I ought to be sorry that you were lonesome—but I'm afraid I'm not, for now you'll know just how I felt, so you won't mind if I'm a little wild and erratic. You see, the tension has snapped," she added laughingly, as she seated herself.

"Tension?"

"The wedding, you know. For so many weeks we've been seeing just December twelfth, that we'd apparently forgotten all about the thirteenth that came after it; so when I got up this morning I felt just as you do when the clock has stopped ticking. But it was a lovely wedding, Mr. Arkwright. I'm sorry you could not be here."

"Thank you; so am I—though usually, I will confess, I'm not much good at attending 'functions' and meeting strangers. As perhaps you've guessed, Miss Neilson, I'm not particularly a society chap."

"Of course you aren't! People who are doing things—real things—seldom are. But we aren't the society kind ourselves, you know—not the capital S kind. We like sociability, which is vastly different from liking Society. Oh, we have friends, to be sure, who dote on 'pink teas and purple pageants,' as Cyril calls them; and we even go ourselves sometimes. But if you had been here yesterday, Mr. Arkwright, you'd have met lots like yourself, men and women who are doing things: singing, playing, painting, illustrating, writing. Why, we even had a poet, sir—only he didn't have long hair, so he didn't look the part a bit," she finished laughingly.

"Is long hair—necessary—for poets?" Arkwright's smile was quizzical.

"Dear me, no; not now. But it used to be, didn't it? And for painters, too. But now they look just like—folks."

Arkwright laughed.

"It isn't possible that you are sighing for the velvet coats and flowing ties of the past, is it, Miss Neilson?"

"I'm afraid it is," dimpled Billy. "I love velvet coats and flowing ties!"

"May singers wear them? I shall don them at once, anyhow, at a venture," declared the man, promptly.

Billy smiled and shook her head.

"I don't think you will. You all like your horrid fuzzy tweeds and worsteds too well!"

"You speak with feeling. One would almost suspect that you already had tried to bring about a reform—and failed. Perhaps Mr. Cyril, now, or Mr. Bertram—" Arkwright stopped with a whimsical smile.

Billy flushed a little. As it happened, she had, indeed, had a merry tilt with Bertram on that very subject, and he had laughingly promised that his wedding present to her would be a velvet house coat for himself. It was on the point of Billy's tongue now to say this to Arkwright; but another glance at the provoking smile on his lips drove the words back in angry confusion. For the second time, in the presence of this man, Billy found herself unable to refer to her engagement to Bertram Henshaw—though this time she did not in the least doubt that Arkwright already knew of it.

With a little gesture of playful scorn she rose and went to the piano.

"Come, let us try some duets," she suggested. "That's lots nicer than quarrelling over velvet coats; and Aunt Hannah will be down presently to hear us sing."

Before she had ceased speaking, Arkwright was at her side with an exclamation of eager acquiescence.

It was after the second duet that Arkwright asked, a little diffidently.

"Have you written any new songs lately?"

"No."

"You're going to?"

"Perhaps—if I find one to write."

"You mean—you have no words?"

"Yes—and no. I have some words, both of my own and other people's; but I haven't found in any one of them, yet—a melody."

Arkwright hesitated. His right hand went almost to his inner coat pocket—then fell back at his side. The next moment he picked up a sheet of music.

"Are you too tired to try this?" he asked.

A puzzled frown appeared on Billy's face.

"Why, no, but—"

"Well, children, I've come down to hear the music," announced Aunt Hannah, smilingly, from the doorway; "only—Billy, will you run up and get my pink shawl, too? This room is colder than I thought, and there's only the white one down here."

"Of course," cried Billy, rising at once. "You shall have a dozen shawls, if you like," she laughed, as she left the room.

What a cozy time it was—the hour that followed, after Billy returned with the pink shawl! Outside, the wind howled at the windows and flung the snow against the glass in sleety crashes. Inside, the man and the girl sang duets until they were tired; then, with Aunt Hannah, they feasted royally on the buttered toast, tea, and frosted cakes that Rosa served on a little table before the roaring fire. It was then that Arkwright talked of himself, telling them something of his studies, and of the life he was living.

"After all, you see there's just this difference between my friends and yours," he said, at last. "Your friends are doing things. They've succeeded. Mine haven't, yet—they're only trying."

"But they will succeed," cried Billy.

"Some of them," amended the man.

"Not—all of them?" Billy looked a little troubled.

Arkwright shook his head slowly.

"No. They couldn't—all of them, you know. Some haven't the talent, some haven't the perseverance, and some haven't the money."

"But all that seems such a pity-when they've tried," grieved Billy.

"It is a pity, Miss Neilson. Disappointed hopes are always a pity, aren't they?"

"Y-yes," sighed the girl. "But—if there were only something one could do to—help!"

Arkwright's eyes grew deep with feeling, but his voice, when he spoke, was purposely light.

"I'm afraid that would be quite too big a contract for even your generosity, Miss Neilson—to mend all the broken hopes in the world," he prophesied.

"I have known great good to come from great disappointments," remarked Aunt Hannah, a bit didactically.

"So have I," laughed Arkwright, still determined to drive the troubled shadow from the face he was watching so intently. "For instance: a fellow I know was feeling all cut up last Friday because he was just too late to get into Symphony Hall on the twenty-five-cent admission. Half an hour afterwards his disappointment was turned to joy—a friend who had an orchestra chair couldn't use his ticket that day, and so handed it over to him."

Billy turned interestedly.

"What are those twenty-five-cent tickets to the Symphony?"

"Then—you don't know?"

"Not exactly. I've heard of them, in a vague fashion."

"Then you've missed one of the sights of Boston if you haven't ever seen that long line of patient waiters at the door of Symphony Hall of a Friday morning."

"Morning! But the concert isn't till afternoon!"

"No, but the waiting is," retorted Arkwright. "You see, those admissions are limited—five hundred and five, I believe—and they're rush seats, at that. First come, first served; and if you're too late you aren't served at all. So the first arrival comes bright and early. I've heard that he has been known to come at peep of day when there's a Paderewski or a Melba for a drawing card. But I've got my doubts of that. Anyhow, I never saw them there much before half-past eight. But many's the cold, stormy day I've seen those steps in front of the Hall packed for hours, and a long line reaching away up the avenue."

Billy's eyes widened.

"And they'll stand all that time and wait?"

"To be sure they will. You see, each pays twenty-five cents at the door, until the limit is reached, then the rest are turned away. Naturally they don't want to be turned away, so they try to get there early enough to be among the fortunate five hundred and five. Besides, the earlier you are, the better seat you are likely to get."

"But only think of standing all that time!"

"Oh, they bring camp chairs, sometimes, I've heard, and then there are the steps. You don't know what a really fine seat a stone step is—if you have a big enough bundle of newspapers to cushion it with! They bring their luncheons, too, with books, papers, and knitting work for fine days, I've been told—some of them. All the comforts of home, you see," smiled Arkwright.

"Why, how—how dreadful!" stammered Billy.

"Oh, but they don't think it's dreadful at all," corrected Arkwright, quickly. "For twenty-five cents they can hear all that you hear down in your orchestra chair, for which you've paid so high a premium."

"But who—who are they? Where do they come from? Who would go and stand hours like that to get a twenty-five-cent seat?" questioned Billy.

"Who are they? Anybody, everybody, from anywhere? everywhere; people who have the music hunger but not the money to satisfy it," he rejoined. "Students, teachers, a little milliner from South Boston, a little dressmaker from Chelsea, a housewife from Cambridge, a stranger from the uttermost parts of the earth; maybe a widow who used to sit downstairs, or a professor who has seen better days. Really to know that line, you should see it for yourself, Miss Neilson," smiled Arkwright, as he reluctantly rose to go. "Some Friday, however, before you take your seat, just glance up at that packed top balcony and judge by the faces you see there whether their owners think they're getting their twenty-five-cents' worth, or not."

"I will," nodded Billy, with a smile; but the smile came from her lips only, not her eyes: Billy was wishing, at that moment, that she owned the whole of Symphony Hall—to give away. But that was like Billy. When she was seven years old she had proposed to her Aunt Ella that they take all the thirty-five orphans from the Hampden Falls Orphan Asylum to live with them, so that little Sallie Cook and the other orphans might have ice cream every day, if they wanted it. Since then Billy had always been trying—in a way—to give ice cream to some one who wanted it.

Arkwright was almost at the door when he turned abruptly. His face was an abashed red. From his pocket he had taken a small folded paper.

"Do you suppose—in this—you might find—that melody?" he stammered in a low voice. The next moment he was gone, having left in Billy's fingers a paper upon which was written in a clear-cut, masculine hand six four-line stanzas.

Billy read them at once, hurriedly, then more carefully.

"Why, they're beautiful," she breathed, "just beautiful! Where did he get them, I wonder? It's a love song—and such a pretty one! I believe there is a melody in it," she exulted, pausing to hum a line or two. "There is—I know there is; and I'll write it—for Bertram," she finished, crossing joyously to the piano.

Half-way down Corey Hill at that moment, Arkwright was buffeting the wind and snow. He, too, was thinking joyously of those stanzas—joyously, yet at the same time fearfully. Arkwright himself had written those lines—though not for Bertram.

CHAPTER XV. "MR. BILLY" AND "MISS MARY JANE"

On the fourteenth of December Billy came down-stairs alert, interested, and happy. She had received a dear letter from Bertram (mailed on the way to New York), the sun was shining, and her fingers were fairly tingling to put on paper the little melody that was now surging riotously through her brain. Emphatically, the restlessness of the day before was gone now. Once more Billy's "clock" had "begun to tick."

After breakfast Billy went straight to the telephone and called up Arkwright. Even one side of the conversation Aunt Hannah did not hear very clearly; but in five minutes a radiant-faced Billy danced into the room.

"Aunt Hannah, just listen! Only think—Mary Jane wrote the words himself, so of course I can use them!"

"Billy, dear, can't you say 'Mr. Arkwright'?" pleaded Aunt Hannah.

Billy laughed and gave the anxious-eyed little old lady an impulsive hug.

"Of course! I'll say 'His Majesty' if you like, dear," she chuckled. "But did you hear—did you realize? They're his own words, so there's no question of rights or permission, or anything. And he's coming up this afternoon to hear my melody, and to make a few little changes in the words, maybe. Oh, Aunt Hannah, you don't know how good it seems to get into my music again!"

"Yes, yes, dear, of course; but—" Aunt Hannah's sentence ended in a vaguely troubled pause.

Billy turned in surprise.

"Why, Aunt Hannah, aren't you glad? You said you'd be glad!"

"Yes, dear; and I am—very glad. It's only—if it doesn't take too much time—and if Bertram doesn't mind."

Billy flushed. She laughed a little bitterly.

"No, it won't take too much time, I fancy, and—so far as Bertram is concerned—if what Sister Kate says is true, Aunt Hannah, he'll be glad to have me occupy a little of my time with something besides himself."

"Fiddlededee!" bristled Aunt Hannah.

"What did she mean by that?"

Billy smiled ruefully.

"Well, probably I did need it. She said it night before last just before she went home with Uncle William. She declared that I seemed to forget entirely that Bertram belonged to his Art first, before he belonged to me; and that it was exactly as she had supposed it would be—a perfect absurdity for Bertram to think of marrying anybody."

"Fiddlededee!" ejaculated the irate Aunt Hannah, even more sharply. "I hope you have too much good sense to mind what Kate says, Billy."

"Yes, I know," sighed the girl; "but of course I can see some things for myself, and I suppose I did make—a little fuss about his going to New York the other night. And I will own that I've had a real struggle with myself sometimes, lately, not to mind—his giving so much time to his portrait painting. And of course both of those are very reprehensible—in an artist's wife," she finished, a little tremulously.

"Humph! Well, I don't think I should worry about that," observed Aunt Hannah with grim positiveness.

"No, I don't mean to," smiled Billy, wistfully. "I only told you so you'd understand that it was just as well if I did have something to take up my mind—besides Bertram. And of course music would be the most natural thing."

"Yes, of course," agreed Aunt Hannah.

"And it seems actually almost providential that Mary—I mean Mr. Arkwright is here to help me, now that Cyril is gone," went on Billy, still a little wistfully.

"Yes, of course. He isn't like—a stranger," murmured Aunt Hannah. Aunt Hannah's voice sounded as if she were trying to convince herself—of something.

"No, indeed! He seems just like one of the family to me, almost as if he were really—your niece, Mary Jane," laughed Billy.

Aunt Hannah moved restlessly.

"Billy," she hazarded, "he knows, of course, of your engagement?"

"Why, of course he does, Aunt Hannah everybody does!" Billy's eyes were plainly surprised.

"Yes, yes, of course—he must," subsided Aunt Hannah, confusedly, hoping that Billy would not divine the hidden reason behind her question. She was relieved when Billy's next words showed that she had not divined it.

"I told you, didn't I? He's coming up this afternoon. He can't get here till five, though; but he's so interested! He's about as crazy over the thing as I am. And it's going to be fine, Aunt Hannah, when it's done. You just wait and see!" she finished gayly, as she tripped from the room.

Left to herself, Aunt Hannah drew a long breath.

"I'm glad she didn't suspect," she was thinking. "I believe she'd consider even the question disloyal to Bertram—dear child! And of course Mary"—Aunt Hannah corrected herself with cheeks aflame—"I mean Mr. Arkwright does—know."

It was just here, however, that Aunt Hannah was mistaken. Mr. Arkwright did not—know. He had not reached Boston when the engagement was announced. He knew none of Billy's friends in town save the Henshaw brothers. He had not heard from Calderwell since he came to Boston. The very evident intimacy of Billy with the Henshaw brothers he accepted as a matter of course, knowing the history of their acquaintance, and the fact that Billy was Mr. William Henshaw's namesake. As to Bertram being Billy's lover—that idea had long ago been killed at birth by Calderwell's emphatic assertion that the artist would never care for any girl—except to paint. Since coming to Boston, Arkwright had seen little of the two together. His work, his friends, and his general mode of life precluded that. Because of all this, therefore, Arkwright did not—know; which was a pity—for Arkwright, and for some others.

Promptly at five o'clock that afternoon, Arkwright rang Billy's doorbell, and was admitted by Rosa to the living-room, where Billy was at the piano.

Billy sprang to her feet with a joyous word of greeting.

"I'm so glad you've come," she sighed happily. "I want you to hear the melody your pretty words have sung to me. Though, maybe, after all, you won't like it, you know," she finished with arch wistfulness.

"As if I could help liking it," smiled the man, trying to keep from his voice the ecstatic delight that the touch of her hand had brought him.

Billy shook her head and seated herself again at the piano.

"The words are lovely," she declared, sorting out two or three sheets of manuscript music from the quantity on the rack before her. "But there's one place—the rhythm, you know—if you could change it. There!—but listen. First I'm going to play it straight through to you."

And she dropped her fingers to the keyboard. The next moment a tenderly sweet melody—with only a chord now and then for accompaniment—filled Arkwright's soul with rapture. Then Billy began to sing, very softly, the words!

No wonder Arkwright's soul was filled with rapture. They were his words, wrung straight from his heart; and they were being sung by the girl for whom they were written. They were being sung with feeling, too—so evident a feeling that the man's pulse quickened, and his eyes flashed a sudden fire. Arkwright could not know, of course, that Billy, in her own mind, was singing that song—to Bertram Henshaw.

The fire was still in Arkwright's eyes when the song was ended; but Billy very plainly did not see it. With a frowning sigh and a murmured "There!" she began to talk of "rhythm" and "accent" and "cadence"; and to point out with anxious care why three syllables instead of two were needed at the end of a certain line. From this she passed eagerly to the accompaniment, and Arkwright at once found himself lost in a maze of "minor thirds" and "diminished sevenths," until he was forced to turn from the singer to the song. Still, watching her a little later, he noticed her absorbed face and eager enthusiasm, her earnest pursuance of an elusive harmony, and he wondered: did she, or did she not sing that song with feeling a little while before?

Arkwright had not settled this question to his own satisfaction when Aunt Hannah came in at half-past five, and he was conscious of a vague disappointment as he rose to greet her. Billy, however, turned an untroubled face to the newcomer.

"We're doing finely, Aunt Hannah," she cried. Then, suddenly, she flung a laughing question to the man. "How about it, sir? Are we going to put on the title-page: 'Words by Mary Jane Arkwright'—or will you unveil the mystery for us now?"

"Have you guessed it?" he bantered.

"No—unless it's 'Methuselah John.' We did think of that the other day."

"Wrong again!" he laughed.

"Then it'll have to be 'Mary Jane,'" retorted Billy, with calm naughtiness, refusing to meet Aunt Hannah's beseechingly reproving eyes. Then suddenly she chuckled. "It would be a combination, wouldn't it? 'Words by Mary Jane Arkwright. Music by Billy Neilson'! We'd have sighing swains writing to 'Dear Miss Arkwright,' telling how touching were her words; and lovelorn damsels thanking Mr. Neilson for his soul-inspiring music!"

"Billy, my dear!" remonstrated Aunt Hannah, faintly.

"Yes, yes, I know; that was bad—and I won't again, truly," promised Billy. But her eyes danced, and the next moment she had whirled about on the piano stool and dashed into a Chopin waltz. The room itself, then, seemed to be full of the twinkling feet of elves.

CHAPTER XVI. A GIRL AND A BIT OF LOWESTOFT

Immediately after breakfast the next morning, Billy was summoned to the telephone.
"Oh, good morning, Uncle William," she called, in answer to the masculine voice that replied to her "Hullo."
"Billy, are you very busy this morning?"
"No, indeed—not if you want me."
"Well, I do, my dear." Uncle William's voice was troubled. "I want you to go with me, if you can, to see a Mrs. Greggory. She's got a teapot I want. It's a genuine Lowestoft, Harlow says. Will you go?"
"Of course I will! What time?"
"Eleven if you can, at Park Street. She's at the West End. I don't dare to put it off for fear I'll lose it. Harlow says others will have to know of it, of course. You see, she's just made up her mind to sell it, and asked him to find a customer. I wouldn't trouble you, but he says they're peculiar—the daughter, especially—and may need some careful handling. That's why I wanted you—though I wanted you to see the tea-pot, too,—it'll be yours some day, you know."
Billy, all alone at her end of the line, blushed. That she was one day to be mistress of the Strata and all it contained was still anything but "common" to her.
"I'd love to see it, and I'll come gladly; but I'm afraid I won't be much help, Uncle William," she worried.
"I'll take the risk of that. You see, Harlow says that about half the time she isn't sure she wants to sell it, after all."
"Why, how funny! Well, I'll come. At eleven, you say, at Park Street?"
"Yes; and thank you, my dear. I tried to get Kate to go, too; but she wouldn't. By the way, I'm going to bring you home to luncheon. Kate leaves this afternoon, you know, and it's been so snowy she hasn't thought best to try to get over to the house. Maybe Aunt Hannah would come, too, for luncheon. Would she?"
"I'm afraid not," returned Billy, with a rueful laugh. "She's got three shawls on this morning, and you know that always means that she's felt a draft somewhere—poor dear. I'll tell her, though, and I'll see you at eleven," finished Billy, as she hung up the receiver.
Promptly at the appointed time Billy met Uncle William at Park Street, and together they set out for the West End street named on the paper in his pocket. But when the shabby house on the narrow little street was reached, the man looked about him with a troubled frown.
"I declare, Billy, I'm not sure but we'd better turn back," he fretted. "I didn't mean to take you to such a place as this."
Billy shivered a little; but after one glance at the man's disappointed face she lifted a determined chin.
"Nonsense, Uncle William! Of course you won't turn back. I don't mind—for myself; but only think of the people whose homes are here," she finished, just above her breath.
Mrs. Greggory was found to be living in two back rooms at the top of four flights of stairs, up which William Henshaw toiled with increasing weariness and dismay, punctuating each flight with a despairing: "Billy, really, I think we should turn back!"
But Billy would not turn back, and at last they found themselves in the presence of a white-haired, sweet-faced woman who said yes, she was Mrs. Greggory; yes, she was. Even as she uttered the words, however, she looked fearfully over her shoulders as if expecting to hear from the hall behind them a voice denying her assertion.
Mrs. Greggory was a cripple. Her slender little body was poised on two once-costly crutches. Both the worn places on the crutches, and the skill with which the little woman swung herself about the room testified that the crippled condition was not a new one.

Billy's eyes were brimming with pity and dismay. Mechanically she had taken the chair toward which Mrs. Greggory had motioned her. She had tried not to seem to look about her; but there was not one detail of the bare little room, from its faded rug to the patched but spotless tablecloth, that was not stamped on her brain.

Mrs. Greggory had seated herself now, and William Henshaw had cleared his throat nervously. Billy did not know whether she herself were the more distressed or the more relieved to hear him stammer:

"We—er—I came from Harlow, Mrs. Greggory. He gave me to understand you had an—er—teapot that—er—" With his eyes on the cracked white crockery pitcher on the table, William Henshaw came to a helpless pause.

A curious expression, or rather, series of expressions crossed Mrs. Greggory's face. Terror, joy, dismay, and relief seemed, one after the other to fight for supremacy. Relief in the end conquered, though even yet there was a second hurriedly apprehensive glance toward the door before she spoke.

"The Lowestoft! Yes, I'm so glad!—that is, of course I must be glad. I'll get it." Her voice broke as she pulled herself from her chair. There was only despairing sorrow on her face now.

The man rose at once.

"But, madam, perhaps—don't let me—" I he began stammeringly. "Of course—Billy!" he broke off in an entirely different voice. "Jove! What a beauty!"

Mrs. Greggory had thrown open the door of a small cupboard near the collector's chair, disclosing on one of the shelves a beautifully shaped teapot, creamy in tint, and exquisitely decorated in a rose design. Near it set a tray-like plate of the same ware and decoration.

"If you'll lift it down, please, yourself," motioned Mrs. Greggory. "I don't like to—with these," she explained, tapping the crutches at her side.

With fingers that were almost reverent in their appreciation, the collector reached for the teapot. His eyes sparkled.

"Billy, look, what a beauty! And it's a Lowestoft, too, the real thing—the genuine, true soft paste! And there's the tray—did you notice?" he exulted, turning back to the shelf. "You don't see that every day! They get separated, most generally, you know."

"These pieces have been in our family for generations," said Mrs. Greggory with an accent of pride. "You'll find them quite perfect, I think."

"Perfect! I should say they were," cried the man.

"They are, then—valuable?" Mrs. Greggory's voice shook.

"Indeed they are! But you must know that."

"I have been told so. Yet to me their chief value, of course, lies in their association. My mother and my grandmother owned that teapot, sir." Again her voice broke.

William Henshaw cleared his throat.

"But, madam, if you do not wish to sell—" He stopped abruptly. His longing eyes had gone back to the enticing bit of china.

Mrs. Greggory gave a low cry.

"But I do—that is, I must. Mr. Harlow says that it is valuable, and that it will bring in money; and we need—money." She threw a quick glance toward the hall door, though she did not pause in her remarks. "I can't do much at work that pays. I sew"—she nodded toward the machine by the window—"but with only one foot to make it go—You see, the other is—is inclined to shirk a little," she finished with a wistful whimsicality.

Billy turned away sharply. There was a lump in her throat and a smart in her eyes. She was conscious suddenly of a fierce anger against—she did not know what, exactly; but she fancied it was against the teapot, or against Uncle William for wanting the teapot, or for not wanting it—if he did not buy it.

"And so you see, I do very much wish to sell."

Mrs. Greggory said then. "Perhaps you will tell me what it would be worth to you," she concluded tremulously.

The collector's eyes glowed. He picked up the teapot with careful rapture and examined it. Then he turned to the tray. After a moment he spoke.

"I have only one other in my collection as rare," he said. "I paid a hundred dollars for that. I shall be glad to give you the same for this, madam."

Mrs. Greggory started visibly.

"A hundred dollars? So much as that?" she cried almost joyously. "Why, nothing else that we've had has brought—Of course, if it's worth that to you—" She paused suddenly. A quick step had sounded in the hall outside. The next moment the door flew open and a young woman, who looked to be about twenty-three or twenty-four years old, burst into the room.

"Mother, only think, I've—" She stopped, and drew back a little. Her startled eyes went from one face to another, then dropped to the Lowestoft teapot in the man's hands. Her expression changed at once. She shut the door quickly and hurried forward.

"Mother, what is it? Who are these people?" she asked sharply.

Billy lifted her chin the least bit. She was conscious of a feeling which she could not name: Billy was not used to being called "these people" in precisely that tone of voice. William Henshaw, too, raised his chin. He, also, was not in the habit of being referred to as "these people."

"My name is Henshaw, Miss—Greggory, I presume," he said quietly. "I was sent here by Mr. Harlow."

"About the teapot, my dear, you know," stammered Mrs. Greggory, wetting her lips with an air of hurried apology and conciliation. "This gentleman says he will be glad to buy it. Er—my daughter, Alice, Mr. Henshaw," she hastened on, in embarrassed introduction; "and Miss—"

"Neilson," supplied the man, as she looked at Billy, and hesitated.

A swift red stained Alice Greggory's face. With barely an acknowledgment of the introductions she turned to her mother.

"Yes, dear, but that won't be necessary now. As I started to tell you when I came in, I have two new pupils; and so"—turning to the man again "I thank you for your offer, but we have decided not to sell the teapot at present." As she finished her sentence she stepped one side as if to make room for the strangers to reach the door.

William Henshaw frowned angrily—that was the man; but his eyes—the collector's eyes—sought the teapot longingly. Before either the man or the collector could speak, however, Mrs. Greggory interposed quick words of remonstrance.

"But, Alice, my dear," she almost sobbed. "You didn't wait to let me tell you. Mr. Henshaw says it is worth a hundred dollars to him. He will give us—a hundred dollars."

"A hundred dollars!" echoed the girl, faintly.

It was plain to be seen that she was wavering. Billy, watching the little scene, with mingled emotions, saw the glance with which the girl swept the bare little room; and she knew that there was not a patch or darn or poverty spot in sight, or out of sight, which that glance did not encompass.

Billy was wondering which she herself desired more—that Uncle William should buy the Lowestoft, or that he should not. She knew she wished Mrs. Greggory to have the hundred dollars. There was no doubt on that point. Then Uncle William spoke. His words carried the righteous indignation of the man who thinks he has been unjustly treated, and the final plea of the collector who sees a coveted treasure slipping from his grasp.

"I am very sorry, of course, if my offer has annoyed you," he said stiffly. "I certainly should not have made it had I not had Mrs. Greggory's assurance that she wished to sell the teapot."

Alice Greggory turned as if stung.

"Wished to sell!" She repeated the words with superb disdain. She was plainly very angry. Her blue-gray eyes gleamed with scorn, and her whole face was suffused with a red that had swept to the roots of her soft hair. "Do you think a woman wishes to sell a thing that she's treasured all her life, a thing that is perhaps the last visible reminder of the days when she was living—not merely existing?"

"Alice, Alice, my love!" protested the sweet-faced cripple, agitatedly.

"I can't help it," stormed the girl, hotly. "I know how much you think of that teapot that was grandmother's. I know what it cost you to make up your mind to sell it at all. And then to hear these people talk about your wishing to sell it! Perhaps they think, too, we wish to live in a place like this; that we wish to have rugs that are darned, and chairs that are broken, and garments that are patches instead of clothes!"

"Alice!" gasped Mrs. Greggory in dismayed horror.

With a little outward fling of her two hands Alice Greggory stepped back. Her face had grown white again.

"I beg your pardon, of course," she said in a voice that was bitterly quiet. "I should not have spoken so. You are very kind, Mr. Henshaw, but I do not think we care to sell the Lowestoft to-day."

Both words and manner were obviously a dismissal; and with a puzzled sigh William Henshaw picked up his hat. His face showed very clearly that he did not know what to do, or what to say; but it showed, too, as clearly, that he longed to do something, or say something. During the brief minute that he hesitated, however, Billy sprang forward.

"Mrs. Greggory, please, won't you let me buy the teapot? And then—won't you keep it for me—here? I haven't the hundred dollars with me, but I'll send it right away. You will let me do it, won't you?"

It was an impulsive speech, and a foolish one, of course, from the standpoint of sense and logic and reasonableness; but it was one that might be expected, perhaps, from Billy.

Mrs. Greggory must have divined, in a way, the spirit that prompted it, for her eyes grew wet, and with a choking "Dear child!" she reached out and caught Billy's hand in both her own—even while she shook her head in denial.

Not so her daughter. Alice Greggory flushed scarlet. She drew herself proudly erect.

"Thank you," she said with crisp coldness; "but, distasteful as darns and patches are to us, we prefer them, infinitely, to—charity!"

"Oh, but, please, I didn't mean—you didn't understand," faltered Billy.

For answer Alice Greggory walked deliberately to the door and held it open.

"Oh, Alice, my dear," pleaded Mrs. Greggory again, feebly.

"Come, Billy! We'll bid you good morning, ladies," said William Henshaw then, decisively. And Billy, with a little wistful pat on Mrs. Greggory's clasped hands, went.

Once down the long four flights of stairs and out on the sidewalk, William Henshaw drew a long breath.

"Well, by Jove! Billy, the next time I take you curio hunting, it won't be to this place," he fumed.

"Wasn't it awful!" choked Billy.

"Awful! The girl was the most stubborn, unreasonable, vixenish little puss I ever saw. I didn't want her old Lowestoft if she didn't want to sell it! But to practically invite me there, and then treat me like that!" scolded the collector, his face growing red with anger. "Still, I was sorry for the poor little old lady. I wish, somehow, she could have that hundred dollars!" It was the man who said this, not the collector.

"So do I," rejoined Billy, dolefully. "But that girl was so—so queer!" she sighed, with a frown. Billy was puzzled. For the first time, perhaps, in her life, she knew what it was to have her proffered "ice cream" disdainfully refused.

CHAPTER XVII. ONLY A LOVE SONG, BUT—

Kate and little Kate left for the West on the afternoon of the fifteenth, and Bertram arrived from New York that evening. Notwithstanding the confusion of all this, Billy still had time to give some thought to her experience of the morning with Uncle William. The forlorn little room with its poverty-stricken furnishings and its crippled mistress was very vivid in Billy's memory. Equally vivid were the flashing eyes of Alice Greggory as she had opened the door at the last.

"For," as Billy explained to Bertram that evening, after she had told him the story of the morning's adventure, "you see, dear, I had never been really turned out of a house before!"

"I should think not," scowled her lover, indignantly; "and it's safe to say you never will again. The impertinence of it! But then, you won't see them any more, sweetheart, so we'll just forget it."

"Forget it! Why, Bertram, I couldn't! You couldn't, if you'd been there. Besides, of course I shall see them again!"

Bertram's jaw dropped.

"Why, Billy, you don't mean that Will, or you either, would try again for that trumpery teapot!"

"Of course not," flashed Billy, heatedly. "It isn't the teapot—it's that dear little Mrs. Greggory. Why, dearie, you don't know how poor they are! Everything in sight is so old and thin and worn it's enough to break your heart. The rug isn't anything but darns, nor the tablecloth, either—except patches. It's awful, Bertram!"

"I know, darling; but you don't expect to buy them new rugs and new tablecloths, do you?"

Billy gave one of her unexpected laughs.

"Mercy!" she chuckled. "Only picture Miss Alice's face if I should try to buy them rugs and tablecloths! No, dear," she went on more seriously, "I sha'n't do that, of course—though I'd like to; but I shall try to see Mrs. Greggory again, if it's nothing more than a rose or a book or a new magazine that I can take to her."

"Or a smile—which I fancy will be the best gift of the lot," amended Bertram, fondly.

Billy dimpled and shook her head.

"Smiles—my smiles—are not so valuable, I'm afraid—except to you, perhaps," she laughed.

"Self-evident facts need no proving," retorted Bertram. "Well, and what else has happened in all these ages I've been away?"

Billy brought her hands together with a sudden cry.

"Oh, and I haven't told you!" she exclaimed. "I'm writing a new song—a love song. Mary Jane wrote the words. They're beautiful."

Bertram stiffened.

"Indeed! And is—Mary Jane a poet, with all the rest?" he asked, with affected lightness.

"Oh, no, of course not," smiled Billy; "but these words are pretty. And they just sang themselves into the dearest little melody right away. So I'm writing the music for them."

"Lucky Mary Jane!" murmured Bertram, still with a lightness that he hoped would pass for indifference. (Bertram was ashamed of himself, but deep within him was a growing consciousness that he knew the meaning of the vague irritation that he always felt at the mere mention of Arkwright's name.) "And will the title-page say, 'Words by Mary Jane Arkwright'?" he finished.

"That's what I asked him," laughed Billy.

"I even suggested 'Methuselah John' for a change. Oh, but, dearie," she broke off with shy eagerness, "I just want you to hear a little of what I've done with it. You see, really, all the time, I suspect, I've been singing it—to you," she confessed with an endearing blush, as she sprang lightly to her feet and hurried to the piano.

It was a bad ten minutes that Bertram Henshaw spent then. How he could love a song and hate it at the same time he did not understand; but he knew that he was doing exactly that. To hear Billy carol "Sweetheart, my sweetheart!" with that joyous tenderness was bliss unspeakable—until he remembered that Arkwright wrote the "Sweetheart, my sweetheart!" then it was—(Even in his thoughts Bertram bit the word off short. He was not a swearing man.) When he looked at Billy now at the piano, and thought of her singing—as she said she had sung—that song to him all through the last three days, his heart glowed. But when he looked at her and thought of Arkwright, who had made possible that singing, his heart froze with terror.

From the very first it had been music that Bertram had feared. He could not forget that Billy herself had once told him that never would she love any man better than she loved her music; that she was not going to marry. All this had been at the first—the very first. He had boldly scorned the idea then, and had said:

"So it's music—a cold, senseless thing of spidery marks on clean white paper—that is my only rival!"

He had said, too, that he was going to win. And he had won—but not until after long weeks of fearing, hoping, striving, and despairing—this last when Kate's blundering had nearly made her William's wife. Then, on that memorable day in September, Billy had walked straight into his arms; and he knew that he had, indeed, won. That is, he had supposed that he knew—until Arkwright came.

Very sharply now, as he listened to Billy's singing, Bertram told himself to be reasonable, to be sensible; that Billy did, indeed, love him. Was she not, according to her own dear assertion, singing that song to him? But it was Arkwright's song. He remembered that, too—and grew faint at the thought. True, he had won when his rival, music, had been a "cold, senseless thing of spidery marks" on paper; but would that winning stand when "music" had become a thing of flesh and blood—a man of undeniable charm, good looks, and winsomeness; a man whose thoughts, aims, and words were the personification of the thing Billy, in the long ago, had declared she loved best of all—music?

Bertram shivered as with a sudden chill; then Billy rose from the piano.

"There!" she breathed, her face shyly radiant with the glory of the song. "Did you—like it?"

Bertram did his best; but, in his state of mind, the very radiance of her face was only an added torture, and his tongue stumbled over the words of praise and appreciation that he tried to say. He saw, then, the happy light in Billy's eyes change to troubled questioning and grieved disappointment; and he hated himself for a jealous brute. More earnestly than ever, now, he tried to force the ring of sincerity into his voice; but he knew that he had miserably failed when he heard her falter:

"Of course, dear, I—I haven't got it nearly perfected yet. It'll be much better, later."

"But it s{sic} fine, now, sweetheart—indeed it is," protested Bertram, hurriedly.

"Well, of course I'm glad—if you like it," murmured Billy; but the glow did not come back to her face.

CHAPTER XVIII. SUGARPLUMS

Those short December days after Bertram's return from New York were busy ones for everybody. Miss Winthrop was not in town to give sittings for her portrait, it is true; but her absence only afforded Bertram time and opportunity to attend to other work that had been more or less delayed and neglected. He was often at Hillside, however, and the lovers managed to snatch many an hour of quiet happiness from the rush and confusion of the Christmas preparations.

Bertram was assuring himself now that his jealous fears of Arkwright were groundless. Billy seldom mentioned the man, and, as the days passed, she spoke only once of his being at the house. The song, too, she said little of; and Bertram—though he was ashamed to own it to himself—breathed more freely.

The real facts of the case were that Billy had told Arkwright that she should have no time to give attention to the song until after Christmas; and her manner had so plainly shown him that she considered himself synonymous with the song, that he had reluctantly taken the hint and kept away.

"I'll make her care for me sometime—for something besides a song," he told himself with fierce consolation—but Billy did not know this.

Aside from Bertram, Christmas filled all of Billy's thoughts these days. There were such a lot of things she wished to do.

"But, after all, they're only sugarplums, you know, that I'm giving, dear," she declared to Bertram one day, when he had remonstrated with with her for so taxing her time and strength. "I can't really do much."

"Much!" scoffed Bertram.

"But it isn't much, honestly—compared to what there is to do," argued Billy. "You see, dear, it's just this," she went on, her bright face sobering a little. "There are such a lot of people in the world who aren't really poor. That is, they have bread, and probably meat, to eat, and enough clothes to keep them warm. But when you've said that, you've said it all. Books, music, fun, and frosting on their cake they know nothing about—except to long for them."

"But there are the churches and the charities, and all those long-named Societies—I thought that was what they were for," declared Bertram, still a little aggrievedly, his worried eyes on Billy's tired face.

"Oh, but the churches and charities don't frost cakes nor give sugarplums," smiled Billy. "And it's right that they shouldn't, too," she added quickly. "They have more than they can do now with the roast beef and coal and flannel petticoats that are really necessary."

"And so it's just frosting and sugarplums, is it—these books and magazines and concert tickets and lace collars for the crippled boy, the spinster lady, the little widow, and all the rest of those people who were here last summer?"

Billy turned in confused surprise.

"Why, Bertram, however in the world did you find out about all—that?"

"I didn't. I just guessed it—and it seems 'the boy guessed right the very first time,'" laughed Bertram, teasingly, but with a tender light in his eyes. "Oh, and I suppose you'll be sending a frosted cake to the Lowestoft lady, too, eh?"

Billy's chin rose to a defiant stubbornness.

"I'm going to try to—if I can find out what kind of frosting she likes."

"How about the Alice lady—or perhaps I should say, the Lady Alice?" smiled the man.

Billy relaxed visibly.

"Yes, I know," she sighed. "There is—the Lady Alice. But, anyhow, she can't call a Christmas present 'charity'—not if it's only a little bit of frosting!" Billy's chin came up again.

"And you're going to, really, dare to send her something?"

"Yes," avowed Billy. "I'm going down there one of these days, in the morning—"

"You're going down there! Billy—not alone?"

"Yes. Why not?"

"But, dearie, you mustn't. It was a horrid place, Will says."

"So it was horrid—to live in. It was everything that was cheap and mean and forlorn. But it was quiet and respectable. 'Tisn't as if I didn't know the way, Bertram; and I'm sure that where that poor crippled woman and daughter are safe, I shall be. Mrs. Greggory is a lady, Bertram, well-born and well-bred, I'm sure—and that's the pity of it, to have to live in a

153

place like that! They have seen better days, I know. Those pitiful little worn crutches of hers were mahogany, I'm sure, Bertram, and they were silver mounted."

Bertram made a restless movement.

"I know, dear; but if you had some one with you! It wouldn't do for Will, of course, nor me—under the circumstances. But there's Aunt Hannah—" He paused hopefully.

Billy chuckled.

"Bless your dear heart! Aunt Hannah would call for a dozen shawls in that place—if she had breath enough to call for any after she got to the top of those four flights!"

"Yes, I suppose so," rejoined Bertram, with an unwilling smile. "Still—well, you can take Rosa," he concluded decisively.

"How Miss Alice would like that—to catch me going 'slumming' with my maid!" cried Billy, righteous indignation in her voice. "Honestly, Bertram, I think even gentle Mrs. Greggory wouldn't stand for that."

"Then leave Rosa outside in the hall," planned Bertram, promptly; and after a few more arguments, Billy finally agreed to this.

It was with Rosa, therefore, that she set out the next morning for the little room up four flights on the narrow West End street.

Leaving the maid on the top stair of the fourth flight, Billy tapped at Mrs. Greggory's door. To her joy Mrs. Greggory herself answered the knock.

"Oh! Why—why, good morning," murmured the lady, in evident embarrassment. "Won't you—come m?"

"Thank you. May I?—just a minute?" smiled Billy, brightly.

As she entered the room, Billy threw a hasty look about her. There was no one but themselves present. With a sigh of satisfaction, therefore, the girl took the chair Mrs. Greggory offered, and began to speak.

"I was down this way—that is, I came this way this morning," she began a little hastily; "and I wanted just to come up and tell you how sorry I was about—about that teapot the other day. We didn't want it, of course—if you didn't want us to have it."

A swift change crossed Mrs. Greggory's perturbed face.

"Oh, then you didn't come for it again—to-day," she said. "I'm so glad! I didn't want to refuse—you."

"Indeed I didn't come for it—and we sha'n't again. Don't worry about that, please."

Mrs. Greggory sighed.

"I'm afraid you thought me very rude and—and impossible the other day," she stammered. "And please let me take this opportunity right now to apologize for my daughter. She was overwrought and excited. She didn't know what she was saying or doing, I'm sure. She was ashamed, I think after you left."

Billy raised a quick hand of protest.

"Don't, please don't, Mrs. Greggory," she begged.

"But it was our fault that you came. We asked you to come—through Mr. Harlow," rejoined the other, hurriedly. "And Mr. Henshaw—was that his name?—was so kind in every way. I'm glad of this chance to tell you how much we really did appreciate it—and your offer, too, which we could not, of course, accept," she finished, the bright color flooding her delicate face.

Again Billy raised a protesting hand; but the little woman in the opposite chair hurried on. There was still more, evidently, that she wished to say.

"I hope Mr. Henshaw did not feel too disappointed—about the Lowestoft. We didn't want to let it go if we could help it; and we hope now to keep it."

"Of course," murmured Billy, sympathetically.

"My daughter knew, you see, how much I have always thought of it, and she was determined that I should not give it up. She said I should have that much left, anyway. You see—my daughter is very unreconciled, still, to things as they are; and no wonder, perhaps. They are so different—from what they were!" Her voice broke a little.

"Of course," said Billy again, and this time the words were tinged with impatient indignation. "If only there were something one could do to help!"

"Thank you, my dear, but there isn't—indeed there isn't," rejoined the other, quickly; and Billy, looking into the proudly lifted face, realized suddenly that daughter Alice had perhaps inherited some traits from mother. "We shall get along very well, I am sure. My daughter has still another pupil. She will be home soon to tell you herself, perhaps."

Billy rose with a haste so marked it was almost impolite, as she murmured:

"Will she? I'm afraid, though, that I sha'n't see her, after all, for I must go. And may I leave these, please?" she added, hurriedly unpinning the bunch of white carnations from her coat. "It seems a pity to let them wilt, when you can put them in water right here." Her studiously casual voice gave no hint that those particular pinks had been bought less than half an hour before of a Park Street florist so that Mrs. Greggory might put them in water—right there.

"Oh, oh, how lovely!" breathed Mrs. Greggory, her face deep in the feathery bed of sweetness. Before she could half say "Thank you," however? she found herself alone.

CHAPTER XIX. ALICE GREGGORY

Christmas came and went; and in a flurry of snow and sleet January arrived. The holidays over, matters and things seemed to settle down to the winter routine.

Miss Winthrop had prolonged her visit in Washington until after Christmas, but she had returned to Boston now—and with her she had brought a brand-new idea for her portrait; an idea that caused her to sweep aside with superb disdain all poses and costumes and sketches to date, and announce herself with disarming winsomeness as "all ready now to really begin!"

Bertram Henshaw was vexed, but helpless. Decidedly he wished to paint Miss Marguerite Winthrop's portrait; but to attempt to paint it when all matters were not to the lady's liking were worse than useless, unless he wished to hang this portrait in the gallery of failures along with Anderson's and Fullam's—and that was not the goal he had set for it. As to the sordid money part of the affair—the great J. G. Winthrop himself had come to the artist, and in one terse sentence had doubled the original price and expressed himself as hopeful that Henshaw would put up with "the child's notions." It was the old financier's next sentence, however, that put the zest of real determination into Bertram, for because of it, the artist saw what this portrait was going to mean to the stern old man, and how dear was the original of it to a heart that was commonly reported "on the street" to be made of stone.

Obviously, then, indeed, there was nothing for Bertram Henshaw to do but to begin the new portrait. And he began it—though still, it must be confessed, with inward questionings. Before a week had passed, however, every trace of irritation had fled, and he was once again the absorbed artist who sees the vision of his desire taking palpable shape at the end of his brush.

"It's all right," he said to Billy then, one evening. "I'm glad she changed. It's going to be the best, the very best thing I've ever done—I think! by the sketches."

"I'm so glad!" exclaimed Billy. "I'm so glad!" The repetition was so vehement that it sounded almost as if she were trying to convince herself as well as Bertram of something that was not true.

But it was true—Billy told herself very indignantly that it was; indeed it was! Yet the very fact that she had to tell herself this, caused her to know how perilously near she was to being actually jealous of that portrait of Marguerite Winthrop. And it shamed her.

Very sternly these days Billy reminded herself of what Kate had said about Bertram's belonging first to his Art. She thought with mortification, too, that it did look as if she were not the proper wife for an artist if she were going to feel like this—always. Very resolutely, then, Billy turned to her music. This was all the more easily done, for, not only did she have her usual concerts and the opera to enjoy, but she had become interested in an operetta her club was about to give; also she had taken up the new song again. Christmas being over, Mr. Arkwright had been to the house several times. He had changed some of the words and she had improved the melody. The work on the accompaniment was progressing finely now, and Billy was so glad!—when she was absorbed in her music she forgot sometimes that she was ever so unfit an artist's sweetheart as to be—jealous of a portrait.

It was quite early in the month that the usually expected "January thaw" came, and it was on a comparatively mild Friday at this time that a matter of business took Billy into the neighborhood of Symphony Hall at about eleven o'clock in the morning. Dismissing John and the car upon her arrival, she said that she would later walk to the home of a friend near by, where she would remain until it was time for the Symphony Concert.

This friend was a girl whom Billy had known at school. She was studying now at the Conservatory of Music; and she had often urged Billy to come and have luncheon with her in her tiny apartment, which she shared with three other girls and a widowed aunt for housekeeper. On this particular Friday it had occurred to Billy that, owing to her business appointment at eleven and the Symphony Concert at half-past two, the intervening time would give her just the opportunity she had been seeking to enable her to accept her friend's invitation. A question asked, and enthusiastically answered in the affirmative, over the telephone that morning, therefore, had speedily completed arrangements, and she had agreed to be at her friend's door by twelve o'clock, or before.

As it happened, business did not take quite so long as she had expected, and half-past eleven found her well on her way to Miss Henderson's home.

In spite of the warm sunshine and the slushy snow in the streets, there was a cold, raw wind, and Billy was beginning to feel thankful that she had not far to go when she rounded a corner and came upon a long line of humanity that curved itself back and forth on the wide expanse of steps before Symphony Hall and then stretched itself far up the Avenue.

"Why, what—" she began under her breath; then suddenly she understood. It was Friday. A world-famous pianist was to play with the Symphony Orchestra that afternoon. This must be the line of patient waiters for the twenty-five-cent balcony seats that Mr. Arkwright had told about. With sympathetic, interested eyes, then, Billy stepped one side to watch the line, for a moment.

Almost at once two girls brushed by her, and one was saying:

"What a shame!—and after all our struggles to get here! If only we hadn't lost that other train!"

"We're too late—you no need to hurry!" the other wailed shrilly to a third girl who was hastening toward them. "The line is 'way beyond the Children's Hospital and around the corner now—and the ones there never get in!"

At the look of tragic disappointment that crossed the third girl's face, Billy's heart ached. Her first impulse, of course, was to pull her own symphony ticket from her muff and hurry forward with a "Here, take mine!" But that would hardly do, she knew—though she would like to see Aunt Hannah's aghast face if this girl in the red sweater and white tam-o'-shanter should suddenly emerge from among the sumptuous satins and furs and plumes that afternoon and claim the adjacent orchestra chair. But it was out of the question, of course. There was only one seat, and there were three girls, besides all those others. With a sigh, then, Billy turned her eyes back to those others—those many others that made up the long line stretching its weary length up the Avenue.

There were more women than men, yet the men were there: jolly young men who were plainly students; older men whose refined faces and threadbare overcoats hinted at cultured minds and starved bodies; other men who showed no hollows in their cheeks nor near-holes in their garments. It seemed to Billy that women of almost all sorts were there, young, old, and middle-aged; students in tailored suits, widows in crape and veil; girls that were members of a merry party, women that were plainly forlorn and alone.

Some in the line shuffled restlessly; some stood rigidly quiet. One had brought a camp stool; many were seated on the steps. Beyond, where the line passed an open lot, a wooden fence afforded a convenient prop. One read a book, another a paper. Three were studying what was probably the score of the symphony or of the concerto they expected to hear that afternoon.

A few did not appear to mind the biting wind, but most of them, by turned-up coat-collars or bent heads, testified to the contrary. Not far from Billy a woman nibbled a sandwich furtively, while beyond her a group of girls were hilariously merry over four triangles of pie which they held up where all might see.

Many of the faces were youthful, happy, and alert with anticipation; but others carried a wistfulness and a weariness that made Billy's heart ache. Her eyes, indeed, filled with quick tears. Later she turned to go, and it was then that she saw in the line a face that she knew—a face that drooped with such a white misery of spent strength that she hurried straight toward it with a low cry.

"Miss Greggory!" she exclaimed, when she reached the girl. "You look actually ill. Are you ill?"

For a brief second only dazed questioning stared from the girl's blue-gray eyes. Billy knew when the recognition came, for she saw the painful color stain the white face red.

"Thank you, no. I am not ill, Miss Neilson," said the girl, coldly.

"But you look so tired out!"

"I have been standing here some time; that is all."

Billy threw a hurried glance down the far-reaching line that she knew had formed since the girl's two tired feet had taken their first position.

"But you must have come—so early! It isn't twelve o'clock yet," she faltered.

A slight smile curved Alice Greggory's lips.

"Yes, it was early," she rejoined a little bitterly; "but it had to be, you know. I wanted to hear the music; and with this soloist, and this weather, I knew that many others—would want to hear the music, too."

"But you look so white! How much longer—when will they let you in?" demanded Billy, raising indignant eyes to the huge, gray-pillared building before her, much as if she would pull down the walls if she could, and make way for this tired girl at her side.

Miss Greggory's thin shoulders rose and fell in an expressive shrug.

"Half-past one."

Billy gave a dismayed cry.

"Half-past one—almost two hours more! But, Miss Greggory, you can't—how can you stand it till then? You've shivered three times since I came, and you look as if you were going to faint away."

Miss Greggory shook her head.

"It is nothing, really," she insisted. "I am quite well. It is only—I didn't happen to feel like eating much breakfast this morning; and that, with no luncheon—" She let a gesture finish her sentence.

"No luncheon! Why—oh, you couldn't leave your place, of course," frowned Billy.

"No, and"—Alice Greggory lifted her head a little proudly—"I do not care to eat—here." Her scornful eyes were on one of the pieces of pie down the line—no longer a triangle.

"Of course not," agreed Billy, promptly. She paused, frowned, and bit her lip. Suddenly her face cleared. "There! the very thing," she exulted. "You shall have my ticket this afternoon, Miss Greggory, then you won't have to stay here another minute. Meanwhile, there is an excellent restaurant—"

"Thank you—no. I couldn't do that," cut in the other, sharply, but in a low voice.

"But you'll take my ticket," begged Billy.

Miss Greggory shook her head.

"Certainly not."

"But I want you to, please. I shall be very unhappy if you don't," grieved Billy.

The other made a peremptory gesture.

"I should be very unhappy if I did," she said with cold emphasis. "Really, Miss Neilson," she went on in a low voice, throwing an apprehensive glance at the man ahead, who was apparently absorbed in his newspaper, "I'm afraid I shall have to ask you to let me go on in my own way. You are very kind, but there is nothing you can do; nothing. You were very kind, too, of course, to send the book and the flowers to mother at Christmas; but—"

"Never mind that, please," interrupted Billy, hurriedly. Billy's head was lifted now. Her eyes were no longer pleading. Her round little chin looked square and determined. "If you simply will not take my ticket this afternoon, you must do this. Go to some restaurant near here and get a good luncheon—something that will sustain you. I will take your place here."

"Miss Neilson!"

Billy smiled radiantly. It was the first time she had ever seen Alice Greggory's haughtily cold reserve break into anything like naturalness—the astonished incredulity of that "Miss Neilson!" was plainly straight from the heart; so, too, were the amazed words that followed.

"You—will stand here?"

"Certainly; I will keep your place. Don't worry. You sha'n't lose it." Billy spoke with a smiling indifference that was meant to convey the impression that standing in line for a twenty-five-cent seat was a daily habit of hers. "There's a restaurant only a little way—right down there," she finished. And before the dazed Alice Greggory knew quite what was happening she found herself outside the line, and the other in her place.

"But, Miss Neilson, I can't—you mustn't—" she stammered; then, because of something in the unyieldingness of the square young chin above the sealskin coat, and because she could not (she knew) use actual force to drag the owner of that chin out of the line, she bowed her head in acquiescence.

"Well, then—I will, long enough for some coffee and maybe a sandwich. And—thank you," she choked, as she turned and hurried away.

Billy drew the deep breath of one who has triumphed after long struggles—but the breath broke off short in a gasp of dismay: coming straight up the Avenue toward her was the one person in the world Billy wished least to see at that moment—Bertram Henshaw. Billy remembered then that she had twice lately heard her lover speak of calling at the Boston Opera House concerning a commission to paint an ideal head to represent "Music" for some decorative purpose. The Opera House was only a short distance up the Avenue. Doubtless he was on his way there now.

He was very near by this time, and Billy held her breath suspended. There was a chance, of course, that he might not notice her; and Billy was counting on that chance—until a gust of wind whirled a loose half-sheet of newspaper from the hands of the man in front of her, and naturally attracted Bertram's eyes to its vicinity—and to hers. The next moment he was at her side and his dumfounded but softly-breathed "Billy!" was in her ears.

Billy bubbled into low laughter—there were such a lot of funny situations in the world, and of them all this one was about the drollest, she thought.

"Yes, I know," she gurgled. "You don't have to say it-your face is saying even more than your tongue could! This is just for a girl I know. I'm keeping her place."

Bertram frowned. He looked as if he were meditating picking Billy up and walking off with her.

"But, Billy," he protested just above his breath, "this isn't sugarplums nor frosting; it's plain suicide—standing out in this wind like this! Besides—" He stopped with an angrily despairing glance at her surroundings.

"Yes, I know," she nodded, a little soberly, understanding the look and answering that first; "it isn't pleasant nor comfortable, in lots of ways—but she's had it all the morning. As for the cold—I'm as warm as toast. It won't be long, anyway; she's just gone to get something to eat. Then I'm going to May Henderson's for luncheon."

Bertram sighed impatiently and opened his lips—only to close them with the words unsaid. There was nothing he could do, and he had already said too much, he thought, with a savage glance at the man ahead who still had enough of his paper left to serve for a pretence at reading. As Bertram could see, however, the man was not reading a word—he was too acutely conscious of the handsome young woman in the long sealskin coat behind him. Billy was already the cynosure of dozens of eyes, and Bertram knew that his own arrival on the scene had not lessened the interest of the owners of those eyes. He only hoped devoutly that no one in the line knew him ar Billy, and that no one quite knew what had happened. He did not wish to see himself and his fiancée the subject of inch-high headlines in some evening paper figuring as:

"Talented young composer and her famous artist lover take poor girl's place in a twenty-five-cent ticket line."

He shivered at the thought.

"Are you cold?" worried Billy. "If you are, don't stand here, please!"

He shook his head silently. His eyes were searching the street for the only one whose coming could bring him relief.

It must have been but a coffee-and-sandwich luncheon for the girl, for soon she came. The man surmised that it was she, as soon as he saw her, and stepped back at once. He had no wish for introductions. A moment later the girl was in Billy's place, and Billy herself was at his side.

"That was Alice Greggory, Bertram," she told him, as they walked on swiftly; "and Bertram, she was actually almost crying when she took my place."

"Humph! Well, I should think she'd better be," growled Bertram, perversely.

"Pooh! It didn't hurt me any, dearie," laughed Billy with a conciliatory pat on his arm as they turned down the street upon which her friend lived. "And now can you come in and see May a minute?"

"I'm afraid not," regretted Bertram. "I wish I could, but I'm busier than busy to-day—and I was supposed to be already late when I saw you. Jove, Billy, I just couldn't believe my eyes!"

"You looked it," twinkled Billy. "It was worth a farm just to see your face!"

"I'd want the farm—if I was going through that again," retorted the man, grimly—Bertram was still seeing that newspaper heading.

But Billy only laughed again.

CHAPTER XX. ARKWRIGHT TELLS A STORY

Arkwright called Monday afternoon by appointment; and together he and Billy put the finishing touches to the new song.

It was when, with Aunt Hannah, they were having tea before the fire a little later, that Billy told of her adventure the preceding Friday afternoon in front of Symphony Hall.

"You knew the girl, of course—I think you said you knew the girl," ventured Arkwright.

"Oh, yes. She was Alice Greggory. I met her with Uncle William first, over a Lowestoft teapot. Maybe you'd like to know how I met her," smiled Billy.

"Alice Greggory?" Arkwright's eyes showed a sudden interest. "I used to know an Alice Greggory, but it isn't the same one, probably. Her mother was a cripple."

Billy gave a little cry.

"Why, it is—it must be! My Alice Greggory's mother is a cripple. Oh, do you know them, really?"

"Well, it does look like it," rejoined Arkwright, showing even deeper interest. "I haven't seen them for four or five years. They used to live in our town. The mother was a little sweet-faced woman with young eyes and prematurely white hair."

"That describes my Mrs. Greggory exactly," cried Billy's eager voice. "And the daughter?"

"Alice? Why—as I said, it's been four years since I've seen her." A touch of constraint had come into Arkwright's voice which Billy's keen ear was quick to detect. "She was nineteen then and very pretty."

"About my height, and with light-brown hair and big blue-gray eyes that look steely cold when she's angry?" questioned Billy.

"I reckon that's about it," acknowledged the man, with a faint smile.

"Then they are the ones," declared the girl, plainly excited. "Isn't that splendid? Now we can know them, and perhaps do something for them. I love that dear little mother already, and I think I should the daughter—if she didn't put out so many prickers that I couldn't get near her! But tell us about them. How did they come here? Why didn't you know they were here?"

"Are you good at answering a dozen questions at once?" asked Aunt Hannah, turning smiling eyes from Billy to the man at her side.

"Well, I can try," he offered. "To begin with, they are Judge Greggory's widow and daughter. They belong to fine families on both sides, and they used to be well off—really wealthy, for a small town. But the judge was better at money-making than he was at money-keeping, and when he came to die his income stopped, of course, and his estate was found to be in bad shape through reckless loans and worthless investments. That was eight years ago. Things went from bad to worse then, until there was almost nothing left."

"I knew there was some such story as that back of them," declared Billy. "But how do you suppose they came here?"

"To get away from—everybody, I suspect," replied Arkwright. "That would be like them. They were very proud; and it isn't easy, you know, to be nobody where you've been somebody. It doesn't hurt quite so hard—to be nobody where you've never been anything but nobody."

"I suppose so," sighed Billy. "Still—they must have had friends."

"They did, of course; but when the love of one's friends becomes too highly seasoned with pity, it doesn't make a pleasant morsel to swallow, specially if you don't like the taste of the pity—and there are people who don't, you know. The Greggorys were that kind. They were morbidly so. From their cheap little cottage, where they did their own work, they stepped out in their shabby garments and old-fashioned hats with heads even more proudly erect than in the old days when their home and their gowns and their doings were the admiration and envy of the town. You see, they didn't want—that pity."

"I do see," cried Billy, her face aglow with sudden understanding; "and I don't believe pity would be—nice!" Her own chin was held high as she spoke.

"It must have been hard, indeed," murmured Aunt Hannah with a sigh, as she set down her teacup.

"It was," nodded Arkwright. "Of course Mrs. Greggory, with her crippled foot, could do nothing to bring in any money except to sew a little. It all depended on Alice; and when matters got to their worst she began to teach. She was fond of music, and could play the piano well; and of course she had had the best instruction she could get from city teachers only twenty miles away from our home town. Young as she was—about seventeen when she began to teach, I think—she got a few beginners right away, and in two years she had worked up quite a class, meanwhile keeping on with her own studies, herself.

"They might have carried the thing through, maybe," continued Arkwright, "and never apparently known that the 'pity' existed, if it hadn't been for some ugly rumors that suddenly arose attacking the Judge's honesty in an old matter that somebody raked up. That was too much. Under this last straw their courage broke utterly. Alice dismissed every pupil, sold almost all their remaining goods—they had lots of quite valuable heirlooms; I suspect that's where your Lowestoft teapot came in—and with the money thus gained they left town. Until they could go, they scarcely showed themselves once on the street, they were never at home to callers, and they left without telling one soul where they were going, so far as we could ever learn."

"Why, the poor dears!" cried Billy. "How they must have suffered! But things will be different now. You'll go to see them, of course, and—" At the look that came into Arkwright's face, she stopped in surprise.

"You forget; they wouldn't wish to see me," demurred the man. And again Billy noticed the odd constraint in his voice.

"But they wouldn't mind you—here," argued Billy.

"I'm afraid they would. In fact, I'm sure they'd refuse entirely to see me."

Billy's eyes grew determined.

"But they can't refuse—if I bring about a meeting just casually, you know," she challenged.

Arkwright laughed.

"Well, I won't pretend to say as to the consequences of that," he rejoined, rising to his feet; "but they might be disastrous. Wasn't it you yourself who were telling me a few minutes ago how steely cold Miss Alice's eyes got when she was angry?"

Billy knew by the way the man spoke that, for some reason, he did not wish to prolong the subject of his meeting the Greggorys. She made a quick shift, therefore, to another phase of the matter.

"But tell me, please, before you go, how did those rumors come out—about Judge Greggory's honesty, I mean?"

"Why, I never knew, exactly," frowned Arkwright, musingly. "Yet it seems, too, that mother did say in one letter, while I was in Paris, that some of the accusations had been found to be false, and that there was a prospect that the Judge's good name might be saved, after all."

"Oh, I wish it might," sighed Billy. "Think what it would mean to those women!"

"'Twould mean everything," cried Arkwright, warmly; "and I'll write to mother to-night, I will, and find out just what there is to it-if anything. Then you can tell them," he finished a little stiffly.

"Yes—or you," nodded Billy, lightly. And because she began at once to speak of something else, the first part of her sentence passed without comment.

The door had scarcely closed behind Arkwright when Billy turned to Aunt Hannah a beaming face.

"Aunt Hannah, did you notice?" she cried, "how Mary Jane looked and acted whenever Alice Greggory was spoken of? There was something between them—I'm sure there was; and they quarrelled, probably."

"Why, no, dear; I didn't see anything unusual," murmured the elder lady.

"Well, I did. And I'm going to be the fairy godmother that straightens everything all out, too. See if I'm not! They'd make a splendid couple, Aunt Hannah. I'm going right down there to-morrow."

"Billy, my dear!" exclaimed the more conservative old lady, "aren't you taking things a little too much for granted? Maybe they don't wish for—for a fairy godmother!"

"Oh, they won't know I'm a fairy godmother—not one of them; and of course I wouldn't mention even a hint to anybody," laughed Billy. "I'm just going down to get acquainted with the Greggorys; that's all. Only think, Aunt Hannah, what they must have suffered! And look at the place they're living in now—gentlewomen like them!"

"Yes, yes, poor things, poor things!" sighed Aunt Hannah.

"I hope I'll find out that she's really good—at teaching, I mean—the daughter," resumed Billy, after a moment's pause. "If she is, there's one thing I can do to help, anyhow. I can get some of Marie's old pupils for her. I know some of them haven't begun with a new teacher, yet; and Mrs. Carleton told me last Friday that neither she nor her sister was at all satisfied with the one their girls have taken. They'd change, I know, in a minute, at my recommendation—that is, of course, if I can give the recommendation," continued Billy, with a troubled frown. "Anyhow, I'm going down to begin operations to-morrow."

CHAPTER XXI. A MATTER OF STRAIGHT BUSINESS

True to her assertion, Billy went down to the Greggorys' the next day. This time she did not take Rosa with her. Even Aunt Hannah conceded that it would not be necessary. She had not been gone ten minutes, however, when the telephone bell rang, and Rosa came to say that Mr. Bertram Henshaw wanted to speak with Mrs. Stetson.

"Rosa says that Billy's not there," called Bertram's aggrieved voice, when Aunt Hannah had said, "Good morning, my boy."

"Dear me, no, Bertram. She's in a fever of excitement this morning. She'll probably tell you all about it when you come out here to-night. You are coming out to-night, aren't you?"

"Yes; oh, yes! But what is it? Where's she gone?"

Aunt Hannah laughed softly.

"Well, she's gone down to the Greggorys'."

"The Greggorys'! What—again?"

"Oh, you might as well get used to it, Bertram," bantered Aunt Hannah, "for there'll be a good many 'agains,' I fancy."

"Why, Aunt Hannah, what do you mean?" Bertram's voice was not quite pleased.

"Oh, she'll tell you. It's only that the Greggorys have turned out to be old friends of Mr. Arkwright's."

"Friends of Arkwright's!" Bertram's voice was decidedly displeased now.

"Yes; and there's quite a story to it all, as well. Billy is wildly excited, as you'd know she would be. You'll hear all about it to-night, of course."

"Yes, of course," echoed Bertram. But there was no ring of enthusiasm in his voice, neither then, nor when he said good-by a moment later.

Billy, meanwhile, on her way to the Greggory home, was, as Aunt Hannah had said, "wildly excited." It seemed so strange and wonderful and delightful—the whole affair: that she should have found them because of a Lowestoft teapot, that Arkwright should know them, and that there should be the chance now that she might help them—in some way; though this last, she knew, could be accomplished only through the exercise of the greatest tact and delicacy. She had not forgotten that Arkwright had told her of their hatred of pity.

In the sober second thought of the morning, Billy was not sure now of a possible romance in connection with Arkwright and the daughter, Alice; but she had by no means abandoned the idea, and she meant to keep her eyes open—and if there should be a chance to bring such a thing about—! Meanwhile, of course, she should not mention the matter, even to Bertram.

Just what would be her method of procedure this first morning, Billy had not determined. The pretty potted azalea in her hand would be excuse for her entrance into the room. After that, circumstances must decide for themselves.

Mrs. Greggory was found to be alone at home as before, and Billy was glad. She would rather begin with one than two, she thought. The little woman greeted her cordially, gave misty-eyed thanks for the beautiful plant, and also for Billy's kind thoughtfulness Friday afternoon. From that she was very skilfully led to talk more of the daughter; and soon Billy was getting just the information she wanted—information concerning the character, aims, and daily life of Alice Greggory.

"You see, we have some money—a very little," explained Mrs. Greggory, after a time; "though to get it we have had to sell all our treasures—but the Lowestoft," with a quick glance into Billy's eyes. "We need not, perhaps, live in quite so poor a place; but we prefer—just now—to spend the little money we have for something other than imitation comfort—lessons, for instance, and an occasional concert. My daughter is studying even while she is teaching. She hopes to train herself for an accompanist, and for a teacher. She does not aspire to concert solo work. She understands her limitations."

"But she is probably—very good—at teaching." Billy hesitated a little.

"She is; very good. She has the best of recommendations." A little proudly Mrs. Greggory gave the names of two Boston pianists—names that would carry weight anywhere.

Unconsciously Billy relaxed. She did not know until that moment how she had worried for fear she could not, conscientiously, recommend this Alice Greggory.

"Of course," resumed the mother, "Alice's pupils are few, and they pay low prices; but she is gaining. She goes to the houses, of course. She herself practises two hours a day at a house up on Pinckney Street. She gives lessons to a little girl in return."

"I see," nodded Billy, brightly; "and I've been thinking, Mrs. Greggory—maybe I know of some pupils she could get. I have a friend who has just given hers up, owing to her marriage. Sometime, soon, I'm going to talk to your daughter, if I may, and—"

"And here she is right now," interposed Mrs. Greggory, as the door opened under a hurried hand.

Billy flushed and bit her lip. She was disturbed and disappointed. She did not particularly wish to see Alice Greggory just then. She wished even less to see her when she noted the swift change that came to the girl's face at sight of herself.

"Oh! Why-good morning, Miss Neilson," murmured Miss Greggory with a smile so forced that her mother hurriedly looked to the azalea in search of a possible peacemaker.

"My dear, see," she stammered, "what Miss Neilson has brought me. And it's so full of blossoms, too! And she says it'll remain so for a long, long time—if we'll only keep it wet."

Alice Greggory murmured a low something—a something that she tried, evidently, very hard to make politely appropriate and appreciative. Yet her manner, as she took off her hat and coat and sat down, so plainly said: "You are very kind, of course, but I wish you would keep yourself and your plants at home!" that Mrs. Greggory began a hurried apology, much as if the words had indeed been spoken.

"My daughter is really ill this morning. You mustn't mind—that is, I'm afraid you'll think— you see, she took cold last week; a bad cold—and she isn't over it, yet," finished the little woman in painful embarrassment.

"Of course she took cold—standing all those hours in that horrid wind, Friday!" cried Billy, indignantly.

A quick red flew to Alice Greggory's face. Billy saw it at once and fervently wished she had spoken of anything but that Friday afternoon. It looked almost as if she were reminding them of what she had done that day. In her confusion, and in her anxiety to say something—anything that would get their minds off that idea—she uttered now the first words that came into her head. As it happened, they were the last words that sober second thought would have told her to say.

"Never mind, Mrs. Greggory. We'll have her all well and strong soon; never fear! Just wait till I send Peggy and Mary Jane to take her out for a drive one of these mild, sunny days. You have no idea how much good it will do her!"

Alice Greggory got suddenly to her feet. Her face was very white now. Her eyes had the steely coldness that Billy knew so well. Her voice, when she spoke, was low and sternly controlled.

"Miss Neilson, you will think me rude, of course, especially after your great kindness to me the other day; but I can't help it. It seems to me best to speak now before it goes any further."

"Alice, dear," remonstrated Mrs. Greggory, extending a frightened hand.

The girl did not turn her head nor hesitate; but she caught the extended hand and held it warmly in both her own, with gentle little pats, while she went on speaking.

"I'm sure mother agrees with me that it is best, for the present, that we keep quite to ourselves. I cannot question your kindness, of course, after your somewhat unusual favor the other day; but I am very sure that your friends, Miss Peggy, and Miss Mary Jane, have no real desire to make my acquaintance, nor—if you'll pardon me—have I, under the circumstances, any wish to make theirs."

"Oh, Alice, Alice," began the little mother, in dismay; but a rippling laugh from their visitor brought an angry flush even to her gentle face.

Billy understood the flush, and struggled for self-control.

"Please—please, forgive me!" she choked. "But you see—you couldn't, of course, know that Mary Jane and Peggy aren't girls. They're just a man and an automobile!"

An unwilling smile trembled on Alice Greggory's lips; but she still stood her ground.

"After all, girls, or men and automobiles, Miss Neilson—it makes little difference. They're—charity. And it's not so long that we've been objects of charity that we quite really enjoy it—yet."

There was a moment's hush. Billy's eyes had filled with tears.

"I never even thought—charity," said Billy, so gently that a faint red stole into the white cheeks opposite.

For a tense minute Alice Greggory held herself erect; then, with a complete change of manner and voice, she released her mother's hand, dropped into her own chair again, and said wearily:

"I know you didn't, Miss Neilson. It's all my foolish pride, of course. It's only that I was thinking how dearly I would love to meet girls again—just as girls! But—I no longer have any business with pride, of course. I shall be pleased, I'm sure," she went on dully, "to accept anything you may do for us, from automobile rides to—to red flannel petticoats."

Billy almost—but not quite—laughed. Still, the laugh would have been near to a sob, had it been given. Surprising as was the quick transition in the girl's manner, and absurd as was the juxtaposition of automobiles and red flannel petticoats, the white misery of Alice Greggory's face and the weary despair of her attitude were tragic—specially to one who knew her story as did Billy Neilson. And it was because Billy did know her story that she did not make the mistake now of offering pity. Instead, she said with a bright smile, and a casual manner that gave no hint of studied labor:

"Well, as it happens, Miss Greggory, what I want to-day has nothing whatever to do with automobiles or red flannel petticoats. It's a matter of straight business." (How Billy blessed the thought that had so suddenly come to her!) "Your mother tells me you play accompaniments. Now a girls' club, of which I am a member, is getting up an operetta for charity, and we need an accompanist. There is no one in the club who is able, and at the same time willing, to spend the amount of time necessary for practice and rehearsals. So we had decided to hire one outside, and I have been given the task of finding one. It has occurred to me that perhaps you would be willing to undertake it for us. Would you?"

Billy knew, at once, from the quick change in the other's face and manner, that she had taken exactly the right course to relieve the strain of the situation. Despair and lassitude fell away from Alice Greggory almost like a garment. Her countenance became alert and interested.

"Indeed I would! I should be glad to do it."

"Good! Then can you come out to my home sometime to-morrow, and go over the music with me? Rehearsals will not begin until next week; but I can give you the music, and tell you something of what we are planning to do."

"Yes. I could come at ten in the morning for an hour, or at three in the afternoon for two hours or more," replied Miss Greggory, after a moment's hesitation.

"Suppose we call it in the afternoon, then," smiled Billy, as she rose to her feet. "And now I must go—and here's my address," she finished, taking out her card and laying it on the table near her.

For reasons of her own Billy went away that morning without saying anything more about the proposed new pupils. New pupils were not automobile rides nor petticoats, to be sure—but she did not care to risk disturbing the present interested happiness of Alice Greggory's face by mentioning anything that might be construed as too officious an assistance.

On the whole, Billy felt well pleased with her morning's work. To Aunt Hannah, upon her return, she expressed herself thus:

"It's splendid—even better than I hoped. I shall have a chance to-morrow, of course, to see for myself just how well she plays, and all that. I'm pretty sure, though, from what I hear, that that part will be all right. Then the operetta will give us a chance to see a good deal of her, and to bring about a natural meeting between her and Mary Jane. Oh, Aunt Hannah, I couldn't have planned it better—and there the whole thing just tumbled into my hands! I knew it had the minute I remembered about the operetta. You know I'm chairman, and they left me to get the accompanist; and like a flash it came to me, when I was wondering what to say or do to get her out of that awful state she was in—'Ask her to be your accompanist.' And I did. And I'm so glad I did! Oh, Aunt Hannah, it's coming out lovely!—I know it is."

CHAPTER XXII. PLANS AND PLOTTINGS

To Billy, Alice Greggory's first visit to Hillside was in every way a delight and a satisfaction. To Alice, it was even more than that. For the first time in years she found herself welcomed into a home of wealth, culture, and refinement as an equal; and the frank cordiality and naturalness of her hostess's evident expectation of meeting a congenial companion was like balm to a sensitive soul rendered morbid by long years of superciliousness and snubbing.

No wonder that under the cheery friendliness of it all, Alice Greggory's cold reserve vanished, and that in its place came something very like her old ease and charm of manner. By the time Aunt Hannah—according to previous agreement—came into the room, the two girls were laughing and chatting over the operetta as if they had known each other for years.

Much to Billy's delight, Alice Greggory, as a musician, proved to be eminently satisfactory. She was quick at sight reading, and accurate. She played easily, and with good expression. Particularly was she a good accompanist, possessing to a marked degree that happy faculty of accompanying a singer: which means that she neither led the way nor lagged behind, being always exactly in sympathetic step—than which nothing is more soul-satisfying to the singer.

It was after the music for the operetta had been well-practised and discussed that Alice Greggory chanced to see one of Billy's own songs lying near her. With a pleased smile she picked it up.

"Oh, you know this, too!" she cried. "I played it for a lady only the other day. It's so pretty, I think—all of hers are, that I have seen. Billy Neilson is a girl, you know, they say, in spite of—" She stopped abruptly. Her eyes grew wide and questioning. "Miss Neilson—it can't be—you don't mean—is your name—it is—you!" she finished joyously, as the telltale color dyed Billy's face. The next moment her own cheeks burned scarlet. "And to think of my letting you stand in line for a twenty-five-cent admission!" she scorned.

"Nonsense!" laughed Billy. "It didn't hurt me any more than it did you. Come!"—in looking about for a quick something to take her guest's attention, Billy's eyes fell on the manuscript copy of her new song, bearing Arkwright's name. Yielding to a daring impulse, she drew it hastily forward. "Here's a new one—a brand-new one, not even printed yet. Don't you think the words are pretty?" she asked.

As she had hoped, Alice Greggory's eyes, after they had glanced half-way through the first page, sought the name at the left side below the title.

"'Words by M. J.—'"—there was a visible start, and a pause before the "'Arkwright'" was uttered in a slightly different tone.

Billy noted both the start and the pause—and gloried in them.

"Yes; the words are by M. J. Arkwright," she said with smooth unconcern, but with a covert glance at the other's face. "Ever hear of him?"

Alice Greggory gave a short little laugh.

"Probably not—this one. I used to know an M. J. Arkwright, long ago; but he wasn't—a poet, so far as I know," she finished, with a little catch in her breath that made Billy long to take her into a warm embrace.

Alice Greggory turned then to the music. She had much to say of this—very much; but she had nothing more whatever to say of Mr. M. J. Arkwright in spite of the tempting conversation bait that Billy dropped so freely. After that, Rosa brought in tea and toast, and the little frosted cakes that were always such a favorite with Billy's guests. Then Alice Greggory said good-by—her eyes full of tears that Billy pretended not to see.

"There!" breathed Billy, as soon as she had Aunt Hannah to herself again. "What did I tell you? Did you see Miss Greggory's start and blush and hear her sigh just over the name of M. J. Arkwright? Just as if—! Now I want them to meet; only it must be casual, Aunt Hannah—casual! And I'd rather wait till Mary Jane hears from his mother, if possible, so if there is anything good to tell the poor girl, he can tell it."

"Yes, of course. Dear child!—I hope he can," murmured Aunt Hannah. (Aunt Hannah had ceased now trying to make Billy refrain from the reprehensible "Mary Jane." In fact, if the truth were known, Aunt Hannah herself in her thoughts—and sometimes in her words—called him "Mary Jane.") "But, indeed, my dear, I didn't see anything stiff, or—or repelling about Miss Greggory, as you said there was."

"There wasn't—to-day," smiled Billy. "Honestly, Aunt Hannah, I should never have known her for the same girl—who showed me the door that first morning," she finished merrily, as she turned to go up-stairs.

It was the next day that Cyril and Marie came home from their honeymoon. They went directly to their pretty little apartment on Beacon Street, Brookline, within easy walking distance of Billy's own cozy home.

Cyril intended to build in a year or two. Meanwhile they had a very pretty, convenient home which was, according to Bertram, "electrified to within an inch of its life, and equipped with everything that was fireless, smokeless, dustless, and laborless." In it Marie had a spotlessly white kitchen where she might make puddings to her heart's content.

Marie had—again according to Bertram—"a visiting acquaintance with a maid." In other words, a stout woman was engaged to come two days in the week to wash, iron, and scrub;

also to come in each night to wash the dinner dishes, thus leaving Marie's evenings free—"for the shaded lamp," Billy said.

Marie had not arrived at this—to her, delightful—arrangement of a "visiting acquaintance" without some opposition from her friends. Even Billy had stood somewhat aghast.

"But, my dear, won't it be hard for you, to do so much?" she argued one day. "You know you aren't very strong."

"I know; but it won't be hard, as I've planned it," replied Marie, "specially when I've been longing for years to do this very thing. Why, Billy, if I had to stand by and watch a maid do all these things I want to do myself, I should feel just like—like a hungry man who sees another man eating up his dinner! Oh, of course," she added plaintively, after Billy's laughter had subsided, "I sha'n't do it always. I don't expect to. Of course, when we have a house—I'm not sure, then, though, that I sha'n't dress up the maid and order her to receive the calls and go to the pink teas, while I make her puddings," she finished saucily, as Billy began to laugh again.

The bride and groom, as was proper, were, soon after their arrival, invited to dine at both William's and Billy's. Then, until Marie's "At Homes" should begin, the devoted couple settled down to quiet days by themselves, with only occasional visits from the family to interrupt—"interrupt" was Bertram's word, not Marie's. Though it is safe to say it was not far different from the one Cyril used—in his thoughts.

Bertram himself, these days, was more than busy. Besides working on Miss Winthrop's portrait, and on two or three other commissions, he was putting the finishing touches to four pictures which he was to show in the exhibition soon to be held by a prominent Art Club of which he was the acknowledged "star" member. Naturally, therefore, his time was well occupied. Naturally, too, Billy, knowing this, lashed herself more sternly than ever into a daily reminder of Kate's assertion that he belonged first to his Art.

In pursuance of this idea, Billy was careful to see that no engagement with herself should in any way interfere with the artist's work, and that no word of hers should attempt to keep him at her side when ART called. (Billy always spelled that word now in her mind with tall, black letters—the way it had sounded when it fell from Kate's lips.) That these tactics on her part were beginning to fill her lover with vague alarm and a very definite unrest, she did not once suspect. Eagerly, therefore,—even with conscientious delight—she welcomed the new song-words that Arkwright brought—they would give her something else to take up her time and attention. She welcomed them, also, for another reason: they would bring Arkwright more often to the house, and this would, of course, lead to that "casual meeting" between him and Alice Greggory when the rehearsals for the operetta should commence—which would be very soon now. And Billy did so long to bring about that meeting!

To Billy, all this was but "occupying her mind," and playing Cupid's assistant to a worthy young couple torn cruelly apart by an unfeeling fate. To Bertram—to Bertram it was terror, and woe, and all manner of torture; for in it Bertram saw only a growing fondness on the part of Billy for Arkwright, Arkwright's music, Arkwright's words, and Arkwright's friends.

The first rehearsal for the operetta came on Wednesday evening. There would be another on Thursday afternoon. Billy had told Alice Greggory to arrange her pupils so that she could stay Wednesday night at Hillside, if the crippled mother could get along alone—and she could, Alice had said. Thursday forenoon, therefore, Alice Greggory would, in all probability, be at Hillside, specially as there would doubtless be an appointment or two for private rehearsal with some nervous soloist whose part was not progressing well. Such being the case, Billy had a plan she meant to carry out. She was highly pleased, therefore, when Thursday morning came, and everything, apparently, was working exactly to her mind.

Alice was there. She had an appointment at quarter of eleven with the leading tenor, and another later with the alto. After breakfast, therefore, Billy said decisively:

"Now, if you please, Miss Greggory, I'm going to put you up-stairs on the couch in the sewing-room for a nap."

"But I've just got up," remonstrated Miss Greggory.

"I know you have," smiled Billy; "but you were very late to bed last night, and you've got a hard day before you. I insist upon your resting. You will be absolutely undisturbed there, and you must shut the door and not come down-stairs till I send for you. Mr. Johnson isn't due till quarter of eleven, is he?"

"N-no."

"Then come with me," directed Billy, leading the way up-stairs. "There, now, don't come down till I call you," she went on, when they had reached the little room at the end of the hall. "I'm going to leave Aunt Hannah's door open, so you'll have good air—she isn't in there. She's writing letters in my room, Now here's a book, and you may read, but I should prefer you to sleep," she nodded brightly as she went out and shut the door quietly. Then, like the guilty conspirator she was, she went down-stairs to wait for Arkwright.

It was a fine plan. Arkwright was due at ten o'clock—Billy had specially asked him to come at that hour. He would not know, of course, that Alice Greggory was in the house; but soon after his arrival Billy meant to excuse herself for a moment, slip up-stairs and send Alice Greggory down for a book, a pair of scissors, a shawl for Aunt Hannah—anything would do for a pretext, anything so that the girl might walk into the living-room and find Arkwright waiting for her alone. And then—What happened next was, in Billy's mind, very vague, but very attractive as a nucleus for one's thoughts, nevertheless.

All this was, indeed, a fine plan; but—(If only fine plans would not so often have a "but"!) In Billy's case the "but" had to do with things so apparently unrelated as were Aunt Hannah's clock and a negro's coal wagon. The clock struck eleven at half-past ten, and the wagon dumped itself to destruction directly in front of a trolley car in which sat Mr. M. J. Arkwright, hurrying to keep his appointment with Miss Billy Neilson. It was almost half-past ten when Arkwright finally rang the bell at Hillside. Billy greeted him so eagerly, and at the same time with such evident disappointment at his late arrival, that Arkwright's heart sang with joy.

"But there's a rehearsal at quarter of eleven," exclaimed Billy, in answer to his hurried explanation of the delay; "and this gives so little time for—for—so little time, you know," she finished in confusion, casting frantically about in her mind for an excuse to hurry up-stairs and send Alice Greggory down before it should be quite too late.

No wonder that Arkwright, noting the sparkle in her eye, the agitation in her manner, and the embarrassed red in her cheek, took new courage. For so long had this girl held him at the end of a major third or a diminished seventh; for so long had she blithely accepted his every word and act as devotion to music, not herself—for so long had she done all this that he had come to fear that never would she do anything else. No wonder then, that now, in the soft radiance of the strange, new light on her face, his own face glowed ardently, and that he leaned forward with an impetuous rush of eager words.

"But there is time, Miss Billy—if you'd give me leave—to say—"

"I'm afraid I kept you waiting," interrupted the hurried voice of Alice Greggory from the hall doorway. "I was asleep, I think, when a clock somewhere, striking eleven—Why, Mr.—Arkwright!"

Not until Alice Greggory had nearly crossed the room did she see that the man standing by her hostess was—not the tenor she had expected to find—but an old acquaintance. Then it was that the tremulous "Mr.-Arkwright!" fell from her lips.

Billy and Arkwright had turned at her first words. At her last, Arkwright, with a half-despairing, half-reproachful glance at Billy, stepped forward.

"Miss Greggory!—you are Miss Alice Greggory, I am sure," he said pleasantly.

At the first opportunity Billy murmured a hasty excuse and left the room. To Aunt Hannah she flew with a woebegone face.

"Oh, Aunt Hannah, Aunt Hannah," she wailed, half laughing, half crying; "that wretched little fib-teller of a clock of yours spoiled it all!"

"Spoiled it! Spoiled what, child?"

"My first meeting between Mary Jane and Miss Greggory. I had it all arranged that they were to have it alone; but that miserable little fibber up-stairs struck eleven at half-past ten, and Miss Greggory heard it and thought she was fifteen minutes late. So down she hurried, half awake, and spoiled all my plans. Now she's sitting in there with him, in chairs the length of the room apart, discussing the snowstorm last night or the moonrise this morning—or some other such silly thing. And I had it so beautifully planned!"

"Well, well, dear, I'm sorry, I'm sure," smiled Aunt Hannah; "but I can't think any real harm is done. Did Mary Jane have anything to tell her—about her father, I mean?"

Only the faintest flicker of Billy's eyelid testified that the everyday accustomedness of that "Mary Jane" on Aunt Hannah's lips had not escaped her.

"No, nothing definite. Yet there was a little. Friends are still trying to clear his name, and I believe are meeting with increasing success. I don't know, of course, whether he'll say anything about it to-day—now. To think I had to be right round under foot like that when they met!" went on Billy, indignantly. "I shouldn't have been, in a minute more, though. I was just trying to think up an excuse to come up and send down Miss Greggory, when Mary Jane began to tell me something—I haven't the faintest idea what—then she appeared, and it was all over. And there's the doorbell, and the tenor, I suppose; so of course it's all over now," she sighed, rising to go down-stairs.

As it chanced, however, it was not the tenor, but a message from him—a message that brought dire consternation to the Chairman of the Committee of Arrangements. The tenor had thrown up his part. He could not take it; it was too difficult. He felt that this should be told—at once rather than to worry along for another week or two, and then give up. So he had told it.

"But what shall we do, Miss Greggory?" appealed Billy. "It is a hard part, you know; but if Mr. Tobey can't take it, I don't know who can. We don't want to hire a singer for it, if we can help it. The profits are to go to the Home for Crippled Children, you know," she explained, turning to Arkwright, "and we decided to hire only the accompanist."

An odd expression flitted across Miss Greggory's face.

"Mr. Arkwright used to sing—tenor," she observed quietly.

"As if he didn't now—a perfectly glorious tenor," retorted Billy. "But as if he would take this!"

For only a brief moment did Arkwright hesitate; then blandly he suggested:

"Suppose you try him, and see."

Billy sat suddenly erect.

"Would you, really? Could you—take the time, and all?" she cried.

"Yes, I think I would—under the circumstances," he smiled. "I think I could, too, though I might not be able to attend all the rehearsals. Still, if I find I have to ask permission, I'll endeavor to convince the powers-that-be that singing in this operetta will be just the stepping-stone I need to success in Grand Opera."

"Oh, if you only would take it," breathed Billy, "we'd be so glad!"

"Well," said Arkwright, his eyes on Billy's frankly delighted face, "as I said before—under the circumstances I think I would."

"Thank you! Then it's all beautifully settled," rejoiced Billy, with a happy sigh; and unconsciously she gave Alice Greggory's hand near her a little pat.

In Billy's mind the "circumstances" of Arkwright's acceptance of the part were Alice Greggory and her position as accompanist, of course. Billy would have been surprised indeed—and dismayed—had she known that in Arkwright's mind the "circumstances" were herself, and the fact that she, too, had a part in the operetta, necessitating her presence at rehearsals, and hinting at a delightful comradeship impossible, perhaps, otherwise.

CHAPTER XXIII. THE CAUSE AND BERTRAM

February came The operetta, for which Billy was working so hard, was to be given the twentieth. The Art Exhibition, for which Bertram was preparing his four pictures, was to open the sixteenth, with a private view for specially invited friends the evening before.

On the eleventh day of February Mrs. Greggory and her daughter arrived at Hillside for a ten-days' visit. Not until after a great deal of pleading and argument, however, had Billy been able to bring this about.

"But, my dears, both of you," Billy had at last said to them; "just listen. We shall have numberless rehearsals during those last ten days before the thing comes off. They will be at all hours, and of all lengths. You, Miss Greggory, will have to be on hand for them all, of course, and will have to stay all night several times, probably. You, Mrs. Greggory, ought not to be alone down here. There is no sensible, valid reason why you should not both come out to the house for those ten days; and I shall feel seriously hurt and offended if you do not consent to do it."

"But—my pupils," Alice Greggory had demurred.

"You can go in town from my home at any time to give your lessons, and a little shifting about and arranging for those ten days will enable you to set the hours conveniently one after another, I am sure, so you can attend to several on one trip. Meanwhile your mother will be having a lovely time teaching Aunt Hannah how to knit a new shawl; so you won't have to be worrying about her."

After all, it had been the great good and pleasure which the visit would bring to Mrs. Greggory that had been the final straw to tip the scales. On the eleventh of February, therefore, in the company of the once scorned "Peggy and Mary Jane," Alice Greggory and her mother had arrived at Hillside.

Ever since the first meeting of Alice Greggory and Arkwright, Billy had been sorely troubled by the conduct of the two young people. She had, as she mournfully told herself, been able to make nothing of it. The two were civility itself to each other, but very plainly they were not at ease in each other's company; and Billy, much to her surprise, had to admit that Arkwright did not appear to appreciate the "circumstances" now that he had them. The pair called each other, ceremoniously, "Mr. Arkwright," and "Miss Greggory"—but then, that, of course, did not "signify," Billy declared to herself.

"I suppose you don't ever call him 'Mary Jane,'" she said to the girl, a little mischievously, one day.

"'Mary Jane'? Mr. Arkwright? No, I don't," rejoined Miss Greggory, with an odd smile. Then, after a moment, she added: "I believe his brothers and sisters used to, however."

"Yes, I know," laughed Billy. "We thought he was a real Mary Jane, once." And she told the story of his arrival. "So you see," she finished, when Alice Greggory had done laughing over the tale, "he always will be 'Mary Jane' to us. By the way, what is his name?"

Miss Greggory looked up in surprise.

"Why, it's—" She stopped short, her eyes questioning. "Why, hasn't he ever told you?" she queried.

Billy lifted her chin.

"No. He told us to guess it, and we have guessed everything we can think of, even up to 'Methuselah John'; but he says we haven't hit it yet."

"'Methuselah John,' indeed!" laughed the other, merrily.

"Well, I'm sure that's a nice, solid name," defended Billy, her chin still at a challenging tilt. "If it isn't 'Methuselah John,' what is it, then?"

But Alice Greggory shook her head. She, too, it seemed, could be firm, on occasion. And though she smiled brightly, all she would say, was:

"If he hasn't told you, I sha'n't. You'll have to go to him."

"Oh, well, I can still call him 'Mary Jane,'" retorted Billy, with airy disdain.

All this, however, so far as Billy could see, was not in the least helping along the cause that had become so dear to her—the reuniting of a pair of lovers. It occurred to her then, one day, that perhaps, after all, they were not lovers, and did not wish to be reunited. At this disquieting thought Billy decided, suddenly, to go almost to headquarters. She would speak to Mrs. Greggory if ever the opportunity offered. Great was her joy, therefore, when, a day or two after the Greggorys arrived at the house, Mrs. Greggory's chance reference to Arkwright and her daughter gave Billy the opportunity she sought.

"They used to know each other long ago, Mr. Arkwright tells me," Billy began warily.

"Yes."

The quietly polite monosyllable was not very encouraging, to be sure; but Billy, secure in her conviction that her cause was a righteous one, refused to be daunted.

"I think it was so romantic—their running across each other like this, Mrs. Greggory," she murmured. "And there was a romance, wasn't there? I have just felt in my bones that there was—a romance!"

Billy held her breath. It was what she had meant to say, but now that she had said it, the words seemed very fearsome indeed—to say to Mrs. Greggory. Then Billy remembered her Cause, and took heart—Billy was spelling it now with a capital C.

For a long minute Mrs. Greggory did not answer—for so long a minute that Billy's breath dropped into a fluttering sigh, and her Cause became suddenly "IMPERTINENCE" spelled in black capitals. Then Mrs. Greggory spoke slowly, a little sadly.

"I don't mind saying to you that I did hope, once, that there would be a romance there. They were the best of friends, and they were well-suited to each other in tastes and temperament. I think, indeed, that the romance was well under way (though there was never an engagement) when—" Mrs. Greggory paused and wet her lips. Her voice, when she resumed, carried the stern note so familiar to Billy in her first acquaintance with this woman and her daughter. "As I presume Mr. Arkwright has told you, we have met with many changes in our life—changes which necessitated a new home and a new mode of living. Naturally, under those circumstances, old friends—and old romances—must change, too."

"But, Mrs. Greggory," stammered Billy, "I'm sure Mr. Arkwright would want—" An uplifted hand silenced her peremptorily.

"Mr. Arkwright was very kind, and a gentleman, always," interposed the lady, coldly; "but Judge Greggory's daughter would not allow herself to be placed where apologies for her father would be necessary—ever! There, please, dear Miss Neilson, let us not talk of it any more," begged Mrs. Greggory, brokenly.

"No, indeed, of course not!" cried Billy; but her heart rejoiced.

She understood it all now. Arkwright and Alice Greggory had been almost lovers when the charges against the Judge's honor had plunged the family into despairing humiliation. Then had come the time when, according to Arkwright's own story, the two women had shut themselves indoors, refused to see their friends, and left town as soon as possible. Thus had come the breaking of whatever tie there was between Alice Greggory and Arkwright. Not to have broken it would have meant, for Alice, the placing of herself in a position where, sometime, apologies must be made for her father. This was what Mrs. Greggory had meant—and again, as Billy thought of it, Billy's heart rejoiced.

Was not her way clear now before her? Did she not have it in her power, possibly—even probably—to bring happiness where only sadness was before? As if it would not be a simple thing to rekindle the old flame—to make these two estranged hearts beat as one again!

Not now was the Cause an IMPERTINENCE in tall black letters. It was, instead, a shining beacon in letters of flame guiding straight to victory.

Billy went to sleep that night making plans for Alice Greggory and Arkwright to be thrown together naturally—"just as a matter of course, you know," she said drowsily to herself, all in the dark.

Some three or four miles away down Beacon Street at that moment Bertram Henshaw, in the Strata, was, as it happened, not falling asleep. He was lying broadly and unhappily awake Bertram very frequently lay broadly and unhappily awake these days—or rather nights. He told himself, on these occasions, that it was perfectly natural—indeed it was!—that Billy should be with Arkwright and his friends, the Greggorys, so much. There were the new songs, and the operetta with its rehearsals as a cause for it all. At the same time, deep within his fearful soul was the consciousness that Arkwright, the Greggorys, and the operetta were but Music—Music, the spectre that from the first had dogged his footsteps.

With Billy's behavior toward himself, Bertram could find no fault. She was always her sweet, loyal, lovable self, eager to hear of his work, earnestly solicitous that it should be a success. She even—as he sometimes half-irritably remembered—had once told him that she realized he belonged to Art before he did to himself; and when he had indignantly denied this, she had only laughed and thrown a kiss at him, with the remark that he ought to hear his sister Kate's opinion of that matter. As if he wanted Kate's opinion on that or anything else that concerned him and Billy!

Once, torn by jealousy, and exasperated at the frequent interruptions of their quiet hours together, he had complained openly.

"Actually, Billy, it's worse than Marie's wedding," he declared, "Then it was tablecloths and napkins that could be dumped in a chair. Now it's a girl who wants to rehearse, or a woman that wants a different wig, or a telephone message that the sopranos have quarrelled again. I loathe that operetta!"

Billy laughed, but she frowned, too.

"I know, dear; I don't like that part. I wish they would let me alone when I'm with you! But as for the operetta, it is really a good thing, dear, and you'll say so when you see it. It's going to be a great success—I can say that because my part is only a small one, you know. We shall make lots of money for the Home, too, I'm sure."

"But you're wearing yourself all out with it, dear," scowled Bertram.

"Nonsense! I like it; besides, when I'm doing this I'm not telephoning you to come and amuse me. Just think what a lot of extra time you have for your work!"

"Don't want it," avowed Bertram.

"But the work may," retorted Billy, showing all her dimples. "Never mind, though; it'll all be over after the twentieth. This isn't an understudy like Marie's wedding, you know," she finished demurely.

"Thank heaven for that!" Bertram had breathed fervently. But even as he said the words he grew sick with fear. What if, after all, this were an understudy to what was to come later when Music, his rival, had really conquered?

Bertram knew that however secure might seem Billy's affection for himself, there was still in his own mind a horrid fear lest underneath that security were an unconscious, growing fondness for something he could not give, for some one that he was not—a fondness that would one day cause Billy to awake. As Bertram, in his morbid fancy pictured it, he realized only too well what that awakening would mean to himself.

CHAPTER XXIV. THE ARTIST AND HIS ART

The private view of the paintings and drawings of the Brush and Pencil Club on the evening of the fifteenth was a great success. Society sent its fairest women in frocks that were pictures in themselves. Art sent its severest critics and its most ardent devotees. The Press sent reporters that the World might know what Art and Society were doing, and how they did it.

Before the canvases signed with Bertram Henshaw's name there was always to be found an admiring group representing both Art and Society with the Press on the outskirts to report. William Henshaw, coming unobserved upon one such group, paused a moment to smile at the various more or less disconnected comments.

"What a lovely blue!"

"Marvellous color sense!"

"Now those shadows are—"

"He gets his high lights so—"

"I declare, she looks just like Blanche Payton!"

"Every line there is full of meaning."

"I suppose it's very fine, but—"

"Now, I say, Henshaw is—"

"Is this by the man that's painting Margy Winthrop's portrait?"

"It's idealism, man, idealism!"

"I'm going to have a dress just that shade of blue."

"Isn't that just too sweet!"

"Now for realism, I consider Henshaw—"

"There aren't many with his sensitive, brilliant touch."

"Oh, what a pretty picture!"

William moved on then.

Billy was rapturously proud of Bertram that evening. He was, of course, the centre of congratulations and hearty praise. At his side, Billy, with sparkling eyes, welcomed each smiling congratulation and gloried in every commendatory word she heard.

"Oh, Bertram, isn't it splendid! I'm so proud of you," she whispered softly, when a moment's lull gave her opportunity.

"They're all words, words, idle words," he laughed; but his eyes shone.

"Just as if they weren't all true!" she bridled, turning to greet William, who came up at that moment. "Isn't it fine, Uncle William?" she beamed. "And aren't we proud of him?"

"We are, indeed," smiled the man. "But if you and Bertram want to get the real opinion of this crowd, you should go and stand near one of his pictures five minutes. As a sort of crazy—quilt criticism it can't be beat."

"I know," laughed Bertram. "I've done it, in days long gone."

"Bertram, not really?" cried Billy.

"Sure! As if every young artist at the first didn't don goggles or a false mustache and study the pictures on either side of his own till he could paint them with his eyes shut!"

"And what did you hear?" demanded the girl.

"What didn't I hear?" laughed her lover. "But I didn't do it but once or twice. I lost my head one day and began to argue the question of perspective with a couple of old codgers who were criticizing a bit of foreshortening that was my special pet. I forgot my goggles and sailed in. The game was up then, of course; and I never put them on again. But it was worth a farm to see their faces when I stood 'discovered' as the stage-folk say."

"Serves you right, sir—listening like that," scolded Billy.

Bertram laughed and shrugged his shoulders.

"Well, it cured me, anyhow. I haven't done it since," he declared.

It was some time later, on the way home, that Bertram said:

"It was gratifying, of course, Billy, and I liked it. It would be absurd to say I didn't like the many pleasant words of apparently sincere appreciation I heard to-night. But I couldn't help thinking of the next time—always the next time."

"The next time?" Billy's eyes were slightly puzzled.

"That I exhibit, I mean. The Bohemian Ten hold their exhibition next month, you know. I shall show just one picture—the portrait of Miss Winthrop."

"Oh, Bertram!"

"It'll be 'Oh, Bertram!' then, dear, if it isn't a success," he sighed. "I don't believe you realize yet what that thing is going to mean for me."

"Well, I should think I might," retorted Billy, a little tremulously, "after all I've heard about it. I should think everybody knew you were doing it, Bertram. Actually, I'm not sure Marie's scrub-lady won't ask me some day how Mr. Bertram's picture is coming on!"

"That's the dickens of it, in a way," sighed Bertram, with a faint smile. "I am amazed—and a little frightened, I'll admit—at the universality of the interest. You see, the Winthrops have been pleased to spread it, for one reason or another, and of course many already know of the failures of Anderson and Fullam. That's why, if I should fail—"

"But you aren't going to fail," interposed the girl, resolutely.

"No, I know I'm not. I only said 'if,'" fenced the man, his voice not quite steady.

"There isn't going to be any 'if,'" settled Billy. "Now tell me, when is the exhibition?"

"March twentieth—the private view. Mr. Winthrop is not only willing, but anxious, that I show it. I wasn't sure that he'd want me to—in an exhibition. But it seems he does. His daughter says he has every confidence in the portrait and wants everybody to see it."

"That's where he shows his good sense," declared Billy. Then, with just a touch of constraint, she asked: "And how is the new, latest pose coming on?"

"Very well, I think," answered Bertram, a little hesitatingly. "We've had so many, many interruptions, though, that it is surprising how slow it is moving. In the first place, Miss Winthrop is gone more than half the time (she goes again to-morrow for a week!), and in this portrait I'm not painting a stroke without my model before me. I mean to take no chances, you see; and Miss Winthrop is perfectly willing to give me all the sittings I wish for. Of course, if she hadn't changed the pose and costume so many times, it would have been done long ago—and she knows it."

"Of course—she knows it," murmured Billy, a little faintly, but with a peculiar intonation in her voice.

"And so you see," sighed Bertram, "what the twentieth of March is going to mean for me."

"It's going to mean a splendid triumph!" asserted Billy; and this time her voice was not faint, and it carried only a ring of loyal confidence.

"You blessed comforter!" murmured Bertram, giving with his eyes the caress that his lips would so much have preferred to give—under more propitious circumstances.

CHAPTER XXV. THE OPERETTA

The sixteenth, seventeenth, and eighteenth of February were, for Billy, and for all concerned in the success of the operetta, days of hurry, worry, and feverish excitement, as was to be expected, of course. Each afternoon and every evening saw rehearsals in whole, or in parts. A friend of the Club-president's sister-in-law-a woman whose husband was stage manager of a Boston theatre—had consented to come and "coach" the performers. At her appearance the performers—promptly thrown into nervous spasms by this fearsome nearness to the "real thing"—forgot half their cues, and conducted themselves generally like frightened school children on "piece day," much to their own and every one else's despair. Then, on the evening of the nineteenth, came the final dress rehearsal on the stage of the pretty little hall that had been engaged for the performance of the operetta.

The dress rehearsal, like most of its kind, was, for every one, nothing but a nightmare of discord, discouragement, and disaster. Everybody's nerves were on edge, everybody was sure the thing would be a "flat failure." The soprano sang off the key, the alto forgot to shriek "Beware, beware!" until it was so late there was nothing to beware of; the basso stepped on Billy's trailing frock and tore it; even the tenor, Arkwright himself, seemed to have lost every bit of vim from his acting. The chorus sang "Oh, be joyful!" with dirge-like solemnity, and danced as if legs and feet were made of wood. The lovers, after the fashion of amateur actors from time immemorial, "made love like sticks."

Billy, when the dismal thing had dragged its way through the final note, sat "down front," crying softly in the semi-darkness while she was waiting for Alice Greggory to "run it through just once more" with a pair of tired-faced, fluffy-skirted fairies who could not learn that a duet meant a duet—not two solos, independently hurried or retarded as one's fancy for the moment dictated.

To Billy, just then, life did not look to be even half worth the living. Her head ached, her throat was going-to-be-sore, her shoe hurt, and her dress—the trailing frock that had been under the basso's foot—could not possibly be decently repaired before to-morrow night, she was sure.

Bad as these things were, however, they were only the intimate, immediate woes. Beyond and around them lay others many others. To be sure, Bertram and happiness were supposed to be somewhere in the dim and uncertain future; but between her and them lay all these other woes, chief of which was the unutterable tragedy of to-morrow night.

It was to be a failure, of course. Billy had calmly made up her mind to that, now. But then, she was used to failures, she told herself. Was she not plainly failing every day of her life to bring about even friendship between Alice Greggory and Arkwright? Did they not emphatically and systematically refuse to be "thrown together," either naturally, or unnaturally? And yet—whenever again could she expect such opportunities to further her Cause as had been hers the past few weeks, through the operetta and its rehearsals? Certainly, never again! It had been a failure like all the rest; like the operetta, in particular.

Billy did not mean that any one should know she was crying. She supposed that all the performers except herself and the two earth-bound fairies by the piano with Alice Greggory were gone. She knew that John with Peggy was probably waiting at the door outside, and she hoped that soon the fairies would decide to go home and go to bed, and let other people do the same. For her part, she did not see why they were struggling so hard, anyway. Why needn't they go ahead and sing their duet like two solos if they wanted to? As if a little thing like that could make a feather's weight of difference in the grand total of to-morrow night's wretchedness when the final curtain should have been rung down on their shame!

"Miss Neilson, you aren't—crying!" exclaimed a low voice; and Billy turned to find Arkwright standing by her side in the dim light.

"Oh, no—yes—well, maybe I was, a little," stammered Billy, trying to speak very unconcernedly. "How warm it is in here! Do you think it's going to rain?—that is, outdoors, of course, I mean."

Arkwright dropped into the seat behind Billy and leaned forward, his eyes striving to read the girl's half-averted face. If Billy had turned, she would have seen that Arkwright's own face showed white and a little drawn-looking in the feeble rays from the light by the piano. But Billy did not turn. She kept her eyes steadily averted; and she went on speaking—airy, inconsequential words.

"Dear me, if those girls would only pull together! But then, what's the difference? I supposed you had gone home long ago, Mr. Arkwright."

"Miss Neilson, you are crying!" Arkwright's voice was low and vibrant. "As if anything or anybody in the world could make you cry! Please—you have only to command me, and I will sally forth at once to slay the offender." His words were light, but his voice still shook with emotion.

Billy gave an hysterical little giggle. Angrily she brushed the persistent tears from her eyes.

"All right, then; I'll dub you my Sir Knight," she faltered. "But I'll warn you—you'll have your hands full. You'll have to slay my headache, and my throat-ache, and my shoe that hurts, and the man who stepped on my dress, and—and everybody in the operetta, including myself."

"Everybody—in the operetta!" Arkwright did look a little startled, at this wholesale slaughter.

"Yes. Did you ever see such an awful, awful thing as that was to-night?" moaned the girl.

Arkwright's face relaxed.

"Oh, so that's what it is!" he laughed lightly. "Then it's only a bogy of fear that I've got to slay, after all; and I'll despatch that right now with a single blow. Dress rehearsals always go like that to-night. I've been in a dozen, and I never yet saw one go half decent. Don't you worry. The worse the rehearsal, the better the performance, every time!"

Billy blinked off the tears and essayed a smile as she retorted:

"Well, if that's so, then ours to-morrow night ought to be a—a—"

"A corker," helped out Arkwright, promptly; "and it will be, too. You poor child, you're worn out; and no wonder! But don't worry another bit about the operetta. Now is there anything else I can do for you? Anything else I can slay?"

Billy laughed tremulously.

"N-no, thank you; not that you can—slay, I fancy," she sighed. "That is—not that you will," she amended wistfully, with a sudden remembrance of the Cause, for which he might do so much—if he only would.

Arkwright bent a little nearer. His breath stirred the loose, curling hair behind Billy's ear. His eyes had flashed into sudden fire.

"But you don't know what I'd do if I could," he murmured unsteadily. "If you'd let me tell you—if you only knew the wish that has lain closest to my heart for—"

"Miss Neilson, please," called the despairing voice of one of the earth-bound fairies; "Miss Neilson, you are there, aren't you?"

"Yes, I'm right here," answered Billy, wearily. Arkwright answered, too, but not aloud—which was wise.

"Oh dear! you're tired, I know," wailed the fairy, "but if you would please come and help us just a minute! Could you?"

"Why, yes, of course." Billy rose to her feet, still wearily.

Arkwright touched her arm. She turned and saw his face. It was very white—so white that her eyes widened in surprised questioning.

As if answering the unspoken words, the man shook his head.

"I can't, now, of course," he said. "But there is something I want to say—a story I want to tell you—after to-morrow, perhaps. May I?"

To Billy, the tremor of his voice, the suffering in his eyes, and the "story" he was begging to tell could have but one interpretation: Alice Greggory. Her face, therefore, was a glory of tender sympathy as she reached out her hand in farewell.

"Of course you may," she cried. "Come any time after to-morrow night, please," she smiled encouragingly, as she turned toward the stage.

Behind her, Arkwright stumbled twice as he walked up the incline toward the outer door—stumbled, not because of the semi-darkness of the little theatre, but because of the blinding radiance of a girl's illumined face which he had, a moment before, read all unknowingly exactly wrong.

A little more than twenty-four hours later, Billy Neilson, in her own room, drew a long breath of relief. It was twelve o'clock on the night of the twentieth, and the operetta was over.

To Billy, life was eminently worth living to-night. Her head did not ache, her throat was not sore, her shoe did not hurt, her dress had been mended so successfully by Aunt Hannah, and with such comforting celerity, that long before night one would never have suspected the filmy thing had known the devastating tread of any man's foot. Better yet, the soprano had sung exactly to key, the alto had shrieked "Beware!" to thrilling purpose, Arkwright had shown all his old charm and vim, and the chorus had been prodigies of joyousness and marvels of lightness. Even the lovers had lost their stiffness, while the two earth-bound fairies of the night before had found so amiable a meeting point that their solos sounded, to the uninitiated, very like, indeed, a duet. The operetta was, in short, a glorious and gratifying success, both artistically and financially. Nor was this all that, to Billy, made life worth the living: Arkwright had begged permission that evening to come up the following afternoon to tell her his "story"; and Billy, who was so joyously confident that this story meant the final crowning of her Cause with victory, had given happy consent.

Bertram was to come up in the evening, and Billy was anticipating that, too, particularly: it had been so long since they had known a really free, comfortable evening together, with nothing to interrupt. Doubtless, too, after Arkwright's visit of the afternoon, she would be in a position to tell Bertram the story of the suspended romance between Arkwright and Miss Greggory, and perhaps something, also, of her own efforts to bring the couple together again. On the whole, life did, indeed, look decidedly worth the living as Billy, with a contented sigh, turned over to go to sleep.

CHAPTER XXVI. ARKWRIGHT TELLS ANOTHER STORY

Promptly at the suggested hour on the day after the operetta, Arkwright rang Billy Neilson's doorbell. Promptly, too, Billy herself came into the living-room to greet him.

Billy was in white to-day—a soft, creamy white wool with a touch of black velvet at her throat and in her hair. The man thought she had never looked so lovely: Arkwright was still under the spell wrought by the soft radiance of Billy's face the two times he had mentioned his "story."

Until the night before the operetta Arkwright had been more than doubtful of the way that story would be received, should he ever summon the courage to tell it. Since then his fears had been changed to rapturous hopes. It was very eagerly, therefore, that he turned now to greet Billy as she came into the room.

"Suppose we don't have any music to-day. Suppose we give the whole time up to the story," she smiled brightly, as she held out her hand.

Arkwright's heart leaped; but almost at once it throbbed with a vague uneasiness. He would have preferred to see her blush and be a little shy over that story. Still—there was a chance, of course, that she did not know what the story was. But if that were the case, what of the radiance in her face? What of—Finding himself in a tangled labyrinth that led apparently only to disappointment and disaster, Arkwright pulled himself up with a firm hand.

"You are very kind," he murmured, as he relinquished her fingers and seated himself near her. "You are sure, then, that you wish to hear the story?"

"Very sure," smiled Billy.

Arkwright hesitated. Again he longed to see a little embarrassment in the bright face opposite. Suddenly it came to him, however, that if Billy knew what he was about to say, it would manifestly not be her part to act as if she knew! With a lighter heart, then, he began his story.

"You want it from the beginning?"

"By all means! I never dip into books, nor peek at the ending. I don't think it's fair to the author."

"Then I will, indeed, begin at the beginning," smiled Arkwright, "for I'm specially anxious that you shall be—even more than 'fair' to me." His voice shook a little, but he hurried on. "There's a—girl—in it; a very dear, lovely girl."

"Of course—if it's a nice story," twinkled Billy.

"And—there's a man, too. It's a love story, you see."

"Again of course—if it's interesting." Billy laughed mischievously, but she flushed a little.

"Still, the man doesn't amount to much, after all, perhaps. I might as well own up at the beginning—I'm the man."

"That will do for you to say, as long as you're telling the story," smiled Billy. "We'll let it pass for proper modesty on your part. But I shall say—the personal touch only adds to the interest."

Arkwright drew in his breath.

"We'll hope—it'll really be so," he murmured.

There was a moment's silence. Arkwright seemed to be hesitating what to say.

"Well?" prompted Billy, with a smile. "We have the hero and the heroine; now what happens next? Do you know," she added, "I have always thought that part must bother the story-writers—to get the couple to doing interesting things, after they'd got them introduced."

Arkwright sighed.

"Perhaps—on paper; but, you see, my story has been lived, so far. So it's quite different."

"Very well, then—what did happen?" smiled Billy.

"I was trying to think—of the first thing. You see it began with a picture, a photograph of the girl. Mother had it. I saw it, and wanted it, and—" Arkwright had started to say "and took it." But he stopped with the last two words unsaid. It was not time, yet, he deemed, to tell this girl how much that picture had been to him for so many months past. He hurried on a little precipitately. "You see, I had heard about this girl a lot; and I liked—what I heard."

"You mean—you didn't know her—at the first?" Billy's eyes were surprised. Billy had supposed that Arkwright had always known Alice Greggory.

"No, I didn't know the girl—till afterwards. Before that I was always dreaming and wondering what she would be like."

"Oh!" Billy subsided into her chair, still with the puzzled questioning in her eyes.

"Then I met her."

"Yes?"

"And she was everything and more than I had pictured her."

"And you fell in love at once?" Billy's voice had grown confident again.

"Oh, I was already in love," sighed Arkwright. "I simply sank deeper."

"Oh-h!" breathed Billy, sympathetically. "And the girl?"

"She didn't care—or know—for a long time. I'm not really sure she cares—or knows—even now." Arkwright's eyes were wistfully fixed on Billy's face.

"Oh, but you can't tell, always, about girls," murmured Billy, hurriedly. A faint pink had stolen to her forehead. She was thinking of Alice Greggory, and wondering if, indeed, Alice did care; and if she, Billy, might dare to assure this man—what she believed to be true—that his sweetheart was only waiting for him to come to her and tell her that he loved her.

Arkwright saw the color sweep to Billy's forehead, and took sudden courage. He leaned forward eagerly. A tender light came to his eyes. The expression on his face was unmistakable.

"Billy, do you mean, really, that there is—hope for me?" he begged brokenly.

Billy gave a visible start. A quick something like shocked terror came to her eyes. She drew back and would have risen to her feet had the thought not come to her that twice before she had supposed a man was making love to her, when subsequent events proved that she had been mortifyingly mistaken: once when Cyril had told her of his love for Marie; and again when William had asked her to come back as a daughter to the house she had left desolate.

Telling herself sternly now not to be for the third time a "foolish little simpleton," she summoned all her wits, forced a cheery smile to her lips, and said:

"Well, really, Mr. Arkwright, of course I can't answer for the girl, so I'm not the one to give hope; and—"

"But you are the one," interrupted the man, passionately. "You're the only one! As if from the very first I hadn't loved you, and—"

"No, no, not that—not that! I'm mistaken! I'm not understanding what you mean," pleaded a horror-stricken voice. Billy was on her feet now, holding up two protesting hands, palms outward.

"Miss Neilson, you don't mean—that you haven't known—all this time—that it was you?" The man, now, was on his feet, his eyes hurt and unbelieving, looking into hers.

Billy paled. She began slowly to back away. Her eyes, still fixed on his, carried the shrinking terror of one who sees a horrid vision.

"But you know—you must know that I am not yours to win!" she reproached him sharply. "I'm to be Bertram Henshaw's—wife." From Billy's shocked young lips the word dropped with a ringing force that was at once accusatory and prohibitive. It was as if, by the mere utterance of the word, wife, she had drawn a sacred circle about her and placed herself in sanctuary.

From the blazing accusation in her eyes Arkwright fell back.

"Wife! You are to be Bertram Henshaw's wife!" he exclaimed. There was no mistaking the amazed incredulity on his face.

Billy caught her breath. The righteous indignation in her eyes fled, and a terrified appeal took its place.

"You don't mean that you didn't—know?" she faltered.

There was a moment's silence. A power quite outside herself kept Billy's eyes on Arkwright's face, and forced her to watch the change there from unbelief to belief, and from belief to set misery.

"No, I did not know," said the man then, dully, as he turned, rested his arm on the mantel behind him, and half shielded his face with his hand.

Billy sank into a low chair. Her fingers fluttered nervously to her throat. Her piteous, beseeching eyes were on the broad back and bent head of the man before her.

"But I—I don't see how you could have helped—knowing," she stammered at last. "I don't see how such a thing could have happened that you shouldn't know!"

"I've been trying to think, myself," returned the man, still in a dull, emotionless voice.

"It's been so—so much a matter of course. I supposed everybody knew it," maintained Billy.

"Perhaps that's just it—that it was—so much a matter of course," rejoined the man. "You see, I know very few of your friends, anyway—who would be apt to mention it to me."

"But the announcements—oh, you weren't here then," moaned Billy. "But you must have known that—that he came here a good deal—that we were together so much!"

"To a certain extent, yes," sighed Arkwright. "But I took your friendship with him and his brothers as—as a matter of course. That was my 'matter of course,' you see," he went on bitterly. "I knew you were Mr. William Henshaw's namesake, and Calderwell had told me the story of your coming to them when you were left alone in the world. Calderwell had said, too, that—" Arkwright paused, then hurried on a little constrainedly—"well, he said something that led me to think Mr. Bertram Henshaw was not a marrying man, anyway."

Billy winced and changed color. She had noticed the pause, and she knew very well what it was that Calderwell had said to occasion that pause. Must always she be reminded that no one expected Bertram Henshaw to love any girl—except to paint?

"But—but Mr. Calderwell must know about the engagement—now," she stammered.

"Very likely, but I have not happened to hear from him since my arrival in Boston. We do not correspond."

There was a long silence, then Arkwright spoke again.

"I think I understand now—many things. I wonder I did not see them before; but I never thought of Bertram Henshaw's being—If Calderwell hadn't said—" Again Arkwright stopped with his sentence half complete, and again Billy winced. "I've been a blind fool. I was so intent on my own—I've been a blind fool; that's all," repeated Arkwright, with a break in his voice.

Billy tried to speak, but instead of words, there came only a choking sob.

Arkwright turned sharply.

"Miss Neilson, don't—please," he begged. "There is no need that you should suffer—too."

"But I am so ashamed that such a thing could happen," she faltered. "I'm sure, some way, I must be to blame. But I never thought. I was blind, too. I was wrapped up in my own affairs. I never suspected. I never even thought to suspect! I thought of course you knew. It was just the music that brought us together, I supposed; and you were just like one of the family, anyway. I always thought of you as Aunt Hannah's—" She stopped with a vivid blush.

"As Aunt Hannah's niece, Mary Jane, of course," supplied Arkwright, bitterly, turning back to his old position. "And that was my own fault, too. My name, Miss Neilson, is Michael Jeremiah," he went on wearily, after a moment's hesitation, his voice showing his utter abandonment to despair. "When a boy at school I got heartily sick of the 'Mike' and the 'Jerry' and the even worse 'Tom and Jerry' that my young friends delighted in; so as soon as possible I sought obscurity and peace in 'M. J.' Much to my surprise and annoyance the initials proved to be little better, for they became at once the biggest sort of whet to people's curiosity. Naturally, the more determined persistent inquirers were to know the name, the more determined I became that they shouldn't. All very silly and very foolish, of course. Certainly it seems so now," he finished.

Billy was silent. She was trying to find something, anything, to say, when Arkwright began speaking again, still in that dull, hopeless voice that Billy thought would break her heart.

"As for the 'Mary Jane'—that was another foolishness, of course. My small brothers and sisters originated it; others followed, on occasion, even Calderwell. Perhaps you did not know, but he was the friend who, by his laughing question, 'Why don't you, Mary Jane?' put into my head the crazy scheme of writing to Aunt Hannah and letting her think I was a real Mary Jane. You see what I stooped to do, Miss Neilson, for the chance of meeting and knowing you."

Billy gave a low cry. She had suddenly remembered the beginning of Arkwright's story. For the first time she realized that he had been talking then about herself, not Alice Greggory.

"But you don't mean that you—cared—that I was the—" She could not finish.

Arkwright turned from the mantel with a gesture of utter despair.

"Yes, I cared then. I had heard of you. I had sung your songs. I was determined to meet you. So I came—and met you. After that I was more determined than ever to win you. Perhaps you see, now, why I was so blind to—to any other possibility. But it doesn't do any good—to talk like this. I understand now. Only, please, don't blame yourself," he begged as he saw her eyes fill with tears. The next moment he was gone.

Billy had turned away and was crying softly, so she did not see him go.

CHAPTER XXVII. THE THING THAT WAS THE TRUTH

Bertram called that evening. Billy had no story now to tell—nothing of the interrupted romance between Alice Greggory and Arkwright. Billy carefully, indeed, avoided mentioning Arkwright's name.

Ever since the man's departure that afternoon, Billy had been frantically trying to assure herself that she was not to blame; that she would not be supposed to know he cared for her; that it had all been as he said it was—his foolish blindness. But even when she had partially comforted herself by these assertions, she could not by any means escape the haunting vision of the man's stern-set, suffering face as she had seen it that afternoon; nor could she keep from weeping at the memory of the words he had said, and at the thought that never again could their pleasant friendship be quite the same—if, indeed, there could be any friendship at all between them.

But if Billy expected that her red eyes, pale cheeks, and generally troubled appearance and unquiet manner were to be passed unnoticed by her lover's keen eyes that evening, she found herself much mistaken.

"Sweetheart, what is the matter?" demanded Bertram resolutely, at last, when his more indirect questions had been evasively turned aside. "You can't make me think there isn't something the trouble, because I know there is!"

"Well, then, there is, dear," smiled Billy, tearfully; "but please just don't let us talk of it. I—I want to forget it. Truly I do."

"But I want to know so I can forget it," persisted Bertram. "What is it? Maybe I could help."

She shook her head with a little frightened cry.

"No, no—you can't help—really."

"But, sweetheart, you don't know. Perhaps I could. Won't you tell me about it?"

Billy looked distressed.

"I can't, dear—truly. You see, it isn't quite mine—to tell."

"Not yours!"

"Not—entirely."

"But it makes you feel bad?"

"Yes—very."

"Then can't I know that part?"

"Oh, no—no, indeed, no! You see—it wouldn't be fair—to the other."

Bertram stared a little. Then his mouth set into stern lines.

"Billy, what are you talking about? Seems to me I have a right to know."

Billy hesitated. To her mind, a girl who would tell of the unrequited love of a man for herself, was unspeakably base. To tell Bertram Arkwright's love story was therefore impossible. Yet, in some way, she must set Bertram's mind at rest.

"Dearest," she began slowly, her eyes wistfully pleading, "just what it is, I can't tell you. In a way it's another's secret, and I don't feel that I have the right to tell it. It's just something that I learned this afternoon."

"But it has made you cry!"

"Yes. It made me feel very unhappy."

"Then—it was something you couldn't help?"

To Bertram's surprise, the face he was watching so intently flushed scarlet.

"No, I couldn't help it—now; though I might have—once." Billy spoke this last just above her breath. Then she went on, beseechingly: "Bertram, please, please don't talk of it any more. It—it's just spoiling our happy evening together!"

Bertram bit his lip, and drew a long sigh.

"All right, dear; you know best, of course—since I don't know anything about it," he finished a little stiffly.

Billy began to talk then very brightly of Aunt Hannah and her shawls, and of a visit she had made to Cyril and Marie that morning.

"And, do you know? Aunt Hannah's clock has done a good turn, at last, and justified its existence. Listen," she cried gayly. "Marie had a letter from her mother's Cousin Jane. Cousin Jane couldn't sleep nights, because she was always lying awake to find out just what time it was; so Marie had written her about Aunt Hannah's clock. And now this Cousin Jane has fixed her clock, and she sleeps like a top, just because she knows there'll never be but half an hour that she doesn't know what time it is!"

Bertram smiled, and murmured a polite "Well, I'm sure that's fine!"; but the words were plainly abstracted, and the frown had not left his brow. Nor did it quite leave till some time later, when Billy, in answer to a question of his about another operetta, cried, with a shudder:

"Mercy, I hope not, dear! I don't want to hear the word 'operetta' again for a year!"

Bertram smiled, then, broadly. He, too, would be quite satisfied not to hear the word "operetta" for a year. Operetta, to Bertram, meant interruptions, interferences, and the constant presence of Arkwright, the Greggorys, and innumerable creatures who wished to rehearse or to change wigs—all of which Bertram abhorred. No wonder, therefore, that he smiled, and that the frown disappeared from his brow. He thought he saw, ahead, serene, blissful days for Billy and himself.

As the days, however, began to pass, one by one, Bertram Henshaw found them to be anything but serene and blissful. The operetta, with its rehearsals and its interruptions, was gone, certainly; but he was becoming seriously troubled about Billy.

Billy did not act natural. Sometimes she seemed like her old self; and he breathed more freely, telling himself that his fears were groundless. Then would come the haunting shadow to her eyes, the droop to her mouth, and the nervousness to her manner that he so dreaded. Worse yet, all this seemed to be connected in some strange way with Arkwright. He found this out by accident one day. She had been talking and laughing brightly about something, when he chanced to introduce Arkwright's name.

"By the way, where is Mary Jane these days?" he asked then.

"I don't know, I'm sure. He hasn't been here lately," murmured Billy, reaching for a book on the table.

At a peculiar something in her voice, he had looked up quickly, only to find, to his great surprise, that her face showed a painful flush as she bent over the book in her hand.

He had said nothing more at the time, but he had not forgotten. Several times, after that, he had introduced the man's name, and never had it failed to bring a rush of color, a biting of the lip, or a quick change of position followed always by the troubled eyes and nervous manner that he had learned to dread. He noticed then that never, of her own free will, did she herself mention the man; never did she speak of him with the old frank lightness as "Mary Jane."

By casual questions asked from time to time, Bertram had learned that Arkwright never came there now, and that the song-writing together had been given up. Curiously enough, this discovery, which would once have filled Bertram with joy, served now only to deepen his distress. That there was anything inconsistent in the fact that he was more frightened now at the man's absence than he had been before at his presence, did not occur to him. He knew only that he was frightened, and badly frightened.

Bertram had not forgotten the evening after the operetta, and Billy's tear-stained face on that occasion. He dated the whole thing, in fact, from that evening. He fell to wondering one day if that, too, had anything to do with Arkwright. He determined then to find out. Shamelessly—for the good of the cause—he set a trap for Billy's unwary feet.

Very adroitly one day he led the talk straight to Arkwright; then he asked abruptly:

"Where is the chap, I wonder! Why, he hasn't shown up once since the operetta, has he?"

Billy, always truthful,—and just now always embarrassed when Arkwright's name was mentioned,—walked straight into the trap.

"Oh, yes; well, he was here once—the day after the operetta. I haven't seen him since."

Bertram answered a light something, but his face grew a little white. Now that the trap had been sprung and the victim caught, he almost wished that he had not set any trap at all.

He knew now it was true. Arkwright had been with Billy the day after the operetta, and her tears and her distress that evening had been caused by something Arkwright had said. It was Arkwright's secret that she could not tell. It was Arkwright to whom she must be fair. It was Arkwright's sorrow that she "could not help—now."

Naturally, with these tools in his hands, and aided by days of brooding and nights of sleeplessness, it did not take Bertram long to fashion The Thing that finally loomed before him as The Truth.

He understood it all now. Music had conquered. Billy and Arkwright had found that they loved each other. On the day after the operetta, they had met, and had had some sort of scene together—doubtless Arkwright had declared his love. That was the "secret" that Billy could not tell and be "fair." Billy, of course,—loyal little soul that she was,—had sent him away at once. Was her hand not already pledged? That was why she could not "help it-now." (Bertram writhed in agony at the thought.) Since that meeting Arkwright had not been near the house. Billy had found, however, that her heart had gone with Arkwright; hence the shadow in her eyes, the nervousness in her manner, and the embarrassment that she always showed at the mention of his name.

That Billy was still outwardly loyal to himself, and that she still kept to her engagement, did not surprise Bertram in the least. That was like Billy. Bertram had not forgotten how, less than a year before, this same Billy had held herself loyal and true to an engagement with William, because a wretched mistake all around had caused her to give her promise to be William's wife under the impression that she was carrying out William's dearest wish. Bertram remembered her face as it had looked all those long summer days while her heart was being slowly broken; and he thought he could see that same look in her eyes now. All of which only goes to prove with what woeful skill Bertram had fashioned this Thing that was looming before him as The Truth.

The exhibition of "The Bohemian Ten" was to open with a private view on the evening of the twentieth of March. Bertram Henshaw's one contribution was to be his portrait of Miss Marguerite Winthrop—the piece of work that had come to mean so much to him; the piece of work upon which already he felt the focus of multitudes of eyes.

Miss Winthrop was in Boston now, and it was during these early March days that Bertram was supposed to be putting in his best work on the portrait; but, unfortunately, it was during these same early March days that he was engaged, also, in fashioning The Thing—and the two did not harmonize.

The Thing, indeed, was a jealous creature, and would brook no rival. She filled his eyes with horrid visions, and his brain with sickening thoughts. Between him and his model she flung a veil of fear; and she set his hand to trembling, and his brush to making blunders with the paints on his palette.

Bertram saw The Thing, and saw, too, the grievous result of her presence. Despairingly he fought against her and her work; but The Thing had become full grown now, and was The Truth. Hence she was not to be banished. She even, in a taunting way, seemed sometimes to be justifying her presence, for she reminded him:

"After all, what's the difference? What do you care for this, or anything again if Billy is lost to you?"

But the artist told himself fiercely that he did care—that he must care—for his work; and he struggled—how he struggled!—to ignore the horrid visions and the sickening thoughts, and to pierce the veil of fear so that his hand might be steady and his brush regain its skill.

And so he worked. Sometimes he let his work remain. Sometimes one hour saw only the erasing of what the hour before had wrought. Sometimes the elusive something in Marguerite Winthrop's face seemed right at the tip of his brush—on the canvas, even. He saw success then so plainly that for a moment it almost—but not quite—blotted out The Thing. At other times that elusive something on the high-bred face of his model was a veritable will-o'-the-wisp, refusing to be caught and held, even in his eye. The artist knew then that his picture would be hung with Anderson's and Fullam's.

But the portrait was, irrefutably, nearing completion, and it was to be exhibited the twentieth of the month. Bertram knew these for facts.

CHAPTER XXVIII. BILLY TAKES HER TURN

If for Billy those first twenty days of March did not carry quite the tragedy they contained for Bertram, they were, nevertheless, not really happy ones. She was vaguely troubled by a curious something in Bertram's behavior that she could not name; she was grieved over Arkwright's sorrow, and she was constantly probing her own past conduct to see if anywhere she could find that she was to blame for that sorrow. She missed, too, undeniably, Arkwright's cheery presence, and the charm and inspiration of his music. Nor was she finding it easy to give satisfactory answers to the questions Aunt Hannah, William, and Bertram so often asked her as to where Mary Jane was.

Even her music was little comfort to her these days. She was not writing anything. There was no song in her heart to tempt her to write. Arkwright's new words that he had brought her were out of the question, of course. They had been put away with the manuscript of the completed song, which had not, fortunately, gone to the publishers. Billy had waited, intending to send them together. She was so glad, now, that she had waited. Just once, since Arkwright's last call, she had tried to sing that song. But she had stopped at the end of the first two lines. The full meaning of those words, as coming from Arkwright, had swept over her then, and she had snatched up the manuscript and hidden it under the bottom pile of music in her cabinet ... And she had presumed to sing that love song to Bertram!

Arkwright had written Billy once—a kind, courteous, manly note that had made her cry. He had begged her again not to blame herself, and he had said that he hoped he should be strong enough sometime to wish to call occasionally—if she were willing—and renew their pleasant hours with their music; but, for the present, he knew there was nothing for him to do but to stay away. He had signed himself "Michael Jeremiah Arkwright"; and to Billy that was the most pathetic thing in the letter—it sounded so hopeless and dreary to one who knew the jaunty "M. J."

Alice Greggory, Billy saw frequently. Billy and Aunt Hannah were great friends with the Greggorys now, and had been ever since the Greggorys' ten-days' visit at Hillside. The cheery little cripple, with the gentle tap, tap, tap of her crutches, had won everybody's heart the very first day; and Alice was scarcely less of a favorite, after the sunny friendliness of Hillside had thawed her stiff reserve into naturalness.

Billy had little to say to Alice Greggory of Arkwright. Billy was no longer trying to play Cupid's assistant. The Cause, for which she had so valiantly worked, had been felled by Arkwright's own hand—but that there were still some faint stirrings of life in it was evidenced by Billy's secret delight when one day Alice Greggory chanced to mention that Arkwright had called the night before upon her and her mother.

"He brought us news of our old home," she explained a little hurriedly, to Billy. "He had heard from his mother, and he thought some things she said would be interesting to us."

"Of course," murmured Billy, carefully excluding from her voice any hint of the delight she felt, but hoping, all the while, that Alice would continue the subject.

Alice, however, had nothing more to say; and Billy was left in entire ignorance of what the news was that Arkwright had brought. She suspected, though, that it had something to do with Alice's father—certainly she hoped that it had; for if Arkwright had called to tell it, it must be good.

Billy had found a new home for the Greggorys; although at first they had drawn sensitively back, and had said that they preferred to remain where they were, they had later gratefully accepted it. A little couple from South Boston, to whom Billy had given a two weeks' outing the summer before, had moved into town and taken a flat in the South End. They had two extra rooms which they had told Billy they would like to let for light house-keeping, if only they knew just the right people to take into such close quarters with themselves. Billy at once thought of the Greggorys, and spoke of them. The little couple were delighted, and the Greggorys were scarcely less so when they at last became convinced that only a very little more money than they were already paying would give themselves a much pleasanter home, and would at the same time be a real boon to two young people who were trying to meet expenses. So the change was made, and general happiness all round had resulted—so much so, that Bertram had said to Billy, when he heard of it:

"It looks as if this was a case where your cake is frosted on both sides."

"Nonsense! This isn't frosting—it's business," Billy had laughed.

"And the new pupils you have found for Miss Alice—they're business, too, I suppose?"

"Certainly," retorted Billy, with decision. Then she had given a low laugh and said: "Mercy! If Alice Greggory thought it was anything but business, I verily believe she would refuse every one of the new pupils, and begin to-night to carry back the tables and chairs herself to those wretched rooms she left last month!"

Bertram had smiled, but the smile had been a fleeting one, and the brooding look of gloom that Billy had noticed so frequently, of late, had come back to his eyes.

Billy was not a little disturbed over Bertram these days. He did not seem to be his natural, cheery self at all. He talked little, and what he did say seldom showed a trace of his usually whimsical way of putting things. He was kindness itself to her, and seemed particularly anxious to please her in every way; but she frequently found his eyes fixed on her with a sombre questioning that almost frightened her. The more she thought of it, the more she wondered what the question was, that he did not dare to ask; and whether it was of herself or himself that he would ask it—if he did dare. Then, with benumbing force, one day, a possible solution of the mystery came to her, he had found out that it was true (what all his friends had declared of him)—he did not really love any girl, except to paint!

The minute this thought came to her, Billy thrust it indignantly away. It was disloyal to Bertram and unworthy of herself, even to think such a thing. She told herself then that it was only the portrait of Miss Winthrop that was troubling him. She knew that he was worried over that. He had confessed to her that actually sometimes he was beginning to fear his hand had lost its cunning. As if that were not enough to bring the gloom to any man's face—to any artist's!

No sooner, however, had Billy arrived at this point in her mental argument, than a new element entered—her old lurking jealousy, of which she was heartily ashamed, but which she had never yet been able quite to subdue; her jealousy of the beautiful girl with the beautiful name (not Billy), whose portrait had needed so much time and so many sittings to finish. What if Bertram had found that he loved her? What if that were why his hand had lost its cunning—because, though loving her, he realized that he was bound to another, Billy herself?

This thought, too, Billy cast from her at once as again disloyal and unworthy. But both thoughts, having once entered her brain, had made for themselves roads over which the second passing was much easier than the first—as Billy found to her sorrow. Certainly, as the days went by, and as Bertram's face and manner became more and more a tragedy of suffering, Billy found it increasingly difficult to keep those thoughts from wearing their roads of suspicion into horrid deep ruts of certainty.

Only with William and Marie, now, could Billy escape from it all. With William she sought new curios and catalogued the old. With Marie she beat eggs and whipped cream in the shining kitchen, and tried to think that nothing in the world mattered except that the cake in the oven should not fall.

CHAPTER XXIX. KATE WRITES A LETTER

Bertram feared that he knew, before the portrait was hung, that it was a failure. He was sure that he knew it on the evening of the twentieth when he encountered the swiftly averted eyes of some of his artist friends, and saw the perplexed frown on the faces of others. But he knew, afterwards, that he did not really know it—till he read the newspapers during the next few days.

There was praise—oh, yes; the faint praise that kills. There was some adverse criticism, too; but it was of the light, insincere variety that is given to mediocre work by unimportant artists. Then, here and there, appeared the signed critiques of the men whose opinion counted—and Bertram knew that he had failed. Neither as a work of art, nor as a likeness, was the portrait the success that Henshaw's former work would seem to indicate that it should have been. Indeed, as one caustic pen put it, if this were to be taken as a sample of what was to follow—then the famous originator of "The Face of a Girl" had "a most distinguished future behind him."

Seldom, if ever before, had an exhibited portrait attracted so much attention. As Bertram had said, uncounted eyes were watching for it before it was hung, because it was a portrait of the noted beauty, Marguerite Winthrop, and because two other well-known artists had failed where he, Bertram Henshaw, was hoping to succeed. After it was hung, and the uncounted eyes had seen it—either literally, or through the eyes of the critics—interest seemed rather to grow than to lessen, for other uncounted eyes wanted to see what all the fuss was about, anyway. And when these eyes had seen, their owners talked. Nor did they, by any means, all talk against the portrait. Some were as loud in its praise as were others in its condemnation; all of which, of course, but helped to attract more eyes to the cause of it all.

For Bertram and his friends these days were, naturally, trying ones. William finally dreaded to open his newspaper. (It had become the fashion, when murders and divorces were scarce, occasionally to "feature" somebody's opinion of the Henshaw portrait, on the first page—something that had almost never been known to happen before.) Cyril, according to Marie, played "perfectly awful things on his piano every day, now." Aunt Hannah had said "Oh, my grief and conscience!" so many times that it melted now into a wordless groan whenever a new unfriendly criticism of the portrait met her indignant eyes.

Of all Bertram's friends, Billy, perhaps not unnaturally, was the angriest. Not only did she, after a time, refuse to read the papers, but she refused even to allow certain ones to be brought into the house, foolish and unreasonable as she knew this to be.

As to the artist himself, Bertram's face showed drawn lines and his eyes sombre shadows, but his words and manner carried a stolid indifference that to Billy was at once heartbreaking and maddening.

"But, Bertram, why don't you do something? Why don't you say something? Why don't you act something?" she burst out one day.

The artist shrugged his shoulders.

"But, my dear, what can I say, or do, or act?" he asked.

"I don't know, of course," sighed Billy. "But I know what I'd like to do. I should like to go out and—fight somebody!"

So fierce were words and manner, coupled as they were with a pair of gentle eyes ablaze and two soft little hands doubled into menacing fists, that Bertram laughed.

"What a fiery little champion it is, to be sure," he said tenderly. "But as if fighting could do any good—in this case!"

Billy's tense muscles relaxed. Her eyes filled with tears.

"No, I don't suppose it would," she choked, beginning to cry, so that Bertram had to turn comforter.

"Come, come, dear," he begged; "don't take it so to heart. It's not so bad, after all. I've still my good right hand left, and we'll hope there's something in it yet—that'll be worth while."

"But this one isn't bad," stormed Billy. "It's splendid! I'm sure, I think it's a b-beautiful portrait, and I don't see what people mean by talking so about it!"

Bertram shook his head. His eyes grew sombre again.

"Thank you, dear. But I know—and you know, really—that it isn't a splendid portrait. I've done lots better work than that."

"Then why don't they look at those, and let this alone?" wailed Billy, with indignation.

"Because I deliberately put up this for them to see," smiled the artist, wearily.

Billy sighed, and twisted in her chair.

"What does—Mr. Winthrop say?" she asked at last, in a faint voice.

Bertram lifted his head.

"Mr. Winthrop's been a trump all through, dear. He's already insisted on paying for this—and he's ordered another."

"Another!"

"Yes. The old fellow never minces his words, as you may know. He came to me one day, put his hand on my shoulder, and said tersely: 'Will you give me another, same terms? Go in, boy, and win. Show 'em! I lost the first ten thousand I made. I didn't the next!' That's all he said. Before I could even choke out an answer he was gone. Gorry! talk about his having a 'heart of stone'! I don't believe another man in the country would have done that—and done it in the way he did—in the face of all this talk," finished Bertram, his eyes luminous with feeling.

Billy hesitated.

"Perhaps—his daughter—influenced him—some."

"Perhaps," nodded Bertram. "She, too, has been very kind, all the way through."

Billy hesitated again.

"But I thought—it was going so splendidly," she faltered, in a half-stifled voice.

"So it was—at the first."

"Then what—ailed it, at the last, do you suppose?" Billy was holding her breath till he should answer.

The man got to his feet.

"Billy, don't—don't ask me," he begged. "Please don't let's talk of it any more. It can't do any good! I just flunked—that's all. My hand failed me. Maybe I tried too hard. Maybe I was tired. Maybe something—troubled me. Never mind, dear, what it was. It can do no good even to think of that—now. So just let's—drop it, please, dear," he finished, his face working with emotion.

And Billy dropped it—so far as words were concerned; but she could not drop it from her thoughts—specially after Kate's letter came.

Kate's letter was addressed to Billy, and it said, after speaking of various other matters:

"And now about poor Bertram's failure." (Billy frowned. In Billy's presence no one was allowed to say "Bertram's failure"; but a letter has a most annoying privilege of saying what it pleases without let or hindrance, unless one tears it up—and a letter destroyed unread remains always such a tantalizing mystery of possibilities! So Billy let the letter talk.) "Of course we have heard of it away out here. I do wish if Bertram must paint such famous people, he would manage to flatter them up—in the painting, I mean, of course—enough so that it might pass for a success!

"The technical part of all this criticism I don't pretend to understand in the least; but from what I hear and read, he must, indeed, have made a terrible mess of it, and of course I'm very sorry—and some surprised, too, for usually he paints such pretty pictures!

"Still, on the other hand, Billy, I'm not surprised. William says that Bertram has been completely out of fix over something, and as gloomy as an owl, for weeks past; and of course, under those circumstances, the poor boy could not be expected to do good work.

Now William, being a man, is not supposed to understand what the trouble is. But I, being a woman, can see through a pane of glass when it's held right up before me; and I can guess, of course, that a woman is at the bottom of it—she always is!—and that you, being his special fancy at the moment" (Billy almost did tear the letter now—but not quite), "are that woman.

"Now, Billy, you don't like such frank talk, of course; but, on the other hand, I know you do not want to ruin the dear boy's career. So, for heaven's sake, if you two have been having one of those quarrels that lovers so delight in—do, please, for the good of the cause, make up quick, or else quarrel harder and break it off entirely—which, honestly, would be the better way, I think, all around.

"There, there, my dear child, don't bristle up! I am very fond of you, and would dearly love to have you for a sister—if you'd only take William, as you should! But, as you very well know, I never did approve of this last match at all, for either of your sakes.

"He can't make you happy, my dear, and you can't make him happy. Bertram never was—and never will be—a marrying man. He's too temperamental—too thoroughly wrapped up in his Art. Girls have never meant anything to him but a beautiful picture to paint. And they never will. They can't. He's made that way. Listen! I can prove it to you. Up to this winter he's always been a care-free, happy, jolly fellow, and you know what beautiful work he has done. Never before has he tied himself to any one girl till last fall. Then you two entered into this absurd engagement.

"Now what has it been since? William wrote me himself not a fortnight ago that he'd been worried to death over Bertram for weeks past, he's been so moody, so irritable, so fretted over his work, so unlike himself. And his picture has failed dismally. Of course William doesn't understand; but I do. I know you've probably quarrelled, or something. You know how flighty and unreliable you can be sometimes, Billy, and I don't say that to mean anything against you, either—that's your way. You're just as temperamental in your art, music, as Bertram is in his. You're utterly unsuited to him. If Bertram is to marry anybody, it should be some quiet, staid, sensible girl who would be a help to him. But when I think of you two flyaway flutterbudgets marrying—!

"Now, for heaven's sake, Billy, do make up or something—and do it now. Don't, for pity's sake, let Bertram ever put out another such a piece of work to shame us all like this. Do you want to ruin his career?

"Faithfully yours,
"KATE HARTWELL.
"P. S. I think William's the one for you. He's devoted to you, and his quiet, sensible affection is just what your temperament needs. I always thought William was the one for you. Think it over.
"P. S. No. 2. You can see by the above that it isn't you I'm objecting to, my dear. It's just you-and-Bertram.
"K."

CHAPTER XXX. "I'VE HINDERED HIM"

Billy was shaking with anger and terror by the time she had finished reading Kate's letter. Anger was uppermost at the moment, and with one sweeping wrench of her trembling fingers she tore the closely written sheets straight through the middle, and flung them into the little wicker basket by her desk. Then she went down-stairs and played her noisiest, merriest Tarantella, and tried to see how fast she could make her fingers fly.

But Billy could not, of course, play tarantellas all day; and even while she did play them she could not forget that waste-basket up-stairs, and the horror it contained. The anger was still uppermost, but the terror was prodding her at every turn, and demanding to know just what it was that Kate had written in that letter, anyway. It is not strange then, perhaps, that before two hours passed, Billy went up-stairs, took the letter from the basket, matched together the torn half-sheets and forced her shrinking eyes to read every word again-just to satisfy that terror which would not be silenced.

At the end of the second reading, Billy reminded herself with stern calmness that it was only Kate, after all; that nobody ought to mind what Kate said; that certainly she, Billy, ought not—after the experience she had already had with her unpleasant interference! Kate did not know what she was talking about, anyway. This was only another case of her trying "to manage." She did so love to manage—everything!

At this point Billy got out her pen and paper and wrote to Kate.

It was a formal, cold little letter, not at all the sort that Billy's friends usually received. It thanked Kate for her advice, and for her "kind willingness" to have Billy for a sister; but it hinted that perhaps Kate did not realize that as long as Billy was the one who would have to live with the chosen man, it would be pleasanter to take the one Billy loved, which happened in this case to be Bertram—not William. As for any "quarrel" being the cause of whatever fancied trouble there was with the new picture—the letter scouted that idea in no uncertain terms. There had been no suggestion of a quarrel even once since the engagement.

Then Billy signed her name and took the letter out to post immediately.

For the first few minutes after the letter had been dropped into the green box at the corner, Billy held her head high, and told herself that the matter was now closed. She had sent Kate a courteous, dignified, conclusive, effectual answer, and she thought with much satisfaction of the things she had said.

Very soon, however, she began to think—not so much of what she had said—but of what Kate had said. Many of Kate's sentences were unpleasantly vivid in her mind. They seemed, indeed, to stand out in letters of flame, and they began to burn, and burn, and burn. These were some of them:

"William says that Bertram has been completely out of fix over something, and as gloomy as an owl for weeks past."

"A woman is at the bottom of it—... you are that woman."

"You can't make him happy."

"Bertram never was—and never will be—a marrying man."

"Girls have never meant anything to him but a beautiful picture to paint. And they never will."

"Up to this winter he's always been a carefree, happy, jolly fellow, and you know what beautiful work he has done. Never before has he tied himself to any one girl until last fall."

"Now what has it been since?"

"He's been so moody, so irritable, so fretted over his work, so unlike himself; and his picture has failed, dismally."

"Do you want to ruin his career?"

Billy began to see now that she had not really answered Kate's letter at all. The matter was not closed. Her reply had been, perhaps, courteous and dignified—but it had not been conclusive nor effectual.

Billy had reached home now, and she was crying. Bertram had acted strangely, of late. Bertram had seemed troubled over something. His picture had—With a little shudder Billy tossed aside these thoughts, and dug at her teary eyes with a determined hand. Fiercely she told herself that the matter was settled. Very scornfully she declared that it was "only Kate," after all, and that she would not let Kate make her unhappy again! Forthwith she picked up a current magazine and began to read.

As it chanced, however, even here Billy found no peace; for the first article she opened to was headed in huge black type:

"MARRIAGE AND THE ARTISTIC TEMPERAMENT."

With a little cry Billy flung the magazine far from her, and picked up another. But even "The Elusiveness of Chopin," which she found here, could not keep her thoughts nor her eyes from wandering to the discarded thing in the corner, lying ignominiously face down with crumpled, out-flung leaves.

Billy knew that in the end she should go over and pick that magazine up, and read that article from beginning to end. She was not surprised, therefore, when she did it—but she was not any the happier for having done it.

The writer of the article did not approve of marriage and the artistic temperament. He said the artist belonged to his Art, and to posterity through his Art. The essay fairly bristled with many-lettered words and high-sounding phrases, few of which Billy really understood. She did understand enough, however, to feel, guiltily, when the thing was finished, that already she had married Bertram, and by so doing had committed a Crime. She had slain Art, stifled Ambition, destroyed Inspiration, and been a nuisance generally. In consequence of which Bertram would henceforth and forevermore be doomed to Littleness.

Naturally, in this state of mind, and with this vision before her, Billy was anything but her bright, easy self when she met Bertram an hour or two later. Naturally, too, Bertram, still the tormented victim of the bugaboo his jealous fears had fashioned, was just in the mood to place the worst possible construction on his sweetheart's very evident unhappiness. With sighs, unspoken questions, and frequently averted eyes, therefore, the wretched evening passed, a pitiful misery to them both.

During the days that followed, Billy thought that the world itself must be in league with Kate, so often did she encounter Kate's letter masquerading under some thin disguise. She did not stop to realize that because she was so afraid she would find it, she did find it. In the books she read, in the plays she saw, in the chance words she heard spoken by friend or stranger—always there was something to feed her fears in one way or another. Even in a yellowed newspaper that had covered the top shelf in her closet she found one day a symposium on whether or not an artist's wife should be an artist; and she shuddered—but she read every opinion given.

Some writers said no, and some, yes; and some said it all depended—on the artist and his wife. Billy found much food for thought, some for amusement, and a little that made for peace of mind. On the whole it opened up a new phase of the matter, perhaps. At all events, upon finishing it she almost sobbed:

"One would think that just because I write a song now and then, I was going to let Bertram starve, and go with holes in his socks and no buttons on his clothes!"

It was that afternoon that Billy went to see Marie; but even there she did not escape, for the gentle Marie all unknowingly added her mite to the woeful whole.

Billy found Marie in tears.

"Why, Marie!" she cried in dismay.

"Sh-h!" warned Marie, turning agonized eyes toward the closed door of Cyril's den.

"But, dear, what is it?" begged Billy, with no less dismay, but with greater caution.

"Sh-h!" admonished Marie again.

On tiptoe, then, she led the way to a room at the other end of the tiny apartment. Once there; she explained in a more natural tone of voice:

"Cyril's at work on a new piece for the piano."

"Well, what if he is?" demanded Billy. "That needn't make you cry, need it?"

"Oh, no—no, indeed," demurred Marie, in a shocked voice.

"Well, then, what is it?"

Marie hesitated; then, with the abandon of a hurt child that longs for sympathy, she sobbed:

"It—it's just that I'm afraid, after all, that I'm not good enough for Cyril."

Billy stared frankly.

"Not good enough, Marie Henshaw! Whatever in the world do you mean?"

"Well, not good for him, then. Listen! To-day, I know, in lots of ways I must have disappointed him. First, he put on some socks that I'd darned. They were the first since our marriage that I'd found to darn, and I'd been so proud and—and happy while I was darning them. But—but he took 'em off right after breakfast and threw 'em in a corner. Then he put on a new pair, and said that I—I needn't darn any more; that it made—bunches. Billy, my darns—bunches!" Marie's face and voice were tragic.

"Nonsense, dear! Don't let that fret you," comforted Billy, promptly, trying not to laugh too hard. "It wasn't your darns; it was just darns—anybody's darns. Cyril won't wear darned socks. Aunt Hannah told me so long ago, and I said then there'd be a tragedy when you found it out. So don't worry over that."

"Oh, but that isn't all," moaned Marie. "Listen! You know how quiet he must have everything when he's composing—and he ought to have it, too! But I forgot, this morning, and put on some old shoes that didn't have any rubber heels, and I ran the carpet sweeper, and I rattled tins in the kitchen. But I never thought a thing until he opened his door and asked me please to change my shoes and let the—the confounded dirt go, and didn't I have any dishes in the house but what were made of that abominable tin s-stuff," she finished in a wail of misery.

Billy burst into a ringing laugh, but Marie's aghast face and upraised hand speedily reduced it to a convulsive giggle.

"You dear child! Cyril's always like that when he's composing," soothed Billy. "I supposed you knew it, dear. Don't you fret! Run along and make him his favorite pudding, and by night both of you will have forgotten there ever were such things in the world as tins and shoes and carpet sweepers that clatter."

Marie shook her head. Her dismal face did not relax.

"You don't understand," she moaned. "It's myself. I've hindered him!" She brought out the word with an agony of slow horror. "And only to-day I read—here, look!" she faltered, going to the table and picking up with shaking hands a magazine.

Billy recognized it by the cover at once—another like it had been flung not so long ago by her own hand into the corner. She was not surprised, therefore, to see very soon at the end of Marie's trembling finger:

"Marriage and the Artistic Temperament."

Billy did not give a ringing laugh this time. She gave an involuntary little shudder, though she tried valiantly to turn it all off with a light word of scorn, and a cheery pat on Marie's heaving shoulders. But she went home very soon; and it was plain to be seen that her visit to Marie had not brought her peace.

Billy knew Kate's letter, by heart, now, both in the original, and in its different versions, and she knew that, despite her struggles, she was being forced straight toward Kate's own verdict: that she, Billy, was the cause, in some way, of the deplorable change in Bertram's appearance, manner, and work. Before she would quite surrender to this heart-sickening belief, however, she determined to ask Bertram himself. Falteringly, but resolutely, therefore, one day, she questioned him.

"Bertram, once you hinted that the picture did not go right because you were troubled over something; and I've been wondering—was it about—me, in any way, that you were troubled?"

Billy had her answer before the man spoke. She had it in the quick terror that sprang to his eyes, and the dull red that swept from his neck to his forehead. His reply, so far as words went did not count, for it evaded everything and told nothing. But Billy knew without words. She knew, too, what she must do. For the time being she took Bertram's evasive answer as he so evidently wished it to be taken; but that evening, after he had gone, she wrote him a little note and broke the engagement. So heartbroken was she—and so fearful was she that he should suspect this—that her note, when completed, was a cold little thing of few words, which carried no hint that its very coldness was but the heart-break in the disguise of pride.

This was like Billy in all ways. Billy, had she lived in the days of the Christian martyrs, would have been the first to walk with head erect into the Arena of Sacrifice. The arena now was just everyday living, the lions were her own devouring misery, and the cause was Bertram's best good.

From Bertram's own self she had it now—that she had been the cause of his being troubled; so she could doubt no longer. The only part that was uncertain was the reason why he had been troubled. Whether his bond to her had become irksome because of his love for another, or because of his love for no girl—except to paint, Billy did not know. But that it was irksome she did not doubt now. Besides, as if she were going to slay his Art, stifle his Ambition, destroy his Inspiration, and be a nuisance generally just so that she might be happy! Indeed, no! Hence she broke the engagement.

This was the letter:

"DEAR BERTRAM:—You won't make the move, so I must. I knew, from the way you spoke to-day, that it was about me that you were troubled, even though you generously tried to make me think it was not. And so the picture did not go well.

"Now, dear, we have not been happy together lately. You have seen it; so have I. I fear our engagement was a mistake, so I'm going to send back your ring to-morrow, and I'm writing this letter to-night. Please don't try to see me just yet. You know what I am doing is best—all round.

"Always your friend,
"BILLY."

CHAPTER XXXI. FLIGHT

Billy feared if she did not mail the letter at once she would not have the courage to mail it at all. So she slipped down-stairs very quietly and went herself to the post box a little way down the street; then she came back and sobbed herself to sleep—though not until after she had sobbed awake for long hours of wretchedness.

When she awoke in the morning, heavy-eyed and unrested, there came to her first the vague horror of some shadow hanging over her, then the sickening consciousness of what that shadow was. For one wild minute Billy felt that she must run to the telephone, summon Bertram, and beseech him to return unread the letter he would receive from her that day. Then there came to her the memory of Bertram's face as it had looked the night before when she had asked him if she were the cause of his being troubled. There came, too, the memory of Kate's scathing "Do you want to ruin his career?" Even the hated magazine article and Marie's tragic "I've hindered him!" added their mite; and Billy knew that she should not go to the telephone, nor summon Bertram.

The one fatal mistake now would be to let Bertram see her own distress. If once he should suspect how she suffered in doing this thing, there would be a scene that Billy felt she had not the courage to face. She must, therefore, manage in some way not to see Bertram—not to let him see her until she felt more sure of her self-control no matter what he said. The easiest way to do this was, of course, to go away. But where? How? She must think. Meanwhile, for these first few hours, she would not tell any one, even Aunt Hannah, what had happened. There must no one speak to her of it, yet. That she could not endure. Aunt Hannah would, of course, shiver, groan "Oh, my grief and conscience!" and call for another shawl; and Billy just now felt as if she should scream if she heard Aunt Hannah say "Oh, my grief and conscience!"—over that. Billy went down to breakfast, therefore, with a determination to act exactly as usual, so that Aunt Hannah should not know—yet.

When people try to "act exactly as usual," they generally end in acting quite the opposite; and Billy was no exception to the rule. Hence her attempted cheerfulness became flippantness, and her laughter giggles that rang too frequently to be quite sincere—though from Aunt Hannah it all elicited only an affectionate smile at "the dear child's high spirits."

A little later, when Aunt Hannah was glancing over the morning paper—now no longer barred from the door—she gave a sudden cry.

"Billy, just listen to this!" she exclaimed, reading from the paper in her hand. "'A new tenor in "The Girl of the Golden West." Appearance of Mr. M. J. Arkwright at the Boston Opera House to-night. Owing to the sudden illness of Dubassi, who was to have taken the part of Johnson tonight, an exceptional opportunity has come to a young tenor singer, one of the most promising pupils at the Conservatory school. Arkwright is said to have a fine voice, a particularly good stage presence, and a purity of tone and smoothness of execution that few of his age and experience can show. Only a short time ago he appeared as the duke at one of the popular-priced Saturday night performances of "Rigoletto"; and his extraordinary success on that occasion, coupled with his familiarity with, and fitness for the part of Johnson in "The Girl of the Golden West," led to his being chosen to take Dubassi's place to-night. His performance is awaited with the greatest of interest.' Now isn't that splendid for Mary Jane? I'm so glad!" beamed Aunt Hannah.

"Of course we're glad!" cried Billy. "And didn't it come just in time? This is the last week of opera, anyway, you know."

"But it says he sang before—on a Saturday night," declared Aunt Hannah, going back to the paper in her hand. "Now wouldn't you have thought we'd have heard of it, or read of it? And wouldn't you have thought he'd have told us?"

"Oh, well, maybe he didn't happen to see us so he could tell us," returned Billy with elaborate carelessness.

"I know it; but it's so funny he hasn't seen us," contended Aunt Hannah, frowning. "You know how much he used to be here."

Billy colored, and hurried into the fray.

"Oh, but he must have been so busy, with all this, you know. And of course we didn't see it in the paper—because we didn't have any paper at that time, probably. Oh, yes, that's my fault, I know," she laughed; "and I was silly, I'll own. But we'll make up for it now. We'll go, of course, I wish it had been on our regular season-ticket night, but I fancy we can get seats somewhere; and I'm going to ask Alice Greggory and her mother, too. I'll go down there this morning to tell them, and to get the tickets. I've got it all planned."

Billy had, indeed, "got it all planned." She had been longing for something that would take her away from the house—and if possible away from herself. This would do the one easily, and might help on the other. She rose at once.

"I'll go right away," she said.

"But, my dear," frowned Aunt Hannah, anxiously, "I don't believe I can go to-night—though I'd love to, dearly."

"But why not?"

"I'm tired and half sick with a headache this morning. I didn't sleep, and I've taken cold somewhere," sighed the lady, pulling the top shawl a little higher about her throat.

"Why, you poor dear, what a shame!"

"Won't Bertram go?" asked Aunt Hannah.

Billy shook her head—but she did not meet Aunt Hannah's eyes.

"Oh, no. I sha'n't even ask him. He said last night he had a banquet on for to-night—one of his art clubs, I believe." Billy's voice was casualness itself.

"But you'll have the Greggorys—that is, Mrs. Greggory can go, can't she?" inquired Aunt Hannah.

"Oh, yes; I'm sure she can," nodded Billy. "You know she went to the operetta, and this is just the same—only bigger."

"Yes, yes, I know," murmured Aunt Hannah.

"Dear me! How can she get about so on those two wretched little sticks? She's a perfect marvel to me."

"She is to me, too," sighed Billy, as she hurried from the room.

Billy was, indeed, in a hurry. To herself she said she wanted to get away—away! And she got away as soon as she could.

She had her plans all made. She would go first to the Greggorys' and invite them to attend the opera with her that evening. Then she would get the tickets. Just what she would do with the rest of the day she did not know. She knew only that she would not go home until time to dress for dinner and the opera. She did not tell Aunt Hannah this, however, when she left the house. She planned to telephone it from somewhere down town, later. She told herself that she could not stay all day under the sharp eyes of Aunt Hannah—but she managed, nevertheless, to bid that lady a particularly blithe and bright-faced good-by.

Billy had not been long gone when the telephone bell rang. Aunt Hannah answered it.

"Why, Bertram, is that you?" she called, in answer to the words that came to her across the wire. "Why, I hardly knew your voice!"

"Didn't you? Well, is—is Billy there?"

"No, she isn't. She's gone down to see Alice Greggory."

"Oh!" So evident was the disappointment in the voice that Aunt Hannah added hastily:

"I'm so sorry! She hasn't been gone ten minutes. But—is there any message?"

"No, thank you. There's no—message." The voice hesitated, then went on a little constrainedly. "How—how is Billy this morning? She—she's all right, isn't she?"

Aunt Hannah laughed in obvious amusement.

"Bless your dear heart, yes, my boy! Has it been such a long time since last evening—when you saw her yourself? Yes, she's all right. In fact, I was thinking at the breakfast table how pretty she looked with her pink cheeks and her bright eyes. She seemed to be in such high spirits."

An inarticulate something that Aunt Hannah could not quite catch came across the line; then a somewhat hurried "All right. Thank you. Good-by."

The next time Aunt Hannah was called to the telephone, Billy spoke to her.

"Aunt Hannah, don't wait luncheon for me, please. I shall get it in town. And don't expect me till five o'clock. I have some shopping to do."

"All right, dear," replied Aunt Hannah. "Did you get the tickets?"

"Yes, and the Greggorys will go. Oh, and Aunt Hannah!"

"Yes, dear."

"Please tell John to bring Peggy around early enough to-night so we can go down and get the Greggorys. I told them we'd call for them."

"Very well, dear. I'll tell him."

"Thank you. How's the poor head?"

"Better, a little, I think."

"That's good. Won't you repent and go, too?"

"No—oh, no, indeed!"

"All right, then; good-by. I'm sorry!"

"So'm I. Good-by," sighed Aunt Hannah, as she hung up the receiver and turned away.

It was after five o'clock when Billy got home, and so hurried were the dressing and the dinner that Aunt Hannah forgot to mention Bertram's telephone call till just as Billy was ready to start for the Greggorys'.

"There! and I forgot," she confessed. "Bertram called you up just after you left this morning, my dear."

"Did he?" Billy's face was turned away, but Aunt Hannah did not notice that.

"Yes. Oh, he didn't want anything special," smiled the lady, "only—well, he did ask if you were all right this morning," she finished with quiet mischief.

"Did he?" murmured Billy again. This time there was a little sound after the words, which Aunt Hannah would have taken for a sob if she had not known that it must have been a laugh.

Then Billy was gone.

At eight o'clock the doorbell rang, and a minute later Rosa came up to say that Mr. Bertram Henshaw was down-stairs and wished to see Mrs. Stetson.

Mrs. Stetson went down at once.

"Why, my dear boy," she exclaimed, as she entered the room; "Billy said you had a banquet on for to-night!"

"Yes, I know; but—I didn't go." Bertram's face was pale and drawn. His voice did not sound natural.

"Why, Bertram, you look ill! Are you ill?" The man made an impatient gesture.

"No, no, I'm not ill—I'm not ill at all. Rosa says—Billy's not here."

"No; she's gone to the opera with the Greggorys."

"The opera!" There was a grieved hurt in Bertram's voice that Aunt Hannah quite misunderstood. She hastened to give an apologetic explanation.

"Yes. She would have told you—she would have asked you to join them, I'm sure, but she said you were going to a banquet. I'm sure she said so."

"Yes, I did tell her so—last night," nodded Bertram, dully.

Aunt Hannah frowned a little. Still more anxiously she endeavored to explain to this disappointed lover why his sweetheart was not at home to greet him.

"Well, then, of course, my boy, she'd never think of your coming here to-night; and when she found Mr. Arkwright was going to sing—"

"Arkwright!" There was no listlessness in Bertram's voice or manner now.

"Yes. Didn't you see it in the paper? Such a splendid chance for him! His picture was there, too."

"No. I didn't see it."

"Then you don't know about it, of course," smiled Aunt Hannah. "But he's to take the part of Johnson in 'The Girl of the Golden West.' Isn't that splendid? I'm so glad! And Billy was, too. She hurried right off this morning to get the tickets and to ask the Greggorys."

"Oh!" Bertram got to his feet a little abruptly, and held out his hand. "Well, then, I might as well say good-by then, I suppose," he suggested with a laugh that Aunt Hannah thought was a bit forced. Before she could remind him again, though, that Billy was really not to blame for not being there to welcome him, he was gone. And Aunt Hannah could only go up-stairs and meditate on the unreasonableness of lovers in general, and of Bertram in particular.

Aunt Hannah had gone to bed, but she was still awake, when Billy came home, so she heard the automobile come to a stop before the door, and she called to Billy when the girl came upstairs.

"Billy, dear, come in here. I'm awake! I want to hear about it. Was it good?"

Billy stopped in the doorway. The light from the hall struck her face. There was no brightness in her eyes now, no pink in her cheeks.

"Oh, yes, it was good—very good," she replied listlessly.

"Why, Billy, how queer you answer! What was the matter? Wasn't Mary Jane—all right?"

"Mary Jane? Oh!—oh, yes; he was very good, Aunt Hannah."

"'Very good,' indeed!" echoed the lady, indignantly. "He must have been!—when you speak as if you'd actually forgotten that he sang at all, anyway!"

Billy had forgotten—almost. Billy had found that, in spite of her getting away from the house, she had not got away from herself once, all day. She tried now, however, to summon her acting powers of the morning.

"But it was splendid, really, Aunt Hannah," she cried, with some show of animation. "And they clapped and cheered and gave him any number of curtain calls. We were so proud of him! But you see, I am tired," she broke off wearily.

"You poor child, of course you are, and you look like a ghost! I won't keep you another minute. Run along to bed. Oh—Bertram didn't go to that banquet, after all. He came here," she added, as Billy turned to go.

"Bertram!" The girl wheeled sharply.

"Yes. He wanted you, of course. I found I didn't do, at all," chuckled Aunt Hannah. "Did you suppose I would?"

There was no answer. Billy had gone.

In the long night watches Billy fought it out with herself. (Billy had always fought things out with herself.) She must go away. She knew that. Already Bertram had telephoned, and called. He evidently meant to see her—and she could not see him. She dared not. If she did—Billy knew now how pitifully little it would take to make her actually willing to slay Bertram's Art, stifle his Ambition, destroy his Inspiration, and be a nuisance generally—if only she could have Bertram while she was doing it all. Sternly then she asked herself if she had no pride; if she had forgotten that it was because of her that the Winthrop portrait had not been a success—because of her, either for the reason that he loved now Miss Winthrop, or else that he loved no girl—except to paint.

Very early in the morning a white-faced, red-eyed Billy appeared at Aunt Hannah's bedside.

"Billy!" exclaimed Aunt Hannah, plainly appalled.

Billy sat down on the edge of the bed.

"Aunt Hannah," she began in a monotonous voice as if she were reciting a lesson she had learned by heart, "please listen, and please try not to be too surprised. You were saying the other day that you would like to visit your old home town. Well, I think that's a very nice idea. If you don't mind we'll go to-day."

Aunt Hannah pulled herself half erect in bed.

"To-day—child?"

"Yes," nodded Billy, unsmilingly. "We shall have to go somewhere to-day, and I thought you would like that place best."

"But—Billy!—what does this mean?"

Billy sighed heavily.

"Yes, I understand. You'll have to know the rest, of course. I've broken my engagement. I don't want to see Bertram. That's why I'm going away."

Aunt Hannah fell nervelessly back on the pillow. Her teeth fairly chattered.

"Oh, my grief and conscience—Billy! Won't you please pull up that blanket," she moaned. "Billy, what do you mean?"

Billy shook her head and got to her feet.

"I can't tell any more now, really, Aunt Hannah. Please don't ask me; and don't—talk. You will—go with me, won't you?" And Aunt Hannah, with her terrified eyes on Billy's piteously agitated face, nodded her head and choked:

"Why, of course I'll go—anywhere—with you, Billy; but—why did you do it, why did you do it?"

A little later, Billy, in her own room, wrote this note to Bertram:

"DEAR BERTRAM:—I'm going away to-day. That'll be best all around. You'll agree to that, I'm sure. Please don't try to see me, and please don't write. It wouldn't make either one of us any happier. You must know that.

"As ever your friend,

"BILLY."

Bertram, when he read it, grew only a shade more white, a degree more sick at heart. Then he kissed the letter gently and put it away with the other.

To Bertram, the thing was very clear. Billy had come now to the conclusion that it would be wrong to give herself where she could not give her heart. And in this he agreed with her—bitter as it was for him. Certainly he did not want Billy, if Billy did not want him, he told himself. He would now, of course, accede to her request. He would not write to her—and make her suffer more. But to Bertram, at that moment, it seemed that the very sun in the heavens had gone out.

CHAPTER XXXII. PETE TO THE RESCUE

One by one the weeks passed and became a month. Then other weeks became other months. It was July when Billy, homesick and weary, came back to Hillside with Aunt Hannah.

Home looked wonderfully good to Billy, in spite of the fact that she had so dreaded to see it. Billy had made up her mind, however, that, come sometime she must. She could not, of course, stay always away. Perhaps, too, it would be just as easy at home as it was away. Certainly it could not be any harder. She was convinced of that. Besides, she did not want Bertram to think—

Billy had received only meagre news from Boston since she went away. Bertram had not written at all. William had written twice—hurt, grieved, puzzled, questioning letters that were very hard to answer. From Marie, too, had come letters of much the same sort. By far the cheeriest epistles had come from Alice Greggory. They contained, indeed, about the only comfort Billy had known for weeks, for they showed very plainly to Billy that Arkwright's heart had been caught on the rebound; and that in Alice Greggory he was finding the sweetest sort of balm for his wounded feelings. From these letters Billy learned, too, that Judge Greggory's honor had been wholly vindicated; and, as Billy told Aunt Hannah, "anybody could put two and two together and make four, now."

It was eight o'clock on a rainy July evening that Billy and Aunt Hannah arrived at Hillside; and it was only a little past eight that Aunt Hannah was summoned to the telephone. When she came back to Billy she was crying and wringing her hands.

Billy sprang to her feet.

"Why, Aunt Hannah, what is it? What's the matter?" she demanded.

Aunt Hannah sank into a chair, still wringing her hands.

"Oh, Billy, Billy, how can I tell you, how can I tell you?" she moaned.

"You must tell me! Aunt Hannah, what is it?"

"Oh—oh—oh! Billy, I can't—I can't!"

"But you'll have to! What is it, Aunt Hannah?"

"It's—B-Bertram!"

"Bertram!" Billy's face grew ashen. "Quick, quick—what do you mean?"

For answer, Aunt Hannah covered her face with her hands and began to sob aloud. Billy, almost beside herself now with terror and anxiety, dropped on her knees and tried to pull away the shaking hands.

"Aunt Hannah, you must tell me! You must—you must!"

"I can't, Billy. It's Bertram. He's—hurt!" choked Aunt Hannah, hysterically.

"Hurt! How?"

"I don't know. Pete told me."

"Pete!"

"Yes. Rosa had told him we were coming, and he called me up. He said maybe I could do something. So he told me."

"Yes, yes! But told you what?"

"That he was hurt."

"How?"

"I couldn't hear all, but I think 'twas an accident—automobile. And, Billy, Billy—Pete says it's his arm—his right arm—and that maybe he can't ever p-paint again!"

"Oh-h!" Billy fell back as if the words had been a blow. "Not that, Aunt Hannah—not that!"

"That's what Pete said. I couldn't get all of it, but I got that. And, Billy, he's been out of his head—though he isn't now, Pete says—and—and—and he's been calling for you."

"For—me?" A swift change came to Billy's face.

"Yes. Over and over again he called for you—while he was crazy, you know. That's why Pete told me. He said he didn't rightly understand what the trouble was, but he didn't believe there was any trouble, really, between you two; anyway, that you wouldn't think there was, if you could hear him, and know how he wanted you, and—why, Billy!"

Billy was on her feet now. Her fingers were on the electric push-button that would summon Rosa. Her face was illumined. The next moment Rosa appeared.

"Tell John to bring Peggy to the door at once, please," directed her mistress.

"Billy!" gasped Aunt Hannah again, as the maid disappeared. Billy was tremblingly putting on the hat she had but just taken off. "Billy, what are you going to do?"

Billy turned in obvious surprise.

"Why, I'm going to Bertram, of course."

"To Bertram! But it's nearly half-past eight, child, and it rains, and everything!"

"But Bertram wants me!" exclaimed Billy. "As if I'd mind rain, or time, or anything else, now!"

"But—but—oh, my grief and conscience!" groaned Aunt Hannah, beginning to wring her hands again.

Billy reached for her coat. Aunt Hannah stirred into sudden action.

"But, Billy, if you'd only wait till to-morrow," she quavered, putting out a feebly restraining hand.

"To-morrow!" The young voice rang with supreme scorn. "Do you think I'd wait till to-morrow—after all this? I say Bertram wants me." Billy picked up her gloves.

"But you broke it off, dear—you said you did; and to go down there to-night—like this—"

Billy lifted her head. Her eyes shone. Her whole face was a glory of love and pride.

"That was before. I didn't know. He wants me, Aunt Hannah. Did you hear? He wants me! And now I won't even—hinder him, if he can't—p-paint again!" Billy's voice broke. The glory left her face. Her eyes brimmed with tears, but her head was still bravely uplifted. "I'm going to Bertram!"

Blindly Aunt Hannah got to her feet. Still more blindly she reached for her bonnet and cloak on the chair near her.

"Oh, will you go, too?" asked Billy, abstractedly, hurrying to the window to look for the motor car.

"Will I go, too!" burst out Aunt Hannah's indignant voice. "Do you think I'd let you go alone, and at this time of night, on such a wild-goose chase as this?"

"I don't know, I'm sure," murmured Billy, still abstractedly, peering out into the rain.

"Don't know, indeed! Oh, my grief and conscience!" groaned Aunt Hannah, setting her bonnet hopelessly askew on top of her agitated head.

But Billy did not even answer now. Her face was pressed hard against the window-pane.

CHAPTER XXXIII. BERTRAM TAKES THE REINS

With stiffly pompous dignity Pete opened the door. The next moment he fell back in amazement before the impetuous rush of a starry-eyed, flushed-cheeked young woman who demanded:

"Where is he, Pete?"

"Miss Billy!" gasped the old man. Then he saw Aunt Hannah—Aunt Hannah with her bonnet askew, her neck-bow awry, one hand bare, and the other half covered with a glove wrong side out. Aunt Hannah's cheeks, too, were flushed, and her eyes starry, but with dismay and anger—the last because she did not like the way Pete had said Miss Billy's name. It was one matter for her to object to this thing Billy was doing—but quite another for Pete to do it.

"Of course it's she!" retorted Aunt Hannah, testily. "As if you yourself didn't bring her here with your crazy messages at this time of night!"

"Pete, where is he?" interposed Billy. "Tell Mr. Bertram I am here—or, wait! I'll go right in and surprise him."

"Billy!" This time it was Aunt Hannah who gasped her name.

Pete had recovered himself by now, but he did not even glance toward Aunt Hannah. His face was beaming, and his old eyes were shining.

"Miss Billy, Miss Billy, you're an angel straight from heaven, you are—you are! Oh, I'm so glad you came! It'll be all right now—all right! He's in the den, Miss Billy."

Billy turned eagerly, but before she could take so much as one step toward the door at the end of the hall, Aunt Hannah's indignant voice arrested her.

"Billy-stop! You're not an angel; you're a young woman—and a crazy one, at that! Whatever angels do, young women don't go unannounced and unchaperoned into young men's rooms! Pete, go tell your master that we are here, and ask if he will receive us."

Pete's lips twitched. The emphatic "we" and "us" were not lost on him. But his face was preternaturally grave when he spoke.

"Mr. Bertram is up and dressed, ma'am. He's in the den. I'll speak to him."

Pete, once again the punctilious butler, stalked to the door of Bertram's den and threw it wide open.

Opposite the door, on a low couch, lay Bertram, his head bandaged, and his right arm in a sling. His face was turned toward the door, but his eyes were closed. He looked very white, and his features were pitifully drawn with suffering.

"Mr. Bertram," began Pete—but he got no further. A flying figure brushed by him and fell on its knees by the couch, with a low cry.

Bertram's eyes flew open. Across his face swept such a radiant look of unearthly joy that Pete sobbed audibly and fled to the kitchen. Dong Ling found him there a minute later polishing a silver teaspoon with a fringed napkin that had been spread over Bertram's tray. In the hall above Aunt Hannah was crying into William's gray linen duster that hung on the hall-rack—Aunt Hannah's handkerchief was on the floor back at Hillside.

In the den neither Billy nor Bertram knew or cared what had become of Aunt Hannah and Pete. There were just two people in their world—two people, and unutterable, incredible, overwhelming rapture and peace. Then, very gradually it dawned over them that there was, after all, something strange and unexplained in it all.

"But, dearest, what does it mean—you here like this?" asked Bertram then. As if to make sure that she was "here, like this," he drew her even closer—Bertram was so thankful that he did have one arm that was usable.

Billy, on her knees by the couch, snuggled into the curve of the one arm with a contented little sigh.

"Well, you see, just as soon as I found out to-night that you wanted me, I came," she said.

"You darling! That was—" Bertram stopped suddenly. A puzzled frown showed below the fantastic bandage about his head. "'As soon as,'" he quoted then scornfully. "Were you ever by any possible chance thinking I didn't want you?"

Billy's eyes widened a little.

"Why, Bertram, dear, don't you see? When you were so troubled that the picture didn't go well, and I found out it was about me you were troubled—I—"

"Well?" Bertram's voice was a little strained.

"Why, of—of course," stammered Billy, "I couldn't help thinking that maybe you had found out you didn't want me."

"Didn't want you!" groaned Bertram, his tense muscles relaxing. "May I ask why?"

Billy blushed.

"I wasn't quite sure why," she faltered; "only, of course, I thought of—of Miss Winthrop, you know, or that maybe it was because you didn't care for any girl, only to paint—oh, oh, Bertram! Pete told us," she broke off wildly, beginning to sob.

"Pete told you that I didn't care for any girl, only to paint?" demanded Bertram, angry and mystified.

"No, no," sobbed Billy, "not that. It was all the others that told me that! Pete told Aunt Hannah about the accident, you know, and he said—he said—Oh, Bertram, I can't say it! But that's one of the things that made me know I could come now, you see, because I—I wouldn't hinder you, nor slay your Art, nor any other of those dreadful things if—if you couldn't ever—p-paint again," finished Billy in an uncontrollable burst of grief.

"There, there, dear," comforted Bertram, patting the bronze-gold head on his breast. "I haven't the faintest idea what you're talking about—except the last; but I know there can't be anything that ought to make you cry like that. As for my not painting again—you didn't understand Pete, dearie. That was what they were afraid of at first—that I'd lose my arm; but that danger is all past now. I'm loads better. Of course I'm going to paint again—and better than ever before—now!"

Billy lifted her head. A look that was almost terror came to her eyes. She pulled herself half away from Bertram's encircling arm.

"Why, Billy," cried the man, in pained surprise. "You don't mean to say you're sorry I'm going to paint again!"

"No, no! Oh, no, Bertram—never that!" she faltered, still regarding him with fearful eyes. "It's only—for me, you know. I can't go back now, and not have you—after this!—even if I do hinder you, and—"

"Hinder me! What are you talking about, Billy?"

Billy drew a quivering sigh.

"Well, to begin with, Kate said—"

"Good heavens! Is Kate in this, too?" Bertram's voice was savage now.

"Well, she wrote a letter."

"I'll warrant she did! Great Scott, Billy! Don't you know Kate by this time?"

"Y-yes, I said so, too. But, Bertram, what she wrote was true. I found it everywhere, afterwards—in magazines and papers, and even in Marie."

"Humph! Well, dearie, I don't know yet what you found, but I do know you wouldn't have found it at all if it hadn't been for Kate—and I wish I had her here this minute!"

Billy giggled hysterically.

"I don't—not right here," she cooed, nestling comfortably against her lover's arm. "But you see, dear, she never has approved of the marriage."

"Well, who's doing the marrying—she, or I?" "That's what I said, too—only in another way," sighed Billy. "But she called us flyaway flutterbudgets, and she said I'd ruin your career, if I did marry you."

"Well, I can tell you right now, Billy, you will ruin it if you don't!" declared Bertram. "That's what ailed me all the time I was painting that miserable portrait. I was so worried—for fear I'd lose you."

"Lose me! Why, Bertram Henshaw, what do you mean?"

A shamed red crept to the man's forehead.

"Well, I suppose I might as well own up now as any time. I was scared blue, Billy, with jealousy of—Arkwright."

Billy laughed gayly—but she shifted her position and did not meet her lover's eyes.

"Arkwright? Nonsense!" she cried. "Why, he's going to marry Alice Greggory. I know he is! I can see it as plain as day in her letters. He's there a lot."

"And you never did think for a minute, Billy, that you cared for him?" Bertram's gaze searched Billy's face a little fearfully. He had not been slow to mark that swift lowering of her eyelids. But Billy looked him now straight in the face—it was a level, frank gaze of absolute truth.

"Never, dear," she said firmly. (Billy was so glad Bertram had turned the question on her love instead of Arkwright's!) "There has never really been any one but you."

"Thank God for that," breathed Bertram, as he drew the bright head nearer and held it close.

After a minute Billy stirred and sighed happily.

"Aren't lovers the beat'em for imagining things?" she murmured.

"They certainly are."

"You see—I wasn't in love with Mr. Arkwright."

"I see—I hope."

"And—and you didn't care specially for—for Miss Winthrop?"

"Eh? Well, no!" exploded Bertram. "Do you mean to say you really—"

Billy put a soft finger on his lips.

"Er—'people who live in glass houses,' you know," she reminded him, with roguish eyes.

Bertram kissed the finger and subsided.

"Humph!" he commented.

There was a long silence; then, a little breathlessly, Billy asked:

"And you don't—after all, love me—just to paint?"

"Well, what is that? Is that Kate, too?" demanded Bertram, grimly.

Billy laughed.

"No—oh, she said it, all right, but, you see, everybody said that to me, Bertram; and that's what made me so—so worried sometimes when you talked about the tilt of my chin, and all that."

"Well, by Jove!" breathed Bertram.

There was another silence. Then, suddenly, Bertram stirred.

"Billy, I'm going to marry you to-morrow," he announced decisively.

Billy lifted her head and sat back in palpitating dismay.

"Bertram! What an absurd idea!"

"Well, I am. I don't know as I can trust you out of my sight till then! You'll read something, or hear something, or get a letter from Kate after breakfast to-morrow morning, that will set you 'saving me' again; and I don't want to be saved—that way. I'm going to marry you to-morrow. I'll get—" He stopped short, with a sudden frown. "Confound that law! I forgot. Great Scott, Billy, I'll have to trust you five days, after all! There's a new law about the license. We've got to wait five days—and maybe more, counting in the notice, and all."

Billy laughed softly.

"Five days, indeed, sir! I wonder if you think I can get ready to be married in five days."

"Don't want you to get ready," retorted Bertram, promptly. "I saw Marie get ready, and I had all I wanted of it. If you really must have all those miles of tablecloths and napkins and doilies and lace rufflings we'll do it afterwards,—not before."

"But—"

"Besides, I need you to take care of me," cut in Bertram, craftily.

"Bertram, do you—really?"

The tender glow on Billy's face told its own story, and Bertram's eager eyes were not slow to read it.

"Sweetheart, see here, dear," he cried softly, tightening his good left arm. And forthwith he began to tell her how much he did, indeed, need her.

"Billy, my dear!" It was Aunt Hannah's plaintive voice at the doorway, a little later. "We must go home; and William is here, too, and wants to see you."

Billy rose at once as Aunt Hannah entered the room.

"Yes, Aunt Hannah, I'll come; besides"—she glanced at Bertram mischievously—"I shall need all the time I've got to prepare for—my wedding."

"Your wedding! You mean it'll be before—October?" Aunt Hannah glanced from one to the other uncertainly. Something in their smiling faces sent a quick suspicion to her eyes.

"Yes," nodded Billy, demurely. "It's next Tuesday, you see."

"Next Tuesday! But that's only a week away," gasped Aunt Hannah.

"Yes, a week."

"But, child, your trousseau—the wedding—the—the—a week!" Aunt Hannah could not articulate further.

"Yes, I know; that is a good while," cut in Bertram, airily. "We wanted it to-morrow, but we had to wait, on account of the new license law. Otherwise it wouldn't have been so long, and—"

But Aunt Hannah was gone. With a low-breathed "Long! Oh, my grief and conscience—William!" she had fled through the hall door.

"Well, it is long," maintained Bertram, with tender eyes, as he reached out his hand to say good-night.

MISS BILLY—MARRIED

CHAPTER I. SOME OPINIONS AND A WEDDING

"I, Bertram, take thee, Billy," chanted the white-robed clergyman.
"'I, Bertram, take thee, Billy,'" echoed the tall young bridegroom, his eyes gravely tender.
"To my wedded wife."
"'To my wedded wife.'" The bridegroom's voice shook a little.
"To have and to hold from this day forward."
"'To have and to hold from this day forward.'" Now the young voice rang with triumph. It had grown strong and steady.
"For better for worse."
"'For better for worse.'"
"For richer for poorer," droned the clergyman, with the weariness of uncounted repetitions.
"'For richer for poorer,'" avowed the bridegroom, with the decisive emphasis of one to whom the words are new and significant.
"In sickness and in health."
"'In sickness and in health.'"
"To love and to cherish."
"'To love and to cherish.'" The younger voice carried infinite tenderness now.
"Till death us do part."
"'Till death us do part,'" repeated the bridegroom's lips; but everybody knew that what his heart said was: "Now, and through all eternity."
"According to God's holy ordinance."
"'According to God's holy ordinance.'"
"And thereto I plight thee my troth."
"'And thereto I plight thee my troth.'"
There was a faint stir in the room. In one corner a white-haired woman blinked tear-wet eyes and pulled a fleecy white shawl more closely about her shoulders. Then the minister's voice sounded again.
"I, Billy, take thee, Bertram."
"'I, Billy, take thee, Bertram.'"
This time the echoing voice was a feminine one, low and sweet, but clearly distinct, and vibrant with joyous confidence, on through one after another of the ever familiar, but ever impressive phrases of the service that gives into the hands of one man and of one woman the future happiness, each of the other.
The wedding was at noon. That evening Mrs. Kate Hartwell, sister of the bridegroom, wrote the following letter:
BOSTON, July 15th.
"MY DEAR HUSBAND:—Well, it's all over with, and they're married. I couldn't do one thing to prevent it. Much as ever as they would even listen to what I had to say—and when they knew how I had hurried East to say it, too, with only two hours' notice!
"But then, what can you expect? From time immemorial lovers never did have any sense; and when those lovers are such irresponsible flutterbudgets as Billy and Bertram—!
"And such a wedding! I couldn't do anything with that, either, though I tried hard. They had it in Billy's living-room at noon, with nothing but the sun for light. There was no maid of honor, no bridesmaids, no wedding cake, no wedding veil, no presents (except from the family, and from that ridiculous Chinese cook of brother William's, Ding Dong, or whatever his name is. He tore in just before the wedding ceremony, and insisted upon seeing Billy to give her a wretched little green stone idol, which he declared would bring her 'heap plenty velly good luckee' if she received it before she 'got married.' I wouldn't have

the hideous, grinning thing around, but William says it's real jade, and very valuable, and of course Billy was crazy over it—or pretended to be). There was no trousseau, either, and no reception. There was no anything but the bridegroom; and when I tell you that Billy actually declared that was all she wanted, you will understand how absurdly in love she is—in spite of all those weeks and weeks of broken engagement when I, at least, supposed she had come to her senses, until I got that crazy note from Bertram a week ago saying they were to be married today.

"I can't say that I've got any really satisfactory explanation of the matter. Everything has been in such a hubbub, and those two ridiculous children have been so afraid they wouldn't be together every minute possible, that any really rational conversation with either of them was out of the question. When Billy broke the engagement last spring none of us knew why she had done it, as you know; and I fancy we shall be almost as much in the dark as to why she has—er—mended it now, as you might say. As near as I can make out, however, she thought he didn't want her, and he thought she didn't want him. I believe matters were still further complicated by a girl Bertram was painting, and a young fellow that used to sing with Billy—a Mr. Arkwright.

"Anyhow, things came to a head last spring, Billy broke the engagement and fled to parts unknown with Aunt Hannah, leaving Bertram here in Boston to alternate between stony despair and reckless gayety, according to William; and it was while he was in the latter mood that he had that awful automobile accident and broke his arm—and almost his neck. He was wildly delirious, and called continually for Billy.

"Well, it seems Billy didn't know all this; but a week ago she came home, and in some way found out about it, I think through Pete—William's old butler, you know. Just exactly what happened I can't say, but I do know that she dragged poor old Aunt Hannah down to Bertram's at some unearthly hour, and in the rain; and Aunt Hannah couldn't do a thing with her. All Billy would say, was, 'Bertram wants me.' And Aunt Hannah told me that if I could have seen Billy's face I'd have known that she'd have gone to Bertram then if he'd been at the top of the Himalaya Mountains, or at the bottom of the China Sea. So perhaps it's just as well—for Aunt Hannah's sake, at least—that he was in no worse place than on his own couch at home. Anyhow, she went, and in half an hour they blandly informed Aunt Hannah that they were going to be married to-day.

"Aunt Hannah said she tried to stop that, and get them to put it off till October (the original date, you know), but Bertram was obdurate. And when he declared he'd marry her the next day if it wasn't for the new license law, Aunt Hannah said she gave up for fear he'd get a special dispensation, or go to the Governor or the President, or do some other dreadful thing. (What a funny old soul Aunt Hannah is!) Bertram told me that he should never feel safe till Billy was really his; that she'd read something, or hear something, or think something, or get a letter from me (as if anything I could say would do any good-or harm!), and so break the engagement again.

"Well, she's his now, so I suppose he's satisfied; though, for my part, I haven't changed my mind at all. I still say that they are not one bit suited to each other, and that matrimony will simply ruin his career. Bertram never has loved and never will love any girl long—except to paint. But if he simply would get married, why couldn't he have taken a nice, sensible domestic girl that would have kept him fed and mended?

"Not but that I'm very fond of Billy, as you know, dear; but imagine Billy as a wife—worse yet, a mother! Billy's a dear girl, but she knows about as much of real life and its problems as—as our little Kate. A more impulsive, irresponsible, regardless-of-consequences young woman I never saw. She can play divinely, and write delightful songs, I'll acknowledge; but what is that when a man is hungry, or has lost a button?

"Billy has had her own way, and had everything she wanted for years now—a rather dangerous preparation for marriage, especially marriage to a fellow like Bertram who has had his own way and everything he's wanted for years. Pray, what's going to happen when those ways conflict, and neither one gets the thing wanted?

"And think of her ignorance of cooking—but, there! What's the use? They're married now, and it can't be helped.

"Mercy, what a letter I've written! But I, had to talk to some one; besides, I'd promised I to let you know how matters stood as soon as I could. As you see, though, my trip East has been practically useless. I saw the wedding, to be sure, but I didn't prevent it, or even postpone it—though I meant to do one or the other, else I should never have made that tiresome journey half across the continent at two hours' notice.

"However, we shall see what we shall see. As for me, I'm dead tired. Good night.

"Affectionately yours,

"KATE."

Quite naturally, Mrs. Kate Hartwell was not the only one who was thinking that evening of the wedding. In the home of Bertram's brother Cyril, Cyril himself was at the piano, but where his thoughts were was plain to be seen—or rather, heard; for from under his fingers there came the Lohengrin wedding march until all the room seemed filled with the scent of orange blossoms, the mistiness of floating veils, and the echoing peals of far-away organs heralding the "Fair Bride and Groom."

Over by the table in the glowing circle of the shaded lamp, sat Marie, Cyril's wife, a dainty sewing-basket by her side. Her hands, however, lay idly across the stocking in her lap.

As the music ceased, she drew a long sigh.

What a perfectly beautiful wedding that was! she breathed.

Cyril whirled about on the piano stool.

"It was a very sensible wedding," he said with emphasis.

"They looked so happy—both of them," went on Marie, dreamily; "so—so sort of above and beyond everything about them, as if nothing ever, ever could trouble them—now."

Cyril lifted his eyebrows.

"Humph! Well, as I said before, it was a very sensible wedding," he declared.

This time Marie noticed the emphasis. She laughed, though her eyes looked a little troubled.

"I know, dear, of course, what you mean. I thought our wedding was beautiful; but I would have made it simpler if I'd realized in time how you—you—"

"How I abhorred pink teas and purple pageants," he finished for her, with a frowning smile. "Oh, well, I stood it—for the sake of what it brought me." His face showed now only the smile; the frown had vanished. For a man known for years to his friends as a "hater of women and all other confusion," Cyril Henshaw was looking remarkably well-pleased with himself.

His wife of less than a year colored as she met his gaze. Hurriedly she picked up her needle. The man laughed happily at her confusion.

"What are you doing? Is that my stocking?" he demanded.

A look, half pain, half reproach, crossed her face.

"Why, Cyril, of course not! You—you told me not to, long ago. You said my darns made—bunches.

"Ho! I meant I didn't want to wear them," retorted the man, upon whom the tragic wretchedness of that half-sobbed "bunches" had been quite lost. "I love to see you mending them," he finished, with an approving glance at the pretty little picture of domesticity before him.

A peculiar expression came to Marie's eyes.

"Why, Cyril, you mean you like to have me mend them just for—for the sake of seeing me do it, when you know you won't ever wear them?"

"Sure!" nodded the man, imperturbably. Then, with a sudden laugh, he asked: "I wonder now, does Billy love to mend socks?"

Marie smiled, but she sighed, too, and shook her head.

"I'm afraid not, Cyril."

"Nor cook?"

Marie laughed outright this time. The vaguely troubled look had fled from her eyes

"Oh, Billy's helped me beat eggs and butter sometimes, but I never knew her to cook a thing or want to cook a thing, but once; then she spent nearly two weeks trying to learn to make puddings—for you."

"For me!"

Marie puckered her lips queerly.

"Well, I supposed they were for you at the time. At all events she was trying to make them for some one of you boys; probably it was really for Bertram, though."

"Humph!" grunted Cyril. Then, after a minute, he observed: "I judge Kate thinks Billy'll never make them—for anybody. I'm afraid Sister Kate isn't pleased."

"Oh, but Mrs. Hartwell was—was disappointed in the wedding," apologized Marie, quickly. "You know she wanted it put off anyway, and she didn't like such a simple one.

"Hm-m; as usual Sister Kate forgot it wasn't her funeral—I mean, her wedding," retorted Cyril, dryly. "Kate is never happy, you know, unless she's managing things."

"Yes, I know," nodded Marie, with a frowning smile of recollection at certain features of her own wedding.

"She doesn't approve of Billy's taste in guests, either," remarked Cyril, after a moment's silence.

"I thought her guests were lovely," spoke up Marie, in quick defense. "Of course, most of her social friends are away—in July; but Billy is never a society girl, you know, in spite of the way Society is always trying to lionize her and Bertram."

"Oh, of course Kate knows that; but she says it seems as if Billy needn't have gone out and gathered in the lame and the halt and the blind."

"Nonsense!" cried Marie, with unusual sharpness for her. "I suppose she said that just because of Mrs. Greggory's and Tommy Dunn's crutches."

"Well, they didn't make a real festive-looking wedding party, you must admit," laughed Cyril; "what with the bridegroom's own arm in a sling, too! But who were they all, anyway?"

"Why, you knew Mrs. Greggory and Alice, of course—and Pete," smiled Marie. "And wasn't Pete happy? Billy says she'd have had Pete if she had no one else; that there wouldn't have been any wedding, anyway, if it hadn't been for his telephoning Aunt Hannah that night."

"Yes; Will told me."

"As for Tommy and the others—most of them were those people that Billy had at her home last summer for a two weeks' vacation—people, you know, too poor to give themselves one, and too proud to accept one from ordinary charity. Billy's been following them up and doing little things for them ever since—sugarplums and frosting on their cake, she calls it; and they adore her, of course. I think it was lovely of her to have them, and they did have such a good time! You should have seen Tommy when you played that wedding march for Billy to enter the room. His poor little face was so transfigured with joy that I almost cried, just to look at him. Billy says he loves music—poor little fellow!"

"Well, I hope they'll be happy, in spite of Kate's doleful prophecies. Certainly they looked happy enough to-day," declared Cyril, patting a yawn as he rose to his feet. "I fancy Will and Aunt Hannah are lonesome, though, about now," he added.

"Yes," smiled Marie, mistily, as she gathered up her work. "I know what Aunt Hannah's doing. She's helping Rosa put the house to rights, and she's stopping to cry over every slipper and handkerchief of Billy's she finds. And she'll do that until that funny clock of hers strikes twelve, then she'll say 'Oh, my grief and conscience—midnight!' But the next minute she'll remember that it's only half-past eleven, after all, and she'll send Rosa to bed and sit patting Billy's slipper in her lap till it really is midnight by all the other clocks."

Cyril laughed appreciatively.

"Well, I know what Will is doing," he declared.

"Will is in Bertram's den dozing before the fireplace with Spunkie curled up in his lap."

As it happened, both these surmises were not far from right. In the Strata, the Henshaws' old Beacon Street home, William was sitting before the fireplace with the cat in his lap, but he was not dozing. He was talking.

"Spunkie," he was saying, "your master, Bertram, got married to-day—and to Miss Billy. He'll be bringing her home one of these days—your new mistress. And such a mistress! Never did cat or house have a better!

"Just think; for the first time in years this old place is to know the touch of a woman's hand—and that's what it hasn't known for almost twenty years, except for those few short months six years ago when a dark-eyed girl and a little gray kitten (that was Spunk, your predecessor, you know) blew in and blew out again before we scarcely knew they were here. That girl was Miss Billy, and she was a dear then, just as she is now, only now she's coming here to stay. She's coming home, Spunkie; and she'll make it a home for you, for me, and for all of us. Up to now, you know, it hasn't really been a home, for years—just us men, so. It'll be very different, Spunkie, as you'll soon find out. Now mind, madam! We must show that we appreciate all this: no tempers, no tantrums, no showing of claws, no leaving our coats—either yours or mine—on the drawing-room chairs, no tracking in of mud on clean rugs and floors! For we're going to have a home, Spunkie—a home!"

At Hillside, Aunt Hannah was, indeed, helping Rosa to put the house to rights, as Marie had said. She was crying, too, over a glove she had found on Billy's piano; but she was crying over something else, also. Not only had she lost Billy, but she had lost her home.

To be sure, nothing had been said during that nightmare of a week of hurry and confusion about Aunt Hannah's future; but Aunt Hannah knew very well how it must be. This dear little house on the side of Corey Hill was Billy's home, and Billy would not need it any longer. It would be sold, of course; and she, Aunt Hannah, would go back to a "second-story front" and loneliness in some Back Bay boarding-house; and a second story front and loneliness would not be easy now, after these years of home—and Billy.

No wonder, indeed, that Aunt Hannah sat crying and patting the little white glove in her hand. No wonder, too, that—being Aunt Hannah—she reached for the shawl near by and put it on, shiveringly. Even July, to-night, was cold—to Aunt Hannah.

In yet another home that evening was the wedding of Billy Neilson and Bertram Henshaw uppermost in thought and speech. In a certain little South-End flat where, in two rented rooms, lived Alice Greggory and her crippled mother, Alice was talking to Mr. M. J. Arkwright, commonly known to his friends as "Mary Jane," owing to the mystery in which he had for so long shrouded his name.

Arkwright to-night was plainly moody and ill at ease.

"You're not listening. You're not listening at all," complained Alice Greggory at last, reproachfully.

With a visible effort the man roused himself.

"Indeed I am," he maintained.

"I thought you'd be interested in the wedding. You used to be friends—you and Billy." The girl's voice still vibrated with reproach.

There was a moment's silence; then, a little harshly, the man said:

"Perhaps—because I wanted to be more than—a friend—is why you're not satisfied with my interest now."

A look that was almost terror came to Alice Greggory's eyes. She flushed painfully, then grew very white.

"You mean—"

"Yes," he nodded dully, without looking up. "I cared too much for her. I supposed Henshaw was just a friend—till too late."

There was a breathless hush before, a little unsteadily, the girl stammered:

"Oh, I'm so sorry—so very sorry! I—I didn't know."

"No, of course you didn't. I've almost told you, though, lots of times; you've been so good to me all these weeks." He raised his head now, and looked at her, frank comradeship in his eyes.

The girl stirred restlessly. Her eyes swerved a little under his level gaze.

"Oh, but I've done nothing—n-nothing," she stammered. Then, at the light tap of crutches on a bare floor she turned in obvious relief. "Oh, here's mother. She's been in visiting with Mrs. Delano, our landlady. Mother, Mr. Arkwright is here."

Meanwhile, speeding north as fast as steam could carry them, were the bride and groom. The wondrousness of the first hour of their journey side by side had become a joyous certitude that always it was to be like this now.

"Bertram," began the bride, after a long minute of eloquent silence.

"Yes, love."

"You know our wedding was very different from most weddings."

"Of course it was!"

"Yes, but really it was. Now listen." The bride's voice grew tenderly earnest. "I think our marriage is going to be different, too."

"Different?"

"Yes." Billy's tone was emphatic. "There are so many common, everyday marriages where—where—Why, Bertram, as if you could ever be to me like—like Mr. Carleton is, for instance!"

"Like Mr. Carleton is—to you?" Bertram's voice was frankly puzzled.

"No, no! As Mr. Carleton is to Mrs. Carleton, I mean."

"Oh!" Bertram subsided in relief.

"And the Grahams and Whartons, and the Freddie Agnews, and—and a lot of others. Why, Bertram, I've seen the Grahams and the Whartons not even speak to each other a whole evening, when they've been at a dinner, or something; and I've seen Mrs. Carleton not even seem to know her husband came into the room. I don't mean quarrel, dear. Of course we'd never quarrel! But I mean I'm sure we shall never get used to—to you being you, and I being I."

"Indeed we sha'n't," agreed Bertram, rapturously.

"Ours is going to be such a beautiful marriage!"

"Of course it will be."

"And we'll be so happy!"

"I shall be, and I shall try to make you so."

"As if I could be anything else," sighed Billy, blissfully. "And now we can't have any misunderstandings, you see."

"Of course not. Er—what's that?"

"Why, I mean that—that we can't ever repeat hose miserable weeks of misunderstanding. Everything is all explained up. I know, now, that you don't love Miss Winthrop, or just girls—any girl—to paint. You love me. Not the tilt of my chin, nor the turn of my head; but me."

"I do—just you." Bertram's eyes gave the caress his lips would have given had it not been for the presence of the man in the seat across the aisle of the sleeping-car.

"And you—you know now that I love you—just you?"

"Not even Arkwright?"

"Not even Arkwright," smiled Billy.

There was the briefest of hesitations; then, a little constrainedly, Bertram asked:

"And you said you—you never had cared for Arkwright, didn't you?"

For the second time in her life Billy was thankful that Bertram's question had turned upon her love for Arkwright, not Arkwright's love for her. In Billy's opinion, a man's unrequited love for a girl was his secret, not hers, and was certainly one that the girl had no right to tell.

Once before Bertram had asked her if she had ever cared for Arkwright, and then she had answered emphatically, as she did now:

"Never, dear."

"I thought you said so," murmured Bertram, relaxing a little.

"I did; besides, didn't I tell you?" she went on airily, "I think he'll marry Alice Greggory. Alice wrote me all the time I was away, and—oh, she didn't say anything definite, I'll admit," confessed Billy, with an arch smile; "but she spoke of his being there lots, and they used to know each other years ago, you see. There was almost a romance there, I think, before the Greggorys lost their money and moved away from all their friends."

"Well, he may have her. She's a nice girl—a mighty nice girl," answered Bertram, with the unmistakably satisfied air of the man who knows he himself possesses the nicest girl of them all.

Billy, reading unerringly the triumph in his voice, grew suddenly grave. She regarded her husband with a thoughtful frown; then she drew a profound sigh.

"Whew!" laughed Bertram, whimsically. "So soon as this?"

"Bertram!" Billy's voice was tragic.

"Yes, my love." The bridegroom pulled his face into sobriety; then Billy spoke, with solemn impressiveness.

"Bertram, I don't know a thing about—cooking—except what I've been learning in Rosa's cook-book this last week."

Bertram laughed so loud that the man across the aisle glanced over the top of his paper surreptitiously.

"Rosa's cook-book! Is that what you were doing all this week?"

"Yes; that is—I tried so hard to learn something," stammered Billy. "But I'm afraid I didn't—much; there were so many things for me to think of, you know, with only a week. I believe I could make peach fritters, though. They were the last thing I studied."

Bertram laughed again, uproariously; but, at Billy's unchangingly tragic face, he grew suddenly very grave and tender.

"Billy, dear, I didn't marry you to—to get a cook," he said gently.

Billy shook her head.

"I know; but Aunt Hannah said that even if I never expected to cook, myself, I ought to know how it was done, so to properly oversee it. She said that—that no woman, who didn't know how to cook and keep house properly, had any business to be a wife. And, Bertram, I did try, honestly, all this week. I tried so hard to remember when you sponged bread and when you kneaded it."

"I don't ever need—yours," cut in Bertram, shamelessly; but he got only a deservedly stern glance in return.

"And I repeated over and over again how many cupfuls of flour and pinches of salt and spoonfuls of baking-powder went into things; but, Bertram, I simply could not keep my mind on it. Everything, everywhere was singing to me. And how do you suppose I could remember how many pinches of flour and spoonfuls of salt and cupfuls of baking-powder went into a loaf of cake when all the while the very teakettle on the stove was singing: 'It's all right—Bertram loves me—I'm going to marry Bertram!'?"

"You darling!" (In spite of the man across the aisle Bertram did almost kiss her this time.)

"As if anybody cared how many cupfuls of baking-powder went anywhere—with that in your heart!"

"Aunt Hannah says you will—when you're hungry. And Kate said—"

Bertram uttered a sharp word behind his teeth.

"Billy, for heaven's sake don't tell me what Kate said, if you want me to stay sane, and not attempt to fight somebody—broken arm, and all. Kate thinks she's kind, and I suppose she means well; but—well, she's made trouble enough between us already. I've got you now, sweetheart. You're mine—all mine—" his voice shook, and dropped to a tender whisper—"'till death us do part.'"

"Yes; 'till death us do part,'" breathed Billy.

And then, for a time, they fell silent.

"'I, Bertram, take thee, Billy,'" sang the whirring wheels beneath them, to one.

"'I, Billy, take thee, Bertram,'" sang the whirring wheels beneath them, to the other. While straight ahead before them both, stretched fair and beautiful in their eyes, the wondrous path of life which they were to tread together.

CHAPTER II. FOR WILLIAM—A HOME

On the first Sunday after the wedding Pete came up-stairs to tell his master, William, that Mrs. Stetson wanted to see him in the drawing-room.

William went down at once.

"Well, Aunt Hannah," he began, reaching out a cordial hand. "Why, what's the matter?" he broke off concernedly, as he caught a clearer view of the little old lady's drawn face and troubled eyes.

"William, it's silly, of course," cried Aunt Hannah, tremulously, "but I simply had to go to some one. I—I feel so nervous and unsettled! Did—did Billy say anything to you—what she was going to do?"

"What she was going to do? About what? What do you mean?"

"About the house—selling it," faltered Aunt Hannah, sinking wearily back into her chair.

William frowned thoughtfully.

"Why, no," he answered. "It was all so hurried at the last, you know. There was really very little chance to make plans for anything—except the wedding," he finished, with a smile.

"Yes, I know," sighed Aunt Hannah. "Everything was in such confusion! Still, I didn't know but she might have said something—to you."

"No, she didn't. But I imagine it won't be hard to guess what she'll do. When they get back from their trip I fancy she won't lose much time in having what things she wants brought down here. Then she'll sell the rest and put the house on the market."

"Yes, of—of course," stammered Aunt Hannah, pulling herself hastily to a more erect position. "That's what I thought, too. Then don't you think we'd better dismiss Rosa and close the house at once?"

"Why—yes, perhaps so. Why not? Then you'd be all settled here when she comes home. I'm sure, the sooner you come, the better I'll be pleased," he smiled.

Aunt Hannah turned sharply.

"Here!" she ejaculated. "William Henshaw, you didn't suppose I was coming here to live, did you?"

It was William's turn to look amazed.

"Why, of course you're coming here! Where else should you go, pray?"

"Where I was before—before Billy came—to you," returned Aunt Hannah a little tremulously, but with a certain dignity. "I shall take a room in some quiet boarding-house, of course."

"Nonsense, Aunt Hannah! As if Billy would listen to that! You came before; why not come now?"

Aunt Hannah lifted her chin the fraction of an inch.

"You forget. I was needed before. Billy is a married woman now. She needs no chaperon."

"Nonsense!" scowled William, again. "Billy will always need you."

Aunt Hannah shook her head mournfully.

"I like to think—she wants me, William, but I know, in my heart, it isn't best."

"Why not?"

There was a moment's pause; then, decisively came the answer.

"Because I think young married folks should not have outsiders in the home."

William laughed relievedly.

"Oh, so that's it! Well, Aunt Hannah, you're no outsider. Come, run right along home and pack your trunk."

Aunt Hannah was plainly almost crying; but she held her ground.

"William, I can't," she reiterated.

"But—Billy is such a child, and—"

For once in her circumspect life Aunt Hannah was guilty of an interruption.

"Pardon me, William, she is not a child. She is a woman now, and she has a woman's problems to meet."

"Well, then, why don't you help her meet them?" retorted William, still with a whimsical smile.

But Aunt Hannah did not smile. For a minute she did not speak; then, with her eyes studiously averted, she said:

"William, the first four years of my married life were—were spoiled by an outsider in our home. I don't mean to spoil Billy's."

William relaxed visibly. The smile fled from his face.

"Why—Aunt—Hannah!" he exclaimed.

The little old lady turned with a weary sigh.

"Yes, I know. You are shocked, of course. I shouldn't have told you. Still, it is all past long ago, and—I wanted to make you understand why I can't come. He was my husband's eldest brother—a bachelor. He was good and kind, and meant well, I suppose; but—he interfered with everything. I was young, and probably headstrong. At all events, there was constant friction. He went away once and stayed two whole months. I shall never forget the utter freedom and happiness of those months for us, with the whole house to ourselves. No, William, I can't come." She rose abruptly and turned toward the door. Her eyes were wistful, and her face was still drawn with suffering; but her whole frail little self quivered plainly with high resolve. "John has Peggy outside. I must go."

"But—but, Aunt Hannah," began William, helplessly.

She lifted a protesting hand.

"No, don't urge me, please. I can't come here. But—I believe I won't close the house till Billy gets home, after all," she declared. The next moment she was gone, and William, dazedly, from the doorway, was watching John help her into Billy's automobile, called by Billy and half her friends, "Peggy," short for "Pegasus."

Still dazedly William turned back into the house and dropped himself into the nearest chair. What a curious call it had been! Aunt Hannah had not acted like herself at all. Not once had she said "Oh, my grief and conscience!" while the things she had said—! Someway, he had never thought of Aunt Hannah as being young, and a bride. Still, of course she must have been—once. And the reason she gave for not coming there to live—the pitiful story of that outsider in her home! But she was no outsider! She was no interfering brother of Billy's—

William caught his breath suddenly, and held it suspended. Then he gave a low ejaculation and half sprang from his chair.

Spunkie, disturbed from her doze by the fire, uttered a purring "me-o-ow," and looked up inquiringly.

For a long minute William gazed dumbly into the cat's yellow, sleepily contented eyes; then he said with tragic distinctness:

"Spunkie, it's true: Aunt Hannah isn't Billy's husband's brother, but—I am! Do you hear? I am!"

"Pur-r-me-ow!" commented Spunkie; and curled herself for another nap.

211

There was no peace for William after that. In vain he told himself that he was no "interfering" brother, and that this was his home and had been all his life; in vain did he declare emphatically that he could not go, he would not go; that Billy would not wish him to go: always before his eyes was the vision of that little bride of years long gone; always in his ears was the echo of Aunt Hannah's "I shall never forget the utter freedom and happiness of those months for us, with the whole house to ourselves." Nor, turn which way he would, could he find anything to comfort him. Simply because he was so fearfully looking for it, he found it—the thing that had for its theme the wretchedness that might be expected from the presence of a third person in the new home.

Poor William! Everywhere he met it—the hint, the word, the story, the song, even; and always it added its mite to the woeful whole. Even the hoariest of mother-in-law jokes had its sting for him; and, to make his cup quite full, he chanced to remember one day what Marie had said when he had suggested that she and Cyril come to the Strata to live: "No; I think young folks should begin by themselves."

Unhappy, indeed, were these days for William. Like a lost spirit he wandered from room to room, touching this, fingering that. For long minutes he would stand before some picture, or some treasured bit of old mahogany, as if to stamp indelibly upon his mind a thing that was soon to be no more. At other times, like a man without a home, he would go out into the Common or the Public Garden and sit for hours on some bench—thinking.

All this could have but one ending, of course. Before the middle of August William summoned Pete to his rooms.

"Oh, Pete, I'm going to move next week," he began nonchalantly. His voice sounded as if moving were a pleasurable circumstance that occurred in his life regularly once a month. "I'd like you to begin to pack up these things, please, to-morrow."

The old servant's mouth fell open.

"You're goin' to—to what, sir?" he stammered.

"Move—move, I said." William spoke with unusual harshness.

Pete wet his lips.

"You mean you've sold the old place, sir?—that we—we ain't goin' to live here no longer?"

"Sold? Of course not! I'm going to move away; not you."

If Pete could have known what caused the sharpness in his master's voice, he would not have been so grieved—or, rather, he would have been grieved for a different reason. As it was he could only falter miserably:

"You are goin' to move away from here!"

"Yes, yes, man! Why, Pete, what ails you? One would think a body never moved before."

"They didn't—not you, sir."

William turned abruptly, so that his face could not be seen. With stern deliberation he picked up an elaborately decorated teapot; but the valuable bit of Lowestoft shook so in his hand that he set it down at once. It clicked sharply against its neighbor, betraying his nervous hand.

Pete stirred.

"But, Mr. William," he stammered thickly; "how are you—what'll you do without—There doesn't nobody but me know so well about your tea, and the two lumps in your coffee; and there's your flannels that you never put on till I get 'em out, and the woolen socks that you'd wear all summer if I didn't hide 'em. And—and who's goin' to take care of these?" he finished, with a glance that encompassed the overflowing cabinets and shelves of curios all about him.

His master smiled sadly. An affection that had its inception in his boyhood days shone in his eyes. The hand in which the Lowestoft had shaken rested now heavily on an old man's bent shoulder—a shoulder that straightened itself in unconscious loyalty under the touch.

"Pete, you have spoiled me, and no mistake. I don't expect to find another like you. But maybe if I wear the woolen socks too late you'll come and hunt up the others for me. Eh?"

And, with a smile that was meant to be quizzical, William turned and began to shift the teapots about again.

"But, Mr. William, why—that is, what will Mr. Bertram and Miss Billy do—without you?" ventured the old man.

There was a sudden tinkling crash. On the floor lay the fragments of a silver-luster teapot. The servant exclaimed aloud in dismay, but his master did not even glance toward his once treasured possession on the floor.

"Nonsense, Pete!" he was saying in a particularly cheery voice. "Have you lived all these years and not found out that newly-married folks don't need any one else around? Come, do you suppose we could begin to pack these teapots to-night?" he added, a little feverishly. "Aren't there some boxes down cellar?"

"I'll see, sir," said Pete, respectfully; but the expression on his face as he turned away showed that he was not thinking of teapots—nor of boxes in which to pack them.

CHAPTER III. BILLY SPEAKS HER MIND

Mr. and Mrs. Bertram Henshaw were expected home the first of September. By the thirty-first of August the old Beacon Street homestead facing the Public Garden was in spick-and-span order, with Dong Ling in the basement hovering over a well-stocked larder, and Pete searching the rest of the house for a chair awry, or a bit of dust undiscovered.

Twice before had the Strata—as Bertram long ago dubbed the home of his boyhood—been prepared for the coming of Billy, William's namesake: once, when it had been decorated with guns and fishing-rods to welcome the "boy" who turned out to be a girl; and again when with pink roses and sewing-baskets the three brothers got joyously ready for a feminine Billy who did not even come at all.

The house had been very different then. It had been, indeed, a "strata," with its distinctive layers of fads and pursuits as represented by Bertram and his painting on one floor, William and his curios on another, and Cyril with his music on a third. Cyril was gone now. Only Pete and his humble belongings occupied the top floor. The floor below, too, was silent now, and almost empty save for a rug or two, and a few pieces of heavy furniture that William had not cared to take with him to his new quarters on top of Beacon Hill. Below this, however, came Billy's old rooms, and on these Pete had lavished all his skill and devotion.

Freshly laundered curtains were at the windows, dustless rugs were on the floor. The old work-basket had been brought down from the top-floor storeroom, and the long-closed piano stood invitingly open. In a conspicuous place, also, sat the little green god, upon whose exquisitely carved shoulders was supposed to rest the "heap plenty velly good luckee" of Dong Ling's prophecy.

On the first floor Bertram's old rooms and the drawing-room came in for their share of the general overhauling. Even Spunkie did not escape, but had to submit to the ignominy of a bath. And then dawned fair and clear the first day of September, bringing at five o'clock the bride and groom.

Respectfully lined up in the hall to meet them were Pete and Dong Ling: Pete with his wrinkled old face alight with joy and excitement; Dong Ling grinning and kotowing, and chanting in a high-pitched treble:

"Miss Billee, Miss Billee—plenty much welcome, Miss Billee!"

"Yes, welcome home, Mrs. Henshaw!" bowed Bertram, turning at the door, with an elaborate flourish that did not in the least hide his tender pride in his new wife.

Billy laughed and colored a pretty pink.

"Thank you—all of you," she cried a little unsteadily. "And how good, good everything does look to me! Why, where's Uncle William?" she broke off, casting hurriedly anxious eyes about her.

"Well, I should say so," echoed Bertram. "Where is he, Pete? He isn't sick, is he?"

A quick change crossed the old servant's face. He shook his head dumbly.

Billy gave a gleeful laugh.

"I know—he's asleep!" she caroled, skipping to the bottom of the stairway and looking up.

"Ho, Uncle William! Better wake up, sir. The folks have come!"

Pete cleared his throat.

"Mr. William isn't here, Miss—ma'am," he corrected miserably.

Billy smiled, but she frowned, too.

"Not here! Well, I like that," she pouted; "—and when I've brought him the most beautiful pair of mirror knobs he ever saw, and all the way in my bag, too, so I could give them to him the very first thing," she added, darting over to the small bag she had brought in with her. "I'm glad I did, too, for our trunks didn't come," she continued laughingly. "Still, if he isn't here to receive them—There, Pete, aren't they beautiful?" she cried, carefully taking from their wrappings two exquisitely decorated porcelain discs mounted on two long spikes. "They're Batterseas—the real article. I know enough for that; and they're finer than anything he's got. Won't he be pleased?"

"Yes, Miss—ma'am, I mean," stammered the old man.

"These new titles come hard, don't they, Pete?" laughed Bertram.

Pete smiled faintly.

"Never mind, Pete," soothed his new mistress. "You shall call me 'Miss Billy' all your life if you want to. Bertram," she added, turning to her husband, "I'm going to just run up-stairs and put these in Uncle William's rooms so they'll be there when he comes in. We'll see how soon he discovers them!"

Before Pete could stop her she was half-way up the first flight of stairs. Even then he tried to speak to his young master, to explain that Mr. William was not living there; but the words refused to come. He could only stand dumbly waiting.

In a minute it came—Billy's sharp, startled cry.

"Bertram! Bertram!"

Bertram sprang for the stairway, but he had not reached the top when he met his wife coming down. She was white-faced and trembling.

"Bertram—those rooms—there's not so much as a teapot there! Uncle William's—gone!"

"Gone!" Bertram wheeled sharply. "Pete, what is the meaning of this? Where is my brother?" To hear him, one would think he suspected the old servant of having hidden his master.

Pete lifted a shaking hand and fumbled with his collar.

"He's moved, sir."

"Moved! Oh, you mean to other rooms—to Cyril's." Bertram relaxed visibly. "He's upstairs, maybe."

Pete shook his head.

"No, sir. He's moved away—out of the house, sir."

For a brief moment Bertram stared as if he could not believe what his ears had heard. Then, step by step, he began to descend the stairs.

"Do you mean—to say—that my brother—has moved-gone away—left—his home?" he demanded.

"Yes, sir."

Billy gave a low cry.

"But why—why?" she choked, almost stumbling headlong down the stairway in her effort to reach the two men at the bottom. "Pete, why did he go?"

There was no answer.

"Pete,"—Bertram's voice was very sharp—"what is the meaning of this? Do you know why my brother left his home?"

The old man wet his lips and swallowed chokingly, but he did not speak.

"I'm waiting, Pete."

Billy laid one hand on the old servant's arm—in the other hand she still tightly clutched the mirror knobs.

"Pete, if you do know, won't you tell us, please?" she begged.

Pete looked down at the hand, then up at the troubled young face with the beseeching eyes. His own features worked convulsively. With a visible effort he cleared his throat.

"I know—what he said," he stammered, his eyes averted.

"What was it?"

There was no answer.

"Look here, Pete, you'll have to tell us, you know," cut in Bertram, decisively, "so you might as well do it now as ever."

Once more Pete cleared his throat. This time the words came in a burst of desperation.

"Yes, sir. I understand, sir. It was only that he said—he said as how young folks didn't need any one else around. So he was goin'."

"Didn't need any one else!" exclaimed Bertram, plainly not comprehending.

"Yes, sir. You two bein' married so, now." Pete's eyes were still averted.

Billy gave a low cry.

"You mean—because I came?" she demanded.

"Why, yes, Miss—no—that is—" Pete stopped with an appealing glance at Bertram.

"Then it was—it was—on account of me," choked Billy.

Pete looked still more distressed

"No, no!" he faltered. "It was only that he thought you wouldn't want him here now."

"Want him here!" ejaculated Bertram.

"Want him here!" echoed Billy, with a sob.

"Pete, where is he?" As she asked the question she dropped the mirror knobs into her open bag, and reached for her coat and gloves—she had not removed her hat.

Pete gave the address.

"It's just down the street a bit and up the hill," he added excitedly, divining her purpose. "It's a sort of a boarding-house, I reckon."

"A boarding-house—for Uncle William!" scorned Billy, her eyes ablaze. "Come, Bertram, we'll see about that."

Bertram reached out a detaining hand.

"But, dearest, you're so tired," he demurred. "Hadn't we better wait till after dinner, or till to-morrow?"

"After dinner! To-morrow!" Billy's eyes blazed anew. "Why, Bertram Henshaw, do you think I'd leave that dear man even one minute longer, if I could help it, with a notion in his blessed old head that we didn't want him?"

"But you said a little while ago you had a headache, dear," still objected Bertram. "If you'd just eat your dinner!"

"Dinner!" choked Billy. "I wonder if you think I could eat any dinner with Uncle William turned out of his home! I'm going to find Uncle William." And she stumbled blindly toward the door.

Bertram reached for his hat. He threw a despairing glance into Pete's eyes.

"We'll be back—when we can," he said, with a frown.

"Yes, sir," answered Pete, respectfully. Then, as if impelled by some hidden force, he touched his master's arm. "It was that way she looked, sir, when she came to you—that night last July—with her eyes all shining," he whispered.

A tender smile curved Bertram's lips. The frown vanished from his face.

"Bless you, Pete—and bless her, too!" he whispered back. The next moment he had hurried after his wife.

The house that bore the number Pete had given proved to have a pretentious doorway, and a landlady who, in response to the summons of the neat maid, appeared with a most impressive rustle of black silk and jet bugles.

No, Mr. William Henshaw was not in his rooms. In fact, he was very seldom there. His business, she believed, called him to State Street through the day. Outside of that, she had been told, he spent much time sitting on a bench in the Common. Doubtless, if they cared to search, they could find him there now.

"A bench in the Common, indeed!" stormed Billy, as she and Bertram hurried down the wide stone steps. "Uncle William—on a bench!"

"But surely now, dear," ventured her husband, "you'll come home and get your dinner!"

Billy turned indignantly.

"And leave Uncle William on a bench in the Common? Indeed, no! Why, Bertram, you wouldn't, either," she cried, as she turned resolutely toward one of the entrances to the Common.

And Bertram, with the "eyes all shining" still before him, could only murmur: "No, of course not, dear!" and follow obediently where she led.

Under ordinary circumstances it would have been a delightful hour for a walk. The sun had almost set, and the shadows lay long across the grass. The air was cool and unusually bracing for a day so early in September. But all this was lost on Bertram. Bertram did not wish to take a walk. He was hungry. He wanted his dinner; and he wanted, too, his old home with his new wife flitting about the rooms as he had pictured this first evening together. He wanted William, of course. Certainly he wanted William; but if William would insist on running away and sitting on park benches in this ridiculous fashion, he ought to take the consequences—until to-morrow.

Five, ten, fifteen minutes passed. Up one path and down another trudged the anxious-eyed Billy and her increasingly impatient husband. Then when the fifteen weary minutes had become a still more weary half-hour, the bonds Bertram had set on his temper snapped.

"Billy," he remonstrated despairingly, "do, please, come home! Don't you see how highly improbable it is that we should happen on William if we walked like this all night? He might move—change his seat—go home, even. He probably has gone home. And surely never before did a bride insist on spending the first evening after her return tramping up and down a public park for hour after hour like this, looking for any man. Won't you come home?"

But Billy had not even heard. With a glad little cry she had darted to the side of the humped-up figure of a man alone on a park bench just ahead of them.

"Uncle William! Oh, Uncle William, how could you?" she cried, dropping herself on to one end of the seat and catching the man's arm in both her hands.

"Yes, how could you?" demanded Bertram, with just a touch of irritation, dropping himself on to the other end of the seat, and catching the man's other arm in his one usable hand.

The bent shoulders and bowed head straightened up with a jerk.

"Well, well, bless my soul! If it isn't our little bride," cried Uncle William, fondly. "And the happy bridegroom, too. When did you get home?"

"We haven't got home," retorted Bertram, promptly, before his wife could speak. "Oh, we looked in at the door an hour or so back; but we didn't stay. We've been hunting for you ever since."

"Nonsense, children!" Uncle William spoke with gay cheeriness; but he refused to meet either Billy's or Bertram's eyes.

"Uncle William, how could you do it?" reproached Billy, again.

"Do what?" Uncle William was plainly fencing for time.

"Leave the house like that?"

"Ho! I wanted a change."

"As if we'd believe that!" scoffed Billy.

"All right; let's call it you've had the change, then," laughed Bertram, "and we'll send over for your things to-morrow. Come—now let's go home to dinner."

William shook his head. He essayed a gay smile.

"Why, I've only just begun. I'm going to stay—oh, I don't know how long I'm going to stay," he finished blithely.

Billy lifted her chin a little.

"Uncle William, you aren't playing square. Pete told us what you said when you left."

"Eh? What?" William looked up with startled eyes.

"About—about our not needing you. So we know, now, why you left; and we sha'n't stand it."

"Pete? That? Oh, that—that's nonsense I—I'll settle with Pete."

Billy laughed softly.

"Poor Pete! Don't. We simply dragged it out of him. And now we're here to tell you that we do want you, and that you must come back."

Again William shook his head. A swift shadow crossed his face.

"Thank you, no, children," he said dully.

"You're very kind, but you don't need me. I should be just an interfering elder brother. I should spoil your young married life." (William's voice now sounded as if he were reciting a well-learned lesson.) "If I went away and stayed two months, you'd never forget the utter freedom and joy of those two whole months with the house all to yourselves."

"Uncle William," gasped Billy, "what are you talking about?"

"About—about my not going back, of course."

"But you are coming back," cut in Bertram, almost angrily. "Oh, come, Will, this is utter nonsense, and you know it! Come, let's go home to dinner."

A stern look came to the corners of William's mouth—a look that Bertram understood well.

"All right, I'll go to dinner, of course; but I sha'n't stay," said William, firmly. "I've thought it all out. I know I'm right. Come, we'll go to dinner now, and say no more about it," he finished with a cheery smile, as he rose to his feet. Then, to the bride, he added: "Did you have a nice trip, little girl?"

Billy, too, had risen, now, but she did not seem to have heard his question. In the fast falling twilight her face looked a little white.

"Uncle William," she began very quietly, "do you think for a minute that just because I married your brother I am going to live in that house and turn you out of the home you've lived in all your life?"

"Nonsense, dear! I'm not turned out. I just go," corrected Uncle William, gayly.

With superb disdain Billy brushed this aside.

"Oh, no, you won't," she declared; "but—I shall."

"Billy!" gasped Bertram.

"My—my dear!" expostulated William, faintly.

"Uncle William! Bertram! Listen," panted Billy. "I never told you much before, but I'm going to, now. Long ago, when I went away with Aunt Hannah, your sister Kate showed me how dear the old home was to you—how much you thought of it. And she said—she said that I had upset everything." (Bertram interjected a sharp word, but Billy paid no attention.) "That's why I went; and I shall go again—if you don't come home to-morrow to stay, Uncle William. Come, now let's go to dinner, please. Bertram's hungry," she finished, with a bright smile.

There was a tense moment of silence. William glanced at Bertram; Bertram returned the glance—with interest.

"Er—ah—yes; well, we might go to dinner," stammered William, after a minute.

"Er—yes," agreed Bertram. And the three fell into step together.

CHAPTER IV. "JUST LIKE BILLY"

Billy did not leave the Strata this time. Before twenty-four hours had passed, the last cherished fragment of Mr. William Henshaw's possessions had been carefully carried down the imposing steps of the Beacon Hill boarding-house under the disapproving eyes of its bugle-adorned mistress, who found herself now with a month's advance rent and two vacant "parlors" on her hands. Before another twenty-four hours had passed her quondam boarder, with a tired sigh, sank into his favorite morris chair in his old familiar rooms, and looked about him with contented eyes. Every treasure was in place, from the traditional four small stones of his babyhood days to the Batterseas Billy had just brought him. Pete, as of yore, was hovering near with a dust-cloth. Bertram's gay whistle sounded from the floor below. William Henshaw was at home again.

This much accomplished, Billy went to see Aunt Hannah.

Aunt Hannah greeted her affectionately, though with tearfully troubled eyes. She was wearing a gray shawl to-day topped with a black one—sure sign of unrest, either physical or mental, as all her friends knew.

"I'd begun to think you'd forgotten—me," she faltered, with a poor attempt at gayety. "You've been home three whole days."

"I know, dearie," smiled Billy; "and 'twas a shame. But I have been so busy! My trunks came at last, and I've been helping Uncle William get settled, too."

Aunt Hannah looked puzzled.

"Uncle William get settled? You mean—he's changed his room?"

Billy laughed oddly, and threw a swift glance into Aunt Hannah's face.

"Well, yes, he did change," she murmured; "but he's moved back now into the old quarters. Er—you haven't heard from Uncle William then, lately, I take it."

"No." Aunt Hannah shook her head abstractedly. "I did see him once, several weeks ago; but I haven't, since. We had quite a talk, then; and, Billy, I've been wanting to speak to you," she hurried on, a little feverishly. "I didn't like to leave, of course, till you did come home, as long as you'd said nothing about your plans; but—"

"Leave!" interposed Billy, dazedly. "Leave where? What do you mean?"

"Why, leave here, of course, dear. I mean. I didn't like to get my room while you were away; but I shall now, of course, at once."

"Nonsense, Aunt Hannah! As if I'd let you do that," laughed Billy.

Aunt Hannah stiffened perceptibly. Her lips looked suddenly thin and determined. Even the soft little curls above her ears seemed actually to bristle with resolution.

"Billy," she began firmly, "we might as well understand each other at once. I know your good heart, and I appreciate your kindness. But I can not come to live with you. I shall not. It wouldn't be best. I should be like an interfering elder brother in your home. I should spoil your young married life; and if I went away for two months you'd never forget the utter joy and freedom of those two months with the whole house all to yourselves."

At the beginning of this speech Billy's eyes had still carried their dancing smile, but as the peroration progressed on to the end, a dawning surprise, which soon became a puzzled questioning, drove the smile away. Then Billy sat suddenly erect.

"Why, Aunt Hannah, that's exactly what Uncle William—" Billy stopped, and regarded Aunt Hannah with quick suspicion. The next moment she burst into gleeful laughter.

Aunt Hannah looked grieved, and not a little surprised; but Billy did not seem to notice this.

"Oh, oh, Aunt Hannah—you, too! How perfectly funny!" she gurgled. "To think you two old blesseds should get your heads together like this!"

Aunt Hannah stirred restively, and pulled the black shawl more closely about her.

"Indeed, Billy, I don't know what you mean by that," she sighed, with a visible effort at self-control; "but I do know that I can not go to live with you."

"Bless your heart, dear, I don't want you to," soothed Billy, with gay promptness.

"Oh! O-h-h," stammered Aunt Hannah, surprise, mortification, dismay, and a grieved hurt bringing a flood of color to her face. It is one thing to refuse a home, and quite another to have a home refused you.

"Oh! O-h-h, Aunt Hannah," cried Billy, turning very red in her turn. "Please, please don't look like that. I didn't mean it that way. I do want you, dear, only—I want you somewhere else more. I want you—here."

"Here!" Aunt Hannah looked relieved, but unconvinced.

"Yes. Don't you like it here?"

"Like it! Why, I love it, dear. You know I do. But you don't need this house now, Billy."

"Oh, yes, I do," retorted Billy, airily. "I'm going to keep it up, and I want you here.

"Fiddlededee, Billy! As if I'd let you keep up this house just for me," scorned Aunt Hannah.

"'Tisn't just for you. It's for—for lots of folks."

"My grief and conscience, Billy! What are you talking about?"

Billy laughed, and settled herself more comfortably on the hassock at Aunt Hannah's feet.

"Well, I'll tell you. Just now I want it for Tommy Dunn, and the Greggorys if I can get them, and maybe one or two others. There'll always be somebody. You see, I had thought I'd have them at the Strata."

"Tommy Dunn—at the Strata!"

Billy laughed again ruefully.

"O dear! You sound just like Bertram," she pouted. "He didn't want Tommy, either, nor any of the rest of them."

"The rest of them!"

"Well, I could have had a lot more, you know, the Strata is so big, especially now that Cyril has gone, and left all those empty rooms. I got real enthusiastic, but Bertram didn't. He just laughed and said 'nonsense!' until he found I was really in earnest; then he—well, he said 'nonsense,' then, too—only he didn't laugh," finished Billy, with a sigh.

Aunt Hannah regarded her with fond, though slightly exasperated eyes.

"Billy, you are, indeed, a most extraordinary young woman—at times. Surely, with you, a body never knows what to expect—except the unexpected."

"Why, Aunt Hannah!—and from you, too!" reproached Billy, mischievously; but Aunt Hannah had yet more to say.

"Of course Bertram thought it was nonsense. The idea of you, a bride, filling up your house with—with people like that! Tommy Dunn, indeed!"

"Oh, Bertram said he liked Tommy all right," sighed Billy; "but he said that that didn't mean he wanted him for three meals a day. One would think poor Tommy was a breakfast food! So that is when I thought of keeping up this house, you see, and that's why I want you here—to take charge of it. And you'll do that—for me, won't you?"

Aunt Hannah fell back in her chair.

"Why, y-yes, Billy, of course, if—if you want it. But what an extraordinary idea, child!"

Billy shook her head. A deeper color came to her cheeks, and a softer glow to her eyes.

"I don't think so, Aunt Hannah. It's only that I'm so happy that some of it has just got to overflow somewhere, and this is going to be the overflow house—a sort of safety valve for me, you see. I'm going to call it the Annex—it will be an annex to our home. And I want to keep it full, always, of people who—who can make the best use of all that extra happiness that I can't possibly use myself," she finished a little tremulously. "Don't you see?"

"Oh, yes, I see," replied Aunt Hannah, with a fond shake of the head.

"But, really, listen—it's sensible," urged Billy. "First, there's Tommy. His mother died last month. He's at a neighbor's now, but they're going to send him to a Home for Crippled Children; and he's grieving his heart out over it. I'm going to bring him here to a real home—the kind that doesn't begin with a capital letter. He adores music, and he's got real talent, I think. Then there's the Greggorys."

Aunt Hannah looked dubious.

"You can't get the Greggorys to—to use any of that happiness, Billy. They're too proud."

Billy smiled radiantly.

"I know I can't get them to use it, Aunt Hannah, but I believe I can get them to give it," she declared triumphantly. "I shall ask Alice Greggory to teach Tommy music, and I shall ask Mrs. Greggory to teach him books; and I shall tell them both that I positively need them to keep you company."

"Oh, but Billy," bridled Aunt Hannah, with prompt objection.

"Tut, tut!—I know you'll be willing to be thrown as a little bit of a sop to the Greggorys' pride," coaxed Billy. "You just wait till I get the Overflow Annex in running order. Why, Aunt Hannah, you don't know how busy you're going to be handing out all that extra happiness that I can't use!"

"You dear child!" Aunt Hannah smiled mistily. The black shawl had fallen unheeded to the floor now. "As if anybody ever had any more happiness than one's self could use!"

"I have," avowed Billy, promptly, "and it's going to keep growing and growing, I know."

"Oh, my grief and conscience, Billy, don't!" exclaimed Aunt Hannah, lifting shocked hands of remonstrance. "Rap on wood—do! How can you boast like that?"

Billy dimpled roguishly and sprang to her feet.

"Why, Aunt Hannah, I'm ashamed of you! To be superstitious like that—you, a good Presbyterian!"

Aunt Hannah subsided shamefacedly.

"Yes, I know, Billy, it is silly; but I just can't help it."

"Oh, but it's worse than silly, Aunt Hannah," teased Billy, with a remorseless chuckle. "It's really heathen! Bertram told me once that it dates 'way back to the time of the Druids—appealing to the god of trees, or something like that—when you rap on wood, you know."

"Ugh!" shuddered Aunt Hannah. "As if I would, Billy! How is Bertram, by the by?"

A swift shadow crossed Billy's bright face.

"He's lovely—only his arm."

"His arm! But I thought that was better."

"Oh, it is," drooped Billy, "but it gets along so slowly, and it frets him dreadfully. You know he never can do anything with his left hand, he says, and he just hates to have things done for him—though Pete and Dong Ling are quarreling with each other all the time to do things for him, and I'm quarreling with both of them to do them for him myself! By the way, Dong Ling is going to leave us next week. Did you know it?"

"Dong Ling—leave!"

"Yes. Oh, he told Bertram long ago he should go when we were married; that he had plenty much money, and was going back to China, and not be Melican man any longer. But I don't think Bertram thought he'd do it. William says Dong Ling went to Pete, however, after we left, and told him he wanted to go; that he liked the little Missee plenty well, but that there'd be too much hen-talk when she got back, and—"

"Why, the impudent creature!"

Billy laughed merrily.

"Yes; Pete was furious, William says, but Dong Ling didn't mean any disrespect, I'm sure. He just wasn't used to having petticoats around, and didn't want to take orders from them; that's all."

"But, Billy, what will you do?"

"Oh, Pete's fixed all that lovely," returned Billy, nonchalantly. "You know his niece lives over in South Boston, and it seems she's got a daughter who's a fine cook and will be glad to come. Mercy! Look at the time," she broke off, glancing at the clock. "I shall be late to dinner, and Dong Ling loathes anybody who's late to his meals—as I found out to my sorrow the night we got home. Good-by, dear. I'll be out soon again and fix it all up—about the Annex, you know." And with a bright smile she was gone.

"Dear me," sighed Aunt Hannah, stooping to pick up the black shawl; "dear me! Of course everything will be all right—there's a girl coming, even if Dong Ling is going. But—but—Oh, my grief and conscience, what an extraordinary child Billy is, to be sure—but what a dear one!" she added, wiping a quick tear from her eye. "An Overflow Annex, indeed, for her 'extra happiness'! Now isn't that just like Billy?"

CHAPTER V. TIGER SKINS

September passed and October came, bringing with it cool days and clear, crisp evenings royally ruled over by a gorgeous harvest moon. According to Billy everything was just perfect—except, of course, poor Bertram's arm; and even the fact that that gained so slowly was not without its advantage (again according to Billy), for it gave Bertram more time to be with her.

"You see, dear, as long as you can't paint," she told him earnestly, one day, "why, I'm not really hindering you by keeping you with me so much."

"You certainly are not," he retorted, with a smile.

"Then I may be just as happy as I like over it," settled Billy, comfortably.

"As if you ever could hinder me," he ridiculed.

"Oh, yes, I could," nodded Billy, emphatically. "You forget, sir. That was what worried me so. Everybody, even the newspapers and magazines, said I would do it, too. They said I'd slay your Art, stifle your Ambition, destroy your Inspiration, and be a nuisance generally. And Kate said—"

"Yes. Well, never mind what Kate said," interrupted the man, savagely.

Billy laughed, and gave his ear a playful tweak.

"All right; but I'm not going to do it, you know—spoil your career, sir. You just wait," she continued dramatically. "The minute your arm gets so you can paint, I myself shall conduct you to your studio, thrust the brushes into your hand, fill your palette with all the colors of the rainbow, and order you to paint, my lord, paint! But—until then I'm going to have you all I like," she finished, with a complete change of manner, nestling into the ready curve of his good left arm.

"You witch!" laughed the man, fondly. "Why, Billy, you couldn't hinder me. You'll be my inspiration, dear, instead of slaying it. You'll see. This time Marguerite Winthrop's portrait is going to be a success."

Billy turned quickly.

"Then you are—that is, you haven't—I mean, you're going to—paint it?"

"I just am," avowed the artist. "And this time it'll be a success, too, with you to help."

Billy drew in her breath tremulously.

"I didn't know but you'd already started it," she faltered.

He shook his head.

"No. After the other one failed, and Mr. Winthrop asked me to try again, I couldn't then. I was so troubled over you. That's the time you did hinder me," he smiled. "Then came your note breaking the engagement. Of course I knew too much to attempt a thing like that portrait then. But now—now—!" The pause and the emphasis were eloquent.

"Of course, now," nodded Billy, brightly, but a little feverishly. "And when do you begin?"

"Not till January. Miss Winthrop won't be back till then. I saw J. G. last week, and I told him I'd accept his offer to try again."

"What did he say?"

"He gave my left hand a big grip and said: 'Good!—and you'll win out this time.'"

"Of course you will," nodded Billy, again, though still a little feverishly. "And this time I sha'n't mind a bit if you do stay to luncheon, and break engagements with me, sir," she went on, tilting her chin archly, "for I shall know it's the portrait and not the sitter that's really keeping you. Oh, you'll see what a fine artist's wife I'll make!"

"The very best," declared Bertram so ardently that Billy blushed, and shook her head in reproof.

"Nonsense! I wasn't fishing. I didn't mean it that way," she protested. Then, as he tried to catch her, she laughed and danced teasingly out of his reach.

Because Bertram could not paint, therefore, Billy had him quite to herself these October days; nor did she hesitate to appropriate him. Neither, on his part, was Bertram loath to be appropriated. Like two lovers they read and walked and talked together, and like two children, sometimes, they romped through the stately old rooms with Spunkie, or with Tommy Dunn, who was a frequent guest. Spunkie, be it known, was renewing her kittenhood, so potent was the influence of the dangling strings and rolling balls that she encountered everywhere; and Tommy Dunn, with Billy's help, was learning that not even a pair of crutches need keep a lonely little lad from a frolic. Even William, roused from his after-dinner doze by peals of laughter, was sometimes inveigled into activities that left him breathless, but curiously aglow. While Pete, polishing silver in the dining-room down-stairs, smiled indulgently at the merry clatter above—and forgot the teasing pain in his side.

But it was not all nonsense with Billy, nor gay laughter. More often it was a tender glow in the eyes, a softness in the voice, a radiant something like an aura of joy all about her, that told how happy indeed were these days for her. There was proof by word of mouth, too—long talks with Bertram in the dancing firelight when they laid dear plans for the future, and when she tried so hard to make her husband understand what a good, good wife she intended to be, and how she meant never to let anything come between them.

It was so earnest and serious a Billy by this time that Bertram would turn startled, dismayed eyes on his young wife; whereupon, with a very Billy-like change of mood, she would give him one of her rare caresses, and perhaps sigh:

"Goosey—it's only because I'm so happy, happy, happy! Why, Bertram, if it weren't for that Overflow Annex I believe I—I just couldn't live!"

It was Bertram who sighed then, and who prayed fervently in his heart that never might he see a real shadow cloud that dear face.

Thus far, certainly, the cares of matrimony had rested anything but heavily upon the shapely young shoulders of the new wife. Domestic affairs at the Strata moved like a piece of well-oiled machinery. Dong Ling, to be sure, was not there; but in his place reigned Pete's grandniece, a fresh-faced, capable young woman who (Bertram declared) cooked like an angel and minded her own business like a man. Pete, as of yore, had full charge of the house; and a casual eye would see few changes. Even the brothers themselves saw few, for that matter.

True, at the very first, Billy had donned a ruffled apron and a bewitching dust-cap, and had traversed the house from cellar to garret with a prettily important air of "managing things," as she suggested changes right and left. She had summoned Pete, too, for three mornings in succession, and with great dignity had ordered the meals for the day. But when Bertram was discovered one evening tugging back his favorite chair, and when William had asked if Billy were through using his pipe-tray, the young wife had concluded to let things remain about as they were. And when William ate no breakfast one morning, and Bertram aggrievedly refused dessert that night at dinner, Billy—learning through an apologetic Pete that Master William always had to have eggs for breakfast no matter what else there was, and that Master Bertram never ate boiled rice—gave up planning the meals. True, for three more mornings she summoned Pete for "orders," but the orders were nothing more nor less than a blithe "Well, Pete, what are we going to have for dinner to-day?" By the end of a week even this ceremony was given up, and before a month had passed, Billy was little more than a guest in her own home, so far as responsibility was concerned.

Billy was not idle, however; far from it. First, there were the delightful hours with Bertram. Then there was her music: Billy was writing a new song—the best she had ever written, Billy declared.

"Why, Bertram, it can't help being that," she said to her husband, one day. "The words just sang themselves to me right out of my heart; and the melody just dropped down from the sky. And now, everywhere, I'm hearing the most wonderful harmonies. The whole universe is singing to me. If only now I can put it on paper what I hear! Then I can make the whole universe sing to some one else!"

Even music, however, had to step one side for the wedding calls which were beginning to be received, and which must be returned, in spite of the occasional rebellion of the young husband. There were the more intimate friends to be seen, also, and Cyril and Marie to be visited. And always there was the Annex.

The Annex was in fine running order now, and was a source of infinite satisfaction to its founder and great happiness to its beneficiaries. Tommy Dunn was there, learning wonderful things from books and still more wonderful things from the piano in the living-room. Alice Greggory and her mother were there, too—the result of much persuasion. Indeed, according to Bertram, Billy had been able to fill the Annex only by telling each prospective resident that he or she was absolutely necessary to the welfare and happiness of every other resident. Not that the house was full, either. There were still two unoccupied rooms.

"But then, I'm glad there are," Billy had declared, "for there's sure to be some one that I'll want to send there."

"Some one, did you say?" Bertram had retorted, meaningly; but his wife had disdained to answer this.

Billy herself was frequently at the Annex. She told Aunt Hannah that she had to come often to bring the happiness—it accumulated so fast. Certainly she always found plenty to do there, whenever she came. There was Aunt Hannah to be read to, Mrs. Greggory to be sung to, and Tommy Dunn to be listened to; for Tommy Dunn was always quivering with eagerness to play her his latest "piece."

Billy knew that some day at the Annex she would meet Mr. M. J. Arkwright; and she told herself that she hoped she should.

Billy had not seen Arkwright (except on the stage of the Boston Opera House) since the day he had left her presence in white-faced, stony-eyed misery after declaring his love for her, and learning of her engagement to Bertram. Since then, she knew, he had been much with his old friend, Alice Greggory. She did not believe, should she see him now, that he would be either white-faced, or stony-eyed. His heart, she was sure, had gone where it ought to have gone in the first place—to Alice. Such being, in her opinion, the case, she longed to get the embarrassment of a first meeting between themselves over with, for, after that, she was sure, their old friendship could be renewed, and she would be in a position to further this pretty love affair between him and Alice. Very decidedly, therefore, Billy wished to meet Arkwright. Very pleased, consequently, was she when, one day, coming into the living-room at the Annex, she found the man sitting by the fire.

Arkwright was on his feet at once.

"Miss—Mrs. H—Henshaw," he stammered

"Oh, Mr. Arkwright," she cried, with just a shade of nervousness in her voice as she advanced, her hand outstretched. "I'm glad to see you."

"Thank you. I wanted to see Miss Greggory," he murmured. Then, as the unconscious rudeness of his reply dawned on him, he made matters infinitely worse by an attempted apology. "That is, I mean—I didn't mean—" he began to stammer miserably.

Some girls might have tossed the floundering man a straw in the shape of a light laugh intended to turn aside all embarrassment—but not Billy. Billy held out a frankly helping hand that was meant to set the man squarely on his feet at her side.

"Mr. Arkwright, don't, please," she begged earnestly. "You and I don't need to beat about the bush. I am glad to see you, and I hope you're glad to see me. We're going to be the best of friends from now on, I'm sure; and some day, soon, you're going to bring Alice to see me, and we'll have some music. I left her up-stairs. She'll be down at once, I dare say—I met Rosa going up with your card. Good-by," she finished with a bright smile, as she turned and walked rapidly from the room.

Outside, on the steps, Billy drew a long breath.

"There," she whispered; "that's over—and well over!" The next minute she frowned vexedly. She had missed her glove. "Never mind! I sha'n't go back in there for it now, anyway," she decided.

In the living-room, five minutes later, Alice Greggory found only a hastily scrawled note waiting for her.

"If you'll forgive the unforgivable," she read "you'll forgive me for not being here when you come down. 'Circumstances over which I have no control have called me away.' May we let it go at that?

"M. J. ARKWRIGHT."

As Alice Greggory's amazed, questioning eyes left the note they fell upon the long white glove on the floor by the door. Half mechanically she crossed the room and picked it up; but almost at once she dropped it with a low cry.

"Billy! He—saw—Billy!" Then a flood of understanding dyed her face scarlet as she turned and fled to the blessedly unseeing walls of her own room.

Not ten minutes later Rosa tapped at her door with a note.

"It's from Mr. Arkwright, Miss. He's downstairs." Rosa's eyes were puzzled, and a bit startled.

"Mr. Arkwright!"

"Yes, Miss. He's come again. That is, I didn't know he'd went—but he must have, for he's come again now. He wrote something in a little book; then he tore it out and gave it to me. He said he'd wait, please, for an answer."

"Oh, very well, Rosa."

Miss Greggory took the note and spoke with an elaborate air of indifference that was meant to express a calm ignoring of the puzzled questioning in the other's eyes. The next moment she read this in Arkwright's peculiar scrawl:

"If you've already forgiven the unforgivable, you'll do it again, I know, and come down-stairs. Won't you, please? I want to see you."

Miss Greggory lifted her head with a jerk. Her face was a painful red.

"Tell Mr. Arkwright I can't possibly—" She came to an abrupt pause. Her eyes had encountered Rosa's, and in Rosa's eyes the puzzled questioning was plainly fast becoming a shrewd suspicion.

There was the briefest of hesitations; then, lightly, Miss Greggory tossed the note aside.

"Tell Mr. Arkwright I'll be down at once, please," she directed carelessly, as she turned back into the room.

But she was not down at once. She was not down until she had taken time to bathe her red eyes, powder her telltale nose, smoothe her ruffled hair, and whip herself into the calm, steady-eyed, self-controlled young woman that Arkwright finally rose to meet when she came into the room.

"I thought it was only women who were privileged to change their mind," she began brightly; but Arkwright ignored her attempt to conventionalize the situation.

"Thank you for coming down," he said, with a weariness that instantly drove the forced smile from the girl's lips. "I—I wanted to—to talk to you."

"Yes?" She seated herself and motioned him to a chair near her. He took the seat, and then fell silent, his eyes out the window.

"I thought you said you—you wanted to talk, she reminded him nervously, after a minute.

"I did." He turned with disconcerting abruptness. "Alice, I'm going to tell you a story."

"I shall be glad to listen. People always like stories, don't they?"

"Do they?" The somber pain in Arkwright's eyes deepened. Alice Greggory did not know it, but he was thinking of another story he had once told in that same room. Billy was his listener then, while now—A little precipitately he began to speak.

"When I was a very small boy I went to visit my uncle, who, in his young days, had been quite a hunter. Before the fireplace in his library was a huge tiger skin with a particularly lifelike head. The first time I saw it I screamed, and ran and hid. I refused then even to go into the room again. My cousins urged, scolded, pleaded, and laughed at me by turns, but I was obdurate. I would not go where I could see the fearsome thing again, even though it was, as they said, 'nothing but a dead old rug!'

"Finally, one day, my uncle took a hand in the matter. By sheer will-power he forced me to go with him straight up to the dreaded creature, and stand by its side. He laid one of my shrinking hands on the beast's smooth head, and thrust the other one quite into the open red mouth with its gleaming teeth.

"'You see,' he said, 'there's absolutely nothing to fear. He can't possibly hurt you. Just as if you weren't bigger and finer and stronger in every way than that dead thing on the floor!'

"Then, when he had got me to the point where of my own free will I would walk up and touch the thing, he drew a lesson for me.

"'Now remember,' he charged me. 'Never run and hide again. Only cowards do that. Walk straight up and face the thing. Ten to one you'll find it's nothing but a dead skin masquerading as the real thing. Even if it isn't if it's alive—face it. Find a weapon and fight it. Know that you are going to conquer it and you'll conquer. Never run. Be a man. Men don't run, my boy!'"

Arkwright paused, and drew a long breath. He did not look at the girl in the opposite chair. If he had looked he would have seen a face transfigured.

"Well," he resumed, "I never forgot that tiger skin, nor what it stood for, after that day when Uncle Ben thrust my hand into its hideous, but harmless, red mouth. Even as a kid I began, then, to try—not to run. I've tried ever since But to-day—I did run."

Arkwright's voice had been getting lower and lower. The last three words would have been almost inaudible to ears less sensitively alert than were Alice Greggory's. For a moment after the words were uttered, only the clock's ticking broke the silence; then, with an obvious effort, the man roused himself, as if breaking away from some benumbing force that held him.

"Alice, I don't need to tell you, after what I said the other night, that I loved Billy Neilson. That was bad enough, for I found she was pledged to another man. But to-day I discovered something worse: I discovered that I loved Billy Henshaw—another man's wife. And—I ran. But I've come back. I'm going to face the thing. Oh, I'm not deceiving myself! This love of mine is no dead tiger skin. It's a beast, alive and alert—God pity me!—to destroy my very soul. But I'm going to fight it; and—I want you to help me."

The girl gave a half-smothered cry. The man turned, but he could not see her face distinctly. Twilight had come, and the room was full of shadows. He hesitated, then went on, a little more quietly.

"That's why I've told you all this—so you would help me. And you will, won't you?"

There was no answer. Once again he tried to see her face, but it was turned now quite away from him.

"You've been a big help already, little girl. Your friendship, your comradeship—they've been everything to me. You're not going to make me do without them—now?"

"No—oh, no!" The answer was low and a little breathless; but he heard it.

"Thank you. I knew you wouldn't." He paused, then rose to his feet. When he spoke again his voice carried a note of whimsical lightness that was a little forced. "But I must go—else you will take them from me, and with good reason. And please don't let your kind heart grieve too much—over me. I'm no deep-dyed villain in a melodrama, nor wicked lover in a ten-penny novel, you know. I'm just an everyday man in real life; and we're going to fight this thing out in everyday living. That's where your help is coming in. We'll go together to see Mrs. Bertram Henshaw. She's asked us to, and you'll do it, I know. We'll have music and everyday talk. We'll see Mrs. Bertram Henshaw in her own home with her husband, where she belongs; and—I'm not going to run again. But—I'm counting on your help, you know," he smiled a little wistfully, as he held out his hand in good-by.

One minute later Alice Greggory, alone, was hurrying up-stairs.

"I can't—I can't—I know I can't," she was whispering wildly. Then, in her own room, she faced herself in the mirror. "Yes—you—can, Alice Greggory," she asserted, with swift change of voice and manner. "This is your tiger skin, and you're going to fight it. Do you understand?—fight it! And you're going to win, too. Do you want that man to know you—care?"

CHAPTER VI. "THE PAINTING LOOK"

It was toward the last of October that Billy began to notice her husband's growing restlessness. Twice, when she had been playing to him, she turned to find him testing the suppleness of his injured arm. Several times, failing to receive an answer to her questions, she had looked up to discover him gazing abstractedly at nothing in particular.

They read and walked and talked together, to be sure, and Bertram's devotion to her lightest wish was beyond question; but more and more frequently these days Billy found him hovering over his sketches in his studio; and once, when he failed to respond to the dinner-bell, search revealed him buried in a profound treatise on "The Art of Foreshortening."

Then came the day when Billy, after an hour's vain effort to imprison within notes a tantalizing melody, captured the truant and rain down to the studio to tell Bertram of her victory.

But Bertram did not seem even to hear her. True, he leaped to his feet and hurried to meet her, his face radiantly aglow; but she had not ceased to speak before he himself was talking.

"Billy, Billy, I've been sketching," he cried. "My hand is almost steady. See, some of those lines are all right! I just picked up a crayon and—" He stopped abruptly, his eyes on Billy's face. A vaguely troubled shadow crossed his own. "Did—did you—were you saying anything in—in particular, when you came in?" he stammered.

For a short half-minute Billy looked at her husband without speaking. Then, a little queerly, she laughed.

"Oh, no, nothing at all in particular," she retorted airily. The next moment, with one of her unexpected changes of manner, she darted across the room, picked up a palette, and a handful of brushes from the long box near it. Advancing toward her husband she held them out dramatically. "And now paint, my lord, paint!" she commanded him, with stern insistence, as she thrust them into his hands.

Bertram laughed shamefacedly.

"Oh, I say, Billy," he began; but Billy had gone.

Out in the hall Billy was speeding up-stairs, talking fiercely to herself.

"We'll, Billy Neilson Henshaw, it's come! Now behave yourself. That was the painting look! You know what that means. Remember, he belongs to his Art before he does to you. Kate and everybody says so. And you—you expected him to tend to you and your silly little songs. Do you want to ruin his career? As if now he could spend all his time and give all his thoughts to you! But I—I just hate that Art!"

"What did you say, Billy?" asked William, in mild surprise, coming around the turn of the balustrade in the hall above. "Were you speaking to me, my dear?"

Billy looked up. Her face cleared suddenly, and she laughed—though a little ruefully.

"No, Uncle William, I wasn't talking to you," she sighed. "I was just—just administering first aid to the injured," she finished, as she whisked into her own room.

"Well, well, bless the child! What can she mean by that?" puzzled Uncle William, turning to go down the stairway.

Bertram began to paint a very little the next day. He painted still more the next, and yet more again the day following. He was like a bird let out of a cage, so joyously alive was he. The old sparkle came back to his eye, the old gay smile to his lips. Now that they had come back Billy realized what she had not been conscious of before: that for several weeks past they had not been there; and she wondered which hurt the more—that they had not been there before, or that they were there now. Then she scolded herself roundly for asking the question at all.

They were not easy—those days for Billy, though always to Bertram she managed to show a cheerfully serene face. To Uncle William, also, and to Aunt Hannah she showed a smiling countenance; and because she could not talk to anybody else of her feelings, she talked to herself. This, however, was no new thing for Billy to do From earliest childhood she had fought things out in like manner.

"But it's so absurd of you, Billy Henshaw," she berated herself one day, when Bertram had become so absorbed in his work that he had forgotten to keep his appointment with her for a walk. "Just because you have had his constant attention almost every hour since you were married is no reason why you should have it every hour now, when his arm is better! Besides, it's exactly what you said you wouldn't do—object—to his giving proper time to his work."

"But I'm not objecting," stormed the other half of herself. "I'm telling him to do it. It's only that he's so—so pleased to do it. He doesn't seem to mind a bit being away from me. He's actually happy!"

"Well, don't you want him to be happy in his work? Fie! For shame! A fine artist's wife you are. It seems Kate was right, then; you are going to spoil his career!"

"Ho!" quoth Billy, and tossed her head. Forthwith she crossed the room to her piano and plumped herself down hard on to the stool. Then, from under her fingers there fell a rollicking melody that seemed to fill the room with little dancing feet. Faster and faster sped Billy's fingers; swifter and swifter twinkled the little dancing feet. Then a door was jerked open, and Bertram's voice called:

"Billy!"

The music stopped instantly. Billy sprang from her seat, her eyes eagerly seeking the direction from which had come the voice. Perhaps—perhaps Bertram wanted her. Perhaps he was not going to paint any longer that morning, after all. "Billy!" called the voice again. "Please, do you mind stopping that playing just for a little while? I'm a brute, I know, dear, but my brush will try to keep time with that crazy little tune of yours, and you know my hand is none too steady, anyhow, and when it tries to keep up with that jiggety, jig, jig, jiggety, jig, jig—! Do you mind, darling, just—just sewing, or doing something still for a while?"

All the light fled from Billy's face, but her voice, when she spoke, was the quintessence of cheery indifference.

"Why, no, of course not, dear."

"Thank you. I knew you wouldn't," sighed Bertram. Then the door shut.

For a long minute Billy stood motionless before she glanced at her watch and sped to the telephone.

"Is Miss Greggory there, Rosa?" she called when the operator's ring was answered.

"Mis' Greggory, the lame one?"

"No; Miss Greggory—Miss Alice."

"Oh! Yes'm."

"Then won't you ask her to come to the telephone, please."

There was a moment's wait, during which Billy's small, well-shod foot beat a nervous tattoo on the floor.

"Oh, is that you, Alice?" she called then. "Are you going to be home for an hour or two?"

"Why, y-yes; yes, indeed."

"Then I'm coming over. We'll play duets, sing—anything. I want some music."

"Do! And—Mr. Arkwright is here. He'll help."

"Mr. Arkwright? You say he's there? Then I won't—Yes, I will, too." Billy spoke with renewed firmness. "I'll be there right away. Good-by." And she hung up the receiver, and went to tell Pete to order John and Peggy at once.

"I suppose I ought to have left Alice and Mr. Arkwright alone together," muttered the young wife feverishly, as she hurriedly prepared for departure. "But I'll make it up to them later. I'm going to give them lots of chances. But to-day—to-day I just had to go—somewhere!"

At the Annex, with Alice Greggory and Arkwright, Billy sang duets and trios, and reveled in a sonorous wilderness of new music to her heart's content. Then, rested, refreshed, and at peace with all the world, she hurried home to dinner and to Bertram.

"There! I feel better," she sighed, as she took off her hat in her own room; "and now I'll go find Bertram. Bless his heart—of course he didn't want me to play when he was so busy!"

Billy went straight to the studio, but Bertram was not there. Neither was he in William's room, nor anywhere in the house. Down-stairs in the dining-room Pete was found looking rather white, leaning back in a chair. He struggled at once to his feet, however, as his mistress entered the room.

Billy hurried forward with a startled exclamation.

"Why, Pete, what is it? Are you sick?" she cried, her glance encompassing the half-set table.

"No, ma'am; oh, no, ma'am!" The old man stumbled forward and began to arrange the knives and forks. "It's just a pesky pain—beggin' yer pardon—in my side. But I ain't sick. No, Miss—ma'am."

Billy frowned and shook her head. Her eyes were on Pete's palpably trembling hands.

"But, Pete, you are sick," she protested. "Let Eliza do that."

Pete drew himself stiffly erect. The color had begun to come back to his face.

"There hain't no one set this table much but me for more'n fifty years, an' I've got a sort of notion that nobody can do it just ter suit me. Besides, I'm better now. It's gone—that pain."

"But, Pete, what is it? How long have you had it?"

"I hain't had it any time, steady. It's the comin' an' goin' kind. It seems silly ter mind it at all; only, when it does come, it sort o' takes the backbone right out o' my knees, and they double up so's I have ter set down. There, ye see? I'm pert as a sparrer, now!" And, with stiff celerity, Pete resumed his task.

His mistress still frowned.

"That isn't right, Pete," she demurred, with a slow shake of her head. "You should see a doctor."

The old man paled a little. He had seen a doctor, and he had not liked what the doctor had told him. In fact, he stubbornly refused to believe what the doctor had said. He straightened himself now a little aggressively.

"Humph! Beggin' yer pardon, Miss—ma'am, but I don't think much o' them doctor chaps."

Billy shook her head again as she smiled and turned away. Then, as if casually, she asked:

"Oh, did Mr. Bertram go out, Pete?"

"Yes, Miss; about five o'clock. He said he'd be back to dinner."

"Oh! All right."

From the hall the telephone jangled sharply.

"I'll go," said Pete's mistress, as she turned and hurried up-stairs. It was Bertram's voice that answered her opening "Hullo."

"Oh, Billy, is that you, dear? Well, you're just the one I wanted. I wanted to say—that is, I wanted to ask you—" The speaker cleared his throat a little nervously, and began all over again. "The fact is, Billy, I've run across a couple of old classmates on from New York, and they are very anxious I should stay down to dinner with them. Would you mind—very much if I did?"

A cold hand seemed to clutch Billy's heart. She caught her breath with a little gasp and tried to speak; but she had to try twice before the words came.

"Why, no—no, of course not!" Billy's voice was very high-pitched and a little shaky, but it was surpassingly cheerful.

"You sure you won't be—lonesome?" Bertram's voice was vaguely troubled.

"Of course not!"

"You've only to say the word, little girl," came Bertram's anxious tones again, "and I won't stay."

Billy swallowed convulsively. If only, only he would stop and leave her to herself! As if she were going to own up that she was lonesome for him—if he was not lonesome for her!

"Nonsense! of course you'll stay," called Billy, still in that high-pitched, shaky treble. Then, before Bertram could answer, she uttered a gay "Good-by!" and hung up the receiver.

Billy had ten whole minutes in which to cry before Pete's gong sounded for dinner; but she had only one minute in which to try to efface the woefully visible effects of those ten minutes before William tapped at her door, and called:

"Gone to sleep, my dear? Dinner's ready. Didn't you hear the gong?"

"Yes, I'm coming, Uncle William." Billy spoke with breezy gayety, and threw open the door; but she did not meet Uncle William's eyes. Her head was turned away. Her hands were fussing with the hang of her skirt.

"Bertram's dining out, Pete tells me," observed William, with cheerful nonchalance, as they went down-stairs together.

Billy bit her lip and looked up sharply. She had been bracing herself to meet with disdainful indifference this man's pity—the pity due a poor neglected wife whose husband preferred to dine with old classmates rather than with herself. Now she found in William's face, not pity, but a calm, even jovial, acceptance of the situation as a matter of course. She had known she was going to hate that pity; but now, curiously enough, she was conscious only of anger that the pity was not there—that she might hate it.

She tossed her head a little. So even William—Uncle William—regarded this monstrous thing as an insignificant matter of everyday experience. Maybe he expected it to occur frequently—every night, or so. Doubtless he did expect it to occur every night, or so. Indeed! Very well. As if she were going to show now that she cared whether Bertram were there or not! They should see.

So with head held high and eyes asparkle, Billy marched into the dining-room and took her accustomed place.

CHAPTER VII. THE BIG BAD QUARREL

It was a brilliant dinner—because Billy made it so. At first William met her sallies of wit with mild surprise; but it was not long before he rose gallantly to the occasion, and gave back full measure of retort. Even Pete twice had to turn his back to hide a smile, and once his hand shook so that the tea he was carrying almost spilled. This threatened catastrophe, however, seemed to frighten him so much that his face was very grave throughout the rest of the dinner.

Still laughing and talking gayly, Billy and Uncle William, after the meal was over, ascended to the drawing-room. There, however, the man, in spite of the young woman's gay badinage, fell to dozing in the big chair before the fire, leaving Billy with only Spunkie for company—Spunkie, who, disdaining every effort to entice her into a romp, only winked and blinked stupid eyes, and finally curled herself on the rug for a nap.

Billy, left to her own devices, glanced at her watch.

Half-past seven! Time, almost, for Bertram to be coming. He had said "dinner"; and, of course, after dinner was over he would be coming home—to her. Very well; she would show him that she had at least got along without him as well as he had without her. At all events he would not find her forlornly sitting with her nose pressed against the window-pane! And forthwith Billy established herself in a big chair (with its back carefully turned toward the door by which Bertram would enter), and opened a book.

Five, ten, fifteen minutes passed. Billy fidgeted in her chair, twisted her neck to look out into the hall—and dropped her book with a bang.

Uncle William jerked himself awake, and Spunkie opened sleepy eyes. Then both settled themselves for another nap. Billy sighed, picked up her book, and flounced back into her chair. But she did not read. Disconsolately she sat staring straight ahead—until a quick step on the sidewalk outside stirred her into instant action. Assuming a look of absorbed interest she twitched the book open and held it before her face.... But the step passed by the door: and Billy saw then that her book was upside down.

Five, ten, fifteen more minutes passed. Billy still sat, apparently reading, though she had not turned a page. The book now, however, was right side up. One by one other minutes passed till the great clock in the hall struck nine long strokes.

"Well, well, bless my soul!" mumbled Uncle William, resolutely forcing himself to wake up. "What time was that?"

"Nine o'clock." Billy spoke with tragic distinctness, yet very cheerfully.

"Eh? Only nine?" blinked Uncle William. "I thought it must be ten. Well, anyhow, I believe I'll go up-stairs. I seem to be unusually sleepy."

Billy said nothing. "'Only nine,' indeed!" she was thinking wrathfully.

At the door Uncle William turned.

"You're not going to sit up, my dear, of course," he remarked.

For the second time that evening a cold hand seemed to clutch Billy's heart.

Sit up! Had it come already to that? Was she even now a wife who had need to sit up for her husband?

"I really wouldn't, my dear," advised Uncle William again. "Good night."

"Oh, but I'm not sleepy at all, yet," Billy managed to declare brightly. "Good night."

Then Uncle William went up-stairs.

Billy turned to her book, which happened to be one of William's on "Fake Antiques."

"'To collect anything, these days, requires expert knowledge, and the utmost care and discrimination,'" read Billy's eyes. "So Uncle William expected Bertram was going to spend the whole evening as well as stay to dinner!" ran Billy's thoughts. "'The enormous quantity of bijouterie, Dresden and Battersea enamel ware that is now flooding the market, is made on the Continent—and made chiefly for the American trade,'" continued the book.

"Well, who cares if it is," snapped Billy, springing to her feet and tossing the volume aside. "Spunkie, come here! You've simply got to play with me. Do you hear? I want to be gay—gay—GAY! He's gay. He's down there with those men, where he wants to be. Where he'd rather be than be with me! Do you think I want him to come home and find me moping over a stupid old book? Not much! I'm going to have him find me gay, too. Now, come,

Spunkie; hurry—wake up! He'll be here right away, I'm sure." And Billy shook a pair of worsted reins, hung with little soft balls, full in Spunkie's face.

But Spunkie would not wake up, and Spunkie would not play. She pretended to. She bit at the reins, and sank her sharp claws into the dangling balls. For a fleeting instant, even, something like mischief gleamed in her big yellow eyes. Then the jaws relaxed, the paws turned to velvet, and Spunkie's sleek gray head settled slowly back into lazy comfort. Spunkie was asleep.

Billy gazed at the cat with reproachful eyes.

"And you, too, Spunkie," she murmured. Then she got to her feet and went back to her chair. This time she picked up a magazine and began to turn the leaves very fast, one after another.

Half-past nine came, then ten. Pete appeared at the door to get Spunkie, and to see that everything was all right for the night.

"Mr. Bertram is not in yet?" he began doubtfully.

Billy shook her head with a bright smile.

"No, Pete. Go to bed. I expect him every minute. Good night."

"Thank you, ma'am. Good night."

The old man picked up the sleepy cat and went down-stairs. A little later Billy heard his quiet steps coming back through the hall and ascending the stairs. She listened until from away at the top of the house she heard his door close. Then she drew a long breath.

Ten o'clock—after ten o'clock, and Bertram not there yet! And was this what he called dinner? Did one eat, then, till ten o'clock, when one dined with one's friends?

Billy was angry now—very angry. She was too angry to be reasonable. This thing that her husband had done seemed monstrous to her, smarting, as she was, under the sting of hurt pride and grieved loneliness—the state of mind into which she had worked herself. No longer now did she wish to be gay when her husband came. No longer did she even pretend to assume indifference. Bertram had done wrong. He had been unkind, cruel, thoughtless, inconsiderate of her comfort and happiness. Furthermore he did not love her as well as she did him or he never, never could have done it! She would let him see, when he came, just how hurt and grieved she was—and how disappointed, too.

Billy was walking the floor now, back and forth, back and forth.

Half-past ten came, then eleven. As the eleven long strokes reverberated through the silent house Billy drew in her breath and held it suspended. A new look came to her eyes. A growing terror crept into them and culminated in a frightened stare at the clock.

Billy ran then to the great outer door and pulled it open. A cold wind stung her face, and caused her to shut the door quickly. Back and forth she began to pace the floor again; but in five minutes she had run to the door once more. This time she wore a heavy coat of Bertram's which she caught up as she passed the hall-rack.

Out on to the broad top step Billy hurried, and peered down the street. As far as she could see not a person was in sight. Across the street in the Public Garden the wind stirred the gray tree-branches and set them to casting weird shadows on the bare, frozen ground. A warning something behind her sent Billy scurrying into the house just in time to prevent the heavy door's closing and shutting her out, keyless, in the cold.

Half-past eleven came, and again Billy ran to the door. This time she put the floor-mat against the casing so that the door could not close. Once more she peered wildly up and down the street, and across into the deserted, wind-swept Garden.

There was only terror now in Billy's face. The anger was all gone. In Billy's mind there was not a shadow of doubt—something had happened to Bertram.

Bertram was ill—hurt—dead! And he was so good, so kind, so noble; such a dear, dear husband! If only she could see him once. If only she could ask his forgiveness for those wicked, unkind, accusing thoughts. If only she could tell him again that she did love him. If only—

Far down the street a step rang sharply on the frosty air. A masculine figure was hurrying toward the house. Retreating well into the shadow of the doorway, Billy watched it, her heart pounding against her side in great suffocating throbs. Nearer and nearer strode the approaching figure until Billy had almost sprung to meet it with a glad cry—almost, but not quite; for the figure neither turned nor paused, but marched straight on—and Billy saw then, under the arc light, a brown-bearded man who was not Bertram at all.

Three times during the next few minutes did the waiting little bride on the doorstep watch with palpitating yearning a shadowy form appear, approach—and pass by. At the third heart-breaking disappointment, Billy wrung her hands helplessly.

"I don't see how there can be—so many—utterly useless people in the world!" she choked. Then, thoroughly chilled and sick at heart, she went into the house and closed the door.

Once again, back and forth, back and forth, Billy took up her weary vigil. She still wore the heavy coat. She had forgotten to take it off. Her face was pitifully white and drawn. Her eyes were wild. One of her hands was nervously caressing the rough sleeve of the coat as it hung from her shoulder.

One—two—three—

Billy gave a sharp cry and ran into the hall.

Yes, it was twelve o'clock. And now, always, all the rest of the dreary, useless hours that that clock would tick away through an endless existence, she would have to live—without Bertram. If only she could see him once more! But she could not. He was dead. He must be dead, now. Here it was twelve o'clock, and—

There came a quick step, the click of a key in the lock, then the door swung back and Bertram, big, strong, and merry-eyed, stood before her.

"Well, well, hullo," he called jovially. "Why, Billy, what's the matter?" he broke off, in quite a different tone of voice.

And then a curious thing happened. Billy, who, a minute before, had been seeing only a dear, noble, adorable, lost Bertram, saw now suddenly only the man that had stayed happily till midnight with two friends, while she—she—

"Matter! Matter!" exclaimed Billy sharply, then. "Is this what you call staying to dinner, Bertram Henshaw?"

Bertram stared. A slow red stole to his forehead. It was his first experience of coming home to meet angry eyes that questioned his behavior—and he did not like it. He had been, perhaps, a little conscience-smitten when he saw how late he had stayed; and he had intended to say he was sorry, of course. But to be thus sharply called to account for a perfectly innocent good time with a couple of friends—! To come home and find Billy making a ridiculous scene like this—! He—he would not stand for it! He—

Bertram's lips snapped open. The angry retort was almost spoken when something in the piteously quivering chin and white, drawn face opposite stopped it just in time.

"Why, Billy—darling!" he murmured instead.

It was Billy's turn to change. All the anger melted away before the dismayed tenderness in those dear eyes and the grieved hurt in that dear voice.

"Well, you—you—I—" Billy began to cry.

It was all right then, of course, for the next minute she was crying on Bertram's big, broad shoulder; and in the midst of broken words, kisses, gentle pats, and inarticulate croonings, the Big, Bad Quarrel, that had been all ready to materialize, faded quite away into nothingness.

"I didn't have such an awfully good time, anyhow," avowed Bertram, when speech became rational. "I'd rather have been home with you."

"Nonsense!" blinked Billy, valiantly. "Of course you had a good time; and it was perfectly right you should have it, too! And I—I hope you'll have it again."

"I sha'n't," emphasized Bertram, promptly, "—not and leave you!"

Billy regarded him with adoring eyes.

"I'll tell you; we'll have 'em come here," she proposed gayly.

"Sure we will," agreed Bertram.

"Yes; sure we will," echoed Billy, with a contented sigh. Then, a little breathlessly, she added: "Anyhow, I'll know—where you are. I won't think you're—dead!"

"You—blessed—little-goose!" scolded Bertram, punctuating each word with a kiss.

Billy drew a long sigh.

"If this is a quarrel I'm going to have them often," she announced placidly.

"Billy!" The young husband was plainly aghast.

"Well, I am—because I like the making-up," dimpled Billy, with a mischievous twinkle as she broke from his clasp and skipped ahead up the stairway.

CHAPTER VIII. BILLY CULTIVATES A "COMFORTABLE INDIFFERENCE"

The next morning, under the uncompromising challenge of a bright sun, Billy began to be uneasily suspicious that she had been just a bit unreasonable and exacting the night before. To make matters worse she chanced to run across a newspaper criticism of a new book bearing the ominous title: "When the Honeymoon Wanes A Talk to Young Wives."

Such a title, of course, attracted her supersensitive attention at once; and, with a curiously faint feeling, she picked up the paper and began to read.

As the most of the criticism was taken up with quotations from the book, it was such sentences as these that met her startled eyes:

"Perhaps the first test comes when the young wife awakes to the realization that while her husband loves her very much, he can still make plans with his old friends which do not include herself.... Then is when the foolish wife lets her husband see how hurt she is that he can want to be with any one but herself.... Then is when the husband—used all his life to independence, perhaps—begins to chafe under these new bonds that hold him so fast.... No man likes to be held up at the end of a threatened scene and made to give an account of himself.... Before a woman has learned to cultivate a comfortable indifference to her husband's comings and goings, she is apt to be tyrannical and exacting."

"'Comfortable indifference,' indeed!" stormed Billy to herself. "As if I ever could be comfortably indifferent to anything Bertram did!"

She dropped the paper; but there were still other quotations from the book there, she knew; and in a moment she was back at the table reading them.

"No man, however fondly he loves his wife, likes to feel that she is everlastingly peering into the recesses of his mind, and weighing his every act to find out if he does or does not love her to-day as well as he did yesterday at this time.... Then, when spontaneity is dead, she is the chief mourner at its funeral.... A few couples never leave the Garden of Eden. They grow old hand in hand. They are the ones who bear and forbear; who have learned to adjust themselves to the intimate relationship of living together.... A certain amount of liberty, both of action and thought, must be allowed on each side.... The family shut in upon itself grows so narrow that all interest in the outside world is lost.... No two people are ever fitted to fill each other's lives entirely. They ought not to try to do it. If they do try, the process is belittling to each, and the result, if it is successful, is nothing less than a tragedy; for it could not mean the highest ideals, nor the truest devotion.... Brushing up against other interests and other personalities is good for both husband and wife. Then to each other they bring the best of what they have found, and each to the other continues to be new and interesting.... The young wife, however, is apt to be jealous of everything that turns her husband's attention for one moment away from herself. She is jealous of his thoughts, his words, his friends, even his business.... But the wife who has learned to be the clinging vine when her husband wishes her to cling, and to be the sturdy oak when clinging vines would be tiresome, has solved a tremendous problem."

At this point Billy dropped the paper. She flung it down, indeed, a bit angrily. There were still a few more words in the criticism, mostly the critic's own opinion of the book; but Billy did not care for this. She had read quite enough—boo much, in fact. All that sort of talk might be very well, even necessary, perhaps (she told herself), for ordinary husbands and wives! but for her and Bertram—

Then vividly before her rose those initial quoted words:

"Perhaps the first test comes when the young wife awakes to the realization that while her husband loves her very much, he can still make plans with his old friends which do not include herself."

Billy frowned, and put her finger to her lips. Was that then, last night, a "test"? Had she been "tyrannical and exacting"? Was she "everlastingly peering into the recesses" of Bertram's mind and "weighing his every act"? Was Bertram already beginning to "chafe" under these new bonds that held him?

No, no, never that! She could not believe that. But what if he should sometime begin to chafe? What if they two should, in days to come, degenerate into just the ordinary, everyday married folk, whom she saw about her everywhere, and for whom just such horrid books as this must be written? It was unbelievable, unthinkable. And yet, that man had said—

With a despairing sigh Billy picked up the paper once more and read carefully every word again. When she had finished she stood soberly thoughtful, her eyes out of the window.

After all, it was nothing but the same old story. She was exacting. She did want her husband's every thought. She gloried in peering into every last recess of his mind if she had half a chance. She was jealous of his work. She had almost hated his painting—at times. She had held him up with a threatened scene only the night before and demanded that he should give an account of himself. She had, very likely, been the clinging vine when she should have been the sturdy oak.

Very well, then. (Billy lifted her head and threw back her shoulders.) He should have no further cause for complaint. She would be an oak. She would cultivate that comfortable indifference to his comings and goings. She would brush up against other interests and personalities so as to be "new" and "interesting" to her husband. She would not be tyrannical, exacting, or jealous. She would not threaten scenes, nor peer into recesses. Whatever happened, she would not let Bertram begin to chafe against those bonds!

Having arrived at this heroic and (to her) eminently satisfactory state of mind, Billy turned from the window and fell to work on a piece of manuscript music.

"Brush up against other interests," she admonished herself sternly, as she reached for her pen.

Theoretically it was beautiful; but practically—

Billy began at once to be that oak. Not an hour after she had first seen the fateful notice of "When the Honeymoon Wanes," Bertram's ring sounded at the door down-stairs.

Bertram always let himself in with his latchkey; but, from the first of Billy's being there, he had given a peculiar ring at the bell which would bring his wife flying to welcome him if she were anywhere in the house. To-day, when the bell sounded, Billy sprang as usual to her feet, with a joyous "There's Bertram!" But the next moment she fell back.

"Tut, tut, Billy Neilson Henshaw! Learn to cultivate a comfortable indifference to your husband's comings and goings," she whispered fiercely. Then she sat down and fell to work again.

A moment later she heard her husband's voice talking to some one—Pete, she surmised. "Here? You say she's here?" Then she heard Bertram's quick step on the stairs. The next minute, very quietly, he came to her door.

"Ho!" he ejaculated gayly, as she rose to receive his kiss. "I thought I'd find you asleep, when you didn't hear my ring."

Billy reddened a little.

"Oh, no, I wasn't asleep."

"But you didn't hear—" Bertram stopped abruptly, an odd look in his eyes. "Maybe you did hear it, though," he corrected.

Billy colored more confusedly. The fact that she looked so distressed did not tend to clear Bertram's face.

"Why, of course, Billy, I didn't mean to insist on your coming to meet me," he began a little stiffly; but Billy interrupted him.

"Why, Bertram, I just love to go to meet you," she maintained indignantly. Then, remembering just in time, she amended: "That is, I did love to meet you, until—" With a sudden realization that she certainly had not helped matters any, she came to an embarrassed pause.

A puzzled frown showed on Bertram's face.

"You did love to meet me until—" he repeated after her; then his face changed. "Billy, you aren't—you can't be laying up last night against me!" he reproached her a little irritably.

"Last night? Why, of course not," retorted Billy, in a panic at the bare mention of the "test" which—according to "When the Honeymoon Wanes"—was at the root of all her misery. Already she thought she detected in Bertram's voice signs that he was beginning to chafe against those "bonds." "It is a matter of—of the utmost indifference to me what time you come home at night, my dear," she finished airily, as she sat down to her work again.

Bertram stared; then he frowned, turned on his heel and left the room. Bertram, who knew nothing of the "Talk to Young Wives" in the newspaper at Billy's feet, was surprised, puzzled, and just a bit angry.

Billy, left alone, jabbed her pen with such force against her paper that the note she was making became an unsightly blot.

"Well, if this is what that man calls being 'comfortably indifferent,' I'd hate to try the uncomfortable kind," she muttered with emphasis.

CHAPTER IX. THE DINNER BILLY TRIED TO GET

Notwithstanding what Billy was disposed to regard as the non-success of her first attempt to profit by the "Talk to Young Wives;" she still frantically tried to avert the waning of her honeymoon. Assiduously she cultivated the prescribed "indifference," and with at least apparent enthusiasm she sought the much-to-be-desired "outside interests." That is, she did all this when she thought of it when something reminded her of the sword of destruction hanging over her happiness. At other times, when she was just being happy without question, she was her old self impulsive, affectionate, and altogether adorable.

Naturally, under these circumstances, her conduct was somewhat erratic. For three days, perhaps, she would fly to the door at her husband's ring, and hang upon his every movement. Then, for the next three, she would be a veritable will-o'-the-wisp for elusiveness, caring, apparently, not one whit whether her husband came or went until poor Bertram, at his wit's end, scourged himself with a merciless catechism as to what he had done to vex her. Then, perhaps, just when he had nerved himself almost to the point of asking her what was the trouble, there would come another change, bringing back to him the old Billy, joyous, winsome, and devoted, plainly caring nothing for anybody or anything but himself. Scarcely, however, would he become sure that it was his Billy back again before she was off once more, quite beyond his reach, singing with Arkwright and Alice Greggory, playing with Tommy Dunn, plunging into some club or church work—anything but being with him.

That all this was puzzling and disquieting to Bertram, Billy not once suspected. Billy, so far as she was concerned, was but cultivating a comfortable indifference, brushing up against outside interests, and being an oak.

December passed, and January came, bringing Miss Marguerite Winthrop to her Boston home. Bertram's arm was "as good as ever" now, according to its owner; and the sittings for the new portrait began at once. This left Billy even more to her own devices, for Bertram entered into his new work with an enthusiasm born of a glad relief from forced idleness, and a consuming eagerness to prove that even though he had failed the first time, he could paint a portrait of Marguerite Winthrop that would be a credit to himself, a conclusive retort to his critics, and a source of pride to his once mortified friends. With his whole heart, therefore, he threw himself into the work before him, staying sometimes well into the afternoon on the days Miss Winthrop could find time between her social engagements to give him a sitting.

It was on such a day, toward the middle of the month, that Billy was called to the telephone at half-past twelve o'clock to speak to her husband.

"Billy, dear," began Bertram at once, "if you don't mind I'm staying to luncheon at Miss Winthrop's kind request. We've changed the pose—neither of us was satisfied, you know—but we haven't quite settled on the new one. Miss Winthrop has two whole hours this afternoon that she can give me if I'll stay; and, of course, under the circumstances, I want to do it."

"Of course," echoed Billy. Billy's voice was indomitably cheerful.

"Thank you, dear. I knew you'd understand," sighed Bertram, contentedly. "You see, really, two whole hours, so—it's a chance I can't afford to lose."

"Of course you can't," echoed Billy, again.

"All right then. Good-by till to-night," called the man.

"Good-by," answered Billy, still cheerfully. As she turned away, however, she tossed her head. "A new pose, indeed!" she muttered, with some asperity. "Just as if there could be a new pose after all those she tried last year!"

Immediately after luncheon Pete and Eliza started for South Boston to pay a visit to Eliza's mother, and it was soon after they left the house that Bertram called his wife up again.

"Say, dearie, I forgot to tell you," he began, "but I met an old friend in the subway this morning, and I—well, I remembered what you said about bringing 'em home to dinner next time, so I asked him for to-night. Do you mind? It's—"

"Mind? Of course not! I'm glad you did," plunged in Billy, with feverish eagerness. (Even now, just the bare mention of anything connected with that awful "test" night was enough to set Billy's nerves to tingling.) "I want you to always bring them home, Bertram."

"All right, dear. We'll be there at six o'clock then. It's—it's Calderwell, this time. You remember Calderwell, of course."

"Not—Hugh Calderwell?" Billy's question was a little faint.

"Sure!" Bertram laughed oddly, and lowered his voice. "I suspect once I wouldn't have brought him home to you. I was too jealous. But now—well, now maybe I want him to see what he's lost."

"Bertram!"

But Bertram only laughed mischievously, and called a gay "Good-by till to-night, then!"

Billy, at her end of the wires, hung up the receiver and backed against the wall a little palpitatingly.

Calderwell! To dinner—Calderwell! Did she remember Calderwell? Did she, indeed! As if one could easily forget the man that, for a year or two, had proposed marriage as regularly (and almost as lightly!) as he had torn a monthly leaf from his calendar! Besides, was it not he, too, who had said that Bertram would never love any girl, really; that it would be only the tilt of her chin or the turn of her head that he loved—to paint? And now he was coming to dinner—and with Bertram.

Very well, he should see! He should see that Bertram did love her; her—not the tilt of her chin nor the turn of her head. He should see how happy they were, what a good wife she made, and how devoted and satisfied Bertram was in his home. He should see! And forthwith Billy picked up her skirts and tripped up-stairs to select her very prettiest house-gown to do honor to the occasion. Up-stairs, however, one thing and another delayed her, so that it was four o'clock when she turned her attention to her toilet; and it was while she was hesitating whether to be stately and impressive in royally sumptuous blue velvet and ermine, or cozy and tantalizingly homy{sic} in bronze-gold crêpe de Chine and swan's-down, that the telephone bell rang again.

Eliza and Pete had not yet returned; so, as before, Billy answered it. This time Eliza's shaking voice came to her.

"Is that you, ma'am?"

"Why, yes, Eliza?"

"Yes'm, it's me, ma'am. It's about Uncle Pete. He's give us a turn that's 'most scared us out of our wits."

"Pete! You mean he's sick?"

"Yes, ma'am, he was. That is, he is, too—only he's better, now, thank goodness," panted Eliza. "But he ain't hisself yet. He's that white and shaky! Would you—could you—that is, would you mind if we didn't come back till into the evenin', maybe?"

"Why, of course not," cried Pete's mistress, quickly. "Don't come a minute before he's able, Eliza. Don't come until to-morrow."

Eliza gave a trembling little laugh.

"Thank you, ma'am; but there wouldn't be no keepin' of Uncle Pete here till then. If he could take five steps alone he'd start now. But he can't. He says he'll be all right pretty quick, though. He's had 'em before—these spells—but never quite so bad as this, I guess; an' he's worryin' somethin' turrible 'cause he can't start for home right away."

"Nonsense!" cut in Mrs. Bertram Henshaw.

"Yes'm. I knew you'd feel that way," stammered Eliza, gratefully. "You see, I couldn't leave him to come alone, and besides, anyhow, I'd have to stay, for mother ain't no more use than a wet dish-rag at such times, she's that scared herself. And she ain't very well, too. So if—if you could get along—"

"Of course we can! And tell Pete not to worry one bit. I'm so sorry he's sick!"

"Thank you, ma'am. Then we'll be there some time this evenin'," sighed Eliza.

From the telephone Billy turned away with a troubled face.

"Pete is ill," she was saying to herself. "I don't like the looks of it; and he's so faithful he'd come if—" With a little cry Billy stopped short. Then, tremblingly, she sank into the nearest chair. "Calderwell—and he's coming to dinner!" she moaned.

For two benumbed minutes Billy sat staring at nothing. Then she ran to the telephone and called the Annex.

Aunt Hannah answered.

"Aunt Hannah, for heaven's sake, if you love me," pleaded Billy, "send Rosa down instanter! Pete is sick over to South Boston, and Eliza is with him; and Bertram is bringing Hugh Calderwell home to dinner. Can you spare Rosa?"

"Oh, my grief and conscience, Billy! Of course I can—I mean I could—but Rosa isn't here, dear child! It's her day out, you know."

"O dear, of course it is! I might have known, if I'd thought; but Pete and Eliza have spoiled me. They never take days out at meal time—both together, I mean—until to-night."

"But, my dear child, what will you do?"

"I don't know. I've got to think. I must do something!"

"Of course you must! I'd come over myself if it wasn't for my cold."

"As if I'd let you!"

237

"There isn't anybody here, only Tommy. Even Alice is gone. Oh, Billy, Billy, this only goes to prove what I've always said, that no woman ought to be a wife until she's an efficient housekeeper; and—"

"Yes, yes, Aunt Hannah, I know," moaned Billy, frenziedly. "But I am a wife, and I'm not an efficient housekeeper; and Hugh Calderwell won't wait for me to learn. He's coming to-night. To-night! And I've got to do something. Never mind. I'll fix it some way. Good-by!"

"But, Billy, Billy! Oh, my grief and conscience," fluttered Aunt Hannah's voice across the wires as Billy snapped the receiver into place.

For the second time that day Billy backed palpitatingly against the wall. Her eyes sought the clock fearfully.

Fifteen minutes past four. She had an hour and three quarters. She could, of course, telephone Bertram to dine Calderwell at a club or some hotel. But to do this now, the very first time, when it had been her own suggestion that he "bring them home"—no, no, she could not do that! Anything but that! Besides, very likely she could not reach Bertram, anyway. Doubtless he had left the Winthrops' by this time.

There was Marie. She could telephone Marie. But Marie could not very well come just now, she knew; and then, too, there was Cyril to be taken into consideration. How Cyril would gibe at the wife who had to call in all the neighbors just because her husband was bringing home a friend to dinner! How he would—Well, he shouldn't! He should not have the chance. So, there!

With a jerk Mrs. Bertram Henshaw pulled herself away from the wall and stood erect. Her eyes snapped, and the very poise of her chin spelled determination.

Very well, she would show them. Was not Bertram bringing this man home because he was proud of her? Mighty proud he would be if she had to call in half of Boston to get his dinner for him! Nonsense! She would get it herself. Was not this the time, if ever, to be an oak? A vine, doubtless, would lean and cling and telephone, and whine "I can't!" But not an oak. An oak would hold up its head and say "I can!" An oak would go ahead and get that dinner. She would be an oak. She would get that dinner.

What if she didn't know how to cook bread and cake and pies and things? One did not have to cook bread and cake and pies just to get a dinner—meat and potatoes and vegetables! Besides, she could make peach fritters. She knew she could. She would show them!

And with actually a bit of song on her lips, Billy skipped up-stairs for her ruffled apron and dust-cap—two necessary accompaniments to this dinner-getting, in her opinion.

Billy found the apron and dust-cap with no difficulty; but it took fully ten of her precious minutes to unearth from its obscure hiding-place the blue-and-gold "Bride's Helper" cookbook, one of Aunt Hannah's wedding gifts.

On the way to the kitchen, Billy planned her dinner. As was natural, perhaps, she chose the things she herself would like to eat.

"I won't attempt anything very elaborate," she said to herself. "It would be wiser to have something simple, like chicken pie, perhaps. I love chicken pie! And I'll have oyster stew first—that is, after the grapefruit. Just oysters boiled in milk must be easier than soup to make. I'll begin with grapefruit with a cherry in it, like Pete fixes it. Those don't have to be cooked, anyhow. I'll have fish—Bertram loves the fish course. Let me see, halibut, I guess, with egg sauce. I won't have any roast; nothing but the chicken pie. And I'll have squash and onions. I can have a salad, easy—just lettuce and stuff. That doesn't have to be cooked. Oh, and the peach fritters, if I get time to make them. For dessert—well, maybe I can find a new pie or pudding in the cookbook. I want to use that cookbook for something, after hunting all this time for it!"

In the kitchen Billy found exquisite neatness, and silence. The first brought an approving light to her eyes; but the second, for some unapparent reason, filled her heart with vague misgiving. This feeling, however, Billy resolutely cast from her as she crossed the room, dropped her book on to the table, and turned toward the shining black stove.

There was an excellent fire. Glowing points of light showed that only a good draft was needed to make the whole mass of coal red-hot. Billy, however, did not know this. Her experience of fires was confined to burning wood in open grates—and wood in open grates had to be poked to make it red and glowing. With confident alacrity now, therefore, Billy caught up the poker, thrust it into the mass of coals and gave them a fine stirring up. Then she set back the lid of the stove and went to hunt up the ingredients for her dinner.

By the time Billy had searched five minutes and found no chicken, no oysters, and no halibut, it occurred to her that her larder was not, after all, an open market, and that one's provisions must be especially ordered to fit one's needs. As to ordering them now—Billy glanced at the clock and shook her head.

"It's almost five, already, and they'd never get here in time," she sighed regretfully. "I'll have to have something else."

Billy looked now, not for what she wanted, but for what she could find. And she found: some cold roast lamb, at which she turned up her nose; an uncooked beefsteak, which she appropriated doubtfully; a raw turnip and a head of lettuce, which she hailed with glee; and some beets, potatoes, onions, and grapefruit, from all of which she took a generous supply. Thus laden she went back to the kitchen.

Spread upon the table they made a brave show.

"Oh, well, I'll have quite a dinner, after all," she triumphed, cocking her head happily. "And now for the dessert," she finished, pouncing on the cookbook.

It was while she was turning the leaves to find the pies and puddings that she ran across the vegetables and found the word "beets" staring her in the face. Mechanically she read the line below.

"Winter beets will require three hours to cook. Use hot water."

Billy's startled eyes sought the clock.

Three hours—and it was five, now!

Frenziedly, then, she ran her finger down the page.

"Onions, one and one-half hours. Use hot water. Turnips require a long time, but if cut thin they will cook in an hour and a quarter."

"An hour and a quarter, indeed!" she moaned.

"Isn't there anything anywhere that doesn't take forever to cook?"

"Early peas—... green corn—... summer squash—..." mumbled Billy's dry lips. "But what do folks eat in January—January?"

It was the apparently inoffensive sentence, "New potatoes will boil in thirty minutes," that brought fresh terror to Billy's soul, and set her to fluttering the cookbook leaves with renewed haste. If it took new potatoes thirty minutes to cook, how long did it take old ones? In vain she searched for the answer. There were plenty of potatoes. They were mashed, whipped, scalloped, creamed, fried, and broiled; they were made into puffs, croquettes, potato border, and potato snow. For many of these they were boiled first— "until tender," one rule said.

"But that doesn't tell me how long it takes to get 'em tender," fumed Billy, despairingly. "I suppose they think anybody ought to know that—but I don't!" Suddenly her eyes fell once more on the instructions for boiling turnips, and her face cleared. "If it helps to cut turnips thin, why not potatoes?" she cried. "I can do that, anyhow; and I will," she finished, with a sigh of relief, as she caught up half a dozen potatoes and hurried into the pantry for a knife. A few minutes later, the potatoes, peeled, and cut almost to wafer thinness, were dumped into a basin of cold water.

"There! now I guess you'll cook," nodded Billy to the dish in her hand as she hurried to the stove.

Chilled by an ominous unresponsiveness, Billy lifted the stove lid and peered inside. Only a mass of black and graying coals greeted her. The fire was out.

"To think that even you had to go back on me like this!" upbraided Billy, eyeing the dismal mass with reproachful gaze.

This disaster, however, as Billy knew, was not so great as it seemed, for there was still the gas stove. In the old days, under Dong Ling's rule, there had been no gas stove. Dong Ling disapproved of "devil stoves" that had "no coalee, no woodee, but burned like hellee." Eliza, however, did approve of them; and not long after her arrival, a fine one had been put in for her use. So now Billy soon had her potatoes with a brisk blaze under them.

In frantic earnest, then, Billy went to work. Brushing the discarded onions, turnip, and beets into a pail under the table, she was still confronted with the beefsteak, lettuce, and grapefruit. All but the beefsteak she pushed to one side with gentle pats.

"You're all right," she nodded to them. "I can use you. You don't have to be cooked, bless your hearts! But you—!" Billy scowled at the beefsteak and ran her finger down the index of the "Bride's Helper"—Billy knew how to handle that book now.

"No, you don't—not for me!" she muttered, after a minute, shaking her finger at the tenderloin on the table. "I haven't got any 'hot coals,' and I thought a 'gridiron' was where they played football; though it seems it's some sort of a dish to cook you in, here—but I shouldn't know it from a teaspoon, probably, if I should see it. No, sir! It's back to the refrigerator for you, and a nice cold sensible roast leg of lamb for me, that doesn't have to be cooked. Understand? Cooked," she finished, as she carried the beefsteak away and took possession of the hitherto despised cold lamb.

Once more Billy made a mad search through cupboards and shelves. This time she bore back in triumph a can of corn, another of tomatoes, and a glass jar of preserved peaches. In the kitchen a cheery bubbling from the potatoes on the stove greeted her. Billy's spirits rose with the steam.

"There, Spunkie," she said gayly to the cat, who had just uncurled from a nap behind the stove. "Tell me I can't get up a dinner! And maybe we'll have the peach fritters, too," she chirped. "I've got the peach-part, anyway."

But Billy did not have the peach fritters, after all. She got out the sugar and the flour, to be sure, and she made a great ado looking up the rule; but a hurried glance at the clock sent her into the dining-room to set the table, and all thought of the peach fritters was given up.

CHAPTER X. THE DINNER BILLY GOT

At five minutes of six Bertram and Calderwell came. Bertram gave his peculiar ring and let himself in with his latchkey; but Billy did not meet him in the hall, nor in the drawing-room. Excusing himself, Bertram hurried up-stairs. Billy was not in her room, nor anywhere on that floor. She was not in William's room. Coming down-stairs to the hall again, Bertram confronted William, who had just come in.

"Where's Billy?" demanded the young husband, with just a touch of irritation, as if he suspected William of having Billy in his pocket.

William stared slightly.

"Why, I don't know. Isn't she here?"

"I'll ask Pete," frowned Bertram.

In the dining-room Bertram found no one, though the table was prettily set, and showed half a grapefruit at each place. In the kitchen—in the kitchen Bertram found a din of rattling tin, an odor of burned food—, a confusion of scattered pots and pans, a frightened cat who peered at him from under a littered stove, and a flushed, disheveled young woman in a blue dust-cap and ruffled apron, whom he finally recognized as his wife.

"Why, Billy!" he gasped.

Billy, who was struggling with something at the sink, turned sharply.

"Bertram Henshaw," she panted, "I used to think you were wonderful because you could paint a picture. I even used to think I was a little wonderful because I could write a song. Well, I don't any more! But I'll tell you who is wonderful. It's Eliza and Rosa, and all the rest of those women who can get a meal on to the table all at once, so it's fit to eat!"

"Why, Billy!" gasped Bertram again, falling back to the door he had closed behind him. "What in the world does this mean?"

"Mean? It means I'm getting dinner," choked Billy. "Can't you see?"

"But—Pete! Eliza!"

"They're sick—I mean he's sick; and I said I'd do it. I'd be an oak. But how did I know there wasn't anything in the house except stuff that took hours to cook—only potatoes? And how did I know that they cooked in no time, and then got all smushy and wet staying in the water? And how did I know that everything else would stick on and burn on till you'd used every dish there was in the house to cook 'em in?"

"Why, Billy!" gasped Bertram, for the third time. And then, because he had been married only six months instead of six years, he made the mistake of trying to argue with a woman whose nerves were already at the snapping point. "But, dear, it was so foolish of you to do all this! Why didn't you telephone? Why didn't you get somebody?"

Like an irate little tigress, Billy turned at bay.

"Bertram Henshaw," she flamed angrily, "if you don't go up-stairs and tend to that man up there, I shall scream. Now go! I'll be up when I can."

And Bertram went.

It was not so very long, after all, before Billy came in to greet her guest. She was not stately and imposing in royally sumptuous blue velvet and ermine; nor yet was she cozy and homy in bronze-gold crêpe de Chine and swan's-down. She was just herself in a pretty little morning house gown of blue gingham. She was minus the dust-cap and the ruffled apron, but she had a dab of flour on the left cheek, and a smutch of crock on her forehead. She had, too, a cut finger on her right hand, and a burned thumb on her left. But she was Billy—and being Billy, she advanced with a bright smile and held out a cordial hand—not even wincing when the cut finger came under Calderwell's hearty clasp.

"I'm glad to see you," she welcomed him. "You'll excuse my not appearing sooner, I'm sure, for—didn't Bertram tell you?—I'm playing Bridget to-night. But dinner is ready now, and we'll go down, please," she smiled, as she laid a light hand on her guest's arm.

Behind her, Bertram, remembering the scene in the kitchen, stared in sheer amazement. Bertram, it might be mentioned again, had been married six months, not six years.

What Billy had intended to serve for a "simple dinner" that night was: grapefruit with cherries, oyster stew, boiled halibut with egg sauce, chicken pie, squash, onions, and potatoes, peach fritters, a "lettuce and stuff" salad, and some new pie or pudding. What she did serve was: grapefruit (without the cherries), cold roast lamb, potatoes (a mush of sogginess), tomatoes (canned, and slightly burned), corn (canned, and very much burned), lettuce (plain); and for dessert, preserved peaches and cake (the latter rather dry and stale). Such was Billy's dinner.

The grapefruit everybody ate. The cold lamb too, met with a hearty reception, especially after the potatoes, corn, and tomatoes were served—and tasted. Outwardly, through it all, Billy was gayety itself. Inwardly she was burning up with anger and mortification. And because she was all this, there was, apparently, no limit to her laughter and sparkling repartee as she talked with Calderwell, her guest—the guest who, according to her original plans, was to be shown how happy she and Bertram were, what a good wife she made, and how devoted and satisfied Bertram was in his home.

William, picking at his dinner—as only a hungry man can pick at a dinner that is uneatable—watched Billy with a puzzled, uneasy frown. Bertram, choking over the few mouthfuls he ate, marked his wife's animated face and Calderwell's absorbed attention, and settled into gloomy silence.

But it could not continue forever. The preserved peaches were eaten at last, and the stale cake left. (Billy had forgotten the coffee—which was just as well, perhaps.) Then the four trailed up-stairs to the drawing-room.

At nine o'clock an anxious Eliza and a remorseful, apologetic Pete came home and descended to the horror the once orderly kitchen and dining-room had become. At ten, Calderwell, with very evident reluctance, tore himself away from Billy's gay badinage, and said good night. At two minutes past ten, an exhausted, nerve-racked Billy was trying to cry on the shoulders of both Uncle William and Bertram at once.

"There, there, child, don't! It went off all right," patted Uncle William.

"Billy, darling," pleaded Bertram, "please don't cry so! As if I'd ever let you step foot in that kitchen again!"

At this Billy raised a tear-wet face, aflame with indignant determination.

"As if I'd ever let you keep me from it, Bertram Henshaw, after this!" she contested. "I'm not going to do another thing in all my life but cook! When I think of the stuff we had to eat, after all the time I took to get it, I'm simply crazy! Do you think I'd run the risk of such a thing as this ever happening again?"

CHAPTER XI. CALDERWELL DOES SOME QUESTIONING

On the day after his dinner with Mr. and Mrs. Bertram Henshaw, Hugh Calderwell left Boston and did not return until more than a month had passed. One of his first acts, when he did come, was to look up Mr. M. J. Arkwright at the address which Billy had given him.

Calderwell had not seen Arkwright since they parted in Paris some two years before, after a six-months tramp through Europe together. Calderwell liked Arkwright then, greatly, and he lost no time now in renewing the acquaintance.

The address, as given by Billy, proved to be an attractive but modest apartment hotel near the Conservatory of Music; and Calderwell was delighted to find Arkwright at home in his comfortable little bachelor suite.

Arkwright greeted him most cordially.

"Well, well," he cried, "if it isn't Calderwell! And how's Mont Blanc? Or is it the Killarney Lakes this time, or maybe the Sphinx that I should inquire for, eh?"

"Guess again," laughed Calderwell, throwing off his heavy coat and settling himself comfortably in the inviting-looking morris chair his friend pulled forward.

"Sha'n't do it," retorted Arkwright, with a smile. "I never gamble on palpable uncertainties, except for a chance throw or two, as I gave a minute ago. Your movements are altogether too erratic, and too far-reaching, for ordinary mortals to keep track of."

"Well, maybe you're right," grinned Calderwell, appreciatively. "Anyhow, you would have lost this time, sure thing, for I've been working."

"Seen the doctor yet?" queried Arkwright, coolly, pushing the cigars across the table.

"Thanks—for both," sniffed Calderwell, with a reproachful glance, helping himself. "Your good judgment in some matters is still unimpaired, I see," he observed, tapping the little gilded band which had told him the cigar was an old favorite. "As to other matters, however,—you're wrong again, my friend, in your surmise. I am not sick, and I have been working."

"So? Well, I'm told they have very good specialists here. Some one of them ought to hit your case. Still—how long has it been running?" Arkwright's face showed only grave concern.

"Oh, come, let up, Arkwright," snapped Calderwell, striking his match alight with a vigorous jerk. "I'll admit I haven't ever given any special indication of an absorbing passion for work. But what can you expect of a fellow born with a whole dozen silver spoons in his mouth? And that's what I was, according to Bertram Henshaw. According to him again, it's a wonder I ever tried to feed myself; and perhaps he's right—with my mouth already so full."

"I should say so," laughed Arkwright.

"Well, be that as it may. I'm going to feed myself, and I'm going to earn my feed, too. I haven't climbed a mountain or paddled a canoe, for a year. I've been in Chicago cultivating the acquaintance of John Doe and Richard Roe."

"You mean—law?"

"Sure. I studied it here for a while, before that bout of ours a couple of years ago. Billy drove me away, then."

"Billy!—er—Mrs. Henshaw?"

"Yes. I thought I told you. She turned down my tenth-dozen proposal so emphatically that I lost all interest in Boston and took to the tall timber again. But I've come back. A friend of my father's wrote me to come on and consider a good opening there was in his law office. I came on a month ago, and considered. Then I went back to pack up. Now I've come for good, and here I am. You have my history to date. Now tell me of yourself. You're looking as fit as a penny from the mint, even though you have discarded that 'lovely' brown beard. Was that a concession to—er—Mary Jane?"

Arkwright lifted a quick hand of protest.

"'Michael Jeremiah,' please. There is no 'Mary Jane,' now," he said a bit stiffly.

The other stared a little. Then he gave a low chuckle.

"'Michael Jeremiah,'" he repeated musingly, eyeing the glowing tip of his cigar. "And to think how that mysterious 'M. J.' used to tantalize me! Do you mean," he added, turning slowly, "that no one calls you 'Mary Jane' now?"

"Not if they know what is best for them."

"Oh!" Calderwell noted the smouldering fire in the other's eyes a little curiously. "Very well. I'll take the hint—Michael Jeremiah."

"Thanks." Arkwright relaxed a little. "To tell the truth, I've had quite enough now—of Mary Jane."

"Very good. So be it," nodded the other, still regarding his friend thoughtfully. "But tell me—what of yourself?"

Arkwright shrugged his shoulders.

"There's nothing to tell. You've seen. I'm here."

"Humph! Very pretty," scoffed Calderwell. "Then if you won't tell, I will. I saw Billy a month ago, you see. It seems you've hit the trail for Grand Opera, as you threatened to that night in Paris; but you haven't brought up in vaudeville, as you prophesied you would do—though, for that matter, judging from the plums some of the stars are picking on the vaudeville stage, nowadays, that isn't to be sneezed at. But Billy says you've made two or three appearances already on the sacred boards themselves—one of them a subscription performance—and that you created no end of a sensation."

"Nonsense! I'm merely a student at the Opera School here," scowled Arkwright.

"Oh, yes, Billy said you were that, but she also said you wouldn't be, long. That you'd already had one good offer—I'm not speaking of marriage—and that you were going abroad next summer, and that they were all insufferably proud of you."

"Nonsense!" scowled Arkwright, again, coloring like a girl. "That is only some of—of Mrs. Henshaw's kind flattery."

Calderwell jerked the cigar from between his lips, and sat suddenly forward in his chair.

"Arkwright, tell me about them. How are they making it go?"

Arkwright frowned.

"Who? Make what go?" he asked.

"The Henshaws. Is she happy? Is he—on the square?"

Arkwright's face darkened.

"Well, really," he began; but Calderwell interrupted.

"Oh, come; don't be squeamish. You think I'm butting into what doesn't concern me; but I'm not. What concerns Billy does concern me. And if he doesn't make her happy, I'll—I'll kill him."

In spite of himself Arkwright laughed. The vehemence of the other's words, and the fierceness with which he puffed at his cigar as he fell back in his chair were most expressive.

"Well, I don't think you need to load revolvers nor sharpen daggers, just yet," he observed grimly.

Calderwell laughed this time, though without much mirth.

"Oh, I'm not in love with Billy, now," he explained. "Please don't think I am. I shouldn't see her if I was, of course."

Arkwright changed his position suddenly, bringing his face into the shadow. Calderwell talked on without pausing.

"No, I'm not in love with Billy. But Billy's a trump. You know that."

"I do." The words were low, but steadily spoken.

"Of course you do! We all do. And we want her happy. But as for her marrying Bertram—you could have bowled me over with a soap bubble when I heard she'd done it. Now understand: Bertram is a good fellow, and I like him. I've known him all his life, and he's all right. Oh, six or eight years ago, to be sure, he got in with a set of fellows—Bob Seaver and his clique—that were no good. Went in for Bohemianism, and all that rot. It wasn't good for Bertram. He's got the confounded temperament that goes with his talent, I suppose—though why a man can't paint a picture, or sing a song, and keep his temper and a level head I don't see!"

"He can," cut in Arkwright, with curt emphasis.

"Humph! Well, that's what I think. But, about this marriage business. Bertram admires a pretty face wherever he sees it—to paint, and always has. Not but that he's straight as a string with women—I don't mean that; but girls are always just so many pictures to be picked up on his brushes and transferred to his canvases. And as for his settling down and marrying anybody for keeps, right along—Great Scott! imagine Bertram Henshaw as a domestic man!"

Arkwright stirred restlessly as he spoke up in quick defense:

"Oh, but he is, I assure you. I—I've seen them in their home together—many times. I think they are—very happy." Arkwright spoke with decision, though still a little diffidently.

Calderwell was silent. He had picked up the little gilt band he had torn from his cigar and was fingering it musingly.

"Yes; I've seen them—once," he said, after a minute. "I took dinner with them when I was on, a month ago."

"I heard you did."

At something in Arkwright's voice, Calderwell turned quickly.

"What do you mean? Why do you say it like that?"

Arkwright laughed. The constraint fled from his manner.

"Well, I may as well tell you. You'll hear of it. It's no secret. Mrs. Henshaw herself tells of it everywhere. It was her friend, Alice Greggory, who told me of it first, however. It seems the cook was gone, and the mistress had to get the dinner herself."

"Yes, I know that."

"But you should hear Mrs. Henshaw tell the story now, or Bertram. It seems she knew nothing whatever about cooking, and her trials and tribulations in getting that dinner on to the table were only one degree worse than the dinner itself, according to her story. Didn't you—er—notice anything?"

"Notice anything!" exploded Calderwell. "I noticed that Billy was so brilliant she fairly radiated sparks; and I noticed that Bertram was so glum he—he almost radiated thunderclaps. Then I saw that Billy's high spirits were all assumed to cover a threatened burst of tears, and I laid it all to him. I thought he'd said something to hurt her; and I could have punched him. Great Scott! Was that what ailed them?"

"I reckon it was. Alice says that since then Mrs. Henshaw has fairly haunted the kitchen, begging Eliza to teach her everything, every single thing she knows!"

Calderwell chuckled.

"If that isn't just like Billy! She never does anything by halves. By George, but she was game over that dinner! I can see it all now."

"Alice says she's really learning to cook, in spite of old Pete's horror, and Eliza's pleadings not to spoil her pretty hands."

"Then Pete is back all right? What a faithful old soul he is!"

Arkwright frowned slightly.

"Yes, he's faithful, but he isn't all right, by any means. I think he's a sick man, myself."

"What makes Billy let him work, then?"

"Let him!" sniffed Arkwright. "I'd like to see you try to stop him! Mrs. Henshaw begs and pleads with him to stop, but he scouts the idea. Pete is thoroughly and unalterably convinced that the family would starve to death if it weren't for him; and Mrs. Henshaw says that she'll admit he has some grounds for his opinion when one remembers the condition of the kitchen and dining-room the night she presided over them."

"Poor Billy!" chuckled Calderwell. "I'd have gone down into the kitchen myself if I'd suspected what was going on."

Arkwright raised his eyebrows.

"Perhaps it's well you didn't—if Bertram's picture of what he found there when he went down is a true one. Mrs. Henshaw acknowledges that even the cat sought refuge under the stove."

"As if the veriest worm that crawls ever needed to seek refuge from Billy!" scoffed Calderwell. "By the way, what's this Annex I hear of? Bertram mentioned it, but I couldn't get either of them to tell what it was. Billy wouldn't, and Bertram said he couldn't—not with Billy shaking her head at him like that. So I had my suspicions. One of Billy's pet charities?"

"She doesn't call it that." Arkwright's face and voice softened. "It is Hillside. She still keeps it open. She calls it the Annex to her home. She's filled it with a crippled woman, a poor little music teacher, a lame boy, and Aunt Hannah."

"But how—extraordinary!"

"She doesn't think so. She says it's just an overflow house for the extra happiness she can't use."

There was a moment's silence. Calderwell laid down his cigar, pulled out his handkerchief, and blew his nose furiously. Then he got to his feet and walked to the fireplace. After a minute he turned.

"Well, if she isn't the beat 'em!" he spluttered. "And I had the gall to ask you if Henshaw made her—happy! Overflow house, indeed!"

"The best of it is, the way she does it," smiled Arkwright. "They're all the sort of people ordinary charity could never reach; and the only way she got them there at all was to make each one think that he or she was absolutely necessary to the rest of them. Even as it is, they all pay a little something toward the running expenses of the house. They insisted on that, and Mrs. Henshaw had to let them. I believe her chief difficulty now is that she has not less than six people whom she wishes to put into the two extra rooms still unoccupied, and she can't make up her mind which to take. Her husband says he expects to hear any day of an Annexette to the Annex."

"Humph!" grunted Calderwell, as he turned and began to walk up and down the room. "Bertram is still painting, I suppose."

"Oh, yes."

"What's he doing now?"

"Several things. He's up to his eyes in work. As you probably have heard, he met with a severe accident last summer, and lost the use of his right arm for many months. I believe they thought at one time he had lost it forever. But it's all right now, and he has several commissions for portraits. Alice says he's doing ideal heads again, too."

"Same old 'Face of a Girl'?"

"I suppose so, though Alice didn't say. Of course his special work just now is painting the portrait of Miss Marguerite Winthrop. You may have heard that he tried it last year and—and didn't make quite a success of it."

"Yes. My sister Belle told me. She hears from Billy once in a while. Will it be a go, this time?"

"We'll hope so—for everybody's sake. I imagine no one has seen it yet—it's not finished; but Alice says—"

Calderwell turned abruptly, a quizzical smile on his face.

"See here, my son," he interposed, "it strikes me that this Alice is saying a good deal—to you! Who is she?"

Arkwright gave a light laugh.

"Why, I told you. She is Miss Alice Greggory, Mrs. Henshaw's friend—and mine. I have known her for years."

"Hm-m; what is she like?"

"Like? Why, she's like—like herself, of course. You'll have to know Alice. She's the salt of the earth—Alice is," smiled Arkwright, rising to his feet with a remonstrative gesture, as he saw Calderwell pick up his coat. "What's your hurry?"

"Hm-m," commented Calderwell again, ignoring the question. "And when, may I ask, do you intend to appropriate this—er—salt—to—er—ah, season your own life with, as I might say—eh?"

Arkwright laughed. There was not the slightest trace of embarrassment in his face.

"Never. You're on the wrong track, this time. Alice and I are good friends—always have been, and always will be, I hope."

"Nothing more?"

"Nothing more. I see her frequently. She is musical, and the Henshaws are good enough to ask us there often together. You will meet her, doubtless, now, yourself. She is frequently at the Henshaw home."

"Hm-m." Calderwell still eyed his host shrewdly. "Then you'll give me a clear field, eh?"

"Certainly." Arkwright's eyes met his friend's gaze without swerving.

"All right. However, I suppose you'll tell me, as I did you, once, that a right of way in such a case doesn't mean a thoroughfare for the party interested. If my memory serves me, I gave you right of way in Paris to win the affections of a certain elusive Miss Billy here in Boston, if you could. But I see you didn't seem to improve your opportunities," he finished teasingly.

Arkwright stooped, of a sudden, to pick up a bit of paper from the floor.

"No," he said quietly. "I didn't seem to improve my opportunities." This time he did not meet Calderwell's eyes.

The good-byes had been said when Calderwell turned abruptly at the door.

"Oh, I say, I suppose you're going to that devil's carnival at Jordan Hall to-morrow night."

"Devil's carnival! You don't mean—Cyril Henshaw's piano recital!"

"Sure I do," grinned Calderwell, unabashed. "And I'll warrant it'll be a devil's carnival, too. Isn't Mr. Cyril Henshaw going to play his own music? Oh, I know I'm hopeless, from your standpoint, but I can't help it. I like mine with some go in it, and a tune that you can find without hunting for it. And I don't like lost spirits gone mad that wail and shriek through ten perfectly good minutes, and then die with a gasping moan whose home is the tombs. However, you're going, I take it."

"Of course I am," laughed the other. "You couldn't hire Alice to miss one shriek of those spirits. Besides, I rather like them myself, you know."

"Yes, I suppose you do. You're brought up on it—in your business. But me for the 'Merry Widow' and even the hoary 'Jingle Bells' every time! However, I'm going to be there—out of respect to the poor fellow's family. And, by the way, that's another thing that bowled me over—Cyril's marriage. Why, Cyril hates women!"

"Not all women—we'll hope," smiled Arkwright. "Do you know his wife?"

"Not much. I used to see her a little at Billy's. Music teacher, wasn't she? Then she's the same sort, I suppose."

"But she isn't," laughed Arkwright. "Oh, she taught music, but that was only because of necessity, I take it. She's domestic through and through, with an overwhelming passion for making puddings and darning socks, I hear. Alice says she believes Mrs. Cyril knows every dish and spoon by its Christian name, and that there's never so much as a spool of thread out of order in the house."

"But how does Cyril stand it—the trials and tribulations of domestic life? Bertram used to declare that the whole Strata was aquiver with fear when Cyril was composing, and I remember him as a perfect bear if anybody so much as whispered when he was in one of his moods. I never forgot the night Bertram and I were up in William's room trying to sing 'When Johnnie comes marching home,' to the accompaniment of a banjo in Bertram's hands, and a guitar in mine. Gorry! it was Hugh that went marching home that night."

"Oh, well, from reports I reckon Mrs. Cyril doesn't play either a banjo or a guitar," smiled Arkwright. "Alice says she wears rubber heels on her shoes, and has put hushers on all the chair-legs, and felt-mats between all the plates and saucers. Anyhow, Cyril is building a new house, and he looks as if he were in a pretty healthy condition, as you'll see to-morrow night."

"Humph! I wish he'd make his music healthy, then," grumbled Calderwell, as he opened the door.

CHAPTER XII. FOR BILLY—SOME ADVICE

February brought busy days. The public opening of the Bohemian Ten Club Exhibition was to take place the sixth of March, with a private view for invited guests the night before; and it was at this exhibition that Bertram planned to show his portrait of Marguerite Winthrop. He also, if possible, wished to enter two or three other canvases, upon which he was spending all the time he could get.

Bertram felt that he was doing very good work now. The portrait of Marguerite Winthrop was coming on finely. The spoiled idol of society had at last found a pose and a costume that suited her, and she was graciously pleased to give the artist almost as many sittings as he wanted. The "elusive something" in her face, which had previously been so baffling, was now already caught and held bewitchingly on his canvas. He was confident that the portrait would be a success. He was also much interested in another piece of work which he intended to show called "The Rose." The model for this was a beautiful young girl he had found selling flowers with her father in a street booth at the North End.

On the whole, Bertram was very happy these days. He could not, to be sure, spend quite so much time with Billy as he wished; but she understood, of course, as did he, that his work must come first. He knew that she tried to show him that she understood it. At the same time, he could not help thinking, occasionally, that Billy did sometimes mind his necessary absorption in his painting.

To himself Bertram owned that Billy was, in some ways, a puzzle to him. Her conduct was still erratic at times. One day he would seem to be everything to her; the next—almost nothing, judging by the ease with which she relinquished his society and substituted that of some one else: Arkwright, or Calderwell, for instance.

And that was another thing. Bertram was ashamed to hint even to himself that he was jealous of either of those men. Surely, after what had happened, after Billy's emphatic assertion that she had never loved any one but himself, it would seem not only absurd, but disloyal, that he should doubt for an instant Billy's entire devotion to him, and yet—there were times when he wished he could come home and not always find Alice Greggory, Calderwell, Arkwright, or all three of them strumming the piano in the drawing-room! At such times, always, though, if he did feel impatient, he immediately demanded of himself: "Are you, then, the kind of husband that begrudges your wife young companions of her own age and tastes to help her while away the hours that you cannot possibly spend with her yourself?"

This question, and the answer that his better self always gave to it, were usually sufficient to send him into some florists for a bunch of violets for Billy, or into a candy shop on a like atoning errand.

As to Billy—Billy, too, was busy these days chief of her concerns being, perhaps, attention to that honeymoon of hers, to see that it did not wane. At least, the most of her thoughts, and many of her actions, centered about that object.

Billy had the book, now—the "Talk to Young Wives." For a time she had worked with only the newspaper criticism to guide her; but, coming at last to the conclusion that if a little was good, more must be better, she had shyly gone into a bookstore one day and, with a pink blush, had asked for the book. Since bringing it home she had studied assiduously (though never if Bertram was near), keeping it well-hidden, when not in use, in a remote corner of her desk.

There was a good deal in the book that Billy did not like, and there were some statements that worried her; but yet there was much that she tried earnestly to follow. She was still striving to be the oak, and she was still eagerly endeavoring to brush up against those necessary outside interests. She was so thankful, in this connection, for Alice Greggory, and for Arkwright and Hugh Calderwell. It was such a help that she had them! They were not only very pleasant and entertaining outside interests, but one or another of them was almost always conveniently within reach.

Then, too, it pleased her to think that she was furthering the pretty love story between Alice and Mr. Arkwright. And she was furthering it. She was sure of that. Already she could see how dependent the man was on Alice, how he looked to her for approbation, and appealed to her on all occasions, exactly as if there was not a move that he wanted to make without her presence near him. Billy was very sure, now, of Arkwright. She only wished she were as much so of Alice. But Alice troubled her. Not but that Alice was kindness itself to the man, either. It was only a peculiar something almost like fear, or constraint, that Billy thought she saw in Alice's eyes, sometimes, when Arkwright made a particularly intimate appeal. There was Calderwell, too. He, also, worried Billy. She feared he was going to complicate matters still more by falling in love with Alice, himself; and this, certainly, Billy did not want at all. As this phase of the matter presented itself, indeed, Billy determined to appropriate Calderwell a little more exclusively to herself, when the four were together, thus leaving Alice for Arkwright. After all, it was rather entertaining—this playing at Cupid's assistant. If she could not have Bertram all the time, it was fortunate that these outside interests were so pleasurable.

Most of the mornings Billy spent in the kitchen, despite the remonstrances of both Pete and Eliza. Almost every meal, now, was graced with a palatable cake, pudding, or muffin that Billy would proudly claim as her handiwork. Pete still served at table, and made strenuous efforts to keep up all his old duties; but he was obviously growing weaker, and really serious blunders were beginning to be noticeable. Bertram even hinted once or twice that perhaps it would be just as well to insist on his going; but to this Billy would not give her consent. Even when one night his poor old trembling hands spilled half the contents of a soup plate over a new and costly evening gown of Billy's own, she still refused to have him dismissed.

"Why, Bertram, I wouldn't do it," she declared hotly; "and you wouldn't, either. He's been here more than fifty years. It would break his heart. He's really too ill to work, and I wish he would go of his own accord, of course; but I sha'n't ever tell him to go—not if he spills soup on every dress I've got. I'll buy more—and more, if it's necessary. Bless his dear old heart! He thinks he's really serving us—and he is, too."

"Oh, yes, you're right, he is!" sighed Bertram, with meaning emphasis, as he abandoned the argument.

In addition to her "Talk to Young Wives," Billy found herself encountering advice and comment on the marriage question from still other quarters—from her acquaintances (mostly the feminine ones) right and left. Continually she was hearing such words as these:

"Oh, well, what can you expect, Billy? You're an old married woman, now."

"Never mind, you'll find he's like all the rest of the husbands. You just wait and see!"

"Better begin with a high hand, Billy. Don't let him fool you!"

"Mercy! If I had a husband whose business it was to look at women's beautiful eyes, peachy cheeks, and luxurious tresses, I should go crazy! It's hard enough to keep a man's eyes on yourself when his daily interests are supposed to be just lumps of coal and chunks of ice, without flinging him into the very jaws of temptation like asking him to paint a pretty girl's picture!"

In response to all this, of course, Billy could but laugh, and blush, and toss back some gay reply, with a careless unconcern. But in her heart she did not like it. Sometimes she told herself that if there were not any advice or comment from anybody—either book or woman—if there were not anybody but just Bertram and herself, life would be just one long honeymoon forever and forever.

Once or twice Billy was tempted to go to Marie with this honeymoon question; but Marie was very busy these days, and very preoccupied. The new house that Cyril was building on Corey Hill, not far from the Annex, was almost finished, and Marie was immersed in the subject of house-furnishings and interior decoration. She was, too, still more deeply engrossed in the fashioning of tiny garments of the softest linen, lace, and woolen; and there was on her face such a look of beatific wonder and joy that Billy did not like to so much as hint that there was in the world such a book as "When the Honeymoon Wanes: A Talk to Young Wives."

Billy tried valiantly these days not to mind that Bertram's work was so absorbing. She tried not to mind that his business dealt, not with lumps of coal and chunks of ice, but with beautiful women like Marguerite Winthrop who asked him to luncheon, and lovely girls like his model for "The Rose" who came freely to his studio and spent hours in the beloved presence, being studied for what Bertram declared was absolutely the most wonderful poise of head and shoulders that he had ever seen.

Billy tried, also, these days, to so conduct herself that not by any chance could Calderwell suspect that sometimes she was jealous of Bertram's art. Not for worlds would she have had Calderwell begin to get the notion into his head that his old-time prophecy concerning Bertram's caring only for the turn of a girl's head or the tilt of her chin—to paint, was being fulfilled. Hence, particularly gay and cheerful was Billy when Calderwell was near. Nor could it be said that Billy was really unhappy at any time. It was only that, on occasion, the very depth of her happiness in Bertram's love frightened her, lest it bring disaster to herself or Bertram.

Billy still went frequently to the Annex. There were yet two unfilled rooms in the house. Billy was hesitating which two of six new friends of hers to choose as occupants; and it was one day early in March, after she had been talking the matter over with Aunt Hannah, that Aunt Hannah said:

"Dear me, Billy, if you had your way I believe you'd open another whole house!"

"Do you know?—that's just what I'm thinking of," retorted Billy, gravely. Then she laughed at Aunt Hannah's shocked gesture of protest. "Oh, well, I don't expect to," she added. "I haven't lived very long, but I've lived long enough to know that you can't always do what you want to."

"Just as if there were anything you wanted to do that you don't do, my dear," reproved Aunt Hannah, mildly.

"Yes, I know." Billy drew in her breath with a little catch. "I have so much that is lovely; and that's why I need this house, you know, for the overflow," she nodded brightly. Then, with a characteristic change of subject, she added: "My, but you should have tasted of the popovers I made for breakfast this morning!"

"I should like to," smiled Aunt Hannah. "William says you're getting to be quite a cook."

"Well, maybe," conceded Billy, doubtfully. "Oh, I can do some things all right; but just wait till Pete and Eliza go away again, and Bertram brings home a friend to dinner. That'll tell the tale. I think now I could have something besides potato-mush and burned corn—but maybe I wouldn't, when the time came. If only I could buy everything I needed to cook with, I'd be all right. But I can't, I find."

"Can't buy what you need! What do you mean?"

Billy laughed ruefully.

"Well, every other question I ask Eliza, she says: 'Why, I don't know; you have to use your judgment.' Just as if I had any judgment about how much salt to use, or what dish to take! Dear me, Aunt Hannah, the man that will grow judgment and can it as you would a mess of peas, has got his fortune made!"

"What an absurd child you are, Billy," laughed Aunt Hannah. "I used to tell Marie—By the way, how is Marie? Have you seen her lately?"

"Oh, yes, I saw her yesterday," twinkled Billy. "She had a book of wall-paper samples spread over the back of a chair, two bunches of samples of different colored damasks on the table before her, a 'Young Mother's Guide' propped open in another chair, and a pair of baby's socks in her lap with a roll each of pink, and white, and blue ribbon. She spent most of the time, after I had helped her choose the ribbon, in asking me if I thought she ought to let the baby cry and bother Cyril, or stop its crying and hurt the baby, because her 'Mother's Guide' says a certain amount of crying is needed to develop a baby's lungs."

Aunt Hannah laughed, but she frowned, too.

"The idea! I guess Cyril can stand proper crying—and laughing, too—from his own child!" she said then, crisply.

"Oh, but Marie is afraid he can't," smiled Billy. "And that's the trouble. She says that's the only thing that worries her—Cyril."

"Nonsense!" ejaculated Aunt Hannah.

"Oh, but it isn't nonsense to Marie," retorted Billy. "You should see the preparations she's made and the precautions she's taken. Actually, when I saw those baby's socks in her lap, I didn't know but she was going to put rubber heels on them! They've built the new house with deadening felt in all the walls, and Marie's planned the nursery and Cyril's den at opposite ends of the house; and she says she shall keep the baby there all the time—the nursery, I mean, not the den. She says she's going to teach it to be a quiet baby and hate noise. She says she thinks she can do it, too."

"Humph!" sniffed Aunt Hannah, scornfully.

"You should have seen Marie's disgust the other day," went on Billy, a bit mischievously. "Her Cousin Jane sent on a rattle she'd made herself, all soft worsted, with bells inside. It was a dear; but Marie was horror-stricken. 'My baby have a rattle?' she cried. 'Why, what would Cyril say? As if he could stand a rattle in the house!' And if she didn't give that rattle to the janitor's wife that very day, while I was there!"

"Humph!" sniffed Aunt Hannah again, as Billy rose to go. "Well, I'm thinking Marie has still some things to learn in this world—and Cyril, too, for that matter."

"I wouldn't wonder," laughed Billy, giving Aunt Hannah a good-by kiss.

CHAPTER XIII. PETE

Bertram Henshaw had no disquieting forebodings this time concerning his portrait of Marguerite Winthrop when the doors of the Bohemian Ten Club Exhibition were thrown open to members and invited guests. Just how great a popular success it was destined to be, he could not know, of course, though he might have suspected it when he began to receive the admiring and hearty congratulations of his friends and fellow-artists on that first evening.

Nor was the Winthrop portrait the only jewel in his crown on that occasion. His marvelously exquisite "The Rose," and his smaller ideal picture, "Expectation," came in for scarcely less commendation. There was no doubt now. The originator of the famous "Face of a Girl" had come into his own again. On all sides this was the verdict, one long-haired critic of international fame even claiming openly that Henshaw had not only equaled his former best work, but had gone beyond it, in both artistry and technique.

It was a brilliant gathering. Society, as usual, in costly evening gowns and correct swallow-tails rubbed elbows with names famous in the world of Art and Letters. Everywhere were gay laughter and sparkling repartee. Even the austere-faced J. G. Winthrop unbent to the extent of grim smiles in response to the laudatory comments bestowed upon the pictured image of his idol, his beautiful daughter.

As to the great financier's own opinion of the work, no one heard him express it except, perhaps, the artist; and all that he got was a grip of the hand and a "Good! I knew you'd fetch it this time, my boy!" But that was enough. And, indeed, no one who knew the stern old man needed to more than look into his face that evening to know of his entire satisfaction in this portrait soon to be the most recent, and the most cherished addition to his far-famed art collection.

As to Bertram—Bertram was pleased and happy and gratified, of course, as was natural; but he was not one whit more so than was Bertram's wife. Billy fairly radiated happiness and proud joy. She told Bertram, indeed, that if he did anything to make her any prouder, it would take an Annex the size of the Boston Opera House to hold her extra happiness.

"Sh-h, Billy! Some one will hear you," protested Bertram, tragically; but, in spite of his horrified voice, he did not look displeased.

For the first time Billy met Marguerite Winthrop that evening. At the outset there was just a bit of shyness and constraint in the young wife's manner. Billy could not forget her old insane jealousy of this beautiful girl with the envied name of Marguerite. But it was for only a moment, and soon she was her natural, charming self.

Miss Winthrop was fascinated, and she made no pretense of hiding it. She even turned to Bertram at last, and cried:

"Surely, now, Mr. Henshaw, you need never go far for a model! Why don't you paint your wife?"

Billy colored. Bertram smiled.

"I have," he said. "I have painted her many times. In fact, I have painted her so often that she once declared it was only the tilt of her chin and the turn of her head that I loved—to paint," he said merrily, enjoying Billy's pretty confusion, and not realizing that his words really distressed her. "I have a whole studio full of 'Billys' at home."

"Oh, have you, really?" questioned Miss Winthrop, eagerly. "Then mayn't I see them? Mayn't I, please, Mrs. Henshaw? I'd so love to!"

"Why, of course you may," murmured both the artist and his wife.

"Thank you. Then I'm coming right away. May I? I'm going to Washington next week, you see. Will you let me come to-morrow at—at half-past three, then? Will it be quite convenient for you, Mrs. Henshaw?"

"Quite convenient. I shall be glad to see you," smiled Billy. And Bertram echoed his wife's cordial permission.

"Thank you. Then I'll be there at half-past three," nodded Miss Winthrop, with a smile, as she turned to give place to an admiring group, who were waiting to pay their respects to the artist and his wife.

There was, after all, that evening, one fly in Billy's ointment.

It fluttered in at the behest of an old acquaintance—one of the "advice women," as Billy termed some of her too interested friends.

"Well, they're lovely, perfectly lovely, of course, Mrs. Henshaw," said this lady, coming up to say good-night. "But, all the same, I'm glad my husband is just a plain lawyer. Look out, my dear, that while Mr. Henshaw is stealing all those pretty faces for his canvases—just look out that the fair ladies don't turn around and steal his heart before you know it. Dear me, but you must be so proud of him!"

"I am," smiled Billy, serenely; and only the jagged split that rent the glove on her hand, at that moment, told of the fierce anger behind that smile.

"As if I couldn't trust Bertram!" raged Billy passionately to herself, stealing a surreptitious glance at her ruined glove. "And as if there weren't ever any perfectly happy marriages—even if you don't ever hear of them, or read of them!"

Bertram was not home to luncheon on the day following the opening night of the Bohemian Ten Club. A matter of business called him away from the house early in the morning; but he told his wife that he surely would be on hand for Miss Winthrop's call at half-past three o'clock that afternoon.

"Yes, do," Billy had urged. "I think she's lovely, but you know her so much better than I do that I want you here. Besides, you needn't think I'm going to show her all those Billys of yours. I may be vain, but I'm not quite vain enough for that, sir!"

"Don't worry," her husband had laughed. "I'll be here."

As it chanced, however, something occurred an hour before half-past three o'clock that drove every thought of Miss Winthrop's call from Billy's head.

For three days, now, Pete had been at the home of his niece in South Boston. He had been forced, finally, to give up and go away. News from him the day before had been anything but reassuring, and to-day, Bertram being gone, Billy had suggested that Eliza serve a simple luncheon and go immediately afterward to South Boston to see how her uncle was. This suggestion Eliza had followed, leaving the house at one o'clock.

Shortly after two Calderwell had dropped in to bring Bertram, as he expressed it, a bunch of bouquets he had gathered at the picture show the night before. He was still in the drawing-room, chatting with Billy, when the telephone bell rang.

"If that's Bertram, tell him to come home; he's got company," laughed Calderwell, as Billy passed into the hall.

A moment later he heard Billy give a startled cry, followed by a few broken words at short intervals. Then, before he could surmise what had happened, she was back in the drawing-room again, her eyes full of tears.

"It's Pete," she choked. "Eliza says he can't live but a few minutes. He wants to see me once more. What shall I do? John's got Peggy out with Aunt Hannah and Mrs. Greggory. It was so nice to-day I made them go. But I must get there some way—Pete is calling for me.

Uncle William is going, and I told Eliza where she might reach Bertram; but what shall I do? How shall I go?"

Calderwell was on his feet at once.

"I'll get a taxi. Don't worry—we'll get there. Poor old soul—of course he wants to see you! Get on your things. I'll have it here in no time," he finished, hurrying to the telephone.

"Oh, Hugh, I'm so glad I've got you here," sobbed Billy, stumbling blindly toward the stairway. "I'll be ready in two minutes."

And she was; but neither then, nor a little later when she and Calderwell drove hurriedly away from the house, did Billy once remember that Miss Marguerite Winthrop was coming to call that afternoon to see Mrs. Bertram Henshaw and a roomful of Billy pictures.

Pete was still alive when Calderwell left Billy at the door of the modest little home where Eliza's mother lived.

"Yes, you're in time, ma'am," sobbed Eliza; "and, oh, I'm so glad you've come. He's been askin' and askin' for ye."

From Eliza Billy learned then that Mr. William was there, but not Mr. Bertram. They had not been able to reach Mr. Bertram, or Mr. Cyril.

Billy never forgot the look of reverent adoration that came into Pete's eyes as she entered the room where he lay.

"Miss Billy—my Miss Billy! You were so good-to come," he whispered faintly.

Billy choked back a sob.

"Of course I'd come, Pete," she said gently, taking one of the thin, worn hands into both her soft ones.

It was more than a few minutes that Pete lived. Four o'clock came, and five, and he was still with them. Often he opened his eyes and smiled. Sometimes he spoke a low word to William or Billy, or to one of the weeping women at the foot of the bed. That the presence of his beloved master and mistress meant much to him was plain to be seen.

"I'm so sorry," he faltered once, "about that pretty dress—I spoiled, Miss Billy. But you know—my hands—"

"I know, I know," soothed Billy; "but don't worry. It wasn't spoiled, Pete. It's all fixed now."

"Oh, I'm so glad," sighed the sick man. After another long interval of silence he turned to William.

"Them socks—the medium thin ones—you'd oughter be puttin' 'em on soon, sir, now. They're in the right-hand corner of the bottom drawer—you know."

"Yes, Pete; I'll attend to it," William managed to stammer, after he had cleared his throat.

Eliza's turn came next.

"Remember about the coffee," Pete said to her, "—the way Mr. William likes it. And always eggs, you know, for—for—" His voice trailed into an indistinct murmur, and his eyelids drooped wearily.

One by one the minutes passed. The doctor came and went: there was nothing he could do. At half-past five the thin old face became again alight with consciousness. There was a good-by message for Bertram, and one for Cyril. Aunt Hannah was remembered, and even little Tommy Dunn. Then, gradually, a gray shadow crept over the wasted features. The words came more brokenly. The mind, plainly, was wandering, for old Pete was young again, and around him were the lads he loved, William, Cyril, and Bertram. And then, very quietly, soon after the clock struck six, Pete fell into the beginning of his long sleep.

CHAPTER XIV. WHEN BERTRAM CAME HOME

It was a little after half-past three o'clock that afternoon when Bertram Henshaw hurried up Beacon Street toward his home. He had been delayed, and he feared that Miss Winthrop would already have reached the house. Mindful of what Billy had said that morning, he knew how his wife would fret if he were not there when the guest arrived. The sight of what he surmised to be Miss Winthrop's limousine before his door hastened his steps still more. But as he reached the house, he was surprised to find Miss Winthrop herself turning away from the door.

"Why, Miss Winthrop," he cried, "you're not going now! You can't have been here any— yet!"

"Well, no, I—I haven't," retorted the lady, with heightened color and a somewhat peculiar emphasis. "My ring wasn't answered."

"Wasn't answered!" Bertram reddened angrily. "Why, what can that mean? Where's the maid? Where's my wife? Mrs. Henshaw must be here! She was expecting you."

Bertram, in his annoyed amazement, spoke loudly, vehemently. Hence he was quite plainly heard by the group of small boys and girls who had been improving the mild weather for a frolic on the sidewalk, and who had been attracted to his door a moment before by the shining magnet of the Winthrop limousine with its resplendently liveried chauffeur. As Bertram spoke, one of the small girls, Bessie Bailey, stepped forward and piped up a shrill reply.

"She ain't, Mr. Henshaw! She ain't here. I saw her go away just a little while ago."

Bertram turned sharply.

"You saw her go away! What do you mean?"

Small Bessie swelled with importance. Bessie was thirteen, in spite of her diminutive height. Bessie's mother was dead, and Bessie's caretakers were gossiping nurses and servants, who frequently left in her way books that were much too old for Bessie to read—but she read them.

"I mean she ain't here—your wife, Mr. Henshaw. She went away. I saw her. I guess likely she's eloped, sir."

"Eloped!"

Bessie swelled still more importantly. To her experienced eyes the situation contained all the necessary elements for the customary flight of the heroine in her story-books, as here, now, was the irate, deserted husband.

"Sure! And 'twas just before you came—quite a while before. A big shiny black automobile like this drove up—only it wasn't quite such a nice one—an' Mrs. Henshaw an' a man came out of your house an' got in, an' drove right away quick! They just ran to get into it, too— didn't they?" She appealed to her young mates grouped about her.

A chorus of shrill exclamations brought Mr. Bertram Henshaw suddenly to his senses. By a desperate effort he hid his angry annoyance as he turned to the manifestly embarrassed young woman who was already descending the steps.

"My dear Miss Winthrop," he apologized contritely, "I'm sure you'll forgive this seeming great rudeness on the part of my wife. Notwithstanding the lurid tales of our young friends here, I suspect nothing more serious has happened than that my wife has been hastily summoned to Aunt Hannah, perhaps. Or, of course, she may not have understood that you were coming to-day at half-past three—though I thought she did. But I'm so sorry—when you were so kind as to come—" Miss Winthrop interrupted with a quick gesture.

"Say no more, I beg of you," she entreated. "Mrs. Henshaw is quite excusable, I'm sure. Please don't give it another thought," she finished, as with a hurried direction to the man who was holding open the door of her car, she stepped inside and bowed her good-byes.

Bertram, with stern self-control, forced himself to walk nonchalantly up his steps, leisurely take out his key, and open his door, under the interested eyes of Bessie Bailey and her friends; but once beyond their hateful stare, his demeanor underwent a complete change. Throwing aside his hat and coat, he strode to the telephone.

"Oh, is that you, Aunt Hannah?" he called crisply, a moment later. "Well, if Billy's there will you tell her I want to speak to her, please?"

"Billy?" answered Aunt Hannah's slow, gentle tones. "Why, my dear boy, Billy isn't here!"

"She isn't? Well, when did she leave? She's been there, hasn't she?"

"Why, I don't think so, but I'll see, if you like. Mrs. Greggory and I have just this minute come in from an automobile ride. We would have stayed longer, but it began to get chilly, and I forgot to take one of the shawls that I'd laid out."

"Yes; well, if you will see, please, if Billy has been there, and when she left," said Bertram, with grim self-control.

"All right. I'll see," murmured Aunt Hannah. In a few moments her voice again sounded across the wires. "Why, no, Bertram, Rosa says she hasn't been here since yesterday. Isn't she there somewhere about the house? Didn't you know where she was going?"

"Well, no, I didn't—else I shouldn't have been asking you," snapped the irate Bertram and hung up the receiver with most rude haste, thereby cutting off an astounded "Oh, my grief and conscience!" in the middle of it.

The next ten minutes Bertram spent in going through the whole house, from garret to basement. Needless to say, he found nothing to enlighten him, or to soothe his temper. Four o'clock came, then half-past, and five. At five Bertram began to look for Eliza, but in vain. At half-past five he watched for William; but William, too, did not come.

Bertram was pacing the floor now, nervously. He was a little frightened, but more mortified and angry. That Billy should have allowed Miss Winthrop to call by appointment only to find no hostess, no message, no maid, even, to answer her ring—it was inexcusable! Impulsiveness, unconventionality, and girlish irresponsibility were all very delightful, of course—at times; but not now, certainly. Billy was not a girl any longer. She was a married woman. Something was due to him, her husband! A pretty picture he must have made on those steps, trying to apologize for a truant wife, and to laugh off that absurd Bessie Bailey's preposterous assertion at the same time! What would Miss Winthrop think? What could she think? Bertram fairly ground his teeth with chagrin, at the situation in which he found himself.

Nor were matters helped any by the fact that Bertram was hungry. Bertram's luncheon had been meager and unsatisfying. That the kitchen down-stairs still remained in silent, spotless order instead of being astir with the sounds and smells of a good dinner (as it should have been) did not improve his temper. Where Billy was he could not imagine. He thought, once or twice, of calling up some of her friends; but something held him back from that— though he did try to get Marie, knowing very well that she was probably over to the new house and would not answer. He was not surprised, therefore, when he received no reply to his ring.

That there was the slightest truth in Bessie Bailey's absurd "elopement" idea, Bertram did not, of course, for an instant believe. The only thing that rankled about that was the fact that she had suggested such a thing, and that Miss Winthrop and those silly children had heard her. He recognized half of Bessie's friends as neighborhood youngsters, and he knew very well that there would be many a quiet laugh at his expense around various Beacon Street dinner-tables that night. At the thought of those dinner-tables, he scowled again. He had no dinner-table—at least, he had no dinner on it!

Who the man might be Bertram thought he could easily guess. It was either Arkwright or Calderwell, of course; and probably that tiresome Alice Greggory was mixed up in it somehow. He did wish Billy—

Six o'clock came, then half-past. Bertram was indeed frightened now, but he was more angry, and still more hungry. He had, in fact, reached that state of blind unreasonableness said to be peculiar to hungry males from time immemorial.

At ten minutes of seven a key clicked in the lock of the outer door, and William and Billy entered the hall.

It was almost dark. Bertram could not see their faces. He had not lighted the hall at all.

"Well," he began sharply, "is this the way you receive your callers, Billy? I came home and found Miss Winthrop just leaving—no one here to receive her! Where've you been? Where's Eliza? Where's my dinner? Of course I don't mean to scold, Billy, but there is a limit to even my patience—and it's reached now. I can't help suggesting that if you would tend to your husband and your home a little more, and go gallivanting off with Calderwell and Arkwright and Alice Greggory a little less, that—Where is Eliza, anyway?" he finished irritably, switching on the lights with a snap.

There was a moment of dead silence. At Bertram's first words Billy and William had stopped short. Neither had moved since. Now William turned and began to speak, but Billy interrupted. She met her husband's gaze steadily.

"I will be down at once to get your dinner," she said quietly. "Eliza will not come to-night. Pete is dead."

Bertram started forward with a quick cry.

"Dead! Oh, Billy! Then you were—there! Billy!"

But his wife did not apparently hear him. She passed him without turning her head, and went on up the stairs, leaving him to meet the sorrowful, accusing eyes of William.

CHAPTER XV. AFTER THE STORM

The young husband's apologies were profuse and abject. Bertram was heartily ashamed of himself, and was man enough to acknowledge it. Almost on his knees he begged Billy to forgive him; and in a frenzy of self-denunciation he followed her down into the kitchen that night, piteously beseeching her to speak to him, to just look at him, even, so that he might know he was not utterly despised—though he did, indeed, deserve to be more than despised, he moaned.

At first Billy did not speak, or even vouchsafe a glance in his direction. Very quietly she went about her preparations for a simple meal, paying apparently no more attention to Bertram than as if he were not there. But that her ears were only seemingly, and not really deaf, was shown very clearly a little later, when, at a particularly abject wail on the part of the babbling shadow at her heels, Billy choked into a little gasp, half laughter, half sob. It was all over then. Bertram had her in his arms in a twinkling, while to the floor clattered and rolled a knife and a half-peeled baked potato.

Naturally, after that, there could be no more dignified silences on the part of the injured wife. There were, instead, half-smiles, tears, sobs, a tremulous telling of Pete's going and his messages, followed by a tearful listening to Bertram's story of the torture he had endured at the hands of Miss Winthrop, Bessie Bailey, and an empty, dinnerless house. And thus, in one corner of the kitchen, some time later, a hungry, desperate William found them, the half-peeled, cold baked potato still at their feet.

Torn between his craving for food and his desire not to interfere with any possible peacemaking, William was obviously hesitating what to do, when Billy glanced up and saw him. She saw, too, at the same time, the empty, blazing gas-stove burner, and the pile of half-prepared potatoes, to warm which the burner had long since been lighted. With a little cry she broke away from her husband's arms.

"Mercy! and here's poor Uncle William, bless his heart, with not a thing to eat yet!"

They all got dinner then, together, with many a sigh and quick-coming tear as everywhere they met some sad reminder of the gentle old hands that would never again minister to their comfort.

It was a silent meal, and little, after all, was eaten, though brave attempts at cheerfulness and naturalness were made by all three. Bertram, especially, talked, and tried to make sure that the shadow on Billy's face was at least not the one his own conduct had brought there.

"For you do—you surely do forgive me, don't you?" he begged, as he followed her into the kitchen after the sorry meal was over.

"Why, yes, dear, yes," sighed Billy, trying to smile.

"And you'll forget?"

There was no answer.

"Billy! And you'll forget?" Bertram's voice was insistent, reproachful.

Billy changed color and bit her lip. She looked plainly distressed.

"Billy!" cried the man, still more reproachfully.

"But, Bertram, I can't forget—quite yet," faltered Billy.

Bertram frowned. For a minute he looked as if he were about to take up the matter seriously and argue it with her; but the next moment he smiled and tossed his head with jaunty playfulness—Bertram, to tell the truth, had now had quite enough of what he privately termed "scenes" and "heroics"; and, manlike, he was very ardently longing for the old easy-going friendliness, with all unpleasantness banished to oblivion.

"Oh, but you'll have to forget," he claimed, with cheery insistence, "for you've promised to forgive me—and one can't forgive without forgetting. So, there!" he finished, with a smilingly determined "now-everything-is-just-as-it-was-before" air.

Billy made no response. She turned hurriedly and began to busy herself with the dishes at the sink. In her heart she was wondering: could she ever forget what Bertram had said? Would anything ever blot out those awful words: "If you would tend to your husband and your home a little more, and go gallivanting off with Calderwell and Arkwright and Alice Greggory a little less—"? It seemed now that always, for evermore, they would ring in her ears; always, for evermore, they would burn deeper and deeper into her soul. And not once, in all Bertram's apologies, had he referred to them—those words he had uttered. He had not said he did not mean them. He had not said he was sorry he spoke them. He had ignored them; and he expected that now she, too, would ignore them. As if she could!" If you would tend to your husband and your home a little more, and go gallivanting off with Calderwell and Arkwright and Alice Greggory a little less—" Oh, if only she could, indeed,—forget!

When Billy went up-stairs that night she ran across her "Talk to Young Wives" in her desk. With a half-stifled cry she thrust it far back out of sight.

"I hate you, I hate you—with all your old talk about 'brushing up against outside interests'!" she whispered fiercely. "Well, I've 'brushed'—and now see what I've got for it!"

Later, however, after Bertram was asleep, Billy crept out of bed and got the book. Under the carefully shaded lamp in the adjoining room she turned the pages softly till she came to the sentence: "Perhaps it would be hard to find a more utterly unreasonable, irritable, irresponsible creature than a hungry man." With a long sigh she began to read; and not until some minutes later did she close the book, turn off the light, and steal back to bed.

During the next three days, until after the funeral at the shabby little South Boston house, Eliza spent only about half of each day at the Strata. This, much to her distress, left many of the household tasks for her young mistress to perform. Billy, however, attacked each new duty with a feverish eagerness that seemed to make the performance of it very like some glad penance done for past misdeeds. And when—on the day after they had laid the old servant in his last resting place—a despairing message came from Eliza to the effect that now her mother was very ill, and would need her care, Billy promptly told Eliza to stay as long as was necessary; that they could get along all right without her.

"But, Billy, what are we going to do?" Bertram demanded, when he heard the news. "We must have somebody!"

"I'm going to do it."

"Nonsense! As if you could!" scoffed Bertram.

Billy lifted her chin.

"Couldn't I, indeed," she retorted. "Do you realize, young man, how much I've done the last three days? How about those muffins you had this morning for breakfast, and that cake last night? And didn't you yourself say that you never ate a better pudding than that date puff yesterday noon?"

Bertram laughed and shrugged his shoulders.

"My dear love, I'm not questioning your ability to do it," he soothed quickly. "Still," he added, with a whimsical smile, "I must remind you that Eliza has been here half the time, and that muffins and date puffs, however delicious, aren't all there is to running a big house like this. Besides, just be sensible, Billy," he went on more seriously, as he noted the rebellious gleam coming into his young wife's eyes; "you'd know you couldn't do it, if you'd just stop to think. There's the Carletons coming to dinner Monday, and my studio Tea to-morrow, to say nothing of the Symphony and the opera, and the concerts you'd lose because you were too dead tired to go to them. You know how it was with that concert yesterday afternoon which Alice Greggory wanted you to go to with her."

"I didn't—want—to go," choked Billy, under her breath.

"And there's your music. You haven't done a thing with that for days, yet only last week you told me the publishers were hurrying you for that last song to complete the group."

"I haven't felt like—writing," stammered Billy, still half under her breath.

"Of course you haven't," triumphed Bertram. "You've been too dead tired. And that's just what I say. Billy, you can't do it all yourself!"

"But I want to. I want to—to tend to things," faltered Billy, with a half-fearful glance into her husband's face.

Billy was hearing very loudly now that accusing "If you'd tend to your husband and your home a little more—" Bertram, however, was not hearing it, evidently. Indeed, he seemed never to have heard it—much less to have spoken it.

"'Tend to things,'" he laughed lightly. "Well, you'll have enough to do to tend to the maid, I fancy. Anyhow, we're going to have one. I'll just step into one of those—what do you call 'em?—intelligence offices on my way down and send one up," he finished, as he gave his wife a good-by kiss.

An hour later Billy, struggling with the broom and the drawing-room carpet, was called to the telephone. It was her husband's voice that came to her.

"Billy, for heaven's sake, take pity on me. Won't you put on your duds and come and engage your maid yourself?"

"Why, Bertram, what's the matter?"

"Matter? Holy smoke! Well, I've been to three of those intelligence offices—though why they call them that I can't imagine. If ever there was a place utterly devoid of intelligence—but never mind! I've interviewed four fat ladies, two thin ones, and one medium with a wart. I've cheerfully divulged all our family secrets, promised every other half-hour out, and taken oath that our household numbers three adult members, and no more; but I simply can't remember how many handkerchiefs we have in the wash each week. Billy, will you come? Maybe you can do something with them. I'm sure you can!"

"Why, of course I'll come," chirped Billy. "Where shall I meet you?"

Bertram gave the street and number.

"Good! I'll be there," promised Billy, as she hung up the receiver.

Quite forgetting the broom in the middle of the drawing-room floor, Billy tripped up-stairs to change her dress. On her lips was a gay little song. In her heart was joy.

"I rather guess now I'm tending to my husband and my home!" she was crowing to herself.

Just as Billy was about to leave the house the telephone bell jangled again. It was Alice Greggory.

"Billy, dear," she called, "can't you come out? Mr. Arkwright and Mr. Calderwell are here, and they've brought some new music. We want you. Will you come?"

"I can't, dear. Bertram wants me. He's sent for me. I've got some housewifely duties to perform to-day," returned Billy, in a voice so curiously triumphant that Alice, at her end of the wires, frowned in puzzled wonder as she turned away from the telephone.

CHAPTER XVI. INTO TRAINING FOR MARY ELLEN

Bertram told a friend afterwards that he never knew the meaning of the word "chaos" until he had seen the Strata during the weeks immediately following the laying away of his old servant.

"Every stratum was aquiver with apprehension," he declared; "and there was never any telling when the next grand upheaval would rock the whole structure to its foundations."

Nor was Bertram so far from being right. It was, indeed, a chaos, as none knew better than did Bertram's wife.

Poor Billy! Sorry indeed were these days for Billy; and, as if to make her cup of woe full to overflowing, there were Sister Kate's epistolary "I told you so," and Aunt Hannah's ever recurring lament: "If only, Billy, you were a practical housekeeper yourself, they wouldn't impose on you so!"

Aunt Hannah, to be sure, offered Rosa, and Kate, by letter, offered advice—plenty of it. But Billy, stung beyond all endurance, and fairly radiating hurt pride and dogged determination, disdained all assistance, and, with head held high, declared she was getting along very well, very well indeed!

And this was the way she "got along."

First came Nora. Nora was a blue-eyed, black-haired Irish girl, the sixth that the despairing Billy had interviewed on that fateful morning when Bertram had summoned her to his aid. Nora stayed two days. During her reign the entire Strata echoed to banged doors, dropped china, and slammed furniture. At her departure the Henshaws' possessions were less by four cups, two saucers, one plate, one salad bowl, two cut glass tumblers, and a teapot—the latter William's choicest bit of Lowestoft.

Olga came next. Olga was a Treasure. She was low-voiced, gentle-eyed, and a good cook. She stayed a week. By that time the growing frequency of the disappearance of sundry small articles of value and convenience led to Billy's making a reluctant search of Olga's room—and to Olga's departure; for the room was, indeed, a treasure house, the Treasure having gathered unto itself other treasures.

Following Olga came a period of what Bertram called "one night stands," so frequently were the dramatis personæ below stairs changed. Gretchen drank. Christine knew only four words of English: salt, good-by, no, and yes; and Billy found need occasionally of using other words. Mary was impertinent and lazy. Jennie could not even boil a potato properly, much less cook a dinner. Sarah (colored) was willing and pleasant, but insufferably untidy. Bridget was neatness itself, but she had no conception of the value of time. Her meals were always from thirty to sixty minutes late, and half-cooked at that. Vera sang—when she wasn't whistling—and as she was generally off the key, and always off the tune, her almost frantic mistress dismissed her before twenty-four hours had passed. Then came Mary Ellen. Mary Ellen began well. She was neat, capable, and obliging; but it did not take her long to discover just how much—and how little—her mistress really knew of practical housekeeping. Matters and things were very different then. Mary Ellen became argumentative, impertinent, and domineering. She openly shirked her work, when it pleased her so to do, and demanded perquisites and privileges so insolently that even William asked Billy one day whether Mary Ellen or Billy herself were the mistress of the Strata: and Bertram, with mock humility, inquired how soon Mary Ellen would be wanting the house. Billy, in weary despair, submitted to this bullying for almost a week; then, in a sudden accession of outraged dignity that left Mary Ellen gasping with surprise, she told the girl to go.

And thus the days passed. The maids came and the maids went, and, to Billy, each one seemed a little worse than the one before. Nowhere was there comfort, rest, or peacefulness. The nights were a torture of apprehension, and the days an even greater torture of fulfilment. Noise, confusion, meals poorly cooked and worse served, dust, disorder, and uncertainty. And this was home, Billy told herself bitterly. No wonder that Bertram telephoned more and more frequently that he had met a friend, and was dining in town. No wonder that William pushed back his plate almost every meal with his food scarcely touched, and then wandered about the house with that hungry, homesick, homeless look that nearly broke her heart. No wonder, indeed!

And so it had come. It was true. Aunt Hannah and Kate and the "Talk to Young Wives" were right. She had not been fit to marry Bertram. She had not been fit to marry anybody. Her honeymoon was not only waning, but going into a total eclipse. Had not Bertram already declared that if she would tend to her husband and her home a little more—

Billy clenched her small hands and set her round chin squarely.

Very well, she would show them. She would tend to her husband and her home. She fancied she could learn to run that house, and run it well! And forthwith she descended to the kitchen and told the then reigning tormentor that her wages would be paid until the end of the week, but that her services would be immediately dispensed with.

Billy was well aware now that housekeeping was a matter of more than muffins and date puffs. She could gauge, in a measure, the magnitude of the task to which she had set herself. But she did not falter; and very systematically she set about making her plans.

With a good stout woman to come in twice a week for the heavier work, she believed she could manage by herself very well until Eliza could come back. At least she could serve more palatable meals than the most of those that had appeared lately; and at least she could try to make a home that would not drive Bertram to club dinners, and Uncle William to hungry wanderings from room to room. Meanwhile, all the time, she could be learning, and in due course she would reach that shining goal of Housekeeping Efficiency, short of which—according to Aunt Hannah and the "Talk to Young Wives"—no woman need hope for a waneless honeymoon.

So chaotic and erratic had been the household service, and so quietly did Billy slip into her new role, that it was not until the second meal after the maid's departure that the master of the house discovered what had happened. Then, as his wife rose to get some forgotten article, he questioned, with uplifted eyebrows:

"Too good to wait upon us, is my lady now, eh?"

"My lady is waiting on you," smiled Billy.

"Yes, I see this lady is," retorted Bertram, grimly; "but I mean our real lady in the kitchen. Great Scott, Billy, how long are you going to stand this?"

Billy tossed her head airily, though she shook in her shoes. Billy had been dreading this moment.

"I'm not standing it. She's gone," responded Billy, cheerfully, resuming her seat. "Uncle William, sha'n't I give you some more pudding?"

"Gone, so soon?" groaned Bertram, as William passed his plate, with a smiling nod. "Oh, well," went on Bertram, resignedly, "she stayed longer than the last one. When is the next one coming?"

"She's already here."

Bertram frowned.

"Here? But—you served the dessert, and—" At something in Billy's face, a quick suspicion came into his own. "Billy, you don't mean that you—you—"

"Yes," she nodded brightly, "that's just what I mean. I'm the next one."

"Nonsense!" exploded Bertram, wrathfully. "Oh, come, Billy, we've been all over this before. You know I can't have it."

"Yes, you can. You've got to have it," retorted Billy, still with that disarming, airy cheerfulness. "Besides, 'twon't be half so bad as you think. Wasn't that a good pudding to-night? Didn't you both come back for more? Well, I made it."

"Puddings!" ejaculated Bertram, with an impatient gesture. "Billy, as I've said before, it takes something besides puddings to run this house."

"Yes, I know it does," dimpled Billy, "and I've got Mrs. Durgin for that part. She's coming twice a week, and more, if I need her. Why, dearie, you don't know anything about how comfortable you're going to be! I'll leave it to Uncle William if—"

But Uncle William had gone. Silently he had slipped from his chair and disappeared. Uncle William, it might be mentioned in passing, had never quite forgotten Aunt Hannah's fateful call with its dire revelations concerning a certain unwanted, superfluous, third-party husband's brother. Remembering this, there were times when he thought absence was both safest and best. This was one of the times.

"But, Billy, dear," still argued Bertram, irritably, "how can you? You don't know how. You've had no experience."

Billy threw back her shoulders. An ominous light came to her eyes. She was no longer airily playful.

"That's exactly it, Bertram. I don't know how—but I'm going to learn. I haven't had experience—but I'm going to get it. I can't make a worse mess of it than we've had ever since Eliza went, anyway!"

"But if you'd get a maid—a good maid," persisted Bertram, feebly.

"I had one—Mary Ellen. She was a good maid—until she found out how little her mistress knew; then—well, you know what it was then. Do you think I'd let that thing happen to me again? No, sir! I'm going into training for—my next Mary Ellen!" And with a very majestic air Billy rose from the table and began to clear away the dishes.

CHAPTER XVII. THE EFFICIENCY STAR—AND BILLY

Billy was not a young woman that did things by halves. Long ago, in the days of her childhood, her Aunt Ella had once said of her: "If only Billy didn't go into things all over, so; but whether it's measles or mud pies, I always know that she'll be the measliest or the muddiest of any child in town!" It could not be expected, therefore, that Billy would begin to play her new rôle now with any lack of enthusiasm. But even had she needed any incentive, there was still ever ringing in her ears Bertram's accusing: "If you'd tend to your husband and your home a little more—" Billy still declared very emphatically that she had forgiven Bertram; but she knew, in her heart, that she had not forgotten.

Certainly, as the days passed, it could not be said that Billy was not tending to her husband and her home. From morning till night, now, she tended to nothing else. She seldom touched her piano—save to dust it—and she never touched her half-finished song-manuscript, long since banished to the oblivion of the music cabinet. She made no calls except occasional flying visits to the Annex, or to the pretty new home where Marie and Cyril were now delightfully settled. The opera and the Symphony were over for the season, but even had they not been, Billy could not have attended them. She had no time. Surely she was not doing any "gallivanting" now, she told herself sometimes, a little aggrievedly.

There was, indeed, no time. From morning until night Billy was busy, flying from one task to another. Her ambition to have everything just right was equalled only by her dogged determination to "just show them" that she could do this thing. At first, of course, hampered as she was by ignorance and inexperience, each task consumed about twice as much time as was necessary. Yet afterwards, when accustomedness had brought its reward of speed, there was still for Billy no time; for increased knowledge had only opened the way to other paths, untrodden and alluring. Study of cookbooks had led to the study of food values. Billy discovered suddenly that potatoes, beef, onions, oranges, and puddings were something besides vegetables, meat, fruit, and dessert. They possessed attributes known as proteids, fats, and carbohydrates. Faint memories of long forgotten school days hinted that these terms had been heard before; but never, Billy was sure, had she fully realized what they meant.

It was at this juncture that Billy ran across a book entitled "Correct Eating for Efficiency." She bought it at once, and carried it home in triumph. It proved to be a marvelous book. Billy had not read two chapters before she began to wonder how the family had managed to live thus far with any sort of success, in the face of their dense ignorance and her own criminal carelessness concerning their daily bill of fare.

At dinner that night Billy told Bertram and William of her discovery, and, with growing excitement, dilated on the wonderful good that it was to bring to them.

"Why, you don't know, you can't imagine what a treasure it is!" she exclaimed. "It gives a complete table for the exact balancing of food."

"For what?" demanded Bertram, glancing up.

"The exact balancing of food; and this book says that's the biggest problem that modern scientists have to solve."

"Humph!" shrugged Bertram. "Well, you just balance my food to my hunger, and I'll agree not to complain."

"Oh, but, Bertram, it's serious, really," urged Billy, looking genuinely distressed. "Why, it says that what you eat goes to make up what you are. It makes your vital energies. Your brain power and your body power come from what you eat. Don't you see? If you're going to paint a picture you need something different from what you would if you were going to—to saw wood; and what this book tells is—is what I ought to give you to make you do each one, I should think, from what I've read so far. Now don't you see how important it is? What if I should give you the saw-wood kind of a breakfast when you were just going up-stairs to paint all day? And what if I should give Uncle William a—a soldier's breakfast when all he is going to do is to go down on State Street and sit still all day?"

"But—but, my dear," began Uncle William, looking slightly worried, "there's my eggs that I always have, you know."

"For heaven's sake, Billy, what have you got hold of now?" demanded Bertram, with just a touch of irritation.

Billy laughed merrily.

"Well, I suppose I didn't sound very logical," she admitted. "But the book—you just wait. It's in the kitchen. I'm going to get it." And with laughing eagerness she ran from the room. In a moment she had returned, book in hand.

"Now listen. This is the real thing—not my garbled inaccuracies. 'The food which we eat serves three purposes: it builds the body substance, bone, muscle, etc., it produces heat in the body, and it generates vital energy. Nitrogen in different chemical combinations contributes largely to the manufacture of body substances; the fats produce heat; and the starches and sugars go to make the vital energy. The nitrogenous food elements we call proteins; the fats and oils, fats; and the starches and sugars (because of the predominance of carbon), we call carbohydrates. Now in selecting the diet for the day you should take care to choose those foods which give the proteins, fats, and carbohydrates in just the right proportion.'"

"Oh, Billy!" groaned Bertram.

"But it's so, Bertram," maintained Billy, anxiously. "And it's every bit here. I don't have to guess at it at all. They even give the quantities of calories of energy required for different sized men. I'm going to measure you both to-morrow; and you must be weighed, too," she continued, ignoring the sniffs of remonstrance from her two listeners. "Then I'll know just how many calories to give each of you. They say a man of average size and weight, and sedentary occupation, should have at least 2,000 calories—and some authorities say 3,000—in this proportion: proteins, 300 calories, fats, 350 calories, carbohydrates, 1,350 calories. But you both are taller than five feet five inches, and I should think you weighed more than 145 pounds; so I can't tell just yet how many calories you will need."

"How many we will need, indeed!" ejaculated Bertram.

"But, my dear, you know I have to have my eggs," began Uncle William again, in a worried voice.

"Of course you do, dear; and you shall have them," soothed Billy, brightly. "It's only that I'll have to be careful and balance up the other things for the day accordingly. Don't you see? Now listen. We'll see what eggs are." She turned the leaves rapidly. "Here's the food table. It's lovely. It tells everything. I never saw anything so wonderful. A—b—c—d—e—here we are. 'Eggs, scrambled or boiled, fats and proteins, one egg, 100.' If it's poached it's only 50; but you like yours boiled, so we'll have to reckon on the 100. And you always have two, so that means 200 calories in fats and proteins. Now, don't you see? If you can't have but 300 proteins and 350 fats all day, and you've already eaten 200 in your two eggs, that'll leave just—er—450 for all the rest of the day,—of fats and proteins, you understand. And you've no idea how fast that'll count up. Why,—just one serving of butter is 100 of fats, and eight almonds is another, while a serving of lentils is 100 of proteins. So you see how it'll go."

"Yes, I see," murmured Uncle William, casting a mournful glance about the generously laden table, much as if he were bidding farewell to a departing friend. "But if I should want more to eat—" He stopped helplessly, and Bertram's aggrieved voice filled the pause.

"Look here, Billy, if you think I'm going to be measured for an egg and weighed for an almond, you're much mistaken; because I'm not. I want to eat what I like, and as much as I like, whether it's six calories or six thousand!"

Billy chuckled, but she raised her hands in pretended shocked protest.

"Six thousand! Mercy! Bertram, I don't know what would happen if you ate that quantity; but I'm sure you couldn't paint. You'd just have to saw wood and dig ditches to use up all that vital energy."

"Humph!" scoffed Bertram.

"Besides, this is for efficiency," went on Billy, with an earnest air. "This man owns up that some may think a 2,000 calory ration is altogether too small, and he advises such to begin with 3,000 or even 3,500—graded, of course, according to a man's size, weight, and occupation. But he says one famous man does splendid work on only 1,800 calories, and another on even 1,600. But that is just a matter of chewing. Why, Bertram, you have no idea what perfectly wonderful things chewing does."

"Yes, I've heard of that," grunted Bertram; "ten chews to a cherry, and sixty to a spoonful of soup. There's an old metronome up-stairs that Cyril left. You might bring it down and set it going on the table—so many ticks to a mouthful, I suppose. I reckon, with an incentive like that to eat, just about two calories would do me. Eh, William?"

"Bertram! Now you're only making fun," chided Billy; "and when it's really serious, too. Now listen," she admonished, picking up the book again. "'If a man consumes a large amount of meat, and very few vegetables, his diet will be too rich in protein, and too lacking in carbohydrates. On the other hand, if he consumes great quantities of pastry, bread, butter, and tea, his meals will furnish too much energy, and not enough building material.' There, Bertram, don't you see?"

"Oh, yes, I see," teased Bertram. "William, better eat what you can to-night. I foresee it's the last meal of just food we'll get for some time. Hereafter we'll have proteins, fats, and carbohydrates made into calory croquettes, and—"

"Bertram!" scolded Billy.

But Bertram would not be silenced.

"Here, just let me take that book," he insisted, dragging the volume from Billy's reluctant fingers. "Now, William, listen. Here's your breakfast to-morrow morning: strawberries, 100 calories; whole-wheat bread, 75 calories; butter, 100 calories (no second helping, mind you, or you'd ruin the balance and something would topple); boiled eggs, 200 calories; cocoa, 100 calories—which all comes to 570 calories. Sounds like an English bill of fare with a new kind of foreign money, but 'tisn't, really, you know. Now for luncheon you can have tomato soup, 50 calories; potato salad—that's cheap, only 30 calories, and—" But Billy pulled the book away then, and in righteous indignation carried it to the kitchen.

"You don't deserve anything to eat," she declared with dignity, as she returned to the dining-room.

"No?" queried Bertram, his eyebrows uplifted. "Well, as near as I can make out we aren't going to get—much."

But Billy did not deign to answer this.

In spite of Bertram's tormenting gibes, Billy did, for some days, arrange her meals in accordance with the wonderful table of food given in "Correct Eating for Efficiency." To be sure, Bertram, whatever he found before him during those days, anxiously asked whether he were eating fats, proteins, or carbohydrates; and he worried openly as to the possibility of his meal's producing one calory too much or too little, thus endangering his "balance."

Billy alternately laughed and scolded, to the unvarying good nature of her husband. As it happened, however, even this was not for long, for Billy ran across a magazine article on food adulteration; and this so filled her with terror lest, in the food served, she were killing her family by slow poison, that she forgot all about the proteins, fats, and carbohydrates. Her talk these days was of formaldehyde, benzoate of soda, and salicylic acid.

Very soon, too, Billy discovered an exclusive Back Bay school for instruction in household economics and domestic hygiene. Billy investigated it at once, and was immediately aflame with enthusiasm. She told Bertram that it taught everything, everything she wanted to know; and forthwith she enrolled herself as one of its most devoted pupils, in spite of her husband's protests that she knew enough, more than enough, already. This school attendance, to her consternation, Billy discovered took added time; but in some way she contrived to find it to take.

And so the days passed. Eliza's mother, though better, was still too ill for her daughter to leave her. Billy, as the warm weather approached, began to look pale and thin. Billy, to tell the truth, was working altogether too hard; but she would not admit it, even to herself. At first the novelty of the work, and her determination to conquer at all costs, had given a fictitious strength to her endurance. Now that the novelty had become accustomedness, and the conquering a surety, Billy discovered that she had a back that could ache, and limbs that, at times, could almost refuse to move from weariness. There was still, however, one spur that never failed to urge her to fresh endeavor, and to make her, at least temporarily, forget both ache and weariness; and that was the comforting thought that now, certainly, even Bertram himself must admit that she was tending to her home and her husband.

As to Bertram—Bertram, it is true, had at first uttered frequent and vehement protests against his wife's absorption of both mind and body in "that plaguy housework," as he termed it. But as the days passed, and blessed order superseded chaos, peace followed discord, and delicious, well-served meals took the place of the horrors that had been called meals in the past, he gradually accepted the change with tranquil satisfaction, and forgot to question how it was brought about; though he did still, sometimes, rebel because Billy was always too tired, or too busy, to go out with him. Of late, however, he had not done even this so frequently, for a new "Face of a Girl" had possessed his soul; and all his thoughts and most of his time had gone to putting on canvas the vision of loveliness that his mind's eye saw.

By June fifteenth the picture was finished. Bertram awoke then to his surroundings. He found summer was upon him with no plans made for its enjoyment. He found William had started West for a two weeks' business trip. But what he did not find one day—at least at first—was his wife, when he came home unexpectedly at four o'clock. And Bertram especially wanted to find his wife that day, for he had met three people whose words had disquieted him not a little. First, Aunt Hannah. She had said:

"Bertram, where is Billy? She hasn't been out to the Annex for a week; and the last time she was there she looked sick. I was real worried about her."

Cyril had been next.

"Where's Billy?" he had asked abruptly. "Marie says she hasn't seen her for two weeks. Marie's afraid she's sick. She says Billy didn't look well a bit, when she did see her."

Calderwell had capped the climax. He had said:

"Great Scott, Henshaw, where have you been keeping yourself? And where's your wife? Not one of us has caught more than a glimpse of her for weeks. She hasn't sung with us, nor played for us, nor let us take her anywhere for a month of Sundays. Even Miss Greggory says she hasn't seen much of her, and that Billy always says she's too busy to go anywhere. But Miss Greggory says she looks pale and thin, and that she thinks she's worrying too much over running the house. I hope she isn't sick!"

"Why, no, Billy isn't sick. Billy's all right," Bertram had answered. He had spoken lightly, nonchalantly, with an elaborate air of carelessness; but after he had left Calderwell he had turned his steps abruptly and a little hastily toward home.

And he had not found Billy—at least, not at once. He had gone first down into the kitchen and dining-room. He remembered then, uneasily, that he had always looked for Billy in the kitchen and dining-room, of late. To-day, however, she was not there.

On the kitchen table Bertram did see a book wide open, and, mechanically, he picked it up. It was a much-thumbed cookbook, and it was open where two once-blank pages bore his wife's handwriting. On the first page, under the printed heading "Things to Remember," he read these sentences:

"That rice swells till every dish in the house is full, and that spinach shrinks till you can't find it.

"That beets boil dry if you look out the window.

"That biscuits which look as if they'd been mixed up with a rusty stove poker haven't really been so, but have only got too much undissolved soda in them."

There were other sentences, but Bertram's eyes chanced to fall on the opposite page where the "Things to Remember" had been changed to "Things to Forget"; and here Billy had written just four words: "Burns," "cuts," and "yesterday's failures."

Bertram dropped the book then with a spasmodic clearing of his throat, and hurriedly resumed his search. When he did find his wife, at last, he gave a cry of dismay—she was on her own bed, huddled in a little heap, and shaking with sobs.

"Billy! Why, Billy!" he gasped, striding to the bedside.

Billy sat up at once, and hastily wiped her eyes.

"Oh, is it you, B-Bertram? I didn't hear you come in. You—you s-said you weren't coming till six o'clock!" she choked.

"Billy, what is the meaning of this?"

"N-nothing. I—I guess I'm just tired."

"What have you been doing?" Bertram spoke sternly, almost sharply. He was wondering why he had not noticed before the little hollows in his wife's cheeks. "Billy, what have you been doing?"

"Why, n-nothing extra, only some sweeping, and cleaning out the refrigerator."

"Sweeping! Cleaning! You! I thought Mrs. Durgin did that."

"She does. I mean she did. But she couldn't come. She broke her leg—fell off the stepladder where she was three days ago. So I had to do it. And to-day, someway, everything went wrong. I burned me, and I cut me, and I used two sodas with not any cream of tartar, and I should think I didn't know anything, not anything!" And down went Billy's head into the pillows again in another burst of sobs.

With gentle yet uncompromising determination, Bertram gathered his wife into his arms and carried her to the big chair. There, for a few minutes, he soothed and petted her as if she were a tired child—which, indeed, she was.

"Billy, this thing has got to stop," he said then. There was a very inexorable ring of decision in his voice.

"What thing?"

"This housework business."

Billy sat up with a jerk.

"But, Bertram, it isn't fair. You can't—you mustn't—just because of to-day! I can do it. I have done it. I've done it days and days, and it's gone beautifully—even if they did say I couldn't!"

"Couldn't what?"

"Be an e-efficient housekeeper."

"Who said you couldn't?"

"Aunt Hannah and K-Kate."

Bertram said a savage word under his breath.

"Holy smoke, Billy! I didn't marry you for a cook or a scrub-lady. If you had to do it, that would be another matter, of course; and if we did have to do it, we wouldn't have a big house like this for you to do it in. But I didn't marry for a cook, and I knew I wasn't getting one when I married you."

Billy bridled into instant wrath.

"Well, I like that, Bertram Henshaw! Can't I cook? Haven't I proved that I can cook?"

Bertram laughed, and kissed the indignant lips till they quivered into an unwilling smile.

"Bless your spunky little heart, of course you have! But that doesn't mean that I want you to do it. You see, it so happens that you can do other things, too; and I'd rather you did those. Billy, you haven't played to me for a week, nor sung to me for a month. You're too tired every night to talk, or read together, or go anywhere with me. I married for companionship—not cooking and sweeping!"

Billy shook her head stubbornly. Her mouth settled into determined lines.

"That's all very well to say. You aren't hungry now, Bertram. But it's different when you are, and they said 'twould be."

"Humph! 'They' are Aunt Hannah and Kate, I suppose."

"Yes—and the 'Talk to Young Wives.'"

"The w-what?"

Billy choked a little. She had forgotten that Bertram did not know about the "Talk to Young Wives." She wished that she had not mentioned the book, but now that she had, she would make the best of it. She drew herself up with dignity.

"It's a book; a very nice book. It says lots of things—that have come true."

"Where is that book? Let me see it, please."

With visible reluctance Billy got down from her perch on Bertram's knee, went to her desk and brought back the book.

Bertram regarded it frowningly, so frowningly that Billy hastened to its defense.

"And it's true—what it says in there, and what Aunt Hannah and Kate said. It is different when they're hungry! You said yourself if I'd tend to my husband and my home a little more, and—"

Bertram looked up with unfeigned amazement.

"I said what?" he demanded.

In a voice shaken with emotion, Billy repeated the fateful words.

"I never—when did I say that?"

"The night Uncle William and I came home from—Pete's."

For a moment Bertram stared dumbly; then a shamed red swept to his forehead.

"Billy, did I say that? I ought to be shot if I did. But, Billy, you said you'd forgiven me!"

"I did, dear—truly I did; but, don't you see?—it was true. I hadn't tended to things. So I've been doing it since."

A sudden comprehension illuminated Bertram's face.

"Heavens, Billy! And is that why you haven't been anywhere, or done anything? Is that why Calderwell said to-day that you hadn't been with them anywhere, and that—Great Scott, Billy! Did you think I was such a selfish brute as that?"

"Oh, but when I was going with them I was following the book—I thought," quavered Billy; and hurriedly she turned the leaves to a carefully marked passage. "It's there—about the outside interests. See? I was trying to brush up against them, so that I wouldn't interfere with your Art. Then, when you accused me of gallivanting off with—" But Bertram swept her back into his arms, and not for some minutes could Billy make a coherent speech again. Then Bertram spoke.

"See here, Billy," he exploded, a little shakily, "if I could get you off somewhere on a desert island, where there weren't any Aunt Hannahs or Kates, or Talks to Young Wives, I think there'd be a chance to make you happy; but—"

"Oh, but there was truth in it," interrupted Billy, sitting erect again. "I didn't know how to run a house, and it was perfectly awful while we were having all those dreadful maids, one after the other; and no woman should be a wife who doesn't know—"

"All right, all right, dear," interrupted Bertram, in his turn. "We'll concede that point, if you like. But you do know now. You've got the efficient housewife racket down pat even to the last calory your husband should be fed; and I'll warrant there isn't a Mary Ellen in Christendom who can find a spot of ignorance on you as big as a pinhead! So we'll call that settled. What you need now is a good rest; and you're going to have it, too. I'm going to have six Mary Ellens here to-morrow morning. Six! Do you hear? And all you've got to do is to get your gladdest rags together for a trip to Europe with me next month. Because we're going. I shall get the tickets to-morrow, after I send the six Mary Ellens packing up here. Now come, put on your bonnet. We're going down town to dinner."

CHAPTER XVIII. BILLY TRIES HER HAND AT "MANAGING"

Bertram did not engage six Mary Ellens the next morning, nor even one, as it happened; for that evening, Eliza—who had not been unaware of conditions at the Strata—telephoned to say that her mother was so much better now she believed she could be spared to come to the Strata for several hours each day, if Mrs. Henshaw would like to have her begin in that way.

Billy agreed promptly, and declared herself as more than willing to put up with such an arrangement. Bertram, it is true, when he heard of the plan, rebelled, and asserted that what Billy needed was a rest, an entire rest from care and labor. In fact, what he wanted her to do, he said, was to gallivant—to gallivant all day long.

"Nonsense!" Billy had laughed, coloring to the tips of her ears. "Besides, as for the work, Bertram, with just you and me here, and with all my vast experience now, and Eliza here for several hours every day, it'll be nothing but play for this little time before we go away. You'll see!"

"All right, I'll see, then," Bertram had nodded meaningly. "But just make sure that it is play for you!"

"I will," laughed Billy; and there the matter had ended.

Eliza began work the next day, and Billy did indeed soon find herself "playing" under Bertram's watchful insistence. She resumed her music, and brought out of exile the unfinished song. With Bertram she took drives and walks; and every two or three days she went to see Aunt Hannah and Marie. She was pleasantly busy, too, with plans for her coming trip; and it was not long before even the remorseful Bertram had to admit that Billy was looking and appearing quite like her old self.

At the Annex Billy found Calderwell and Arkwright, one day. They greeted her as if she had just returned from a far country.

"Well, if you aren't the stranger lady," began Calderwell, looking frankly pleased to see her. "We'd thought of advertising in the daily press somewhat after this fashion: 'Lost, strayed, or stolen, one Billy; comrade, good friend, and kind cheerer-up of lonely hearts. Any information thankfully received by her bereft, sorrowing friends.'"

Billy joined in the laugh that greeted this sally, but Arkwright noticed that she tried to change the subject from her own affairs to a discussion of the new song on Alice Greggory's piano. Calderwell, however, was not to be silenced.

"The last I heard of this elusive Billy," he resumed, with teasing cheerfulness, "she was running down a certain lost calory that had slipped away from her husband's breakfast, and—"

Billy wheeled sharply.

"Where did you get hold of that?" she demanded.

"Oh, I didn't," returned the man, defensively. "I never got hold of it at all. I never even saw the calory—though, for that matter, I don't think I should know one if I did see it! What we feared was, that, in hunting the lost calory, you had lost yourself, and—" But Billy would hear no more. With her disdainful nose in the air she walked to the piano.

"Come, Mr. Arkwright," she said with dignity. "Let's try this song."

Arkwright rose at once and accompanied her to the piano.

They had sung the song through twice when Billy became uneasily aware that, on the other side of the room, Calderwell and Alice Greggory were softly chuckling over something they had found in a magazine. Billy frowned, and twitched the corners of a pile of music, with restless fingers.

"I wonder if Alice hasn't got some quartets here somewhere," she murmured, her disapproving eyes still bent on the absorbed couple across the room.

Arkwright was silent. Billy, throwing a hurried glance into his face, thought she detected a somber shadow in his eyes. She thought, too, she knew why it was there. So possessed had Billy been, during the early winter, of the idea that her special mission in life was to inaugurate and foster a love affair between disappointed Mr. Arkwright and lonely Alice Greggory, that now she forgot, for a moment, that Arkwright himself was quite unaware of her efforts. She thought only that the present shadow on his face must be caused by the same thing that brought worry to her own heart—the manifest devotion of Calderwell to Alice Greggory just now across the room. Instinctively, therefore, as to a coworker in a common cause, she turned a disturbed face to the man at her side.

"It is, indeed, high time that I looked after something besides lost calories," she said significantly. Then, at the evident uncomprehension in Arkwright's face, she added: "Has it been going on like this—very long?"

Arkwright still, apparently, did not understand.

"Has—what been going on?" he questioned.

"That—over there," answered Billy, impatiently, scarcely knowing whether to be more irritated at the threatened miscarriage of her cherished plans, or at Arkwright's (to her) wilfully blind insistence on her making her meaning more plain. "Has it been going on long—such utter devotion?"

As she asked the question Billy turned and looked squarely into Arkwright's face. She saw, therefore, the great change that came to it, as her meaning became clear to him. Her first feeling was one of shocked realization that Arkwright had, indeed, been really blind. Her second—she turned away her eyes hurriedly from what she thought she saw in the man's countenance.

With an assumedly gay little cry she sprang to her feet.

"Come, come, what are you two children chuckling over?" she demanded, crossing the room abruptly. "Didn't you hear me say I wanted you to come and sing a quartet?"

Billy blamed herself very much for what she called her stupidity in so baldly summoning Arkwright's attention to Calderwell's devotion to Alice Greggory. She declared that she ought to have known better, and she asked herself if this were the way she was "furthering matters" between Alice Greggory and Arkwright.

Billy was really seriously disturbed. She had never quite forgiven herself for being so blind to Arkwright's feeling for herself during those days when he had not known of her engagement to Bertram. She had never forgotten, either, the painful scene when he had hopefully told of his love, only to be met with her own shocked repudiation. For long weeks after that, his face had haunted her. She had wished, oh, so ardently, that she could do something in some way to bring him happiness. When, therefore, it had come to her knowledge afterward that he was frequently with his old friend, Alice Greggory, she had been so glad. It was very easy then to fan hope into conviction that here, in this old friend, he had found sweet balm for his wounded heart; and she determined at once to do all that she could do to help. So very glowing, indeed, was her eagerness in the matter, that it looked suspiciously as if she thought, could she but bring this thing about, that old scores against herself would be erased.

Billy told herself, virtuously, however, that not only for Arkwright did she desire this marriage to take place, but for Alice Greggory. In the very nature of things Alice would one day be left alone. She was poor, and not very strong. She sorely needed the shielding love and care of a good husband. What more natural than that her old-time friend and almost-sweetheart, M. J. Arkwright, should be that good husband?

That really it was more Arkwright and less Alice that was being considered, however, was proved when the devotion of Calderwell began to be first suspected, then known for a fact. Billy's distress at this turn of affairs indicated very plainly that it was not just a husband, but a certain one particular husband that she desired for Alice Greggory. All the more disturbed was she, therefore, when to-day, seeing her three friends together again for the first time for some weeks, she discovered increased evidence that her worst fears were to be realized. It was to be Alice and Calderwell, not Alice and Arkwright. Arkwright was again to be disappointed in his dearest hopes.

Telling herself indignantly that it could not be, it should not be, Billy determined to remain after the men had gone, and speak to Alice. Just what she would say she did not know. Even what she could say, she was not sure. But certainly there must be something, some little thing that she could say, which would open Alice's eyes to what she was doing, and what she ought to do.

It was in this frame of mind, therefore, that Billy, after Arkwright and Calderwell had gone, spoke to Alice. She began warily, with assumed nonchalance.

"I believe Mr. Arkwright sings better every time I hear him."

There was no answer. Alice was sorting music at the piano.

"Don't you think so?" Billy raised her voice a little.

Alice turned almost with a start.

"What's that? Oh, yes. Well, I don't know; maybe I do."

"You would—if you didn't hear him any oftener than I do," laughed Billy. "But then, of course you do hear him oftener."

"I? Oh, no, indeed. Not so very much oftener." Alice had turned back to her music. There was a slight embarrassment in her manner. "I wonder—where—that new song—is," she murmured.

Billy, who knew very well where the song lay, was not to be diverted.

"Nonsense! As if Mr. Arkwright wasn't always telling how Alice liked this song, and didn't like that one, and thought the other the best yet! I don't believe he sings a thing that he doesn't first sing to you. For that matter, I fancy he asks your opinion of everything, anyway."

"Why, Billy, he doesn't!" exclaimed Alice, a deep red flaming into her cheeks. "You know he doesn't."

Billy laughed gleefully. She had not been slow to note the color in her friend's face, or to ascribe to it the one meaning she wished to ascribe to it. So sure, indeed, was she now that her fears had been groundless, that she flung caution to the winds.

"Ho! My dear Alice, you can't expect us all to be blind," she teased. "Besides, we all think it's such a lovely arrangement that we're just glad to see it. He's such a fine fellow, and we like him so much! We couldn't ask for a better husband for you than Mr. Arkwright, and—" From sheer amazement at the sudden white horror in Alice Greggory's face, Billy stopped short. "Why, Alice!" she faltered then.

With a visible effort Alice forced her trembling lips to speak.

"My husband—Mr. Arkwright! Why, Billy, you couldn't have seen—you haven't seen—there's nothing you could see! He isn't—he wasn't—he can't be! We—we're nothing but friends, Billy, just good friends!"

Billy, though dismayed, was still not quite convinced.

"Friends! Nonsense! When—"

But Alice interrupted feverishly. Alice, in an agony of fear lest the true state of affairs should be suspected, was hiding behind a bulwark of pride.

"Now, Billy, please! Say no more. You're quite wrong, entirely. You'll never, never hear of my marrying Mr. Arkwright. As I said before, we're friends—the best of friends; that is all. We couldn't be anything else, possibly!"

Billy, plainly discomfited, fell back; but she threw a sharp glance into her friend's flushed countenance.

"You mean—because of—Hugh Calderwell?" she demanded. Then, for the second time that afternoon throwing discretion to the winds, she went on plaintively: "You won't listen, of course. Girls in love never do. Hugh is all right, and I like him; but there's more real solid worth in Mr. Arkwright's little finger than there is in Hugh's whole self. And—" But a merry peal of laughter from Alice Greggory interrupted.

"And, pray, do you think I'm in love with Hugh Calderwell?" she demanded. There was a curious note of something very like relief in her voice.

"Well, I didn't know," began Billy, uncertainly.

"Then I'll tell you now," smiled Alice. "I'm not. Furthermore, perhaps it's just as well that you should know right now that I don't intend to marry—ever."

"Oh, Alice!"

"No." There was determination, and there was still that curious note of relief in the girl's voice. It was as if, somewhere, a great danger had been avoided. "I have my music. That is enough. I'm not intending to marry."

"Oh, but Alice, while I will own up I'm glad it isn't Hugh Calderwell, there is Mr. Arkwright, and I did hope—" But Alice shook her head and turned resolutely away. At that moment, too, Aunt Hannah came in from the street, so Billy could say no more.

Aunt Hannah dropped herself a little wearily into a chair.

"I've just come from Marie's," she said.

"How is she?" asked Billy.

Aunt Hannah smiled, and raised her eyebrows.

"Well, just now she's quite exercised over another rattle—from her cousin out West, this time. There were four little silver bells on it, and she hasn't got any janitor's wife now to give it to."

Billy laughed softly, but Aunt Hannah had more to say.

"You know she isn't going to allow any toys but Teddy bears and woolly lambs, of which, I believe, she has already bought quite an assortment. She says they don't rattle or squeak. I declare, when I see the woolen pads and rubber hushers that that child has put everywhere all over the house, I don't know whether to laugh or cry. And she's so worried! It seems Cyril must needs take just this time to start composing a new opera or symphony, or something; and never before has she allowed him to be interrupted by anything on such an occasion. But what he'll do when the baby comes she says she doesn't know, for she says she can't—she just can't keep it from bothering him some, she's afraid. As if any opera or symphony that ever lived was of more consequence than a man's own child!" finished Aunt Hannah, with an indignant sniff, as she reached for her shawl.

CHAPTER XIX. A TOUGH NUT TO CRACK FOR CYRIL

It was early in the forenoon of the first day of July that Eliza told her mistress that Mrs. Stetson was asking for her at the telephone. Eliza's face was not a little troubled.

"I'm afraid, maybe, it isn't good news," she stammered, as her mistress hurriedly arose. "She's at Mr. Cyril Henshaw's—Mrs. Stetson is—and she seemed so terribly upset about something that there was no making real sense out of what she said. But she asked for you, and said to have you come quick."

Billy, her own face paling, was already at the telephone.

"Yes, Aunt Hannah. What is it?"

"Oh, my grief and conscience, Billy, if you can, come up here, please. You must come! Can't you come?"

"Why, yes, of course. But—but—Marie! The—the baby!"

A faint groan came across the wires.

"Oh, my grief and conscience, Billy! It isn't the baby. It's babies! It's twins—boys. Cyril has them now—the nurse hasn't got here yet."

"Twins! Cyril has them!" broke in Billy, hysterically.

"Yes, and they're crying something terrible. We've sent for a second nurse to come, too, of course, but she hasn't got here yet, either. And those babies—if you could hear them! That's what we want you for, to—"

But Billy was almost laughing now.

"All right, I'll come out—and hear them," she called a bit wildly, as she hung up the receiver.

Some little time later, a palpably nervous maid admitted Billy to the home of Mr. and Mrs. Cyril Henshaw. Even as the door was opened, Billy heard faintly, but unmistakably, the moaning wails of two infants.

"Mrs. Stetson says if you will please to help Mr. Henshaw with the babies," stammered the maid, after the preliminary questions and answers. "I've been in when I could, and they're all right, only they're crying. They're in his den. We had to put them as far away as possible—their crying worried Mrs. Henshaw so."

"Yes, I see," murmured Billy. "I'll go to them at once. No, don't trouble to come. I know the way. Just tell Mrs. Stetson I'm here, please," she finished, as she tossed her hat and gloves on to the hall table, and turned to go upstairs.

Billy's feet made no sound on the soft rugs. The crying, however, grew louder and louder as she approached the den. Softly she turned the knob and pushed open the door. She stopped short, then, at what she saw.

Cyril had not heard her, nor seen her. His back was partly toward the door. His coat was off, and his hair stood fiercely on end as if a nervous hand had ruffled it. His usually pale face was very red, and his forehead showed great drops of perspiration. He was on his feet, hovering over the couch, at each end of which lay a rumpled roll of linen, lace, and flannel, from which emerged a prodigiously puckered little face, two uncertainly waving rose-leaf fists, and a wail of protesting rage that was not uncertain in the least.

In one hand Cyril held a Teddy bear, in the other his watch, dangling from its fob chain. Both of these he shook feebly, one after the other, above the tiny faces.

"Oh, come, come, pretty baby, good baby, hush, hush," he begged agitatedly.

In the doorway Billy clapped her hands to her lips and stifled a laugh. Billy knew, of course, that what she should do was to go forward at once, and help this poor, distracted man; but Billy, just then, was not doing what she knew she ought to do.

With a muttered ejaculation (which Billy, to her sorrow, could not catch) Cyril laid down the watch and flung the Teddy bear aside. Then, in very evident despair, he gingerly picked up one of the rumpled rolls of flannel, lace, and linen, and held it straight out before him. After a moment's indecision he began awkwardly to jounce it, teeter it, rock it back and forth, and to pat it jerkily.

"Oh, come, come, pretty baby, good baby, hush, hush," he begged again, frantically.

Perhaps it was the change of position; perhaps it was the novelty of the motion, perhaps it was only utter weariness, or lack of breath. Whatever the cause, the wailing sobs from the bundle in his arms dwindled suddenly to a gentle whisper, then ceased altogether.

With a ray of hope illuminating his drawn countenance, Cyril carefully laid the baby down and picked up the other. Almost confidently now he began the jouncing and teetering and rocking as before.

"There, there! Oh, come, come, pretty baby, good baby, hush, hush," he chanted again.

This time he was not so successful. Perhaps he had lost his skill. Perhaps it was merely the world-old difference in babies. At all events, this infant did not care for jerks and jounces, and showed it plainly by emitting loud and yet louder wails of rage—wails in which his brother on the couch speedily joined.

"Oh, come, come, pretty baby, good baby, hush, hush—confound it, HUSH, I say!" exploded the frightened, weary, baffled, distracted man, picking up the other baby, and trying to hold both his sons at once.

Billy hurried forward then, tearfully, remorsefully, her face all sympathy, her arms all tenderness.

"Here, Cyril, let me help you," she cried.

Cyril turned abruptly.

"Thank God, some one's come," he groaned, holding out both the babies, with an exuberance of generosity. "Billy, you've saved my life!"

Billy laughed tremulously.

"Yes, I've come, Cyril, and I'll help every bit I can; but I don't know a thing—not a single thing about them myself. Dear me, aren't they cunning? But, Cyril, do they always cry so?"

The father-of-an-hour drew himself stiffly erect.

"Cry? What do you mean? Why shouldn't they cry?" he demanded indignantly. "I want you to understand that Doctor Brown said those were A number 1 fine boys! Anyhow, I guess there's no doubt they've got lungs all right," he added, with a grim smile, as he pulled out his handkerchief and drew it across his perspiring brow.

Billy did not have an opportunity to show Cyril how much or how little she knew about babies, for in another minute the maid had appeared with the extra nurse; and that young woman, with trained celerity and easy confidence, assumed instant command, and speedily had peace and order restored.

Cyril, freed from responsibility, cast longing eyes, for a moment, upon his work; but the next minute, with a despairing glance about him, he turned and fled precipitately.

Billy, following the direction of his eyes, suppressed a smile. On the top of Cyril's manuscript music on the table lay a hot-water bottle. Draped over the back of his favorite chair was a pink-bordered baby blanket. On the piano-stool rested a beribboned and beruffled baby's toilet basket. From behind the sofa pillow leered ridiculously the Teddy bear, just as it had left Cyril's desperate hand.

No wonder, indeed, that Billy smiled. Billy was thinking of what Marie had said not a week before:

"I shall keep the baby, of course, in the nursery. I've been in homes where they've had baby things strewn from one end of the house to the other; but it won't be that way here. In the first place, I don't believe in it; but, even if I did, I'd have to be careful on account of Cyril. Imagine Cyril's trying to write his music with a baby in the room! No! I shall keep the baby in the nursery, if possible; but wherever it is, it won't be anywhere near Cyril's den, anyway."

Billy suppressed many a smile during the days that immediately followed the coming of the twins. Some of the smiles, however, refused to be suppressed. They became, indeed, shamelessly audible chuckles.

Billy was to sail the tenth, and, naturally, during those early July days, her time was pretty much occupied with her preparations for departure; but nothing could keep her from frequent, though short, visits to the home of her brother-in-law.

The twins were proving themselves to be fine, healthy boys. Two trained maids, and two trained nurses ruled the household with a rod of iron. As to Cyril—Billy declared that Cyril was learning something every day of his life now.

"Oh, yes, he's learning things," she said to Aunt Hannah, one morning; "lots of things. For instance: he has his breakfast now, not when he wants it, but when the maid wants to give it to him—which is precisely at eight o'clock every morning. So he's learning punctuality. And for the first time in his life he has discovered the astounding fact that there are several things more important in the world than is the special piece of music he happens to be composing—chiefly the twins' bath, the twins' nap, the twins' airing, and the twins' colic."

Aunt Hannah laughed, though she frowned, too.

"But, surely, Billy, with two nurses and the maids, Cyril doesn't have to—to—" She came to a helpless pause.

"Oh, no," laughed Billy; "Cyril doesn't have to really attend to any of those things—though I have seen each of the nurses, at different times, unhesitatingly thrust a twin into his arms and bid him hold the child till she comes back. But it's this way. You see, Marie must be kept quiet, and the nursery is very near her room. It worries her terribly when either of the children cries. Besides, the little rascals have apparently fixed up some sort of labor-union compact with each other, so that if one cries for something or nothing, the other promptly joins in and helps. So the nurses have got into the habit of picking up the first disturber of the peace, and hurrying him to quarters remote; and Cyril's den being the most remote of all, they usually fetch up there."

"You mean—they take those babies into Cyril's den—now?" Even Aunt Hannah was plainly aghast.

"Yes," twinkled Billy. "I fancy their Hygienic Immaculacies approved of Cyril's bare floors, undraped windows, and generally knick-knackless condition. Anyhow, they've made his den a sort of—of annex to the nursery."

"But—but Cyril! What does he say?" stammered the dumfounded Aunt Hannah. "Think of Cyril's standing a thing like that! Doesn't he do anything—or say anything?"

Billy smiled, and lifted her brows quizzically.

"My dear Aunt Hannah, did you ever know many people to have the courage to 'say things' to one of those becapped, beaproned, bespotless creatures of loftily superb superiority known as trained nurses? Besides, you wouldn't recognize Cyril now. Nobody would. He's as meek as Moses, and has been ever since his two young sons were laid in his reluctant, trembling arms. He breaks into a cold sweat at nothing, and moves about his own home as if he were a stranger and an interloper, endured merely on sufferance in this abode of strange women and strange babies."

"Nonsense!" scoffed Aunt Hannah.

"But it's so," maintained Billy, merrily. "Now, for instance. You know Cyril always has been in the habit of venting his moods on the piano (just as I do, only more so) by playing exactly as he feels. Well, as near as I can gather, he was at his usual trick the next day after the twins arrived; and you can imagine about what sort of music it would be, after what he had been through the preceding forty-eight hours.

"Of course I don't know exactly what happened, but Julia—Marie's second maid, you know—tells the story. She's been with them long enough to know something of the way the whole household always turns on the pivot of the master's whims; so she fully appreciated the situation. She says she heard him begin to play, and that she never heard such queer, creepy, shivery music in her life; but that he hadn't been playing five minutes before one of the nurses came into the living-room where Julia was dusting, and told her to tell whoever was playing to stop that dreadful noise, as they wanted to take the twins in there for their nap.

"'But I didn't do it, ma'am,' Julia says. 'I wa'n't lookin' for losin' my place, an' I let the young woman do the job herself. An' she done it, pert as you please. An' jest as I was seekin' a hidin'-place for the explosion, if Mr. Henshaw didn't come out lookin' a little wild, but as meek as a lamb; an' when he sees me he asked wouldn't I please get him a cup of coffee, good an' strong. An' I got it.'

"So you see," finished Billy, "Cyril is learning things—lots of things."

"Oh, my grief and conscience! I should say he was," half-shivered Aunt Hannah. "Cyril looking meek as a lamb, indeed!"

Billy laughed merrily.

"Well, it must be a new experience—for Cyril. For a man whose daily existence for years has been rubber-heeled and woolen-padded, and whose family from boyhood has stood at attention and saluted if he so much as looked at them, it must be quite a change, as things are now. However, it'll be different, of course, when Marie is on her feet again."

"Does she know at all how things are going?"

"Not very much, as yet, though I believe she has begun to worry some. She confided to me one day that she was glad, of course, that she had two darling babies, instead of one; but that she was afraid it might be hard, just at first, to teach them both at once to be quiet; for she was afraid that while she was teaching one, the other would be sure to cry, or do something noisy."

"Do something noisy, indeed!" ejaculated Aunt Hannah.

"As for the real state of affairs, Marie doesn't dream that Cyril's sacred den is given over to Teddy bears and baby blankets. All is, I hope she'll be measurably strong before she does find it out," laughed Billy, as she rose to go.

CHAPTER XX. ARKWRIGHT'S EYES ARE OPENED

William came back from his business trip the eighth of July, and on the ninth Billy and Bertram went to New York. Eliza's mother was so well now that Eliza had taken up her old quarters in the Strata, and the household affairs were once more running like clockwork. Later in the season William would go away for a month's fishing trip, and the house would be closed.

Mr. and Mrs. Bertram Henshaw were not expected to return until the first of October; but with Eliza to look after the comfort of William, the mistress of the house did no worrying. Ever since Pete's going, Eliza had said that she preferred to be the only maid, with a charwoman to come in for the heavier work; and to this arrangement her mistress had willingly consented, for the present.

Marie and the babies were doing finely, and Aunt Hannah's health, and affairs at the Annex, were all that could be desired. As Billy, indeed, saw it, there was only one flaw to mar her perfect content on this holiday trip with Bertram, and that was her disappointment over the very evident disaster that had come to her cherished matrimonial plans for Arkwright and Alice Greggory. She could not forget Arkwright's face that day at the Annex, when she had so foolishly called his attention to Calderwell's devotion; and she could not forget, either, Alice Greggory's very obvious perturbation a little later, and her suspiciously emphatic assertion that she had no intention of marrying any one, certainly not Arkwright. As Billy thought of all this now, she could not but admit that it did look dark for Arkwright—poor Arkwright, whom she, more than any one else in the world, perhaps, had a special reason for wishing to see happily married.

There was, then, this one cloud on Billy's horizon as the big boat that was to bear her across the water steamed down the harbor that beautiful July day.

As it chanced, naturally, perhaps, not only was Billy thinking of Arkwright that morning, but Arkwright was thinking of Billy.

Arkwright had thought frequently of Billy during the last few days, particularly since that afternoon meeting at the Annex when the four had renewed their old good times together. Up to that day Arkwright had been trying not to think of Billy. He had been "fighting his tiger skin." Sternly he had been forcing himself to meet her, to see her, to talk with her, to sing with her, or to pass her by—all with the indifference properly expected to be shown in association with Mrs. Bertram Henshaw, another man's wife. He had known, of course, that deep down in his heart he loved her, always had loved her, and always would love her. Hopelessly and drearily he accepted this as a fact even while with all his might fighting that tiger skin. So sure was he, indeed, of this, so implicitly had he accepted it as an unalterable certainty, that in time even his efforts to fight it became almost mechanical and unconscious in their stern round of forced indifference.

Then came that day at the Annex—and the discovery: the discovery which he had made when Billy called his attention to Calderwell and Alice Greggory across the room in the corner; the discovery which had come with so blinding a force, and which even now he was tempted to question as to its reality; the discovery that not Billy Neilson, nor Mrs. Bertram Henshaw, nor even the tender ghost of a lost love held the center of his heart—but Alice Greggory.

The first intimation of all this had come with his curious feeling of unreasoning hatred and blind indignation toward Calderwell as, through Billy's eyes, he had seen the two together. Then had come the overwhelming longing to pick up Alice Greggory and run off with her—somewhere, anywhere, so that Calderwell could not follow.

At once, however, he had pulled himself up short with the mental cry of "Absurd!" What was it to him if Calderwell did care for Alice Greggory? Surely he himself was not in love with the girl. He was in love with Billy; that is—

It was all confusion then, in his mind, and he was glad indeed when he could leave the house. He wanted to be alone. He wanted to think. He must, in some way, thrash out this astounding thing that had come to him.

Arkwright did not visit the Annex again for some days. Until he was more nearly sure of himself and of his feelings, he did not wish to see Alice Greggory. It was then that he began to think of Billy, deliberately, purposefully, for it must be, of course, that he had made a mistake, he told himself. It must be that he did, really, still care for Billy—though of course he ought not to.

Arkwright made another discovery then. He learned that, however deliberately he started in to think of Billy, he ended every time in thinking of Alice. He thought of how good she had been to him, and of how faithful she had been in helping him to fight his love for Billy. Just here he decided, for a moment, that probably, after all, his feeling of anger against Calderwell was merely the fear of losing this helpful comradeship that he so needed. Even with himself, however, Arkwright could not keep up this farce long, and very soon he admitted miserably that it was not the comradeship of Alice Greggory that he wanted or needed, but the love.

He knew it now. No longer was there any use in beating about the bush. He did love Alice Greggory; but so curiously and unbelievably stupid had he been that he had not found it out until now. And now it was too late. Had not even Billy called his attention to the fact of Calderwell's devotion? Besides, had not he himself, at the very first, told Calderwell that he might have a clear field?

Fool that he had been to let another thus lightly step in and win from under his very nose what might have been his if he had but known his own mind before it was too late!

But was it, after all, quite too late? He and Alice were old friends. Away back in their young days in their native town they had been, indeed, almost sweethearts, in a boy-and-girl fashion. It would not have taken much in those days, he believed, to have made the relationship more interesting. But changes had come. Alice had left town, and for years they had drifted apart. Then had come Billy, and Billy had found Alice, thus bringing about the odd circumstance of their renewing of acquaintanceship. Perhaps, at that time, if he had not already thought he cared for Billy, there would have been something more than acquaintanceship.

But he had thought he cared for Billy all these years; and now, at this late day, to wake up and find that he cared for Alice! A pretty mess he had made of things! Was he so inconstant then, so fickle? Did he not know his own mind five minutes at a time? What would Alice Greggory think, even if he found the courage to tell her? What could she think? What could anybody think?

Arkwright fairly ground his teeth in impotent wrath—and he did not know whether he were the most angry that he did not love Billy, or that he had loved Billy, or that he loved somebody else now.

It was while he was in this unenviable frame of mind that he went to see Alice. Not that he had planned definitely to speak to her of his discovery, nor yet that he had planned not to. He had, indeed, planned nothing. For a man usually so decided as to purpose and energetic as to action, he was in a most unhappy state of uncertainty and changeableness. One thing only was unmistakably clear to him, and that was that he must see Alice.

For months, now, he had taken to Alice all his hopes and griefs, perplexities and problems; and never had he failed to find comfort in the shape of sympathetic understanding and wise counsel. To Alice, therefore, now he turned as a matter of course, telling himself vaguely that, perhaps, after he had seen Alice, he would feel better.

Just how intimately this particular problem of his concerned Alice herself, he did not stop to realize. He did not, indeed, think of it at all from Alice's standpoint—until he came face to face with the girl in the living-room at the Annex. Then, suddenly, he did. His manner became at once, consequently, full of embarrassment and quite devoid of its usual frank friendliness.

As it happened, this was perhaps the most unfortunate thing that could have occurred, so far as it concerned the attitude of Alice Greggory, for thereby innumerable tiny sparks of suspicion that had been tormenting the girl for days were instantly fanned into consuming flames of conviction.

Alice had not been slow to note Arkwright's prolonged absence from the Annex. Coming as it did so soon after her most disconcerting talk with Billy in regard to her own relations with him, it had filled her with frightened questionings.

If Billy had seen things to make her think of linking their names together, perhaps Arkwright himself had heard some such idea put forth somewhere, and that was why he was staying away—to show the world that there was no foundation for such rumors. Perhaps he was even doing it to show her that—

Even in her thoughts Alice could scarcely bring herself to finish the sentence. That Arkwright should ever suspect for a moment that she cared for him was intolerable. Painfully conscious as she was that she did care for him, it was easy to fear that others must be conscious of it, too. Had she not already proof that Billy suspected it? Why, then, might not it be quite possible, even probable, that Arkwright suspected it, also; and, because he did suspect it, had decided that it would be just as well, perhaps, if he did not call so often.

In spite of Alice's angry insistence to herself that, after all, this could not be the case—that the man knew she understood he still loved Billy—she could not help fearing, in the face of Arkwright's unusual absence, that it might yet be true. When, therefore, he finally did appear, only to become at once obviously embarrassed in her presence, her fears instantly became convictions. It was true, then. The man did believe she cared for him, and he had been trying to teach her—to save her.

To teach her! To save her, indeed! Very well, he should see! And forthwith, from that moment, Alice Greggory's chief reason for living became to prove to Mr. M. J. Arkwright that he needed not to teach her, to save her, nor yet to sympathize with her.

"How do you do?" she greeted him, with a particularly bright smile. "I'm sure I hope you are well, such a beautiful day as this."

"Oh, yes, I'm well, I suppose. Still, I have felt better in my life," smiled Arkwright, with some constraint.

"Oh, I'm sorry," murmured the girl, striving so hard to speak with impersonal unconcern that she did not notice the inaptness of her reply.

"Eh? Sorry I've felt better, are you?" retorted Arkwright, with nervous humor. Then, because he was embarrassed, he said the one thing he had meant not to say: "Don't you think I'm quite a stranger? It's been some time since I've been here."

Alice, smarting under the sting of what she judged to be the only possible cause for his embarrassment, leaped to this new opportunity to show her lack of interest.

"Oh, has it?" she murmured carelessly. "Well, I don't know but it has, now that I come to think of it."

Arkwright frowned gloomily. A week ago he would have tossed back a laughingly aggrieved remark as to her unflattering indifference to his presence. Now he was in no mood for such joking. It was too serious a matter with him.

"You've been busy, no doubt, with—other matters," he presumed forlornly, thinking of Calderwell.

"Yes, I have been busy," assented the girl. "One is always happier, I think, to be busy. Not that I meant that I needed the work to be happy," she added hastily, in a panic lest he think she had a consuming sorrow to kill.

"No, of course not," he murmured abstractedly, rising to his feet and crossing the room to the piano. Then, with an elaborate air of trying to appear very natural, he asked jovially: "Anything new to play to me?"

Alice arose at once.

"Yes. I have a little nocturne that I was playing to Mr. Calderwell last night."

"Oh, to Calderwell!" Arkwright had stiffened perceptibly.

"Yes. He didn't like it. I'll play it to you and see what you say," she smiled, seating herself at the piano.

"Well, if he had liked it, it's safe to say I shouldn't," shrugged Arkwright.

"Nonsense!" laughed the girl, beginning to appear more like her natural self. "I should think you were Mr. Cyril Henshaw! Mr. Calderwell is partial to ragtime, I'll admit. But there are some good things he likes."

"There are, indeed, some good things he likes," returned Arkwright, with grim emphasis, his somber eyes fixed on what he believed to be the one especial object of Calderwell's affections at the moment.

Alice, unaware both of the melancholy gaze bent upon herself and of the cause thereof, laughed again merrily.

"Poor Mr. Calderwell," she cried, as she let her fingers slide into soft, introductory chords. "He isn't to blame for not liking what he calls our lost spirits that wail. It's just the way he's made."

Arkwright vouchsafed no reply. With an abrupt gesture he turned and began to pace the room moodily. At the piano Alice slipped from the chords into the nocturne. She played it straight through, then, with a charm and skill that brought Arkwright's feet to a pause before it was half finished.

"By George, that's great!" he breathed, when the last tone had quivered into silence.

"Yes, isn't it—beautiful?" she murmured.

The room was very quiet, and in semi-darkness. The last rays of a late June sunset had been filling the room with golden light, but it was gone now. Even at the piano by the window, Alice had barely been able to see clearly enough to read the notes of her nocturne.

To Arkwright the air still trembled with the exquisite melody that had but just left her fingers. A quick fire came to his eyes. He forgot everything but that it was Alice there in the half-light by the window—Alice, whom he loved. With a low cry he took a swift step toward her.

"Alice!"

Instantly the girl was on her feet. But it was not toward him that she turned. It was away—resolutely, and with a haste that was strangely like terror.

Alice, too, had forgotten, for just a moment. She had let herself drift into a dream world where there was nothing but the music she was playing and the man she loved. Then the music had stopped, and the man had spoken her name.

Alice remembered then. She remembered Billy, whom this man loved. She remembered the long days just passed when this man had stayed away, presumably to teach her—to save her. And now, at the sound of his voice speaking her name, she had almost bared her heart to him.

No wonder that Alice, with a haste that looked like terror, crossed the floor and flooded the room with light.

"Dear me!" she shivered, carefully avoiding Arkwright's eyes. "If Mr. Calderwell were here now he'd have some excuse to talk about our lost spirits that wail. That is a creepy piece of music when you play it in the dark!" And, for fear that he should suspect how her heart was aching, she gave a particularly brilliant and joyous smile.

Once again at the mention of Calderwell's name Arkwright stiffened perceptibly. The fire left his eyes. For a moment he did not speak; then, gravely, he said:

"Calderwell? Yes, perhaps he would; and—you ought to be a judge, I should think. You see him quite frequently, don't you?"

"Why, yes, of course. He often comes out here, you know."

"Yes; I had heard that he did—since you came."

His meaning was unmistakable. Alice looked up quickly. A prompt denial of his implication was on her lips when the thought came to her that perhaps just here lay a sure way to prove to this man before her that there was, indeed, no need for him to teach her, to save her, or yet to sympathize with her. She could not affirm, of course; but she need not deny—yet.
"Nonsense!" she laughed lightly, pleased that she could feel what she hoped would pass for a telltale color burning her cheeks. "Come, let us try some duets," she proposed, leading the way to the piano. And Arkwright, interpreting the apparently embarrassed change of subject exactly as she had hoped that he would interpret it, followed her, sick at heart.
"'O wert thou in the cauld blast,'" sang Arkwright's lips a few moments later.
"I can't tell her now—when I know she cares for Calderwell," gloomily ran his thoughts, the while. "It would do no possible good, and would only make her unhappy to grieve me."
"'O wert thou in the cauld blast,'" chimed in Alice's alto, low and sweet.
"I reckon now he won't be staying away from here any more just to save me!" ran Alice's thoughts, palpitatingly triumphant.

CHAPTER XXI. BILLY TAKES HER TURN AT QUESTIONING

Arkwright did not call to see Alice Greggory for some days. He did not want to see Alice now. He told himself wearily that she could not help him fight this tiger skin that lay across his path, The very fact of her presence by his side would, indeed, incapacitate himself for fighting. So he deliberately stayed away from the Annex until the day before he sailed for Germany. Then he went out to say good-by.
Chagrined as he was at what he termed his imbecile stupidity in not knowing his own heart all these past months, and convinced, as he also was, that Alice and Calderwell cared for each other, he could see no way for him but to play the part of a man of kindliness and honor, leaving a clear field for his preferred rival, and bringing no shadow of regret to mar the happiness of the girl he loved.
As for being his old easy, frank self on this last call, however, that was impossible; so Alice found plenty of fuel for her still burning fires of suspicion—fires which had, indeed, blazed up anew at this second long period of absence on the part of Arkwright. Naturally, therefore, the call was anything but a joy and comfort to either one. Arkwright was nervous, gloomy, and abnormally gay by turns. Alice was nervous and abnormally gay all the time. Then they said good-by and Arkwright went away. He sailed the next day, and Alice settled down to the summer of study and hard work she had laid out for herself.
On the tenth of September Billy came home. She was brown, plump-cheeked, and smiling. She declared that she had had a perfectly beautiful time, and that there couldn't be anything in the world nicer than the trip she and Bertram had taken—just they two together. In answer to Aunt Hannah's solicitous inquiries, she asserted that she was all well and rested now. But there was a vaguely troubled questioning in her eyes that Aunt Hannah did not quite like. Aunt Hannah, however, said nothing even to Billy herself about this.
One of the first friends Billy saw after her return was Hugh Calderwell. As it happened Bertram was out when he came, so Billy had the first half-hour of the call to herself. She was not sorry for this, as it gave her a chance to question Calderwell a little concerning Alice Greggory—something she had long ago determined to do at the first opportunity.
"Now tell me everything—everything about everybody," she began diplomatically, settling herself comfortably for a good visit.
"Thank you, I'm well, and have had a passably agreeable summer, barring the heat, sundry persistent mosquitoes, several grievous disappointments, and a felon on my thumb," he began, with shameless imperturbability. "I have been to Revere once, to the circus once, to

Nantasket three times, and to Keith's and the 'movies' ten times, perhaps—to be accurate. I have also—But perhaps there was some one else you desired to inquire for," he broke off, turning upon his hostess a bland but unsmiling countenance.

"Oh, no, how could there be?" twinkled Billy. "Really, Hugh, I always knew you had a pretty good opinion of yourself, but I didn't credit you with thinking you were everybody. Go on. I'm so interested!"

Hugh chuckled softly; but there was a plaintive tone in his voice as he answered.

"Thanks, no. I've rather lost my interest now. Lack of appreciation always did discourage me. We'll talk of something else, please. You enjoyed your trip?"

"Very much. It just couldn't have been nicer!"

"You were lucky. The heat here has been something fierce!"

"What made you stay?"

"Reasons too numerous, and one too heart-breaking, to mention. Besides, you forget," with dignity. "There is my profession. I have joined the workers of the world now, you know."

"Oh, fudge, Hugh!" laughed Billy. "You know very well you're as likely as not to start for the ends of the earth to-morrow morning!"

Hugh drew himself up.

"I don't seem to succeed in making people understand that I'm serious," he began aggrievedly. "I—" With an expressive flourish of his hands he relaxed suddenly, and fell back in his chair. A slow smile came to his lips. "Well, Billy, I'll give up. You've hit it," he confessed. "I have thought seriously of starting to-morrow morning for half-way to the ends of the earth—Panama."

"Hugh!"

"Well, I have. Even this call was to be a good-by—if I went."

"Oh, Hugh! But I really thought—in spite of my teasing—that you had settled down, this time."

"Yes, so did I," sighed the man, a little soberly. "But I guess it's no use, Billy. Oh, I'm coming back, of course, and link arms again with their worthy Highnesses, John Doe and Richard Roe; but just now I've got a restless fit on me. I want to see the wheels go 'round. Of course, if I had my bread and butter and cigars to earn, 'twould be different. But I haven't, and I know I haven't; and I suspect that's where the trouble lies. If it wasn't for those natal silver spoons of mine that Bertram is always talking about, things might be different. But the spoons are there, and always have been; and I know they're all ready to dish out mountains to climb and lakes to paddle in, any time I've a mind to say the word. So—I just say the word. That's all."

"And you've said it now?"

"Yes, I think so; for a while."

"And—those reasons that have kept you here all summer," ventured Billy, "they aren't in—er—commission any longer?"

"No."

Billy hesitated, regarding her companion meditatively. Then, with the feeling that she had followed a blind alley to its termination, she retreated and made a fresh start.

"Well, you haven't yet told me everything about everybody, you know," she hinted smilingly. "You might begin that—I mean the less important everybodies, of course, now that I've heard about you."

"Meaning—"

"Oh, Aunt Hannah, and the Greggorys, and Cyril and Marie, and the twins, and Mr. Arkwright, and all the rest."

"But you've had letters, surely."

"Yes, I've had letters from some of them, and I've seen most of them since I came back. It's just that I wanted to know your viewpoint of what's happened through the summer."

"Very well. Aunt Hannah is as dear as ever, wears just as many shawls, and still keeps her clock striking twelve when it's half-past eleven. Mrs. Greggory is just as sweet as ever—and a little more frail, I fear,—bless her heart! Mr. Arkwright is still abroad, as I presume you know. I hear he is doing great stunts over there, and will sing in Berlin and Paris this winter. I'm thinking of going across from Panama later. If I do I shall look him up. Mr. and Mrs. Cyril are as well as could be expected when you realize that they haven't yet settled on a pair of names for the twins."

"I know it—and the poor little things three months old, too! I think it's a shame. You've heard the reason, I suppose. Cyril declares that naming babies is one of the most serious and delicate operations in the world, and that, for his part, he thinks people ought to select their own names when they've arrived at years of discretion. He wants to wait till the twins are eighteen, and then make each of them a birthday present of the name of their own choosing."

"Well, if that isn't the limit!" laughed Calderwell. "I'd heard some such thing before, but I hadn't supposed it was really so."

"Well, it is. He says he knows more tomboys and enormous fat women named 'Grace' and 'Lily,' and sweet little mouse-like ladies staggering along under a sonorous 'Jerusha Theodosia' or 'Zenobia Jane'; and that if he should name the boys 'Franz' and 'Felix' after Schubert and Mendelssohn as Marie wants to, they'd as likely as not turn out to be men who hated the sound of music and doted on stocks and dry goods."

"Humph!" grunted Calderwell. "I saw Cyril last week, and he said he hadn't named the twins yet, but he didn't tell me why. I offered him two perfectly good names myself, but he didn't seem interested."

"What were they?"

"Eldad and Bildad."

"Hugh!" protested Billy.

"Well, why not?" bridled the man. "I'm sure those are new and unique, and really musical, too—'way ahead of your Franz and Felix."

"But those aren't really names!"

"Indeed they are."

"Where did you get them?"

"Off our family tree, though they're Bible names, Belle says. Perhaps you didn't know, but Sister Belle has been making the dirt fly quite lively of late around that family tree of ours, and she wrote me some of her discoveries. It seems two of the roots, or branches—say, are ancestors roots, or branches?—were called Eldad and Bildad. Now I thought those names were good enough to pass along, but, as I said before, Cyril wasn't interested."

"I should say not," laughed Billy. "But, honestly, Hugh, it's really serious. Marie wants them named something, but she doesn't say much to Cyril. Marie wouldn't really breathe, you know, if she thought Cyril disapproved of breathing. And in this case Cyril does not hesitate to declare that the boys shall name themselves."

"What a situation!" laughed Calderwell.

"Isn't it? But, do you know, I can sympathize with it, in a way, for I've always mourned so over my name. 'Billy' was always such a trial to me! Poor Uncle William wasn't the only one that prepared guns and fishing rods to entertain the expected boy. I don't know, though, I'm afraid if I'd been allowed to select my name I should have been a 'Helen Clarabella' all my days, for that was the name I gave all my dolls, with 'first,' 'second,' 'third,' and so on, added to them for distinction. Evidently I thought that 'Helen Clarabella' was the most feminine appellation possible, and the most foreign to the despised 'Billy.' So you see I can sympathize with Cyril to a certain extent."

"But they must call the little chaps something, now," argued Hugh.

Billy gave a sudden merry laugh.

"They do," she gurgled, "and that's the funniest part of it. Oh, Cyril doesn't. He always calls them impersonally 'they' or 'it.' He doesn't see much of them anyway, now, I understand. Marie was horrified when she realized how the nurses had been using his den as a nursery annex and she changed all that instanter, when she took charge of things again. The twins stay in the nursery now, I'm told. But about the names—the nurses, it seems, have got into the way of calling them 'Dot' and 'Dimple.' One has a dimple in his cheek, and the other is a little smaller of the two. Marie is no end distressed, particularly as she finds that she herself calls them that; and she says the idea of boys being 'Dot' and 'Dimple'!"

"I should say so," laughed Calderwell. "Not I regard that as worse than my 'Eldad' and 'Bildad.'"

"I know it, and Alice says—By the way, you haven't mentioned Alice, but I suppose you see her occasionally."

Billy paused in evident expectation of a reply. Billy was, in fact, quite pluming herself on the adroit casualness with which she had introduced the subject nearest her heart.

Calderwell raised his eyebrows.

"Oh, yes, I see her."

"But you hadn't mentioned her."

There was the briefest of pauses; then with a half-quizzical dejection, there came the remark:

"You seem to forget. I told you that I stayed here this summer for reasons too numerous, and one too heart-breaking, to mention. She was the one."

"You mean—"

"Yes. The usual thing. She turned me down. Oh, I haven't asked her yet as many times as I did you, but—"

"Hugh!"

Hugh tossed her a grim smile and went on imperturbably.

"I'm older now, of course, and know more, perhaps. Besides, the finality of her remarks was not to be mistaken."

Billy, in spite of her sympathy for Calderwell, was conscious of a throb of relief that at least one stumbling-block was removed from Arkwright's possible pathway to Alice's heart.

"Did she give any special reason?" hazarded Billy, a shade too anxiously.

"Oh, yes. She said she wasn't going to marry anybody—only her music."

"Nonsense!" ejaculated Billy, falling back in her chair a little.

"Yes, I said that, too," gloomed the man; "but it didn't do any good. You see, I had known another girl who'd said the same thing once." (He did not look up, but a vivid red flamed suddenly into Billy's cheeks.) "And she—when the right one came—forgot all about the music, and married the man. So I naturally suspected that Alice would do the same thing. In fact, I said so to her. I was bold enough to even call the man by name—I hadn't been jealous of Arkwright for nothing, you see—but she denied it, and flew into such an indignant allegation that there wasn't a word of truth in it, that I had to sue for pardon before I got anything like peace."

"Oh-h!" said Billy, in a disappointed voice, falling quite back in her chair this time.

"And so that's why I'm wanting especially just now to see the wheels go 'round," smiled Calderwell, a little wistfully. "Oh, I shall get over it, I suppose. It isn't the first time, I'll own—but some day I take it there will be a last time. Enough of this, however! You haven't told me a thing about yourself. How about it? When I come back, are you going to give me a dinner cooked by your own fair hands? Going to still play Bridget?"

Billy laughed and shook her head.

"No; far from it. Eliza has come back, and her cousin from Vermont is coming as second girl to help her. But I could cook a dinner for you if I had to now, sir, and it wouldn't be potato-mush and cold lamb," she bragged shamelessly, as there sounded Bertram's peculiar ring, and the click of his key in the lock.

It was the next afternoon that Billy called on Marie. From Marie's, Billy went to the Annex, which was very near Cyril's new house; and there, in Aunt Hannah's room, she had what she told Bertram afterwards was a perfectly lovely visit.

Aunt Hannah, too, enjoyed the visit very much, though yet there was one thing that disturbed her—the vaguely troubled look in Billy's eyes, which to-day was more apparent than ever. Not until just before Billy went home did something occur to give Aunt Hannah a possible clue as to what was the meaning of it. That something was a question from Billy.

"Aunt Hannah, why don't I feel like Marie did? why don't I feel like everybody does in books and stories? Marie went around with such a detached, heavenly, absorbed look in her eyes, before the twins came to her home. But I don't. I don't find anything like that in my face, when I look in the glass. And I don't feel detached and absorbed and heavenly. I'm happy, of course; but I can't help thinking of the dear, dear times Bertram and I have together, just we two, and I can't seem to imagine it at all with a third person around."

"Billy! Third person, indeed!"

"There! I knew 'twould shock you," mourned Billy. "It shocks me. I want to feel detached and heavenly and absorbed."

"But Billy, dear, think of it—calling your own baby a third person!"

Billy sighed despairingly.

"Yes, I know. And I suppose I might as well own up to the rest of it too. I—I'm actually afraid of babies, Aunt Hannah! Well, I am," she reiterated, in answer to Aunt Hannah's gasp of disapproval. "I'm not used to them at all. I never had any little brothers and sisters, and I don't know how to treat babies. I—I'm always afraid they'll break, or something. I'm just as afraid of the twins as I can be. How Marie can handle them, and toss them about as she does, I don't see."

"Toss them about, indeed!"

"Well, it looks that way to me," sighed Billy. "Anyhow, I know I can never get to handle them like that—and that's no way to feel! And I'm ashamed of myself because I can't be detached and heavenly and absorbed," she added, rising to go. "Everybody always is, it seems, but just me."

"Fiddledeedee, my dear!" scoffed Aunt Hannah, patting Billy's downcast face. "Wait till a year from now, and we'll see about that third-person bugaboo you're worrying about. I'm not worrying now; so you'd better not!"

CHAPTER XXII. A DOT AND A DIMPLE

On the day Cyril Henshaw's twins were six months old, a momentous occurrence marked the date with a flaming red letter of remembrance; and it all began with a baby's smile.

Cyril, in quest of his wife at about ten o'clock that morning, and not finding her, pursued his search even to the nursery—a room he very seldom entered. Cyril did not like to go into the nursery. He felt ill at ease, and as if he were away from home—and Cyril was known to abhor being away from home since he was married. Now that Marie had taken over the reins of government again, he had been obliged to see very little of those strange women and babies. Not but that he liked the babies, of course. They were his sons, and he was proud of them. They should have every advantage that college, special training, and travel could give them. He quite anticipated what they would be to him—when they really knew anything. But, of course, now, when they could do nothing but cry and wave their absurd little fists, and wobble their heads in so fearsome a manner, as if they simply did not know the meaning of the word backbone—and, for that matter, of course they didn't—why, he could not be expected to be anything but relieved when he had his den to himself again, with a reasonable chance of finding his manuscript as he had left it, and not cut up into a ridiculous string of paper dolls holding hands, as he had once found it, after a visit from a woman with a small girl.

Since Marie had been at the helm, however, he had not been troubled in such a way. He had, indeed, known almost his old customary peace and freedom from interruption, with only an occasional flitting across his path of the strange women and babies—though he had realized, of course, that they were in the house, especially in the nursery. For that reason, therefore, he always avoided the nursery when possible. But to-day he wanted his wife, and his wife was not to be found anywhere else in the house. So, reluctantly, he turned his steps toward the nursery, and, with a frown, knocked and pushed open the door.

"Is Mrs. Henshaw here?" he demanded, not over gently.

Absolute silence greeted his question. The man saw then that there was no one in the room save a baby sitting on a mat in the middle of the floor, barricaded on all sides with pillows.

With a deeper frown the man turned to go, when a gleeful "Ah—goo!" halted his steps midway. He wheeled sharply.

"Er—eh?" he queried, uncertainly eyeing his small son on the floor.

"Ah—goo!" observed the infant (who had been very lonesome), with greater emphasis; and this time he sent into his father's eyes the most bewitching of smiles.

"Well, by George!" murmured the man, weakly, a dawning amazement driving the frown from his face.

"Spgggh—oo—wah!" gurgled the boy, holding out two tiny fists.

A slow smile came to the man's face.

"Well, I'll—be—darned," he muttered half-shamefacedly, wholly delightedly. "If the rascal doesn't act as if he—knew me!"

"Ah—goo—spggghh!" grinned the infant, toothlessly, but entrancingly.

With almost a stealthy touch Cyril closed the door back of him, and advanced a little dubiously toward his son. His countenance carried a mixture of guilt, curiosity, and dogged determination so ludicrous that it was a pity none but baby eyes could see it. As if to meet more nearly on a level this baffling new acquaintance, Cyril got to his knees—somewhat stiffly, it must be confessed—and faced his son.

"Goo—eee—ooo—yah!" crowed the baby now, thrashing legs and arms about in a transport of joy at the acquisition of this new playmate.

"Well, well, young man, you—you don't say so!" stammered the growingly-proud father, thrusting a plainly timid and unaccustomed finger toward his offspring. "So you do know me, eh? Well, who am I?"

"Da—da!" gurgled the boy, triumphantly clutching the outstretched finger, and holding on with a tenacity that brought a gleeful chuckle to the lips of the man.

"Jove! but aren't you the strong little beggar, though! Needn't tell me you don't know a good thing when you see it! So I'm 'da-da,' am I?" he went on, unhesitatingly accepting as the pure gold of knowledge the shameless imitation vocabulary his son was foisting upon him. "Well, I expect I am, and—"

"Oh, Cyril!" The door had opened, and Marie was in the room. If she gave a start of surprise at her husband's unaccustomed attitude, she quickly controlled herself. "Julia said you wanted me. I must have been going down the back stairs when you came up the front, and—"

"Please, Mrs. Henshaw, is it Dot you have in here, or Dimple?" asked a new voice, as the second nurse entered by another door.

Before Mrs. Henshaw could answer, Cyril, who had got to his feet, turned sharply.

"Is it—who?" he demanded.

"Oh! Oh, Mr. Henshaw," stammered the girl. "I beg your pardon. I didn't know you were here. It was only that I wanted to know which baby it was. We thought we had Dot with us, until—"

"Dot! Dimple!" exploded the man. "Do you mean to say you have given my sons the ridiculous names of 'Dot' and 'Dimple'?"

"Why, no—yes—well, that is—we had to call them something," faltered the nurse, as with a despairing glance at her mistress, she plunged through the doorway.

Cyril turned to his wife.

"Marie, what is the meaning of this?" he demanded.

"Why, Cyril, dear, don't—don't get so wrought up," she begged. "It's only as Mary said, we had to call them something, and—"

"Wrought up, indeed!" interrupted Cyril, savagely. "Who wouldn't be? 'Dot' and 'Dimple'! Great Scott! One would think those boys were a couple of kittens or puppies; that they didn't know anything—didn't have any brains! But they have—if the other is anything like this one, at least," he declared, pointing to his son on the floor, who, at this opportune moment joined in the conversation to the extent of an appropriate "Ah—goo—da—da!"

"There, hear that, will you?" triumphed the father. "What did I tell you? That's the way he's been going on ever since I came into the room; The little rascal knows me—so soon!"

Marie clapped her fingers to her lips and turned her back suddenly, with a spasmodic little cough; but her husband, if he noticed the interruption, paid no heed.

"Dot and Dimple, indeed!" he went on wrathfully. "That settles it. We'll name those boys to-day, Marie, to-day! Not once again will I let the sun go down on a Dot and a Dimple under my roof."

Marie turned with a quick little cry of happiness.

"Oh, Cyril, I'm so glad! I've so wanted to have them named, you know! And shall we call them Franz and Felix, as we'd talked?"

"Franz, Felix, John, James, Paul, Charles—anything, so it's sane and sensible! I'd even adopt Calderwell's absurd Bildad and—er—Tomdad, or whatever it was, rather than have those poor little chaps insulted a day longer with a 'Dot' and a 'Dimple.' Great Scott!" And, entirely forgetting what he had come to the nursery for, Cyril strode from the room.

"Ah—goo—spggggh!" commented baby from the middle of the floor.

It was on a very windy March day that Bertram Henshaw's son, Bertram, Jr., arrived at the Strata. Billy went so far into the Valley of the Shadow of Death for her baby that it was some days before she realized in all its importance the presence of the new member of her family. Even when the days had become weeks, and Bertram, Jr., was a month and a half old, the extreme lassitude and weariness of his young mother was a source of ever-growing anxiety to her family and friends. Billy was so unlike herself, they all said.

"If something could only rouse her," suggested the Henshaw's old family physician one day. "A certain sort of mental shock—if not too severe—would do the deed, I think, and with no injury—only benefit. Her physical condition is in just the state that needs a stimulus to stir it into new life and vigor."

As it happened, this was said on a certain Monday. Two days later Bertram's sister Kate, on her way with her husband to Mr. Hartwell's old home in Vermont, stopped over in Boston for a two days' visit. She made her headquarters at Cyril's home, but very naturally she went, without much delay, to pay her respects to Bertram, Jr.

"Mr. Hartwell's brother isn't well," she explained to Billy, after the greetings were over. "You know he's the only one left there, since Mother and Father Hartwell came West. We shall go right on up to Vermont in a couple of days, but we just had to stay over long enough to see the baby; and we hadn't ever seen the twins, either, you know. By the way, how perfectly ridiculous Cyril is over those boys!"

"Is he?" smiled Billy, faintly.

"Yes. One would think there were never any babies born before, to hear him talk. He thinks they're the most wonderful things in the world—and they are cunning little fellows, I'll admit. But Cyril thinks they know so much," went on Kate, laughingly. "He's always bragging of something one or the other of them has done. Think of it—Cyril! Marie says it all started from the time last January when he discovered the nurses had been calling them Dot and Dimple."

"Yes, I know," smiled Billy again, faintly, lifting a thin, white, very un-Billy-like hand to her head.

Kate frowned, and regarded her sister-in-law thoughtfully.

"Mercy! how you look, Billy!" she exclaimed, with cheerful tactlessness. "They said you did, but, I declare, you look worse than I thought."

Billy's pale face reddened perceptibly.

"Nonsense! It's just that I'm so—so tired," she insisted. "I shall be all right soon. How did you leave the children?"

"Well, and happy—'specially little Kate, because mother was going away. Kate is mistress, you know, when I'm gone, and she takes herself very seriously."

"Mistress! A little thing like her! Why, she can't be more than ten or eleven," murmured Billy.

"She isn't. She was ten last month. But you'd think she was forty, the airs she gives herself, sometimes. Oh, of course there's Nora, and the cook, and Miss Winton, the governess, there to really manage things, and Mother Hartwell is just around the corner; but little Kate thinks she's managing, so she's happy."

Billy suppressed a smile. Billy was thinking that little Kate came naturally by at least one of her traits.

"Really, that child is impossible, sometimes," resumed Mrs. Hartwell, with a sigh. "You know the absurd things she was always saying two or three years ago, when we came on to Cyril's wedding."

"Yes, I remember."

"Well, I thought she would get over it. But she doesn't. She's worse, if anything; and sometimes her insight, or intuition, or whatever you may call it, is positively uncanny. I never know what she's going to remark next, when I take her anywhere; but it's safe to say, whatever it is, it'll be unexpected and usually embarrassing to somebody. And—is that the baby?" broke off Mrs. Hartwell, as a cooing laugh and a woman's voice came from the next room.

"Yes. The nurse has just brought him in, I think," said Billy.

"Then I'll go right now and see him," rejoined Kate, rising to her feet and hurrying into the next room.

Left alone, Billy lay back wearily in her reclining-chair. She wondered why Kate always tired her so. She wished she had had on her blue kimono, then perhaps Kate would not have thought she looked so badly. Blue was always more becoming to her than—

Billy turned her head suddenly. From the next room had come Kate's clear-cut, decisive voice.

"Oh, no, I don't think he looks a bit like his father. That little snubby nose was never the Henshaw nose."

Billy drew in her breath sharply, and pulled herself half erect in her chair. From the next room came Kate's voice again, after a low murmur from the nurse.

"Oh, but he isn't, I tell you. He isn't one bit of a Henshaw baby! The Henshaw babies are always pretty ones. They have more hair, and they look—well, different."

Billy gave a low cry, and struggled to her feet.

"Oh, no," spoke up Kate, in answer to another indistinct something from the nurse. "I don't think he's near as pretty as the twins. Of course the twins are a good deal older, but they have such a bright look,—and they did have, from the very first. I saw it in their tiniest baby pictures. But this baby—"

"This baby is mine, please," cut in a tremulous, but resolute voice; and Mrs. Hartwell turned to confront Bertram, Jr.'s mother, manifestly weak and trembling, but no less manifestly blazing-eyed and determined.

"Why, Billy!" expostulated Mrs. Hartwell, as Billy stumbled forward and snatched the child into her arms.

"Perhaps he doesn't look like the Henshaw babies. Perhaps he isn't as pretty as the twins. Perhaps he hasn't much hair, and does have a snub nose. He's my baby just the same, and I shall not stay calmly by and see him abused! Besides, I think he's prettier than the twins ever thought of being; and he's got all the hair I want him to have, and his nose is just exactly what a baby's nose ought to be!" And, with a superb gesture, Billy turned and bore the baby away.

CHAPTER XXIII. BILLY AND THE ENORMOUS RESPONSIBILITY

When the doctor heard from the nurse of Mrs. Hartwell's visit and what had come of it, he only gave a discreet smile, as befitted himself and the occasion; but to his wife privately, that night, the doctor said, when he had finished telling the story:

"And I couldn't have prescribed a better pill if I'd tried!"

"Pill—Mrs. Hartwell! Oh, Harold," reproved the doctor's wife, mildly.

But the doctor only chuckled the more, and said:

"You wait and see."

If Billy's friends were worried before because of her lassitude and lack of ambition, they were almost as worried now over her amazing alertness and insistent activity. Day by day, almost hour by hour, she seemed to gain in strength; and every bit she acquired she promptly tested almost to the breaking point, so plainly eager was she to be well and strong. And always, from morning until night, and again from night until morning, the pivot of her existence, around which swung all thoughts, words, actions, and plans, was the sturdy little plump-cheeked, firm-fleshed atom of humanity known as Bertram, Jr. Even Aunt Hannah remonstrated with her at last.

"But, Billy, dear," she exclaimed, "one would almost get the idea that you thought there wasn't a thing in the world but that baby!"

Billy laughed.

"Well, do you know, sometimes I 'most think there isn't," she retorted unblushingly.

"Billy!" protested Aunt Hannah; then, a little severely, she demanded: "And who was it that just last September was calling this same only-object-in-the-world a third person in your home?"

"Third person, indeed! Aunt Hannah, did I? Did I really say such a dreadful thing as that? But I didn't know, then, of course. I couldn't know how perfectly wonderful a baby is, especially such a baby as Bertram, Jr., is. Why, Aunt Hannah, that little thing knows a whole lot already. He's known me for weeks; I know he has. And ages and ages ago he began to give me little smiles when he saw me. They were smiles—real smiles! Oh, yes, I know nurse said they weren't smiles at the first," admitted Billy, in answer to Aunt Hannah's doubting expression. "I know nurse said it was only wind on his stomach. Think of it—wind on his stomach! Just as if I didn't know the difference between my own baby's smile and wind on his stomach! And you don't know how soon he began to follow my moving finger with his eyes!"

"Yes, I tried that one day, I remember," observed Aunt Hannah demurely. "I moved my finger. He looked at the ceiling—fixedly."

"Well, probably he wanted to look at the ceiling, then," defended the young mother, promptly. "I'm sure I wouldn't give a snap for a baby if he didn't sometimes have a mind of his own, and exercise it!"

"Oh, Billy, Billy," laughed Aunt Hannah, with a shake of her head as Billy turned away, chin uptilted.

By the time Bertram, Jr., was three months old, Billy was unmistakably her old happy, merry self, strong and well. Affairs at the Strata once more were moving as by clockwork—only this time it was a baby's hand that set the clock, and that wound it, too.

Billy told her husband very earnestly that now they had entered upon a period of Enormous Responsibility. The Life, Character, and Destiny of a Human Soul was intrusted to their care, and they must be Wise, Faithful, and Efficient. They must be at once Proud and Humble at this their Great Opportunity. They must Observe, Learn, and Practice. First and foremost in their eyes must always be this wonderful Important Trust.

Bertram laughed at first very heartily at Billy's instructions, which, he declared, were so bristling with capitals that he could fairly see them drop from her lips. Then, when he found how really very much in earnest she was, and how hurt she was at his levity, he managed to pull his face into something like sobriety while she talked to him, though he did persist in dropping kisses on her cheeks, her chin, her finger-tips, her hair, and the little pink lobes of her ears—"just by way of punctuation" to her sentences, he said. And he told her that he wasn't really slighting her lips, only that they moved so fast he could not catch them. Whereat Billy pouted, and told him severely that he was a bad, naughty boy, and that he did not deserve to be the father of the dearest, most wonderful baby in the world.

"No, I know I don't," beamed Bertram, with cheerful unrepentance; "but I am, just the same," he finished triumphantly. And this time he contrived to find his wife's lips.

"Oh, Bertram," sighed Billy, despairingly.

"You're an old dear, of course, and one just can't be cross with you; but you don't, you just don't realize your Immense Responsibility."

"Oh, yes, I do," maintained Bertram so seriously that even Billy herself almost believed him.

In spite of his assertions, however, it must be confessed that Bertram was much more inclined to regard the new member of his family as just his son rather than as an Important Trust; and there is little doubt that he liked to toss him in the air and hear his gleeful crows of delight, without any bother of Observing him at all. As to the Life and Character and Destiny intrusted to his care, it is to be feared that Bertram just plain gloried in his son, poked him in the ribs, and chuckled him under the chin whenever he pleased, and gave never so much as a thought to Character and Destiny. It is to be feared, too, that he was Proud without being Humble, and that the only Opportunity he really appreciated was the chance to show off his wife and baby to some less fortunate fellow-man.

But not so Billy. Billy joined a Mothers' Club and entered a class in Child Training with an elaborate system of Charts, Rules, and Tests. She subscribed to each new "Mothers' Helper," and the like, that she came across, devouring each and every one with an eagerness that was tempered only by a vague uneasiness at finding so many differences of opinion among Those Who Knew.

Undeniably Billy, if not Bertram, was indeed realizing the Enormous Responsibility, and was keeping ever before her the Important Trust.

In June Bertram took a cottage at the South Shore, and by the time the really hot weather arrived the family were well settled. It was only an hour away from Boston, and easy of access, but William said he guessed he would not go; he would stay in Boston, sleeping at the house, and getting his meals at the club, until the middle of July, when he was going down in Maine for his usual fishing trip, which he had planned to take a little earlier than usual this year.

"But you'll be so lonesome, Uncle William," Billy demurred, "in this great house all alone!"

"Oh, no, I sha'n't," rejoined Uncle William. "I shall only be sleeping here, you know," he finished, with a slightly peculiar smile.

It was well, perhaps, that Billy did not exactly realize the significance of that smile, nor the unconscious emphasis on the word "sleeping," for it would have troubled her not a little.

William, to tell the truth, was quite anticipating that sleeping. William's nights had not been exactly restful since the baby came. His evenings, too, had not been the peaceful things they were wont to be.

Some of Billy's Rules and Tests were strenuously objected to on the part of her small son, and the young man did not hesitate to show it. Billy said that it was good for the baby to cry, that it developed his lungs; but William was very sure that it was not good for him. Certainly, when the baby did cry, William never could help hovering near the center of disturbance, and he always had to remind Billy that it might be a pin, you know, or some cruel thing that was hurting. As if he, William, a great strong man, could sit calmly by and smoke a pipe, or lie in his comfortable bed and sleep, while that blessed little baby was crying his heart out like that! Of course, if one did not know he was crying—Hence William's anticipation of those quiet, restful nights when he could not know it.

Very soon after Billy's arrival at the cottage, Aunt Hannah and Alice Greggory came down for a day's visit. Aunt Hannah had been away from Boston for several weeks, so it was some time since she had seen the baby.

"My, but hasn't he grown!" she exclaimed, picking the baby up and stooping to give him a snuggling kiss. The next instant she almost dropped the little fellow, so startling had been Billy's cry.

"No, no, wait, Aunt Hannah, please," Billy was entreating, hurrying to the little corner cupboard. In a moment she was back with a small bottle and a bit of antiseptic cotton. "We always sterilize our lips now before we kiss him—it's so much safer, you know."

Aunt Hannah sat down limply, the baby still in her arms.

"Fiddlededee, Billy! What an absurd idea! What have you got in that bottle?"

"Why, Aunt Hannah, it's just a little simple listerine," bridled Billy, "and it isn't absurd at all. It's very sensible. My 'Hygienic Guide for Mothers' says—"

"Well, I suppose I may kiss his hand," interposed Aunt Hannah, just a little curtly, "without subjecting myself to a City Hospital treatment!"

Billy laughed shamefacedly, but she still held her ground.

"No, you can't—nor even his foot. He might get them in his mouth. Aunt Hannah, why does a baby think that everything, from his own toes to his father's watch fob and the plush balls on a caller's wrist-bag, is made to eat? As if I could sterilize everything, and keep him from getting hold of germs somewhere!"

"You'll have to have a germ-proof room for him," laughed Alice Greggory, playfully snapping her fingers at the baby in Aunt Hannah's lap.

Billy turned eagerly.

"Oh, did you read about that, too?" she cried. "I thought it was so interesting, and I wondered if I could do it."

Alice stared frankly.

"You don't mean to say they actually have such things," she challenged.

"Well, I read about them in a magazine," asserted Billy, "—how you could have a germ-proof room. They said it was very simple, too. Just pasteurize the air, you know, by heating it to one hundred and ten and one-half degrees Fahrenheit for seventeen and one-half minutes. I remember just the figures."

"Simple, indeed! It sounds so," scoffed Aunt Hannah, with uplifted eyebrows.

"Oh, well, I couldn't do it, of course," admitted Billy, regretfully. "Bertram never'd stand for that in the world. He's always rushing in to show the baby off to every Tom, Dick and Harry and his wife that comes; and of course if you opened the nursery door, that would let in those germ things, and you couldn't very well pasteurize your callers by heating them to one hundred and ten and one-half degrees for seventeen and one-half minutes! I don't see how you could manage such a room, anyway, unless you had a system of—of rooms like locks, same as they do for water in canals."

"Oh, my grief and conscience—locks, indeed!" almost groaned Aunt Hannah. "Here, Alice, will you please take this child—that is, if you have a germ-proof certificate about you to show to his mother. I want to take off my bonnet and gloves."

"Take him? Of course I'll take him," laughed Alice; "and right under his mother's nose, too," she added, with a playful grimace at Billy. "And we'll make pat-a-cakes, and send the little pigs to market, and have such a beautiful time that we'll forget there ever was such a thing in the world as an old germ. Eh, babykins?"

"Babykins" cooed his unqualified approval of this plan; but his mother looked troubled.

"That's all right, Alice. You may play with him," she frowned doubtfully; "but you mustn't do it long, you know—not over five minutes."

"Five minutes! Well, I like that, when I've come all the way from Boston purposely to see him," pouted Alice. "What's the matter now? Time for his nap?"

"Oh, no, not for—thirteen minutes," replied Billy, consulting the watch at her belt. "But we never play with Baby more than five minutes at a time. My 'Scientific Care of Infants' says it isn't wise; that with some babies it's positively dangerous, until after they're six months old. It makes them nervous, and forces their mind, you know," she explained anxiously. "So of course we'd want to be careful. Bertram, Jr., isn't quite four, yet."

"Why, yes, of course," murmured Alice, politely, stopping a pat-a-cake before it was half baked.

The infant, as if suspecting that he was being deprived of his lawful baby rights, began to fret and whimper.

"Poor itty sing," crooned Aunt Hannah, who, having divested herself of bonnet and gloves, came hurriedly forward with outstretched hands. "Do they just 'buse 'em? Come here to your old auntie, sweetems, and we'll go walkee. I saw a bow-wow—such a tunnin' ickey wickey bow-wow on the steps when I came in. Come, we go see ickey wickey bow-wow?"

"Aunt Hannah, please!" protested Billy, both hands upraised in horror. "Won't you say 'dog,' and leave out that dreadful 'ickey wickey'? Of course he can't understand things now, really, but we never know when he'll begin to, and we aren't ever going to let him hear baby-talk at all, if we can help it. And truly, when you come to think of it, it is absurd to expect a child to talk sensibly and rationally on the mental diet of 'moo-moos' and 'choo-choos' served out to them. Our Professor of Metaphysics and Ideology in our Child Study Course says that nothing is so receptive and plastic as the Mind of a Little Child, and that it is perfectly appalling how we fill it with trivial absurdities that haven't even the virtue of being accurate. So that's why we're trying to be so careful with Baby. You didn't mind my speaking, I know, Aunt Hannah."

"Oh, no, of course not, Billy," retorted Aunt Hannah, a little tartly, and with a touch of sarcasm most unlike her gentle self. "I'm sure I shouldn't wish to fill this infant's plastic mind with anything so appalling as trivial inaccuracies. May I be pardoned for suggesting, however," she went on as the baby's whimper threatened to become a lusty wail, "that this young gentleman cries as if he were sleepy and hungry?"

"Yes, he is," admitted Billy.

"Well, doesn't your system of scientific training allow him to be given such trivial absurdities as food and naps?" inquired the lady, mildly.

"Of course it does, Aunt Hannah," retorted Billy, laughing in spite of herself. "And it's almost time now. There are only a few more minutes to wait."

"Few more minutes to wait, indeed!" scorned Aunt Hannah. "I suppose the poor little fellow might cry and cry, and you wouldn't set that clock ahead by a teeny weeny minute!"

"Certainly not," said the young mother, decisively. "My 'Daily Guide for Mothers' says that a time for everything and everything in its time, is the very A B C and whole alphabet of

Right Training. He does everything by the clock, and to the minute," declared Billy, proudly.

Aunt Hannah sniffed, obviously skeptical and rebellious. Alice Greggory laughed.

"Aunt Hannah looks as if she'd like to bring down her clock that strikes half an hour ahead," she said mischievously; but Aunt Hannah did not deign to answer this.

"How long do you rock him?" she demanded of Billy. "I suppose I may do that, mayn't I?"

"Mercy, I don't rock him at all, Aunt Hannah," exclaimed Billy.

"Nor sing to him?"

"Certainly not."

"But you did—before I went away. I remember that you did."

"Yes, I know I did," admitted Billy, "and I had an awful time, too. Some evenings, every single one of us, even to Uncle William, had to try before we could get him off to sleep. But that was before I got my 'Efficiency of Mother and Child,' or my 'Scientific Training,' and, oh, lots of others. You see, I didn't know a thing then, and I loved to rock him, so I did it—though the nurse said it wasn't good for him; but I didn't believe her. I've had an awful time changing; but I've done it. I just put him in his little crib, or his carriage, and after a while he goes to sleep. Sometimes, now, he doesn't cry hardly any. I'm afraid, to-day, though, he will," she worried.

"Yes, I'm afraid he will," almost screamed Aunt Hannah, in order to make herself heard above Bertram, Jr., who, by this time, was voicing his opinion of matters and things in no uncertain manner.

It was not, after all, so very long before peace and order reigned; and, in due course, Bertram, Jr., in his carriage, lay fast asleep. Then, while Aunt Hannah went to Billy's room for a short rest, Billy and Alice went out on to the wide veranda which faced the wonderful expanse of sky and sea.

"Now tell me of yourself," commanded Billy, almost at once. "It's been ages since I've heard or seen a thing of you."

"There's nothing to tell."

"Nonsense! But there must be," insisted Billy. "You know it's months since I've seen anything of you, hardly."

"I know. We feel quite neglected at the Annex," said Alice.

"But I don't go anywhere," defended Billy. "I can't. There isn't time."

"Even to bring us the extra happiness?" smiled Alice.

A quick change came to Billy's face. Her eyes glowed deeply.

"No; though I've had so much that ought to have gone—such loads and loads of extra happiness, which I couldn't possibly use myself! Sometimes I'm so happy, Alice, that—that I'm just frightened. It doesn't seem as if anybody ought to be so happy."

"Oh, Billy, dear," demurred Alice, her eyes filling suddenly with tears.

"Well, I've got the Annex. I'm glad I've got that for the overflow, anyway," resumed Billy, trying to steady her voice. "I've sent a whole lot of happiness up there mentally, if I haven't actually carried it; so I'm sure you must have got it. Now tell me of yourself."

"There's nothing to tell," insisted Alice, as before.

"You're working as hard as ever?"

"Yes—harder."

"New pupils?"

"Yes, and some concert engagements—good ones, for next season. Accompaniments, you know."

Billy nodded.

"Yes; I've heard of you already twice, lately, in that line, and very flatteringly, too."

"Have you? Well, that's good."

"Hm-m." There was a moment's silence, then, abruptly, Billy changed the subject. "I had a letter from Belle Calderwell, yesterday." She paused expectantly, but there was no comment.

"You don't seem interested," she frowned, after a minute.

Alice laughed.

"Pardon me, but—I don't know the Lady, you see. Was it a good letter?"

"You know her brother."

"Very true." Alice's cheeks showed a deeper color. "Did she say anything of him?"

"Yes. She said he was coming back to Boston next winter."

"Indeed!"

"Yes. She says that this time he declares he really is going to settle down to work," murmured Billy, demurely, with a sidelong glance at her companion. "She says he's engaged to be married—one of her friends over there."

There was no reply. Alice appeared to be absorbed in watching a tiny white sail far out at sea.

Again Billy was silent. Then, with studied carelessness, she said:

"Yes, and you know Mr. Arkwright, too. She told of him."

"Yes? Well, what of him?" Alice's voice was studiedly indifferent.

"Oh, there was quite a lot of him. Belle had just been to hear him sing, and then her brother had introduced him to her. She thinks he's perfectly wonderful, in every way, I should judge. In fact, she simply raved over him. It seems that while we've been hearing nothing from him all winter, he's been winning no end of laurels for himself in Paris and Berlin. He's been studying, too, of course, as well as singing; and now he's got a chance to sing somewhere—create a rôle, or something—Belle said she wasn't quite clear on the matter herself, but it was a perfectly splendid chance, and one that was a fine feather in his cap."

"Then he won't be coming home—that is, to Boston—at all this winter, probably," said Alice, with a cheerfulness that sounded just a little forced.

"Not until February. But he is coming then. He's been engaged for six performances with the Boston Opera Company—as a star tenor, mind you! Isn't that splendid?"

"Indeed it is," murmured Alice.

"Belle writes that Hugh says he's improved wonderfully, and that even he can see that his singing is marvelous. He says Paris is wild over him; but—for my part, I wish he'd come home and stay here where he belongs," finished Billy, a bit petulantly.

"Why, why, Billy!" murmured her friend, a curiously startled look coming into her eyes.

"Well, I do," maintained Billy; then, recklessly, she added: "I had such beautiful plans for him, once, Alice. Oh, if you only could have cared for him, you'd have made such a splendid couple!"

A vivid scarlet flew to Alice's face.

"Nonsense!" she cried, getting quickly to her feet and bending over one of the flower boxes along the veranda railing. "Mr. Arkwright never thought of marrying me—and I'm not going to marry anybody but my music."

Billy sighed despairingly.

"I know that's what you say now; but if—" She stopped abruptly. Around the turn of the veranda had appeared Aunt Hannah, wheeling Bertram, Jr., still asleep in his carriage.

"I came out the other door," she explained softly. "And it was so lovely I just had to go in and get the baby. I thought it would be so nice for him to finish his nap out here."

Billy arose with a troubled frown.

"But, Aunt Hannah, he mustn't—he can't stay out here. I'm sorry, but we'll have to take him back."

Aunt Hannah's eyes grew mutinous.

"But I thought the outdoor air was just the thing for him. I'm sure your scientific hygienic nonsense says that!"

"They do—they did—that is, some of them do," acknowledged Billy, worriedly; "but they differ, so! And the one I'm going by now says that Baby should always sleep in an even temperature—seventy degrees, if possible; and that's exactly what the room in there was, when I left him. It's not the same out here, I'm sure. In fact I looked at the thermometer to see, just before I came out myself. So, Aunt Hannah, I'm afraid I'll have to take him back."

"But you used to have him sleep out of doors all the time, on that little balcony out of your room," argued Aunt Hannah, still plainly unconvinced.

"Yes, I know I did. I was following the other man's rules, then. As I said, if only they wouldn't differ so! Of course I want the best; but it's so hard to always know the best, and—"

At this very inopportune moment Master Bertram took occasion to wake up, which brought even a deeper wrinkle of worry to his fond mother's forehead; for she said that, according to the clock, he should have been sleeping exactly ten and one-half more minutes, and that of course he couldn't commence the next thing until those ten and one-half minutes were up, or else his entire schedule for the day would be shattered. So what she should do with him for those should-have-been-sleeping ten minutes and a half, she did not know. All of which drew from Aunt Hannah the astounding exclamation of:

"Oh, my grief and conscience, Billy, if you aren't the—the limit!" Which, indeed, she must have been, to have brought circumspect Aunt Hannah to the point of actually using slang.

CHAPTER XXIV. A NIGHT OFF

The Henshaw family did not return to the Strata until late in September. Billy said that the sea air seemed to agree so well with the baby it would be a pity to change until the weather became really too cool at the shore to be comfortable.

William came back from his fishing trip in August, and resumed his old habit of sleeping at the house and taking his meals at the club. To be sure, for a week he went back and forth between the city and the beach house; but it happened to be a time when Bertram, Jr., was cutting a tooth, and this so wore upon William's sympathy—William still could not help insisting it might be a pin—that he concluded peace lay only in flight. So he went back to the Strata.

Bertram had stayed at the cottage all summer, painting industriously. Heretofore he had taken more of a vacation through the summer months, but this year there seemed to be nothing for him to do but to paint. He did not like to go away on a trip and leave Billy, and she declared she could not take the baby nor leave him, and that she did not need any trip, anyway.

"All right, then, we'll just stay at the beach, and have a fine vacation together," he had answered her.

As Bertram saw it, however, he could detect very little "vacation" to it. Billy had no time for anything but the baby. When she was not actually engaged in caring for it, she was studying how to care for it. Never had she been sweeter or dearer, and never had Bertram loved her half so well. He was proud, too, of her devotion, and of her triumphant success as a mother; but he did wish that sometimes, just once in a while, she would remember she was a wife, and pay a little attention to him, her husband.

Bertram was ashamed to own it, even to himself, but he was feeling just a little abused that summer; and he knew that, in his heart, he was actually getting jealous of his own son, in spite of his adoration of the little fellow. He told himself defensively that it was not to be expected that he should not want the love of his wife, the attentions of his wife, and the companionship of his wife—a part of the time. It was nothing more than natural that occasionally he should like to see her show some interest in subjects not mentioned in Mothers' Guides and Scientific Trainings of Infants; and he did not believe he could be blamed for wanting his residence to be a home for himself as well as a nursery for his offspring.

Even while he thus discontentedly argued with himself, however, Bertram called himself a selfish brute just to think such things when he had so dear and loving a wife as Billy, and so fine and splendid a baby as Bertram, Jr. He told himself, too, that very likely when they were back in their own house again, and when motherhood was not so new to her, Billy would not be so absorbed in the baby. She would return to her old interest in her husband, her music, her friends, and her own personal appearance. Meanwhile there was always, of course, for him, his painting. So he would paint, accepting gladly what crumbs of attention fell from the baby's table, and trust to the future to make Billy none the less a mother, perhaps, but a little more the wife.

Just how confidently he was counting on this coming change, Bertram hardly realized himself; but certainly the family was scarcely settled at the Strata before the husband gayly proposed one evening that he and Billy should go to the theater to see "Romeo and Juliet." Billy was clearly both surprised and shocked.

"Why, Bertram, I can't—you know I can't!" she exclaimed reprovingly.

Bertram's heart sank; but he kept a brave front.

"Why not?"

"What a question! As if I'd leave Baby!"

"But, Billy, dear, you'd be gone less than three hours, and you say Delia's the most careful of nurses."

Billy's forehead puckered into an anxious frown.

"I can't help it. Something might happen to him, Bertram. I couldn't be happy a minute."

"But, dearest, aren't you ever going to leave him?" demanded the young husband, forlornly.

"Why, yes, of course, when it's reasonable and necessary. I went out to the Annex yesterday afternoon. I was gone almost two whole hours."

"Well, did anything happen?"

"N-no; but then I telephoned, you see, several times, so I knew everything was all right."

"Oh, well, if that's all you want, I could telephone, you know, between every act," suggested Bertram, with a sarcasm that was quite lost on the earnest young mother.

"Y-yes, you could do that, couldn't you?" conceded Billy; "and, of course, I haven't been anywhere much, lately."

"Indeed I could," agreed Bertram, with a promptness that carefully hid his surprise at her literal acceptance of what he had proposed as a huge joke. "Come, is it a go? Shall I telephone to see if I can get seats?"

"You think Baby'll surely be all right?"

"I certainly do."

"And you'll telephone home between every act?"

"I will." Bertram's voice sounded almost as if he were repeating the marriage service.

"And we'll come straight home afterwards as fast as John and Peggy can bring us?"

"Certainly."

"Then I think—I'll—go," breathed Billy, tremulously, plainly showing what a momentous concession she thought she was making. "I do love 'Romeo and Juliet,' and I haven't seen it for ages!"

"Good! Then I'll find out about the tickets," cried Bertram, so elated at the prospect of having an old-time evening out with his wife that even the half-hourly telephones did not seem too great a price to pay.

When the time came, they were a little late in starting. Baby was fretful, and though Billy usually laid him in his crib and unhesitatingly left the room, insisting that he should go to sleep by himself in accordance with the most approved rules in her Scientific Training; yet to-night she could not bring herself to the point of leaving the house until he was quiet.

Hurried as they were when they did start, Billy was conscious of Bertram's frowning disapproval of her frock.

"You don't like it, of course, dear, and I don't blame you," she smiled remorsefully.

"Oh, I like it—that is, I did, when it was new," rejoined her husband, with apologetic frankness. "But, dear, didn't you have anything else? This looks almost—well, mussy, you know."

"No—well, yes, maybe there were others," admitted Billy; "but this was the quickest and easiest to get into, and it all came just as I was getting Baby ready for bed, you know. I am a fright, though, I'll acknowledge, so far as clothes go. I haven't had time to get a thing since Baby came. I must get something right away, I suppose."

"Yes, indeed," declared Bertram, with emphasis, hurrying his wife into the waiting automobile.

Billy had to apologize again at the theater, for the curtain had already risen on the ancient quarrel between the houses of Capulet and Montague, and Billy knew her husband's special abhorrence of tardy arrivals. Later, though, when well established in their seats, Billy's mind was plainly not with the players on the stage.

"Do you suppose Baby is all right?" she whispered, after a time.

"Sh-h! Of course he is, dear!"

There was a brief silence, during which Billy peered at her program in the semi-darkness. Then she nudged her husband's arm ecstatically.

"Bertram, I couldn't have chosen a better play if I'd tried. There are five acts! I'd forgotten there were so many. That means you can telephone four times!"

"Yes, dear." Bertram's voice was sternly cheerful.

"You must be sure they tell you exactly how Baby is."

"All right, dear. Sh-h! Here's Romeo."

Billy subsided. She even clapped a little in spasmodic enthusiasm. Presently she peered at her program again.

"There wouldn't be time, I suppose, to telephone between the scenes," she hazarded wistfully. "There are sixteen of those!"

"Well, hardly! Billy, you aren't paying one bit of attention to the play!"

"Why, of course I am," whispered Billy, indignantly. "I think it's perfectly lovely, and I'm perfectly contented, too—since I found out about those five acts, and as long as I can't have the sixteen scenes," she added, settling back in her seat.

As if to prove that she was interested in the play, her next whisper, some time later, had to do with one of the characters on the stage.

"Who's that—the nurse? Mercy! We wouldn't want her for Baby, would we?"

In spite of himself Bertram chuckled this time. Billy, too, laughed at herself. Then, resolutely, she settled into her seat again.

The curtain was not fairly down on the first act before Billy had laid an urgent hand on her husband's arm.

"Now, remember; ask if he's waked up, or anything," she directed. "And be sure to say I'll come right home if they need me. Now hurry."

"Yes, dear." Bertram rose with alacrity. "I'll be back right away."

"Oh, but I don't want you to hurry too much," she called after him, softly. "I want you to take plenty of time to ask questions."

"All right," nodded Bertram, with a quizzical smile, as he turned away.

Obediently Bertram asked all the question she could think of, then came back to his wife. There was nothing in his report that even Billy could disapprove of, or worry about; and with almost a contented look on her face she turned toward the stage as the curtain went up on the second act.

"I love this balcony scene," she sighed happily.

Romeo, however, had not half finished his impassioned love-making when Billy clutched her husband's arm almost fiercely.

"Bertram," she fairly hissed in a tragic whisper, "I've just happened to think! Won't it be awful when Baby falls in love? I know I shall just hate that girl for taking him away from me!"

"Sh-h! Billy!" expostulated her husband, choking with half-stifled laughter. "That woman in front heard you, I know she did!"

"Well, I shall," sighed Billy, mournfully, turning back to the stage.

"'Good night, good night! parting is such sweet sorrow,
   That I shall say good night, till it be morrow,'"

sighed Juliet passionately to her Romeo.

"Mercy! I hope not," whispered Billy flippantly in Bertram's ear. "I'm sure I don't want to stay here till to-morrow! I want to go home and see Baby."

"Billy!" pleaded Bertram so despairingly, that Billy, really conscience-smitten, sat back in her seat and remained, for the rest of the act, very quiet indeed.

Deceived by her apparent tranquillity, Bertram turned as the curtain went down.

"Now, Billy, surely you don't think it'll be necessary to telephone so soon as this again," he ventured.

Billy's countenance fell.

"But, Bertram, you said you would! Of course if you aren't willing to—but I've been counting on hearing all through this horrid long act, and—"

"Goodness me, Billy, I'll telephone every minute for you, of course, if you want me to," cried Bertram, springing to his feet, and trying not to show his impatience.

He was back more promptly this time.

"Everything O. K.," he smiled reassuringly into Billy's anxious eyes. "Delia said she'd just been up, and the little chap was sound asleep."

To the man's unbounded surprise, his wife grew actually white.

"Up! Up!" she exclaimed. "Do you mean that Delia went down-stairs to stay, and left my baby up there alone?"

"But, Billy, she said he was all right," murmured Bertram, softly, casting uneasy sidelong glances at his too interested neighbors.

"'All right'! Perhaps he was, then—but he may not be, later. Delia should stay in the next room all the time, where she could hear the least thing."

"Yes, dear, she will, I'm sure, if you tell her to," soothed Bertram, quickly. "It'll be all right next time."

Billy shook her head. She was obviously near to crying.

"But, Bertram, I can't stand it to sit here enjoying myself all safe and comfortable, and know that Baby is alone up there in that great big room! Please, please won't you go and telephone Delia to go up now and stay there?"

Bertram, weary, sorely tried, and increasingly aware of those annoyingly interested neighbors, was on the point of saying a very decided no; but a glance into Billy's pleading eyes settled it. Without a word he went back to the telephone.

The curtain was up when he slipped into his seat, very red of face. In answer to Billy's hurried whisper he shook his head; but in the short pause between the first and second scenes he said, in a low voice:

"I'm sorry, Billy, but I couldn't get the house at all."

"Couldn't get them! But you'd just been talking with them!"

"That's exactly it, probably. I had just telephoned, so they weren't watching for the bell. Anyhow, I couldn't get them."

"Then you didn't get Delia at all!"

"Of course not."

"And Baby is still—all alone!"

"But he's all right, dear. Delia's keeping watch of him."
For a moment there was silence; then, with clear decisiveness came Billy's voice.
"Bertram, I am going home."
"Billy!"
"I am."
"Billy, for heaven's sake don't be a silly goose! The play's half over already. We'll soon be going, anyway."
Billy's lips came together in a thin little determined line.
"Bertram, I am going home now, please," she said. "You needn't come with me; I can go alone."
Bertram said two words under his breath which it was just as well, perhaps, that Billy—and the neighbors—did not hear; then he gathered up their wraps and, with Billy, stalked out of the theater.
At home everything was found to be absolutely as it should be. Bertram, Jr., was peacefully sleeping, and Delia, who had come up from downstairs, was sewing in the next room.
"There, you see," observed Bertram, a little sourly.
Billy drew a long, contented sigh.
"Yes, I see; everything is all right. But that's exactly what I wanted to do, Bertram, you know—to see for myself," she finished happily.
And Bertram, looking at her rapt face as she hovered over the baby's crib, called himself a brute and a beast to mind anything that could make Billy look like that.

CHAPTER XXV. "SHOULD AULD ACQUAINTANCE BE FORGOT"

Bertram did not ask Billy very soon again to go to the theater. For some days, indeed, he did not ask her to do anything. Then, one evening, he did beg for some music.
"Billy, you haven't played to me or sung to me since I could remember," he complained. "I want some music."
Billy gave a merry laugh and wriggled her fingers experimentally.
"Mercy, Bertram! I don't believe I could play a note. You know I'm all out of practice."
"But why don't you practice?"
"Why, Bertram, I can't. In the first place I don't seem to have any time except when Baby's asleep; and I can't play then-I'd wake him up."
Bertram sighed irritably, rose to his feet, and began to walk up and down the room. He came to a pause at last, his eyes bent a trifle disapprovingly on his wife.
"Billy, dear, don't you wear anything but those wrapper things nowadays?" he asked plaintively.
Again Billy laughed. But this time a troubled frown followed the laugh.
"I know, Bertram, I suppose they do look dowdy, sometimes," she confessed; "but, you see, I hate to wear a really good dress—Baby rumples them up so; and I'm usually in a hurry to get to him mornings, and these are so easy to slip into, and so much more comfortable for me to handle him in!"
"Yes, of course, of course; I see," mumbled Bertram, listlessly taking up his walk again.
Billy, after a moment's silence, began to talk animatedly. Baby had done a wonderfully cunning thing that morning, and Billy had not had a chance yet to tell Bertram. Baby was growing more and more cunning anyway, these days, and there were several things she believed she had not told him; so she told them now.
Bertram listened politely, interestedly. He told himself that he was interested, too. Of course he was interested in the doings of his own child! But he still walked up and down the room

a little restlessly, coming to a halt at last by the window, across which the shade had not been drawn.

"Billy," he cried suddenly, with his old boyish eagerness, "there's a glorious moon. Come on! Let's take a little walk—a real fellow-and-his-best-girl walk! Will you?"

"Mercy! dear, I couldn't," cried Billy springing to her feet. "I'd love to, though, if I could," she added hastily, as she saw disappointment cloud her husband's face. "But I told Delia she might go out. It isn't her regular evening, of course, but I told her I didn't mind staying with Baby a bit. So I'll have to go right up now. She'll be going soon. But, dear, you go and take your walk. It'll do you good. Then you can come back and tell me all about it—only you must come in quietly, so not to wake the baby," she finished, giving her husband an affectionate kiss, as she left the room.

After a disconsolate five minutes of solitude, Bertram got his hat and coat and went out for his walk—but he told himself he did not expect to enjoy it.

Bertram Henshaw knew that the old rebellious jealousy of the summer had him fast in its grip. He was heartily ashamed of himself, but he could not help it. He wanted Billy, and he wanted her then. He wanted to talk to her. He wanted to tell her about a new portrait commission he had just obtained; and he wanted to ask her what she thought of the idea of a brand-new "Face of a Girl" for the Bohemian Ten Exhibition next March. He wanted—but then, what would be the use? She would listen, of course, but he would know by the very looks of her face that she would not be really thinking of what he was saying; and he would be willing to wager his best canvas that in the very first pause she would tell about the baby's newest tooth or latest toy. Not but that he liked to hear about the little fellow, of course; and not but that he was proud as Punch of him, too; but that he would like sometimes to hear Billy talk of something else. The sweetest melody in the world, if dinned into one's ears day and night, became something to be fled from.

And Billy ought to talk of something else, too! Bertram, Jr., wonderful as he was, really was not the only thing in the world, or even the only baby; and other people—outsiders, their friends—had a right to expect that sometimes other matters might be considered—their own, for instance. But Billy seemed to have forgotten this. No matter whether the subject of conversation had to do with the latest novel or a trip to Europe, under Billy's guidance it invariably led straight to Baby's Jack-and-Jill book, or to a perambulator journey in the Public Garden. If it had not been so serious, it would have been really funny the way all roads led straight to one goal. He himself, when alone with Billy, had started the most unusual and foreign subjects, sometimes, just to see if there were not somewhere a little bypath that did not bring up in his own nursery. He never, however, found one.

But it was not funny; it was serious. Was this glorious gift on parenthood to which he had looked forward as the crowning joy of his existence, to be nothing but a tragedy that would finally wreck his domestic happiness? It could not be. It must not be. He must be patient, and wait. Billy loved him. He was sure she did. By and by this obsession of motherhood, which had her so fast in its grasp, would relax. She would remember that her husband had rights as well as her child. Once again she would give him the companionship, love, and sympathetic interest so dear to him. Meanwhile there was his work. He must bury himself in that. And fortunate, indeed, he was, he told himself, that he had something so absorbing.

It was at this point in his meditations that Bertram rounded a corner and came face to face with a man who stopped him short with a jovial:

"Isn't it—by George, it is Bertie Henshaw! Well, what do you think of that for luck?—and me only two days home from 'Gay Paree'!"

"Oh, Seaver! How are you? You are a stranger!" Bertram's voice and handshake were a bit more cordial than they would have been had he not at the moment been feeling so abused and forlorn. In the old days he had liked this Bob Seaver well. Seaver was an artist like himself, and was good company always. But Seaver and his crowd were a little too Bohemian for William's taste; and after Billy came, she, too, had objected to what she called "that horrid Seaver man." In his heart, Bertram knew that there was good foundation for their objections, so he had avoided Seaver for a time; and for some years, now, the man had been abroad, somewhat to Bertram's relief. To-night, however, Seaver's genial smile and hearty friendliness were like a sudden burst of sunshine on a rainy day—and Bertram detested rainy days. He was feeling now, too, as if he had just had a whole week of them.

"Yes, I am something of a stranger here," nodded Seaver. "But I tell you what, little old Boston looks mighty good to me, all the same. Come on! You're just the fellow we want. I'm on my way now to the old stamping ground. Come—right about face, old chap, and come with me!"

Bertram shook his head.

"Sorry—but I guess I can't, to-night," he sighed. Both gesture and words were unhesitating, but the voice carried the discontent of a small boy, who, while the sun is still shining, has been told to come into the house.

"Oh, rats! Yes, you can, too. Come on! Lots of the old crowd will be there—Griggs, Beebe, Jack Jenkins, and Tully. We need you to complete the show."

"Jack Jenkins? Is he here?" A new eagerness had come into Bertram's voice.

"Sure! He came on from New York last night. Great boy, Jenkins! Just back from Paris fairly covered with medals, you know."

"Yes, so I hear. I haven't seen him for four years."

"Better come to-night then."

"No-o," began Bertram, with obvious reluctance. "It's already nine o'clock, and—"

"Nine o'clock!" cut in Seaver, with a broad grin. "Since when has your limit been nine o'clock? I've seen the time when you didn't mind nine o'clock in the morning, Bertie! What's got—Oh, I remember. I met another friend of yours in Berlin; chap named Arkwright—and say, he's some singer, you bet! You're going to hear of him one of these days. Well, he told me all about how you'd settled down now—son and heir, fireside bliss, pretty wife, and all the fixings. But, I say, Bertie, doesn't she let you out—any?"

"Nonsense, Seaver!" flared Bertram in annoyed wrath.

"Well, then, why don't you come to-night? If you want to see Jenkins you'll have to; he's going back to New York to-morrow."

For only a brief minute longer did Bertram hesitate; then he turned squarely about with an air of finality.

"Is he? Well, then, perhaps I will," he said. "I'd hate to miss Jenkins entirely."

"Good!" exclaimed his companion, as they fell into step. "Have a cigar?"

"Thanks. Don't mind if I do."

If Bertram's chin was a little higher and his step a little more decided than usual, it was all merely by way of accompaniment to his thoughts.

Certainly it was right that he should go, and it was sensible. Indeed, it was really almost imperative—due to Billy, as it were—after that disagreeable taunt of Seaver's. As if she did not want him to go when and where he pleased! As if she would consent for a moment to figure in the eyes of his friends as a tyrannical wife who objected to her husband's passing a social evening with his friends! To be sure, in this particular case, she might not favor Seaver's presence, but even she would not mind this once—and, anyhow, it was Jenkins that was the attraction, not Seaver. Besides, he himself was no undeveloped boy now. He was a man, presumably able to take care of himself. Besides, again, had not Billy herself told him to go out and enjoy the evening without her, as she had to stay with the baby? He would telephone her, of course, that he had met some old friends, and that he might be late; then she would not worry.

And forthwith, having settled the matter in his mind, and to his complete satisfaction, Bertram gave his undivided attention to Seaver, who had already plunged into an account of a recent Art Exhibition he had attended in Paris.

CHAPTER XXVI. GHOSTS THAT WALKED FOR BERTRAM

October proved to be unusually mild, and about the middle of the month, Bertram, after much unselfish urging on the part of Billy, went to a friend's camp in the Adirondacks for a week's stay. He came back with an angry, lugubrious face—and a broken arm.

"Oh, Bertram! And your right one, too—the same one you broke before!" mourned Billy, tearfully.

"Of course," retorted Bertram, trying in vain to give an air of jauntiness to his reply. "Didn't want to be too changeable, you know!"

"But how did you do it, dear?"

"Fell into a silly little hole covered with underbrush. But—oh, Billy, what's the use? I did it, and I can't undo it—more's the pity!"

"Of course you can't, you poor boy," sympathized Billy; "and you sha'n't be tormented with questions. We'll just be thankful 'twas no worse. You can't paint for a while, of course; but we won't mind that. It'll just give Baby and me a chance to have you all to ourselves for a time, and we'll love that!'

"Yes, of course," sighed Bertram, so abstractedly that Billy bridled with pretty resentment.

"Well, I like your enthusiasm, sir," she frowned. "I'm afraid you don't appreciate the blessings you do have, young man! Did you realize what I said? I remarked that you could be with Baby and me," she emphasized.

Bertram laughed, and gave his wife an affectionate kiss.

"Indeed I do appreciate my blessings, dear—when those blessings are such treasures as you and Baby, but—" Only his doleful eyes fixed on his injured arm finished his sentence.

"I know, dear, of course, and I understand," murmured Billy, all tenderness at once.

They were not easy for Bertram—those following days. Once again he was obliged to accept the little intimate personal services that he so disliked. Once again he could do nothing but read, or wander disconsolately into his studio and gaze at his half-finished "Face of a Girl." Occasionally, it is true, driven nearly to desperation by the haunting vision in his mind's eye, he picked up a brush and attempted to make his left hand serve his will; but a bare half-dozen irritating, ineffectual strokes were usually enough to make him throw down his brush in disgust. He never could do anything with his left hand, he told himself dejectedly.

Many of his hours, of course, he spent with Billy and his son, and they were happy hours, too; but they always came to be restless ones before the day was half over. Billy was always devotion itself to him—when she was not attending to the baby; he had no fault to find with Billy. And the baby was delightful—he could find no fault with the baby. But the baby was fretful—he was teething, Billy said—and he needed a great deal of attention; so, naturally, Bertram drifted out of the nursery, after a time, and went down into his studio, where were his dear, empty palette, his orderly brushes, and his tantalizing "Face of a Girl." From the studio, generally, Bertram went out on to the street.

Sometimes he dropped into a fellow-artist's studio. Sometimes he strolled into a club or café where he knew he would be likely to find some friend who would help him while away a tiresome hour. Bertram's friends quite vied with each other in rendering this sort of aid, so much so, indeed, that—naturally, perhaps—Bertram came to call on their services more and more frequently.

Particularly was this the case when, after the splints were removed, Bertram found, as the days passed, that his arm was not improving as it should improve. This not only disappointed and annoyed him, but worried him. He remembered sundry disquieting warnings given by the physician at the time of the former break—warnings concerning the probable seriousness of a repetition of the injury. To Billy, of course, Bertram said nothing of all this; but just before Christmas he went to see a noted specialist.

An hour later, almost in front of the learned surgeon's door, Bertram met Bob Seaver.

"Great Scott, Bertie, what's up?" ejaculated Seaver. "You look as if you'd seen a ghost."

"I have," answered Bertram, with grim bitterness. "I've seen the ghost of—of every 'Face of a Girl' I ever painted."

"Gorry! So bad as that? No wonder you look as if you'd been disporting in graveyards," chuckled Seaver, laughing at his own joke "What's the matter—arm on a rampage to day?"

He paused for reply, but as Bertram did not answer at once, he resumed, with gay insistence: "Come on! You need cheering up. Suppose we go down to Trentini's and see who's there."

"All right," agreed Bertram, dully. "Suit yourself."

Bertram was not thinking of Seaver, Trentini's, or whom he might find there. Bertram was thinking of certain words he had heard less than half an hour ago. He was wondering, too, if ever again he could think of anything but those words.

"The truth?" the great surgeon had said. "Well, the truth is—I'm sorry to tell you the truth, Mr. Henshaw, but if you will have it—you've painted the last picture you'll ever paint with your right hand, I fear. It's a bad case. This break, coming as it did on top of the serious injury of two or three years ago, was bad enough; but, to make matters worse, the bone was imperfectly set and wrongly treated, which could not be helped, of course, as you were miles away from skilled surgeons at the time of the injury. We'll do the best we can, of course; but—well, you asked for the truth, you remember; so I had to give it to you."

CHAPTER XXVII. THE MOTHER—THE WIFE

Bertram made up his mind at once that, for the present, at least, he would tell no one what the surgeon had said to him. He had placed himself under the man's care, and there was nothing to do but to take the prescribed treatment and await results as patiently as he could. Meanwhile there was no need to worry Billy, or William, or anybody else with the matter.

Billy was so busy with her holiday plans that she was only vaguely aware of what seemed to be an increase of restlessness on the part of her husband during those days just before Christmas.

"Poor dear, is the arm feeling horrid to-day?" she asked one morning, when the gloom on her husband's face was deeper than usual.

Bertram frowned and did not answer directly.

"Lots of good I am these days!" he exclaimed, his moody eyes on the armful of many-shaped, many-sized packages she carried. "What are those for-the tree?"

"Yes; and it's going to be so pretty, Bertram," exulted Billy. "And, do you know, Baby positively acts as if he suspected things—little as he is," she went on eagerly. "He's as nervous as a witch. I can't keep him still a minute!"

"How about his mother?" hinted Bertram, with a faint smile.

Billy laughed.

"Well, I'm afraid she isn't exactly calm herself," she confessed, as she hurried out of the room with her parcels.

Bertram looked after her longingly, despondently.

"I wonder what she'd say if she—knew," he muttered. "But she sha'n't know—till she just has to," he vowed suddenly, under his breath, striding into the hall for his hat and coat.

Never had the Strata known such a Christmas as this was planned to be. Cyril, Marie, and the twins were to be there, also Kate, her husband and three children, Paul, Egbert, and little Kate, from the West. On Christmas Day there was to be a big family dinner, with Aunt Hannah down from the Annex. Then, in concession to the extreme youth of the young host and his twin cousins, there was to be an afternoon tree. The shades were to be drawn and the candles lighted, however, so that there might be no loss of effect. In the evening the tree was to be once more loaded with fascinating packages and candy-bags, and this time the Greggorys, Tommy Dunn, and all the rest from the Annex were to have the fun all over again.

From garret to basement the Strata was aflame with holly, and aglitter with tinsel. Nowhere did there seem to be a spot that did not have its bit of tissue paper or its trail of red ribbon. And everything—holly, ribbon, tissue, and tinsel—led to the mysteriously closed doors of the great front drawing-room, past which none but Billy and her accredited messengers might venture. No wonder, indeed, that even Baby scented excitement, and that Baby's mother was not exactly calm. No wonder, too, that Bertram, with his helpless right arm, and his heavy heart, felt peculiarly forlorn and "out of it." No wonder, also, that he took himself literally out of it with growing frequency.

Mr. and Mrs. Hartwell and little Kate were to stay at the Strata. The boys, Paul and Egbert, were to go to Cyril's. Promptly at the appointed time, two days before Christmas, they arrived. And from that hour until two days after Christmas, when the last bit of holly, ribbon, tissue, and tinsel disappeared from the floor, Billy moved in a whirl of anxious responsibility that was yet filled with fun, frolic, and laughter.

It was a great success, the whole affair. Everybody seemed pleased and happy—that is, everybody but Bertram; and he very plainly tried to seem pleased and happy. Even Cyril unbent to the extent of not appearing to mind the noise one bit; and Sister Kate (Bertram said) found only the extraordinarily small number of four details to change in the arrangements. Baby obligingly let his teeth-getting go, for the occasion, and he and the twins, Franz and Felix, were the admiration and delight of all. Little Kate, to be sure, was a trifle disconcerting once or twice, but everybody was too absorbed to pay much attention to her. Billy did, however, remember her opening remarks.

"Well, little Kate, do you remember me?" Billy had greeted her pleasantly.

"Oh, yes," little Kate had answered, with a winning smile. "You're my Aunt Billy what married my Uncle Bertram instead of Uncle William as you said you would first."

Everybody laughed, and Billy colored, of course; but little Kate went on eagerly:

"And I've been wanting just awfully to see you," she announced.

"Have you? I'm glad, I'm sure. I feel highly flattered," smiled Billy.

"Well, I have. You see, I wanted to ask you something. Have you ever wished that you had married Uncle William instead of Uncle Bertram, or that you'd tried for Uncle Cyril before Aunty Marie got him?"

"Kate!" gasped her horrified mother. "I told you—You see," she broke off, turning to Billy despairingly. "She's been pestering me with questions like that ever since she knew she was coming. She never has forgotten the way you changed from one uncle to the other. You may remember; it made a great impression on her at the time."

"Yes, I—I remember," stammered Billy, trying to laugh off her embarrassment.

"But you haven't told me yet whether you did wish you'd married Uncle William, or Uncle Cyril," interposed little Kate, persistently.

"No, no, of course not!" exclaimed Billy, with a vivid blush, casting her eyes about for a door of escape, and rejoicing greatly when she spied Delia with the baby coming toward them. "There, look, my dear, here's your new cousin, little Bertram!" she exclaimed. "Don't you want to see him?"

Little Kate turned dutifully.

"Yes'm, Aunt Billy, but I'd rather see the twins. Mother says they're real pretty and cunning."

"Er—y-yes, they are," murmured Billy, on whom the emphasis of the "they're" had not been lost.

Naturally, as may be supposed, therefore, Billy had not forgotten little Kate's opening remarks.

Immediately after Christmas Mr. Hartwell and the boys went back to their Western home, leaving Mrs. Hartwell and her daughter to make a round of visits to friends in the East. For almost a week after Christmas they remained at the Strata; and it was on the last day of their stay that little Kate asked the question that proved so momentous in results.

Billy, almost unconsciously, had avoided tête-á-têtes with her small guest. But to-day they were alone together.

"Aunt Billy," began the little girl, after a meditative gaze into the other's face, "you are married to Uncle Bertram, aren't you?"

"I certainly am, my dear," smiled Billy, trying to speak unconcernedly.

"Well, then, what makes you forget it?"

"What makes me forget—Why, child, what a question! What do you mean? I don't forget it!" exclaimed Billy, indignantly.

"Then what did mother mean? I heard her tell Uncle William myself—she didn't know I heard, though—that she did wish you'd remember you were Uncle Bertram's wife as well as Cousin Bertram's mother."

Billy flushed scarlet, then grew very white. At that moment Mrs. Hartwell came into the room. Little Kate turned triumphantly.

"There, she hasn't forgotten, and I knew she hadn't, mother! I asked her just now, and she said she hadn't."

"Hadn't what?" questioned Mrs. Hartwell, looking a little apprehensively at her sister-in-law's white face and angry eyes.

"Hadn't forgotten that she was Uncle Bertram's wife."

"Kate," interposed Billy, steadily meeting her sister-in-law's gaze, "will you be good enough to tell me what this child is talking about?"

Mrs. Hartwell sighed, and gave an impatient gesture.

"Kate, I've a mind to take you home on the next train," she said to her daughter. "Run away, now, down-stairs. Your Aunt Billy and I want to talk. Come, come, hurry! I mean what I say," she added warningly, as she saw unmistakable signs of rebellion on the small young face.

"I wish," pouted little Kate, rising reluctantly, and moving toward the door, "that you didn't always send me away just when I wanted most to stay!"

"Well, Kate?" prompted Billy, as the door closed behind the little girl.

"Yes, I suppose I'll have to say it now, as long as that child has put her finger in the pie. But I hadn't intended to speak, no matter what I saw. I promised myself I wouldn't, before I came. I know, of course, how Bertram and Cyril, and William, too, say that I'm always interfering in affairs that don't concern me—though, for that matter, if my own brother's affairs don't concern me, I don't know whose should!

"But, as I said, I wasn't going to speak this time, no matter what I saw. And I haven't—except to William, and Cyril, and Aunt Hannah; but I suppose somewhere little Kate got hold of it. It's simply this, Billy. It seems to me it's high time you began to realize that you're Bertram's wife as well as the baby's mother."

"That, I am—I don't think I quite understand," said Billy, unsteadily.

"No, I suppose you don't," sighed Kate, "though where your eyes are, I don't see—or, rather, I do see: they're on the baby, always. It's all very well and lovely, Billy, to be a devoted mother, and you certainly are that. I'll say that much for you, and I'll admit I never thought you would be. But can't you see what you're doing to Bertram?"

"Doing to Bertram!—by being a devoted mother to his son!"

"Yes, doing to Bertram. Can't you see what a change there is in the boy? He doesn't act like himself at all. He's restless and gloomy and entirely out of sorts."

"Yes, I know; but that's his arm," pleaded Billy. "Poor boy—he's so tired of it!"

Kate shook her head decisively.

"It's more than his arm, Billy. You'd see it yourself if you weren't blinded by your absorption in that baby. Where is Bertram every evening? Where is he daytimes? Do you realize that he's been at home scarcely one evening since I came? And as for the days—he's almost never here."

"But, Kate, he can't paint now, you know, so of course he doesn't need to stay so closely at home," defended Billy. "He goes out to find distraction from himself."

"Yes, 'distraction,' indeed," sniffed Kate. "And where do you suppose he finds it? Do you know where he finds it? I tell you, Billy, Bertram Henshaw is not the sort of man that should find too much 'distraction' outside his home. His tastes and his temperament are altogether too Bohemian, and—"

Billy interrupted with a peremptorily upraised hand.

"Please remember, Kate, you are speaking of my husband to his wife; and his wife has perfect confidence in him, and is just a little particular as to what you say."

"Yes; well, I'm speaking of my brother, too, whom I know very well," shrugged Kate. "All is, you may remember sometime that I warned you—that's all. This trusting business is all very pretty; but I think 'twould be a lot prettier, and a vast deal more sensible, if you'd give him a little attention as well as trust, and see if you can't keep him at home a bit more. At least you'll know whom he's with, then. Cyril says he saw him last week with Bob Seaver."

"With—Bob—Seaver?" faltered Billy, changing color.

"Yes. I see you remember him," smiled Kate, not quite agreeably. "Perhaps now you'll take some stock in what I've said, and remember it."

"I'll remember it, certainly," returned Billy, a little proudly. "You've said a good many things to me, in the past, Mrs. Hartwell, and I've remembered them all—every one."

It was Kate's turn to flush, and she did it.

"Yes, I know. And I presume very likely sometimes there hasn't been much foundation for what I've said. I think this time, however, you'll find there is," she finished, with an air of hurt dignity.

Billy made no reply, perhaps because Delia, at that moment, brought in the baby.

Mrs. Hartwell and little Kate left the Strata the next morning. Until then Billy contrived to keep, before them, a countenance serene, and a manner free from unrest. Even when, after dinner that evening, Bertram put on his hat and coat and went out, Billy refused to meet her sister-in-law's meaning gaze. But in the morning, after they had left the house, Billy did not attempt to deceive herself. Determinedly, then, she set herself to going over in her mind the past months since the baby came; and she was appalled at what she found. Ever in her ears, too, was that feared name, "Bob Seaver"; and ever before her eyes was that night years ago when, as an eighteen-year-old girl, she had followed Bertram and Bob Seaver into a glittering café at eleven o'clock at night, because Bertram had been drinking and was not himself. She remembered Bertram's face when he had seen her, and what he had said when she begged him to come home. She remembered, too, what the family had said afterward. But she remembered, also, that years later Bertram had told her what that escapade of hers had really done for him, and that he believed he had actually loved her from that moment. After that night, at all events, he had had little to do with Bob Seaver.

And now Seaver was back again, it seemed—and with Bertram. They had been seen together. But if they had, what could she do? Surely she could hardly now follow them into a public café and demand that Seaver let her husband come home! But she could keep him at home, perhaps. (Billy quite brightened at this thought.) Kate had said that she was so absorbed in Baby that her husband received no attention at all. Billy did not believe this was true; but if it were true, she could at least rectify that mistake. If it were attention that he wanted—he should want no more. Poor Bertram! No wonder that he had sought distraction outside! When one had a horrid broken arm that would not let one do anything, what else could one do?

Just here Billy suddenly remembered the book, "A Talk to Young Wives." If she recollected rightly, there was a chapter that covered the very claim Kate had been making. Billy had not thought of the book for months, but she went at once to get it now. There might be, after all, something in it that would help her.

"The Coming of the First Baby." Billy found the chapter without difficulty and settled herself to read, her countenance alight with interest. In a surprisingly short time, however, a new expression came to her face; and at last a little gasp of dismay fell from her lips. She looked up then, with a startled gaze.

Had her walls possessed eyes and ears all these past months, only to give instructions to an unseen hand that it might write what the eyes and ears had learned? For it was such sentences as these that the conscience-smitten Billy read:

"Maternity is apt to work a miracle in a woman's life, but sometimes it spells disaster so far as domestic bliss is concerned. The young mother, wrapped up in the delights and duties of motherhood, utterly forgets that she has a husband. She lives and moves and has her being in the nursery. She thinks baby, talks baby, knows only baby. She refuses to dress up, because it is easier to take care of baby in a frowzy wrapper. She will not go out with her husband for fear something might happen to the baby. She gives up her music because baby won't let her practice. In vain her husband tries to interest her in his own affairs. She has neither eyes nor ears for him, only for baby.

"Now no man enjoys having his nose put out of joint, even by his own child. He loves his child devotedly, and is proud of him, of course; but that does not keep him from wanting the society of his wife occasionally, nor from longing for her old-time love and sympathetic interest. It is an admirable thing, certainly, for a woman to be a devoted mother; but maternal affection can be carried too far. Husbands have some rights as well as offspring; and the wife who neglects her husband for her babies does so at her peril. Home, with the wife eternally in the nursery, is apt to be a dull and lonely thing to the average husband, so he starts out to find amusement for himself—and he finds it. Then is the time when the new little life that is so precious, and that should have bound the two more closely together, becomes the wedge that drives them apart."

Billy did not read any more. With a little sobbing cry she flung the book back into her desk, and began to pull off her wrapper. Her fingers shook. Already she saw herself a Monster, a Wicked Destroyer of Domestic Bliss with her thoughtless absorption in Baby, until he had become that Awful Thing—a Wedge. And Bertram—poor Bertram, with his broken arm! She had not played to him, nor sung to him, nor gone out with him. And when had they had one of their good long talks about Bertram's work and plans?

But it should all be changed now. She would play, and sing, and go out with him. She would dress up, too. He should see no more wrappers. She would ask about his work, and seem interested. She was interested. She remembered now, that just before he was hurt, he had told her of a new portrait, and of a new "Face of a Girl" that he had planned to do. Lately he had said nothing about these. He had seemed discouraged—and no wonder, with his broken arm! But she would change all that. He should see! And forthwith Billy hurried to her closet to pick out her prettiest house frock.

Long before dinner Billy was ready, waiting in the drawing-room. She had on a pretty little blue silk gown that she knew Bertram liked, and she watched very anxiously for Bertram to come up the steps. She remembered now, with a pang, that he had long since given up his peculiar ring; but she meant to meet him at the door just the same.

Bertram, however, did not come. At a quarter before six he telephoned that he had met some friends, and would dine at the club.

"My, my, how pretty we are!" exclaimed Uncle William, when they went down to dinner together. "New frock?"

"Why, no, Uncle William," laughed Billy, a little tremulously. "You've seen it dozens of times!"

"Have I?" murmured the man. "I don't seem to remember it. Too bad Bertram isn't here to see you. Somehow, you look unusually pretty to-night."

And Billy's heart ached anew.

Billy spent the evening practicing—softly, to be sure, so as not to wake Baby—but practicing.

As the days passed Billy discovered that it was much easier to say she would "change things" than it was really to change them. She changed herself, it is true—her clothes, her habits, her words, and her thoughts; but it was more difficult to change Bertram. In the first place, he was there so little. She was dismayed when she saw how very little, indeed, he was at home—and she did not like to ask him outright to stay. That was not in accordance with her plans. Besides, the "Talk to Young Wives" said that indirect influence was much to be preferred, always, to direct persuasion—which last, indeed, usually failed to produce results.

So Billy "dressed up," and practiced, and talked (of anything but the baby), and even hinted shamelessly once or twice that she would like to go to the theater; but all to little avail. True, Bertram brightened up, for a minute, when he came home and found her in a new or a favorite dress, and he told her how pretty she looked. He appeared to like to have her play to him, too, even declaring once or twice that it was quite like old times, yes, it was. But he never noticed her hints about the theater, and he did not seem to like to talk about his work, even a little bit.

Billy laid this last fact to his injured arm. She decided that he had become blue and discouraged, and that he needed cheering up, especially about his work; so she determinedly and systematically set herself to doing it.

She talked of the fine work he had done, and of the still finer work he would yet do, when his arm was well. She told him how proud she was of him, and she let him see how dear his Art was to her, and how badly she would feel if she thought he had really lost all his interest in his work and would never paint again. She questioned him about the new portrait he was to begin as soon as his arm would let him; and she tried to arouse his enthusiasm in the picture he had planned to show in the March Exhibition of the Bohemian Ten, telling him that she was sure his arm would allow him to complete at least one canvas to hang.

In none of this, however, did Bertram appear in the least interested. The one thing, indeed, which he seemed not to want to talk about, was his work; and he responded to her overtures on the subject with only moody silence, or else with almost irritable monosyllables; all of which not only grieved but surprised Billy very much. For, according to the "Talk to Young Wives," she was doing exactly what the ideal, sympathetic, interested-in-her-husband's-work wife should do.

When February came, bringing with it no change for the better, Billy was thoroughly frightened. Bertram's arm plainly was not improving. He was more gloomy and restless than ever. He seemed not to want to stay at home at all; and Billy knew now for a certainty that he was spending more and more time with Bob Seaver and "the boys."

Poor Billy! Nowhere could she look these days and see happiness. Even the adored baby seemed, at times, almost to give an added pang. Had he not become, according to the "Talk to Young Wives" that awful thing, a Wedge? The Annex, too, carried its sting; for where was the need of an overflow house for happiness now, when there was no happiness to overflow? Even the little jade idol on Billy's mantel Billy could not bear to see these days, for its once bland smile had become a hideous grin, demanding, "Where, now, is your heap plenty velly good luckee?"

But, before Bertram, Billy still carried a bravely smiling face, and to him still she talked earnestly and enthusiastically of his work—which last, as it happened, was the worst course she could have pursued; for the one thing poor Bertram wished to forget, just now, was—his work.

CHAPTER XXVIII. CONSPIRATORS

Early in February came Arkwright's appearance at the Boston Opera House—the first since he had sung there as a student a few years before. He was an immediate and an unquestioned success. His portrait adorned the front page of almost every Boston newspaper the next morning, and captious critics vied with each other to do him honor. His full history, from boyhood up, was featured, with special emphasis on his recent triumphs in New York and foreign capitals. He was interviewed as to his opinion on everything from vegetarianism to woman's suffrage; and his preferences as to pies and pastimes were given headline prominence. There was no doubt of it. Mr. M. J. Arkwright was a star.

All Arkwright's old friends, including Billy, Bertram, Cyril, Marie, Calderwell, Alice Greggory, Aunt Hannah, and Tommy Dunn, went to hear him sing; and after the performance he held a miniature reception, with enough adulation to turn his head completely around, he declared deprecatingly. Not until the next evening, however, did he have an opportunity for what he called a real talk with any of his friends; then, in Calderwell's room, he settled back in his chair with a sigh of content.

For a time his own and Calderwell's affairs occupied their attention; then, after a short pause, the tenor asked abruptly:

"Is there anything—wrong with the Henshaws, Calderwell?"

Calderwell came suddenly erect in his chair.

"Thank you! I hoped you'd introduce that subject; though, for that matter, if you hadn't, I should. Yes, there is—and I'm looking to you, old man, to get them out of it."

"I?" Arkwright sat erect now.

"Yes."

"What do you mean?"

"In a way, the expected has happened—though I know now that I didn't really expect it to happen, in spite of my prophecies. You may remember I was always skeptical on the subject of Bertram's settling down to a domestic hearthstone. I insisted 'twould be the turn of a girl's head and the curve of her cheek that he wanted to paint."

Arkwright looked up with a quick frown.

"You don't mean that Henshaw has been cad enough to find another—"

Calderwell threw up his hand.

"No, no, not that! We haven't that to deal with—yet, thank goodness! There's no woman in it. And, really, when you come right down to it, if ever a fellow had an excuse to seek diversion, Bertram Henshaw has—poor chap! It's just this. Bertram broke his arm again last October."

"Yes, so I hear, and I thought he was looking badly."

"He is. It's a bad business. 'Twas improperly set in the first place, and it's not doing well now. In fact, I'm told on pretty good authority that the doctor says he probably will never use it again."

"Oh, by George! Calderwell!"

"Yes. Tough, isn't it? 'Specially when you think of his work, and know—as I happen to—that he's particularly dependent on his right hand for everything. He doesn't tell this generally, and I understand Billy and the family know nothing of it—how hopeless the case is, I mean. Well, naturally, the poor fellow has been pretty thoroughly discouraged, and to get away from himself he's gone back to his old Bohemian habits, spending much of his time with some of his old cronies that are none too good for him—Seaver, for instance."

"Bob Seaver? Yes, I know him." Arkwright's lips snapped together crisply.

"Yes. He said he knew you. That's why I'm counting on your help."

"What do you mean?"

"I mean I want you to get Henshaw away from him, and keep him away."

Arkwright's face darkened with an angry flush.

"Great Scott, Calderwell! What are you talking about? Henshaw is no kid to be toted home, and I'm no nursery governess to do the toting!"

Calderwell laughed quietly.

"No; I don't think any one would take you for a nursery governess, Arkwright, in spite of the fact that you are still known to some of your friends as 'Mary Jane.' But you can sing a song, man, which will promptly give you a through ticket to their innermost sacred circle. In fact, to my certain knowledge, Seaver is already planning a jamboree with you at the right hand of the toastmaster. There's your chance. Once in, stay in—long enough to get Henshaw out."

"But, good heavens, Calderwell, it's impossible! What can I do?" demanded Arkwright, savagely. "I can't walk up to the man, take him by the ear, and say: 'Here, you, sir—march home!' Neither can I come the 'I-am-holier-than-thou' act, and hold up to him the mirror of his transgressions."

"No, but you can get him out of it some way. You can find a way—for Billy's sake."

There was no answer, and, after a moment, Calderwell went on more quietly.

"I haven't seen Billy but two or three times since I came back to Boston—but I don't need to, to know that she's breaking her heart over something. And of course that something is—Bertram."

There was still no answer. Arkwright got up suddenly, and walked to the window.

"You see, I'm helpless," resumed Calderwell. "I don't paint pictures, nor sing songs, nor write stories, nor dance jigs for a living—and you have to do one or another to be in with that set. And it's got to be a Johnny-on-the-spot with Bertram. All is, something will have to be done to get him out of the state of mind and body he's in now, or—"

Arkwright wheeled sharply.

"When did you say this jamboree was going to be?" he demanded.

"Next week, some time. The date is not settled. They were going to consult you."

"Hm-m," commented Arkwright. And, though his next remark was a complete change of subject, Calderwell gave a contented sigh.

If, when the proposition was first made to him, Arkwright was doubtful of his ability to be a successful "Johnny-on-the-spot," he was even more doubtful of it as the days passed, and he was attempting to carry out the suggestion.

He had known that he was undertaking a most difficult and delicate task, and he soon began to fear that it was an impossible one, as well. With a dogged persistence, however, he adhered to his purpose, ever on the alert to be more watchful, more tactful, more efficient in emergencies.

Disagreeable as was the task, in a way, in another way it was a great pleasure to him. He was glad of the opportunity to do anything for Billy; and then, too, he was glad of something absorbing enough to take his mind off his own affairs. He told himself, sometimes, that this helping another man to fight his tiger skin was assisting himself to fight his own.

Arkwright was trying very hard not to think of Alice Greggory these days. He had come back hoping that he was in a measure "cured" of his "folly," as he termed it; but the first look into Alice Greggory's blue-gray eyes had taught him the fallacy of that idea. In that very first meeting with Alice, he feared that he had revealed his secret, for she was plainly so nervously distant and ill at ease with him that he could but construe her embarrassment and chilly dignity as pity for him and a desire to show him that she had nothing but friendship for him. Since then he had seen but little of her, partly because he did not wish to see her, and partly because his time was so fully occupied. Then, too, in a round-about way he had heard a rumor that Calderwell was engaged to be married; and, though no feminine name had been mentioned in connection with the story, Arkwright had not hesitated to supply in his own mind that of Alice Greggory.

Beginning with the "jamboree," which came off quite in accordance with Calderwell's prophecies, Arkwright spent the most of such time as was not given to his professional duties in deliberately cultivating the society of Bertram and his friends. To this extent he met with no difficulty, for he found that M. J. Arkwright, the new star in the operatic firmament, was obviously a welcome comrade. Beyond this it was not so easy. Arkwright wondered, indeed, sometimes, if he were making any progress at all. But still he persevered. He walked with Bertram, he talked with Bertram, unobtrusively he contrived to be near Bertram almost always, when they were together with "the boys." Gradually he won from him the story of what the surgeon had said to him, and of how black the future looked in consequence. This established a new bond between them, so potent that Arkwright ventured to test it one day by telling Bertram the story of the tiger skin—the first tiger skin in his uncle's library years ago, and of how, since then, any difficulty he had encountered he had tried to treat as a tiger skin. In telling the story he was careful to draw no moral for his listener, and to preach no sermon. He told the tale, too, with all possible whimsical lightness of touch, and immediately at its conclusion he changed the subject. But that he had not failed utterly in his design was evidenced a few days later when Bertram grimly declared that he guessed his tiger skin was a lively beast, all right.

The first time Arkwright went home with Bertram, his presence was almost a necessity. Bertram was not quite himself that night. Billy admitted them. She had plainly been watching and waiting. Arkwright never forgot the look on her face as her eyes met his. There was a curious mixture of terror, hurt pride, relief, and shame, overtopped by a fierce loyalty which almost seemed to say aloud the words: "Don't you dare to blame him!"

Arkwright's heart ached with sympathy and admiration at the proudly courageous way in which Billy carried off the next few painful minutes. Even when he bade her good night a little later, only her eyes said "thank you." Her lips were dumb.

Arkwright often went home with Bertram after that. Not that it was always necessary—far from it. Some time, indeed, elapsed before he had quite the same excuse again for his presence. But he had found that occasionally he could get Bertram home earlier by adroit suggestions of one kind or another; and more and more frequently he was succeeding in getting him home for a game of chess.

Bertram liked chess, and was a fine player. Since breaking his arm he had turned to games with the feverish eagerness of one who looks for something absorbing to fill an unrestful mind. It was Seaver's skill in chess that had at first attracted Bertram to the man long ago; but Bertram could beat him easily—too easily for much pleasure in it now. So they did not play chess often these days. Bertram had found that, in spite of his injury, he could still take part in other games, and some of them, if not so intricate as chess, were at least more apt to take his mind off himself, especially if there was a bit of money up to add zest and interest.

As it happened, however, Bertram learned one day that Arkwright could play chess—and play well, too, as he discovered after their first game together. This fact contributed not a little to such success as Arkwright was having in his efforts to wean Bertram from his undesirable companions; for Bertram soon found out that Arkwright was more than a match for himself, and the occasional games he did succeed in winning only whetted his appetite for more. Many an evening now, therefore, was spent by the two men in Bertram's den, with Billy anxiously hovering near, her eyes longingly watching either her husband's absorbed face or the pretty little red and white ivory figures, which seemed to possess so wonderful a power to hold his attention. In spite of her joy at the chessmen's efficacy in keeping Bertram at home, however, she was almost jealous of them.

"Mr. Arkwright, couldn't you show me how to play, sometime?" she said wistfully, one evening, when the momentary absence of Bertram had left the two alone together. "I used to watch Bertram and Marie play years ago; but I never knew how to play myself. Not that I can see where the fun is in just sitting staring at a chessboard for half an hour at a time, though! But Bertram likes it, and so I—I want to learn to stare with him. Will you teach me?"

"I should be glad to," smiled Arkwright.

"Then will you come, maybe, sometimes when Bertram is at the doctor's? He goes every Tuesday and Friday at three o'clock for treatment. I'd rather you came then for two reasons: first, because I don't want Bertram to know I'm learning, till I can play some; and, secondly, because—because I don't want to take you away—from him."

The last words were spoken very low, and were accompanied by a painful blush. It was the first time Billy had ever hinted to Arkwright, in words, that she understood what he was trying to do.

"I'll come next Tuesday," promised Arkwright, with a cheerfully unobservant air. Then Bertram came in, bringing the book of Chess Problems, for which he had gone up-stairs.

CHAPTER XXIX. CHESS

Promptly at three o'clock Tuesday afternoon Arkwright appeared at the Strata, and for the next hour Billy did her best to learn the names and the moves of the pretty little ivory men. But at the end of the hour she was almost ready to give up in despair.

"If there weren't so many kinds, and if they didn't all insist on doing something different, it wouldn't be so bad," she sighed. "But how can you be expected to remember which goes diagonal, and which crisscross, and which can't go but one square, and which can skip 'way across the board, 'specially when that little pawn-thing can go straight ahead two squares sometimes, and the next minute only one (except when it takes things, and then it goes crooked one square) and when that tiresome little horse tries to go all ways at once, and can jump 'round and hurdle over anybody's head, even the king's—how can you expect folks to remember? But, then, Bertram remembers," she added, resolutely, "so I guess I can."

Whenever possible, after that, Arkwright came on Tuesdays and Fridays, and, in spite of her doubts, Billy did very soon begin to "remember." Spurred by her great desire to play with Bertram and surprise him, Billy spared no pains to learn well her lessons. Even among the baby's books and playthings these days might be found a "Manual of Chess," for Billy pursued her study at all hours; and some nights even her dreams were of ruined castles where kings and queens and bishops disported themselves, with pawns for servants, and where a weird knight on horseback used the castle's highest tower for a hurdle, landing always a hundred yards to one side of where he would be expected to come down.

It was not long, of course, before Billy could play a game of chess, after a fashion, but she knew just enough to realize that she actually knew nothing; and she knew, too, that until she could play a really good game, her moves would not hold Bertram's attention for one minute. Not at present, therefore, was she willing Bertram should know what she was attempting to do.

Billy had not yet learned what the great surgeon had said to Bertram. She knew only that his arm was no better, and that he never voluntarily spoke of his painting. Over her now seemed to be hanging a vague horror. Something was the matter. She knew that. But what it was she could not fathom. She realized that Arkwright was trying to help, and her gratitude, though silent, knew no bounds. Not even to Aunt Hannah or Uncle William could she speak of this thing that was troubling her. That they, too, understood, in a measure, she realized. But still she said no word. Billy was wearing a proud little air of aloofness these days that was heart-breaking to those who saw it and read it aright for what it was: loyalty to Bertram, no matter what happened. And so Billy pored over her chessboard feverishly, tirelessly, having ever before her longing eyes the dear time when Bertram, across the table from her, should sit happily staring for half an hour at a move she had made.

Whatever Billy's chess-playing was to signify, however, in her own life, it was destined to play a part in the lives of two friends of hers that was most unexpected.

During Billy's very first lesson, as it chanced, Alice Greggory called and found Billy and Arkwright so absorbed in their game that they did not at first hear Eliza speak her name.

The quick color that flew to Arkwright's face at sight of herself was construed at once by Alice as embarrassment on his part at being found tête-á-tête with Bertram Henshaw's wife. And she did not like it. She was not pleased that he was there. She was less pleased that he blushed for being there.

It so happened that Alice found him there again several times. Alice gave a piano lesson at two o'clock every Tuesday and Friday afternoon to a little Beacon Street neighbor of Billy's, and she had fallen into the habit of stepping in to see Billy for a few minutes afterward, which brought her there at a little past three, just after the chess lesson was well started.

If, the first time that Alice Greggory found Arkwright opposite Billy at the chess-table, she was surprised and displeased, the second and third times she was much more so. When it finally came to her one day with sickening illumination, that always the tête-á-têtes were during Bertram's hour at the doctor's, she was appalled.

What could it mean? Had Arkwright given up his fight? Was he playing false to himself and to Bertram by trying thus, on the sly, to win the love of his friend's wife? Was this man, whom she had so admired for his brave stand, and to whom all unasked she had given her heart's best love (more the pity of it!)—was this idol of hers to show feet of clay, after all? She could not believe it. And yet—

Sick at heart, but imbued with the determination of a righteous cause, Alice Greggory resolved, for Billy's sake, to watch and wait. If necessary she should speak to some one—though to whom she did not know. Billy's happiness should not be put in jeopardy if she could help it. Indeed, no!

As the weeks passed, Alice came to be more and more uneasy, distressed, and grieved. Of Billy she could believe no evil; but of Arkwright she was beginning to think she could believe everything that was dishonorable and despicable. And to believe that of the man she still loved—no wonder that Alice did not look nor act like herself these days.

Incensed at herself because she did love him, angry at him because he seemed to be proving himself so unworthy of that love, and genuinely frightened at what she thought was the fast-approaching wreck of all happiness for her dear friend, Billy, Alice did not know which way to turn. At the first she had told herself confidently that she would "speak to somebody." But, as time passed, she saw the impracticability of that idea. Speak to somebody, indeed! To whom? When? Where? What should she say? Where was her right to say anything? She was not dealing with a parcel of naughty children who had pilfered the cake jar! She was dealing with grown men and women, who, presumedly, knew their own affairs, and who, certainly, would resent any interference from her. On the other hand, could she stand calmly by and see Bertram lose his wife, Arkwright his honor, Billy her happiness, and herself her faith in human nature, all because to do otherwise would be to meddle in other people's business? Apparently she could, and should. At least that seemed to be the rôle which she was expected to play.

It was when Alice had reached this unhappy frame of mind that Arkwright himself unexpectedly opened the door for her.

The two were alone together in Bertram Henshaw's den. It was Tuesday afternoon. Alice had called to find Billy and Arkwright deep in their usual game of chess. Then a matter of domestic affairs had taken Billy from the room.

"I'm afraid I'll have to be gone ten minutes, or more," she had said, as she rose from the table reluctantly. "But you might be showing Alice the moves, Mr. Arkwright," she had added, with a laugh, as she disappeared.

"Shall I teach you the moves?" he had smiled, when they were alone together.

Alice's reply had been so indignantly short and sharp that Arkwright, after a moment's pause, had said, with a whimsical smile that yet carried a touch of sadness:

"I am forced to surmise from your answer that you think it is you who should be teaching me moves. At all events, I seem to have been making some moves lately that have not suited you, judging by your actions. Have I offended you in any way, Alice?"

The girl turned with a quick lifting of her head. Alice knew that if ever she were to speak, it must be now. Never again could she hope for such an opportunity as this. Suddenly throwing circumspect caution quite aside, she determined that she would speak. Springing to her feet she crossed the room and seated herself in Billy's chair at the chess-table.

"Me! Offend me!" she exclaimed, in a low voice. "As if I were the one you were offending!"

"Why, Alice!" murmured the man, in obvious stupefaction.

Alice raised her hand, palm outward.

"Now don't, please don't pretend you don't know," she begged, almost piteously. "Please don't add that to all the rest. Oh, I understand, of course, it's none of my affairs, and I wasn't going to speak," she choked; "but, to-day, when you gave me this chance, I had to. At first I couldn't believe it," she plunged on, plainly hurrying against Billy's return. "After all you'd told me of how you meant to fight it—your tiger skin. And I thought it merely happened that you were here alone with her those days I came. Then, when I found out they were always the days Mr. Henshaw was away at the doctor's, I had to believe."

She stopped for breath. Arkwright, who, up to this moment had shown that he was completely mystified as to what she was talking about, suddenly flushed a painful red. He was obviously about to speak, but she prevented him with a quick gesture.

"There's a little more I've got to say, please. As if it weren't bad enough to do what you're doing at all, but you must needs take it at such a time as this when—when her husband isn't doing just what he ought to do, and we all know it—it's so unfair to take her now, and try to—to win—And you aren't even fair with him," she protested tremulously. "You pretend to be his friend. You go with him everywhere. It's just as if you were helping to—to pull him down. You're one with the whole bunch." (The blood suddenly receded from Arkwright's face, leaving it very white; but if Alice saw it, she paid no heed.) "Everybody says you are. Then to come here like this, on the sly, when you know he can't be here, I—Oh, can't you see what you're doing?"

There was a moment's pause, then Arkwright spoke. A deep pain looked from his eyes. He was still very pale, and his mouth had settled into sad lines.

"I think, perhaps, it may be just as well if I tell you what I am doing—or, rather, trying to do," he said quietly.

Then he told her.

"And so you see," he added, when he had finished the tale, "I haven't really accomplished much, after all, and it seems the little I have accomplished has only led to my being misjudged by you, my best friend."

Alice gave a sobbing cry. Her face was scarlet. Horror, shame, and relief struggled for mastery in her countenance.

"Oh, but I didn't know, I didn't know," she moaned, twisting her hands nervously. "And now, when you've been so brave, so true—for me to accuse you of—Oh, can you ever forgive me? But you see, knowing that you did care for her, it did look—" She choked into silence, and turned away her head.

He glanced at her tenderly, mournfully.

"Yes," he said, after a minute, in a low voice. "I can see how it did look; and so I'm going to tell you now something I had meant never to tell you. There really couldn't have been anything in that, you see, for I found out long ago that it was gone—whatever love there had been for—Billy."

"But your—tiger skin!"

"Oh, yes, I thought it was alive," smiled Arkwright, sadly, "when I asked you to help me fight it. But one day, very suddenly, I discovered that it was nothing but a dead skin of dreams and memories. But I made another discovery, too. I found that just beyond lay another one, and that was very much alive."

"Another one?" Alice turned to him in wonder. "But you never asked me to help you fight—that one!"

He shook his head.

"No; I couldn't, you see. You couldn't have helped me. You'd only have hindered me."

"Hindered you?"

"Yes. You see, it was my love for—you, that I was fighting—then."

Alice gave a low cry and flushed vividly; but Arkwright hurried on, his eyes turned away.

"Oh, I understand. I know. I'm not asking for—anything. I heard some time ago of your engagement to Calderwell. I've tried many times to say the proper, expected pretty speeches, but—I couldn't. I will now, though. I do. You have all my tenderest best wishes for your happiness—dear. If long ago I hadn't been such a blind fool as not to know my own heart—"

"But—but there's some mistake," interposed Alice, palpitatingly, with hanging head. "I—I'm not engaged to Mr. Calderwell."

Arkwright turned and sent a keen glance into her face.

"You're—not?"

"No."

"But I heard that Calderwell—" He stopped helplessly.

"You heard that Mr. Calderwell was engaged, very likely. But—it so happens he isn't engaged—to me," murmured Alice, faintly.

"But, long ago you said—" Arkwright paused, his eyes still keenly searching her face.

"Never mind what I said—long ago," laughed Alice, trying unsuccessfully to meet his gaze. "One says lots of things, at times, you know."

Into Arkwright's eyes came a new light, a light that plainly needed but a breath to fan it into quick fire.

"Alice," he said softly, "do you mean that maybe now—I needn't try to fight—that other tiger skin?"

There was no answer.

Arkwright reached out a pleading hand.

"Alice, dear, I've loved you so long," he begged unsteadily. "Don't you think that sometime, if I was very, very patient, you could just begin—to care a little for me?"

Still there was no answer. Then, slowly, Alice shook her head. Her face was turned quite away—which was a pity, for if Arkwright could have seen the sudden tender mischief in her eyes, his own would not have become so somber.

"Not even a little bit?"

"I couldn't ever—begin," answered a half-smothered voice.

"Alice!" cried the man, heart-brokenly.

Alice turned now, and for a fleeting instant let him see her eyes, glowing with the love so long kept in relentless exile.

"I couldn't, because, you see-I began—long ago," she whispered.

"Alice!" It was the same single word, but spoken with a world of difference, for into it now was crowded all the glory and the wonder of a great love. "Alice!" breathed the man again; and this time the word was, oh, so tenderly whispered into the little pink and white ear of the girl in his arms.

"I got delayed," began Billy, in the doorway.

"Oh-h!" she broke off, beating a hushed, but precipitate, retreat.

Fully thirty minutes later, Billy came to the door again. This time her approach was heralded by a snatch of song.

"I hope you'll excuse my being gone so long," she smiled, as she entered the room where her two guests sat decorously face to face at the chess-table.

"Well, you know you said you'd be gone ten minutes," Arkwright reminded her, politely.
"Yes, I know I did." And Billy, to her credit, did not even smile at the man who did not know ten minutes from fifty.

CHAPTER XXX. BY A BABY'S HAND

After all, it was the baby's hand that did it, as was proper, and perhaps to be expected; for surely, was it not Bertram, Jr.'s place to show his parents that he was, indeed, no Wedge, but a dear and precious Tie binding two loving, loyal hearts more and more closely together? It would seem, indeed, that Bertram, Jr., thought so, perhaps, and very bravely he set about it; though, to carry out his purpose, he had to turn his steps into an unfamiliar way—a way of pain, and weariness, and danger.

It was Arkwright who told Bertram that the baby was very sick, and that Billy wanted him. Bertram went home at once to find a distracted, white-faced Billy, and a twisted, pain-racked little creature, who it was almost impossible to believe was the happy, laughing baby boy he had left that morning.

For the next two weeks nothing was thought of in the silent old Beacon Street house but the tiny little life hovering so near Death's door that twice it appeared to have slipped quite across the threshold. All through those terrible weeks it seemed as if Billy neither ate nor slept; and always at her side, comforting, cheering, and helping wherever possible was Bertram, tender, loving, and marvelously thoughtful.

Then came the turning point when the universe itself appeared to hang upon a baby's breath. Gradually, almost imperceptibly, came the fluttering back of the tiny spirit into the longing arms stretched so far, far out to meet and hold it. And the father and the mother, looking into each other's sleepless, dark-ringed eyes, knew that their son was once more theirs to love and cherish.

When two have gone together with a dear one down into the Valley of the Shadow of Death, and have come back, either mourning or rejoicing, they find a different world from the one they had left. Things that were great before seem small, and some things that were small seem great. At least Bertram and Billy found their world thus changed when together they came back bringing their son with them.

In the long weeks of convalescence, when the healthy rosiness stole bit by bit into the baby's waxen face, and the light of recognition and understanding crept day by day into the baby's eyes, there was many a quiet hour for heart-to-heart talks between the two who so anxiously and joyously hailed every rosy tint and fleeting sparkle. And there was so much to tell, so much to hear, so much to talk about! And always, running through everything, was that golden thread of joy, beside which all else paled—that they had Baby and each other. As if anything else mattered!

To be sure, there was Bertram's arm. Very early in their talks Billy found out about that. But Billy, with Baby getting well, was not to be daunted, even by this.

"Nonsense, darling—not paint again, indeed! Why, Bertram, of course you will," she cried confidently.

"But, Billy, the doctor said," began Bertram; but Billy would not even listen.

"Very well, what if he did, dear?" she interrupted. "What if he did say you couldn't use your right arm much again?" Billy's voice broke a little, then quickly steadied into something very much like triumph. "You've got your left one!"

Bertram shook his head.

"I can't paint with that."

"Yes, you can," insisted Billy, firmly. "Why, Bertram, what do you suppose you were given two arms for if not to fight with both of them? And I'm going to be ever so much prouder of what you paint now, because I'll know how splendidly you worked to do it. Besides, there's Baby. As if you weren't ever going to paint for Baby! Why, Bertram, I'm going to have you paint Baby, one of these days. Think how pleased he'll be to see it when he grows up! He's nicer, anyhow, than any old 'Face of a Girl' you ever did. Paint? Why, Bertram, darling, of course you're going to paint, and better than you ever did before!"

Bertram shook his head again; but this time he smiled, and patted Billy's cheek with the tip of his forefinger.

"As if I could!" he disclaimed. But that afternoon he went into his long-deserted studio and hunted up his last unfinished picture. For some time he stood motionless before it; then, with a quick gesture of determination, he got out his palette, paints, and brushes. This time not until he had painted ten, a dozen, a score of strokes, did he drop his brush with a sigh and carefully erase the fresh paint on the canvas. The next day he worked longer, and this time he allowed a little, a very little, of what he had done to remain.

The third day Billy herself found him at his easel.

"I wonder—do you suppose I could?" he asked fearfully.

"Why, dearest, of course you can! Haven't you noticed? Can't you see how much more you can do with your left hand now? You've had to use it, you see. I've seen you do a lot of things with it, lately, that you never used to do at all. And, of course, the more you do with it, the more you can!"

"I know; but that doesn't mean that I can paint with it," sighed Bertram, ruefully eyeing the tiny bit of fresh color his canvas showed for his long afternoon's work.

"You wait and see," nodded Billy, with so overwhelming a cheery confidence that Bertram, looking into her glowing face, was conscious of a curious throb of exultation, almost as if already the victory were his.

But it was not always of Bertram's broken arm, nor even of his work that they talked. Bertram, hanging over the baby's crib to assure himself that the rosiness and the sparkle were really growing more apparent every day, used to wonder sometimes how ever in the world he could have been jealous of his son. He said as much one day to Billy.

To Billy it was a most astounding idea.

"You mean you were actually jealous of your own baby?" she gasped. "Why, Bertram, how could—And was that why you—you sought distraction and—Oh, but, Bertram, that was all my f-fault," she quavered remorsefully. "I wouldn't play, nor sing, nor go to walk, nor anything; and I wore horrid frowzy wrappers all the time, and—"

"Oh, come, come, Billy," expostulated the man. "I'm not going to have you talk like that about my wife!"

"But I did—the book said I did," wailed Billy.

"The book? Good heavens! Are there any books in this, too?" demanded Bertram.

"Yes, the same one; the—the 'Talks to Young Wives,'" nodded Billy. And then, because some things had grown small to them, and some others great, they both laughed happily.

But even this was not quite all; for one evening, very shyly, Billy brought out the chessboard.

"Of course I can't play well," she faltered; "and maybe you don't want to play with me at all."

But Bertram, when he found out why she had learned, was very sure he did want very much to play with her.

Billy did not beat, of course. But she did several times experience—for a few blissful minutes—the pleasure of seeing Bertram sit motionless, studying the board, because of a move she had made. And though, in the end, her king was ignominiously trapped with not an unguarded square upon which to set his poor distracted foot, the memory of those blissful minutes when she had made Bertram "stare" more than paid for the final checkmate.

By the middle of June the baby was well enough to be taken to the beach, and Bertram was so fortunate as to secure the same house they had occupied before. Once again William went down in Maine for his fishing trip, and the Strata was closed. In the beach house Bertram was painting industriously—with his left hand. Almost he was beginning to feel Billy's enthusiasm. Almost he was believing that he was doing good work. It was not the "Face of a Girl," now. It was the face of a baby: smiling, laughing, even crying, sometimes; at other times just gazing straight into your eyes with adorable soberness. Bertram still went into Boston twice a week for treatment, though the treatment itself had changed. The great surgeon had sent him to still another specialist.

"There's a chance—though perhaps a small one," he had said. "I'd like you to try it, anyway."

As the summer advanced, Bertram thought sometimes that he could see a slight improvement in his injured arm; but he tried not to think too much about this. He had thought the same thing before, only to be disappointed in the end. Besides, he was undeniably interested just now in seeing if he could paint with his left hand. Billy was so sure, and she had said that she would be prouder than ever of him, if he could—and he would like to make Billy proud! Then, too, there was the baby—he had no idea a baby could be so interesting to paint. He was not sure but that he was going to like to paint babies even better than he had liked to paint his "Face of a Girl" that had brought him his first fame.

In September the family returned to the Strata. The move was made a little earlier this year on account of Alice Greggory's wedding.

Alice was to be married in the pretty living-room at the Annex, just where Billy herself had been married a few short years before; and Billy had great plans for the wedding—not all of which she was able to carry out, for Alice, like Marie before her, had very strong objections to being placed under too great obligations.

"And you see, really, anyway," she told Billy, "I owe the whole thing to you, to begin with—even my husband."

"Nonsense! Of course you don't," disputed Billy.

"But I do. If it hadn't been for you I should never have found him again, and of course I shouldn't have had this dear little home to be married in. And I never could have left mother if she hadn't had Aunt Hannah and the Annex which means you. And if I hadn't found Mr. Arkwright, I might never have known how—how I could go back to my old home (as I am going on my honeymoon trip), and just know that every one of my old friends who shakes hands with me isn't pitying me now, because I'm my father's daughter. And that means you; for you see I never would have known that my father's name was cleared if it hadn't been for you. And—"

"Oh, Alice, please, please," begged Billy, laughingly raising two protesting hands. "Why don't you say that it's to me you owe just breathing, and be done with it?"

"Well, I will, then," avowed Alice, doggedly. "And it's true, too, for, honestly, my dear, I don't believe I would have been breathing to-day, nor mother, either, if you hadn't found us that morning, and taken us out of those awful rooms."

"I? Never! You wouldn't let me take you out," laughed Billy. "You proud little thing! Maybe you've forgotten how you turned poor Uncle William and me out into the cold, cold world that morning, just because we dared to aspire to your Lowestoft teapot; but I haven't!"

"Oh, Billy, please, don't," begged Alice, the painful color staining her face. "If you knew how I've hated myself since for the way I acted that day—and, really, you did take us away from there, you know."

"No, I didn't. I merely found two good tenants for Mr. and Mrs. Delano," corrected Billy, with a sober face.

"Oh, yes, I know all about that," smiled Alice, affectionately; "and you got mother and me here to keep Aunt Hannah company and teach Tommy Dunn; and you got Aunt Hannah here to keep us company and take care of Tommy Dunn; and you got Tommy Dunn here so Aunt Hannah and we could have somebody to teach and take care of; and, as for the others,—" But Billy put her hands to her ears and fled.

The wedding was to be on the fifteenth. From the West Kate wrote that of course it was none of her affairs, particularly as neither of the interested parties was a relation, but still she should think that for a man in Mr. Arkwright's position, nothing but a church wedding would do at all, as, of course, he did, in a way, belong to the public. Alice, however, declared that perhaps he did belong to the public, when he was Don Somebody-or-other in doublet and hose; but when he was just plain Michael Jeremiah Arkwright in a frock coat he was hers, and she did not propose to make a Grand Opera show of her wedding. And as Arkwright, too, very much disapproved of the church-wedding idea, the two were married in the Annex living-room at noon on the fifteenth as originally planned, in spite of Mrs. Kate Hartwell's letter.

It was soon after the wedding that Bertram told Billy he wished she would sit for him with Bertram, Jr.

"I want to try my hand at you both together," he coaxed.

"Why, of course, if you like, dear," agreed Billy, promptly, "though I think Baby is just as nice, and even nicer, alone."

Once again all over Bertram's studio began to appear sketches of Billy, this time a glorified, tender Billy, with the wonderful mother-love in her eyes. Then, after several sketches of trial poses, Bertram began his picture of Billy and the baby together.

Even now Bertram was not sure of his work. He knew that he could not yet paint with his old freedom and ease; he knew that his stroke was not so sure, so untrammeled. But he knew, too, that he had gained wonderfully, during the summer, and that he was gaining now, every day. To Billy he said nothing of all this. Even to himself he scarcely put his hope into words; but in his heart he knew that what he was really painting his "Mother and Child" picture for was the Bohemian Ten Club Exhibition in March—if he could but put upon canvas the vision that was spurring him on.

And so Bertram worked all through those short winter days, not always upon the one picture, of course, but upon some picture or sketch that would help to give his still uncertain left hand the skill that had belonged to its mate. And always, cheering, encouraging, insisting on victory, was Billy, so that even had Bertram been tempted, sometimes, to give up, he could not have done so—and faced Billy's grieved, disappointed eyes. And when at last his work was completed, and the pictured mother and child in all their marvelous life and beauty seemed ready to step from the canvas, Billy drew a long ecstatic breath.

"Oh, Bertram, it is, it is the best work you have ever done." Billy was looking at the baby. Always she had ignored herself as part of the picture. "And won't it be fine for the Exhibition!"

Bertram's hand tightened on the chair-back in front of him. For a moment he could not speak. Then, a bit huskily, he asked:

"Would you dare—risk it?"

"Risk it! Why, Bertram Henshaw, I've meant that picture for the Exhibition from the very first—only I never dreamed you could get it so perfectly lovely. Now what do you say about Baby being nicer than any old 'Face of a Girl' that you ever did?" she triumphed.

And Bertram, who, even to himself, had not dared whisper the word exhibition, gave a tremulous laugh that was almost a sob, so overwhelming was his sudden realization of what faith and confidence had meant to Billy, his wife.

If there was still a lingering doubt in Bertram's mind, it must have been dispelled in less than an hour after the Bohemian Ten Club Exhibition flung open its doors on its opening night. Once again Bertram found his picture the cynosure of all admiring eyes, and himself the center of an enthusiastic group of friends and fellow-artists who vied with each other in hearty words of congratulation. And when, later, the feared critics, whose names and opinions counted for so much in his world, had their say in the daily press and weekly reviews, Bertram knew how surely indeed he had won. And when he read that "Henshaw's work shows now a peculiar strength, a sort of reserve power, as it were, which, beautiful as was his former work, it never showed before," he smiled grimly, and said to Billy:

"I suppose, now, that was the fighting I did with my good left hand, eh, dear?"

But there was yet one more drop that was to make Bertram's cup of joy brim to overflowing. It came just one month after the Exhibition in the shape of a terse dozen words from the doctor. Bertram fairly flew home that day. He had no consciousness of any means of locomotion. He thought he was going to tell his wife at once his great good news; but when he saw her, speech suddenly fled, and all that he could do was to draw her closely to him with his left arm and hide his face.

"Why, Bertram, dearest, what—what is it?" stammered the thoroughly frightened Billy. "Has anything-happened?"

"No, no—yes—yes, everything has happened. I mean, it's going to happen," choked the man. "Billy, that old chap says that I'm going to have my arm again. Think of it—my good right arm that I've lost so long!"

"Oh, Bertram!" breathed Billy. And she, too, fell to sobbing.

Later, when speech was more coherent, she faltered:

"Well, anyway, it doesn't make any difference how many beautiful pictures you p-paint, after this, Bertram, I can't be prouder of any than I am of the one your l—left hand did."

"Oh, but I have you to thank for all that, dear."

"No, you haven't," disputed Billy, blinking teary eyes; "but—" she paused, then went on spiritedly, "but, anyhow, I—I don't believe any one—not even Kate—can say now that—that I've been a hindrance to you in your c-career!"

"Hindrance!" scoffed Bertram, in a tone that left no room for doubt, and with a kiss that left even less, if possible.

Billy, for still another minute, was silent; then, with a wistfulness that was half playful, half serious, she sighed:

"Bertram, I believe being married is something like clocks, you know, 'specially at the first."

"Clocks, dear?"

"Yes. I was out to Aunt Hannah's to-day. She was fussing with her clock—the one that strikes half an hour ahead—and I saw all those quantities of wheels, little and big, that have to go just so, with all the little cogs fitting into all the other little cogs just exactly right. Well, that's like marriage. See? There's such a lot of little cogs in everyday life that have to be fitted so they'll run smoothly—that have to be adjusted, 'specially at the first."

"Oh, Billy, what an idea!"

"But it's so, really, Bertram. Anyhow, I know my cogs were always getting out of place at the first," laughed Billy. "And I was like Aunt Hannah's clock, too, always going off half an hour ahead of time. And maybe I shall be so again, sometimes. But, Bertram,"—her voice shook a little—"if you'll just look at my face you'll see that I tell the right time there, just as Aunt Hannah's clock does. I'm sure, always, I'll tell the right time there, even if I do go off half an hour ahead!"

"As if I didn't know that," answered Bertram, very low and tenderly. "Besides, I reckon I have some cogs of my own that need adjusting!"

Note from the Editor

Odin's Library Classics strives to bring you unedited and unabridged works of classical literature. As such, this is the complete and unabridged version of the original English text unless noted. In some instances, obvious typographical errors have been corrected. This is done to preserve the original text as much as possible. The English language has evolved since the writing and some of the words appear in their original form, or at least the most commonly used form at the time. This is done to protect the original intent of the author. If at any time you are unsure of the meaning of a word, please do your research on the etymology of that word. It is important to preserve the history of the English language.

Taylor Anderson

Made in United States
Troutdale, OR
11/29/2023